That First Year

By

Margaret Kay

Published by Sisters Romance

I0661421

This book is dedicated to Animal House Shelter in Huntley, Illinois.

I thank its founder, Leslie, for allowing me to use the name in this story. We adopted our beloved fur-baby from AHS. Our daughter's family has adopted from them, as has our son. Animal House Shelter is a non-profit, no-kill 501(c)3 shelter for all breeds of dogs and cats. They rescue, care for, and find homes for homeless pets who arrive at AHS for various reasons, including:

- Abuse, neglect, or abandonment
- Owners whose time, income, or situation changes
- Animals scheduled for euthanasia at other clinics

Once rehabilitated and ready, they are carefully matched with homes for adoption or foster care.

https://www.animalhouseshelter.com/

When looking for the next addition to your family, please visit a local shelter and consider one of the many pets looking for homes.

May

Chapter 1—It Arrives

The design was beautiful, sleek, Asian inspired. It was onyx with inlaid mother-of-pearl in a traditional floral tapestry pattern he would have loved. It was cool to the touch and heavy in its weight. Elyse Laramie clutched the urn to herself as she watched the woman from the Solace Crematorium and Funeral Home retreat down her long driveway, the wheels of the black SUV crunching the gravel. The chrome on the car's bumper gleamed in the early afternoon sun.

It was a stunning spring day. The sky was cobalt blue and there wasn't a cloud in sight. The trees and bushes had filled in with dark green leaves and beautiful, brilliant purple- and salmon-colored blooms. They gently swayed in the seventy-degree breeze. The vibrant colors were breathtaking, surreal, life bursting forth; a stark contrast to the life suddenly lost.

When the SUV disappeared behind the wall of purple leaf plum trees and flowering quince shrubs at the end of the drive, only then did she move within her spacious, two-story foyer. Beneath her bare feet, the beige ceramic tile was cool. The tile color matched the paint on the upper portion of the entry walls. The white wainscoting below flowed up the grand staircase that looped around the entire entry, ending on the second floor at the entrance to her master suite, where Tim had seldom slept.

She set the urn on the black entry table beneath the ornate, white wrought iron mirror to the spot she had prepared for it. Dangling from her hand were the four necklaces with charms that each held a small portion of Tim's ashes. Cremation jewelry. *Who thought up such a thing?* She set the necklaces beside the urn.

Beside the urn to the right was her favorite photo of him, taken with her cell phone four and a half months earlier, on Christmas Day. She had printed it on high-grade photo paper and placed it in an eight by ten black frame. On the other side of the urn was the family photo taken the same day. The five of them together. That was a rare event. It was in an identical frame. She admired the balanced appearance the two black picture frames gave the urn presentation against the rich beige wall. *A short white candle in front*, she thought. *That would finish the display beautifully.*

She lifted the family photo, her eyes scanning each of her family members' faces. Tim looked genuinely happy, his arms around each of his girls. Claire to his right, the spitting image of her father in both personality and appearance. Black hair, brown eyes, olive complexion, just like Tim and his mother. Kelsey, Elyse's mini-me on his left; her same auburn-brown hair, sparkling green eyes, high cheekbones, full lips, and a wide, beautiful smile.

Kade, their middle child, the tallest of all five of them, a mix of both his parents. He had Tim's hair and complexion, Elyse's personality, eyes, and lips. He stood towering over them all by nearly a foot. He had his arm draped over Claire's shoulder, the new dragon tattoo on his forearm peeking out from under the rolled up white shirt sleeve. Its yellow eyes appeared to glow, drawing her gaze.

Elyse smiled, remembering how Claire had berated Kade after the photo was taken, angry he hadn't rolled his sleeves down. She'd said his ink ruined the picture, which led into a tirade by Claire about how disgusting tattoos and tattoo parlors were. Elyse wondered how she had raised such a judgmental prude. Elyse was neither judgmental nor was she prudish, and neither was Tim, that she knew of.

Her eyes shifted to the wall to the right, zeroing in on the other family picture taken that day. It was in the middle of the many family photos she had displayed in the large grouping of frames. This picture included Claire's husband, Matthew, who had the same olive complexion, brown eyes, and black hair, as both of their young children did.

Kade's sleeve was rolled down in that shot, she noticed. Her eyes shifted to Kelsey, Elyse's arm around her. Around her twenty-two-year-old. Kelsey had told her that day that she would not be home after she graduated from Old Dominion University that June. She had decided to stay in Norfolk for the summer and then she would settle wherever she went to grad school. Elyse's last child had officially flown the coop. She was proud of all her children. She raised them to become successful adults who could stand on their own two feet, and they were. It was just that, as much as she hated to admit it, she was closest to Kelsey, and she missed her.

Norfolk was only an hour away. Both Claire and Kade lived there as well. Elyse wished one of her children had returned to Franklin to settle into their adult lives. It was a good town, a quaint, small town that she loved. The best years of her life had been spent right there in that house.

She was sad for Tim, taken from this world too soon. She was sad for her children. They'd lost their father. Kelsey would not have her father to walk her down the aisle on her wedding day as Claire had. Claire would no longer receive his guidance in their mutual career field. Tim was very successful, a respected authority in the structural engineering community. He was the go-to guy to investigate any collapse. Claire yearned to be just as successful as her father. She had no idea of the sacrifices her parents had made for her father to acquire the exemplary reputation he had, though. And, sadly, Elyse could see Claire already making the same choices Tim had.

And Kade. Elyse had no idea what the loss of his father at the age of thirty would mean to him. They'd never been close. Tim hadn't been around much when the kids were growing up, always at a construction site or an accident investigation site. He didn't coach Little League or attend Boy Scout campouts with his son. Maybe that was what Elyse was the saddest about. The fact that there would never be the opportunity for Kade to have the relationship with his father that Elyse always hoped for them to have.

But she had no tears for her own loss, because Tim's passing created no loss in her life. He was a ten minute a day Skype session at best, a brief visit once every month or two or three or four. He was more of a roommate during those visits, a good friend. Their relationship couldn't have been called a marriage for a long time.

She did love him, though it was no longer in a romantic way. It had become a relationship neither of them wanted to end, but one neither could change. That was what made her the saddest. There would never be the opportunity to see if the romantic love they'd once shared could be rekindled.

She replaced the picture frame to its spot, pulled her cell phone from her jeans pocket and tapped out a text message in the string that copied all three of her children. *"Dad's urn arrived as planned. We're on for tonight. Please confirm that you're still coming and what time you plan to arrive. I'm making Dad's favorite for dinner in his honor."*

Kelsey's reply chimed in immediately. Typical. She lived on her phone, bringing a smile to Elyse's lips. *"Of course, I'm still coming. I'll be there by four."*

Elyse heard a bark from the rear of the house. She had forgotten about Charlie, confined to the sun porch. She passed through her sunny yellow kitchen and opened the French doors to the sunroom. She greeted him as she stepped into the room, patting his head. He was a mutt, mixed with a little of everything. His coat was mostly black, speckled with brown and white throughout. He had a shepherd's nose and a retriever body. His legs were short like a bulldog. His muzzle was gray, showing his age. He was a cutie, and she had gotten attached to him in the few short weeks she had been fostering him.

She let him out into the backyard and stepped out onto the brick patio, onto her sanctuary. It was a welcoming space, flower pots overflowing with colorful blooms everywhere and hundreds of decorations swaying or spinning in the gentle breeze. It was whimsical, a fairy garden that brought a smile to her lips whenever she viewed the arrangement that had taken her years to create.

"Seriously, the weekend would be better for me. It's a school night. But forget making it convenient for the mother of the young children in the family. Let's all bend over backwards to accommodate King Kade," Claire's normal sarcastic reply displayed.

"This is a group text, dumb-shit. And no one is asking you to accommodate me. I have to work double shifts all weekend to make up some of the time my coworkers covered for me," Kade texted back. *"Besides, your kids go to daycare. They're not even in real school. And it's not like you have to be home tonight. Leave them with the nanny, like usual."*

"Grow up and get a job with normal hours," Claire texted back. *"And preschool is a real school. To get into a good kindergarten, they have to be able to interview well and pass basic tests."*

"Ugh!" Elyse groaned aloud. She typed out a quick reply. *"Will you please both just stop? It's tonight, Claire. And Kade don't call your sister names or judge her parenting, not until you have had two preschoolers."*

"Thank you, Mom," Claire replied. She inserted an emoji with its tongue sticking out, followed by a message. *"So, be nice to me, Kade."*

"And Claire, stop calling your brother King Kade," Elyse added. *"See you both tonight?"*

"Yes, Mom. I'll be there by five," Kade replied.

"Six for me, and yes, I'll have to leave the kids with Lizette. Matthew is out-of-town tonight."

Elyse sighed. Her grandkids spent more time with the nanny than they did a parent. She didn't like it, but it wasn't her place to say anything. *"Great, see you all tonight,"* she fingered into the touchscreen.

Or Claire could just bring the kids with her, she thought. But Claire was just like her father in all ways, just as rigid with schedules. Claire's kids went to bed at eight, always. No exceptions. A dinner to honor their grandfather would not interfere with their routine.

She exited the text message screen and took a seat on the cushioned swing. Charlie had already positioned himself at the edge of the patio, his nose in one of her flower pots.

· · · ·

KELSEY TAPPED HER PHONE to see the time. How had only a half hour passed since she'd last checked it? Her green eyes flickered back to the instructor in the front of the lecture hall. What exactly was he droning on about? Statistical algorisms, yes, that was it. She'd stopped listening over an hour ago. There was less than a month left until graduation. She was already checked out. The thought of several more years of classes to earn her master's degree turned her stomach.

But what else would she do? And everyone expected her to go to grad school. To be able to get a job in the field, she had to have her master's degree. But was that what she really wanted to do with her life? She'd once been sure, but now, she wasn't sure of anything.

Her phone vibrated a new text message. *"Dad's urn arrived...favorite for dinner."*

Kelsey smiled as she typed out a quick reply. *"Of course, I'm still coming. I'll be there by four."*

Lasagna, yum! She loved her mom's lasagna. She loved her mom, was looking forward to spending the evening with her, Kade, and Claire. When this lecture was done, she'd pack a few things and surprise her mom by spending the night at home. She knew these last few weeks had been very difficult for her mom, but she'd handled it all so well, losing her husband, the love of her life. Kelsey thought for a moment about how great a role model her mom had always been. She was a strong woman who Kelsey had always looked up to.

Another text message displayed. *"Weekend...better...accommodate King Kade."* Claire. What a bitch. She knew her mom would be upset that she thought that way about her sister, but the honest truth was that Claire was a self-important, condescending bitch.

"Group text, dumb-shit...working double shifts," came Kade's text. Kelsey chuckled to herself. Way to go Kade! *"Kids go to daycare...leave them with the nanny."*

That was so true. She was glad Kade told her that. Kade was an awesome brother, called Claire on her bullshit. Kelsey would confront Claire when absolutely necessary, but she preferred to fly under the radar and not cause any conflict or get drawn into any of Claire's drama. Kelsey opened the ongoing text message that was between just Kade and herself. *"Why does Claire have to be such a bitch?"*

"She can't help it," Kade's reply came. *"I think it was a class she aced during her engineering program. Principles of the self-absorbed 101."*

Kelsey fought the urge to laugh out loud.

"*Job...normal hours,*" Claire texted back. "*Preschool...real school...interview...pass tests.*"

Kelsey rolled her eyes at that. Those poor kids didn't stand a chance of growing up to be normal with Claire as their mom. Talk about pressure! Testing to get into kindergarten? What the hell?

"*Stop...don't call your sister names...judge parenting...*"

Kelsey almost laughed aloud again. Mom was being diplomatic. She knew her mom felt the same way she and Kade did about Claire's parenting, which was rigid and extreme. The past few weeks had held way too much family time. Four people who were normally only together a few times a year had overdosed on each other's company.

Her attention momentarily went to the instructor again. She rolled her eyes. How could anyone stand up there and talk about this for two hours? She decided in that moment that she couldn't do this for a living. And she absolutely didn't want to commit to several more years of school to study it.

"*Thank you, Mom,*" Claire's text replied. An emoji with its tongue sticking out followed.

Jeez, just stop yourself, Claire, Kelsey thought. She barely skimmed the next few text messages. Kade would be there by five.

"*Six for me...kids...Lizette.*"

Of course, she would, Kelsey thought. Heaven forbid Claire actually spend time with her own children. Two summers ago, she'd lived with Claire and Matthew and played nanny to Claire's kids. It had been the worst summer of her life. She had spent more time with those kids than Claire or Matthew ever did.

"Great, see you all tonight," Mom's text read.

Kelsey closed the lid to her laptop. She hadn't taken a single note on the lecture. Her grade was a solid A. Even if she failed the last few assignments and final test, she already calculated her ending grade would be a B. That was good enough for her. Even though the lecture wasn't over yet, she stood and made her way up the stairs to the exit.

· · · ·

"MAN, THIS IS ONE BEAUTIFUL day," Cletus Taylor said, breaking the quiet in the cab of the ambulance.

Kade knew he'd been poor company for the last few shifts. His mind was on too much family stuff. His eyes shifted to Cletus, a smart, energetic guy. Cletus was his partner and his best friend. Cletus shot him a smile, bright white teeth against his dark skin. "Yeah, it is," he agreed.

They'd just transported a patient to the level one trauma center, cleaned the back of the unit, and were heading back towards their assigned territory. A call came in. An elderly man having chest pains in an apartment complex they were very familiar with. They usually visited the large low-rent area at least once a shift. Kade acknowledged the call, then flipped the switch activating the sirens and lights. The sirens wailed as Cletus expertly weaved the unit through traffic.

Kade's phone vibrated in his hand. He sighed aloud as he read it.

"What?" Cletus asked.

"Dad's urn came. Dinner at my mom's tonight."

"Sorry, man. How's your mom doing, anyway?"

"You know my mom. She's doing fine, as always."

He read Kelsey's reply. *"Be there by four."* He smiled. Had to love his little sister.

Another text message displayed. *"Weekend...better...King Kade."*

"Oh my God, Claire is such a bitch!" Kade read Claire's text to Cletus. "I know it's probably not even worth it, but I'm not going to let her get away with that." He typed out his reply and hit send. He read his reply to Cletus, who laughed aloud.

"How did that stick get stuck so far up her ass?" Cletus asked with a chuckle. "Your mom is a great lady. Kelsey's as cool as you are. Claire must have been adopted or switched at birth at the hospital."

Kade's phone displayed a text in a different conversation with just Kelsey. After he typed out his reply, he smiled to himself.

"Job with normal hours," Claire texted back. *"Preschool is real school...interview...pass tests."*

Kade rolled his eyes at that. He read it aloud to Cletus. "Man, those poor kids. You don't ever think about those kinds of things with your little guy. Do you?"

"Hell no," Cletus replied. "Preschool is for fun. There will be more than enough time for all that bullshit when he gets older."

His mother's text replied. *"Will you please both just stop?...had two preschoolers."*

Kade dismissed his mother's text right away. He wouldn't even respond.

Claire's text replied. An emoji with its tongue sticking out, followed by a message. *"So, be nice to me, Kade."*

Fat chance, he thought.

They were just arriving on-site. "He's in unit twelve," Kade said, pointing in the direction of building twelve. Then he typed out a quick reply to the text before transmitting to dispatch that they were on-site. *"Yes, Mom. I'll be there by five."*

He saw Claire's reply. *"Six for me...leave kids with Lizette."*

Figured.

He pulled himself from the unit, slipped his phone into his pocket, and then opened the back of the truck to get the stretcher and the other gear needed for a possible heart attack. He immediately pushed all thoughts of his family away to focus on the patient who waited in distress within the door that Cletus had gone ahead to and was holding open for him.

He left the stretcher by the door and went in to find a man older than dirt lying on the couch in what he was sure was full cardiac arrest. He and Cletus moved him to the floor and pressed the EKG pads to the various places on his torso needed to get a reading.

They worked on him for just a few minutes and then transferred him to the stretcher. While Cletus drove to the hospital, Kade rode in the back. He started an IV, kept tabs on his vital signs, and comforted the wife, who rode in the back of the ambulance.

• • • •

CLAIRE REPLACED THE picture frame on her desk that she had stared at for at least five minutes. Her dad, her best friend. She missed him so much. His passing left a hole in her heart that she didn't think would ever heal. She knew her husband, Matthew, didn't understand. She hated that they fought that morning before Matthew left on his trip. A long weekend golf trip with his fraternity brothers, this soon after her dad's death. She was angry he wouldn't cancel. She didn't care about the money he'd spent on this weekend. She needed him, and he was letting her down.

Her phone chimed a new text message from her mom. *"Dad's urn...tonight... Dad's favorite."*

Kelsey's reply chimed in immediately. Typical. She had no responsibilities. Claire groaned. Of course, Kelsey could drop everything on a week night. And Kade, with his messed-up work schedule. He was the reason behind this dinner taking place tonight rather than Friday or Saturday night, or even Sunday afternoon, which would have been Claire's preference.

"Weekend would be better...school night...making it convenient...accommodate King Kade," Claire typed out and hit send without rereading it. She didn't care if it sounded harsh. She honestly was so tired of family dinners and holidays being scheduled to accommodate his messed-up schedule.

"Group text, dumb-shit..." Kade texted back.

"Dumb-shit? Seriously. How dare he?" she said aloud.

"Besides...kids...daycare...not school...Leave them with the nanny, like usual."

"You jerk," she grumbled aloud. *"Job with normal hours...preschool is a real school."* She wasn't sure why she even tried to explain it to him. He'd never get it. Kids didn't grow up to be successful by accident. It took careful planning by involved and determined parents, which she was.

Her phone chimed again. *"Kade, don't call your sister...judge her parenting, not until you have had two preschoolers."*

"Thank you, Mom," Claire replied. She was grateful her mom understood. She inserted an emoji with its tongue sticking out, followed by a message. *"Be nice to me, Kade."*

Yes, that would be the day. Kade was such a different person than she was. She was much closer to Kelsey. At least her sister was as dedicated to her future as she was. Kelsey understood wanting the best and realized that sacrifices and hard work were needed to be successful. She was so proud of her little sister, graduating in the top five percent of her class, accepted by three different master's programs in a tight field.

"Claire, stop calling your brother King Kade," her mom added. *"See you both tonight?"*

"Yes...be there by five," Kade replied.

She replied that she'd be there by six. It was embarrassing that Matthew wouldn't be with her. Of course, Kade's girlfriend wouldn't be there either. If she wasn't working, she'd probably be sleeping. That was Kade's normal excuse for Melanie never attending family events. She certainly hoped they never got married. With their schedules, she was surprised their relationship had lasted as long as it had. If they were ever to get married, it would be doomed from the start. Couples who didn't spend much time together just couldn't last.

Claire rubbed the back of her neck. It was tight with stress. These last few weeks had been brutal. She did feel bad that she had been so busy she hadn't reached out to her mom everyday like she'd planned. She was sure her mom felt as lost as she did because of her father's death. And sad. She was just so sad.

She called Lizette to tell her she wouldn't be home until late because of the trip out to Franklin. And then she called the spa and booked herself a massage. She could squeeze it in before driving out to her mom's place. She knew she needed to try to convince her mom to move into Norfolk to live near her and Kade. That would be on the top of her agenda this evening.

• • • •

CHARLIE DIDN'T EVEN bark when Julia approached from the back of the garage. Elyse had almost forgotten that Julia was in the barn, working on the restoration. Julia was dressed in blue jeans and a red t-shirt, both splattered with white paint. A blue bandana around her head held her wild black curls back.

"You look quite patriotic. Did you get any paint on the walls?" Elyse asked with a smile.

"I told you painting isn't my thing," Julia said with a laugh, her eyes scanning the splattered paint on her clothes. She took a seat across from Elyse on one of the black metal chairs. "How are you holding up?" Her brown eyes gazed into Elyse's bright greens, which were a little less sparkling than usual these days.

"I'm okay," Elyse replied with a shrug. "Notifying everyone of Tim's death has taken so much time. I'm sorry I've dumped so much on you," she said.

Julia gave her a dismissive wave and interrupted. "No worries, chica. I've got this. Besides, that plumber you hired is hot! I'll stare at his crack all day," she laughed. "Or his other parts. His butt is mighty fine, though."

Elyse laughed. "And the electrician?"

"He's okay, too blonde for me. I like tall, dark, and steamy better. I just wish he didn't have to have his head under the sink so much. His face is cute too and his scruffy jaw is so manly. I'd so let him examine my pipes any day!" She waggled her eyebrows and laughed.

Elyse laughed again. "By the way, I took Charlie off the website. I'm keeping him."

Julia's eyebrows shot up. "Are you ready for that? Look, Elyse. I'd never pry, you know that, but he's not exactly a young dog. You just lost Thor and Jane Foster, not even six months ago, and now Tim. Do you really want to get attached to another dog that may only have a few years left? If you're ready for another dog, maybe a much younger one would be better?"

Elyse's lips formed a small, sad grin. "Thor and Jane Foster were great dogs. Sixteen years for them both. That's good for German Shepherds. I wasn't ready till now to have another. If Charlie hadn't been staying with me, I wouldn't have seen how great he is, wouldn't have gotten attached. But I'm attached. He's such a good boy. He didn't even bark at you when you came into the yard. He knows you, knows you belong. He's smart and good company for me."

Julia cocked her head. "I know Tim wasn't home much, but you did Skype with him daily. It's understandable that you'd feel lonely not talking to him."

Julia had never asked about Elyse's relationship with her husband, and Elyse had never volunteered any insights. Julia secretly wondered if it was still a marriage, and if it was, how it could survive the long separations. She doubted Elyse had ever been unfaithful, but she seriously suspected Tim had to have been. Come on, he was home so infrequently, and he was a man, after all, so she just assumed even though she didn't know him well.

"I'm sad he's gone." Elyse spoke up, breaking in on Julia's thoughts. "I loved him, but I can't say I miss him. He wasn't here much, wasn't a part of my life, so there is nothing concrete to miss."

Julia's expression was one of shock. She fingered her jaw to see if it had dropped open. She wouldn't be surprised if she sat there with her mouth hanging open. Thankfully, she found her mouth closed. She and Elyse had known each other for six years, since Elyse started the dog rescue and shelter she'd lovingly named Animal House Shelter and Julia had volunteered. It was a charity that became a full-time job for Elyse. She spent her time and money on it. The shelter had taken over Elyse's life, hence the restoration in the barn to transform the building into an actual public animal shelter where they planned to house forty dogs if the county approved their application. Currently, the animals were in a small building that wasn't open to the public and others were scattered in hard-to-find foster homes.

Never in all these years had Elyse ever elaborated on her marriage or her feelings towards her husband. Elyse had opened the door to the conversation, though, so Julia decided to step through. "I've never asked, and I don't want to offend you by prying, but..." She paused, her courage to ask suddenly faltering.

"I'm sorry," Elyse apologized due to Julia's reaction. "We had a complicated relationship."

"I'd say. You've always said you love him, and always seemed happy when he came home, but he was rarely here. What kind of relationship was that?"

"One that just kind of happened over time. It wasn't what either of us set out for it to be."

Julia peered hard at her, rolling Elyse's words around. "I know he traveled constantly. Kelsey's been gone for four years now. Why didn't you just go with him?" There, she said aloud what she had wondered for years.

"It's simple. I wasn't invited," Elyse confessed.

Julia's shock was evident.

"I invited myself on that trip to Dubai last year because I really wanted to see it. It was the same with Singapore the year before, but on both trips, I was basically there alone. He put in sixteen to twenty-hour days at his job site." Elyse's eyes got a faraway look in them. After a few seconds' pause, she added, "and he was dealing with an engineering failure that resulted in the loss of life. He was no joy to be around when he was back at the hotel. I would have thought after all these years it wouldn't affect him that way, but it did. It was as if

20

the details of the people who died in the collapse fueled him to figure out why it happened and how to prevent it from ever happening again. He immersed himself in all of it. It was almost lonelier to be there with him," Elyse confessed. She'd never told a soul about any of this before.

"I'm sorry, El," Julia said. "I didn't mean to pry."

"You didn't," Elyse said with a brave smile. "I didn't blame him. Figuring out disasters was what he did. He was very good at his job. He'd never have been happy living a normal life, with a normal job."

Julia just nodded. Her heart broke for her friend. She had many unsaid thoughts, but voicing them would have been hurtful to Elyse. She didn't know what else to say, so she said nothing. Thankfully, Elyse came to her feet, her gaze directed toward the back corner of the yard that led to the barn, around the flowering bushes.

"Come on, let's go check on the work," Elyse said.

"The work or the workers?" Julia said with a suggestive smile.

Elyse chuckled. "The work. I'm nowhere near ready for a relationship."

Julia raised an eyebrow. "Who said anything about a relationship? Unless I'm mistaken, I saw hay in the barn. You could just go for a roll in it."

Elyse laughed again. Leave it to Julia to know what to say to lighten her mood. Like she would ever just have a roll in the hay, a fling! Julia knew her well enough to know how ridiculous that was.

Chapter 2–Dinner Surprises

"Hey," Kelsey said softly, pulling her sketch pad from her backpack. "I had some time to work on it. Here's what I've come up with so far." She handed it over to Kade. She bit her lip as Kade looked it over.

She had drawn in colored pencils an intricate scrollwork design with fleur de lis at the top, her father's initials, his date of death, and the family coat of arms all incorporated into the vine and leaf design. Blue, his favorite color, was predominant with green, black, and gold used to accent.

"This is good, really good. I like how you incorporated Dad's initials and the date of his death in the detail of the design."

Kelsey smiled. "Do you really think it's good?"

Kade wrapped his arm around her. "It is. Can I tear the whole page out? I want to get it to Ash, my tattoo artist. It's really good, Kelsey."

"Aren't you going to let me work more on it? That's my only copy."

"It's perfect the way it is. No work is needed." He tore it out of the pad and then folded it up and slid it into his back pocket.

Kelsey eyed him suspiciously. She doubted she'd ever see that picture again, least of all tattooed on his arm.

"I have an appointment to get it done Monday afternoon. Why don't you meet me there?"

"What, at the tattoo parlor?"

Kade chuckled. "Yes, at the tattoo parlor. Where do you think?"

"I just didn't realize you were getting it done so soon. What if you hadn't liked it?"

Kade laughed again and playfully drew her in for a tighter hug, almost putting her neck into a choke hold. "Then you would have been working on it all weekend, I guess." He flipped through the next few pages of sketches, admiring Kelsey's artwork. His mom was artistic, too. She painted beautiful landscapes. He pointed to one of the drawings, a dog wrapped in a blanket. "This one is so lifelike. I love the shading. Hey, I know you've drawn pictures of Thor and Jane Foster. Do you think you could do one kind of like this one with them both snug in a blanket? I know Mom would love it."

• • • •

CLAIRE PUT HER CAR in park. As expected, Kelsey's car and Kade's pickup truck were in the driveway. She glanced at the house, performing a mental calculation of the house's value and how much work potentially had to be done for her mom to put it on the market. A townhouse or a condo would be much easier for her mom to manage, and there were several nice communities near her home in Norfolk.

She was sure her father had left her mom well off with his investments and life insurance, but without proper fiscal management, the money wouldn't last as long as her mother would live. She'd not worked outside the home except to volunteer for her silly charities. She'd have to get a real job now. Claire knew that her mom would need her guidance.

She entered the house, and right there on the table in the entry was the urn. Tears filled her eyes. She paused to view the amazing memorial her mom had set up on the table. A picture of her dad was in a frame to one side, one with the five of them on the other side. Why hadn't she used the picture taken that day with Matthew and the kids too, instead of this one? They were as much a part of this family and Dad had loved his grandchildren.

"Hi, Claire," Elyse said, coming into the hallway and wrapping her arms around her. "No tears, sweetie. Tonight is about celebrating his life and remembering the good times."

"I'm just so sad, Mom."

Elyse embraced her more tightly. "I know. We all are. That's why us being together tonight to celebrate him is important."

Claire allowed her mother to guide her into the kitchen, even though she would have preferred to linger in the entryway long enough to fully embrace her feelings and soak in a solemn remembrance of her father. She smelled the incredible aroma of lasagna in the room. She hoped her mom had also made a large salad. No one needed to eat that much pasta.

Kelsey came up and gave her a hug. "Glad you could make it," she said, setting her wine glass on the counter to wrap both arms around her.

Claire noticed that the glass was nearly empty.

"Hi, sis," Kade said. He, too, gave her a hug. He had a beer in his hand.

Great, tonight would be another drink-fest. Her eyes scanned Kade. He wore a plain white t-shirt and his work pants and boots. "You couldn't even change out of your uniform?"

"I came right from work." He knew where this was heading.

"Gross, just gross. Are there any bodily fluids on your clothes?" Claire demanded.

Claire crossed her arms over her chest and gave him that bitchy look she was so good at.

Kade looked down over his clothing. "Look, I started at four a.m. I'm still making up a few shifts that I traded with my coworkers to be at Dad's memorial. There's no blood or other bodily fluids on it. No one peed or threw up on me today."

Claire shot Kelsey a warning scowl when Kelsey laughed at his statement. "That's just gross, Kade," Claire repeated.

"Here, have a glass of wine, Claire, and relax." Elyse handed her a glass of red wine and refilled Kelsey's glass. Then she lifted her own glass in the air. "To Dad."

"To Dad," Claire agreed.

The three wine glasses tapped, along with Kade's beer bottle. Elyse pulled the salad from the refrigerator and set it on the table. She had the good china out. "Let's have our salads. The bread is nearly done."

Garlic bread too? More carbs. Great, thought Claire. They all took their normal seats at the table. Claire couldn't help but focus on her father's empty chair.

"I know we haven't said grace in years, since you were all children, but I think it would be nice to this evening. Claire, would you like to say grace?" Elyse asked.

Claire knew she should. She was the only one in the family who attended church regularly. But she just didn't have the words in her. "I'm at a loss, Mom."

"Then I will," Elyse said.

Claire took Kade's hand from across the table, and Kelsey's beside her. She bowed her head.

"Heavenly Father, thank You for bringing the four of us together this evening to celebrate Tim and his life. We are comforted, knowing he's home in Your Almighty Kingdom. Bless this food and this time for us to be together. May we remember the good times with him, and all find comfort from this time together. Amen."

Claire felt Kade squeeze her hand before he released it. She decided in that moment that it was better that it was just the four of them tonight. This night should be about their nuclear family. Matthew didn't belong here tonight any more than Kade's girlfriend, Melanie, did.

"That was a nice blessing, Mom," Kelsey said.

"Yes, nice, Mom," Kade agreed.

"Why did we stop going to church back when we all lived at home, anyway?" Claire asked.

Elyse laughed. "You really don't remember? You three gave me such a hard time about going and you were each so busy with soccer, horseback riding, and swim team. Practices and meets landed on Sundays. It was crazy for me to run you in three different directions as well as fight with you about going to church. Your father and I agreed you would all go until you each made it through confirmation classes, and you did. I don't even know how."

"You should have just told us no to all the other stuff," Claire said. "Matthew and I agree that certain family things will take precedence and the kids will just not do certain things if it interferes."

Elyse chuckled. "Talk to me in a few years when the kids are older and let me know how that goes." Claire had no clue what was yet to come when her children were school age.

Claire was offended by that comment, but decided not to say anything. Whatever. She was raising her children her way.

"I remember those screaming matches between you and Mom, Claire," Kelsey said. "There was one specifically about going on a Confirmation Retreat that comes to mind." She paused and laughed.

"I remember that one too," Kade jumped in. "You slammed your bedroom door so hard you knocked all the pictures in the hallway off the wall. But in the end, Mom took you to the church and dropped you off with the group, made you go if you wanted to or not."

"I don't remember it quite that way," Claire said.

Everyone else laughed at that statement. Claire did not.

As they talked and reminisced over dinner, Elyse realized that most of the memories they shared, Tim was not a part of. He was rarely home. It was no surprise. She brought up the previous Christmas, when the photos in the hall had been taken, the last time the family was together. They talked about how fun that day had been, even though Elyse remembered more of the awkwardness and tension than the fun. Her eyes went to Kade's tattoos on his arm, and she smiled again, recalling Claire's tirade over them showing in the family pictures they'd taken. Tim had been oblivious to it at the time. Tim had been oblivious to a lot over the years.

Elyse pulled the box of cannoli from the refrigerator as the girls cleared the table. Kade took Charlie out back to have an after-dinner cigarette. She hated that he still smoked. Being a paramedic, he knew of the health risks associated with smoking. He should know better.

When he came back in, she poured the coffee she'd made to go with the cannoli. Then she handed out the cremation jewelry they'd ordered. The girls both chose heart necklaces, each as unique as they were. Hers was an ornately carved silver cross with a gold wedding band looped on it, and Kade had selected a solid, masculine-looking chunky black cross.

They each put their necklaces on. Elyse's gaze swept over each of her children and the necklaces they wore. "Your dad would be happy to see us all wearing these necklaces, keeping him close to our hearts." She rose from the table. "I have something else I want to give you each. I'll be right back." She hurried from the room and up the stairs. She'd meant to bring them down earlier, but had gotten sidetracked when she went out back to the barn.

"I need you two to help me with something," Claire said in a hushed voice when their mom had left the room. "The first thing we have to do is get her out of this house and get her moved to Norfolk near the rest of us. There are a few cute townhome and condo communities she should be able to buy in," she whispered. "Without Dad's income, do you think she will have to get a real job?"

"Don't try to tell her what to do, Claire. She's taken care of everything since we were born. Dad was never around. I'm sure Mom knows what she can afford and what she needs to do," Kade answered, his irritation with Claire going from zero to sixty in two seconds flat.

"I'm sure Dad left her well off, but that money will only go so far. She can't piss it away," Claire countered.

"Claire, stop," Kade moaned. "What Mom decides to do is her business. Don't try to ride roughshod over her." Typical Claire.

"Kade, Mom has never had to work. She's always had Dad and his income to rely on. I'm just trying to look out for her."

"No, you're trying to take over, like usual," Kelsey said. "Kade is right. Let her work it out on her own for a little while. We'll all be here for her if she needs us."

Claire huffed out a sarcastic "huh," and rolled her eyes. "Like you can give her advice. You haven't even graduated from college yet. Look, no offense, but I'm the oldest. It's my job to step in and help. It's what Dad would want."

"Stand back and wait, Claire. I'm telling you; I won't let you try to talk Mom into doing anything she doesn't want to," Kade warned.

"Like what?" Elyse asked from the doorway. She'd heard just enough to get the gist of the conversation, heard each of her kids' last statements.

All eyes swept to her as she walked back into the kitchen.

"What is Claire going to try to talk me into that I won't want to do?" Claire and Kelsey both looked guilty. Kade just looked angry.

"Claire wants us to help talk you into selling the house. She wants you to move to Norfolk," Kade said.

Elyse noticed Claire's angry and outraged stare settle on Kade.

"Don't waste any of your energy on that. I will not be selling my home. Claire, sweetie, I love you and I know you only want what's best for me. But I will be staying in the house."

"Mom, I only meant that it would be nice if you were in Norfolk near all of us instead of alone out here."

Elyse laughed. "Claire, you seem to forget that your father was never home. I've been mostly alone here for four years since Kelsey went to college. I love it here in Franklin. It's my home. My friends are here, my life is here. But thank you for your concern." She handed out the three pieces of paper, one to each of them. "So, here is what I have for you."

Each of the kids studied the statements with checks attached and then turned toward her with questioning stares. She watched as they each eyed what amounts were on each other's checks.

"You each get the same amount," Elyse said. "When Kelsey was little, Dad and I took out these small policies for each of you should anything happen to him. We put a three-thousand-dollar investment on each and they sat there for the last twenty years, accruing interest. I completely forgot about them, but our financial planner submitted Dad's death certificate and I got the checks in the other day for you. I know it's only six thousand dollars, but it will at least pay for a vacation for you, Kelsey, or money to put down on a new truck if you still plan to get one, Kade."

"Was this some kind of weird life insurance policy?" Claire asked.

"More like an after-death gift fund. Dad got a nice bonus that year and we thought why not, when our financial planner told us about this fund."

"I can think of a lot of different investment strategies that would have grown nine thousand dollars to a larger amount over a twenty-year period," Claire criticized.

"It was a gift your father wanted to give you," Elyse said.

"It's nice and very unexpected," Kelsey said, wrapping her arm around her mother. "Thank you, Mom."

"I should probably head home," Claire said. "Mom, why don't you come stay at my house for the weekend? Matthew will be out of town, and I'd love for you to come to church with me. You know, my church has a widow and widower support group that's one of the best in the area. They meet every Wednesday night. If you wanted to try it out, we could make Wednesday night dinner a regular thing at my house and then you could come back and stay the night at my place after the meeting. The kids would love to see you every week."

"I'd love to see them every week, too. I'm not sure about the support group, though. We'll see. Where will Matthew be?"

"His yearly golf trip with his college friends," Claire said, waving it off like it was no big deal. "He actually left this morning. They have an early tee time for their first round tomorrow morning." She smiled to indicate that it didn't bother her at all.

"Good for him," Elyse said. "I know the last few weeks have been rough for all of us. He was so helpful during your dad's memorial service."

"Yes, so helpful," Claire agreed. She gave her mom a hug. "Okay, so you'll come to my house on Saturday and stay the night. I really want you to go to church with me on Sunday."

"I'll let you know, sweetie. If not this weekend, next weekend for sure." Elyse sidestepped committing. She already had plans for the weekend to work more to bring to life her dream of making the barn a shelter.

"I'd better head home, too," Kade said. "Mel goes to work in a few hours, and I want to spend some time with her." He held the check up. "Thanks for this, Mom." He gave her a hug. "I'll give you a call over the weekend sometime." His gaze shifted to Kelsey. "You, too." Then he hugged Kelsey.

"I'm staying the night," Kelsey said.

Claire watched her mom wrap Kelsey in a hug. "What about class tomorrow?" Claire asked.

"I've got solid A's in all subjects. The few lectures I have tomorrow are taped. I can catch up anytime."

Elyse gave Claire a hug. "Drive safely. I'll give you a call towards the end of the week about church on Sunday."

• • • •

KADE PULLED UP BESIDE Mel's car in the assigned spaces outside their apartment building. She should be up getting ready for her shift, which started at midnight. Mel also worked for the city of Norfolk. She was an EMT, and damn good at her job. They'd met through work two years earlier and hit it off instantly.

When he let himself into the apartment, Mel was still in bed. Or, more accurately, she'd gone back to bed after throwing up her stomach contents. He brushed her light brown hair back and felt her forehead. "No fever. Maybe you just ate something bad. All the same, I'm going to sleep on the couch. We can't both be out with the flu."

"Yeah, I feel bad calling out sick. Two others were out with the flu last night," Mel moaned. Originally from South Carolina, she still had a hint of a southern accent.

Kade plopped down on the couch and turned the TV on. He thought about dinner, smiling at the livelier parts of the conversation. The unexpected six-thousand-dollar windfall was a nice surprise. He'd be able to get the rest of his sleeve tattooed sooner than planned. The new truck could wait. Maybe he'd just make some repairs to the old one instead.

Chapter 3–An Up-Close Glimpse

On Saturday, Elyse left Charlie with Julia and she made the drive into Norfolk. A backpack with what she would need to stay the night sat beside her purse on the passenger seat. She was excited to see her grandchildren. She didn't get to see them, nearly often enough. That was why she changed her plans for the weekend. Claire had their time scheduled, with little room for a spontaneous visit. She was looking forward to the rest of the day, the evening and Sunday morning with them and finally attending church as a family before she drove back to Franklin. When her kids were that little, going to church together was enjoyable. It was later when they were pre-teens that it became difficult.

She pulled into the driveway of Claire and Matthew's stately home. It was in a gated community of newly constructed monstrosities, boasting grand staircases and separate quarters for the live-in help. She wasn't sure what all these people did for a living, or how much of this was bought with old money. She knew that Claire and Matthew worked long hours to pay for this house.

Claire answered the door shortly after she rang the bell. "Mom, I'm so glad you came." Claire swung the door wide.

"Thank you for the invitation. I'm looking forward to spending time with you and the kids this afternoon and going to church tomorrow." She glanced around the very quiet entryway and front room. "Where are the kids?"

"Down for their afternoon naps. I thought it best you arrive while they were sleeping so you wouldn't be attacked as you walked in the door."

"I don't mind that," Elyse assured her. Her grandkids' excitement to see her always warmed her heart. She didn't understand why Claire didn't understand that and felt the need to tone down her kids being kids. Depending on how the next two days went, coming every week to see them would be nice. And she wanted to have a closer relationship with Claire.

Claire brought her backpack to the guest room to get it put away immediately. Elyse had to secretly roll her eyes that even with a four-year-old and a two-year-old, Claire didn't like to have any clutter in the house or anything out of place. She fondly remembered her house when her three children were young. She was proud of herself for making sure the toys throughout the house were picked up before bed most nights and the bath toys were put in the toy net she had strung in the corner of the bathtub. She remembered passing out exhausted most nights after the kids were in bed.

Claire got her a glass of iced tea and they sat under the umbrella on Claire's deck. It was a beautiful day. Glancing across the back yards of all her neighbors, she saw the many public-park-sized swing sets boasting tunnel slides and other play equipment. It was three in the afternoon on a gorgeous day, but not a single child could be heard or seen.

"Where are all the kids?" Elyse asked. "On a day like this you, Kade, and Kelsey would be playing outside all day."

"The little ones are probably in taking naps or a quiet time like mine, and I'm sure the older ones are at soccer or softball games, or dance classes. Kids don't just hang out in the neighborhood playing all day like we did," Claire said.

Elyse saw an attitude she didn't like displayed in Claire's reply. "That's too bad."

Claire wouldn't even address her mother's comment. She knew her mother didn't understand today's approach to parenting. "So, I figured while we're at church tomorrow, we can pick up an information brochure on the widow and widower's support group I told you about."

"It wouldn't hurt to check it out, but the truth is, I'm not sure I'm the typical widow. After all, your father was away for work most of the time. It's not like I miss his daily presence in the house, like others who saw their spouses daily would feel."

Claire flashed her a horrified stare. "How can you say that, Mom? I miss Daddy every day." She clutched a hand to her chest. "I miss our daily calls. I miss his career advice and the tips and tricks he shared with me in creating designs. He was my best friend, and I just can't help but feel so incredibly sad."

Elyse knew that Claire and Tim spoke often. She had no idea it was daily. They worked for the same firm, Kensington-Laramie. Tim was a partner. Claire was an associate. She covered Claire's hand with her own and gave it a reassuring squeeze. "Oh, honey, I know you're sad. And I know you were very close to your father, but he wouldn't want you to feel this sad." Maybe Claire was the one who needed the bereavement support group. She wouldn't mention that.

"How are you putting on a brave face and trudging through?" Claire asked.

"You just have to, honey." Though Elyse really didn't feel like she was, or that she had to.

· · · ·

CLAIRE PUT THE CAR in park in front of the megachurch. The building was even bigger than Elyse remembered it being. There had to be over a thousand cars in the parking lot, and there was a stream of people moving towards the building that looked like something out of a Godzilla movie. Claire got the two children from their car seats. Elyse held Aiden's hand as he excitedly pulled her towards the church. She was thrilled to see his eagerness to go to church.

Once inside the large, vaulted atrium that was packed with people hustling in all directions, Aiden pulled her towards the staircase that led downstairs. The doors to the theater were in front of them and she knew entering there put them at ground level. There were no seats downstairs.

"Do you want to come with me to check the kids into their programs?" Claire asked.

"What do you mean, their programs?"

"The children go to age-appropriate classrooms for the church service. It's better this way. They get the sermon on their level. We get to enjoy a church service without too many kids fussing and disrupting the message for us."

Elyse was disappointed. Claire didn't even attend church with her children. They were checked into children's programs, probably nothing more than babysitting. "Yes, I'd love to come down and see these age-appropriate classrooms." She tried very hard to keep the attitude from her voice. She saw this as one more opportunity for Claire to shift the care of her children to someone else.

The wide hallway the stairs emptied into was loud and chaotic. Children of all ages, and many parents, chatted as they went into different rooms. Two pre-teen boys ran up from behind, nearly knocking Aiden over. Elyse pulled him closer to herself.

As they passed the first room, Elyse was shocked to see at least three dozen children within, appearing to be around the age of twelve. A glance at the sign above the door confirmed that age group. It was the room the boys ran into. There were bean bag chairs and a rug, overflowing with the kids. The two boys were already on the far side of the room, near a drum kit and several guitars. This was a Sunday school program? It seemed to Elyse that the inmates had taken over the asylum.

At the door to the room clearly marked 'Two to Four Year Olds' Aiden broke free and ran in, greeting the adult women within with hugs. Emma required a little more coaxing from Claire to go in. Elyse watched Claire sign them in. She was handed what looked like a restaurant pager, and then she thanked the young woman. Elyse took in the room. It had the rug, tables with art supplies, bins of toys, and even a playhouse.

"That's it. They're all checked in," Claire said with a smile. "I'll get notified by this, if there are any issues with the kids. Otherwise, I know they're doing fine." She pointed back down the hall towards the stairs. "Let's go find seats in the auditorium."

Elyse rolled her eyes at Claire's back as she followed her, dodging the many kids who were still streaming down the stairs. She didn't correct her daughter that the place in the church where weekly services took place was called a sanctuary. In Elyse's mind, a sanctuary was a sacred place with an altar to God. The word auditorium brought images of the girls' dance recitals and school concerts. She'd never had these thoughts when she'd attended church with Claire's family on holidays in the past.

They took seats on the main level in the auditorium and Elyse tried to relax and not judge. The stage was always decorated so nicely for the holidays, Easter Sunday, Mother's Day, or Christmas. Today, she noticed, it looked just like the stage of the last concert she'd attended.

The service started with music as a steady line of people entered through the many doors on the four levels of the auditorium. It soon became as crowded as it was for holiday services. That surprised Elyse quite a bit. The church they attended in Franklin was only crowded on holidays.

The other thing that surprised her was that she enjoyed the service. The lyrics for all the songs were displayed on the two large screens that were on either side of the stage. The sermon message from the good-looking young pastor was of finding your joy in everyday moments and being thankful to God for those moments. It was as though he spoke directly to Elyse.

A grand purpose was not needed. It was the little things that made life grand. Wow. She realized that somewhere along the way, she'd forgotten that. The shelter she was trying to create didn't need to be grand. It just needed to serve the animals she wanted to help find homes for. She exited the auditorium, feeling a new sense of peace regarding her plans for the shelter.

"This way, Mom," Claire said as Elyse headed towards the stairs to retrieve the children. She pointed towards the far end of the building. "I figured we'd swing through the outreach booths for the different groups on our way to the coffee shop. I normally meet a few friends there after the service."

"Oh, okay," Elyse said, following her. She thought how nice it was that Claire and a few friends got together after the service. Only then did Elyse notice all the small booths set up along the corridor, displaying different opportunities to join groups at the church. There had to be fifty of them.

Claire ushered her up to one manned by two older women. The banner read 'Widow and Widower Support Group'. "Hello," Claire greeted. "This is my mother, Elyse. She's not a member of the church. She attends occasionally with my family, who are members. We recently lost my father, and I told her about your group."

"Hello, and welcome," one woman said with a small smile. She had to be in her late sixties. "I'm so sorry for your loss."

"Thank you," Elyse said. She had to wonder if she'd be the youngest person there, should she attend a meeting.

"I'm Annie Edison, one of the group's moderators." She reached a hand towards Elyse.

Elyse shook her hand. "Hi, Annie. It's nice to meet you."

"We welcome all to our group, church members and nonmembers alike." She handed Elyse a brochure. "This will tell you about us, where in the church we meet and when each week. We've got a good group of people in all stages of the mourning process. Most find our group to be helpful."

"I'm sure," Elyse replied. "I live in Franklin, but all three of my children live in Norfolk. I'm not sure I could commit to coming every Wednesday. Would that be a problem?"

"No, not at all. We have a lot of members of our group who travel for work and only come when they can. Or they come and go as needed, kind of a check-in type of thing when they feel stuck in one of the stages of grief. I always ask someone who is going to try the meeting to commit to two meetings and then evaluate how they feel about it. We're religious-based, but our meetings aren't like a service." Annie smiled.

"Okay, well, thank you," Elyse said.

"I hope to see you Wednesday night," Annie said.

"Yes, maybe," Elyse said.

Elyse walked with Claire through the maze of people, noticing the group names on the other booths and the people clustered around them. Three booths side by side caught her eye: Alcoholics Anonymous, Al-Anon, Al-ateen. That wasn't very anonymous or discreet, picking up literature and talking with program coordinators here in the open.

They arrived at the coffee shop. "This is pretty nice, a coffee shop and food court right here at the church," she said. On previous visits to the church, they'd never come to this wing. She'd had no idea all this was here.

"This is one of the many things I like about this church,"
Claire said. "It makes it more of a gathering place, and given
that everyone is so busy, it's convenient. Many moms I know
with older children pick their kids up from daycare or sports
practices and only have a half-hour or so until their child's
choir practice or their meeting here on a weeknight. They
can get a quick dinner for themselves and their kids at the
food court. Or they can have lunch here after Sunday church
before running and doing whatever their busy day brings."

"I can see how that would be convenient," Elyse agreed.
"How long will the childcare program downstairs keep the
kids?"

"It's not childcare. It's Sunday School and worship
services that are age-appropriate for them," Claire corrected
her. "So, there's the early service that we just attended and
then there are multiple adult Sunday School opportunities
and the children's Sunday School program runs for the next
hour. I'm not taking part in any of the adult opportunities
right now, so I meet the girls for coffee. And then at
ten-thirty is the late service. We have to get the kids from
their rooms before ten-thirty."

Elyse checked her watch. It was nine-twenty. She saw
Claire smile and wave at four women seated at one of the
casual seating areas in the large coffee shop as they entered.

"I'll buy you a cup, Mom." She pointed at the menu sign.
She had her phone in her hand.

It was a Starbucks. This mega church had a Starbucks in
it!

Claire introduced Elyse to her friends. They all appeared
to be around the same age as Claire. All were dressed nicely

in current trendy clothing, sported large diamond rings on their left hands with professionally manicured fingertips, and had an air of wealth. Elyse soon learned each was a working professional with live-in help. Figured Claire's friends would be just like her.

"I run several charities," Elyse answered when one of the women asked what she did. "The one nearest and dearest to my heart is Animal House Shelter. We take dogs in from several high-kill facilities and find them their forever homes. It's very rewarding to save the animals from death."

"Oh, that is such a noble and wonderful pursuit," Jenna, a platinum blonde with dark eyebrows said. "I hope later in my life, when I'm a grandmother such as yourself, I can do something like that and make a difference. Right now, though, unfortunately, it's all about making the money so my kids can have everything in life that I want them to have."

"And what is it that you do, Jenna?" Elyse asked.

"I'm a lawyer. My firm concentrates mostly on corporate and contract law. It's boring, but it pays well."

Elyse was a bit stunned by her admission. "That's a shame you find your career boring. You spend more awake hours there than with your children. You should enjoy it. Life is too short."

Chapter 4–A Life Changing Confession

Kelsey exited from the map app on her phone and then pulled the door open to Ash's Ink and Blades. She'd never been in a tattoo parlor before. She wasn't sure what she expected, but the room before her definitely was not it.

There were comfortable-looking overstuffed couches and chairs scattered around the room, and tables stacked with photo albums that were open, showcasing pictures of tattoos. Larger pictures of intricate tattoo designs were also displayed in black frames all over the moonlight-blue walls. Higher on the walls were knives, swords, and daggers. They ran around the room in rows like a wallpaper border. There were spotlights focused on them making the metal gleam.

A glass counter divided the front of the store from the back, where she saw what she assumed to be the tattoo workstations. Padded chairs much like you'd see in a dentist's office and flat padded tables were beside desks that were loaded with equipment. Kade and another man stood by the counter. She was glad when Kade turned and smiled.

"And here's my sister, the artist," Kade said.

The word 'artist' hit her, causing mixed feelings. Kade had always supported her artistic interests, but she would never call herself an artist.

The other man stepped forward. His hand was extended. "It's nice to meet you. I'm Ashley. This is my shop."

"Hi, I'm Kelsey."

They shook hands. He beamed a warm smile at her that was surrounded by a nicely trimmed, full black beard and mustache. His eyes were brown like the chocolate diamonds in her favorite necklace. His shake was firm, and she noticed the corded muscles of his forearm beneath the sleeve of colorful ink that adorned his arm all the way down to his wrist. He was a sturdy guy, with broad shoulders and a solid-looking torso.

"The design you drew is good. It'll integrate nicely into the overall sleeve layout I've worked on for the rest of Kade's forearm."

She smiled shyly, always uncomfortable when anyone praised her artwork. She also realized they still held hands. She pulled hers away. "Will it? Do you have the drawings for the rest of his sleeve? I'd like to see what it's going to look like."

Ash realized he'd held on to her hand too long because of how awkwardly she pulled her hand away. He took a step back, giving her space. "Yeah, I do. It's at my station. I had to fit your drawing in."

She wasn't sure if he was bothered by that or not. Was she stepping on his toes by contributing art to the design he had created? That hadn't been her intention.

He stepped behind the counter. Kade followed him. "Are you coming?" Kade asked.

She wasn't sure if she was allowed to go back there, but Kade invited her so she followed. Kade hopped up onto the padded chair with no prompting. Ash pulled a chair up next to Kade and motioned for her to take a seat, and then he sat on the round stool with wheels.

She was fascinated by the tools and ink lined up on the table in front of him. He picked up a piece of paper with drawings all over it and held it near Kelsey's knees. She recognized several of the tattoos that were already on Kade's arms. She smiled as she glanced over it. The drawings were detailed, and brought the individual items together into a cohesive scene.

Her eyes met Ash's. "You're an amazing artist. That is so good."

Ash chuckled, and she realized she must have sounded stupid to him. Of course, his drawings were good. He did this for a living. She wasn't sure how old he was. She guessed over thirty. She probably sounded like a silly little girl to him.

"Thanks. Kade and I have worked on the design a lot to get it right."

She watched as he donned gloves and assembled the tattoo needles. He dispensed the ink into a small disposable tray, explaining to her the hygienic and safety reasons behind what he did. Then he pressed a transfer sheet with her design onto Kade's forearm. Her design was now outlined on his arm.

When he turned on the tattoo instrument, it hummed. She was fascinated with the entire process. He kept referring to her drawing as he applied the ink. He chatted with them both as he worked on the design, pausing to wipe the excess ink and blood from Kade's arm.

After a half-hour of small talk, Ashley paused. "What do you think of it so far?" he asked Kelsey.

She smiled shyly, her eyes locked with his. "It's really cool to see my design come to life on his arm." Her eyes shifted to Kade. "Doesn't that hurt?"

Kade chuckled. "It's a different kind of pain, almost an irritation rather than what you'd think of as pain."

"You don't have one?" Ash asked.

"Me? Oh, no, I don't," she stammered. "I guess I'm a chicken."

"Some places hurt worse than others. You should think about getting this, too. I have time today. We could ink you after Kade's is done. It's to honor your father, right?"

"Yes, he died in a building collapse last month. And thank you, but I'm not sure about getting one."

"Kels, I'll pay for it. Consider it your birthday present. It would be cool if we have the same ink to honor dad."

"My birthday was last month," she argued.

"And I didn't get you anything. Offer stands. Today, tomorrow, or six months from now," Kade said.

"Thanks, I'll think about it."

Ash got back to work on it and Kelsey continued to watch intently.

"Have you decided where you're going to go for grad school?" Kade asked after several quiet minutes.

Kelsey hesitated, and she knew the expression on her face was not the excited one he expected by the questioning gaze he regarded her with. "The thing is, I'm not sure I'm going to go to grad school."

"What?"

"I hate probabilities, statistics, actuarial tables, algorithms, all of it. I can't do it, Kade."

"You can't do what, Kelsey?"

"I can't take one more class that has anything to do with it, and I know I absolutely don't want to work in that field." She breathed out heavily. It felt freeing to say that aloud to someone other than herself.

"You're good at it. You're graduating in the top five percent of your class, and you've been accepted to three different grad school programs." Kade was dumbfounded.

"I know, but I hate it."

"So what are you going to do?"

"Not go to grad school," she said, and then laughed. "I'm not going to grad school," she repeated, taking the words for another test drive.

"Are you going to stay at Old Dominion and study a different major?" Kade asked.

Kelsey shook her head. She hadn't thought about that, didn't have a clue what that major could be. "Honestly, I don't know. I don't want to study anything for a little while. I just spent four intense years. Lectures, papers, tests, projects...no, I'm done going to school."

"Kelsey, what are you going to do?"

"I don't know," she confessed. She didn't want to admit she hadn't thought it out that far.

"What about your art?" Ash asked. He hadn't wanted to get in the middle of their conversation before now. "Have you thought about being a tattoo artist?"

Kelsey laughed aloud. "Me? Make a living off of my drawings? That's not going to happen."

"Why not?" Ash stopped working on Kade's arm. His stare was intense. "Your drawings are good. Really good."

Kelsey knew she turned multiple shades of red. She smiled shyly as she glanced away. "Thanks. They're okay."

"Kelsey, why do you do that?" Kade asked. "Your artwork is really good. Stop discounting how good it is when anyone compliments you."

Kelsey nodded, and twisted her lips between her teeth. She saw Kade's glare reprimand her and realized she had relapsed into a nervous childhood habit of rolling, biting, or twisting her lips. She forced a smile as her eyes met Ash's. "I've never thought of doing anything with art for a career. It's always just been a hobby."

"Think about it," Ash said. "I've been doing this a long time and I can tell you; you have talent." Ash went back to tattooing Kade's arm. A while later, he spoke again. "I could use a smoke break. Kade, you up for a break?"

"Yeah," Kade agreed.

Kelsey followed them through the door at the back of the shop into the back room. She watched Ash grab three beers from a mini fridge. He handed them out and then opened the back door. She followed them outside and took a seat at the picnic table.

Kade admired the work in process on his arm. "Man, this is going to look great." His eyes drifted to Kelsey. "Ash is the best artist in all of Norfolk, if you ask me."

"It's pretty cool watching it get done," Kelsey agreed.

"How long did you stay at Mom's last week?"

"Just the one night."

"How was she after Claire and I left? And the next morning?"

"She was good," Kelsey said, and then took a big drink of her beer. "You know Mom. She's strong. I helped her make a big batch of dog food before I headed back. Oh, hey, did you know she took Charlie down from the website? She's keeping him."

Kade took a deep drag of his cigarette. "No, I didn't know, but I know she does like him. He's a good dog; it'll be good for her to have him."

"Your mom makes dog food?" Ash asked.

Kade laughed. "Yeah, she makes these huge batches for the dogs at the shelter she's involved with."

"She runs the shelter, Kade. She's not involved with it. It's her baby," Kelsey corrected him. "She told me she's redoing the barn to make it into a big shelter for them. She submitted a request to the county to build a public entrance on the west side of the property by the barn for the public to come see and adopt the dogs. She's hoping to house eighty-some dogs in the barn."

"Shit, I didn't know that," Kade said. "Good for her!"

"Just don't tell Claire. She'll be all freaked out about the money Mom is spending."

"The way I see it, it's her business. Not Claire's," Kade said.

"What I realized is that Claire seems more upset than Mom." Kelsey laughed. "When Claire was nagging Mom about going to that bereavement support group, I thought Claire's the one who needs it, not Mom."

Kade laughed hard. He glanced at Ash. "You wouldn't believe our sister. She's not like Kelsey or me. She's so uptight and opinionated. I have a hard time being in the same room with her for more than an hour. Her big thing at dinner last week was that our mom needs to sell her house out in Franklin and move to Norfolk so she's closer to us and not alone. My mom has been alone in that house for four years since Kelsey went to college. My dad was never home, traveled for months at a time my whole life."

"And then Claire was like, she'll probably have to get a job now, too. I'm sure my dad left her very well off. Mom will know what she needs to do. She certainly doesn't need Claire telling her anything. Her know-it-all attitude gets under my skin," Kelsey admitted.

"Yeah, she really pisses me off," Kade agreed. He took another drag from his cigarette.

They lingered, finishing their beers and talking. Part of the conversation was Kade trying to talk Kelsey into getting the tattoo, too.

"That would be really cute on the front of your pelvis, below the jeans line and above where most women's panties hug," Ash said, and then drained his beer.

"Really?" she said with a laugh patting the front of the right hip.

"Yeah, really cute," Ash replied. "And wherever you get your first one, you'll want to make sure it's in a place you can easily reach so you can care for it yourself, unless you live with someone who will rub the lotion on you a few times a day. Would your boyfriend do that for you?"

"I don't have a boyfriend right now," she said, partially embarrassed. Her eyes went to Kade. He knew the circumstances surrounding her break-up. The jerk had been cheating on her.

"You're better off without him. I'm proud you kicked him to the curb," Kade said.

"Definitely his loss," Ash added. "So, get your ink in a place you can reach yourself. Plus, you want to be able to see it without two mirrors. But really consider if you want it or not. Tattoos are permanent."

"Yeah, I still haven't decided if I'm going to get it or not," she said.

"No hurry," Ash said. "I'll be here if you decide you want to get it."

• • • •

A FEW HOURS LATER, Kade and Kelsey had matching tattoos.

"Thanks, man," Kade said to Ash, shaking his hand.

Ash then extended his hand toward Kelsey. "It was great to meet you, Kelsey. Make sure you put the lotion on it twice a day, and call me if you have any questions." He handed her a business card, which she slipped into her back pocket.

"Thanks, Ash, I'm glad I got it too. You're a talented artist."

"You are too. Think about doing something with it."

By Kelsey's car in the parking lot, Kade gave Kelsey a hug. "The ink looks great. I wish Claire would get one, too, but that's never going to happen."

Kelsey let out a snort of laughter. "Yeah, I don't see that happening. I'm glad I got it, but don't tell Mom or Claire. I'll do that in my own time."

"Kelsey, you're an adult. You don't have to justify anything to Mom or anyone else, least of all Claire."

"I know. Thanks for paying for it, Kade. I think I'm going to need every penny of that money Mom gave us from that policy Dad took out to live on the next few months till I figure out what I'm going to do."

"Okay, I'll catch you later," Kade said, and then stepped towards his pickup truck that was parked across the lot.

"Kade, one more thing. Don't say anything to anyone about grad school. Until I figure out what I'm going to do, I'm not telling anyone."

Kade stopped and turned back to face her. "Kelsey, make sure this isn't about anything else before you make your decision."

"What do you mean anything else?"

"We just lost Dad. Are you sure this isn't just grief?"

Kelsey huffed. "Like Dad was even a part of my life that I need to grieve. This isn't about anything except I hate the field and I don't want to do it. I knew it last summer, after my internship. I just didn't know what to do about it."

"Maybe a year off to just work will make a difference. Can you delay any of the acceptances to the programs out a year?"

"Maybe," she agreed, but she knew a year off wouldn't change how she felt.

Chapter 5–Ulterior Motives

At dinner with Claire and her family Wednesday evening, Elyse felt the same awkwardness she always did when she spent time with them. It hadn't been that way over the weekend when Matthew was out of town. Elyse could just feel that something was drastically off in the house; or, more specifically off between Claire and Matthew. She didn't approve of their parenting, but it was more than that.

Matthew had never warmed up to their family. He would come with Claire and the kids for holiday dinners, but rarely any other time. And on the rare occasions that Elyse had been invited to their home over the years, he was polite but never warm and fuzzy. Claire always made excuses. He was exhausted that day from so many hours at work, he didn't feel well, or that something was bothering him. Elyse had wondered what kind of father he was if he was always that exhausted.

She decided that if she liked the widow and widowers support group at all, maybe she would take Claire up on her offer to come for dinner and stay the night every Wednesday to see for herself what was really going on in the house. Although she never had allowed it in the past when Elyse offered, maybe Claire would even allow her to take the kids home on a Thursday and keep them till Sunday morning, when she could drive them back and attend church with Claire and the family. It still bothered her that the kids were basically checked into childcare while there and didn't attend the church service. One battle at a time, she told herself.

"I'll be up when you get back, Mom," Claire said. "As you pull into the driveway, text me and I'll unlock the front door." She gave her mom a hug and closed the door behind her, watching her mom walk to her car through the front window.

"Claire, we should have talked about this," Matthew said in a reprimanding voice.

"About my mother going to a widow support group?"

"About coming for dinner and staying in our guest room every Wednesday night," he clarified in that chastising tone that always started an argument. "Franklin is only an hour away. I don't understand why she can't drive home after the meeting."

"Maybe she will," Claire replied. "I thought it would be nice to offer her a place to stay for the night after the first meeting. I wanted her to give the group a try, and she may not have if she had to drive home after. Besides, she may be emotionally exhausted and want to talk when she gets back from the meeting."

"Don't expect me to get home early for dinner next Wednesday. I did this week for you, but it's not something I can do every Wednesday," Matthew said.

"That's fine. I know not to ask you to do anything to accommodate me."

"What's that supposed to mean? Are you still angry I went on my golf weekend? Get over it, Claire. It's one of the few things I do with my friends every year."

"And I normally don't mind. It was just too soon after my dad died," she said.

"It's been nearly a month, and I was there with you and your family for weeks."

"I don't want to fight, Matthew," she moaned. "You were there when I needed you, and you helped a lot. I appreciate you and everything you did."

Matthew nodded and then left the room without another word spoken. This was how the majority of their fights ended, with a whimper and no real resolution. Claire knew he was stressed, so she never forced issues. They both had strong personalities, and someone had to take a step back when personalities clashed. She was confident enough to be the one to do that, putting the relationship before her ego.

• • • •

"OKAY, ELYSE, JUST GIVE it a chance," she said out loud to herself as she turned the car off.

The parking lot had so many cars in it for a Wednesday night, though, she knew that there were many support groups that met in this section of the church, as well as music groups practicing. She was on the north side of the sprawling complex in front of the wing that housed the meeting rooms.

She felt like she was a child starting a new school as she walked through the doors and into the bustling lobby. Annie Edison was in front of her as she entered, and she beamed a big smile at her. "Elyse, you did decide to come join us! I'm so glad." She stepped up to Elyse and offered her hand, cupping Elyse's hand in both of hers. "Welcome."

"Thank you, Annie. My daughter really wanted me to give this group a try and it was very nice seeing my grandchildren again for dinner tonight. That was an added perk of trying the group out." She smiled at Annie.

"They are such a joy," Annie said knowingly. "It was all the time I spent with my grandchildren that got me through when my husband died. There is something so uplifting about seeing the excited wonderment of little children as they discover all of life's marvels." She led Elyse towards the open doors of meeting room one. There were three other meeting rooms with people entering them as well. "And your little ones are just adorable and so curious. I volunteer in the children's programs during service a few times a month and I just love watching them dance and sing to the service music. Aiden hangs on every word when we tell the bible story every week. And Emma is such a loving little soul. We use stuffed biblical figures like puppets to act out the bible stories we read each week in the under-five rooms. Emma knows who Jesus is, and gives his stuffed doll hugs when we ask her if she loves Jesus."

Elyse wasn't sure how she felt about that, hugging a Jesus stuffed figure? But it was intriguing that they actually read bible stories to the kids, and they listened to the music from the service. "So, do you broadcast the music from the service into the children's rooms?"

"Yes, on closed circuit televisions. And we leave on all the scripture readings. But during the sermon each room instead delivers a bible lesson geared to the children's ages. It follows the same topic of what the pastor preaches, but is brought to their level of understanding."

"That must require a lot of coordination," Elyse said as she entered the room and saw the thirty-some other members of the group who were already inside.

"Yes, we have quite a volunteer network here at Flowing Waters. Did you enjoy the service last week?"

"Yes. I've come with Claire and her family on holidays. I don't attend regularly with them because I do live an hour away, and on weekends, I'm usually busy with my dog shelter. Saturdays and Sundays are prime meet, greet, and adopt days."

Elyse quickly realized that the room full of people was predominately female, twice as many women as men. And most of them were older than she was. There was only a handful of women who looked anywhere near her age. A group of four of them stood near a coffee decanter, engaged in animated and friendly conversation. Annie directed her towards them. She introduced her to them and then stepped away.

They were welcoming and friendly. She learned they became friends in this group and socialized outside of it. They ranged in age from two years younger than her to eight years older.

"We're the youngest members of the group," Bonni, a forty-seven-year-old bookkeeper who had been widowed nearly a year earlier, said. "A few of the older ladies in the group were widowed four or five years ago, and their wisdom has helped a lot to gain perspective."

"They're still in the group five years later?" Elyse asked.

"I think a few stay in it just to socialize, and a few others like to be mentors to the newly widowed. You'll see a few are stuck in different stages of grief, though," Sheryl, a forty-two-year-old cop with three school aged children, answered. Her husband was also a Norfolk police officer who was killed on the job eight months earlier. Her children were all part of the music program and were at rehearsal while she attended this meeting.

"Ladies and gentlemen," Annie called from the chairs, which were set up in a ring of three large circles. "We're ready to get started."

Elyse followed the other ladies to the chairs. They took seats in the back ring. Glancing around, she noticed the room had gotten fuller while she chatted with the four ladies. There had to be fifty people in the room now.

"We'll open with a prayer," Annie said. After she said a short prayer, she introduced herself and stated that she had been widowed for six years. "We have a few newcomers joining us tonight, so I'm going to quickly run through our meeting format and our group's ground rules."

Elyse sat back and listened. It would be a two-hour meeting. After this fifteen-minute opening they would break into groups based on length of time since their loved one passed away for a half-hour discussion, each with a mentor group leader. Then they would reconvene as a group to share highpoints of their conversations for fifteen minutes. At the top of the hour was a fifteen-minute break to get a snack and a beverage. The last forty-five minutes would be a discussion period of them broken into another series of groups based on their ages with a led discussion by a mentor.

The ground rules were common sense and common courtesy that showed respect and empathy to all. But Elyse supposed some needed to be reminded not to talk when others did, and to keep all information that was shared confidential.

"For our first-time visitors, beginning with the inner circle, please stand and introduce yourself, include if you work and what you do, how long you were with your partner, and how long it has been since you were widowed."

Two people stood in the inner circle, then one in the middle, then she and two others stood in the outer ring. They all explained what their spouse had died from—cancer, car accident, heart attack. She didn't like having to do this at all. "Hi, I'm Elyse Laramie. I live out in Franklin where I run an animal rescue, Animal House Shelter, so if anyone is looking to adopt a rescued dog, come see me. We have some great pets looking for homes. My husband of thirty years, Tim, died last month in a building collapse in India," she breathed out heavily, relieved that it was over.

"Welcome Elyse," the crowd responded as she retook her seat.

"You will all find that there is someone here who is going through or has gone through what you all are. There are many stages of grief, and everyone goes through them at their own pace. It's individual and unique. This group is here to support you as you find your footing and your new normal without your loved one," Annie continued. "Our topic for the first part of discussion is May Events." Then she pointed to different corners and announced the length of time one was widowed and which corner to go to.

Elyse found herself with eight other women whose spouse had died within the last six months. The tenth person was a forty-eight-year-old man by the name of Earl. His wife had died in a car accident six years earlier. He was the mentor for the group.

"There aren't many of us men in this group because statistically, we go first. That's why I feel it's important for me to stay involved in this group, to help the men who might need advice from a male perspective. Because let's face it ladies, when it comes to taking care of the kids and things at home, you usually handle the bulk of it. I had never paid a bill or done much housework before my wife, Paula, died. I didn't even know who the kids' doctor was. I was clueless."

Elyse couldn't help but smile and nod in agreement. Had she died and Tim was left, he wouldn't know anything.

"When we say May Events, we're referring to graduations, weddings, confirmations and such that usually occur in May or June. These happy occasions may not be what you're up for."

They proceeded to talk about attending or not attending, and how to plainly tell your family and friends that you just don't feel like going and asking for their understanding. They also discussed times when you absolutely must attend, like for a child or to recognize a life event of someone else who is grieving.

Elyse shared that she hadn't even considered not going to Kelsey's graduation because Tim died, but she understood how some people would want to skip a public event if they were actively grieving, which she didn't really feel she was. She didn't mention that last part.

After the half-hour, as they moved their chairs back to the three circles, she found she'd really gained a lot of different perspectives from the conversation in the group. And once the mentors shared the different thoughts from each group—and for many, it included inviting new significant others to attend the events with them—she understood why this group was so important to many. This was new territory for her. She doubted she would encounter those decisions any time soon, but perhaps she might sometime in the future.

They took a break shortly after, the half-way point of the meeting. Elyse was surprised how fast the night was going. They exited the room back into the open lobby area. All the meetings were taking a break at the same time. Elyse stayed with the ladies she had sat with and made her way into the crowded lobby. There were tables with sweet treats—cookies, brownies, and the like—and a few more with water, lemonade, coffee, and tea.

Several of the ladies went to get cups of coffee. Elyse knew she wouldn't sleep if she had a cup this late, plus she had a specific way she liked her coffee, which wasn't available anywhere but home. She made her own custom additive of a dark, unsweetened chocolate powder that was nearly one hundred percent cacao, along with ground turmeric, cinnamon, and collagen protein powder.

She headed towards the table that had the large decanters of water and lemonade, as well as a plate of what looked like M&M cookies that looked good. She had her gaze focused on the cookies as she stepped towards the table and she didn't see the man moving in from her right until they nearly collided, but the stranger stopped her forward trajectory by grasping her shoulders, much to her surprise.

She let out a quiet yelp. "Oh, my goodness. I'm so sorry," she apologized, gazing up into the face of the attractive man who had kept them from what would have been an embarrassing accident.

"Are you okay?" he asked, still gripping her shoulders.

"Yes, just embarrassed. I guess I wasn't looking where I was walking."

He chuckled as he let go of her shoulders. "Your attention was zeroed in on those cookies."

Elyse laughed with him. "They do look good, and I can't remember the last time I had one of those cookies."

He motioned to the cookies. "By all means, go in front of me. I'll admit I was going to snag a couple of them myself."

She laughed again. "I think there's room at the table for us both."

As they stepped up to the table her eyes took him in. He was about three inches taller than she, which would put him at about five-eight. He had light brown hair worn short, pale green eyes, and a smooth, sun-kissed complexion over very masculine bone structure. He smiled as he grabbed two napkins, handing one to her. As he did, she saw deep creases bracketing his lips and in the corners of his eyes, indicating that he smiled often. She assessed that he was about her age, though she couldn't be sure. She also knew he was not from the widow and widower support group. She wasn't sure what other groups met tonight.

He handed her the napkin and then presented his hand. "Hi, I'm Jake."

She shook his hand. "Hello, I'm Elyse. It's nice to meet you." She selected a cookie and then moved away from the table.

Sheryl stepped up to her. "Hey, I wanted to talk with you about adopting one of the dogs from your organization. For my kids," she said. "The problem is, I'm not sure how they'll be with one. Can I do it on a trial basis?"

"Absolutely," Elyse said. "It's called fostering to adopt. You take one on a trial basis and we take him down from our website as adoptable while you're trying it out. We are always looking for new homes to foster. We currently have a small facility where we house up to twenty or so dogs. It's not open to the public, though, for a variety of reasons. And I have forty-some dogs out in foster homes right now and need more to accommodate a couple of litters of puppies that are coming in a few weeks. I have an application in to create a larger shelter that can be open to the public, so we can house up to eighty dogs there. The need is huge. We don't get to rescue nearly enough from the high-kill shelters, and that just breaks my heart. A lot of the dogs surrendered to those places are good family pets, even litters of puppies."

"That's horrible," Sheryl said. "How do I go about meeting some of the dogs to see who might be compatible?"

"We have an adoption event in Suffolk this weekend. All of our available dogs in foster care will be on-site to hopefully find their fur-ever homes." She smiled as she emphasized the word 'fur'. "Here," she said, digging into her purse. "Let me give you a card. You can check our website for the details. I'll be there Saturday from eight until four."

"We'll be there," Sheryl said. "I'm not on duty."

"Fantastic," Elyse said.

Jake stepped up to them. "I didn't mean to eavesdrop, but I couldn't help but overhear your conversation. You run a shelter?"

"Yes," she replied with a smile.

"I actually am looking for volunteering opportunities for some of the vets, to keep them busy," he said.

"Vets?"

He pointed over his shoulder to one of the other meeting rooms. "The injured veterans' support group. Animal therapy is a widely accepted treatment for PTSD and even TBI, traumatic brain injury. Research has shown that just petting a dog or cat lowers the stress hormone cortisol and increases levels of oxytocin. And they found brain activity increased in people when they had close contact with a dog or cat when a social bond formed. It's beneficial for both the injured vet and the animal."

"Are you a doctor or therapist?" Elyse asked.

"No, and I don't play one on TV either," he joked. "Do you remember the fire aboard the destroyer docked in Norfolk a couple of months ago?"

She did recall hearing about it on the news. She didn't recall how bad it was or if anyone had been killed or injured. She nodded.

"I was onboard and suffered some injuries to my legs, and a significant head trauma. This church's veterans support group is the best in the area. I've been coming for a few weeks. Anyway, I've been talking with command regarding other therapy options and animal therapy for our injured service men and women, was discussed. But the appropriate organization to partner with has not been identified yet," he said.

This was unexpected and the prospect of her organization partnering with the United States Navy or an offshoot of it to help wounded veterans was an exciting thought. Who would have predicted that attending this meeting tonight could lead to new fosters, new homes for adopted dogs, or even the possibility of an influx of volunteers by partnering with another organization?

She reached into her purse and pulled out another card. "Please take my card and take a look at my organization. My email and phone number are on the card also. Don't hesitate to reach out if you have any questions."

His eyes scanned the card. "Elyse Laramie," he read with a smile. "I'll most definitely be in touch."

"I look forward to discussing it further with you," she said, not even sure if he had the authority to discuss it on behalf of the Navy, or whatever group would officially be sponsoring such an outreach or partnering. But he was a starting point.

The break was over, and the masses moved back within the four meeting rooms. Even though she sat in a bereavement support group, Elyse felt downright giddy from her conversation with Jake, only then realizing she didn't get his last name. For some reason, she took him at face value. What would he have to gain from lying? She then suddenly realized she should probably discover what other groups met that night. For all she knew, there could be a compulsive liar's group that he was a part of in the next room.

After the meeting, she approached Annie Edison. "This was a good meeting. I will be back, though I'm not sure of my schedule yet for next week."

"I'm so glad you found value in it," Annie said.

"Can I ask you what other groups meet in this area tonight?"

"Well, there's the veterans' group in room two, and Al-Anon in room three. The last group in room four is the divorce support group. Wednesday evenings are the self-help, support group meetings. The other, more social, groups typically meet every other week on different days."

Elyse felt relieved to hear the run-down on the groups. "I was just curious, thank you."

Elyse drove back to Claire's, still energized from the meeting. It was only nine o'clock. She could easily drive home to Franklin after a meeting, if she continued to come. She would still go to Claire's for dinner before a meeting so she could see her grandchildren, and hopefully form a closer relationship with Claire. The truth was, Claire and Tim had always been close, closer than she was with Claire. Unfortunately, due to Elyse often being overwhelmed with basically being a single parent, Claire, being the oldest, got the least of her attention when both Kade and Kelsey were young. She wasn't sure if she could remedy that now, but she'd like to try.

She put the car in park and texted Claire as requested. Many lights shone through the windows. It looked like the whole house was still awake. As she walked up the brick sidewalk towards the front door, one of the three garage doors opened, spilling light onto the driveway. Matthew's car pulled into the driveway and into the garage as Claire swung the front door open.

"Hi, Mom. How was the meeting?"

Elyse glanced between Claire and the now-closing garage door. "It was fine. Where was Matthew coming home from?"

"He had to go back to the office really quick," Claire said in a dismissive way. "He's going to work from home in the morning and forgot a few things he'll need for a video meeting he has scheduled."

Elyse found it odd. Wasn't everything pretty much on computers these days? And when Matthew came into the house empty-handed from the garage, her suspicion grew. She checked her watch. It was nine-twenty. Where would he have gone in the evening that Claire didn't want to tell her about? Unless Claire didn't know.

"How was your meeting?" he asked Elyse.

"It was good, thank you for asking," she replied.

Claire led her to the kitchen. "Would you like to have a cup of herbal tea with me before bed, Mom?"

"That would be nice," Elyse said, welcoming the opportunity to have another conversation with her daughter. Then she caught sight of Matthew heading towards their first-floor master bedroom suite. He didn't say a word to either one of them.

Elyse took a seat on one of the high stools that lined the island while Claire turned on a kettle on the stove. "I preheated it in case you'd want a cup. It should only take a minute to heat it back up." She presented a box with a dozen herbal tea varieties.

Elyse chose a strawberry pomegranate. "The support group was helpful," she said. "There are people in all stages of coping with the loss of a spouse. I met a woman, younger than me, who is a Norfolk police officer. Her husband also was. He was killed in the line of duty last year. She has three school-aged children. The people attending the meeting are not all older, as I assumed they'd be."

"That's terrible. That poor woman," Claire said. "It makes you grateful for what you have. I'm sure she cannot afford a nanny on a cop's salary. I don't know how in the world, with her job, she can be a single parent."

"Being a single parent is hard, no matter the circumstances," Elyse replied. "Before Kade was born, I worked when you were a baby while Dad was finishing school. He started traveling about six months before Kade was born. Your father was gone all the time, for weeks or a month at a time. It was hard. And after Kade was born and your father was gone, I was left with a newborn and a two-year-old."

"Mom, you cannot even compare yourself to a single parent. You had Dad!" Her tone was scolding.

"Who was never home. And you have to remember, that was at the very beginning of the internet and email use becoming common. We certainly didn't have a computer, access to the internet, or email accounts. I think you were in kindergarten before we got a computer and internet service."

"But there were phones, and I remember Dad calling all the time when I was little."

"Once every week or two," Elyse corrected her. "There were few cell phones back then. And they were expensive.

Dad didn't have one. There were calling cards and long-distance phone charges. And times of certain days that were cheaper to call. Sunday evenings after six is when he'd call, as it was cheapest then. And we still had some phone bills that were doozies."

"His company didn't pay those bills? That should have been part of his expenses," Claire argued as she poured the water into their cups.

Elyse laughed at that. "It wasn't back then. By the time you were in junior high his salary caught up with the money we needed to live on, and his company paid for his cell phone so he could call home. There were a few years that were tough financially. I remember one year before Christmas, when you and Kade were little that I had to decide between Christmas gifts and paying the rent and utility bills. It was the first year we were in that three-bedroom townhouse we rented. I don't know if you remember it. It was the place with that park in front of the complex's pool."

"Yes, I remember it! You and Dad only rented that place? I thought you owned it."

"No, we couldn't afford to buy back then. While we lived there I took kids in, providing daycare to several women whose husbands were in the Navy and deployed who also worked outside the home. Even though your dad wasn't in the Navy he was gone a lot, so the comradery for me of having friends whose husbands were also gone, helped. And I was able to save a lot of money, that combined with a bonus your father got one year, enabled us to buy our first home. It was that little cape cod in Suffolk. We lived there for only a few years, until just after Kelsey was born, before we made the decision to move out to Franklin where the homes were cheaper."

"Wow, I don't ever remember our family being strapped for cash," Claire said.

"Of course you wouldn't. I would never have let on that was the case. Kids shouldn't be burdened with adult issues like that," Elyse said.

"We always did so much. I remember always going to the beach and zoo, and when I was older you never said no to going to the movies, fairs, and shopping with my friends."

"We did a lot of free or low-cost activities like the beach and the zoo, going on bike rides, and to parks when you kids were young. And I kept the food bill low. I also planted gardens to provide fresh vegetables, another cost savings for the family. I budgeted where I could so you kids could do things with your friends; of course, by then, Dad's salary finally met our financial needs. But I still planted the garden every year."

"I hated helping in the garden," Claire said with a laugh. "I had no idea you planted the gardens to save money. Why didn't you just get a job?"

Elyse was taken aback by that question. "Once we had the computer and internet access, I worked from home doing data entry. I got these big batches of promo coupon things in the mail from the marketing company I worked for. It was from a cigarette company, and people would get a free pack of cigarettes for answering the questions on these post cards. It was boring work but it enabled me to be home with you kids, put you on the bus, volunteer at your school, and be there when you got home or when you were home sick, on school holidays, and during the summers."

"Why don't I remember you doing that?" Claire asked.

"I did it mostly while you were at school, or in the evenings after you were in bed. I only did it part time, enough to make the extra money we needed."

"Why not just go out and get a regular job?"

"Claire, your father was never home. How would I have held a regular job with three kids? Who would have taken care of you while I was at work when one of you were sick or when school was out? It just wasn't feasible, and I wanted to be with my kids. I wanted to be the one who raised you."

"Plus, you didn't have a college education, so you probably wouldn't have made enough to afford a nanny or three children in daycare," Claire added.

Elyse was put off by that comment. Surely, Claire hadn't meant to offend her. She was just insensitive. "That's correct. I got pregnant with you when I was eighteen, and Kade when you were six months old. I never had the luxury of going to college. Everything centered on your father finishing his college education and then him establishing himself in his career when you were little. But you're missing the point. I didn't want a nanny or babysitter raising you."

"I know I was an accidental pregnancy, but why on earth did you get pregnant again with Kade right away if money was tight?"

"Because my doctor told me I couldn't get pregnant while breastfeeding you. That was a fallacy. Believe me, having the two of you so close together was not my plan. Having you at nineteen years old was not my plan. I never considered aborting you, though. And I preferred to think of you as a surprise rather than an accident."

"I'm glad you never thought about aborting your pregnancy with me," Claire said, clearly shocked by the revelation that it could have been possible. "I planned my kids to be two years apart. I guess I just always thought you had planned your pregnancy with Kade, too."

Elyse shook her head no while she sipped her tea. She was somewhat surprised they were having this conversation and that there was so much that Claire hadn't known. She smiled, though, realizing she had been successful in keeping adult concerns from her children. "But it all worked out and, looking back, I wouldn't have changed anything. However, I would have liked your father to be there more. He missed out on so much of your lives."

"What he did was important. I always understood that," Claire said.

"Yes, it was important. But so were you kids and all the things with you that he never got to experience." She tried to phrase it delicately, knowing that Claire was following in her father's footsteps. "Kade was a week old when your father made it back and met him. He was at an accident site in Malaysia. That wasn't the plan, but Kade came nearly a month early."

"How come I didn't know that?" Claire asked, dumbfounded.

"I guess it just never came up," Elyse said.

"So, did you have to go through labor and delivery alone, or was Grandma there with you?"

"Grandma and Grandpa were away on vacation when I went into labor. I called one of my girlfriends, Christy, whose husband was in the Navy. He'd gotten home from deployment about a month earlier and was comfortable with taking care of his kids again. You'd met him a few times and never had a problem with him. You stayed with him, and their children and Christy came to the hospital with me."

"You left me with some man, some stranger I'd only met a few times?" Claire demanded in shocked outrage. "How could you do that?"

"I had no choice, Claire. I was alone and eight months pregnant when my water broke, and I was in active labor. Your father was in Malaysia and your grandparents were in Arizona."

"That was very bad planning."

Elyse laughed. "There was no way I could know I would go into labor a month early. Dad was supposed to be home three weeks before Kade came, and so were my parents. They flew in the next morning after Kade was born and took care of you until I was out of the hospital. You were with Patrick alone for only eight or nine hours, and you slept most of that time. I went into labor at seven in the evening."

Claire reached across the counter and took hold of her mother's hand. "I can't even imagine how scared you were or how alone you felt. My God! You were so young, younger than Kelsey is now."

Elyse was impressed that Claire understood. "Thank you, Claire. Yes, it was scary, and I so wanted your dad there. It was just one of many things he missed over the years. He sacrificed a lot to have the career he did. He was good at it, the best, and was happy doing the job he did. I just wish we could have had a better work and family life balance," Elyse admitted. "But that wasn't as much a thing back then, like it is now."

"That's true. We're more aware of it now, and things are different in a lot of ways from when Dad was building his career," Claire said.

"And I had some close friends, built a community around myself. That was one of the reasons we lived so close to the Navy base, because those women were in the same boat as me when their husbands were deployed."

"I don't remember a Christy or Patrick. Whatever happened to them?" Claire asked.

"They moved away about a year later. Patrick got orders to a base in Japan. We stayed in touch for a few years by writing letters, Christmas cards. We lost touch way before the internet and email. I should try to look her up on social media now, though, and see about reconnecting," Elyse said.

"That's sad you lost touch. If you want me to help you search, I'd be happy to," Claire offered, knowing her mom wasn't as social-media-savvy as she was.

"Yes, I'd like that," Elyse said.

"So, do you think you'll come back to the widow support group meeting next week?"

"I've got to check my schedule, but I'd like to. I liked seeing the kids today and having dinner with you before it. Though, I could easily drive home after the meeting. It would be easier with Charlie, so I probably won't stay overnight again."

"That's perfect. I can make Wednesday nights one of my early nights and have dinner with you and the kids. Matthew can't. He's on a golf league on Wednesday nights. He skipped it tonight to be here for dinner with you. But I'd like to spend the time with you regardless." She was pleased that her mom had brought up that she could drive home rather than staying the night. That would make Matthew happy.

"That sounds very nice, Claire," she said. She handed her empty cup back to her. "I think I'm ready for bed now and I'd like to get going tomorrow early. What time do you leave for work?"

"I was planning to go in a little late, after whenever you left. But it would be nice to have breakfast with you and the kids. I have breakfast with them so infrequently."

Elyse wanted to comment on that but stopped herself. If her coming to Norfolk to go to these meetings gave Claire a reason to get home early to have dinner with her kids, or if her staying the night would be the reason Claire went in late to work one morning and had breakfast with her kids, maybe she would stay after all. She reminded herself again that she had to broach these subjects gingerly with Claire, and perhaps by her presence alone Claire would make these changes without anything said.

Elyse slid down from the stool. "Breakfast before I head out tomorrow sounds great. I'm glad we talked. Goodnight, honey," she said, giving Claire a hug. She left the kitchen and went upstairs to the guest room.

Claire lay awake in bed, thinking about the conversation she and her mother just had. How had she not known so much about her own family while she was growing up? She wasn't sure what she was more shocked by, learning her mom did work for many years or that they were strapped financially until she was in junior high. Also, for the first time, just how much her mother had to take care of alone dawned on her.

Claire was lucky. Both she and Matthew made enough money to afford a comfortable home, a live-in nanny, and no stress about paying bills or buying groceries or gifts. She realized she didn't ask her mom which choice she made that year, gifts or expenses. Claire couldn't fathom being faced with that choice. Her mother's life had been much different than hers. An unplanned teen pregnancy would do that. Her mom and dad had overcome a lot that had been thrust on them at young ages, and had built a good life for their family. She was proud of them both. She was glad they had talked.

She was still awake when Matthew came into the room, though she closed her eyes and pretended to sleep. His Wednesday evenings with his partners at Topgolf were becoming weekly occurrences. She always smelled liquor on his breath, so he knew it wasn't just the golf he was partaking in. She wouldn't be concerned if both his partners hadn't divorced in the last year. That was when these golf evenings began. The question was, did they truly discuss business? Or were these evening outings purely social? Why that mattered to her, she wasn't sure.

Chapter 6 – An Unexpected Call

Kade and Cletus were in the middle of another busy shift. Six hours in and they'd already made five runs to the hospital with patients.

Kade's phone vibrated with an incoming call. It was Ash. "Hey man, I can talk for a few minutes. I'm at work, so if a call comes, I'll have to go."

"No problem. I wanted to talk to you about your sister. I was thinking, her art is good, and since she's not sure what she's going to do and I have a position open, I could take her on as an apprentice. But she's your sister and I don't want to cause any problems."

"What she does is her choice. But I agree, her art work is good. I'd have no problem with you hiring her."

"There's something else, Kade. You're my friend and I don't want to cross any lines. I think she's cool and I'd like to get to know her better."

"As in a relationship?" Kade asked, bringing Cletus' attention to him. "You want to date my sister?"

"And have her work for him?" Cletus asked with a laugh. "What could go wrong?"

"Yeah," Ash admitted. "But I do want her to check out her artistic abilities further."

"And you want to date her," Kade added.

Ash chuckled. "Yes, to both."

"She's young, Ash, only twenty-two. And it's not like I think she's innocent or naive, but she's definitely not like the women you're normally with, so if you go there with her be aware of that and go easy."

"Damn, man, you make me sound like a predator," he said, and then gave a little laugh.

"I don't want to see her hurt, Ash."

"I'm not going to hurt her, Kade. I think she's pretty cool. And I'd like to help her check out her art potential."

"Just remember what I said," Kade warned.

"I will. She's your sister, man. I'm not going to be reckless with her."

"Then we don't have a problem. I appreciate you calling me before her, but it's probably best we keep this call between us. I think she'd be pissed if she knew about it."

A call came in and Cletus flipped on the sirens and lights as Kade disconnected the call. "That sounds like trouble if you ask me." Cletus said.

Kade focused on Cletus, rolling his conversation with Ash around in his brain. "Ash is a good guy. If he says he'll be careful, I know he will."

"I know he's a good guy. He's just at a much different place in his life than Kelsey."

Kade gazed out the window, thankful that Cletus drove today. His thoughts were still on the conversation with Ash. Cletus wasn't kidding. Kelsey and Ash were in two different places in their lives. Ash was nine years older than Kelsey, and very experienced with women. And Kelsey was twenty-two and just graduating college without much life experience. Plus, her cheating ex-boyfriend had really done a number on her self-confidence.

• • • •

KELSEY'S PHONE RANG. She didn't recognize the number, so she let it go to voice mail. She played the message when the message chime sounded.

"Hi Kelsey, this is Ash Vincent from Ash's Ink and Blades. I'm calling to see how your ink is healing. Give me a call back, will you?"

Kelsey's lips curved into a smile as she listened to Ash's message. Wow, that was pretty cool. He called just to check on how the tattoo was doing. She wondered if he called all his clients or just first-timers like her. Or was it because she was Kade's sister, and he and Kade were friends? She had a minute, so she hit redial and returned the call.

"Hi, this is Ash," he greeted, fighting to keep his voice even. He had already programmed Kelsey's number into his phone, so he knew it was her returning his call.

"Hi, Ash, this is Kelsey. Kade's sister."

"Hey Kelsey, how's it going?"

"Good. The tattoo is fine."

"Are you remembering to put the lotion on a couple times a day?"

Kelsey giggled. "Yeah. I'm glad I did get it where I could reach it. That was good advice."

"Do you like it? And are you glad you got it?"

"Yeah, it's cool. I like it. Thank you for calling and checking on it. That was really nice of you."

"Kelsey, there's another reason I called."

"There is?"

Ash chuckled. "Yeah, I'd like to talk with you more about coming to work for me at the shop. I think you're a talented artist, and if you'd like to try it out I'd take you on as my apprentice and teach you how to be a tattoo artist. You said you weren't sure what you wanted to do instead of grad school, and I thought you might want to try this out." He breathed out hard and waited, hoping she wouldn't shoot him down flat.

"Wow, um, I don't know what to say. I don't know."

"When can you stop by the shop so we can talk some more about it?" He waited. She was quiet for a few moments longer than he would have liked. "Unless you've figured out what you're going to do."

"No, I haven't figured anything out. Yeah, I'll come talk with you."

"When can you drop by?" he pressed.

"I'll be near there this afternoon. I guess I could come by around four if that works for you."

"Cool, yeah, four is good. Kade said you have a sketch pad full of your drawings. Bring it with. Oh, and if the door is locked when you get there, call or text me."

"Um, okay. If you're not open then, I can come another time."

"No, we open around then. I'll be there."

"Okay, great. Thanks. I'll see you then," she said. Then she said her goodbye and ended the call. That was weird. She couldn't believe he really wanted her to work for him. Her drawings were okay, but they weren't that good.

• • • •

KELSEY PARKED IN THE same place she had the first time she met Kade at this tattoo parlor. She checked her hair and makeup in the rearview mirror and swiped some tinted lip gloss on her lips. She grabbed her purse and her sketch pad and then got out of the car. It was the only one in this section of the lot.

The door was locked when she tugged on it, but before she could pull her phone from her jeans pocket Ash appeared at the door. He unlocked it and opened it, greeting her with a smile. "Hi, thanks for coming," he said as he motioned her in. He locked the door behind her.

No one else was in the store. Kelsey glanced around wondering why he relocked the door. And where were the others who worked here?

Ash motioned to the comfortable chairs in the center of the room. He could see she was getting jumpy. He knew he needed to do something to put her at ease. He sat and leaned forward, his elbows on his knees. He looked her over. She was even prettier than he remembered. He wouldn't even pretend he wasn't very attracted to her. "Let me see your sketch pad."

She reluctantly handed it over; sure he'd flip through it and retract the employment offer.

Ash studied each drawing, making a comment on some aspect before flipping the page, be it the line work, the shading, the color combinations, or the overall balance a drawing had. "These are really good." He pointed to the dog wrapped in the blanket. "This one is so life-like. I'd say animals or portraits are your strongpoint. I don't see much whimsey in your drawings, but I'll bet you drew a lot of whimsical characters when you were younger."

Kelsey smiled and shook her head. She was sure she was blushing. "I went through a phase in high school and drew a lot of fairies and trolls." She shrugged.

"You don't believe that I really like your art work, do you?"

She shook her head, a shy smile curving her lips. "It's okay. Look, don't think you have to do this, offer me a job because you're friends with Kade."

"Let me stop you right there. I'm offering you a job because I have a spot open, and I happen to think you're an amazing artist." He tapped her sketch pad. "I knew you were good when Kade showed me that design you drew. I didn't need to see the rest of these in here, but I wanted to see your range."

Kelsey considered him with suspicion.

He smiled and shook his head at her. "And no, don't protest that."

Kelsey rolled her lips together. Yes, she was about to argue with him. A reflex. "And I don't want you to offer me this because I'm some sort of charity case either."

He laughed harder. "I don't think you're a charity case. I think you need to try something completely different than what you've been studying. You'll either love it or decide the whole actuarial thing isn't so bad."

"I'm pretty sure I don't want to be an actuary or analyze financial risk for organizations, and I'm one-hundred percent sure I don't want to go to grad school."

"Then what do you have to lose? Come give it a shot. I make a good living off it, and you could, too."

"How much will it pay to be your apprentice? I have only a month left in the apartment I share with my girlfriends at school. Then we all move out. I'll either have to move home or be able to afford to rent something cheap."

"There's a vacant apartment upstairs I can let you have as part of your salary. Two of the other artists live here."

"Do you live here, too?"

Ash chuckled. "No, I have a house."

"You have your own house?" she asked, and then immediately regretted how it came out. She sounded surprised or doubting.

He chuckled again. She liked his smile. It was warm and genuine, and his eyes sparkled when he laughed.

"Yes. As I told you, I make a good living. I also own this strip mall; but in all honesty, some of my income comes from my bladesmith work." He motioned to the blades on the wall.

She glanced at them again. "That's really amazing. I've never known anyone who made knives. Where do you do it at?"

"I have a forge in a shed at the back of my property."

"A forge?" A smile spread over her lips.

He nodded yes. "Come on, let's go upstairs. I'll show you the apartment. It's really more of a studio apartment, not terribly big, but it has a small kitchen and a private bathroom. And there's a laundry room for all three apartments to share on the same level."

He led her through the tattooing stations and through the door at the back. Near the door that led outside there was a narrow staircase leading up. She hadn't noticed that when she'd been here before. He went up first. She followed closely behind. At the top of the stairs were four doors.

"Those are where my two other artists live." He unclipped a large key chain from his belt loop and unlocked one of the doors. He swung the door open. "Here it is."

He motioned her in. She stepped in and looked at the small space. It was furnished with a full-sized bed, a loveseat-sized couch, and a small table with two chairs. The kitchen was along one wall, a single sink, a small stove with a microwave above it, and a small refrigerator. There was a counter about the size of a desk with cabinets above and below. Beside it was the door that opened to a small bathroom. No tub, just a small shower.

"It's not big, but it's private and I can make it part of your salary," Ash repeated. "You can paint it or decorate it however you like, if you paint it back white like this when you move out."

"It's nice, lots of light coming through those two windows," she said with a smile. "Yes. I can see myself living here." She looked the room over. "I do have my own bedroom furniture, though."

"We can move that bed out of here and anything else you don't like."

"Okay, yes. Thank you, Ash. I accept your offer." She offered her right hand to him to shake on it.

85

Ash took her hand in a firm shake. He held it in an overfamiliar grasp after. "Kelsey, there's another reason I want to hire you," Ash said, leaning in close to her.

"There is?"

A smile spread over Ash's face. "I'm really attracted to you. I'd like to spend time with you, get to know you better. See if this could go anywhere."

"Go anywhere," she repeated, a doubting smile curving her lips.

"You know, a relationship."

Kelsey had to hold her laughter back. A relationship? He wanted a relationship with her. How had she not seen that coming? And she had been worried he would see her as a silly little girl. Of course, that was a legitimate fear. Jeez, he had to be ten years older than she was. He owned his own business. He owned his own house with a metal forge. Who had a metal forge at their home? He was fit and good-looking. How could he possibly be interested in her?

"Kelsey, say something. You're about to do in my ego," he said jokingly, but inside he felt anything but.

"I'm sorry. Wow." She realized how close he stood. Her heart pounded in her chest. She could feel the heat radiating from him. She knew she was smiling at him like a fool, and she was probably making goo-goo eyes at him. *Cool, real cool.* "I'm very flattered."

He waited a few seconds. "But?"

She shook her head a little. "There's no but. I'm flattered." Her teeth tugged at her bottom lip. He was drawing closer. She was pretty sure he was about to kiss her. That realization created feelings of panic as well as arousal.

"I've never kissed anyone with a full beard and mustache before." She regretted her words as soon as they slipped from her mouth. *Smooth, real smooth. Jeez, just broadcast that you're a silly little girl, already.*

The smile on Ash's face spread wider. "Well, I think we need to remedy that."

His eyes were gazing so deeply into hers she felt stripped naked. She was pretty sure she wasn't breathing, either. And when he gently grasped the sides of her face, the ragged draws of air she pulled in confirmed that she hadn't been.

His lips were soft, his beard and mustache a prickly contradiction yet soft in a different way. She felt his weight press against her, pressing her to the wall. She felt his tongue gently press against the seam of her lips and her knees went weak. Her whole body became pliant including her lips, which eagerly parted and accepted his tongue. The kiss was intense, long, pleasurable.

She was breathless when their lips parted and she discovered her hands were threaded through his hair, unsure how they got there. No one had ever kissed her like that.

"Wow, that was some kiss," he whispered.

She was jealous he had a voice. Hers was broken. She initiated a second kiss like the first. Every part of her was buzzing, screaming for more as she kissed him. She felt his hands travel lightly down her neck, over her shoulders and down her arms. Her skin tingled beneath his touch. When his hands caressed over her ribs as they traveled down her sides, she wasn't sure if she could take any more. She unconsciously arched her back, pressing her pelvis into his hardness, and she gasped aloud.

The kiss was getting intense. Ash forced himself to pull away. "If I don't stop now, I won't," he murmured, voice raspy. Pulling away showed incredible self-control on his part. What he really wanted to do was press her to the bed and make love to her right then and there. But Kade would not be happy about that, and he had promised his friend he would go easy with her. "I like you, Kelsey, and the physical attraction is not all that this is about. I don't want to go too fast, but damn, with kisses like that it's going to be hard not to."

Kelsey smiled wide. That was very flattering. She was glad he had pulled away. Her brain had quit working too.

"What are you doing tonight? Can you come to my house? I'll make us some dinner, cook up some steaks."

"Your house?" she repeated.

"Unless you'd rather go out. I just thought it would be quieter to talk and get to know each other at my place." He paused, seeing the indecision across her face. "I'm safe, I promise. Your brother is a good friend of mine. You can ask him about me if you want. I won't be offended."

She chuckled softly. She didn't want him to think she had to check him out with Kade or anyone else. "No, that's not necessary. Yeah, I can come to your house."

"Do you like wine? I have a couple bottles of this red that goes great with steaks."

She smiled again. A couple bottles? She drank beer and mixed drinks at parties with friends, had done her fair share of clubbing, but had never had more than a few glasses of wine at family dinners. She could see Claire sitting around with friends, drinking wine all night, but not herself. "That sounds nice. Can I bring anything?"

"Just a bag. Plan to stay tonight. We'll be drinking, and there's no reason to risk driving. I promise there will be no pressure to have sex or anything, but I would like to go to sleep holding you tonight."

It was important to him that he was up front with her regarding his intentions. He could see the hesitation in her eyes. Maybe Kade had been more accurate than he originally thought in his assessment of her experience level. She was twenty-two years old, a college senior. Surely, she had slept with and stayed the night with several guys. His invitation couldn't be that far outside of her experience level, could it?

Kelsey wasn't even sure what to say to that. Ash Vincent was unlike any guy she had ever been with. He was truly a man, that was the difference. She suddenly felt like that little girl again. She wasn't a virgin, but she didn't sleep around either. And she certainly had never shared a bed with a guy this soon after meeting him. Her group of friends often slept where they drank–at friends' apartments, her previous boyfriend's frat house, motels–so this wasn't completely abnormal. But this was different because she would be alone with him at his house. She'd be in his bed after kisses like those, kisses that were consuming, kisses that might make her forget to be careful. Yes, this would be something different all together.

"We'll see," she said without making a commitment.

Chapter 7 – A New Life

Kelsey turned onto the tree-lined driveway that the robotic voice from her GPS told her to. Set back from the road was the house, a small, light blue cape cod with a two-car garage on the right side that was attached but set back from the house. It did not appear that it was original to the construction. Two dormers were on the slanted roof of the house, and two more were equally spaced and centered on the matching roof of the garage. It was cute, well maintained, and surrounded by trees.

She put the car in park and glanced at her backpack on the passenger seat. No, she would not bring it in with her. If she decided to stay the night, she could come get it later. She grabbed her purse and got out of the car. Ash stood at the open front door. He descended the two steps from the small porch with a smile on his face. "Hi, hope you found it okay."

"I did, thanks," she said as she approached. She felt a bit awkward, not sure how to greet him.

He solved that for her as he stepped in and took her in an embrace. Then he pulled away just enough to angle his head in to kiss her lips. The kiss was as igniting as those earlier had been.

When their lips parted, he said, "Hi." His voice was soft and raspy.

Her shy smile met his. "Hi yourself."

"No bag?"

"It's in the car."

"Ah, you're leaving it there until you decide if you're staying or not," Ash said with a smile. He still held her in a tight embrace. "Really, I promise, no pressure to have sex. I just thought it would be safer if you stay since we'll be drinking."

"With kisses like those, it's more a matter of intentionally not staying so nothing more happens," Kelsey admitted with a smile.

"You say that like it would be a bad thing." Ash watched her closely. That statement made her tense. "Kelsey, nothing is going to happen that you don't want to. Dinner, wine, conversation. That's it. I really like you, and want to spend tonight getting to know you better."

Besides, her brother would kill him if he pressured her into anything. Kade had warned him that Kelsey was not like the women he usually dated, and that wasn't just due to her age, nearly ten years his junior. There was a sweetness, a naivety to her that was refreshing and attractive.

"I like you, too," she said softly, her eyes still locked on his. "So, you said something about wine."

Ash led her by the hand into his house. He closed the front door behind her. Her eyes swept the comfortable living room. A sectional black leather sofa dominated the room. It faced a big screen television. A few glass-topped end tables and a coffee table crowded against the sofa in the small space. She saw a short hallway to the left, an open bathroom door at the end of it. There was an archway into the kitchen at the right side of the living room.

He ushered her into the kitchen. It was small, but recently updated with granite countertops and stainless-steel appliances. A built-in corner booth surrounded a square table that had a chair on each open side beneath a window just past the door into the laundry room that she assumed led into the garage. On the far wall, a sliding glass door emptied onto an inviting-looking outside patio.

On the table sat an open bottle of red wine, flanked by two stemless glasses. He poured the wine and handed a glass to her. She set her purse on the table and raised the glass to her lips. Ash held his glass out to her. "To new beginnings," he said.

She tapped her glass to his and drank to his toast.

"How's the tattoo?" he asked after he took a drink from his glass.

"It's good. It doesn't itch any longer."

His eyes shifted to the front of her jeans. "Let's have a look." He reached out and took hold of her button. He slowly unbuttoned it and then lowered the zipper, smiling at the silky-looking bright pink panties that greeted him.

She sucked in a breath, shocked by his advances. He dropped to his knees to be eye level with his artwork. She stared at the top of his head as he examined it carefully. His finger gliding over the surface of the tattoo shot pangs of desire through her body.

"It healed nicely. You can stop putting the lotion on it." He placed a soft kiss on it and then slowly re-fastened her pants. He smiled as he came to his feet. "We can both relax now that I've achieved my goal of getting into your pants."

She let out a short burst of laughter, a nervous release.

Then his hands caressed her face and neck. "Seriously though, I'm glad you're here." He leaned close and took her lips again in one of those kisses that made her melt into him.

When he pulled away, her dilated eyes focused on his. A small smile curved her lips. "I'm glad I am, too."

Ash reluctantly stepped back, putting some distance between them. His jeans were tight, painfully so, but he knew he had to take it slow, slower than that. "So, I have baked potatoes on the grill and I made a salad. The potatoes have a little longer before I put the steaks on. I thought I'd show you my forge and then we could sit at the table on the patio. How does that sound?"

"Sounds wonderful." She was amazed he had gone to so much trouble, making a complete dinner.

She followed him from the kitchen, stepping out onto the paver block patio. A glass table with six chairs sat on it. The grill was near the edge to the left, a firepit on the edge to the right. A decent sized yard stretched between the patio and the shed at the rear of the tree-lined property. It was quiet and private. Not a single other house could be seen through all the trees.

She walked beside him across the yard. The shed had a large double door. He opened one side and within was something much like the set of the television show, *Forged in Fire*. He showed her several works in process, his tools, and explained how pieces of steel were transformed from hunks of metal to beautifully crafted pieces of art, as he called it.

She watched his face as he spoke. His eyes sparkled, his passion for and his pride in his workmanship equal to his exuberance towards his tattoo craft. Ashley Vincent didn't do anything halfway, she realized. She felt almost jealous that he found his place in the world, found what made him happy and gave his life meaning. The fact that he had, made him even more attractive to her.

"That is so cool," she said as he swung the door closed. "How did you get interested in metal forging?"

"My grandfather was a farrier. He was also a blacksmith, and made the shoes for the horses and dabbled in blade-smithing. I spent a great deal of time with him when I was younger, before he died, and I learned it from him. He left me all his equipment." He motioned back to the shed.

"I could tell how much you love doing it when you showed me your works in process. You're very artistic all the way around. Thank you for showing me your forge."

His eyes met hers and he nodded in appreciation. She got it, unlike any other woman he'd dated. He didn't elaborate on the connection to his grandfather he felt whenever he worked in his forge, but even that he believed she would understand.

They sat at the table on the patio and sipped their wine as he cooked the steaks. She helped to bring the salad and dishes out when they decided to eat outside. It was a beautiful evening. The sun was just dipping beneath the treetops when he set the plate with the steaks onto the table. The temperature was seventy degrees but would drop quickly after the sun went down. The low was forecast to dip into the low fifties.

"I thought, after dinner, we could light the firepit," he said motioning to it at the edge of the patio.

"That would be nice," she agreed.

He poured her another glass of wine, emptying the bottle.

"I've been pricing hot tubs." He pointed to an area adjacent to the patio. "I could extend the patio there, so the tub would sit up near the house. Maybe build a trellis around and over it for privacy and so I can string some lights. The electric panel is right beneath it, too, in the basement."

"That sounds like a great plan." She sipped her wine. "You'll have to get some plastic wine glasses."

Ash chuckled. "So, if I had my hot tub, you'd come in with me?"

"Of course, I would." She knew she was probably looking at him with puppy dog eyes, because she was completely enamored with him.

After they cleaned up the dishes together Ash pulled two of the chairs over near the firepit, positioning them side by side. And then he arranged kindling in the pit and lit it. He also opened and brought out the second bottle of wine. As he started to pour her a glass, he stopped himself. "Are you staying tonight?"

She smiled wide. "If I'm not, do I not get a refill?"

He shook his head, returning her smile with a flirty one of his own. "No. No more wine for you if you intend to drive." His voice was light and joking.

She laughed. "Go ahead and pour. I'm staying."

"So you've decided I'm safe?"

She laughed harder. "No, I've decided you're definitely not safe."

He chuckled and then leaned over and kissed her. When he pulled back, he poured her wine. She smiled and then her eyes refocused on the fire as she took a drink. They talked for nearly two hours, sipped their wine, and enjoyed each other's company. It was comfortable, and the conversation came easily. But the underlying sexual desire remained potent even without any physical contact.

The logs in the fire were burning down, the flames low over the bed of coals. He had a decision to make; add another log or let it burn itself out. Her eyes were fixed on the dying flames. The warm glow cast shadows on her beautiful face. He pressed a kiss to her heated cheek. When her head turned to meet his stare, he took her glass from her and set it on the ground beside his own and the now empty bottle, and then pulled her into his lap.

The kiss he initiated was lengthy and intense, and she eagerly returned it, her hands caressing over him wherever they'd reach. When he moved his mouth down her neck, kissing a trail to her collar bone, he felt her tremble and heard her pleasure-filled gasps. Yes, she felt what he did, wanting him as much as he wanted her.

He nuzzled her when he ended the kiss, held her tightly and gazed into the fire. This was not taking it slowly, he knew. He wanted to take her up to his bedroom and make love to her, and he was sure she would welcome it, but Kade's words of warning nagged at him.

"I could kiss you like that all night," he whispered.

"I just might want that," she breathed out.

His eyes shifted and locked onto hers. Her half-hooded eyes were dilated, molten green pools of desire that melted his heart and made his uncomfortably tight pants even tighter. "I want to lay with you and hold you. And I want to kiss you like that a lot more."

She nodded, wanting that like she'd never wanted anything.

"Let's go in," he whispered, already moving to help her stand. He doused the fire with a nearby bucket of water. Then he held her hand and walked to the door to the kitchen. He kept hold of her hand as he moved within the house, locking doors, and turning lights off. "Do you need anything from your bag tonight?"

"No, not till morning."

Through the short hallway to the left of the living room, he guided her to the open door that revealed a narrow staircase that led up. Beside the bathroom there were two other open doors, small rooms. One held a desk and twin bed, the other music equipment. He turned on the switch and a soft glow came from above. He motioned her ahead of him and closed the door behind himself as he ascended the stairs behind her.

She came into the space, his master bedroom, which took up nearly the entire second floor of his small house. She saw the large bathroom at the far end of the room that lay on the other side of his king-sized bed. Her eyes, though, were focused on the sloped ceiling which was painted like a night sky, with thousands of glowing stars. The walls themselves were a dark blue.

"Wow, that's incredible," she said. "It's actually glowing."

"Phosphorescent paint," he said. "One of my friends paints murals. This was his idea. He painted my house; I inked his arms."

"Wow," she repeated. "It's beautiful."

He led her over to the bed.

"I need to use the..." she said softly and pointed to the bathroom. And then she stepped away from him.

When she reentered the room he had the dark blue comforter pulled back revealing light blue sheets. She sat nervously on the edge of the bed as he sealed himself within the bathroom. Now that the hormones were calming, she second-guessed coming up here with him. Had they been near this bed before when they were kissing, rational thought wouldn't have kicked in. She was pretty sure she wouldn't stop when they started kissing again, and she did not plan to sleep with him tonight.

Ash saw the indecision in her face when her eyes met his. She was still fully clothed. Other women stripped while he was in the john and waited for him, either butt naked or wearing only sexy bra and panty sets seductively stretched out and posed in his bed. His thoughts drifted to her bright pink panties that he had seen earlier. He wanted to see them again, touch them, take them off her.

He pulled her to her feet and embraced her. "No pressure," he whispered. "I just want to hold you and kiss you." He paused while gazing into her eyes to judge her comfort level. She still looked tense.

He stepped back and undid his jeans. She watched him drop them to the floor, revealing plaid boxer shorts. Then he stripped his t-shirt off, revealing more tattoos on his chest and over his tight abdominal muscles. She watched him with an intense focus, her eyes wandering over his body.

"What are you doing?" she finally forced out.

Ash chuckled. It was low and sexy. "I don't sleep in my clothes." He stepped close to her. "I don't think you do either." He smiled as he watched her roll that around in her head. "May I?" he asked as his hands took hold of her jeans.

She didn't answer. She just stared at him, trying to remember how to breathe.

When she said nothing, he went ahead and undid the button, unzipped them, and then tugged them down her legs. She stepped out of them. She reached behind her back and unfastened her bra. She pulled each strap down each arm and then pulled the whole thing from beneath her shirt. It was beige and lacy.

He found her shy disrobing to be sexier than hell. He guided her to the bed, and she slid in beneath the covers, stopping a foot or two over, leaving just enough space for him to slide in beside her. He turned the light off on the table beside the bed and then took her into his arms. Her body was tense. Her eyes were focused on the glowing stars on the ceiling.

"That really is beautiful," she repeated.

"So are you," he whispered. And then he kissed her again like he had earlier. Her body responded, the stiffness in her form relaxed. They caressed each other and after several pleasurable minutes, he knew it was nearing a point of no return for him. He pulled just an inch away. "Are you okay with this?" he asked.

The glow from the ceiling lit the room just enough that she saw his face hanging barely an inch over her. "I don't ever do this, Ash, sleep with someone I've just met." Her voice was soft, almost pleading.

"I know," he said. That fact made him feel honored that she was in his bed. He knew he wanted her. He had said no pressure several times, but he also knew how igniting the kisses they shared were. When his lips were on hers, he was lost to the passion. Taking it slowly wasn't an option.

"What if we don't work out and I'm living above the tattoo parlor and working for you. This is like the stupidest thing I could ever do," she admitted.

"First of all, all we've done is kiss and hang out tonight. Even if we don't work out at this point, I can keep my personal life and work separate. This isn't stupid. I really like you and I'm very attracted to you, Kelsey. And I think it's mutual. We'll never know if we can work if we don't try."

"We both know if we kiss like that again a lot more is going to happen," she challenged.

His lips tipped into a grin. "I'm not going to lie to you and say I don't want you, but I meant it when I said no pressure. I can hold you, kiss you, and not push for more. I'll wait as long as I have to, until you're ready. But I need to know right now how far you want to go tonight. Do you want me to stop?"

"When you kiss me like that, I don't think about stopping."

"Then don't," he said. "For once in your life just let go and let happen whatever is going to happen." He reached into his bedside table and pulled out a condom. "Are you on the pill?"

"Yes." She knew what she felt. Every part of her was screaming for him to kiss her again, to touch her like he had, to touch her in more intimate places. The weight of his body on hers fueled a desire unlike any she recalled ever feeling. "You'll wear the condom?"

His lips tugged up. "Yes, until we both get tested, but after, I don't want anything between us, least of all a condom. I'm clean, but I will get a test tomorrow to prove it to you." He saw the surprise flash over her face. "I'm a one-woman kind of guy, Kelsey. If we're together, we're together. If we do this, we do it all the way and see where it can go. A relationship is with one woman and one man. Can you commit to that?"

Her last boyfriend had cheated on her. That was why she'd ended the relationship. Ash's declaration was the most seductive thing he could have said. And for some reason, she believed him one hundred percent. "Yes, if you can."

"I don't play games, Kelsey. If I'm sleeping with you, I'm sleeping *only* with you."

"Please be genuine," she begged. She knew she couldn't go through the betrayal again, or the worry about STDs.

"You can trust me," he guaranteed.

And she believed him. She knew this was incredibly stupid, a relationship with the man who was about to become her boss. Sleeping with him this soon, was not anything she had planned on. But he was a good friend of Kade's, which also made her trust him.

And then he kissed her. And he didn't stop. Hands explored over intimate places, clothing got pushed aside, removed. His lips explored her neck, her chest, her breasts. He found tiny nipples and was reminded she'd never had a child. The last three women he was with had, and their breasts showed it. He smiled to himself with that realization.

His hands and his mouth then thoroughly enjoyed her pristine body. He didn't want to rush it. He wanted to make the foreplay last as long as he could. He was surprised when she tried to stop him before she reached her peak. He pinned her to the mattress and continued his focus.

In her head she screamed for him to stop. It was too intense, too much. She grabbed his hand. "I can't take much more," she said. Her chest pounded; her body felt as though it would explode. She felt every muscle in her body tense. "Stop, too much," she said.

"Do you trust me?" he breathed.

"Yes," she moaned.

"Then trust me to make you feel good."

An incredible sensation washed over her and crashed into her, an explosion unlike any she'd ever felt. She cried out, saw bursts of light in her closed eyes and the release of fluids felt like she'd peed the bed. "Oh my God, that's what it's supposed to feel like," she moaned, her breathing ragged.

"You mean you've never had an orgasm?" he whispered, shocked it could be the case.

"If that was one, I guess not," she said, still breathing heavy. "I thought I had, but I've never felt anything that good before."

A smile filled Ash's face. He knew she was genuine. He would never think she lied or was trying to build up his ego. That declaration by her was enough to make him feel like a sex god. A sense of pride washed over him. He had given her her first orgasm ever.

Then another thought crossed his mind. "Are you a virgin?"

"No, I just never felt that before."

He kissed her again, sheathed his hard member with the latex, and then pressed into her tight, drenched heat. It was an out of body experience for him. He tried to angle, so he'd hit her g-spot. He tried to focus on her and make it good for her, but the mind-blowing sensation of being buried in her superseded his thoughts. He became mindlessly lost in her. He finished before he could give it more thought. His own orgasm was intense, making him dizzy and numbing his mind.

He found his face buried in her neck. He lay, joined with her, breathless, and sated. Then he realized she hadn't orgasmed again during the act. He kissed her again and then pulled out and lowered his mouth to the V of her legs. He found her wet, her clit swollen. It didn't take long for her to cry out in another hard orgasm from his intimate kisses.

Then he crawled up her and held her, reveling in the sensation of his body wrapped around hers. Thoughts weren't necessary, nor were words. She was his, and that was a powerful feeling. Contentment washed over him, and he drifted into a peaceful and relaxed slumber.

She stared at the glowing stars on the ceiling, her mind reeling from the orgasms she'd just experienced. How come she'd never felt anything like that before? She heard and felt Ash's quiet breathing against her ear. His whole body was wrapped around hers, holding her tightly, possessively. She truly felt she was his from how he held her, which was a feeling she had never experienced before. His words about commitment and what a relationship was to him–one man one woman—came back to her. No, Ashley Vincent didn't do anything half way.

Her hands caressed his muscled back. She remained awake long after she knew he was asleep. She enjoyed how he held her, appreciated the closeness, and felt good about her decision to sleep with him. She hadn't wanted another relationship yet, had still felt the hurt from how the last one ended, but she felt she could trust Ash with her heart. He was a good guy, a committed guy, and it showed in everything he did. Those were the last thoughts she had before she, too, drifted off to sleep.

When Kelsey awoke, her back was firmly against Ash's chest, his arms were wrapped around her, their legs were entwined. Light flooded the room through the sheer curtains.

She pulled just enough away from him to roll to her back. Her stirring woke him. She watched his eyes open. And then a smile pulled at his lips. "Good morning," she said in almost a whisper.

"Good morning," he replied. His hand rose to gently stroke her cheek. He pressed a soft kiss to her lips. "How'd you sleep?"

Kelsey knew she smiled like a fool. "Good, sound asleep all night."

He leaned into her and kissed her again. Then he pulled back, his face hovering over hers. "I liked waking with you in my arms. I liked going to sleep holding you last night. And I really liked making love to you."

Kelsey's smile broadened. "Me, too." What she really liked was his openness and confidence.

"Thank you for staying," he said.

"Thank you for inviting me."

"Do you think you'd want to do it again tonight?"

She chuckled. "Tonight?"

"I'm serious," he said. His fingers still caressed her face.

"If it's just that you want to sleep with me again, I'm here now and we're both still naked," she invited.

Ash's smile lit his whole face. "Well, I planned on that." He kissed her forehead, the tip of her nose, and then her chin. Then, ever so softly, he brushed his lips over hers. "Kelsey, I was thinking. I don't want you to move into that spare apartment over the shop. Move in with me. Here."

"What? You're crazy!"

"Think about it. I want you in my bed every night and I want to wake to you there the next morning."

"You've known me all of a few days," she said.

"And I want to get to know you a whole lot better. I just feel there could be something really special between us, and I don't want to waste any time while we explore it. I told you, I don't play games."

"We could still spend a lot of time together if I live over the shop, like your other artists."

"You'd spend most of your time here anyway," he said.

If it had been anyone else saying that, she'd have thought their confidence was arrogance. But not Ashley Vincent. There was nothing arrogant about him. "You think so, huh?" *Big talk, coming from the naked girl in his bed*, she thought.

He rolled onto her, settling between her legs. She could feel his hardness up against her. "Yeah, I do. And I don't think you'd want me spending the night at your place above

105

the shop to advertise your sleeping with me in front of the other artists, not that I'd care. They wouldn't care, either, but I think you will. At least until you get to know them."

Kelsey went from turned on to cringing. "See, I knew this would be messy, no matter what you said."

"Not messy for me. I'm just guessing how you'd feel. Kels, I really like you. I want to go all in on this with you to see if we're as compatible as I think we are, to see if the spark I feel is real. And I think you do too. I know exactly what I'm looking for in a woman and I think you have those qualities."

There was more of that confidence. She had to admit it was flattering. "How can you be sure so soon?"

"Just from the short time we spent together while I worked on Kade and you, I know you're a good person. Kind, caring, and loyal. I know you're honest, even with yourself. That's a rare quality in women, trust me. You're intelligent, and you appeal to me on an intellectual level as well as physical."

Kelsey was beyond flattered. She couldn't contain her smile as she gazed into his eyes. "I've never been with anyone like you. I really like you, Ash." She could easily fall for him. "I really enjoyed our conversation last night," she said. "You're easy to talk to, and I feel I can be myself with you."

"How long until you have to be out of your apartment?"

"Three weeks," she replied.

"Spend every minute you can with me here. We'll know if we're compatible before you move in."

She found herself nodding her agreement.

Ashley was elated that she agreed. He kissed her deeply and then made love to her, once again sheathing himself in latex. Them both getting tested was a priority for him. He hated using a condom.

Afterwards, Kelsey lay, contented in his arms. It had been mind-blowing again, and she wondered why she hadn't felt like this with anyone else, ever. The other thing she realized was how comfortable it was to lie there naked. Even though she should get up and get going, as she had class in just over an hour, she was in no hurry to get up.

It was as though he read her mind. "Do you have class today?"

"Yes, a lecture in about an hour. But the instructor records his lectures, and I can watch it anytime. I'm honestly checked out."

Ash rolled onto his forearm and hung his head over hers, gazing into her eyes. "You have what, a few weeks left?"

She nodded.

"Just tough it out the last few weeks. You have a good GPA going. Don't blow it, just in case."

"In case I decide to go to grad school?"

"Or any other education at any point in your life."

"I'll watch the video of the lecture later. And I have one last paper I'm working on. I'll finish it and submit it."

"Can I come to your graduation?"

"Do you really want to?"

"Yes, of course I do!" He watched the thoughts play over her face. "Unless you don't want me to."

"Jeez, Ash, of course I do. It's in just a few weeks, though, and I really should tell my mom and sister about you before you show up."

"I think I should meet your mom before then, so it's not awkward. Surprise, new boyfriend. I assume Kade will be there."

Kelsey smiled. "Yes, he took off for it. So at least you'll be sitting with someone you know. I got four tickets to the ceremony, not knowing if my dad would have been in town or not. He probably wouldn't have."

"I get it. You're at a weird place in your life, about to make a huge change. You have to feel uncertain in your path."

"I'm really not sure if I feel uncertain or not. What I do know is that I'm going to disappoint my mom and my sister by not going to grad school, but I have to do what's right for me."

"Your sister? I understand feeling like you'd disappoint your mom, but why your sister?"

"How do I explain Claire?" she said, and laughed sarcastically. "She thinks she's my best friend, thinks I'm just like her. I'm not. Kade and I are more alike."

"My advice to you is to tell your mom right away and don't worry about your sister. If it's stressing you out, don't put if off. Do it right away."

"I just don't want to add more to my mom's plate to have to worry about. And I absolutely don't want her to think my decision has anything to do with my dad's death, like Kade thought. It doesn't."

"I find it very interesting that you didn't worry about disappointing Kade."

"No, Kade is different than the rest of my family. He and I are close, and he's, he's Kade. I can be myself with him."

"Everyone can be themselves with Kade. He's a good guy, a good friend."

"Yes," Kelsey agreed. "I wonder what Kade will think about us together. Are you worried about that?"

"Kade is fine with it. Kelsey, I called him before I called you. I didn't want to offer you a job or start a relationship with you without Kade being okay with it. He's my friend."

Kelsey evaluated that. Ash was loyal. Of course he'd never have started anything with her if Kade didn't approve. Any anger she may have felt by it vanished. "You're a good person, Ashley Vincent," she said, and then she leaned up and kissed him. "And, I feel so comfortable here with you, like this."

Ash chuckled. "And you really like what I do to your body."

She knew she turned multiple shades of red. "I'm just still so shocked what a real orgasm feels like. I thought I was having them, but it was just the build-up to one I felt. How can that be?"

"I suspect you've been with boys who cared more about getting themselves off than getting you off. We've all been there, but a smart man figures out that the more pleasure you give a woman, the more pleasure she'll give you, and the better it will be for you both."

She was a bit taken aback by his frankness. Even though she lay naked in his bed, that didn't stop her from feeling like that little girl again. But his confidence and honesty were two of the things that made him attractive to her.

"So, when are you planning to talk to your mom? And when can I meet her?"

"I'll see her tomorrow morning. She's doing an adoption event for her shelter, and I promised her I would help for a few hours. There should be time for us to have a private conversation at some point then."

Ash waited, his gaze penetrating hers.

"And I guess any time after that for you to meet her is good. It's a two-day event, so she'll be there all day Sunday, too. What day will work good for you?"

"Where do you want to do it at? Her house, a restaurant? Here at my place for dinner?"

"Your shop closes early on Sundays, doesn't it?" She thought she recalled the hours on his door indicating that it was closed on Wednesdays and closed by five on Sundays. The other days, it was open from various times in the afternoon until late in the evening.

"Yes, and I'm closed on Wednesdays, but any other day that is good for her, if I don't have appointments booked, I can leave my other artists in charge of the shop. I think I'm light on Tuesday of this week. If that's all that works for her, I could shuffle a few appointments."

"Okay, block out Tuesday and we'll see. And Ash, I'm not going to tell her I'm mostly going to be staying here for the next few weeks. I'm going to tell her I plan to move into that apartment over the shop."

"Tell her what you want. I won't say anything to the contrary. If she knew you were going to stay here for a few weeks to try it out, would it be a problem for her?"

"Yes, given that I just met you, it would be a huge problem for her."

Chapter 8 – Adoption Event Confessional

Saturday's adoption event was in full swing when Elyse saw Sheryl, from the grief support group, enter the warehouse through the large, open garage door. She had three school-aged children and an older woman with her. Elyse had been watching for her, Kelsey, and Jake, as they'd all said they'd be there.

"Hi, Sheryl," Elyse greeted, walking up to her.

"Hi, Elyse. This is my mom, Jayne, my daughters, Cheyanne and Savannah, and my son, Wyatt," she introduced, motioning to them as she said their names.

Elyse greeted them each by name.

"We are so excited to possibly take a dog home today," Sheryl said. "Foster to adopt is what you called it, right?"

"Yes. So, here's how it works. You're free to go to each of the pens and meet the dogs. There's a bio on each of the pens that tells you about the dog. With a volunteer's help, you can go in their pens and even take them over to the large play yard, back there," she said as she motioned to the pens and the large fenced in play yard taking up the back half of the warehouse on the right side. "If you find someone you think will be a good fit, I have some paperwork for you to fill out."

"Mom said you have puppies," Cheyanne said.

"Yes, we have all ages of dogs, puppies through old guys and gals who just want a home to live out their remaining days. Their bio will tell you their age, their breed, if they're potty trained, their history if we know it, how long they've been with us, and anything else we know about them. Make sure you take the time to read the bio for the best match," Elyse said. "Puppies are fun, but they're a lot of work to train them. Keep that in mind."

"Remember we talked about that," Sheryl said. "A puppy would be a lot of fun, but we will look at all of them before we make our decision."

Elyse sent them into the row of pens just as Kelsey arrived. Kelsey knew all the volunteers, so she greeted them as she entered while making her way to her mom. They shared a quick embrace.

"Sorry I'm late," she said.

She'd stayed at Ash's place the night before and they'd lingered in bed that morning. After they made love, they talked for over an hour. Kelsey told him all about her mom's dog rescue and how she helped as much as she could. That led into more about her mom from when Kelsey was growing up and why she held her mother up as an incredible role model. The conversations with Ash always came so easily. The two of them talked for hours about so many topics. She'd never found talking with anyone else as comfortable as she did with Ash. She loved how he listened, really listened to her. And he was open, sharing his views and thoughts with her as well.

"No worries, Kels. I'm glad you're here. I always like spending time with you, and I appreciate your help. We're down a couple of volunteers today."

"Looks like you're busy, too." Kelsey smiled. "I hope you find lots of good homes for these guys today."

"Me, too." She pointed out Sheryl and her family. "She's from the widow support group I went to Wednesday. Please go introduce yourself as a volunteer and let them know you'll help them meet any dog they want. They're interested in fostering to adopt. I don't want to hover and make Sheryl uncomfortable."

"Sure, Mom." Kelsey loved this part of it, watching families fall in love with one of the dogs.

Sheryl and her family met 'the one' in the third pen they entered. They all agreed Bo was who they wanted. He was a six-year-old Border Collie mix. The family spent an hour with him before filling out the paperwork.

"See you Wednesday?" Sheryl asked Elyse as she walked them out.

"I'm pretty sure I'll be there," Elyse said. "Have fun with him." She pointed to Bo. "He's a good boy. I'm glad you picked him."

A few more hours passed while Elyse and Kelsey both helped potential adoptive families. It was nearing the time that Kelsey had to go. Kelsey finished up with the family she'd been working with and then stepped back over to her mom. "Mom, before I go, can I talk to you for a second?" Kelsey asked. There was a lull, and she knew Julia and the other volunteers could take care of the few people who were there to meet dogs.

"Of course, honey." Elyse looked at her expectantly.

Kelsey pointed to the far corner of the warehouse, away from everyone. She led her mom to the door in that corner and then opened it and propped it open to provide light and fresh air.

"What's up, honey?" Elyse asked.

"I've made a decision about grad school I wanted to talk to you about."

Elyse smiled. Given her daughter's off and somewhat nervous demeanor, she assumed Kelsey was going to go to the school farthest away. She had hoped she'd stay nearby. "And what have you decided?"

"When I did my internship last summer, I hated the work," Kelsey said. "The classes and topics we covered this year made me like anything to do with risk management, probabilities and statistics, and anything in the actuarial field even less. The truth is, Mom, I can't see me doing anything in the field for a job. I'm good at it, and it comes easy to me, but I hate it."

Elyse was shocked. "Hate is a strong word." Kelsey looked even more nervous. "You're not going to grad school, are you?"

Kelsey shook her head. "And this has nothing to do with Dad dying. I knew I didn't want to do this for a living before he died. I just didn't know what to do about it. But now that I have to decide, I know this is the right decision for me. Please don't be disappointed in me, Mom."

Elyse engulfed her in a hug. "Oh, Kels, of course, I'm not disappointed in you. You have to do what's right for you."

"I'm still going to graduate with honors. I'll always have my education and degree," Kelsey said.

"You will," Elyse agreed. "Have you given any thought to what you are going to do?"

"Yes, I have a job lined up. You know I drew that sketch for Kade's new tattoo, right? I went with him when he got it.

His tattoo artist owns the shop. He really liked my artwork, offered to take me on as his apprentice."

"Tattoo artist?"

"Yes, it's completely different from what I've been doing, which is what I think I need right now. I'll either love it or hate it. Kade thinks I should try to see if I can push out one of the offers for grad school a year, in case I try this and the thought of grad school becomes desirable. I don't think it will."

"You talked about this with Kade?"

"I'm sorry, Mom. I didn't mean to talk with him before you, it just came out while he was getting his tattoo done."

"Oh, honey, it's okay you talked to your brother first. That doesn't bother me at all." She paused and thought about it. "I think it's a good idea if you delay grad school for a year, for at least at one of the schools. Worse case, you decline it if you love being a tattoo artist. I happen to think you're an amazing artist, and I'm excited to see what you'll do with it," she said with a smile.

"Thank you, Mom," Kelsey said, swallowing her up in a hug. She should have known that her mom would be supportive.

"Does that mean you'll be moving back home?" Elyse asked, hoping it was the case.

"No, but I'll probably come home to visit more often. There are a couple of apartments over the shop, and I get one as part of my salary," she said. "The shop is open late several nights, so it'll be super convenient and safer for me not having to drive anywhere at midnight after work."

"That's good," Elyse agreed. "It sounds like you've really thought this out."

"I did. And I talked about it a lot with Ash, the owner. I had dinner at his place the other night and we talked for five hours. He's a great guy and he's a personal friend of Kade's. He actually asked Kade if it would be okay with him if he hired me."

Elyse found that odd. She wasn't sure what, employment-wise, there would be to talk about for that long unless they talked about the training and what it was like to do the job. She felt better about it, though, knowing that this Ash was a friend of Kade's.

"There's one more thing, Mom," Kelsey said hesitantly. "Ash and I are also exploring a personal relationship."

Elyse wasn't sure what that meant. "A personal relationship? As in dating?"

"Yeah, I guess that's what you'd call it. He's this super nice guy, Mom. Wait until you meet him!"

"There's a reason most people don't date their bosses, Kelsey. It's really just not a good idea."

Kelsey laughed nervously. "I know. And if it was anyone else but him, I'd never go there. Reserve judgement until you meet him, Mom. He's sure we can work out, working together and a personal relationship. He's so confident he's made me believe it, too."

"He's a friend of Kade's? How old is this guy?" Elyse asked.

"I'm not sure. He's older, probably around Kade's age. He owns the strip mall the shop is in. He owns his house, and he also does metal working in a forge in a shed at the back of his property. He makes these incredible blades like they make on the TV show, *Forged in Fire*. He's an incredible artist."

Elyse didn't like this one bit. She knew she'd want to talk with Kade about his friend, which she'd do when the adoption event was over. And she also had to wonder if this guy was the reason she'd decided not to go to grad school.

"Mom, what does your week look like? I'd like you to meet him this week. I have the extra ticket for my graduation and Ash would like to come."

"What if Claire already invited Matthew?"

Kelsey rolled her eyes. "Come on, Mom, do you really think Matthew wants to come or is going to come? Besides, it's my graduation and I want Ash there."

"How long have you known this guy, Kels?"

"Since last Monday when I met Kade there to get his tattoo." A big smile pulled at her lips. She scooted the top of her pants down. "I got the same tattoo that day."

Elyse was a bit surprised by that. Kelsey had never expressed any interest in getting a tattoo of her own. She did always admire Kade's, though, so she shouldn't have been surprised. She leaned over and examined it. "Wow, that's beautiful. You drew it?"

Kelsey nodded excitedly. "It was so cool seeing my design come to life on Kade's arm and then on myself."

"I can tell it's your style. You're a talented artist, Kelsey. Don't take my concern over you working there and dating your boss as a lack in confidence of your artistic ability." She offered a reassuring smile to her daughter who was adjusting her pants back into place.

"Thanks, Mom," Kelsey said. "So, what day can we meet you? We could come to Franklin, or meet you at a restaurant someplace. Ash even said he'd love you to come to his house and we could make a nice dinner there. Tomorrow is good, or Ash has a light afternoon and evening at the shop on Tuesday; he could switch some appointments around. The shop is closed on Wednesdays, but I know you're planning to go to Claire's for dinner."

Elyse wanted to slow her down. This was happening too fast. But she didn't think that was possible. "I could do dinner tomorrow night. Or Tuesday is good, too."

"Great, I'll talk to Ash and get back to you. We'll come to the house if you don't mind cooking. Or we could pick up takeout and bring it with us," Kelsey offered.

"Sure, how about you pick up a pizza?" Out of the corner of her eye, she caught sight of a familiar figure who just entered the warehouse through the open garage door. It was Jake, the man she'd talked with during the break during the widow and widower support group meeting.

Kelsey gave her another hug. "Sounds perfect. I'll text you later and let you know which day." Her gaze followed her mom's back to where the others were. "Looks like it's getting busier. I should let you get back to it."

"Yes," Elyse agreed, anxious to talk with Jake. "I'll see you soon, then. I'm looking forward to meeting him. Don't let my concern cloud your excitement over this new chapter in your life. I love you, Kels."

"Love you, too, Mom."

Elyse closed the door after her daughter left. Then she returned to the front of the warehouse where the dogs and people were. Jake was talking with Julia. She smiled as she approached. "Hi. Be careful or Julia will talk you into adopting two or three dogs."

Jake laughed. "Hi, Elyse. Yes, she was trying her best to get me to take a few home."

Julia laughed as well. "People who come here are looking for a dog to adopt. I merely told him that those two shepherds would be a great fit for him." She pointed to the two German Shepherds who were on leashes, whose obedience was being showed off by their foster mom. They'd only been with the organization a few weeks. Had Elyse not already met, fallen in love with, and decided to keep Charlie, she probably would have taken the two in, herself.

"That's our hope," Elyse said. "I'm surprised you did come today," she said to Jake.

"I wanted to look more into your organization. I'm serious about looking for a group to partner with. I'd like to sit down with you at some point and talk about how that could work, about what needs for volunteers you have to see if our injured or disabled veterans' group could fulfill those needs."

Elyse filled Julia in on how she met Jake and what he was looking to accomplish. She left out exactly which church group she was attending the night she met him.

"Foster homes are our primary need right now," Elyse said. "Are your veterans in locations that would allow them to have a dog?"

"Some are, some aren't. For those who can't foster, is there a facility they could visit to walk or play with the dogs? That sort of interaction would be beneficial."

Elyse and Julia exchanged a glance. The current location that housed twenty dogs was not open to the public partially due to insurance reasons. And it wasn't handicapped accessible either. The owner of this currently unused warehouse was one of their sponsors, allowing them to use it on weekends for events. Elyse wondered if they could use it another day or two out of the week. They could set it up to have a place where the volunteers could play with the dogs, provide some basic training, or just interaction.

"Would your veterans have access to vehicles to transport themselves and possibly the dogs to a location to interact with them? The facility they're housed in isn't open to the public, nor is it accessible. But we could see about a specific day of the week or two where we could transport the dogs maybe here, to meet your veterans," Elyse suggested.

"That's possible," Jake said.

"Maybe even on Saturday nights after our adoption events are over. The dogs are already here. It could be a good starting point," Julia threw out.

"That actually could work for starters," Jake said. "In the meantime, I'm here willing to volunteer. What do you need me to do?"

"Since you asked, follow me," Elyse said. She led him to one of the pens. Inside were two very active eight-month-old puppies. Frick and Frack were the names on the pen. They clearly had some Pit Bull in them. "These guys haven't played nearly enough today. They don't have foster homes. They live at our kennel facility and don't get enough attention. If you wanted to take them either together or one at a time over to the play yard and throw the ball or work on basic commands like sit and stay, that would be great."

"Yes, ma'am," Jake said with a smile.

Elyse went about her normal activities, greeting new potential adopting families as they entered, helping them fill out the paperwork necessary to adopt, taking payments and turning over dogs to families who had applied and been approved. It was always a fun and social atmosphere. They took pictures of the dog with their new family, and she'd upload them onto the website later.

The Saturday event always went from ten in the morning until five in the afternoon. The dogs spent the night at the warehouse under volunteer supervision, as it was easier to do that rather than transport them all back to their foster homes or to the facility. Sunday's event always ran from eleven in the morning until four in the afternoon, when they'd transport the animals all back to wherever they stayed. They were lucky that their sponsor who owned the warehouse allowed them to keep the pens and play area set up, as breaking them down and reassembling them would be very time-consuming each event weekend.

By four-thirty the event was winding down, as usual. Elyse glanced across the warehouse to find that Jake still played with the same two dogs in one of the large play yards. She crossed the room and went up to the fence. "Thank you for all your help today," she said to Jake.

"You're welcome. I enjoyed it. I sure wish I was at a place that I could adopt. These two are sweethearts. I don't understand why they haven't found homes yet." He sat on the ground, both dogs on his lap.

"A lot of people don't want Pit Bulls. Most landlords won't allow them, and many insurance policies won't cover them. Some are aggressive, but it's a fallacy that they're all vicious. The breed has gotten a bad rap."

"I'd say so. There is nothing vicious about either of these guys." Then he showed her what they'd worked on. He ran them through sit, stay, shake, down, roll over, and even kiss, which had both of them licking his cheeks.

Elyse was impressed. And after so many hours interacting with him and running off energy playing fetch, they were both quite calm now. "I think Julia may be right that if some of your veterans come here during our weekend events it would be helpful to us and the dogs."

Jake checked his watch. "You're nearly done here, aren't you?"

Elyse nodded.

"How about we go grab some dinner and talk more about it."

"That would be nice," Elyse agreed. "There's a microbrewery around the corner with a great menu."

Chapter 9 – It Gets Personal

An hour and a half later, they'd had a wonderful meal and discussed not only the need the rescue had for volunteers, but how his veterans' group could fill the need. They'd even be able to help on a Saturday night sleep-over at the warehouse. Jake knew of many vets who couldn't sleep at night. They would be perfect to supervise the dogs, as getting volunteers for that was often difficult.

Elyse took the last sip of her wine. "I look forward to this partnership, Jake."

He pointed at her glass. "Do you have to go, or would you like another?"

"I do have to drive home," she said. "If we were going to stay another hour it would be okay for me to have another glass."

"I have nowhere I need to be," he said. He flagged down their server and ordered another round. Then he drained the rest of his beer. "I'd like to hear more about this new facility you have a permit request in for."

Elyse told him about the renovations to her barn and the permit with the county to rezone the property and allow for the public access driveway. "I can still house the dogs there even if the permit doesn't get approved, but there's no point if we still have to transport the dogs for adoption events."

"You'd be able to house more dogs than you currently do."

"True, but then I'd have volunteers coming onto my personal property. I doubt my insurance carrier would like that."

"Could you sell that portion of your land to the rescue? Then you wouldn't have any personal liability," Jake suggested.

"That's part of the permit request, permission to split my property. Which would make that portion commercial rather than residential, which it currently is not zoned for."

"What do you do about insurance for the warehouse?"

"Special event policies cover that. The warehouse's owner helped with that to cover himself as well as our organization."

"I will say I'm impressed. You have it organized well, right down to covering yourself legally."

"Thank you. What about you? We've talked about me all night. You said you were injured in that accident on the ship. Will you be going back to work, or did you get a medical discharge?"

"That's still up in the air, pending my recovery. Besides the cuts and abrasions that I suffered, which are healed, my ACL was torn during the accident. The recovery time after surgery is lengthy. The doc says it looks good, though. I'm still working on my physical therapy. I have to have full bending and straightening in the knee without swelling before I can perform the minimum physical fitness and ability test that I have to pass to return to active duty. I'm not there yet. I'm not ready to retire. I planned on at least another four years."

"Then I hope it works out for you. What exactly do you do in the Navy?"

"Right now, not much," he said with a laugh. "They have me assigned to the office of my destroyer group to keep me working a minimum number of hours around my PT. It's boring office work."

"Would you rather be deployed?"

"I'd rather be assigned to a ship, be it in port or out to sea."

"When my children were young, I lived in Norfolk near the base and had a lot of friends who were Navy wives. My husband traveled all the time, so it was good for me to have comradery with women who were living the same situation I was. My husband wasn't in the Navy," she clarified when she saw his confused expression at what she'd said.

"Do you live here in Suffolk now?"

Elyse wasn't sure she wanted to tell him what town she lived in, but then she remembered the official address for Animal House Shelter was a post office box in Franklin. "No, my home is in Franklin. All of my adult children live in Norfolk, though."

"How many children do you have?"

"Three. What about you, do you have any children?" Her eyes flickered to his left hand. No ring. Then she realized she didn't wear hers, hadn't in two years since she lost it.

"No, no children. I was married once, for about a minute. She decided she didn't like being what she called abandoned when I was out to sea on my first deployment after we were married. Of course, that was before the internet and cell phones. They have it easier now, and they don't even realize it."

"It's hard on relationships, the long separations. And yes, back when we were doing it, it was different than today. My youngest daughter had a roommate during her freshman year of college whose fiancé was in the Navy and deployed. They talked, texted, and Skyped often. I think she saw him more often than my daughter saw her boyfriend who was still in Franklin."

Jake laughed. "And I'm sure she complained nonstop about the separation. I had a young man under my command request emergency leave because his girlfriend couldn't handle the separation just two months into our deployment last year. He was sure if he gave her an engagement ring, it would patch things up and she'd wait for him. I sat him down and set him straight that this was not an emergency, and if she couldn't handle two months she'd never handle a full deployment, ring or no ring."

Elyse laughed. "She sounds like my daughter's old roommate. I don't know if we were just tougher than the young adults now are or what it is."

"Yes, I don't know if it's all the conveniences they have or if it's an instant gratification mindset in so many young adults. I'll tell you, most of them grow up real fast in bootcamp and when assigned to the fleet. Unfortunately, those who don't are usually disciplinary problems."

"It has to be difficult to deal with that. I'm sure you've seen a big change in the young men and women assigned to your command over the last however many years you've been in."

"Yes, I have." He chuckled. "And it's been twenty-six years. If you ever really want to feel old all you have to do is talk to the newly-assigned recruits. I swear they look younger every year."

"I'm sure," she said with a laugh. "If you're cleared medically to return to active duty, will it be here in Norfolk?"

"Most likely. But I'm not sure when I'd deploy again, so I wouldn't be able to adopt Frick and Frack."

"Oh, no, that's not why I was asking," she defended.

Jake laughed again. "I know. I do wish I could, though. I really had fun playing with them today. I sure hope they get a good home."

Elyse shrugged. "Well, if you do end up with a medical discharge, would you be in a position to take them?"

"Julia isn't the only one who's persuasive," he said.

"Who do you think she learned from?" Elyse asked with a smile.

After they finished their second drinks, Jake insisted on paying the bill. "I had a nice time talking with you tonight. Thank you for your company," he said.

"No, thank you. I haven't taken the time to meet new people and have a good time that wasn't completely centered around the rescue in far too long." She suddenly felt embarrassed at how she'd phrased it. This dinner had been about the rescue, but she had let it get personal. "I mean, we did talk about Animal House, but I feel I relaxed and was more myself with you than I let most people see. So thank you for letting this also be somewhat personal for me." She

127

stared into his eyes and only now noticed that they were the softest shade of green she'd ever seen.

"I thank you for that. I truly enjoyed getting to know you better this evening."

At her car, Elyse offered her hand. "I enjoyed getting to know you, too, Jake. Thank you again for your help today and for dinner."

Elyse turned the engine over, smiled at Jake, who stood beside her car, and then reversed out of her parking spot. She waved to him before she pulled away. At the first stop light, she remembered she'd meant to call Kade. She wasn't sure of his work schedule. She was relieved when he answered and didn't tell her right away that he was at work, like he would do if he was.

"What are you doing tonight, Mom? It sounds like you're in your car."

Elyse laughed. "Yes, I am. I went out for dinner with one of the volunteers after the adoption event."

"Nice. How'd it go today?"

"It was good. Five dogs got adopted, and we picked up two more foster homes," Elyse said. "Kelsey came and helped for a few hours, and we talked about grad school and her new career choice of tattoo artist."

"I was as shocked as I'm sure you were when she told me she wasn't going to grad school."

"I'm okay with her following a different path. Kade, I need to ask you about this friend of yours, the tattoo artist."

"Ash is a good guy, Mom. I trust him with her."

"I assume you know about the personal relationship in addition to the work relationship."

Kade let out a soft chuckle. "Ash is a good guy. I trust him with her," he repeated.

"You know the potential issues with her having a relationship with her boss. It's just not smart."

"For anyone else in any other type of job, yes. Tattoo artists are a different breed, though. And Ashley is a stable, reliable guy. He knows what he's looking for and he doesn't play games with women."

For some reason that didn't make her feel any better. "How old is this guy?"

"A couple years older than me," Kade replied. "And before you get all freaked out about that, let me tell you that he spent his twenties building his business. He's one of the best tattoo artists in the state. He's never been married, has no children, and doesn't go out partying or anything. He's very responsible. He called me before calling Kelsey because he's a good friend and wouldn't cross any lines."

Elyse rolled that around in her head for a moment. "It sounds like he's in a very different place in his life than she is."

"Yes, but maybe he's exactly who she needs right now," Kade said. "The one thing I do know about Ash is that he will never cheat on her like that last asshole did."

That was good to hear. Yes, Kelsey's last boyfriend really did a number on her and caused quite a hit to her self-confidence. "Maybe someone who is more mature will be a good fit for her. I'll reserve judgement until I meet him."

"He's a good guy," Kade said for a third time.

She wished he'd stop saying that. "Okay. So, how are you doing?"

129

"I'm good. Mel is at work, so I'm just chilling at home alone tonight."

"Is she feeling better?"

"There is something definitely going around the department. Mel's been hit hard. Every time we think she's feeling better, her stomach revolts again. I've pulled a few extra shifts because so many have called out with the flu but thankfully, so far, I haven't gotten it."

"That's good," Elyse remarked. "That's rough when the first responders are sick, especially when two of them live together."

"Yeah, I haven't slept in our bedroom since the first night she was sick."

"Have you gone out truck shopping yet?" she asked.

"I think I'm going to wait a bit and let that money sit in the bank. My truck is still running, and I have no payment. I'm not anxious to jump into another one."

Elyse was impressed how responsible and mature that was of Kade. Just a year ago, any unexpected cash that landed in his hand would have been spent immediately. "Sounds like a good plan. I thought for sure Kelsey would spend it on a vacation this summer, but now that her plans have changed she even said she's going to sit on it for a while."

"She'll be okay financially, working for Ash and living over the shop. Hey, I meant to ask you, how was that widow support group and the time you spent at Claire's house?"

"Both were good. I enjoyed spending time with the kids. The meeting was better than I thought it would be."

At that Kade chuckled.

"And I wasn't the youngest one there, like I anticipated. One of the women I met there even brought her children to our adoption event today and they took home a dog. Meeting at the same time is a wounded and disabled veterans' group. I think I just picked up a bunch of volunteers from that group, too."

"Mom, only you could go to a grief support group and make it about your rescue organization." He laughed.

"That's not exactly how it went, but of course I'm going to talk about Animal House like anyone else talks about their job."

"Yeah, I see that. And who doesn't want to support a great cause like rescuing puppies. Anyway, back to the reason you called. Don't worry too much about Kelsey and Ash."

"Thanks, Kade."

"One last thing when you meet him. Take him at face value. What you see is what you get with him."

She wasn't sure what that meant. "Okay, I'll do that. I'll talk to you later."

"Love you, Mom."

"Love you, too."

· · · ·

ALL DURING THE SECOND day of the adoption event on Sunday, Elyse watched the entrance into the warehouse. She was hopeful that Jake would come to volunteer again. She had enjoyed talking with him the previous evening. It had been a personal evening for her, and she was attracted to him. She knew it was wrong to feel this way this soon after Tim's death. She told herself that there was nothing wrong with making a new friend. And she had no reason to believe that Jake had any interest in her beyond partnering with her rescue and friendship. Two adults of the opposite sex could be just friends.

By the end of the afternoon, he hadn't come. Well, he'd never said he would. They'd never even discussed it, but he did know they'd be there all day. She, Julia, and the other volunteers loaded the dogs from their facility back into vehicles for transport. The foster families claimed their charges who hadn't been adopted over the weekend. This was the saddest part of an adoption weekend for Elyse, counting the dogs that hadn't found homes. She put three dogs in crates in the back of her car and left Frick and Frack loose in the backseat to drive back to the building they were using as their facility to house the dogs that didn't have foster homes.

Elyse so hoped her zoning request would be approved. It would be so convenient not to have to transport the dogs back and forth like this and people could come with more frequency to meet the dogs if she had a place that could be open to the public. If that was the case, she was sure more dogs would get adopted.

By the time she got home, she was beat. She let Charlie out, popped a microwave dinner in to cook, and then settled on the couch to eat it and watch a television show she had DVRd. She watched little TV, and she always watched recordings. As she sat, her mind couldn't help but be overloaded with thoughts of her conversations on Saturday with Kelsey, Kade, and Jake.

Chapter 10 – A Tale of Two Dinners

Kelsey watched the windshield wipers swipe back and forth at high speed to clear the steady torrent that came down almost sideways. She hoped the crappy weather wouldn't set the mood for this meeting. They'd picked up her mom's favorite pizza from the restaurant in Norfolk that offered their famous Chicago-style deep dish frozen to take home and bake to perfection. An hour in the oven while they talked, and they'd have a pie freshly baked and as yummy as was served in the restaurant. They also had a bottle of her mom's favorite wine to accompany the pizza.

"You're quiet," Ash said, giving her hand a squeeze.

"Just letting you concentrate on your driving. This rain is crazy."

"It's okay to admit you're nervous about your mom and me meeting."

Her gaze flickered to him. "I know she'll like you as much as I do."

"It's just that I'm going to be a shock to her, much different from any of your previous boyfriends."

Kelsey let out a long sigh. Wasn't that the truth. "I think she'll be surprised you're older than me."

"You mean so much older than you. Kelsey, don't sweat it. And don't feel like you need to walk lightly around anything you'd say to me. I know I'm nearly ten years older than you." He paused and then laughed. "It doesn't bother me if it doesn't bother you, and we're the only two that it should matter to."

She returned the squeeze to his hand. "I know that. And no, the age difference between us doesn't matter to me. My mom knows you're older, just not by how many years, and I don't think it will matter to her. She just wants me to be happy. I think she's more concerned with the fact that I'm going to have a romantic relationship with my boss."

Ash laughed again. "I guess I don't really see it that way. I'll be teaching you tattooing, but any money you earn will be from the clients you tattoo, not really directly from me, kind of sort of. Relationships between artists is common. There's a different social structure in this community than what is considered right and wrong, say, in a corporate job. Tattoo shops are usually single proprietors or partnerships, and friends and family are hired all the time, including girlfriends and boyfriends. Disagreements happen and partners separate, it's all part of it."

"Yeah, that's much different than anything my mom is familiar with," Kelsey agreed.

Ash raised her hand to his lips and brushed a kiss across her knuckles. "Relax. Either she likes me or she doesn't. I'm not stressing about it, and neither should you."

She loved his confidence and comfort with letting happen what would happen. He was right. Either her mom would like him as much as she did or she wouldn't. Ash wouldn't be anyone other than who he was to try to sway that outcome. And nor should he. For some reason, thinking of it that way did take all the pressure away.

"You're right," she said, feeling more relaxed. "And I'm sure she will like you. She likes all of Kade's friends."

Ash laughed again. "Oh, is that all I am? Just one of Kade's friends?"

She smacked him playfully and then leaned over and pressed a kiss to his cheek. "You are much more than just one of Kade's friends and you know it."

• • • •

ELYSE SAT IN THE LIVING room, flipping through a magazine and waiting for Kelsey and Ash to arrive. Charlie sat beside her. Thor and Jane Foster were never allowed on the living room couch, but she justified letting Charlie up that he weighed far less and wouldn't damage the cushions.

A newer, dark blue pickup truck with a cover on the back pulled into the driveway. Charlie alerted her with a bark even though she saw it. Through the windshield she saw Kelsey in the passenger seat, beside a man with a full beard and mustache. The rain had let up just a few minutes before. Hopefully they could make it into the house before it picked back up.

She went to the front door and swung it open as the pair exited the truck. They rushed up the sidewalk to dodge the few raindrops that still fell. Kelsey entered first, stepping in far enough so the man behind her could get in and out of the rain as well. And he was a *man*. He did look a few years older than Kade as he'd said. He looked older than Matthew as a matter of fact, but that could have been because of the beard and mustache. Elyse thought that facial hair added years to a man's appearance.

Kelsey wrapped her mom in a hug. One of her hands clutched the bottle of wine. "Hi, Mom." When she broke the embrace, she motioned to him. "This is Ash."

"Hello, Missus Laramie. It's nice to meet you." He presented his hand. "Ashley Vincent, no relation to the famous composer, photographer, or UK footballer who have the same name." He held the pizza box in his other hand.

She didn't know of anyone else with the name, but she'd take his word that his name was shared as he'd said. "Hi Ash, it's nice to meet you, too. I've heard a lot about you. Please come in." She led them to the kitchen. "And thank you for picking up the pizza. I'll get it into the oven right away." She already had the pizza stone sitting on the counter, waiting for it. The oven, too, was preheated.

"And we brought a bottle of your favorite red blend." Kelsey held up the bottle to show her.

Elyse smiled, and nodded to the identical bottle she had open on the counter with three stemless wine glasses beside it. "I also have beer in the fridge if you prefer, Ash. I know Kade prefers beer with his pizza."

"I like both beer and wine," he said. "Kelsey has talked up this wine and how it goes so well with pizza so much that I have to try it."

After Elyse had the pizza in the oven, she poured three glasses of wine from the open bottle. "I had hoped it would be a nice day so we could sit out on the patio when you got here. Kelsey, you pick where you'd like us to sit to get to know each other."

Kelsey and Ash both shrugged off their wet raincoats. Kelsey draped them over two of the kitchen chairs. Elyse saw the colorful tattoos that adorned both of his arms from his wrists all the way up both arms, disappearing under the short sleeves of his black t-shirt. She had expected he would have a lot of tattoos, and she was used to Kade's, so she wasn't surprised.

Ash looked past her and into the sunroom. He saw her painting in progress on the easel as well as the other, completed canvases she had sitting around the room. "Those are some of your work? Kelsey said you paint landscapes. May I?" he asked, taking a step towards the sunroom.

"Yes, certainly," Elyse replied.

He stepped into the room and looked first at the canvas on the easel that was nearly done. He studied it for a minute and then looked over the others. After a few minutes, he turned to face her. "These are really good. You have a good use of color, and it's well balanced and proportionate. The lines are clean and there is no hesitation in your brush strokes. It's the same thing we look for in tattooing. I can see where Kelsey gets her artistic ability. I should hire you to draw any landscape work we get," he said with a smile.

Elyse laughed softly. "I'm not looking for a job."

"Neither was Kelsey," Ash said. "But I saw her talent in the design she drew for Kade's tattoo. And when she told Kade she wasn't going to go to grad school and didn't know what she was going to do, I suggested she do something with her art. I've been doing this long enough that I know true artistic ability when I see it."

"How'd you get into tattooing?" Elyse asked.

Ash took the glass of wine from her. "Thank you. I got my first tattoo when I was eighteen, drew the design myself.

I'd always dabbled in art as well as metalworking with my grandfather. My uncle was a tattoo artist. He inked it." He paused and pointed out a tattoo of a sword on the inner bicep of his left arm. "This is it, my first."

"That's really an intricate and beautiful design," Elyse said. "It looks so real."

"I drew it to honor my grandfather. I had a very close relationship with him. I have many fond memories from my childhood and teen years of hours out in his forge, learning the craft. He was a farrier who also made swords and knives for fun. Anyway, I was fascinated by the whole process. And after I got this first tattoo, I just knew that was what I wanted to do with my art, and I knew I could make a living doing it."

"Kelsey said you also make blades, and you have them up in your shop for sale."

"Yes," Ash said with a smile. "When my grandfather passed away, he left me his metal forge and all the equipment. At first it was a hobby, but I've honed my skills over the years and now I make a decent living off of what I make in the forge in addition to the tattooing."

The one thing that struck Elyse as she listened to him was that he didn't sound boastful, just factual. He was matter of fact and down to earth in how he spoke. This man wasn't trying to impress her. He was just having a discussion with her. "That's great. Very few people can say they're doing what they love and making a living from it. That's why I was glad that Kelsey spoke up and decided not to go to grad school if she knew she didn't want to do that for a living. Life is way too short to do a job you don't like," Elyse said, flashing Kelsey a supportive smile.

Kelsey was surprised by her mom's statement. "Thanks, Mom. I can't tell you how nervous I was to tell you I wasn't going to grad school."

"I know, sweetie," Elyse said, giving Kelsey a brief hug. "Your father loved his job. That's why I didn't demand at any point that he get a different job that would allow him to be home more. He would have hated doing anything else, even in the same field. If he couldn't go to the accident sites, he wouldn't have been as happy. I want the same thing for you. I want you to find something you're passionate about, and I don't want you to ever settle by doing anything less."

"Thanks, Mom," Kelsey repeated. "I don't know if tattooing will be it or not, but I want to explore it to see if it is."

"And I think you should. You have time. Try it. If you like it, great. If not, try something else. You're young and have few bills right now. This is the perfect time for you to explore what's going to do it for you. Later on, when you have bills and a family, that's when you would get trapped in a job you don't like."

"I always thought you expected me to have a plan—college, grad school, career," Kelsey said.

"No, not my expectation, but you had my support when you laid out that path for yourself." Her gaze shifted to Ash. "Kelsey, in addition to having an artistic ability, has always had this mathematical brain. It came very easily to her all through school. When she said she wanted to major in a math field, I never questioned it. I assumed she loved it because she was so good at it."

Ash smiled and nodded. His gaze went to Kelsey. "I think it takes courage to speak up and go against what you think is expected of you and to do what you feel is best for you. I have a lot of friends and clients who finished that degree and got jobs in fields they knew they hated. Fast forward ten years or so and they're bogged down by bills and have families and feel trapped, just like you said, Missus Laramie."

"Please, it's Elyse," she said. Both Matthew and Mel called her by her first name. She judged that Ashley Vincent was going to be a part of their lives for a while, if not permanently, so he might as well call her by her first name as well.

They took seats at the kitchen table and continued to talk as the pizza baked. Soon the mouth-watering aroma of the perfect balance of ingredients filled the room. The conversation came easily and there was a lot of laughter. Elyse saw how comfortable her daughter was with this man, and she saw the fun side of their relationship as they traded barbs playfully and respectfully.

The other thing that was apparent to her was that her daughter was a true equal in the relationship. It was not a boss and doting employee sitting with her. It was two people who seemed to have a lot in common, who talked and laughed with a comfort like old friends had.

By the time they devoured the entire pie and drank most of the two bottles of wine, Elyse had already decided she liked him and approved of the relationship. Kelsey was happy. She was spreading her wings and open to new experiences. Elyse saw a new confidence in her that she liked.

"I know you have to be curious about the age difference between Kelsey and me. It's nearly ten years," Ash said after he'd finished the last sip of his wine.

It was funny, now that they had gotten around to it, it no longer mattered to Elyse. "You know what, Ash? That doesn't bother me at all. I can see that Kelsey is happy with you, and that's all that matters."

Kelsey's smile spread. "Thanks, Mom. Yes, I'm happy. Have you ever met someone, and everything just clicked? That's how I feel with Ash." She flashed him a smile.

"And for the record, it's not one-sided. I knew right away when I met Kelsey that I wanted to get to know her better on a personal level while helping her check out her artistic ability. I'm sure you had to think it was reckless of me to hire her and want to date her. But for me, my art is part of who I am in all facets of my life. There's no division between work and home, employee and friend; or, in Kelsey's case, girlfriend. And that's kind of how it's in general in the tattooing world. Artists are different than anyone in any other profession."

"That's what Kade said, too," Elyse remarked.

"Yeah, Kade gets it," Ash agreed.

The rain had stopped by the time Elyse walked Kelsey and Ash to the front door. Ash presented his hand, but Elyse pulled him in for a hug. "I'm so glad you two came for dinner. I'll see you at Kelsey's graduation."

"I look forward to it." He stepped back and through the front door, allowing space for Kelsey to also give her mother a hug good night.

"I like him," Elyse whispered to Kelsey as they embraced. "Goodnight, sweetie."

Kelsey flashed her a smile as they separated. "Goodnight, Mom. I'll talk to you soon."

"You two drive safe!" Elyse said as they got into the truck.

• • • •

LATE WEDNESDAY AFTERNOON, Elyse again made the drive into Norfolk. She was happy to see her grandchildren and have dinner with them and Claire. Matthew wasn't home. Elyse noticed it felt much more comfortable in the house. The kids were livelier. Claire was more relaxed. She knew she had to talk to Claire about it, somehow, sometime soon. But she knew that Claire would get defensive and make excuses for Matthew, like she always did. She had not planned to spend the night, which Claire was fine with, though she would have liked to be the reason Claire had breakfast with her kids the next morning. Maybe every other week Elyse could stay.

She drove to the church, more eager to see Jake than attend the meeting. Though the meeting had been fine the previous week, she still wasn't sure she needed the support. Was she stuck in some weird stage of grief that denied she was grieving?

She entered the room and greeted the women she'd met the week before, standing in their normal group. Sheryl and her family loved Bo. So far, it was working out great.

The topic for the group she was divided into for the first half of the meeting talked about bringing yourself to purge your deceased spouse's clothes, shoes, and other belongings. Elyse realized she hadn't even thought about doing it. All of Tim's things were where they'd always been. He had very little in their closet and the drawers of his wardrobe. He had naturally purged his out-of-style and wrong-sized clothing each time he was home. He had two suitcases that traveled with him. They currently sat in the garage. Out of sight, out of mind. Tim's partner had claimed them from the hotel and shipped them to Elyse.

The only thing that was kept in their room that he used when he was home was a bathrobe on the back of the bathroom door for when he got out of the shower, a pair of slippers, and two pairs of pajamas. Tim wore the two-piece sets made of a thin jersey material, pants, and a t-shirt. Elyse wasn't sure if she wanted to cry or laugh, thinking about it.

"Elyse?" Annie Edison asked. She was her group's moderator.

"I didn't even think about getting rid of his things," she admitted. "Tim traveled more than he was home for the last thirty years. He was literally never home. I've stared at his bathrobe on the hook on the bathroom door for so long it never occurred to me that I would need to get rid of it."

"It's comfortable there. I get it," Annie said. "I still have my late husband's bathrobe. I wear it. It's a fond reminder of him. There is nothing wrong with selecting a few items you will keep."

"I have David's dress uniform on a hanger on the inside of my closet door," Sheryl offered. "I'm purposely keeping it. I gave the majority of his things to Goodwill, except for the things he prized most, like his band t-shirts. They're in a box for the kids. He always wore them when he was off duty."

"How long after his death did you go through his things, Sheryl?" Annie asked.

"It was about four months before I could bring myself to."

"We all do it in our own time, Elyse. Your heart will tell you when it's time," Annie said.

"I started, but had to stop," Bonni, who had been widowed nearly a year before, said. "With every item I touched, the last time I saw him in it came back and the trip down memory lane was too long."

"How did you get past that?" Elyse asked, doubting that would be an issue for her.

"I didn't. Everything is still in his closet and drawers."

Elyse was shocked. Nearly a year later? Not that she was judging.

"We talk about the seven stages of grief," Annie said. "Shock, denial, anger, bargaining, depression, acceptance and hope, and finally processing that grief. As you know, everyone's journey is unique. You're here, Bonni, you are going to work, you go to lunch with friends. You are moving through those stages. When you are ready to get rid of his things, you will. Another member of our group had her sister come to her house and take care of that task for her. That is a suggestion, if you think it will help you, but don't do it if you're not ready to."

"I have a question about the denial stage," Elyse said. "I think that's where I might be, because I just don't feel devastated that he's gone. God, when I say that out loud it sounds terrible. We talked almost every day for about fifteen minutes, but I can't say I've even missed those calls. My life is full and, honestly, he hasn't been a part of it for so long." She sighed loudly and rubbed her forehead. "That sounds terrible, too."

"Not terrible, just honest. Elyse, when my mother died, I felt the same way. She lived in another state, and I talked to her a few times a week, saw her a few times a year. The grief I felt from her death was very different than the grief I felt when my husband died. I loved them both, but the impact of their deaths was different. Allow yourself the time to grieve in whatever way is appropriate for you."

That made Elyse feel somewhat better. Maybe she wasn't stuck in denial. She wasn't sure why she felt the need to identify what stage of grief she was in, but she did.

The group as a whole reconvened. The other groups had discussed such things as selling the family home or other property and when the timing would be right. They were reminded that grief experts advised people not to make any major life decisions or changes within the first year after a loved one's death. Elyse wasn't sure how that was even possible. Life continued, and making decisions or changes in your life was a constant.

On that note, they adjourned for the break. Elyse felt sad from the conversation in the meeting when she stepped out into the area set up with coffee and treats. The room was full as the three other meeting rooms had begun break before her group did. She glanced around but did not see Jake. She felt even sadder. She went to the water cooler and dispensed a glass for herself. Then she went for a cookie.

A familiar hand reached for the same cookie she was about to grab. "We have to stop meeting like this," Jake said.

"I think we both have a cookie problem," she said, returning his smile.

"Not a problem, just good cookies," he said. "How did your event on Sunday go? Did Frick and Frack get homes?"

"No, I'm afraid they didn't. I drove them back to our facility Sunday afternoon."

"I wish I could have come to help, but I had duty. They have me temporarily assigned to the headquarters of my destroyer group, and I'm working part time for the command when I'm not at physical therapy or other doctor's appointments."

Oh, so he had worked on Sunday. She was glad to know. "I'm glad you were off on Saturday and able to be there."

Jake's gaze drifted behind her. He motioned with his hand. Two other men stepped up to them. "Elyse, these are two of the guys I had in mind to help at your events on the weekends you have them. This is Fergie and Maitland," he introduced.

"Trever Ferguson, ma'am," the first man said. He was a tall guy, mid-thirties, longer black hair and stubble heavily peppering his jaw, with a prosthetic left arm. He presented his right hand to shake hers.

Elyse placed her cookie atop her water cup so she could shake his hand. "It's nice to meet you, Trevor." Her eyes went to the other man who had stepped up to them. "Hi, I'm Elyse Laramie," she said, presenting her hand.

"Miles Maitland," he said with a heavy Southern accent, extending a hand that had severe scars on it. He was clean-shaven, with a shaved head. She noticed a few scars on his head as well. He was a thin guy with dark circles beneath his deep-set brown eyes. "I was a canine handler in the Army. Mr. Tanner told me about his day with your dogs. I'd like to work with them."

"The rescue would be lucky to have you both volunteer." She dug into her purse. "Here's my card." She handed both men one. "Our next adoption event is out in Suffolk a week from Saturday. Text, email, or give me a call by Friday of next week and I'll put you on our schedule."

"I'll be able to be there on Saturday, too," Jake said. "I'll probably give the guys a ride."

"Fantastic, I'll put you on the schedule as well."

"Can you stick around after our meetings end this evening? I wanted to talk with you about one more thing when it's a little quieter," Jake asked.

"Sure," she said.

Through the rest of the meeting, all she could think about was what Jake wanted to talk with her about. Had his command not agreed to the partnering with her organization? Would the volunteers be limited to whoever Jake could personally recruit? Not that even two more volunteers were a bad thing. She'd take as few or as many as he could refer her way.

At nine p.m., she exited the meeting room. As was the case the week before, the area was chaotic. And with all the people from the four rooms leaving at the same time, it was quite noisy. She glanced around and finally caught sight of Jake near the doors that led out into the parking lot. She said her goodbyes to those from her meeting as they all moved towards the door.

Jake opened the door. "Let's talk outside." He held it open for her and then followed her out.

Stepping out into the cool evening air, Elyse slipped her jacket on as they stepped to the side of the doors. The low was predicted to be fifty-nine degrees overnight and it felt as though it had already hit the low. "Thank you for introducing me to Miles and Trevor," she said.

"You're welcome. They're both good men. As you saw, they are both permanently disabled from the wounds they sustained while serving. I think the contact with the dogs will help both men tremendously," Jake said.

"Are the scars on Miles' hands from burns?"

"Yes. He had burns on over forty percent of his body." Jake watched her closely for her reaction.

She cringed. "That poor man. I've heard burns are extremely painful."

"Yes. But on a better note, I wanted to tell you that I submitted the paperwork to command to recognize Animal House Shelter as a partner to refer our injured and disabled servicemen and women to in the same way this church's support group is listed."

"Really? That's fantastic! Thank you so much!" Without thinking what she was doing, she hugged him.

Jake chuckled as he returned her brief embrace. "You're welcome."

She took a step back quickly when she realized what she was doing.

"It can take a few weeks to go through, but until then there are several other people who come to the meetings here that I can refer to you."

"That's great, thank you."

"You let me know how often and how many new volunteers you want, and the frequency of new ones starting. I recognize that too many too soon could overwhelm your organization."

"Yes, and we still need to identify the times of need until we have a larger, physical location that's open to the public. Once we have that, we'll be able to take on a lot of volunteers."

"When do you expect to hear on your zoning petition regarding your property?" Jake asked.

"The next board meeting is on June fifteenth. I expect the answer after that. I've had substantial work done to the barn to get it ready. We could be up and running by July first if it's approved, assuming we could close on the sale of the property by then."

"I guess I'd better get busy finding you some able-bodied volunteers to help move everything," Jake said.

"That would be much appreciated. As of now, all I have is my son and any of his strong friends he can talk into helping." Her thoughts went to Ash. He would probably help, too.

Most of the meeting attendees had all departed, and there were only a few stragglers exiting the building. Inside, the lights all flicked off. "Where are you parked?" Jake asked.

She motioned to the lot on the left. They continued to chat about the work she'd had done on the barn as she led him to her car, which was parked in a section that was quickly emptying of the other cars that had been parked there. By the time they arrived at her car, it was the only one left in the area. It was parked directly beneath a light pole.

"There was one more thing, Elyse," Jake said. "Would you like to have dinner with me this Saturday evening?"

"This Saturday isn't an adoption event weekend."

Jake smiled. "I know it isn't. I'm asking you to dinner, a personal evening, not related to your rescue. I'd really like to get to know you better, Elyse."

"Oh!" Elyse exclaimed, embarrassed that she hadn't understood his intention. He was asking her out on a date. She knew she was both smiling and turning several shades of red. And she was suddenly very warm. It wasn't like it was the first time over the years she had been asked out by a man. But it was the first time since Tim died, and she was no longer married and actually free to go. But was she really ready for this, so soon? Not to mention how inappropriate it would be to go out on a date just over a month after her husband's death. She had to decline.

Jake eyed her, waiting for the reply. "That's okay," he said. "I'm sorry if I made you uncomfortable."

"Oh, no, I'm sorry, that's not it at all. I'd love to have dinner with you on Saturday."

"Okay, great," he said, somewhat surprised. "I have your phone number, but let me send you a text, so you have mine." He pulled his phone from the back pocket of his jeans. He pulled up a text he'd started to her that merely said, Jake Tanner's number. He hit send. "So, around six on Saturday?"

"That will work. Where were you thinking?" she asked.

"I could certainly drive out to Franklin. Do you have any favorite restaurants?"

No, that would not be a good idea, dinner where they'd most likely run into people she knew, people who knew she was recently widowed. "I actually have a favorite Italian restaurant on the outskirts of Norfolk, heading towards Suffolk. You probably passed it on your way last weekend. I could meet you there at six."

"That sounds perfect. Text me the name of it if you will, and I will touch base with you again Saturday morning to confirm."

"I will." She was both thrilled and nervous at the thought of going on an actual date. She knew that she was attracted to him. He was easy to talk with, and there was something about him that appealed to her on a level she had not allowed herself to act on since she'd gotten married. Sure, other men had caught her eye. And she would admit that she probably had even participated in harmless flirtatious moments with other men over the years. But she certainly had never acted on those impulses. She had never scheduled a time alone with a man she found charming or alluring.

She unlocked her car door and swung it open. "I'll see you Saturday."

"Drive safe. Goodnight, Elyse." Jake leaned in and pressed a chaste kiss to her cheek.

She was stunned. Her cheek tingled where he'd kissed. She felt like a teenager again. "Goodnight, Jake."

She pulled herself into the car. He shut her door for her. She watched his back as he walked away, towards the parking lot to the right where his car was the only one left. Then she pulled out of her parking spot, feeling giddy.

"Elyse, what are you thinking?" she asked herself aloud as she drove out of the parking lot. This was crazy. It was too soon.

Chapter 11 – A Dinner to Remember

It took Elyse over an hour to decide what to wear. She pulled ten outfits from her closet, tried all of them on, and didn't like any of them. What did grown women wear on dinner dates? She put the first casual sundress back on. It was a dark green color. She paired it with a sheer, floral kimono duster that hung long to the dress's hemline. Then she added flat sandals. She gazed at her reflection in the full-length mirror for the umpteenth time. She didn't look too dressy, nor did she look too casual, like she hadn't made an effort.

"Good grief," she muttered to herself. "Jewelry." She went to her jewelry box and picked a simple gold pendant and matching earrings. She was going to leave it at that but remembered she did have a bracelet that would look good with it, too. She added the bracelet and made herself leave her room. She was dressed, her makeup was done, just a little heavier than she normally wore it, and she would stop obsessing over her appearance.

Elyse arrived at the restaurant at five till six. She was about to text Jake she was there, but she saw him get out of his car across the parking lot. Taking a deep breath, she blew it out slowly to calm her racing heart. She met him at the door to the restaurant.

"Hi," he said with a smile. "You look lovely this evening." He leaned in and pressed a kiss to her cheek.

This time it didn't fluster her, as bad. "Thank you." She smiled as she looked him over. He wore a multicolored striped dress shirt, worn untucked over dark blue jeans with the sleeves rolled up to his elbows. Kade had told her once that keeping the shirt untucked was to keep it casual. "You look nice, yourself. The green in that shirt really brings out the green of your eyes."

"I was going to say the same about your dress."

She smiled uncomfortably. "I actually picked the dark color to hide any pasta sauce I might spill on myself."

He laughed. "That's why I went with the multicolor scheme. Great minds," he said.

He swung the door open and motioned her in. They were sat at a small table for two flanked by two room dividers, which made the table feel very private.

"Everything here is very good," she said after they'd been presented the menus and the hostess moved away.

"What is your favorite?" he asked.

"They have a good Spinach Rotolo. It comes with either marinara or meat sauce."

He closed his menu. "I'll take your recommendation. Do you have a favorite red wine to go with your pasta?"

"Their house cab is good."

"We'll get a bottle of that as well."

She smiled and set her closed menu atop his as the server delivered warm bread and olives to the table. "Jake, I have to confess to you that I haven't been out like this in a very long time." *In over thirty years*, she thought to herself.

"We just had dinner last Saturday," he said.

She laughed uncomfortably. "I don't consider that the same."

"Ah, so the two of us grabbing a bite to talk about your rescue after the event last week was different than us purposely meeting here to get to know each other better?" His tone was flirty.

"You know it was. And you're teasing me now, aren't you?"

"Guilty as charged, ma'am," he said, then chuckled. "I like you, Elyse. I really enjoyed spending time with you at dinner last week. I didn't think our friendship had to be confined to or centered around the rescue."

"Our friendship," she repeated with a smile. Had she totally misread him? Was friendship his only intention?

"I believe all relationships should begin with friendship. Don't you think? But please don't misunderstand me. My intentions do ultimately go beyond friendship."

Had she said that aloud, she wondered. "I like your frankness. And yes, in any relationship I may have at any point in time, I agree it has to begin with a friendship."

The server returned. They placed their orders, including the bottle of wine.

"I apologize if I'm too blunt. I don't believe there's anything to be gained by not being completely honest." He shrugged. "And I feel the games people sometimes play when they first meet are counterproductive. Not admitting they are attracted to each other or that they have a romantic interest because they don't want to put it out there and get shot down if the other person doesn't feel the same way just feels, I don't know, juvenile. And a waste of time."

155

"I can respect that," she agreed. "Admitting your intentions is a much more mature approach and, as you said, honest."

The server returned with the bottle of wine. She poured a taste in Jake's glass. He sampled it and nodded to her. She then poured a serving in both glasses and set the bottle in the middle of the table.

Jake raised his glass to her. "To friendship."

She smiled and tapped his glass before taking a sip.

After both glasses were returned to the table, Jake spoke again. "So, let me be very frank. I want to get to know you better and consider you a friend, but I also find you very attractive, your personality and physically. I do have romantic intentions."

Elyse just stared at him. His declaration shouldn't have taken her off guard, but it did. A million thoughts ran through her mind. "I have never met anyone like you before," she said, feeling pressure to say something in response.

He chuckled nervously. "Is that good or bad?"

She smiled, regaining her poise. "It's good. I'm excited at the prospect of getting to know you better. I have to warn you, though, we need to take anything romantic slowly. It's been a really long time since I've done this," she repeated, but she still didn't give him any more details. She wasn't ready to.

"Duly noted," he said with a smile. "And, as I said, friendship first. And companionship is a big part of that for me. I've spent more than half of my adult life out at sea. I'm honest enough to admit that now that I'm faced with a possible medical separation, it's been lonely. I'd really like to find a woman who has the same interests I do, to share my life with."

"And if you don't get a medical separation?" she asked.

"I'll be land-based for some time until command comes up with another position for me, and I'd still like to have a relationship with a woman who has the same interests I have."

"And do we have the same interests?" She knew she sounded flirty.

"Let's start with the dog rescue. When I heard you talk about it with that other woman the night we met, I saw how your eyes lit up and I admired how passionate you were about it. I'll admit that got my attention. That is one interest we share, finding homes for abandoned animals."

"What else interests you?" she asked.

"When I'm done with my Naval career, be it now or in four years, I really like the idea of putting down roots in a community and getting involved in the local government or the school board, something that will have me working towards the betterment of that community. I'll have a nice pension, but I see myself working in some capacity still, maybe not a regular forty-hour a week job, but something."

She was impressed by that plan. "I can see you doing something along those lines," she agreed.

"I'm also honest enough to admit that I would like for this potential woman and me to discover new interests together. I'd like us to try new things together and make that discovery an adventure, be it traveling to new places or just taking a sushi-making class."

Elyse laughed. "A sushi-making class?"

"Wouldn't that be fun? I've always wanted to. Do you like sushi?"

"Yes, I do, and a sushi-making class does sound fun."

Their salads arrived and their conversation momentarily halted until the server moved away.

"Okay, so our next dinner will be for sushi," he said.

"That sounds nice," she agreed. "I have several favorite sushi restaurants."

"I discovered one just outside the gates of the base that I've been going to that's pretty good. I'm open to try your favorites."

"How long did you say it would be before you find out if you'll remain on active duty?"

"They have PT booked for me through the end of June. It'll be re-evaluated then, but they may kick the final eval date out later depending on my healing."

"The unknown of it must be very unsettling," she said.

"You know, it was at first. But after my ship sailed without me and I was assigned to the destroyer group while receiving PT, I came to some kind of peace with it. I had been one hundred percent focused on the mission and on my career for so long, it was nice to take a step back and realize that there are other things in life that I've been missing." He paused and smiled. "Like the company of a very interesting woman."

Elyse felt her cheeks heat. "Besides the rescue, I'm not sure what else I do that's interesting."

"What about the church? Are you a member there or active in any other groups?"

"No, and no." She smiled. "My oldest daughter Claire and her family attend the church."

"So, whichever group you're attending, you are there as an attendee and not a host or moderator of the group?"

Elyse felt her mood crash. "Is that what you thought?"

"Yes," he said with a shrug. "I don't want to pry, Elyse, but I know what the three other meetings are, and I guess you just don't fit the profile of someone I'd see needing support from those meetings."

"Well, thank you for that. And you're not prying."

The server returned and removed their salad plates, sliding their entrees in front of them. They both got the Spinach Rotolo. She intended to tell him she was a widow and how recently that had happened after the server moved away. She'd have to sooner or later. It might as well be right away. She wasn't sure how he'd feel about it. This could be their last dinner.

"Wow is this good," Jake said after his first bite.

The conversation switched topics and flowed for the remainder of dinner. Elyse's mood returned to light and flirty. There was a lot of laughter between them when Elyse shared stories of the mishaps with her children when they were younger. At the time, the different situations weren't funny, but now, as she relayed them–including Kade falling off the roof, Claire slamming her bedroom door so hard when she was mad all the photos on the walls fell, followed by the door being taken off its hinges–she could see the humor in them. They both laughed hard when she told him about Kelsey driving off the road three times to avoid hitting squirrels when Elyse was teaching her to drive.

"She hit a tree in one man's yard. It was a little sapling; she drove right over it."

Jake relayed a young sailor being taught to drive a forklift and how he tipped it over with an uneven load. "He damn near put it in the water."

They both laughed. They lingered over dessert and finished the bottle of wine. Jake paid the bill, and they walked out into the cool evening air. They lingered near the side of the building.

"I had a very nice time with you this evening," she said, planning on presenting her hand for a goodnight handshake again.

Jake stepped in close and caressed her cheeks with both hands. "You are a true delight, Elyse Laramie." His hands gently gripped her neck, his thumbs tracing her jawline.

Something Elyse hadn't felt in more years than she could recall, skittered through her.

"Thank you for your companionship this evening. I look forward to our next evening out," he said.

He leaned in and pressed a very soft kiss to her cheek. Elyse thought he was pulling back, but his lips then pressed to hers. Her back was a few inches from the wall. She returned the soft kiss and then stepped back into the wall. Jake followed, filling the space she'd created as he deepened the kiss, parting her lips with his tongue. The sensations that assaulted her senses were overwhelming. Her entire body hummed from the contact. He leaned closer, his body trapping hers against the wall. She was hyperaware of every place their bodies touched.

When one of his hands slid down her shoulder and brushed her breast as he slipped it between her side and her arm to wrap it around her, it was too much. The hand came to rest on her hip. He used that hand to pull her closer to his body until their pelvises touched.

"Jake," she murmured as she pressed the palms of her hands against his solid chest to create enough space for her to break the contact with his lips. "Slow, remember?"

"Sorry, that was so nice, I got carried away," he whispered. He leaned in and pressed another closed mouth kiss to her lips as if to show her he could restrain himself. "I'll behave."

She gave him a forced, slightly embarrassed smile. She felt like an idiot. It had just been a kiss. An amazing kiss that heated her up everywhere. A kiss so intense it frightened her. She hadn't felt anything like that in over fifteen years. What was wrong with her that she couldn't handle a kiss like that from a nice, good-looking man? "I should go."

Jake nodded, motioning toward her car.

She was aware that he followed her the few steps to her car. Her face had to be a bright shade of red by the heat she felt in her cheeks. She owed him an explanation. She owed him an apology. She clearly wasn't ready for this.

Summoning her courage, Elyse turned to face him. "It was the widow and widower support group I was attending. I haven't been with a man other than my husband, and we were married thirty-two years. Since I was eighteen years old," she confessed.

"I'm an idiot. I'm sorry," he said. "That would explain why an incredible woman such as you is single. Just so you know, I aim to change that." He held his hand up in front of him and moved it slowly from one side to the other. "Slow and steady ahead."

She smiled and laughed softly. "You're not an idiot. You didn't know because I didn't tell you."

"It wasn't my business," he said.

"Until you kissed me, and I felt things I haven't felt in more years than I can recall. Thank you for that. If you can be patient and take it slow, I'd love to spend more time with you. But I do want to tell you up front, Jake, my husband traveled for work all the time during all of our marriage. I'm not looking to repeat that relationship. I'm more than a little concerned about starting something with a man who potentially will be leaving for long deployments."

He nodded. "I'll keep that in mind. Thank you for being honest with me. I don't have a crystal ball, Elyse. I don't know what the future holds for my career. Even if I'm cleared for full duty, that doesn't mean I would deploy anytime soon. It could be some time before command assigns me to a boat. I could end up finishing out my thirty years right where I am with no deployments." Even as he said it, he knew it was unlikely. He was the executive officer on a destroyer, a lieutenant commander. There was zero chance he wouldn't deploy again in the next four years.

She nodded. "Again, thank you for a lovely evening. I'll talk to you soon." She pressed a chaste kiss to his cheek and then got into her car. She watched him through her windshield as she pulled from her parking space. In her rearview mirror, she watched him walk towards his car until he was out of sight.

What was she doing? Was she crazy? She clearly wasn't ready for this. It was too soon. And she had chickened out of telling him it was just over a month since she'd been widowed. He'd surely think she was callous, or worse, for dating this soon. But what he wouldn't understand was that her separation from Tim had occurred years before. Besides an occasional quick kiss, she and Tim hadn't shared a passionate kiss in at least fifteen years. It had been nearly that long since they'd made love. They'd devolved to friends and merely roommates when he was in town. There'd been no passion, no sexual desire in her marriage for that long. It was sad, but she'd mourned the loss of the intimacy in her marriage way before his death.

No wonder she felt what she did from Jake's kiss. As she drove home, she couldn't help but think about the feelings his touch and kisses stirred in her. The one thing she couldn't deny was that she was attracted to him, to his personality as well as to him physically. He had a nice smile. And those soft green eyes held so much life.

Chapter 12 – Official Summer Kickoff

It hadn't really dawned on Elyse that it was Memorial Day weekend until Kelsey called to invite her to a barbecue at Ash's house on Monday. Her dinner date with Jake had been the previous evening. She was working at the building that housed the rescued dogs when Kelsey called.

"Oh, Kels, I don't know," Elyse said.

She had text-messaged a bit with Jake that morning and learned he was on duty all day both Sunday and Monday. He had said he would have liked to spend time with her if he wasn't. It seemed as though he was feeling her out to see if she still wanted to see him after the previous evening without coming out and asking. She was okay that he was busy. She was still trying to make sense of her reaction to his kiss and the conversation that followed. Even now, a day later, her thoughts were preoccupied with it and she was thrown for a loop.

"Mom, come on. Kade and Mel are going to be there. They both get off shift at four and should be there by a quarter to five."

"I'm a bit out of your friend's age group, aren't I?"

"No! One of Ash's artists at the shop is forty-five and he'll be there. Some of Ash's clients are invited and they're all ages. Ash would really like it as much as I would if you came."

"Kade and Mel are getting there after four-thirty? Okay, I will too. I planned to work at the rescue for several hours tomorrow. I can do that and then come to your barbecue after."

"Great!" Kelsey said. "Mom, please don't tell Claire. I'm not inviting her. I haven't told her about Ash yet and I don't want too quite yet."

"Kels, your graduation is in less than a week. She'll meet him then."

"Yes, and that's when I want her to meet him. I'll message her midweek with her ticket to the graduation and remind her about dinner for all of us after, and I'll tell her about Ash then, too. I made reservations at Lorenzo's."

Lorenzo's? Great, hopefully we won't have the same server. And if we do, hopefully she won't remember me there with Jake and mention it, Elyse thought. "I won't mention it to Claire, not that they're free. They're spending the day with their friends."

"So, that means you're coming for sure?"

"Yes," Elyse confirmed. "Text me his address."

The text chime sounded immediately after they said their goodbyes. Elyse smiled as she viewed the message from Kelsey with his address.

"Who's having a barbecue?" Julia asked her. They were in the kitchen of the rescue, making dog food for the dogs that had sensitive stomachs. It was Elyse's foolproof recipe.

"Kelsey and her new boyfriend, Ash, at his house." She frowned.

"I thought you said you liked him?" Julia asked.

"I do like him. It's not that."

"Then what is it?" Julia asked.

165

"I'm too old to hang out with them. Kelsey said it will be a group of all ages, but seriously, I'm sure I'll be the oldest."

"Since when has that bothered you?" Julia asked. "Now, why don't you tell me what's really going on? You've been looking at your phone all morning and you seem preoccupied, which is not like you."

Elyse dumped the pot of boiling organ meat and ground turkey into the colander. Protein was an important ingredient for dog food, and she was fortunate that a local farmer donated beef organ meat as well as ground turkey to her rescue. The donation saved her a fortune! She sighed loudly. "Julia, my thoughts have been preoccupied," she admitted. "I have to be one of the biggest idiots ever." Was she really going to do this? Was she going to tell Julia about Jake? She hadn't planned to.

Julia laughed. "Chica, you're talking to the biggest idiot right here. Sorry, I won't give my crown up to you. Now, what's going on?"

Elyse chuckled. "Do you remember that man who came to the adoption event a week ago last Saturday?"

Julia smiled with a lusty grin. "You mean that sexy man who promised to get us more volunteers? Um, no, I barely remember him."

Elyse's laughter grew louder. "Yes, he's the one. He introduced me to two disabled veterans at last Wednesday night's meeting at the church. He's bringing them on Saturday."

"Why does that make you an idiot?"

"I'm not going to be there this week. It's Kelsey's graduation."

"I'll be there. I'll put them to work and watch them. What's the problem?"

Elyse twisted her lips in consideration. "I had dinner with Jake last night."

Julia burst into laughter. "And let me guess, it wasn't to discuss the Animal House volunteers."

"No, it was personal," Elyse confirmed.

"So, why does that make you an idiot?"

"For two reasons. The first is that if he heals and doesn't get a medical discharge, he will be going on deployment. If he stays in, he's planning four more years of active duty and at least half of that would be deployed. Julia, I will not ever have another relationship like I had with Tim. Why would I start anything up with a man whose life situation is a deal-killer for me? And I have to be heartless to have gone on a date this soon after Tim died."

"You went on one date. That doesn't constitute a relationship. And you're not heartless. So, you had dinner with a very nice, really hot man," she said with a smile. "Again, one date. There is absolutely nothing wrong with that, no matter when Tim died. That doesn't make you an idiot."

"And he kissed me, and I just about panicked. I kind of pushed him away. It's all I can think about today."

Julia laughed again. "Okay, now *that* does make you an idiot."

"Thanks."

"I'm kidding, sort of."

"I haven't kissed anyone other than Tim in thirty years. And he and I hadn't kissed like that in probably fifteen. It was some kiss," she admitted, feeling her cheeks heat.

Julia closed her mouth. Yes, Elyse's confession had been jaw-dropping. Then her lips formed a smile. "Sexy and he can kiss, too. You're not an idiot. You're lucky. I'm not surprised, though. I saw the way he looked at you. Chica, he was parched and you were a jug of water."

"You're not helping," Elyse moaned.

"Do you want my advice?" She didn't wait for Elyse to answer. "Just go with it. Do what feels right. Don't worry about how long it's been since Tim died. Don't worry if it's a relationship or just two people spending time together, and don't worry about the future. Just try it on for size and see how it feels. And when it feels amazing, don't push it away. Enjoy it. You deserve it."

"He doesn't even know how long I've been widowed. Can you even imagine what he'll think when I tell him?"

"Tim may have died recently, but you haven't had what would be called a marriage in years. Start with that."

"I know you're right," Elyse said.

"Isn't it exhilarating, the thought of being with him?" she asked in a sexually suggestive way.

"It's terrifying," Elyse admitted.

"I'm not suggesting you hop into bed with him tomorrow, unless you want to," she said, raising one eye brow.

Elyse felt her cheeks get even hotter. "Stop," she moaned with a smile. "He's a very nice man. I really enjoyed dinner last night."

"Tell him that," Julia said. "I assume the text messages today have been from him?"

"Yes. He hasn't come out and asked, but I think he's been feeling me out in the text messages to see if our date last night scared me off. I did tell him I was unsure about starting anything up with a man who had the potential to be gone a lot, as Tim was."

"Okay, so you put it out there. Now just let it sit. At some point today or tonight, try to have a conversation with him, and not over text. If you're right and he's wondering, that means his intentions haven't changed. Have a nice conversation to put his fears to rest."

"That's a good idea," Elyse agreed. "Thanks for your ear and the advice."

It was later than Elyse planned when she left the rescue. The afternoon and early evening volunteer cancelled, so she stayed. Julia had left hours earlier. She was glad she had confided in her friend. She did feel better than she had before they'd talked. The overnight volunteer was in, a college kid who did his homework while he sat in the office so the dogs weren't alone all night.

Elyse drove home with Charlie asleep on the passenger seat beside her. Before she left, she took a few pictures of herself petting Frick and Frack. She messaged those to Jake. She was surprised that she didn't hear back from him.

After she arrived home, she brought a bowl of cereal up with her to her room. Charlie settled on his side of the bed. She clicked the television on and ate her cereal, glancing at her phone every so often. Then she took a much-needed shower. It was past eleven when she settled in bed. She plugged her phone in to charge and then went to sleep.

When she woke at eight a.m. the next morning the 'do not disturb' function on her phone was off and she saw the four text messages from Jake and the missed call with a voicemail from the previous evening. "Dumb," she said aloud, only then realizing that Jake was not in her 'favorites' so his texts and calls were silenced when the phone auto-shifted to 'do not disturb'.

She read his text messages first. The first three, he was commenting on Frick and Frack and the late hour she was leaving the rescue. The fourth said he was concerned because she wasn't answering and to please give him a call. His phone message mirrored that. That message had come in at eleven p.m.

She hit dial on her phone. The call went right to his voicemail. "Hi Jake, this is Elyse. I'm sorry I missed your call and text messages last night. My phone is set to go on do not disturb at ten o'clock each night and anyone who isn't in my favorites is silenced. I hope you have a nice day at work. I'm heading to the rescue soon and then over to my daughter Kelsey's boyfriend's house for a holiday barbecue later. If I don't talk to you before, I'll see you Wednesday night."

Later that afternoon, after she put in a full day at the rescue, she brought Charlie home and took a quick shower. She missed a call from Jake while she was in the shower. They'd been missing each other all day. He apologized that he was incredibly busy at work, which surprised her given that it was a holiday.

She followed the maps program to a quiet neighborhood in a wooded section outside of the city. The quiet tree-lined street hid many of the homes the driveways led to. "You have arrived at your destination," the voice declared.

She turned in to the driveway and immediately saw at least fifty cars parked along the edges of the driveway, off into the grass on both sides of it as well as lined up the length of the driveway that led to the cute little light blue cape cod. She recognized Kelsey's car parked closest to the house. She parked, grabbed the bucket of wings she'd stopped and bought on the way, and then walked up the driveway. A note taped to the front door said 'Party is around back' with an arrow pointing towards the garage.

There were paving stones marking the walkway from the edge of the driveway around the side of the garage. Before she'd made it halfway around she heard music, laughing, and voices. She rounded the corner to see a sea of bodies. There was a volleyball net with people lobbing the ball back and forth towards the back of the yard. Croquet was set up on one side, several rows of bags on the other.

Up close to the house was a patio with tables and chairs set up and groups of people engaged in lively conversation while they ate from paper plates. She saw Ash at one of two grills. She could smell the aroma of burgers and other meats.

Kelsey came out of the house with a tray of various raw meats as Elyse stepped closer to the patio. Kelsey smiled and waved when she saw her mom. Elyse returned her smile and waved as she walked towards her. Elyse noticed that the party attendees were all ages, as Kelsey had promised.

Kelsey was happy to see her mom. She had been waiting all day for the text from her mom sending her regrets. She brought the tray to Ash. "Mom's here," she said.

He turned just as she reached them. "Elyse, happy you came." He gave her a brief hug. "Everyone, this is Kelsey's mom, Elyse," he shouted above the music. "Introduce yourselves when you get the chance."

"Thanks, Ash. You have quite a party going on. And whatever you're cooking smells amazing."

"We have a little bit of everything," he said. He pointed to the man at the grill beside him. "Elyse, this is one of my artists from the shop, Eric."

The man looked to be in his late forties. He had tattoos running up both arms and climbing up his neck. His head was shaved but he had a full beard and mustache and he had gauged earlobes, stretched out to the diameter of a nickel. He reached his right hand towards her. "Elyse, nice to meet you. Your daughter is a total sweetheart. We already love having her work at the shop." His voice was raspy sounding, like he'd smoked way too many cigarettes over the years.

Elyse shook his hand. "It's nice to meet you, too. And I agree, Kelsey is a total sweetheart."

"I'll take this," Kelsey said, taking the wings from her mom. "Come in with me. I'll add them to the buffet and get you a drink."

Elyse followed Kelsey through the door into the small kitchen. Food was lined up on every surface. Kelsey readjusted a few things and added the bucket of wings. Kelsey opened a drawer and pulled out a pair of tongs, adding it to the bucket.

"His house is cute," Elyse said.

"I'll show you where the bathroom is," Kelsey said, motioning her mom through the archway into the living room.

Elyse glanced around the living room. It, too, was small and crowded with black leather furniture and a large television. On one of the end tables, she noticed a picture of Kelsey and Ash embracing. It was a selfie. They smiled and looked happy. It was a digital photo frame as it then switched to a picture of them kissing. The third picture was of them smiling and staring into each other's eyes. There was a line of people chatting. "I'll assume the bathroom is through there."

"Yes," Kelsey answered. "Well, if you need it, just follow the line." She laughed.

They returned to the kitchen. "I made sangria. It's in the fridge. Beer is in a cooler out on the patio, or we have mixers." She tapped the bottles that were on one end of the granite countertop.

"Sangria sounds good," Elyse said.

Kelsey grabbed a red Solo cup from the counter near the hard alcohol and wrote her name on it. Then she dispensed ice cubes into the glass from the panel on the outside of the freezer. She swung the refrigerator open and poured her a glass of the red liquid with berries and fruit in it. "Here you go." She handed the cup to her mom.

Elyse sipped it. "This is good. Thanks, Kels."

"Help yourself whenever you want a refill. Are you hungry yet?" She pointed to the food.

"No, I'll wait a little bit."

MARGARET KAY

They went back out onto the patio. Kelsey brought her to a few people seated close by and introduced her. Kelsey picked up her own glass of sangria which sat on one of the tables. Elyse recognized a few of Kelsey's friends from school and greeted them as well.

It wasn't long before Kade and Melanie arrived. Elyse watched them greet a lot of the other guests as they made their way towards the patio. She watched Kade and Ash embrace and then Ash and Melanie did as well. She judged there was a close relationship there. And then they both came over to Elyse and Kelsey.

"Mom, I'm glad you came," Kade said. He gave her a hug.

"Me, too," she said. Then she embraced Melanie. "It's nice to see you, honey. I'm glad you're feeling better. Kade told me how sick you've been."

"It's the weirdest flu I've ever had. The whole department has been hit hard," Mel said.

Kade dug two beers from the cooler and handed one to Mel.

Ash held an empty platter out to Kelsey. "Babe, can you wash this and bring it back? These are nearly done." He nodded to the grill.

"Sure," she said. She grabbed the platter and returned to the house.

Elyse had a wonderful time. All the people at the party were friendly and talkative. The food was delicious, and there was so much of it. She also enjoyed watching Kelsey and Ash as well as Kade and Melanie interact with each other and with the other guests.

She saw a confident and outgoing side of Kelsey she hadn't seen before. And it also struck her how happy her daughter was. She saw a fun relationship between her and Ash. They teased each other as they and Kade and Melanie squared off against each other as teams in a game of Bags, girls against boys. Elyse also saw a tight, sisterly relationship between Kelsey and Melanie that she'd never noticed before. She'd always liked Melanie and knew she was good for Kade, but seeing this relationship warmed her heart. Melanie was not close with her family, which consisted of divorced parents, both remarried, and two brothers. She was glad that Melanie and Kelsey had formed this bond.

Eric, the man she'd been introduced to while he and Ash cooked, took a seat beside her. "She's good for Ash," he said in his raspy voice. "I've never seen him this happy."

"They do look like they're having a good time," Elyse replied.

"Not just today, but overall. Ashley's a good guy, in case you're worried. He's one of those guys who doesn't do anything half-way. He commits one hundred percent."

Elyse made eye contact with him and smiled. Then her eyes shifted to those gauged ears. *Between the tattoos and those ears, Claire would have a field day with him,* she thought. "Thanks, but I wasn't worried after I met him last week. Plus, my son, Kade, said the same thing."

"Kade's a good guy, too," Eric said. "There's little resemblance between him and Kelsey. She takes after you," he said, and then chuckled. "She could be your younger sister. There's no way I'd guess you're the age you'd have to be to have a son as old as Kade. You look very young for your age. Anyway, I assume Kade takes more after his dad?"

His compliment made Elyse uncomfortable. "Thank you," she said awkwardly. "And Kade is more a mix of his father and me. Their sister takes completely after their father. You would never guess she and Kelsey are sisters."

"I heard he recently passed away. I'm sorry for your loss." He took a drink of his beer, but his eyes remained on her in a way that made her nervous.

Why was she getting the feeling he was hitting on her? "Thank you," she said.

"Take your time to grieve. Don't let anyone tell you what's the right timeframe for anything. I lost my wife going on a year and a half ago. I miss her every day. Several of my friends have asked when I'm going to move on, maybe find a new woman." He paused and shook his head. "They don't get it. We were together ten years. I was addicted to some bad shit when I met her. She helped me get clean. I woulda died of an OD I'm sure if it weren't for her. You don't get past that and move on this soon. She was my life."

"I'm so sorry," Elyse said, now feeling foolish thinking this man was hitting on her. "She had to have loved you very much to stay with you through addiction and after."

"She was special. And now she's an angel watching over me."

"Did you ever go to a bereavement support group? I'm attending one at Flowing Waters, you know, that megachurch? I didn't think it would be for me, but there are so many different types and ages of people there in all stages of the mourning process."

"Nah, I haven't gone to anything like that. Not sure it's for me."

"If you ever want to try it out, let me know and you can go with me. The meetings are every Wednesday night from seven till nine."

He lit a cigarette, inhaled deeply, and blew the smoke straight up. "I don't know, but if I decide to I'll let you know."

Elyse's phone vibrated in her pocket. It was Jake asking if now was a good time to talk. She felt bad, but she typed out her reply that it wasn't. She said she'd text when she was leaving the party and maybe they could talk as she drove home.

"There's not a problem at the shelter, is there?" Kelsey asked as she approached her.

"No, why would you think that?"

"You've been on your phone more today than I've ever seen you," Kelsey said.

Elyse smiled. Guilty as charged. She and Jake kept missing each other, but she wouldn't mention him to Kelsey yet. "No, not a problem with Animal House, just trying to coordinate and schedule some new volunteers for this weekend's adoption event."

"You're not working Saturday before my graduation, are you?"

"No, that's one of the reasons for the text messages, to coordinate coverage since I won't be there."

"Okay, good," Kelsey said.

The rest of the day flew by, and Elyse legitimately had a great time. Kelsey and Ash even convinced her to play bags and a game of volleyball. As the party broke up, she helped clean up as well. It was well after dark before she said her goodbyes to the half-dozen guests who sat on the patio around the firepit. Kelsey and Ash walked her back into the house. She'd leave out the front door.

"Oh, hey, I almost forgot," Ash said. "I made something for you, Elyse. Kelsey, where is that blade I made for her?"

Kelsey pointed at the ceiling. "I saw it on your nightstand when we went to bed last night."

"That's right," he kissed her forehead. "Thanks, babe." His gaze went to Elyse. "Don't go yet. I'm going to run up and get it."

After he opened the door near the bathroom and went up the stairs, Elyse's eyes went to Kelsey. Should she bring up what Kelsey had just said? She'd just said they were sleeping together. How did she feel about that? Was it even her business?

"I didn't mean to just blurt that out," Kelsey said after watching the thoughts play out across her mom's face. "But certainly, it doesn't shock you that Ash and I are sleeping together. As a matter of fact, Mom, I'm probably going to just move in here when I have to be out of my apartment, instead of over the shop." She shrugged. "I'll probably spend all my time off work here, anyway. And Ashley and I are really compatible. Mom, I really like him. Dad's death has made me realize that there are no guarantees in how long any of us will be here, so waiting to do anything is stupid."

Elyse held her hand up. "Kels, please stop right there. You're an adult. You do not need to ask my permission for anything. I would never judge you or your decisions, and you certainly don't have to explain them to me or anyone else." She took hold of Kelsey's hands. "Besides, I like him. I see a different side of you when you're with him. You're genuinely happy. And I like the self-confidence I see in you."

Kelsey felt relieved. She loved her mom and didn't want to lie to her about anything, especially something as big as where she would be living. "I'm happy," she said with a smile. "I spent the last year at odds with my path and my future. It's crazy how at peace I feel about it now."

Ash came back into the living room. "Here it is," he said, holding up a beautifully detailed small dagger, about the size of a butter knife. "I made it for you, Elyse. You can use it as a letter opener if you want."

Elyse took it from him. She was in awe of the craftmanship and detail in the piece. "Ash, this is beautiful," she said. "The scroll-work on the handle alone had to take hours. It's so small and dainty, and perfect."

"Yeah, I spent a few days working on it," he said. "I've made a few similar to that one over the years, but I wanted to try out some new detailing on the handle, different than anything I've ever done. I like how it came out."

"Wow, Ash, just wow! This is incredible. I can't believe you made it." She pointed to the blades he had displayed on the living room walls. "And I can't believe you made those either. You're very talented. Thank you for this. I will always treasure it."

"Aw, thanks," Ash said. He gave her a hug. "Drive safely on your way home."

Kelsey hugged her next. "Yes, Mom, drive safe. We'll see you Saturday at my graduation." She was all smiles.

"Yes," Elyse agreed. "And thank you for the invitation to your party."

As she drove home, she waited for the phone to ring. She had remembered to text Jake before she left. And she'd added him to her favorites so his calls or text messages wouldn't be silenced during the do not disturb hours. They talked as she drove. She told him about the party, the blade Ash made her, and Kelsey's admission that she planned to move in with him and how she felt about it. It was so refreshing to have a man in her life to talk with about, well, life.

Chapter 13 – Chicken Breasts and a Broken Wing

C laire opened the front door as Elyse approached it. Elyse noticed that she seemed kind of flustered. "Hi, sweetie," she greeted her.

"Hi Mom, come in. I have to log into a work call in two minutes. Lizette is off, so I'm glad you're here to be with the kids. They're in the playroom. I have dinner in the oven. I'll be off my call in twenty minutes."

They walked towards the kitchen together. Claire turned off, heading to her home office to the right. Elyse went through the kitchen to the playroom. "Hi guys," she said as she entered the playroom. It was a big room with just about every age-appropriate toy imaginable stored neatly in rows of bins and shelves. There were riding toys, a LEGO table, and a kid-size table and chair set that was currently set up for a tea party with stuffed animal guests, a play kitchen behind it.

"Grandma!" both kids squealed, and ran towards her.

She loved greetings like this! And she loved seeing them every week. Spending time with these two would keep her coming to the grief support meetings, whether she felt she needed them or not. She had again evaluated if she really needed the meeting during her drive in. This week, she would admit that, again, an opportunity to see Jake and talk with him was more the lure than the meeting was. Especially since their dinner date the Saturday before. She planned to ask him if he wanted to go get ice cream after the meeting.

MARGARET KAY

She wanted to talk with him face to face. She'd thought a lot about the kiss and her conversation with Julia about it.

Emma took her by the hand and led her to the play table and chairs. She knocked a large purple bunny from it. "Play, Grandma," she said.

Elyse sat in the little chair. She'd played tea party many times when her kids were young. She was glad kids still played this way. She had a great half-hour in the playroom with them before Claire appeared in the door to tell them dinner was ready.

The table was set for the four of them. No Matthew again. But at least Claire was home and eating dinner with her kids. Elyse helped the kids wash their hands for dinner and then helped Emma climb into her booster seat while Claire plated the food. The kids used divided plastic plates that were similar to what she used when her kids were young. It warmed her heart that just maybe something from Claire's youth had mattered to her.

Elyse took the last bite of her chicken breast. "Dinner was good. Thank you for cooking, Claire. I have really enjoyed seeing you three and having dinner with you the last three weeks."

"Me, too, Mom. And the kids are getting used to you coming every week. I'm glad that meeting at the church is working for you. I may not be available next week, though. I may be going on my first on-site to a building in Atlanta that's under construction. Michael asked me if I'm ready to step up and take over some of Dad's old workload. Chris has decided he will only travel fifty percent of the time." She said the last part with an attitude of disapproval.

Michael Kensington had been Tim's partner. Chris Barton was an associate at KL, the same title Claire held. Elyse was annoyed that Michael had asked that of her and she could pretty much guess on-sites at collapses would come next. She was a mother of two young children. He should know better. "Good for Chris," Elyse said. "How does Matthew feel about you traveling?"

"He doesn't know yet, but he knows I have always wanted to go on-site like Dad did." She helped Emma down from her booster seat. "Aiden, sit down. We don't stand on our chairs."

Just then he leapt from the chair, landed on the floor, and executed a roll like a parachuter would. He didn't tuck his arm, though, and as he rolled the arm twisted in a weird way, accompanied by his sudden pain-filled shriek. He stayed on the floor, rolled in a ball howling in pain.

Claire and Elyse both ran to him. Every time Claire tried to touch his arm, he cried louder. Elyse went to the freezer and brought over a bag of peas. She pressed it to his arm where it seemed to hurt him the worst. Then she conducted an examination of his arm. "I think it could be broken, Claire. I'll drive you to the hospital or urgent care."

"No, it can't be broken," Claire argued.

When Aiden showed no signs of calming, even when hugging Mister Quack, his favorite stuffed animal, Elyse prodded Claire to get her purse. "I'll drop you and Aiden at the ER and then bring Emma home so she can get to bed on time. Where's Matthew tonight?"

"With his partners; Topgolf night," Claire admitted.

"Will he be able to meet you there?"

"If he hears his phone, but I'm sure I'll be there a few hours, so probably."

"Call me and I'll bring Emma back with me to pick you up when you're done if you can't reach Matthew," Elyse said as she pulled up in front of the Emergency Room doors.

Elyse had driven Claire's Cadillac Escalade so the kids could be in their car seats. Claire sat in the backseat beside Aiden. Emma thought it was cool she got to sit in the third row, usually Aiden's seat. Aiden had cried or whimpered most of the way there. Claire was frazzled. Elyse was calm. It had been many years, but she had driven an injured, crying child to the ER more times than she wanted to admit to. Kade had been a daredevil who didn't pull his stunts off quite as planned.

"I will," Claire said. She got out of the car and then helped Aiden from his car seat. "Thank you, Mom." She carried Aiden through the doors.

Elyse gazed at Emma in the rearview mirror. She looked sad and on the verge of tears herself. She certainly didn't understand what was going on. "Hey, Emma, how about we go for ice cream? Won't that be fun?"

They stopped at a neighborhood ice cream shop near Claire's home. She let Emma get a sundae with sprinkles. They sat in the shop, eating their ice cream. When they got home Elyse knew it was Emma's bedtime, but she had this nagging feeling that Claire wouldn't be able to reach Matthew and that she'd be going back to pick them up. It would be a lot easier if Emma was still up.

She was right. Two hours later her phone rang. It was Claire. She had text messaged and called and hadn't been able to contact Matthew. And Aiden's arm was broken. They had set it, splinted and wrapped it, but she'd have to take him to an orthopedic doctor to evaluate it for surgery or just cast it the next day.

Emma fell asleep in the car as Elyse drove back to the hospital. She only then realized that the meetings at the church were just getting out as well. She hadn't text messaged or called Jake to tell him she wouldn't be there. She placed a call to him, disappointed it went straight to voicemail.

"Hi Jake, it's Elyse. I couldn't make it tonight. My grandson jumped from a chair after dinner and broke his arm. I'm heading back to the hospital to pick up him and his mom, almost there now. I'll text when I'm leaving their house later tonight and maybe we can talk if you're up. I don't know what time that will be."

As she turned into the hospital entrance, her voicemail chimed. He must have called at the same time she had called him, as his call went to her voicemail, too. She tucked her phone away. She'd check it later. Claire exited the doors as she pulled in front of them. She helped Aiden into his seat. He was still awake.

"You look much better, buddy," Elyse said to him, turning in her seat to look at him. "How did Mister Quack do? Was he afraid?" Elyse could see a Band-Aid on Mister Quack's wing.

Aiden frowned and nodded. "Mister Quack has a broken wing."

"Does he feel better now than he did when you went into the hospital?"

Aiden nodded his head.

Claire took a seat in the front passenger seat. "You don't mind driving home, do you, Mom? I'm emotionally beat from this." She turned and viewed Emma sleeping in the car seat. "I hate that her sleep had to be interrupted, too."

"They'll both get back on schedule," Elyse said. "Emma was good tonight. I changed her into her pajamas but kept her up, suspecting we would be heading back out to get you. If I remember correctly, Topgolf is kind of loud, so I doubted Matthew would hear his phone if he had it put away in his golf bag."

"I don't even want to talk about him," Claire whispered. "I'm so disgusted I couldn't reach him."

Elyse momentarily glanced at her daughter. She saw anger in her daughter's features. After they got home and got the kids to bed, Elyse would stay and try to get Claire to talk to her about what was going on with Matthew and their relationship. She hoped her daughter would open up.

"Mom, tonight was just one more example of Matthew not being there for us when we need him," Claire said as she opened a bottle of wine. The kids were tucked into their beds. "These damn Wednesday night golf meetings," she said, making air quotes while saying the word, 'meetings'. She poured the wine and handed Elyse's glass to her. She pointed to the living room. "Let's sit in there."

Elyse followed her to her formal living room.

"I like this room, and rarely use it," Claire said. She kicked her shoes off and pulled her legs beneath herself on the white couch. She rubbed her forehead. "I can't believe

Aiden stood on and jumped from the chair. He knows that's against the rules. And I didn't act fast enough to stop him."

Elyse took a seat beside her. "These things happen quickly. Don't beat yourself up that you didn't prevent it."

"The people at the hospital first thought I did something to break his arm, and then, when they were sure he caused it himself with reckless behavior, they looked at me like I was this terrible mother who doesn't supervise her child."

"They have to be sure all injuries to children are not child abuse. That's their job, Claire. And I'm sure they didn't think you're a bad mother. Kids do dumb things and cause injuries to themselves all the time. All it means is that they're normal kids. I was at the ER with Kade so many times." She paused and chuckled. "And I had to drag you and Kelsey along most of the time. I think the ER staff knew us all by name. The nurses used to keep you and Kels occupied while the doctor was in with Kade and me."

Claire laughed as well. "I remember that. I used to sit beside the nurse who checked everyone in as they arrived. I was her assistant."

"You walked in like you owned the place," Elyse said.

Claire laughed at that but then turned serious. "How did you do it? And you did it basically alone."

Elyse was glad she realized it. This was the first time that Claire acknowledged that fact that she could recall. "Yes, I did. I'm sure the first few ER trips I was as drained as you feel right now. It's horrible seeing your child in pain. And these things always happen at inopportune times."

"Oh jeez, you missed your meeting tonight because of it. I'm sorry, Mom," Claire said, only now realizing it.

"That's okay. I'm glad I was here."

"Matthew is going to be so pissed when he finds out this happened." She frowned and shook her head.

"What's going on with him, Claire?"

Claire flashed her mom a panicked expression. She didn't want to tell her what was going on in her marriage. And then the anger she felt bubbled back to the surface. "As I said, he's never here when we need him. He started going to these Wednesday night golf nights with his partners a few months ago, after they both got divorced. And it's not like he's home on time any other night."

"You need to talk to Matthew if the Wednesday night golf outings are bothering you. You two need to come to an understanding of expectations."

"I thought when the kids were older it would be easier than when they were babies," Claire lamented. "It's getting harder, though."

Elyse smiled knowingly. "No, when they're babies it's easier. There's a saying; bigger kids, bigger problems."

"Mom, I don't think he wants to spend time with the kids." It was hard for Claire to admit this to her mom.

Elyse was surprised by her statement. Wasn't that a perfect example of the pot calling the kettle black? "Why do you say that?"

"I think Lizette has a boyfriend. She's recently asked to renegotiate her employment terms so she has more time off. I've committed to being home on Wednesdays by five so she can have the evening off. She gets back on Thursday mornings by seven. Not only would Matthew not agree to switch off every other week with me, but he also wouldn't even commit to coming home before eleven to help me with the kids, tuck them in bed, or spend time all four of us as a family."

"So, is he usually out until eleven every Wednesday evening?"

"Yes, he's playing in a Wednesday night league at Topgolf with his partners. They have dinner and drinks while they play."

"I know you both work long hours, Claire," Elyse said, considering how to phrase what she wanted to ask so she didn't put her daughter on the defensive. "How many days a week do the four of you eat breakfast or dinner as a family? That time together is important for children."

Claire paused and rubbed her forehead again. "We always have Sunday dinner together. Lizette is off on Sundays unless we have something planned, a special circumstance that necessitates us being away. Matthew used to play with the kids on Sundays. He hasn't in months. He spends a lot of his time in his office when the kids are up."

"Is his workload that great? Or is his company in trouble, so he feels he needs to work that much? That could explain it if it isn't that he doesn't want to spend time with the kids."

Claire shrugged. "I don't know."

"If it's the kids, maybe he needs to spend time with them each one on one for an hour or so each time. Maybe he's getting overwhelmed by them both at the same time," Elyse offered.

"I don't even know how to bring it up," Claire said. "He gets defensive when I say anything."

"Maybe if you model the behavior you want to see from him. You could start by having a few hours a week alone with each of your kids, take one of them out for ice cream, or out for lunch on a Saturday, just the two of you. And then you tell Matthew how nice it was and encourage him to do the same. I took Emma out for ice cream tonight after we left you at the ER and she loved it. Aiden is old enough for Matthew to start sharing what he enjoys with him. He could take Aiden to Topgolf. Maybe one child at a time is what's best for him right now."

"Yes, that could work," Claire agreed.

"And what about you and Matthew? Are you satisfied with your marriage?" Elyse asked, deciding to broach this topic.

Claire sighed and looked away, not wanting to admit to her mom the state of her marriage.

Elyse knew her daughter well enough to know from her reaction that the answer to her question was no. "You know, sweetie, marriage relationships ebb and flow, continually changing. People grow and face new challenges all their lives. Sometimes, even the best marriages have a cool period while one or both of the partners comes to terms with whatever challenges they may be facing. You've been grieving the loss of your father. Maybe Matthew is just stepping back and giving you room to grieve."

Claire stared straight ahead and nodded. It was around the time her dad died that she felt Matthew pull back. Maybe her mom was right.

"Straight and honest communication is usually what does the trick to resolve these cool periods. My advice is to plan a night out with Matthew, just the two of you, someplace quiet where you can talk. Bring up your issues and invite him to as well. And really listen to what he has to say. And then talk about the expectations you both have of the other and see if you can come to an agreement."

Claire nodded again. "Thanks, Mom," she said, finally looking her mom in the eye. "I'm thinking maybe a night away. I could book a hotel room for the night and that way we could both really relax."

"If you need me to babysit, just let me know."

"Thanks, Mom."

"You know, Claire, if you can't get him to talk and things don't resolve when you tell him how you feel, it could be something deeper and you may want to consider marriage counseling. The longer things fester, the more detrimental it is to your marriage. When you talk to him use a lot of 'I' statements. I feel this or I feel that. Don't tell him that you don't like how he handles whatever the issue is. That'll put him off."

Claire frowned, annoyed by her mom's advice. Of course, she knew to use 'I' statements and not attack him in how she phrased it. Did her mom think she was stupid? "I think you're right that he's stepping back because I've been grieving. All our issues basically started when Dad died."

Elyse doubted that. "And see about building a few more meals with the four of you eating together into your schedule. It's so important for children to have that time with their parents, no matter how busy at work they both are."

"I remember we always had dinner together, and breakfast most days before school, too," Claire admitted.

Elyse was happy she remembered that. Hopefully, it was remembered fondly. "It's a simple way to build a strong family bond, which is important for kids. They need to know they're part of something. That they belong."

Claire yawned. She was exhausted. And she'd have to take off work the next day to get Aiden's arm looked at by an orthopedic specialist.

"I should go and let you get to sleep," Elyse said. She'd finished her glass of wine. "I hope Aiden sleeps all night."

Claire stood and hugged her mom. "Thank you for being here tonight."

"Of course, sweetie," Elyse said.

After Claire closed and locked the front door, her cell phone chimed a text from Matthew. "*Are you still at the ER?*"

"*No, my mom came back and picked us up,*" she messaged back.

"*Sorry, I just saw this.*"

"How convenient," she said aloud.

"*Is he okay?*"

"No, his arm is broken," Claire continued with her solo conversation. "*He's sleeping.*"

"*Okay, good. I'll see you when I get home.*"

It was nearly eleven. He was probably just leaving, and had just checked his phone.

• • • •

ELYSE SENT JAKE A TEXT telling him that she was just leaving when she reached the stop sign down the street from

Claire's house. It was late. She doubted he would reply. She was surprised when her phone rang. "Hi, I'm glad you were still awake."

"Me, too. I missed seeing you tonight," Jake said.

Elyse smiled into the phone. "I was going to ask you to go get ice cream with me after the meeting. I took my granddaughter instead."

Jake laughed. "I'm jealous of her. How's your grandson?"

"He was more comfortable when they left the hospital. He broke his right ulna. It was his first ER trip. My daughter was quite frazzled. I stayed and we talked for a while after we got back to her house and put the kids to bed."

"I'm sure she appreciated that you were there."

"Yes, she did. As I told you, my daughter Claire and I aren't that close, but I think tonight may have changed that."

"That's good to hear," Jake said. "Well worth the time spent there this evening then."

Elyse chuckled. "I don't think my daughter or grandson would agree with that."

"I mean for you, missing your meeting." Jake laughed as well.

"I'm glad I gave the meetings a chance. I wasn't going to. But it's been nice seeing Claire and my grandkids every week, and of course meeting you there as well."

"I was hoping you'd add that last part," Jake said.

"I've been thinking a lot about our conversation at dinner last weekend," Elyse began. "It's been very nice to get to know you as a friend. I was genuinely disappointed I didn't go to the meeting, as I wouldn't see you tonight."

"I like the sound of that. Keep talking," he joked.

She laughed. "That's pretty much it. I enjoy spending time with you. I just wanted to tell you that."

"You know I feel the same," he said.

"Oh, and I forgot to tell you. I won't be at the adoption event on Saturday. Kelsey, my youngest, graduates from college on Saturday. We have the ceremony in the afternoon and then we're going out to dinner as a family."

"Now I'm the one who's disappointed that I won't see you again."

"I hope you will still volunteer at the adoption event. Julia is expecting you."

"Yes, ma'am, I'll be there."

"Perfect. Are you working on Sunday?"

"Yes, I have duty," Jake said.

She wasn't sure what that meant or what exactly he did in the Navy. She hadn't asked because it seemed insensitive to ask him about his career that could be ended due to the injury and not by his choice. "So, I guess I'll see you again next Wednesday."

"I guess so. My schedule is quite booked the beginning of the week," he said.

They chatted until she arrived home.

• • • •

CLAIRE HAD ANOTHER glass of wine and waited in the kitchen for Matthew to get home. Her heartbeat sped up when she heard the garage door open. The anger that she felt towards him because he hadn't replied to her messages or come to the hospital, resurged. She took a deep breath as she recalled the conversation with her mom. Attacking him wouldn't help the situation.

Matthew stepped into the kitchen. "How in the hell did it happen?"

Claire didn't like his tone. He was definitely blaming her. "He stood on the kitchen chair and jumped off, pretending to be a parachuter."

"And you let him?"

"No, I didn't let him. I was helping Emma down, saw him stand, and told him to sit down. He jumped before I could get over to him."

"Where would he even get the idea to do that?" Matthew asked.

"Probably a cartoon," Claire said.

"Lizette is going to have to preview everything they watch to make sure there's nothing in there he'd want to try," Matthew said.

"Do you have any idea how stupid that sounds?" Claire demanded. "It's not feasible. It's not even logical. I think after this he'll be less daring, realizing now that he can get hurt."

"I'm sorry if I'm more upset by this than you are and want to do what we can to prevent it from happening again," Matthew said.

He'd said it with an attitude that immediately got under Claire's skin. "Excuse me? More upset? I don't think so! I was very upset about this. I was the one there with him. I wasn't having drinks with my buddies."

"Yes, you were the one who was there with him when it happened," he reminded her with more of the same attitude.

She ignored him and what he was insinuating. "I'm just thankful it wasn't more serious, given that I couldn't reach you."

"I'm sorry about that, Claire. We purposefully leave our phones put away so that we have one night away from the clients."

"I get that," Claire acknowledged.

"I'll leave it out from now on."

"Thank you. Aiden is fine and Emma was fine with my mom while we were at the hospital. I have to call in the morning and get him into an orthopedic specialist. The ER doctor is pretty sure he won't need surgery and that the orthopedic doctor will just cast him."

"Thank God for that," Matthew said.

"It really happened so fast," Claire said. "I'm glad I was here with him and not Lizette. I probably would have wanted to fire her for letting Aiden get hurt."

"I'm sure I would have, too," Matthew seconded.

"What time are you planning to go in to work tomorrow? Aiden was asking for you tonight. It would be nice if you could be home to have breakfast with him tomorrow morning. He knows he has to go to the doctor to get a cast and I think he needs some daddy time before it."

"Yeah, I could be home to have breakfast with him," Matthew said. "I can't take any time to go to the doctor with you, if that's where you're going with this."

"No, that's not where I was going," Claire said in a controlled tone, to stop the anger she again felt towards him from coming out in her words. "One of us taking time away from work is enough."

June
Chapter 14 – The Graduation Surprise

Claire arrived at the auditorium, feeling frazzled. She had to park farther away than she planned, and hadn't worn the correct shoes for the long walk. Per their text messages, Kade and her mom were already at their seats. Kelsey had electronically sent each of them their tickets so they would not have to arrive together or meet someplace outside. That had been a good plan. She put home and the fight with Matthew before she left out of her thoughts. Today was about Kelsey.

Her sister had scored some good seats directly off the aisle in a new elevated section, giving them a great view of the stage that the graduates would walk across. She was all smiles when she approached her mom and Kade. Kelsey's new boyfriend was supposed to be there, too. He must have been running even later than she had been. Kade stood a few steps further down the row, clearly out of their range of seats, talking with two men she didn't know.

"Hi, Mom," she greeted her with a hug. "I had to park so far away!"

"Yes, me, too. It doesn't help when people like us all drive separate."

Claire glanced around the nearly full auditorium. "Yes, I imagine everyone else is like us, coming from different directions to be here. But this is nice. I'm glad we can be here to support Kels. I just wish Dad could have been here today." She frowned.

Elyse took her hand. "He's here with us, Claire. Don't you feel his presence?"

"Oh, Mom, that is so nice. Yes, but I wish he was here in the flesh. I miss him so much."

Elyse hugged her. She hoped Claire would get to a better place regarding his death soon. Kade and Ash stepped back over. When they'd found their seats they also found a mutual friend of theirs, seated at the end of the row and they had stepped over to talk to him.

"Claire, I want to introduce you to Kelsey's new boyfriend."

Claire's gaze went to the stairs as the men approached through the row of seats. She glanced back at her mom, seeing Kade and the other man reach her. "Hi, Kade."

Kade leaned past his mom and gave Claire a quick embrace. "Hi, Claire."

Kade now had tattoos on his other arm. She knew where the unexpected windfall they'd received from their father went, wastefully on ink injected into his skin. Yuck. Just yuck.

"And this is Ashley Vincent, Kelsey's boyfriend. Ash, this is Claire," Elyse introduced.

Claire stared at him for minute. Oh, dear Lord, he was a carbon copy of Kade! He also had tattoos up each arm. Just like Kade, he wore a dress shirt, with the sleeves rolled up to his elbows and blue jeans. Blue jeans? They couldn't wear anything nicer to the graduation? And he was far too old for Kelsey. What was Kelsey thinking? And what was her mother thinking, supporting this relationship? She forced a pleasant expression. "Ash, nice to meet you." She extended her hand to him.

"Hi, Claire. I've heard a lot about you. It's nice to meet you."

Just then the music began, announcing the impending procession into the auditorium. They took their seats and watched the steady stream of dark blue cap-and-gown-clad graduates fill the seating on the ground floor of the auditorium. Kelsey, like other graduates, searched the stands for her family. Upon seeing them, she smiled and waved.

The ceremony was long, as there were so many graduates who crossed the stage to get their degrees. The speeches were short and not horrible. Kelsey did her best to be in the moment, enjoying this celebration of her accomplishment. Her gaze kept going to her family in the stands. She wondered how Claire meeting Ash went. She knew her mom liked him and supported their relationship, and of course Kade and Ash were friends, so Claire was outnumbered.

Kelsey felt incredibly proud, crossing the stage to get her diploma. Around her neck were the cords indicating she graduated with honors. She'd done it. Four years of dedication and hard work paid off. After shaking everyone's hands on the stage, as she exited she held the diploma high above her head in triumph. Then she switched the tassel on her hat to the other side.

After the graduates exited the auditorium, she found her group of friends and they all hugged, took pictures, and promised to stay in touch. She hadn't told any of them of her future plans. They exited the grad area into the hallway to go find their families. The noise in the hallway was deafening. She'd already made plans with her mom that they would meet up by the sculpture in front of the auditorium. She made her way there.

Pushing through the front doors, she came out into the beautiful, sunny day. Her eyes took a second to adjust to the bright light. She found them in the sea of people milling around. Evidently, she wasn't the only graduate who had designated this as the meeting spot.

She greeted her family with smiles and hugs.

Claire handed Kelsey the bouquet of flowers and then embraced her. "I'm so proud of you!"

"Thanks," she replied with a big smile. "They're beautiful. Are Matthew and the kids going to meet us at the restaurant?"

"We decided it would just be easier if they skipped it," Claire said dismissively, as though it didn't bother her. "Graduations always run over, so the coordination to meet would be a challenge with the kids. The last thing we'd want is for him to drag two cranky kids who missed their naps in to disrupt your special day."

"I'm disappointed. I was looking forward to seeing them," Kelsey said.

"You're out of school now and free. Drop over at the house any day this week. I'll let Lizette know you're planning to visit the kids."

Elyse got that feeling again, that feeling she hated. Claire was either missing the point of a family celebration or she really just didn't want her children with the family. The other possibility was that it was Matthew's decision. Yes, it would be easier for Matthew to not bring the kids. Elyse would bet that, even though it was Saturday and Lizette was normally off, Lizette was with the kids. She just didn't see Matthew spending all day with them while Claire was here.

"Let's head over to the restaurant," Elyse said.

"Kade, is Mel joining us at the restaurant?" Claire asked, betting she wouldn't be as usual.

"No, she's at work today."

Claire snickered. No one better give her anymore grief that Matthew and the kids weren't coming either.

Kelsey rode with Ash to the restaurant, her favorite Italian ristorante, which lay on the outskirts of Norfolk, heading towards Suffolk and Franklin. It was early so they nearly had the place to themselves. They were seated at a round table in the corner. Elyse ordered a bottle of red for the table.

As they looked over the menus, the server brought bread and olives. "Welcome back," the server said to Elyse.

"Thank you," she said, hoping the server wouldn't say anything more or ask about the man she'd been in with just last week.

After the server poured the wine and took their orders, Elyse raised her glass. "To Kelsey. Congratulations on your graduation. You worked hard and it shows. I'm excited for you to experience the next chapter of your life."

"Hear, hear," Claire said.

They tapped glasses and drank to the toast. Even Kade had a glass of wine tonight.

"So, Kels, have you decided which grad school program you're going to yet?" Claire asked.

Kelsey took another sip of her wine. "I'm not."

Claire waited for more, her questioning gaze on her sister. "What do you mean, you're not?"

Beneath the table, Kelsey felt Ash squeeze her thigh. "I'm not going to grad school. I've hated my major for some time. I knew I didn't want to do anything like it after my internship last summer."

"What do you mean you hate it? Kelsey, you're a math genius," Claire argued.

"Maybe, but I absolutely cannot sit through one more lecture on the subject. I'm going to try something different." Her gaze shifted to her mom. "I was able to delay the acceptance to one of the programs until next year. I just have to let them know by March if I'll be attending the following fall."

"That's good to keep your options open," Elyse said. Her gaze then shifted to Claire. "I think it's good that Kelsey had the courage to speak up and say she doesn't think grad school is the best fit for her. Exploring a different option now while she can, without many bills or a family, is smart."

"What option?" Claire asked. "What are you going to do?"

Kelsey had rehearsed this moment. And since she had her mom's support, surprisingly she wasn't the least bit nervous telling Claire, and she wasn't worried about letting her down. This was her life, not Claire's. Her sister got no vote in her life. "Ash is taking me on as his apprentice. I'm going to be a tattoo artist."

Claire nearly choked on the sip of wine she just took. She coughed a few times, trying to redirect the liquid to the correct pipe and swallow it. "Tattoo artist?" Claire repeated when she could speak.

"Ash is the best tattoo artist in the state," Kade said.

"We met when I went with Kade to get the tattoo to honor Dad that I drew," Kelsey said.

Kade sat next to Claire. He rolled his arm and pointed at it. "This is it. Kels did an amazing job drawing it. Ash, of course, noticed her talent."

"And I noticed her," Ash added with a grin. He leaned in and pressed a kiss to Kelsey's cheek.

"I got the same tattoo that day, too," Kelsey said. "You should consider getting it, Claire, to honor Dad."

"No, wait. This is a planned joke on me, isn't it?" Claire said.

"No joke. Why would you think that?" Kelsey asked. "Claire, I'm not going to grad school. I'm going to give tattooing a try. I've always loved drawing, but I never thought I could do something with my art for a living. After I saw Kade get my drawing tattooed on his arm, I knew I could. It was really the coolest thing, seeing my drawing on his arm."

"You're serious?" Claire asked, dumbfounded.

"She is," Elyse answered. "And we all support Kelsey's decision, Claire."

Claire made eye contact with her mom. Oh, so that was her approach, support Kelsey's lunacy and try to dissuade her quietly. That's what it had to be. Certainly, her mom didn't support Kelsey throwing away her education to pursue this.

And certainly, her mom didn't support her relationship with this man who was way too old for her, who was going to also be her boss. Okay, yes, she could do that, too. "Of course we do, Kels. Whatever is going to make you happy."

"Thanks, Claire. Yes, I've already worked a few shifts with Ash in the shop. There's a lot to learn, but it's really cool, and all his clients so far have been so nice."

Claire forced a smile and nodded.

The subject got dropped and the rest of the meal was filled with other conversation. To Claire, it felt like she was trapped in some bizzarro world. Of course, Kade supported Kelsey's direction on her life. It was with one of his friends in the tattoo world. But her mom, pretending to support this, all smiles and comfortable with all this. Claire was glad that Matthew hadn't come with the kids. She couldn't wait to tell Matthew about it later after they both got home.

Dinner ended and they all exited the restaurant together. Immediately outside the door both Kade and Ash lit up. *Oh gross, he smokes cigarettes, too*, thought Claire. Thankfully Kelsey didn't join them. Had she, Claire would not have been able to remain silent.

It was hugs all around, and everyone moved towards their own vehicles. Claire followed her mom to hers. "Mom, are you coming Wednesday night for dinner?" she asked to delay her as the others got into the two pickup trucks parked beside each other.

"Yes, I'm looking forward to it," Elyse answered, turning to face Claire.

They waved as the others drove out of the lot.

"What the hell?" Claire demanded now that they were alone.

Elyse shrugged. "I'm looking forward to dinner with you and the kids."

"Not about that. About that guy Kelsey is throwing her life away for!"

"Kelsey's decision not to go to grad school has nothing to do with Ash," Elyse said. "She decided that before she met him."

"Her not going to grad school is crazy! She needs a master's degree to get a decent job and support herself."

"Claire, she says she hates her major. She wants to give this a try. It may be what makes her happy. It might not, and if that's the case, she can try something different."

"She'll be way behind the curve if she hops professions, not that I'll say tattoo artist is a profession. Kelsey is way too smart to do this. I think this is the grief talking. She's distraught about Dad and she's making reckless and horrible decisions. We have to get through to her," Claire urged.

"We will do nothing of the sort," Elyse said in her harshest reprimanding voice. "Claire, your sister knows what she wants and what she doesn't. I do not think this has anything to do with Dad dying. I've talked with her several times and her head is screwed on straight. The worst thing that will happen is she'll decide she really liked her major and she'll go to that grad program next year. In the meantime, she explores her art and explores her relationship with Ashley."

"What kind of name is Ashley for a guy?"

"Apparently a very popular one, given that he pointed out to me when I met him that he was not the footballer from the UK, the Canadian composer, or the photographer with the same name," Elyse said with a smile.

"Not funny," Claire snapped. "Seriously, Mom, how old is he? And tell me you seriously are not supporting this insanity!"

Elyse smiled. "Kelsey really likes him, and from what I've seen he adores your sister. His age is irrelevant."

"Irrelevant? Unbelievable!"

"Claire, spend some time with them, watching and listening and not judging. You'll see they have a lot in common and they have fun together. I've never seen your sister as confident as she is now. There's a reason for that."

Claire knew she wouldn't sway her mom. She knew her father would not have approved of this.

"Claire, your sister is happy. That's all that matters," Elyse added.

Claire sighed out loud. "Yeah," she agreed.

Chapter 15 – And the Surprises Keep Coming

Kade was surprised to find Mel's car parked in its spot in front of their apartment building. He entered to find her lying on the couch, watching a movie. "Hey, babe, you're not feeling any better, huh?" he asked. She was supposed to be at work. "Maybe you should go see a doctor tomorrow. This has been going on for over two weeks."

"I feel a little better, and I don't need to go to a doctor. I know what it is." She pulled the pregnancy test stick into sight.

The blue plus sign jumped out at him.

He took a seat beside her, taking the pregnancy test results into his hand. "A baby, wow." He sat stunned. Given that the flu was making the rounds through the department, he never considered her sickness could be caused by her being pregnant.

"Doesn't have to be. I've given this a lot of thought, Kade; this isn't what either of us is ready for right now. I'm not even sure if a child is something I ever want."

"What are you saying, Mel?"

"I'm saying we need to consider not having this baby."

"An abortion?" Kade demanded.

"I don't know. Maybe."

"No, you can't be serious," Kade argued.

"Kade, I just got accepted to the Paramedic Program. I'm already exhausted. I can't imagine working full-time and going to school while I'm pregnant."

"Mel, what if you take a leave and go full-time to the Paramedic Program? Problem solved. Six months of school during the pregnancy. I'm sure you can do your on-the-job hours after the baby is born."

"You know I can't afford that. The cost of the school and then the six months of no paycheck."

"What if I find a way to afford it? You qualified for the Paramedic Program. You want this and you'll make a damn good paramedic."

"You can't afford it, either. We both know it. And neither of us is ready for a baby. With our work schedules, how can we possibly think about having a child?"

"Cletus and Valarie work odd schedules and they manage. We can, too. I just know it."

"They have Val's mom. She lives next door to them. We don't have that," she argued.

"Mel, I love you," Kade swore. "I have a few ideas on how to work this out. Give me three days, that's all I'm asking for, three days to come up with a plan."

Mel wiped the tears from her face. "If you can figure something out, I'll listen. But I'm still not sure I want this, now or ever."

Sunday evening Kade punched in at the garage and was assigned his partner and his unit. He had switched shifts with another paramedic to be able to attend Kelsey's graduation the previous day. He wished it was a regular shift with Cletus. He seriously could use some of his partner's humor and straight talk regarding Mel's pregnancy.

If Mel wasn't sure she wanted kids now or ever, did he have the right to demand otherwise? Afterall, it was her body and her career that would be impacted the most, even though that child was half his, or half created by him. He was wrestling with that. The other serious consideration that was in his thoughts was that maybe this relationship with Mel shouldn't continue. They had never discussed having children, but he always figured he would, they would.

He reported to the unit assigned. His partner for the night, EMT Dan Moody, was already in the back, performing a quick inventory. "Hey," he greeted upon reaching the open back door. "How's it going?"

"Good," Dan replied. "I was happy to see your name assigned with me tonight. It's been a while."

"Yeah, it has," Kade agreed. He went to the cab and dropped his backpack. Then he climbed into the back and helped Dan finish the inventory to be sure they had all the needed supplies. He knew that Dan was doing the part-time Paramedic Program. He was also married and had two young kids. His wife was active-duty Navy, Military Police, stationed at Norfolk. He'd bounce a few things off Dan without divulging Mel's pregnancy.

As Dan drove from the lot, Kade updated the log and got the cab set up how he liked his side arranged. Dan was telling him about his last shift and a bad pile-up on the two-sixty-four heading towards Virginia Beach. "Six cars and a semi, multiple injuries with entrapment, one fatality, and four transports to the trauma center. Even the chief was on-site for it. The only good thing I can say was there was no fire, so Rescue could concentrate on cutting the doors open to get the injured out."

"And it wasn't even raining yesterday," Kade remarked.

"People just won't slow the hell down," Dan grumbled.

The cab fell silent for a few minutes. "How's your paramedic training coming?"

"It's good," Dan said with a smile. "I wish I could do it full-time. It's taking forever and I'm just halfway through. Two years is a long commitment."

"And you have a family. That can't be easy," Kade said.

"No, it's not, but my wife is a saint."

"How do you do it? You both work rotating hours and you're going to school, so there is class time and study time on top of this job." Kade was especially interested to know.

"Yeah, honestly, if I had to do it over again, I probably wouldn't have started the course. Don't get me wrong, I really want the training, and the bump up in pay after I get certified will be nice, but now is just such a rough time with the kids as young as they are. We couldn't do it if we didn't have my little sister living with us. She goes to college full-time. The kids go to daycare part-time. All three of us split up taking care of the kids to make it work. It takes a lot of coordinating schedules and communication."

"I bet it does," Kade agreed, a bit deflated that they had the live-in help. He and Mel wouldn't have that.

"When it was just Kenny and he was a baby, and I was doing the EMT program, it was much easier. My classes were all during the day. My wife's schedule varied, but it didn't matter because I was always available overnight to take care of him. Any other time of day, he could go to daycare."

Kade was glad to hear that with the one child it was easier. "You have two in daycare now. That's not cheap."

"No, but we make it work and they aren't there full-time. It's temporary and I know, in the long run with the bigger salary, we'll be better off. Elinda's enlistment is up next year, and we'd like her to get out. That will line up with my completing the paramedic program."

"You definitely have a plan," Kade said.

Dan laughed. "When you have kids, you have to. You and Mel are living in a completely different world than I am. How I'd love to go home and not be on Dad duty tomorrow. After a full shift, I'm responsible for the kids for at least four hours, no matter how tired I am. I'm not complaining, don't get me wrong. I love my family and wouldn't have it any other way. It's just rough sometimes."

"I didn't think you were complaining."

A call came in. A seventy-year-old man was having chest pains. Kade acknowledged the call as Dan flipped the lights and sirens on. That was the start of a busy shift. It was several calls and several hours later when the worst call of the shift came in. A fifteen-month-old was unconscious and not responding.

They were within a few blocks. They arrived as a police car pulled up as well. "We know this address," one of the cops said. "Been here on domestic as well as drunk and disorderly calls. We'll go in with you."

"Appreciate it," Kade said.

They entered the filthy and overcrowded apartment at eleven p.m. Six children from around age two to what appeared to be around twelve huddled around the woman holding the infant, who was limp. There were two adult males milling around, looking sketchy. Kade was glad the cops were there.

"Hey there, momma," Kade said to the woman. "Let me take him and see what's up." He took the child from her arms. Dan was getting the kids to step back. Kade laid him onto the filthy carpet that he thought had been beige at one point in time. He felt for a pulse, there wasn't one. He checked his pupils. They were pinpricks.

"Is there any way he got a hold of an opioid like heroin or fentanyl?" Kade asked.

"No, I don't know how he coulda," his mom said.

Kade immediately blew a breath into his lungs. They inflated. His windpipe was clear. He administered a small dose of Narcan. The child responded, shuddered awake and cried. "What's his name?" he asked the woman.

"Johnathan."

"Easy there, Johnathan," he said, picking the baby up to comfort him. "Well, momma, he just responded to Narcan, so it was an opioid overdose."

Behind the woman one of the cops stood. He'd heard. He moved to his partner, who stood closer to the two men who were now in the kitchen area of the room. The two men were getting antsy. Kade didn't like their posturing. And with the confirmation of an opioid overdose, the cops were about to go at them.

"We have to transport him to the hospital." His gaze went back to Dan. "I'll carry him to the truck."

"He's awake now, he's fine. You don't need to take him," the woman argued.

"Yes, momma we do. This could be temporary. They need to watch him, as he might stop breathing again."

The police and the two men argued. Kade didn't like the way it was going. "Momma, you and your kids need to step outside with me. Right now." His voice was forceful. It was not a request.

He stood and carried the child out. Dan followed right behind him, also assessing that the scene in the house was beginning to spiral. Kade didn't look back until he was at the back of the ambulance. The woman was just getting the six other children out of the apartment when, from inside the residence, the sound of gunshots blasted the otherwise quiet area. Through the front window, Kade saw the muzzle flashes in concert with the shots. The woman and the kids ran towards them.

"Ten-one, shots fired, shots fired!" Kade broadcasted. "Dispatch, be advised there are gunshots at our location. NPD is in the residence where the shots originated. We are out of the building, will be relocating our unit two blocks east." The women and children were now beside him. "Get them up in the back," he told Dan. "Then get this truck moved at least two blocks."

Kade climbed up inside the back of the unit and placed the child in his mother's arms, directing her to sit on the stretcher. He directed the kids to all sit just as Dan swung the back door closed. He heard more gunshots, three in rapid succession. The ambulance lurched forward.

Kade went back to examining the child. He was conscious, but not by much. He started an IV and then listened to his heart and lungs. He hooked the child up to an EKG machine. His heartrate was still too low. The baby wasn't out of the woods yet. His eyes went back to the woman. "What drugs did he get his hands on?"

"No drugs," she swore.

"I'm not the cops. All I care about is knowing what he took so I can treat him."

"Maybe heroin," she finally said.

"You do realize had we arrived even two minutes later, he'd be dead. Momma, whoever had the drugs there cannot be near these kids, cannot be in your home." His eyes swept over the other children sitting huddled on the bench. It was eleven p.m. These kids should have been in bed.

The baby coded again. Kade administered another small dose of the Narcan. He startled awake, crying and disoriented. "We need to get him to the hospital. Is there someone who can watch your kids?"

"These aren't all mine," she said. "But they're going to have to come with," she said. "There isn't anyone I can leave them with at this hour."

Kade knew that wasn't going to happen. First off, they couldn't be transported unrestrained in the ambulance. Secondly, child protective services would be called. A toddler had overdosed on heroin and nearly died. Plus, there was a shootout with police at the location. Nothing was going back the way it was.

Over the radio Kade heard the codes that the scene was secure. Additional police units had been called in as well as two more ambulances for three injuries, including one of the cops. He also heard Dan transmit the code that they needed child protective services to their location.

"What's your name, momma?"

"Karen."

"Karen, no one rides in the ambulance without seatbelts. We went two blocks to get us out of the line of gunfire, otherwise we wouldn't have moved. The police are sorting out what just happened back there. I need to get this boy to the hospital before he stops breathing again."

Just then he saw the lights of a police car pull up behind him. The back door opened, revealing two uniformed officers. "You're from the ten-one up the street?"

"Yes. I need to transport this child, heroin overdose. I already hit him twice with Narcan," Kade said. "Karen, are you coming with me or staying with the kids and these officers?"

She looked back and forth between Kade, the kids, and the cops.

"Kids, you all need to get out of the ambulance and stay with these officers," Kade said.

They got up and the officers helped them down one by one.

"Karen?" Kade questioned. The kids were all offloaded and she hadn't moved.

"I'm going with."

"Whose children are these?" one of the cops asked.

"Johnathan is mine," she said, glancing at the semi-conscious child she held. "And three of them are mine, the other three are my sister's. She's at work but she can't have her phone at work. I'll text her and she'll see it when she gets off in the morning."

One of the police officers climbed into the truck. He took a full report with names of everyone involved and made her provide her sister's phone number. He even got her place of employment. They'd send a car there. "Send that text." Then he jumped down beside the kids and his partner. "I'll be in touch with you, Karen, if I have any questions." He closed the back doors.

"Dan, we can go," Kade called towards the cab. Seconds later they pulled away from the curb, heading to the nearest trauma center. On the way, the baby coded a third time. Kade hit him again with Narcan and performed CPR on him. He didn't bounce back as quickly after this dose. Kade had a bad feeling he was losing the baby. He gave him another small dose of the life-saving drug, and finally his eyes popped open, and he sucked in a big breath before wailing out a cry that elated Kade. He was back.

Kade and Dan delivered the baby and his mom to the emergency room and were just returning to their unit when another ambulance pulled in, followed by a police car. An injured officer was in that ambulance. Kade and Dan stood back to give them room, but saw the gunshot wound to the man's shoulder as they pulled his gurney from the back. The officer appeared to be conscious. That was a good sign.

They hung around and waited for their coworkers, the EMT and paramedic, to return to their unit. They of course knew them. EMS was a community. They were acquainted with the majority of cops as well. Kade knew the cop they'd pulled from the back of the truck was married with two kids.

Finally, the two men exited the hospital and came back to their unit, which Kade and Dan's was still parked beside.

Their two EMS coworkers filled them in. One of the men in the apartment was DOA at the scene when they arrived. The other had a GSW to his chest. It didn't look good. Another unit transported him to a higher-level trauma center. The cop had taken a bullet to his right shoulder, as they'd seen. He'd remained conscious throughout. After a quick assessment, the emergency room sent him directly to surgery. The second cop on the scene hadn't been injured.

"I heard you guys had just left the residence seconds before the shooting started," Denton, the paramedic, said.

"Yeah, we weren't even to the truck yet," Dan answered.

"Things were starting to go south between the cops and the two men in the apartment, so we got the patient out right away; a toddler, who somehow got a hold of heroin." Kade frowned and shook his head. "They had six other kids in there."

"We got them and the mom out before the shooting started, thank God," Dan added.

Kade's thoughts remained on that infant the rest of the shift. He'd breathed life back into that child several times. It made him think of his child, within Mel. He couldn't let that child go, either. His plan formed on how they could work it out, how Mel could go to the full-time program. Dan was right. A two-year commitment while working was too long, and Mel would never have the baby if that was staring her in the face. Cletus had help with his mother-in-law living next door. Dan had help with his college-aged sister living with them. In both cases, there were three adults stitching together schedules to provide coverage to care for the children. He and Mel would need help. And they needed a much less expensive place to live if they were going to give up Mel's salary. He'd go see his mother in the morning when his shift ended.

• • • •

WHEN ELYSE'S EYES MET Kade's, she knew something was wrong. "Kade, what is it?"

"Mom, I need a favor," he said in a voice Elyse hadn't heard since he was a little boy. It was full of pleading and desperation, along with hope. Now that he was standing here, he felt less sure of his plan than when he'd come up with it in the shotgun seat of the ambulance the previous evening.

"Anything," she replied.

"I need to borrow thirteen thousand dollars, and Mel and I need a place to live rent-free for the next six months to a year."

"Okay," Elyse said without missing a beat.

Kade snorted out a cynical laugh. "Just like that? Okay?"

"Of course, okay. You're my son, who I know to be very responsible. If you say you need it, I know it's important."

Kade wrapped his mother in an embrace. The adrenaline that spiked when he pulled into her driveway was receding. He had felt stressed and was in a fight or flight response as he came through the door, but now he felt exhausted.

"Mel got accepted to the Paramedic Training Program. It's what she's always wanted. It's thirteen thousand dollars. She was going to take out a loan and do the part-time program over the next few years while still working full-time. It would have been super-tight financially, but we would have worked it out somehow. But then she realized that she's pregnant."

"Mel's pregnant?" Elyse asked.

Kade nodded.

"You're going to be a father?"

"Yeah, but Mel thinks she wants to terminate it. She doesn't think she can work and do the part-time Paramedic Program, too. She thinks that will be too much for her. And it probably will be. The morning sickness and exhaustion has been bad. She hasn't checked yet, but she's not sure she can put Paramedic School off a year to have the baby. And if we have this baby, she knows we'll never have the thirteen grand for the program. She sees it as the end of her career."

Elyse was shocked. Mel wanted to terminate the pregnancy. Mel wanted to kill her grandchild. "Kade, what do you want?"

"I want to work it out. If we can live here and not pay rent, we could afford for her to do the training program full-time while she's pregnant. She could take a leave of absence and not have to try to work and go to school. A lot of the EMTs do when they go to the Paramedic Training Program. And after we have the baby, if you'd help us with it a little so we don't have to pay for full-time daycare, we could get back on our feet. I want this baby, Mom. You and Dad were a lot younger than we are when you had us, and I have to believe you were just as unready for it as Mel and I are."

"Kade, this is your home. You know that you are always welcome here, as is Melanie. Let me get my checkbook. I'll write you the check for thirteen thousand right now."

Kade returned to his apartment, feeling so relieved. But now he had to sell the plan to Mel. He sat at the kitchen table with a pad of paper, where he'd detailed out how doable, financially, his plan was. His original assumption of needing time after the baby came to get back on their feet was incorrect. Based on his calculations, they would come out ahead by living at his mom's house. And if they stayed with her for six months after the baby was born and she would let them delay paying back the thirteen thousand for a few years, they may have enough for a down payment on a house. He couldn't believe it. He checked his calculations three times.

"Hi, how was your shift?" he greeted Mel as she came through the front door. She looked beat. But at least she'd made it through her entire shift. She set the cooler she used as her lunchbox onto the counter.

"Busy as usual. How was your shift last night?"

"It was good," he said. He rose from his seat and embraced her. "You look tired."

She exhaled loudly and nodded. Tears were in the corners of her eyes. "I feel like such a wimp. I can barely make it through a shift."

He caressed her back. "You know early pregnancy can cause extreme exhaustion. You're not a wimp." He led her to the table and pulled the chair out for her. "I know you're tired, but I want to show you what I worked on today."

He laid it out for her, beginning with his trip to see his mom earlier that day, omitting his borrowing the money from her. Then he went over his financial calculations and how it would work living at his mom's while Mel went to Paramedic Training full time.

"That's great, Kade, but where is that thirteen grand coming from? If it's me taking the loan, I have to pay it back. So all your numbers there are wrong."

He pulled the check from his mom out from the back of the tablet. "My mom didn't even hesitate to loan us the money. There is no due date from her for us to return it to her."

"Your mom?" Mel was shocked.

"She believes in you and you acing paramedic school. She knows our combined income will be greater and provide more financial stability to our child, to our family in the long run. I love you, Mel, and I want this baby with you. We can do it. We can make this work."

Tears filled her eyes and she found it difficult to breathe. "Your mom loaned us the money for me to go to school? I'm not even her daughter and she'd do that?" Mel had always adored his mom, but this generosity on her part was overwhelming.

"You know my mom loves you. And you are carrying her grandchild," Kade said. He slid from the chair as he pulled the small box from his cargo short's pocket. He dropped to his knees and opened the box, displaying the small diamond ring. "And if you marry me, you'll be her daughter-in-law. I love you, Mel. We can do this together."

Mel flung her arms around his neck and held him close. She moistened his t-shirt with the tears that flowed from her eyes, damned pregnancy hormones making her so emotional. She hated feeling so emotional. But she loved

Kade. He was so confident they could make this work that she allowed herself to believe it. She nodded against him. "I love you, too, Kade."

"My mom and dad were less ready for kids when my mom found out she was pregnant with Claire. She supports us, Mel. We won't be doing this alone."

Mel nodded again. "We can do this," she agreed.

Chapter 16 – Ice Cream Also Melts When It Heats Up

Claire was out of town as she predicted, visiting a client in Pensacola who was planning a major building renovation. She'd left on Tuesday morning, calling her mom on her way to the airport. Claire told her mom it was best she didn't go have dinner with the kids on Wednesday. She didn't want to stress the nanny with that, as she would be on duty with the kids the three full days she'd be gone.

Elyse agreed, but really wanted to go check on the kids. And she had to wonder if Matthew would be spending more time at home during Claire's absence. She doubted it. She ate dinner at home and then drove into Norfolk for the grief support meeting. She contemplated not going, but it had been a week and a half since she'd actually seen Jake, since the night he'd kissed her. Sure, they'd talked on the phone and texted, but that wasn't the same.

Traffic was heavy, and she arrived only minutes before the meetings started. Jake stood in the lobby, just inside the doors. She approached him, glad that he'd waited for her. "Hi, stranger," she greeted with a smile. "It seems like forever since I've seen you."

"It has," he agreed.

"Traffic was heavy. I'll see you at break." There were only a few others left in the lobby and they were all heading to their meeting rooms.

"Yes, ma'am," he said with a smile.

During the break, like usual, they enjoyed a drink and a cookie while chatting, mostly about the rescue with Trevor Ferguson and Miles Maitland. Elyse would really have preferred a few minutes alone with Jake.

After the meeting, Elyse saw Jake waiting by the exit. "Walk me to my car?" she invited as a question.

"I was hoping you'd ask," he said with a flirty smile. As they crossed the parking lot and were a good enough distance away from the other people, he spoke again. "I know it's kind of late, but I was wondering if you'd want to go get a cup of coffee?"

"No," she said flatly. "But I would love to go get some ice cream. There's a little shop not too far from here I like," she added after a pause just long enough to take him aback by her refusal.

"That sounds better than coffee," he said. "Text me the name of it and I'll meet you there."

As Elyse drove towards the ice cream shop, her thoughts threatened to overwhelm her. She knew after she told him how recently she'd been widowed that he may want to call it quits with her. And she wouldn't blame him. But he deserved to know, and she felt dishonest that she hadn't told him yet. She'd also decided that she wanted things to physically progress with him if he wasn't scared away after he knew her little secret.

He pulled into the parking spot beside her car. She already stood in front of it. He quickly exited his car and came up to her, greeting her with a quick kiss on the lips. Then he embraced her. "It's been way too long since we spent time together."

"I agree," she said. "Let's get our ice cream."

She ordered a turtle sundae. He got one with strawberry sauce and whipped cream. Then she led him to a row of picnic tables that faced the Lafyette River. The lights from the other side reflected off the water. It was quiet, beautiful, and private.

"This is nice," he said as he sat on the picnic table beside her.

"Yes." She took a spoonful and placed it in her mouth. "And this is good," she said after she swallowed. "I have a confession I have to make," she said. Might as well get it over with. "But first, I need to tell you about my husband and about my marriage."

"Elyse, really, don't feel you need to."

"No, I do, and you'll understand why in a minute. My husband, Tim, was a structural engineer. He was a building collapse expert. Like the NTSB investigate on-site when there's a crash, Tim went on-site to where there had been a collapse. He investigated after earthquakes, mudslides, sinkholes, or just collapses from unknown origins. He was good. His firm was the go-to firm for any building collapse. He also worked with architects and builders when buildings were going up. He conducted inspections and safety inspections on existing buildings when renovations were taking place. Needless to say, he spent very little time at home. I counted the days. In the last two years, he spent thirty-eight days at home."

"That's not many; worse than being married to someone in the Navy."

"That's about how it had been for the last twenty years. We got married when I was eighteen, a month after my high school graduation. He was twenty-one and in college. I was pregnant with Claire. Everything during those early years was about him finishing school. I worked full-time so he could graduate with his bachelor's degree and then his master's degree while he worked for his first firm. I also got pregnant with Kade during that time. That also wasn't planned. He had already started to go on-site by then. He loved it. He came home so proud of the work he was doing. Over the next few years, his time away increased. By the time Kelsey was born, he was only home for maybe a week in between month-long jobs away. It wasn't the relationship I envisioned. At first, I thought it was a temporary situation until he established himself in his career. But I was wrong. It was the career, and when he did get well established he was gone even more. We became different people. We drifted apart. Our relationship turned into more of a friendship. When he was home, we were more like roommates. About fifteen years ago, we stopped pretending we had a romantic relationship. We hadn't in years. It was a relationship neither of us wanted, but neither of us could change without divorcing, and neither of us wanted that. I secretly hoped that when he retired, that romantic relationship would be rekindled." She stared straight ahead as she spoke.

"Elyse, I'm sorry that was your relationship. I understand now why you told me you weren't sure about starting anything up with me." He was sure she was going to halt their relationship right then. She still gazed straight ahead at the water. She couldn't even look at him.

"That's not why I told you. I need you to understand that I haven't really had a marriage for some time because Tim died recently. In April."

Jake stared at her profile. "This past April, as in two months ago?"

Finally, she turned to face him, afraid to see the expression on his face. "Yes." He looked stunned.

"Oh, good God, Elyse. I'm so sorry. I didn't know."

She pinched her lips, fighting the tears that were starting to fill her eyes. They weren't there for Tim. They were there because she was sure Jake would surely end things with her now that he knew how recently she'd been widowed. "I feel horrible that I can't say I miss him. He was never home. He wasn't a daily presence in my life. I'm sad for him, leaving this world too soon. And I'm sad that my kids lost their father."

"How long had it been since the two of you...," He paused, second guessing this question.

"Since we were intimate? At least fifteen years, maybe more."

Jake was stunned. Her husband had to have been blind, stupid, or gay. Elyse was beautiful. She was both intelligent and personable. He couldn't fathom how any man wouldn't make a marriage with her a priority. He rubbed his forehead. He knew what he wanted to ask, what he needed to know. His gaze must have betrayed him.

"Ask. I don't know what you want to ask but I can see you have something you want to know."

Jake took another spoonful of his ice cream. It was melting. He nodded to hers.

She also ate a spoonful, swallowing it past the lump in her throat.

"It's none of my business."

"Ask," she repeated forcefully.

"Your marriage was dead for a long time. Did you ever...," he began.

She interrupted before he'd finished his question. "Have an affair? God, no. I took a vow."

Jake set his cup of ice cream on the table beside him. Then he took hers and set it beside his. He reached both hands to her face and gently cupped her cheeks. He pressed a very gentle kiss to her lips. When he pulled his lips back, he smiled at her. "Slow and steady ahead."

She smiled as well. "That's all you have to say?"

Jake laughed. "Did you figure out how to prevent getting pregnant yet?"

Elyse laughed harder than she had in a long time. When she squelched her laughter, she finally answered. "Yes, I did. Would you like to come back to my place, and we can see if it works?"

"I'd like that, but I don't want to rush you," he said. "I can wait."

"Well, let's see what happens. Even if we don't make love, if I'm not ready, I'd like to take things further than we have and I'd like to go to sleep with you beside me."

Jake stood and reached a hand towards her, helping her up.

He surprised her by pulling her into his arms and pressing another kiss to her lips. This time, his tongue parted hers immediately. It was a long, passionate kiss. She was breathless when their lips separated. And she was heated in her most intimate places. She knew in that moment she'd made the right decision in telling him everything and inviting him back to her house.

Elyse provided Jake her address. By the time they had made it to the outskirts of Franklin, it began to rain. It was coming down sideways with near gale-force winds when they pulled into the driveway. As the garage door rolled open Elyse called Jake and invited him to pull into the garage as well, so he wouldn't get soaked.

They entered the house and were greeted by Charlie. Jake bent down and showered the pup with attention. "Who are you, fella?"

"That's Charlie. He didn't do so well at the rescue, so I brought him home to foster him. I ended up falling in love with him, so I kept him."

"What a lucky boy you are," Jake said. "You'd like two little brothers, wouldn't you? Yes, I think you would love to have Frick and Frack live here with you."

Elyse chuckled. "Good try but no, I don't think so. Charlie is very happy being an only child and, honestly, those two are just a little bit too much for me right now."

Jake laughed. "You can't blame me for trying. I really like those two." He glanced around at the kitchen as they entered through the laundry room from the garage. "Your home is beautiful, Elyse. This room is so you."

She nodded. "Thank you. I love my home. Claire actually suggested I sell it and move to Norfolk to be nearer to her after Tim died. Why in the world would I do that? This is my home." She liked having someone to share things with other than her children. They had discussed her children several times and she felt comfortable telling Jake about them.

His gaze caught sight of the paintings in the sunroom. He pointed to the one on the easel. "Did you paint that?"

"Yes, I have always painted landscapes." She smiled proudly. "Kind of a hobby."

"So, your daughter, the future tattoo artist, is not the only one with artistic ability," he said. "May I?"

She nodded.

He went into the room and turned the light on. He looked over the paintings. "Wow, Elyse, these are really good. I'm impressed."

Elyse smiled. She had followed him into the room and now stood beside him. "Don't be too impressed. I'm a one trick pony. Landscapes are all I can paint. Kelsey is the one with the real artistic talent. She can draw almost anything."

"Well, I am impressed. These are beautiful." He pressed a kiss to her lips.

"I need to let Charlie out," she said. "Then we can head upstairs."

Jake grasped her by the shoulders. "Are you sure? What happened to taking it slowly?"

"Kelsey is moving in with her new boyfriend, Ash. She told me on Memorial Day. She met him around the same time I met you. A lot of people would think that is way too soon for her to do that. A lot of people would think the same about us sleeping together this soon after Tim's death. And I'll admit that I even thought that we needed to take it slower for that reason, and a few others. But what Kelsey said made so much sense. She said that her father's death made her realize that there are no guarantees in life and putting off spending time with someone is stupid because they could be gone or you could be, and then you'd never get that chance. It made me realize that there is no correct timeframe for me to wait, and what anyone else thinks about it is irrelevant. It also made me realize that worrying about the future, will you or won't you go back on deployment, and letting that question impact if we move ahead in our relationship or not is just as stupid. As you said, there is no crystal ball that will tell us what will or won't happen in the future. I'm not willing to put my life and what I want on hold any longer. Life is made for living in the moment."

Jake followed her up the staircase and into the large master bedroom at the top of the stairs. Charlie jumped up immediately, settling on one of the pillows. Good thing it was a king-sized bed. There'd be room for all three of them.

He pointed to the doorway to the left. "Bathroom?"

"Yes."

When he emerged from the bathroom, she had the bedcovers turned back. She was placing Charlie on the comfortable-looking overstuffed chair in the corner of the room. The low light that was on the table beside the chair was all that now illuminated the room. She met him by the side of the bed, excited at the thought of spending the night with him. She wouldn't lie, she was also nervous. It had been so long since she and Tim had been intimate. And Tim was the only man she'd ever been with.

Jake wrapped her in an embrace and held her, staring into her eyes. She didn't take her eyes off his. She liked how he just held her for a long moment. There was no hurry. They had all night. One of his hands caressed over her face. What she felt was electric, just from his touch. A strong want surged through her. She initiated the kiss that quickly escalated.

The emotions and physical sensations that washed through her were incredible. She felt neither awkward nor panicked by their closeness, even as all their clothes were shed, even as they made love. And after, lying with naked bodies pressed together, she felt comfortable, sated, and another emotion she couldn't put her finger on. Perhaps connected? Whatever the emotion was, it was powerful.

Chapter 17 – And Good Morning to You Too

"**D**o you mind if I get a quick shower?" Jake asked.

His head hung over hers. Their legs were still tangled. Their naked bodies were pressed together. Elyse's eyes were rivetted to his. His hair was disheveled, which, as short as it was, didn't seem possible, but it was. "Sure, I'll be down in the kitchen. I have to let Charlie out and I'll make coffee."

He kissed her again. "Or you could come join me."

"Next time," she promised with a smile. "Charlie needs to go out. I'll see you down there after your shower."

Wow! That was all Elyse could think after he'd gotten up and she watched his tight little behind walk into the bathroom. She'd had a vague memory of what intimacy was like with a man; vague, as it had been so many years. But wow! She obviously had forgotten what she'd been missing out on. It almost made her angry with Tim and herself for allowing this to leave their marriage. Almost, until she reminded herself there was no use in wasting time or emotional energy on what she couldn't change.

She needed to concentrate on the present. And she needed to live fully in the moment from this point forward. She'd made the decision to have this relationship with Jake. It would be dishonest of her to think of Tim and the moments of life she'd lost over the years, while she was with Jake. He deserved more than that, and so did she. Regrets from the past had no place in the present.

Last night, making love with him had been an awakening. Going to sleep while being held in his arms had felt perfect. Waking the same way had been amazing. And making love with him as the sunlight streamed through the sheer curtains over the east facing windows as it rose in the cloudless blue sky, had been incredible.

Charlie jumped onto the bed and nudged her with his nose.

"I know, you need to go out." She got up and pulled on her spaghetti strap pajamas and robe. Both fell mid-thigh. And then she went down the stairs, Charlie racing in front of her.

After letting him out through the back sliding glass door, she went to the kitchen and turned the morning news on the TV. She liked to hear the weather forecast and the top news stories every day. Then she made a full pot of coffee, something she rarely did but she hoped she would have the need for it more often.

She felt legitimately happy. And it wasn't just the sex. It was the friendship she also felt while spending time with Jake. They talked, they laughed, they shared thoughts and experiences. He was good company. Until he spoke about wanting companionship when they had gone out for dinner, she hadn't really considered that she'd missed having a man in her life who she could say offered her it. But his presence in her life shined a bright spotlight on the need that she didn't even realize existed, a need he then fulfilled.

She let Charlie in and fed him his breakfast. Jake entered the room as the coffee finished brewing. She watched his eyes scan her up and down as he smiled. It made her feel good. It made her feel desirable, something she hadn't felt in a long time. She was sure she blushed.

"I feel overdressed," he said.

"And I feel underdressed."

"No, you're dressed perfectly." His smile spread.

"Coffee's ready," she said with an embarrassed smile. She poured them both a cup. "I noticed at the Wednesday meetings you've taken your coffee black, but do you usually use cream or anything?"

"No, I always take it straight."

She laughed as she grabbed the sugar bowl that she had her odd additives mixed in. "This is how I take it," she said as she lifted the lid. "It's a mixture of dark, unsweetened chocolate powder that is nearly one hundred percent cacao, along with ground turmeric, cinnamon, and collagen protein powder." She stirred two teaspoons of the dark powder into her coffee.

"I have to try this," he said. He took the cup from her and tasted it. "Oh, that's bitter," he said.

"It's the unsweetened chocolate. I don't think it's any more bitter than black coffee," she said as she let Charlie back outside, as he had been prancing near the door.

He took another drink. "It's actually not bad." He gave her a kiss as she reached him, still standing near the coffeepot on the counter.

She tasted her cinnamon toothpaste on his lips. She hadn't brushed her teeth yet. She wanted to get back up to her bathroom and do that. "No, it's not. And it's healthier than anything else I could add to it."

"Beautiful and smart," he said, grabbing her and pulling her in for a hug. "And dressed in this sexy little number. I have to be the luckiest man."

Thinking he had to be joking around, Elyse laughed.

"Seriously, Elyse. I am. I could get used to this as a way to start the morning. We haven't talked about what this step means in our relationship, but I want you to know that I don't want to see anyone else, and I hope you feel the same. I don't mean to put you on the spot, but I think we need to talk about it."

She gripped his biceps where her hands had come to rest. "I appreciate you bringing it up. I feel the same way. Honestly, I wasn't sure how to ask you."

"Just like that." He smiled. "Last night meant a lot to me."

The expression she saw on his face proved to her that he understood how big a step it was for her and that he genuinely appreciated it. "Thank you," she whispered. "It meant a lot to me, too. I'm really glad that you're in my life, Jake. I didn't realize what I've been missing and how lonely it's been until you were there, and I was reminded what having someone special in your life is supposed to be like."

"I'm glad I'm that person for you. I knew when I first met you that you were special, but every time I learn more about you, I'm reminded just how special you are. Even how you take your coffee is as unique as you are."

He kissed her again—a deep, passionate, lengthy kiss.

· · · ·

THAT FIRST YEAR

KADE PUT HIS PICKUP in park. He'd come straight to his mom's house from an overnight shift. The drive was never bad. He was sure he could do this daily. He was excited to tell his mom that Mel had agreed to not terminate the pregnancy. She would accept his mom's generous check to pay for the Paramedic Program and they would move in here when their lease was up.

He unlocked and opened the front door. Glancing up the stairs as he passed them, he saw his mom's bedroom door was open, not that he thought she'd still be sleeping. She generally was an early riser. He came into the kitchen and stopped like he'd hit an invisible wall.

"Mom?" Kade exclaimed, shocked to see his mom in her pajamas, kissing some man in her kitchen. "I should have knocked!" He turned and rushed back towards the front door.

"Kade!" she yelled after him.

"Let me, Elyse," Jake said. He jogged through the entry and followed Kade. "Hold up!" Jake called as he cleared the front door. Kade had already opened the door to his pickup truck. "Kade, please don't go."

Kade turned to look at him, shocked this man knew his name.

"My name is Jake Tanner. I've heard a lot about you. It's nice to meet you, Kade." He presented his right hand. He now stood in front of Kade.

Kade let out a loud sigh. He wouldn't be an ass and refuse to shake this man's hand. "I wish I could say the same, but I've heard nothing about you," he said, clasping the proffered hand.

"Your mom didn't want to tell you three anything about me yet. I met her shortly after your father died, at the Wednesday night meetings at the Flowing Waters Church. I volunteered to help at the Animal House adoption events, and I've helped to recruit some other injured and disabled veterans, too. We spent time together to coordinate that and became friends."

"You're the man from the Navy that she told me about. She never mentioned that you have a personal relationship." He lit a cigarette.

"Yes, I'm in the Navy. I was injured a few months ago in an accident on my ship and was assigned to my destroyer group on base while I complete my physical therapy and an evaluation to determine if I can return to regular duty. I also was tasked by the command with checking out a few local charities that offer services to disabled or injured servicemembers and that's how I met your mom. I was attending the veterans' support group at the church the same night she was attending the bereavement support group. I heard her talking with others about her rescue and knew that was a group that I wanted to possibly add to the posted charity list. Animal therapy has helped a lot of injured vets."

"You're an officer," he remarked.

"Yes, a lieutenant commander. Though, knowing your mom, she wouldn't care what my rank is. She's a very special lady."

"Yes, she is," Kade agreed.

"Last night was the first time I was here, if that matters to you."

Kade's gaze shifted away. He took a deep drag from his cigarette. Yeah, that was more than he wanted to know. Walking in to find his mom making out with some man was the last thing he wanted to see. But really, should he be surprised? His father was never home. He had secretly wondered for years what kind of relationship his parents could have. Especially when he noticed on the rare occasions his father was home the lack of physical affection between them. And that was nothing new. It was that way for as long as he could remember, even as a child.

"My mom can do what she wants," he said. And then he took another deep drag of his cigarette. Bad timing. He was coming to tell her that he and Mel were going to move in. But now, he wasn't sure that was a good idea.

"You and your sisters are important to her. She'd never do anything that would hurt you. I'm sorry you walked in on that before she could tell you about me."

Kade snickered. "She doesn't need my permission."

"No, but I'm sure she would like your understanding and acceptance. Will you please come back inside and sit down and have a cup of coffee with us?"

Kade took another drag of his smoke and considered it.

"Your mom deserves happiness and companionship. I like and respect the person she is. Obviously, we're more than just friends," Jake said. "And I'm glad we've met. I plan to be around for a while, and I know you and your girlfriend may be moving in with her. It sure would make it more comfortable all the way around if we get to know each other. By the way, congratulations. Your mom told me you're going to be a father."

"Yeah," Kade agreed. "I'm sorry. Seeing you here was just a shock. You're right. She does deserve to be happy and have companionship. She was alone for a long time."

Kade snuffed out his cigarette and set the unsmoked portion in the ashtray of his truck. Then he led Jake back into the house.

Elyse was just descending the stairs when Kade and Jake entered. She'd hurried to her room and gotten dressed, throwing on the same pair of jeans and t-shirt she wore the night before, hoping Jake would talk Kade into coming back inside. "Kade, I'm sorry you walked in on that," she said.

Kade stepped up to her and gave her a hug, as he always did when entering the house. "You don't need to apologize. I'm sorry I acted as I did. It was a shock to see you and Jake." He stepped back. "He said you have coffee made?" He nodded towards the kitchen.

"Yes, a fresh pot," Elyse said.

The three of them went to the kitchen. She poured Kade a cup and then warmed hers and Jake's.

Kade took a seat at the table. "Mel agreed with my plan. She's going to take a leave of absence from work to do the full-time Paramedic Program. We're going to have the baby," he said with a smile. "But it might not be such a good idea for us to move in here, huh?"

Elyse glanced at Jake and then back at Kade.

"This is your home. If you aren't comfortable with me being around after you move back, I won't be," Jake said.

Elyse's heart warmed from his statement. "But I would hope that you could become comfortable with it at some point. Kade, I can only imagine how you feel about this."

Kade held his hand up to her in a stopping gesture. "I reacted badly and I'm sorry. You deserve to be happy, Mom. I'm really okay with your relationship."

He could be an adult about this. He wasn't sure how he'd feel meeting up with Jake in the hallway outside the bedrooms, but he'd have to deal with it. His mom had always supported his relationship with Mel, and they moved in together shortly after meeting each other. And he knew that Kelsey recently told her that she was moving in with Ash. And Kelsey said she was perfectly fine with it, much to his surprise.

"Thank you, Kade," Elyse said. She and Jake brought their cups to the table and sat with him. "Needless to say, I'm thrilled you and Melanie are having the baby. When will you be moving in?"

"We have to be out of the apartment by August first, so we'd probably move in here that last weekend of July, if that's okay."

"Of course, it is," Elyse said. "If you want to start bringing anything over earlier in the month, please feel free to."

"Yeah, we might. I was thinking, if you don't mind, the bonus room over the garage that you're using for storage, could we move all that stuff out, and could Mel and I use that as a living room? The door to it's beside Claire's old room, which is the biggest of the three bedrooms. Could we move into it?"

"Yes, I was going to suggest that if you wanted to use the bonus room you could, but you also could take over Claire's old room because it's the largest. And after the baby comes, your old room beside it could be converted to the nursery. That'll leave me Kelsey's old room as a guest room."

"Okay," Kade said with a nod and a smile. "We have a plan. Cletus will probably come over with me the next time we're off and we'll take a look at what all we'll have to move so I have an idea of how long it will take."

"Let me know when that will be. I'd love to see Cletus and help you in any way I can. A lot of that stuff might be able to either go right in the trash or be donated to Goodwill."

"If you need any help, let me know," Jake offered.

"Thanks," Kade replied. "So, I take it neither Kelsey nor Claire know about you two?" He was sure both would have called him if they knew.

"No, they don't," Elyse said. "I'm not going to ask you to lie to your sisters, but if you could just not tell them for a little while, I'd appreciate it, out of respect for your father."

"Yeah, I get it. We both know how Claire will react, and Kelsey thinks you had some fairytale love that transcended long separations. How she can think that while admitting that Dad wasn't really a part of our lives is beyond me!" His gaze shifted to Jake. "As I'm sure my mom told you, our dad was never home. I can honestly say I don't think I really knew him. He was a hard man to connect with even if he was sitting in the same room. If you weren't a building that had collapsed, you didn't get his attention."

Kade's statements hurt Elyse's heart. It saddened her that was how Kade felt, even though she knew it was true. "I think he tried his best, but I think he lost touch with his family because he poured himself into his career. He just didn't have the capacity to do both. And, if I'm being completely honest, I made it easy for him to disconnect from the family because I never demanded he be more present, so he wasn't."

"You should tell Claire that. I see both her and Matthew making that same choice," Kade said. He shook his head. "Those poor kids. At least we had you. All they have is whatever nanny Claire hires."

Elyse was shocked that he saw it, too. "Why do you think I've been spending so much time with them? But unfortunately, Claire is so much like your father. I have to tread lightly."

"Claire *is* Dad, without a penis," Kade said with a straight face.

Elyse choked back her laughter.

Jake barely contained his. His gaze went back and forth between them.

"What? It's true," Kade said. "Even Cletus has asked me how that broomstick got shoved so far up her ass."

Elyse knew she should tell Kade not to say these things about his sister. "Kade, language. Please."

Kade laughed. She hadn't said it wasn't true. "Sorry, Mom." His eyes went to Jake. Jake was stifling a laugh. "Just wait till you meet her. You'll see what I mean."

"I look forward to it," Jake said with a smile.

"No, you really don't," Kade said.

Chapter 18 – Goodbye Past Life

Kelsey had worked late into the night to finish packing her belongings. She'd been in this apartment with her girlfriends for two years. She was surprised how much stuff she had. At least she didn't have to pack her clothes, as Ash had told her they'd just pull the drawers out and move it like that. He'd moved his bedroom furniture around and made room for her dresser and her high chest. The rest of her bedroom furniture would be stored in his garage until they figured out where it might fit.

Earlier that week, Ash had shown her blueprints he'd had drawn up a few years earlier to put an addition on his house that would enlarge the kitchen and create a large first-floor family room with bedrooms and another bathroom above it. He had enough land to build it and he'd even had the permit approved by the city at that time. He just never followed through on building it; he'd bought the strip mall his shop was in instead.

Kelsey was close to her roommates, who were also friends. They'd shared almost everything over their college years, including the devastating breakup with her last boyfriend. But Kelsey had not yet shared with all of them the path she'd chosen for her life. She'd only confided this with her best friend, Cathy Kay. The others knew she had a new boyfriend, as she hadn't been at the apartment much over the past three weeks. Besides his name and that he was a friend of her brother's, she hadn't shared much else.

Kade's pickup truck pulled up in front of her apartment and parked on the street, because the driveway was jammed with cars and moving trucks. The apartment was the second floor of a large home that had been divided into three apartments and rented to college kids. It appeared they were all moving out today. Ash pulled up behind him with the rented U-Haul truck. Ash got out of the driver's seat and Eric, the artist from the shop, pulled himself from the passenger seat. Ash had promised her he would get one more guy to help move her. She liked Eric. Talk about not judging a book by its cover! Eric was a total sweetheart, but he looked rough.

She met them at the door that was propped open. Two of her other roommates were nearly finished moving their stuff. Cathy Kay wasn't planning to move out until Sunday morning. She was in the kitchen helping to pack up items, separating them into boxes with each girl's name on it. It was amazing the random things they'd acquired in two years. How did four girls own six corkscrews and eighteen beer bottle openers?

"Hi," Kelsey greeted them with hugs. "I'm so sorry it's so crazy. Two of my roommates are also trying to move out now, too, but they're almost done."

Ash pulled her into an embrace. "It's okay, we'll manage." He kissed the top of her head. "I missed you in bed with me last night," he whispered.

She smiled up at him. "Me, too," she also whispered.

Cathy Kay came into the room at that moment. "Hey, guys," she greeted. She'd been at Ash's Memorial Day barbecue.

"Hey, CK," Kade said. He'd known her for years.

"Hey Ash, Eric," she then said, getting the attention of Danielle, another of their roommates as she came back into the apartment.

Danielle greeted Kade, as all the roommates knew him, but she gave the two new men a visual once over.

"Hi Danielle," Kade replied. Then he shifted his attention back to Kelsey. "Is your bedroom ready for us to start moving your furniture out?"

"Yeah, Ash said you'd just take the drawers from my dresser and chest and carry them down that way, so I didn't pack any of my clothes up."

Kade laughed. "Just as long as you don't have a vibrator or any other sex toys sitting in plain sight."

"Shut up!" Kelsey smacked him, laughing. She also blushed.

"No judgement," Eric said, following Kade into the hall that led to the bedrooms.

"Sex toys, huh?" Ash said with a flirty grin. He then kissed her lips. "Mm, I'm glad your stuff is moving into my house."

"Go lift furniture," she teased back.

He followed the others into the hallway.

"That's him?" Danielle asked, coming close to Kelsey. "Your boyfriend?"

"No, he was just some random guy who kissed me. Of course that's Ash."

"He's so...," She paused searching for the right word.

"Hot, muscular, tatted up?" Kelsey offered her.

"Yeah, and old, too. You said he was one of Kade's friends, but I didn't think he would be as old as Kade," Danielle said.

Kelsey shrugged. "I guess I don't see him that way, just hot and muscular, and sweet, and fun to be around, and smart."

"Did he say you're moving in with him? What about in the fall when school starts? Hey, which grad school program did you pick, anyway?" Kelsey knew Danielle had gotten into her first pick for grad school, for Occupational Therapy, at a college in Southern California.

"I'm not going to grad school. I'm working at Ash's shop and learning to be a tattoo artist."

Danielle stared at her in disbelief. "Seriously?"

"Yes," Kelsey replied, her head high, a smile on her face. "It turns out I'm a good enough artist. And honestly, if I don't ever sit through another lecture, write another paper, or take another stupid test I'll be happy. I'm so done with boring classes."

"Wow, I'm shocked," Danielle said. "I thought you loved all that statistics and risk management shit."

Kelsey shook her head. "I'm excited to try something new."

"With someone new," Danielle added.

The three men emerged from the hallway. Kade and Ash carried her mattress. Eric carried her nightstand.

Danielle went back to her room to finish removing all the clothes from her closet, still on hangers. She made multiple trips, piling them across the backseat of her car. Kelsey planned to do the same thing. The guys made a dozen trips down to the pickup and U-Haul and had the bedroom cleared out quickly. They also helped move out the hanging clothes from her closet. She only made one trip down to her car.

Kelsey stood in the doorway, gazing into her empty bedroom. She felt a mix of emotions she didn't expect. She was excited for the next chapter of her life, but she felt sad for this one closing. She and her friends had shared some great times in this apartment. Cathy Kay sat on her bed, or she sat on Cathy Kay's late into the night on many occasions. They studied. They bitched about their professors. They watched movies and ate popcorn, or they laughed or cried about their love lives in their rooms, in this room.

"Babe?" Ash asked. He came up beside her and saw the tears in her eyes.

"Just saying goodbye to two years of my life," she said. She beamed a smile at him. "But don't let this fool you. I'm excited for my future."

Ash nodded. "I get it." He leaned in and kissed her. "I'm excited for it, too."

"Hey, any other boxes to move?" Kade asked, walking up to them.

"Maybe in the kitchen," Kelsey said.

Eric re-entered the apartment as they passed through the living room. In the kitchen, Cathy Kay had all the cabinets open and continued to place items in the four boxes. "Take a look through this mess," she said to Kelsey. "I think I remember what belongs to who."

"So, where are you heading off to?" Kade asked her

"Back to my mom's house. I got a job with Sentara and could afford to pay rent if Kelsey wasn't moving in with Ash and would have moved in with me. This is better, I guess. I can pay my student loans off faster and maybe next year I can get my own place. I'll be working overnights and sleeping during the day, so I won't see my mom much. It won't be like we're all in each other's business."

Kade laughed. He understood that and would soon have a similar situation. "Congrats, by the way. Kelsey told me you passed your nursing boards on your first try. You'll have to let me know which hospital you're at and which department."

"Thanks," she said. "Yeah, that would be pretty cool to see you once in a while as you transport patients to my hospital."

Kade remembered that he hadn't told Kelsey his news yet. "Kels, I've been meaning to tell you. I'm moving home, too." This statement got everyone's attention.

"Did you and Mel break up?" Kelsey asked.

"No, that isn't it. Mel got accepted to the Paramedic Training Program. It's either two years part-time while she works, or a full year, full-time if she can take a leave of absence. If we don't have rent for a year, we can afford for her to take the leave of absence."

"Wow, that's so awesome of you to make the sacrifice for her," Kelsey said. "It couldn't have been an easy decision."

"Well, given that she's pregnant, it was really an easy one."

"Pregnant?" Kelsey asked with a huge, surprised smile. She hugged him. "You're going to be a dad, Kade?"

"Yes, I'm going to be a dad," he repeated. He hadn't said that aloud to too many people. Besides his mom and Cletus, he hadn't told anyone else. It felt good to tell them. "Mom said she'd help with the baby after it's born."

Everyone congratulated him.

"You know I will, too," Kelsey volunteered.

"We can get a crib and keep it at the house," Ash offered.

"Man, thank you," Kade said, embracing his friend. He hugged Kelsey again. "I was hoping you'd say you'd help."

"Of course! I'm so happy for you and Mel. And I'm going to be an aunt!" she said as she hugged him.

As Kade embraced her, he really wanted to tell her about Jake. But he knew his mom didn't want her or Claire to know yet. He respected that, and he knew that it wasn't his news to share. He hoped his mom would decide to tell them soon. He was sure that Kelsey would pop over to the house unannounced, like he had, and she may walk in on a similar situation like he had. There was no chance of that happening with Claire, but it was a good possibility for Kelsey. He'd talk to his mom about it the next chance he got.

Chapter 19 – Denied

"Hi Elyse, it's Wayne Hall from the Zoning Department."

"Hi Wayne. I know my permit application is on the agenda for tonight's meeting. I plan to be there."

"I'm calling to save you the trip. We've already rendered a decision. I'm sorry, Elyse, but we have to decline the zoning change."

"What? Why, Wayne? That part of the property is currently zoned for agriculture. Are dogs really that different than cattle or farming?"

"It's the public entrance, Elyse, and rezoning it as commercial use. Farms don't have a flow of visitors. That's the sticking point."

"Can I appeal the ruling?"

"There's really no use in doing that. We're not going to reverse the decision. With that curve and the trees to the north of your property, making lefts in and out of there is just not safe. And we're not going to put a stop sign up out there."

She didn't think that it was that unsafe. She'd made lefts in and out of her driveway every day since she'd lived there. "What other options can you offer me?"

"Well, with the agricultural designation you could house the dogs there, just not have the facility open to the public," Wayne said.

Yes, she knew that. True, it would help her house more dogs, but that would be just that many more she'd have to worry about transporting to adoption events. And then she'd have the volunteers accessing her personal property, an insurance liability for sure.

"Thanks, Wayne. I'm very disappointed."

"I'm sure you are. I'm sorry, Elyse."

She sat at her kitchen table just staring at her patio outside the sliding glass door for the longest time. "Shit!" she said out loud, even though she rarely cursed.

Then she got up and went out to the barn. She flipped on the overhead canned lights in the finished portion that had a floor and had been drywalled in to form the large, open main office area. She'd designed it to be a space that would hold many who were there to meet the dogs. Behind it was the finished backroom, bathroom, and medical office space that was roughed out. On the other side of the barn were the roughed in spaces that were to have become pens, runs, spaces to house the dogs with space for outside runs she planned to construct leading out of every pen and run.

This would have been perfect, she thought, tears pooling in her eyes.

She pulled her phone from her shorts pocket and called Julia. "They denied my zoning petition," she said after Julia had picked up with a cheerful greeting.

"Are you serious?" Julia asked.

"Yes. I don't know what we're going to do now."

"And you just put so much money into fixing up the barn. It's so cute out there."

"That's not even the issue at this point. That facility we're in, we can't use for too much longer. It's too small and it's not accessible for some of our volunteers with those steep stairs.

My biggest fear is that Sal sells the warehouse and our free location for the events disappears."

"As far as I knew, he wasn't trying to do anything with it," Julia said.

"That could always change," Elyse said. She massaged her forehead. A doozy of a headache was coming on.

"What are we going to do?" Julia asked.

"Well, maybe we should go back to the original plan of trying to buy something closer to Norfolk. That's where the majority of our adoptive families comes from anyway. We have our annual fundraising gala in August. What if we go all out and make this one huge? Maybe it could fund the new facility."

"Chica, you're counting on numbers we've never seen in amounts donated at any of our galas. Even if we double what we brought in at last year's gala, it still wouldn't be enough."

Elyse's mood crashed further. Julia was right and she knew it. "We'd have to go after corporate donations."

"Do we have time to do that? The gala is only two months away."

"I don't know," she admitted. Her screen flashed with a call from Jake coming in, accompanying the beep on her phone. She'd forgotten that he was coming over. "I have to go. I'll call you later to brainstorm." She clicked over to Jake's call. "Hi, are you here?"

"Yes, but where are you?"

"I'll be back to the house in a minute. I'm in the barn."

"I'll come out to you. I'd love to see what you've done with it."

"Sure," she agreed.

She wiped her eyes so it wouldn't appear she'd been crying. She met him outside the door to enter the office.

"You've been crying?" he asked as he wrapped his arms around her. "What's wrong?"

She let out a heavy sigh, aggravated with herself. "My zoning petition was denied. I can't use this building to be Animal House's public facility."

He patted her back. "Oh, babe, I'm so sorry."

"Me, too. Honestly, Jake, I don't know what I'm going to do now. Julia thinks we should just use this to house the dogs, with only the volunteers coming onto my property, but I really don't want the liability."

"Let's take a look at what you had done to the barn."

After a tour of it, he crossed his arms over his chest as he looked out the large window next to the front door. "This view is beautiful. I could see a little front porch on this place with a swing." He pointed to the corner of the room. "I know you put heat and cooling in, but I see a woodburning stove there in the corner. And this room would be a super cute art studio for your painting. You have a bathroom and a space that could be a little kitchenette."

"Yes, and it could be even more than that. Jake, do you think I could finish it off even more and make a cute little place for Kade and Melanie? The finished space in here is more than double the size of their apartment."

"Yes, you could, but that would be even more of your money not going towards Animal House."

She shrugged. "At this point I don't think it really matters. I'll never raise enough to fill the need. I just talked to Julia, and she grounded me. I thought that we could try to get some corporate sponsors and make our annual gala really big this year, but it's only two months away. There just isn't time." She wiped her tears again. "Okay, big girl panties time. It is what it is. I tried. Now I need to regroup and lower my aim to what I can accomplish."

Chapter 20 – Adoption Event Confessional, Episode Two

Two days later, Elyse arrived early at the warehouse in Suffolk to ready it for the adoption event. She glanced around the outside of it, wondering if they could buy the warehouse, if outdoor runs could be set up coming out of the back of the warehouse, which was the area she'd convert to the pens and runs. She calculated how much that could possibly cost. That was if the area's zoning would allow an animal shelter to operate here. It was fully a commercial development with roads that had stop signs at every intersection.

She went inside and envisioned putting up walls to divide the space into the section that would house the dogs in the back of the building. Offices and a medical evaluation room would be in the front right of the space. The play yards and other meet and greet spaces would be erected in the front left of the area. There was a single bathroom in there. If need be, another could be added next to it. Knowing what she just spent to finish off a portion of her barn, she had a pretty good idea what it would cost to do a space this large.

Since she was notified her zoning petition was denied, she'd been brainstorming different fundraising ideas. She kept coming back to the annual gala and seeking corporate sponsors, beginning with Tim's firm. She'd approach Michael, Tim's old partner, directly. She wouldn't go through Claire. She was banking on Michael feeling guilt over Tim's death. But she would reach out to Matthew and see if he and his partners would do anything. She'd never asked him for a donation. If they wouldn't do a direct donation, maybe they would buy a table at the gala and attend. That would bring her three thousand dollars. And while they were there, if she was able to score some great items for the silent auction, maybe they would bid on them and end up donating more money.

The volunteers began to arrive with the dogs from the current shelter building. The foster parents brought their fosters as well. She'd sent an email and text out to everyone who volunteered and fostered, asking that they come for a meeting before the event started if they could. She said she had important news on the future of Animal House Shelter.

Jake and four new volunteers from the veterans' support group arrived, as did the two original men he'd recruited. Miles Maitland, the former Army canine handler, had turned out to be invaluable. He had insomnia and was usually awake all night. He had become one of the overnight workers at the current building, usually arriving by six every evening to help feed the dogs dinner and then he worked one on one with the dogs who needed the most training. He stayed through the morning to feed them breakfast as well. He came nearly every night. Trever Ferguson, or Fergie as everyone called him, committed to helping on-site at the event every weekend it would run for the next two months, all day both on Saturday and Sunday. And Jake had told her that he thought both men were benefitting greatly from not only the interactions with the dogs, but also with having somewhere to go and something scheduled to do.

After they got all the dogs settled in their pens, Elyse began the meeting. "Thank you all for coming. I know many of you are in when you had not planned to be here today, or this early. I wanted to give you an update on the zoning petition that I've filed to convert my current barn into our shelter facility. Unfortunately, it has been denied."

Murmurs of surprise were heard from those assembled. She could see the disappointment on all of their faces. She knew that a lot of the volunteers had worked hard to make this rescue a reality. Many of them no doubt thought that she was closing the rescue with this news.

"I've given it a lot of thought what we're going to do from this point forward to keep Animal House operational. Our current facility is full. We could not fit another dog in it if we had to. Plus, as you know, the stairs to get into that building are steep and the building has too many issues to fix. It needs its electrical updated, which is a major issue and will be costly. At some point we're going to have to say the building is no longer safe to be in." It had been donated years ago by a supporter when he passed away. It was better than nothing, but even then Elyse knew it was not a long-term solution.

Coming through the warehouse door, Elyse saw Kelsey. She'd forgotten that she promised to help today. She of course had talked with Kelsey since finding out the petition was denied. She and Kelsey talked, or text messaged daily.

"How much revenue could be generated by selling the building and land? Would that net the rescue enough to buy another location?" Tom Wallace, a long-time volunteer who was also the accountant who handled everything financial for Animal House Shelter, spoke up. "If you haven't yet, I think you should have a realtor perform a market analysis for you."

"Thank you, Tom. Yes, I have consulted with a realtor. Due to the extreme state of disrepair of the building, its age, and the unsafety of the entry, she recommended we pay to have it leveled and sell the empty lot. It would cost more to do that and haul the debris away than that lot is worth."

There was a collective sigh heard from the meeting participants.

Elyse became more depressed about the situation as she informed everyone of what she knew and as she saw their reactions. "I see two options. One, I go ahead and finish the conversion of my barn to use it for just the kenneling facility, but we would still need to transport the dogs here in order to hold our adoption events. And while that would mean that, yes, we could house more dogs, that would just increase our transportation dilemma on adoption weekends. Also, the personal liability to me, given it's on my property, would be increased. I have my attorney working on that. No doubt there would be some strong liability waivers any volunteer coming onto my property would have to sign."

"I'd be willing to make more trips to transport the dogs back and forth," Pam, one of the drivers, said.

"Me, too," several others concurred.

"Thank you all. It's an option. But I have to tell you, I'm also concerned that at some point the owner of this facility will find use for it and either lease it out or sell it. That has been my fear for some time and that is why I wanted to have our own facility that would be open to the public. As far as a public adoption venue, this warehouse works well. A choice I think we have to consider is to ask the current owner if he would be willing to donate it or sell it to us for a reduced cost. We would first see if this warehouse would be zoned to operate as a public animal shelter. Even if he would sell it to us at a greatly reduced cost, there's still a lot of work that would be needed to convert this into a full-time animal shelter, and we would still need to raise funds for that to happen. Our annual gala is in exactly eight weeks. The amount we'd need to net from it would be triple what we received last year. And the venue is the same size as it was last year, though our tables are not sold out yet and we could probably fit a few more tables in there."

There were various side conversations that sprang up between the volunteers. "Elyse, I'm sure I speak for everyone when I say I've tapped on my friends and family as much as I can to attend the gala."

"I know, Pam, and I appreciate it. I think we need to use the gala to focus on getting more donations. And we need to go bigger than individual people. We need corporate sponsors, and we need some cool items for our silent auction to drive up the bidding," Elyse said. "And I will need help identifying those potential sponsors." Elyse paused. She knew she wasn't going to get anything definitive today, but she'd planted the seed of need. She'd give it a week or so and see if anything grew. "Okay, that's all I have. If you think of anything that would be helpful, reach out to me. No idea is crazy. For all our volunteers today and tomorrow, thank you! To our overnight volunteers at the facility, thank you! To each and every one of you, thank you!"

Jake and the four new volunteers approached Elyse. She called Julia over. Introductions were made. Jake would of course start his day working with Frick and Frack in one of the pens where he could play fetch with them to tire them out a bit before working on some basic commands. Julia took the four others to complete volunteer paperwork. She'd then put them to work doing something similar to what Jake was doing with several of their more hyper dogs.

"Hi, Mom," Kelsey greeted her with a hug. Her gaze shifted to Jake, who still stood beside Elyse. "Hi, I'm Kelsey, Elyse's daughter."

"Hi, it's nice to meet you, Kelsey. I'm Jake Tanner." He presented his hand.

They shook.

"Jake is the Navy man I told you about," Elyse said.

"Oh, it's very nice to meet you," Kelsey said, her smile getting bigger. "I know my mom really appreciates the volunteers you've steered her way."

"It's helped them as well. Animal therapy is a recognized treatment for injuries from head trauma to PTSD," he said. "And on that note, Frick and Frack await me. I'm going to go get me some of that beneficial animal therapy." He smiled and nodded. "Ladies."

"You have a lot of volunteers here today," Kelsey said, wondering if she was really needed.

"Many are the drivers and they'll be leaving soon. I'm glad you're here."

"Kade helped me move last weekend. He told me about Mel and the baby," she said.

Elyse wondered what else he'd told her. "Yes, I'm going to be a grandmother again. I'm very happy."

"He also told me...," she began, but they were interrupted by one of the volunteers stepping up to them.

"Elyse, sorry to interrupt, but I have to go and I have a good fundraising idea," Tammie said. "My daughter's soccer team did a new uniform fundraiser can-shake. By standing on a busy intersection during rush hour, eight of us collected five thousand dollars in three hours. People donated whatever change or small bills they had handy, and it added up fast. Just imagine if we put sixteen or twenty volunteers out, canvassing many busy intersections. I'm sure we could double or triple that."

"I will add it to the possible list of fundraising ideas. Thanks, Tammie," Elyse said.

Tammie left and Elyse turned back to Kelsey, wondering what else Kade told her. "I'm sorry, you were saying?" She braced herself.

"He told me that he and Mel are moving home," she said.

Elyse was relieved. Her relaxed smile spread over her face. "Yes. I think it will work out just fine. And if they stay for a while after the baby comes, I'll get to spend a lot of time with my grandchild."

"Yeah, unlike Claire's kids. Honestly, Mom, I was so pissed she didn't bring them to the dinner after my graduation. She acts like they're a huge inconvenience. Why did she even have them to begin with? I know Kade and Mel will be totally different parents and they'll be busy, juggling their jobs and the kids with no nanny, and I'm sure they'll be much more involved and hands on. You can believe their kid will go everywhere with them."

Elyse wrapped an arm around Kelsey. "I know, sweetie. Claire is so much like your father was."

"Yeah. And unfortunately, so is Matthew," Kelsey added.

Just as she'd been surprised by Kade's realization of it, it again surprised her that Kelsey also recognized it. Elyse knew she had to talk to Claire soon, especially since she strongly felt that there was more than that wrong at Claire's house. She wouldn't say the kids were being neglected, but there were some issues that she believed would harm the kids that she was sure Claire did not see.

Potential adoptive families began to arrive, and Elyse and Kelsey got pulled into working with them. That conversation would have to rest where it was. The morning was busy. Elyse couldn't help but sneak glances Jake's way every chance she got. He was having so much fun with Frick and Frack. She wished he could adopt them. She considered taking them herself, for him, but then banished the thought as ridiculous. They were a handful, and it wouldn't be fair to Charlie to bring them home.

At lunchtime, Kelsey volunteered to go pick up sandwiches for all the volunteers before she headed back to Norfolk. She was working in the tattoo shop from two that afternoon until closing.

"Thank you, sweetie. Let me get you cash. My purse is in my trunk." A nearby grocery store donated the slightly out of date, unsold sub sandwiches to their organization on adoption days instead of throwing them away. Elyse always paid for several bags of chips to go with the sandwiches.

Jake had just returned Frick and Frack to their pen when he saw Elyse slip out the side door. He followed her, catching up with her by the trunk of her car. "Where are you running off to?"

Elyse turned to face him. "Nowhere, just getting some cash for Kelsey. She's going to go pick up the sandwiches."

Jake leaned in and kissed her lips. "I've been wanting to do that all day."

"I missed you last night," she said.

"I missed you. I'm sorry I had duty. But I'm yours tonight," he said with a smile. He glanced around to be sure no one would see them before he kissed her again.

"All night?" she asked, after their lips separated.

"Yes, ma'am," he replied. Then he kissed her again, also embracing her.

Kelsey figured she'd just go out and meet her mom in the parking lot. She pushed open the side door and froze where she was. Her mom and that Navy guy were kissing, as in arms around each other, lips to lips kissing. She quietly reclosed the door and hurried towards the front of the warehouse's open garage door. She'd wait there.

Her mom re-entered the warehouse, that man following right behind her. Jeez! They weren't even trying to hide that they were outside together. *Oh my God! My mom is already seeing that guy! How is that possible?* Kelsey thought.

"Okay, here you go," Elyse said, handing a twenty to Kelsey. "Just get as many bags as possible of a variety of chips that this will buy you."

Kelsey took the money, flustered. "Sure, I'll be back in a few." She turned to leave.

"Kels, is everything okay?" Elyse asked.

"Yes, everything is fine." She turned and hurried from the warehouse. No, everything was not fine. As soon as she pulled out of the parking lot, she hit dial on her phone. She hoped Kade was available.

Kade sat in the unit beside Cletus. It had been a strangely quiet day, five calls but zero transports. His phone rang. It was Kelsey. "Hi Kels, I'm at work. It's quiet now but if a call comes in...," he said.

"Yes, yes, I know you'll have to go. Kade, I just saw something, OMG! I can't believe it. Mom was just kissing this guy."

Kade sucked in a breath. *Oh shit, Kelsey is not going to take this well,* he thought. His eyes flickered to Cletus. "Kelsey found out about Mom and Jake," he whispered, covering the phone. He'd told him the shift they'd worked together after he'd walked in on his mom and Jake. Now that he'd really had a chance to think about it, and Cletus had imparted some of his jovial wisdom, he was perfectly fine with his mom having a boyfriend.

"She needs to know things were not all wine and roses with your mom and dad. And your mom needs to have this man be a part of her whole life. That life includes Kelsey and broom-stick Claire," Cletus said.

Kade chuckled at Cletus' humor. "Kels, did you ask Mom about it?"

"No, she didn't see me. I was too shocked to say anything."

"Have you met him? He's a nice guy," Kade said.

"What? You know?"

"Yes. I found out last week the same way you did. I had a chance to sit down and talk to them both. He's a nice guy, and he really likes and respects Mom. They were friends first," he added, as though it would make a difference. Kelsey returned silence from her side of the call. "Kels, I know you think Mom and Dad had this great, really close relationship, and I know they loved each other, but when was the last time you saw them kiss? When was the last time he was home? She has fun with Jake. They go out. They talk a lot more than she and Dad ever did. He's a companion and a friend."

"And obviously more than a friend," Kelsey said.

"Kels, when Mel moved in with me after we were only together for a few weeks, Mom never once said anything that it was too fast or anything. I know it was the same for you moving in with Ashley. Why was it okay for both of us, but it's not for Mom? Yeah, it's only been two months since Dad died, but they were basically separated for years."

"They weren't separated as in the marriage is over, separated," Kelsey argued.

"Weren't they?" Kade challenged. "Seriously, Kelsey, think about it. They were two very different people with separate lives. As I said, I'm sure they loved each other, but I doubt it was a romantic love. How could it be?"

"Mom always said he was the love of her life," Kelsey said.

"And I'm sure he was. But that relationship changed over time and I'm sure she was lonely. She isn't now. Doesn't she deserve to be happy? And if not now, when?"

"I'm at the store. I have to go in and pick up sandwiches for Mom."

"Kelsey, think about what I said. You need to talk to Mom and let her know that you know. It'll make things so much easier, and I guarantee you'll feel better about it."

"Okay, thanks. Bye." She disconnected the call, feeling betrayed by Kade. He'd known and he hadn't told her. Her phone rang a callback from Kade. "What?" she said, answering it.

"I didn't tell you because Mom asked me not to tell either you or Claire yet out of respect for Dad's memory. That has to count for something. And Kels, don't tell Claire. She'll go off the deep end."

"That's an understatement. Thanks, Kade."

"Okay, call me back if you want. Bye."

"Bye."

Kade thought about it for only a second and then he hit dial, calling his mom.

"Hi Kade," Elyse greeted.

"Hi Mom. I just had a call from Kelsey. She knows. She saw you and Jake kissing."

"Oh, shit," Elyse swore.

"Language, Mom," Kade teased.

"I knew something was wrong before she left."

"I told her to tell you she knows. I also told her not to tell Claire."

"Was she mad that you knew but didn't tell her?" Elyse asked. She knew her daughter well enough to know it was a possibility.

"At first. I think she's okay now," Kade answered. "I also told her that I think Jake is a nice guy and you deserve to have companionship and be happy."

"Thanks, Kade. And thank you for letting me know she called you. If she doesn't bring it up, I will."

"Can you leave me out of it?"

Elyse sighed. "Yes, I won't tell her you called."

Elyse found Jake and told him. "When she comes back in, I'm going to pull her aside and talk to her if she doesn't bring it up. Do me a favor and give me a few minutes with her and then follow us to wherever we're talking. You worked some magic with Kade. I'm counting on you doing the same with Kelsey."

"I'll try. Kade was easy, we talked man to man."

When Kelsey pulled back into her parking spot at the warehouse, she'd decided she couldn't talk with her mom about this yet. She'd go in, drop the food, and exit as quickly as she could. She wanted to talk with Ash about it and get his opinion. Kade was okay with it. Was she over-reacting?

She brought the bags in. Her mom was standing directly in front of her. "Thank you for picking these up, sweetie."

"You're welcome." She set the bags on the table. "I have to go. I'll see you soon." She turned and stepped out of the warehouse.

Elyse nodded to Jake and then she followed her out. "Kels, can I talk to you for a second?" She caught up with her at her car.

Kelsey turned. "Sure, Mom, what's up?"

"This is going to be kind of like the talk we had when you told me about grad school, tattooing, and Ash. I wanted to tell you that I'm seeing Jake, the man from the Navy. I loved your father, Kelsey, but he was never home, and it's been lonely for me since you went away to school. The relationship we had was not what either of us set out for it to be, but neither of us wanted to end it because we did love and respect each other, but it hadn't been a romantic love in years. And that was fine with us both. But after I met Jake, we became friends. To coordinate his volunteers we went to dinner, we talked. It was comfortable and I really liked his company, which made me realize what I hadn't had in so long. He's a really nice man, Kelsey, and I'm glad he's in my life. I want you to know about it and hopefully be okay with it."

Kelsey sighed and looked away. She didn't want to have this conversation with her about this now. "I don't know if I can be okay with this, Mom."

"I'm sure it's a shock. I'll tell you that Kade also knows. Maybe talk with him about it. He was shocked at first, too, but after he thought about it and we talked, I think he's okay with it. I asked him not to tell either you or Claire, so don't be mad at him that he didn't tell you. He understood this was for me to tell you each when I wanted to, when I felt the time was right."

"So, Claire doesn't know?" Kelsey asked.

"No, she's going to take it the hardest. She won't understand that life is short and there are no guarantees in how long any of us will be here, so waiting to do something that will make you happy is stupid. Spending time with Jake makes me happy."

"I get that, but why can't you just be friends. Why does it have to be romantic?"

"Why couldn't you and Ash just be friends? Why do you have to sleep with him?" Elyse asked but then answered her own question without taking a breath. "Because you feel something more than friendship for him. Because there is a romantic spark there, an attraction."

Kelsey nodded as Jake approached.

"Now let me properly introduce you," Elyse said. "Jake, this is my youngest daughter and my best friend, Kelsey. Kelsey, this is Jake Tanner, a man I've been spending time with who has become special to me."

"Hello again, Kelsey," Jake said. His eyes shifted to Elyse. "Elyse, can you give me a second with Kelsey?"

"Sure." She embraced her daughter. "I love you. Drive safely back to the shop. I'll talk to you later."

"Love you, too, Mom." She watched her mom go back into the warehouse.

"Your mom is an amazing person. I respect her tremendously. Getting to know her over the last few months has reminded me what I've been missing in my life, someone to share it with. Have you ever met someone you feel so comfortable with, who you can just be yourself with? Someone you can talk with and laugh with. Well, that's what I found in your mom."

"I get it," said Kelsey. "It's just a shock, though. My mom said that you make her happy and that's all that matters. I'll warn you, though, my sister Claire isn't going to feel the same way. So good luck with that."

Jake chuckled. "I'm looking forward to meeting her."

"No, you're really not," Kelsey said. She beamed a smile at him. "Tell my mom I'm okay with this and I'll talk to her tomorrow."

"Will do," he said.

Chapter 21 – Planning Session Depression

No matter what Tom Wallace did with the numbers, there was no way they would ever make enough in donations to afford to fix the electric and plumbing. And it would cost as much to level the current shelter location to ready it for sale. And that wasn't where Elyse wanted the money that they would raise from the gala to go. They still needed to fund the rescue for the next year.

Elyse glanced at each person who sat around her kitchen table. Besides Tom, Julia was there. A woman by the name of Cassie Eischen, who had been a professional corporate event planner before her company downsized and she was let go a year earlier, sat beside Julia. After she lost her job was when she started to volunteer at Animal House. Elyse was glad to have her experience on the gala planning committee. Pam, the volunteer who had suggested the can-shake had also said she wanted to be in on the planning. Jake rounded out the six-person committee. Elyse found over the years that six was a good number to plan their fundraisers. There was truth to the saying that too many cooks in the kitchen ruin the stew.

"Okay," Elyse said. "I don't want to put any money into the current building. If we decide where the dogs will go to empty that facility out I say we put it on the market as is, at a rock-bottom price. Any amount we can get out of it's better than putting a dime into it."

"Agreed," Jake seconded. "There's another option I haven't heard discussed. Tom, you'd be able to give a financial opinion on this. Could Elyse split her land and sell or donate the barn and a swath of property to the rescue without it being rezoned as commercial and with no public access expected? That way it could house the rescued animals as planned and the volunteers coming to tend them and pick them up to transport them to events wouldn't be on Elyse's property, eliminating liability to her?"

"Say, Jake, I think you might have something there. It would remain agriculture in the zoning," Tom said. His gaze shifted to Elyse. "If you donated it, you'd have the tax write-off this year and you wouldn't have any funds going to it."

"I could run it by the zoning board, just to make sure it wouldn't be a problem," Elyse said, nodding her head. "This might be the best we can do right now. I think it might be our second-best option if we can't buy a place to house the dogs that will allow the public to meet them there." Even as she said it, she wasn't happy with the idea. It felt like she was settling. It wasn't what she wanted, though what she did want had been a lofty goal. She'd just have to pray that Sal, who owned the warehouse, wouldn't rent it or sell it.

"Okay, so, the gala," Cassie said. "Bring me up to speed on what's already done, so I can make suggestions."

"Thank you, Cassie. We really appreciate your expertise," Elyse said.

For about fifteen minutes, Elyse filled everyone in on the plans that had been made, so far. They had signed a contract the previous year with their venue, a hotel's banquet facility. The owner of the hotel was donating the profit he'd make to the rescue, for the tax deduction, of course; the fee that would normally be collected above and beyond staff and food costs, including linen and cleaning.

They would charge two hundred dollars a plate. The venue's costs came down to one hundred per person, so they would make one hundred on each person who bought a ticket to the gala. So far they only had half of their tickets sold, but this was normal for them. It was usually within the last two months that the remainder of the tickets would sell.

Their title for the evening was the Black and White Gala. It was black tie, formal, meant to be an elegant evening. They took a few minutes and discussed the decorations that Elyse envisioned. Cassie had some great ideas she added. Elyse turned the decorations for the event over to Cassie, with a specified budget.

Their regular emcee, John Harris, was again donating his services in exchange for a receipt to claim on his taxes. He was an engaging and funny host. Elyse had just confirmed with him earlier that morning, so she knew they still had him.

"The problem is entertainment," Elyse said. "We had a great couple booked. They performed with keyboard, guitar, and vocals. They had a great range. I called them to confirm but unfortunately, they no longer live in the area. They moved to Florida in January. They said they'd come if we paid their airfare and all other expenses. I said no."

"You know who you should try to get?" Jake asked. "Eddie Brown."

Elyse looked at him and shook her head. "Who's Eddie Brown?"

"He's the keyboardist and vocalist during the services at Flowing Waters," Jake said.

"You've been to the services?" This was news to her. And he knew him by name?

"A few times," Jake said. "This guy has amazing pipes. You know him, Elyse. He's in your widow support group."

"He is?" She searched her thoughts for a man named Eddie. Only one came to mind. "The white-haired, African-American gentleman?"

"Yes, that's him," Jake said. "Will you be at the meeting on Wednesday? Maybe we can approach him together?"

"Yes, let's do that. But we do need to come up with a short-list of a few more names," Elyse said. "We can spend a few hundred for the entertainment, but obviously, if we can find someone to donate their services, that would be best."

Next, they talked about acquiring great, high-end donated items for the silent auction. This had been especially difficult in the past. "Let me work on this one," Cassie said. "There are some people I know with amazing sports and concert tickets to local venues who never use them or give them away to customers or clients. A few owe me a favor or two."

"That would be amazing," Julia said. "We need things that will drive the bidding high because people actually want them."

"I mentioned this last Saturday, and I really think this could be profitable. We need to solicit corporate sponsors for either a cash donation or for them to sponsor a table or two. They could give the tickets to their employees, clients, customers, whatever. Or they can let us fill the seats," Elyse said.

"I think that's a great idea," Cassie said.

"I have two firms in mind where I have a direct relationship with one of the partners," Elyse said. "I've never tapped either one for a donation. But I will admit I'm at a loss at who else to approach. I don't mind making an appointment with anyone. I'd like to target those who may be inclined to donate, though."

"You want to target animal lovers, businesses needing a tax deduction, or businesses that have gotten bad press lately and need to boost their image," Cassie said. "I'll work on that, too. I also think you need to send a text out to all the volunteers and see if they have any ideas and if anyone would feel comfortable doing the approach."

At the end of the meeting, Elyse felt a little less depressed. They had ideas, which was more than they had when they first sat down. She truly hoped Cassie could deliver on all she had said she would work on. They had a volunteer one year who took on a lot of the task and then, poof, they were gone without providing a single thing. Elyse didn't know why she was skeptical of Cassie, she just was.

She and Jake saw the others to the door. After they left, she wrapped her arms around his neck and dropped her head to his chest. "Thank you for volunteering to help with this."

"You seemed kind of down as we planned," he said.

"I'll still have to put some more money into the barn renovation to house the dogs there, if that's the route we go. I really have my heart set on a location to house them as well as having public access. I guess it's depressing admitting that we'll fall short and not be able to do that."

"You have a good group. You never know what you might accomplish. And I do like Tom. He's smart and straight-forward, and will give you realistic predictions. I'm here to keep your dreams flying, though. Don't give up until the final donation dollars are counted."

She kissed him with appreciation. He was a true partner and encouraged her, encouraged her dreams. She'd never had that with Tim. She'd learned over the years that he was oblivious to most things, especially something that was important to her.

• • • •

IN THE THREE AND A half weeks since Aiden broke his arm, Claire had spent three afternoons alone with each of her kids. She did solo trips with them each to the park and to the ice cream parlor. She took a trip to the zoo with just Emma and had a movie afternoon with Aiden. She'd taken her mom's advice to model the behavior she wanted to see from Matthew, and she had told him how nice the time alone had been. And she hadn't been lying. It was so much more relaxed with only one child. She told him this, too. She encouraged him to as well, but so far he hadn't.

So, she carefully planned an evening away where she had a thought-out agenda of items to discuss and ways to phrase it so she wouldn't put Matthew on the defensive. She wanted to talk with him about his lack of interest in spending time with the kids and about her perception that he was pulling away from her. She had supporting circumstances to relate as well as an admission that she knew she had been difficult to live with since her dad died, and offer him her understanding that maybe he was just stepping back and allowing her the time she needed to grieve. She also would invite him to bring up his issues with her as her mom suggested.

She'd reserved a room at one of their favorite hotels on the beach, but didn't tell him. She merely told him of the dinner reservations. She packed a bag for him. He had gone into work that afternoon to meet with clients, so she met him there. They had a gourmet dinner on the starlit patio while drinking martinis. The temperature outside was perfect.

After dinner she would have loved to go for a walk on the beach to talk, but she knew that was not one of Matthew's favorite places. And tonight was about getting him to open up. By the time dessert came he already seemed calmer, and the conversation between them was comfortable and relaxed. That was when she realized that yes, he had seemed quite stressed when he arrived. And that stressed state had become his normal.

After they'd finished their shared dessert, a decadent white chocolate cheesecake, Claire smiled and held up the room key. "I got us a room for the night."

"What's the occasion?"

"A night and a morning away from the kids, just the two of us. A complete date night."

"We haven't done that in a long time," Matthew said.

"Check-out isn't until eleven. I figured we could order room service for breakfast and lounge around all morning. We've both been working long hours and I've traveled a few times this month. I've missed us. I've enjoyed my afternoons out with each of the kids, one-on-one time, and I realized you and I haven't had that in too long."

Matthew reached across the table and took hold of her hand. "That's nice. I've missed what it was like when it was just us."

Claire waited for him to add something to the effect that he loved the children, but he didn't. "You seem to get, oh, I don't know, overwhelmed with both the kids sometimes." She watched him as she said it to gauge how he felt about it.

He took another drink of his martini. "The constant noise and chattering about absolutely nothing gets on my nerves, especially when my mind is on work."

"I've found the two-hour one-on-one blocks of time with them each to be really helpful in that regard. I think when they're together, they're sometimes trying to out talk the other to get our attention. Another benefit of it is, at four and a half, Aiden is capable of such different things than Emma. Have you given any thought to scheduling one-on-one time when you can shut work off for a few hours maybe on a Sunday afternoon?"

"I haven't thought about it."

Claire was getting annoyed. "Why don't you want to?"

"It's not that I don't want to. I told you, I haven't given it any thought."

Claire took the last drink of her martini. Whew! That was strong. "Are you almost done? I'd like to head up to the room." She wanted to have the part of the conversation where she admitted she'd been moody since her dad died and give Matthew the opportunity to agree with her that he had stepped back to allow her time to grieve and work through it. That would be followed up with a new commitment to each other and coming to an agreement of expectations, in their marriage and as parents. This would be followed by sex, which they hadn't had in over a month.

Matthew pointed to the far end of the patio at the acoustic guitar player who was setting up. "It's early. Don't you want to have another drink and listen to him for a bit?"

"Sure, we could do that," she agreed. "I know I've been moody since my dad died, and I'm sorry for how I've let it impact our marriage. I think I'm working through the grief. It was just such a shock."

"It was," he agreed. Then he flagged down their server and ordered another round.

"Matthew, I appreciate that you have given me the time and space I've needed to grieve, but I feel a distance between us that I think is because of it, and I want things back the way they were," she said in a volume just above a whisper, as she didn't want to be heard at the surrounding tables.

"Were how?" he asked, his voice at a normal level.

Her annoyance level was spiking. "You've seemed stressed lately," she said, still whispering.

He shrugged. "I guess."

The guitar player began his first set and Matthew's attention went to him. Claire didn't know if she was more aggravated or depressed by this. She tucked away the conversation for now. She'd bring things back up once they were in their room.

Several hours and several drinks later, Claire and Matthew stumbled into their room. Claire had initiated no further conversation on her topics for the evening as they listened to the soft rock music of the solo musician. It wasn't too loud, and they did talk a bit about possible vacation plans with and without the children over the next year.

Once they were inside their room and the door was locked, Matthew shifted into sex mode. Claire didn't want to kill the mood by bringing up difficult conversation topics. That could wait until the morning. Sex was always phenomenal, and that night didn't disappoint. As Claire lay in his arms wide awake long after he'd fallen asleep, she tried to turn off the many thoughts that were in her head.

She was still bothered that at no time that evening had Matthew declared that he loved the kids and was glad they had them. Even when she threw out the possibility of a Disney World vacation, Matthew just cringed and didn't acknowledge that the kids would love it. All he did say about any vacation with the kids was that Lizette would have to come, too, so they could enjoy adult time away for dinner in the evening.

The next morning, she woke to Matthew caressing her with intent. She normally would want a cup of coffee first, but she needed him in a good mood for the conversation she would make sure they had over breakfast. No more pussyfooting around. She'd be direct and clear. She got in the mood and the sex was better than she expected without coffee bringing her to a fully alert state.

"Why don't you order us coffee and some breakfast. I need to take a quick rinse-off shower." She pulled herself from his arms and out of the bed.

THAT FIRST YEAR

While in the shower, Claire mentally regrouped, getting her head around the topics they needed to discuss. After she toweled off, she slid on the sexy satin and lace robe she'd brought. She hoped they would eat, talk, come to an agreement, and then make love again before the eleven o'clock checkout time.

When she came out of the bathroom, she found Matthew propped up in bed with the television on. Great, now she'd have to get that distraction turned off. She mounted the bed from the foot of it and crawled up towards him on all fours. She sat, straddling him. "How long until breakfast and coffee are due?"

Matthew shifted her to one side and looked past her. "Should be here in about forty minutes. I'm trying to watch this."

She picked up the remote control and clicked the pause button. "No, you're not. There are a few things I need to talk to you about. I need your attention for just a few minutes."

Matthew's demeanor instantly changed. "I'm listening." His gaze was hard.

"Last night and this morning were so nice. We need to make an effort to do this more often."

His expression softened. "I'd like that."

"You have seemed stressed, like I said last night. And you've been working more at home and on Saturdays than you ever have. Are you overloaded at work, or is the company in trouble?" She waited and watched his eyes shift around. He was silent too long. "Or are you using it to avoid being at home and engaged with us?"

His eyes went wide, and Claire knew she'd guessed it.

281

"It's not entirely that I'm avoiding being with you," he finally said. "The demands are more. We've doubled our client base in three years without hiring any additional staff."

"Are these Wednesday night golf league things working, client-focused outings, or are they purely personal and fun?" She knew she sounded like she was interrogating him, and that hadn't been her intention.

"Both. You know there's no way to be with my partners and not talk work, but it's competitive league play too. I'm not going to lie. It's fun and I really enjoy it."

"There needs to be balance, Matthew. I have no problem with your Wednesday night golf league nights if you have your phone on in case I need you, like the night I had to bring Aiden to the hospital. But I need to spend time with you alone and we need to spend time with the kids, all four of us as a family. And you need to spend time alone with your kids. If they get on your nerves when you're around both, then you need to do one-on-one outings like I have. You can't tell me that you can't carve out four hours a week for your kids."

"Listen to yourself, Claire. It's not just four hours a week. How many hours are we talking that you think all four of us need to be together? And I thought you and I do spend time alone together, and time out with your friends doing couples dinners. And you're always on my back to go to church at least once a month, if not more. How much more time do you need?"

His reply and tone of voice pissed Claire off. She went from zero to sixty in two seconds flat. "Oh, so breakfast and dinner with your family a few times a week is too much to ask? And church, once in a blue moon? Really? You're a father, Matthew. Time with your family comes with the territory."

"If it was pleasant, it wouldn't be an issue. Come on, Claire, you know getting through a dinner without one of the kids throwing a fit or spilling food all over never happens. The whining and negotiating with one of them to try a bite of their beans or finish their chicken nugget is a never-ending battle that I just can't tolerate any longer. And nothing I ever do is good enough for you. I make all the wrong calls with the kids when I'm just trying to keep the peace. You've made it clear that I don't parent as you'd like, so how can you be surprised that I'm done trying?" He pushed her off himself and carried his bag into the bathroom.

Claire sat on the bed, shocked by his declaration. Anger surged through her. And she wanted to cry, she was so hurt. When he came out of the bathroom, fully dressed, and began to pick up the clothes he had on the night before from the floor, she jumped from the bed. "What are you doing?"

"I'm going."

She grabbed his shoes. "You aren't going until we come to an agreement."

"Fine, we have an agreement. What do you want, breakfast three days a week? Great, yes. We'll start our days out with aggravation three days a week. Dinner twice a week, fantastic! I'll elevate my blood pressure two nights a week. And one-on-one time, sure. I'll take Emma to the park every Saturday morning and I'll figure out something Aiden and I can do together for a few hours every Sunday afternoon since you've decided he's old enough to do things I enjoy. And oh yes, keep planning the evenings out with your friends and their husbands. We'll pretend to be the perfect couple."

Claire hated to cry. It was a sign of weakness she seldom allowed to show. But she couldn't stop the tears that streamed down her face. "I thought you enjoyed dinners out with them. You never said you didn't."

Matthew let out a frustrated sigh. He ran both hands through his hair. "I don't mind them. I just wish you'd ask once in a while before you plan and commit us."

Claire looked away and nodded. She still clutched his shoes to her chest. She wanted to throw them at his face, hard. "You know, if we get divorced, you'll have the kids one night a week and every other weekend."

Matthew moaned. "I don't want a divorce."

"I don't want things to continue as they are. Something needs to change, Matthew."

He dropped his bag to the floor and then climbed onto the bed. He wrapped his arms around her. "I don't want a divorce, Claire. I love you and the kids. I'm sure this is just a phase that they're getting on my nerves so badly. I'll try and do the one-on-one time to see if it makes a difference. But I need you to back off for a bit and give me some space. Can you do that?"

Claire nodded.

"And please don't cry."

Chapter 22 – Hardball Home Run

E lyse felt nervous as she put her car into park. It had been months since she'd visited this building. Calling and making the appointment caused her no stress. Driving here, parking, and staring at the familiar five-story beige building with large black windows spiked every stress hormone in her body. Kensington-Laramie was on the fifth floor.

She felt her heart race as she pushed through the lobby doors. The white floors reflected the sun for the moment the door was open, momentarily blinding her since she'd left her sunglasses in her car. She went to the elevator and pressed the up arrow, hoping that when the car arrived it would be empty. Thankfully, it was. She took calming breaths as the elevator rose. Kensington-Laramie was one of three offices on this floor. Its door was tucked around the corner.

She couldn't help but glance over the gold print on the door into their suite. Tim's name remained beneath Michael's. She wondered when Michael would get around to removing it. She pushed the door open and stepped inside the suite, hoping she wouldn't see Claire until at least after her meeting with Michael.

Tara Britton rose from her reception desk as soon as she entered. "Elyse, it's so nice to see you." She came out from behind it and greeted Elyse with a hug. "How have you been? Please know you have been in my thoughts."

"Thank you, Tara. I've been well. How are you?" Elyse asked.

"Good, good," Tara said.

Tara Britton had been the receptionist at the firm for as long as the firm had been in existence. She was older than Elyse, more around Michael's age. Her late husband had been a partner back when the firm was formed. Back then it was Kensington-Britton-Laramie. That was before the firm had crossed out of the red. Grant Britton suffered a massive coronary at the age of forty-five, nearly twenty years before. Tara had since remarried several times. Elyse wasn't sure what she negotiated with Michael and Tim when Grant died, but Elyse was sure it was the job she still occupied, as there were no funds at that time for her to get a cut of, and no guarantee of any funds to come. Certainly none her late husband would have brought to the firm.

"Michael is just finishing up a call," Tara said, moving back behind her desk. "I'll message him and tell him you're here. I'm sure he'll be out momentarily to greet you."

"Thanks, Tara," Elyse said. She paced around and viewed the familiar pictures and technical drawings that were displayed on the walls.

She didn't have to wait long. "Elyse," she heard Michael's scratchy voice say from the hallway that led within the suite.

She turned and smiled. "Hello, Michael." She stepped towards him, and they embraced.

"I was so surprised to see you on my calendar as an appointment. Surely, you know you're welcome to drop by anytime."

"I wanted to be sure you'd be here and available," she said.

Michael led her to his office, which was the first one on the left, a corner office. Tim's had been the other corner office with the junior employees and support staff occupying smaller offices between them. He closed the door and motioned to the comfortable seating to the side of his desk.

Elyse settled on the brown leather sofa.

"I've thought of you often. I'm sorry I haven't called. I've asked Claire often how you're doing, and she's told me you're doing well. Otherwise, I would have reached out."

"Michael, really, it's fine you haven't. I understand life and business never stop. The firm was swamped with work when Tim was alive. I'm sure that hasn't changed."

"No, it hasn't. I've hired a few new young associates, but they are years away from being able to handle even a quarter of the jobs Tim did. The one thing they have going for them is that they're young and eager. They'll travel with no restrictions. Chris Barton took over Tim's work for the last few months, but he's just told me he will only travel fifty percent of the time going forward. I know Claire is a mom. I haven't tapped on her before now, but with Chris pulling back I'm going to need to have her pick up some of the slack."

Elyse wondered if that's what he thought her visit was about. "I wasn't going to mention it, Michael, but since you brought it up, I already sacrificed my married life with Tim because he was always away. I sacrificed my husband's life. I won't sacrifice my daughter to this firm. When you schedule her for trips, do not send her to investigate a collapse. I could not bear it if you ever called me to tell me my daughter was crushed to death as you did the news of Tim's death."

"Elyse, Claire was training with Tim for that very purpose. Besides myself, she's the best we've got to investigate collapses."

Elyse shook her head. "No, Michael. Not Claire. Not on-site. You're going to have to get back out in the field and work with one of these young, eager associates. Make one of them your protégé, your expert. Either that or maybe Kensington-Laramie isn't the go-to firm for a few years." She saw shock flash across his face. "But as I said, I wasn't going to bring this up. It's not the purpose of my visit."

"And what is?" he asked, now on the defensive.

"As you know, I run Animal House Shelter. We are funded completely through donations. We are preparing for our Annual Gala, which is our biggest fundraising event of the year. It's on Saturday August twelfth. We have a formal theme this year with a delicious catered dinner, entertainment, dancing, great items up for bid in our silent auction, and of course donations to the organization. I'm looking for corporate sponsors we can list and publicize their generosity. The cost is two hundred per plate, ten at each table, with one hundred of each plate going directly to AHS. Given that the Laramie name is half of this firm, I'm coming to you to ask what I can count on from Kensington-Laramie."

Michael stared at her, dumbfounded. "A donation," he repeated.

"Yes, either a cash donation directly to the organization or you could buy a table or two. You could give the tickets to local clients, your employees, whoever you would like. Or you could sponsor a few tables and let me fill the seats for you." She knew Michael well enough to see the gears turning in his head on how to phrase his decline. "Look, Michael, because Tim died doing this firm's work, the money I would have used from his salary to keep the shelter afloat has been cut off. You and Tim had an old agreement in place that gave you all of this firm at the time of his death. My attorney tells me I could sue and be awarded either a large cash settlement or a piece of this company due to the age of that agreement. It's so old, it still has Grant Britton's name on it. I don't want that. I just want the money I was counting on for operational costs that died with Tim."

Michael scrubbed his hand over his face. "Oh, Elyse, please don't phrase it that way. You know I feel horrible that Tim died while working. But you did receive a large life insurance payout the firm had on him."

"I received the smaller of the two the firm had on him. You received the other, larger payout. And that life insurance amount is not what he would have made until retirement; even less if you account for the increase that will occur in the cost of living each year."

"The payout I received was for staff to replace Tim, the two associates I hired."

"I'm sure they're both making half of what Tim was. We both know Tim was the best in the field, and it was his expertise that brought the clients to Kensington-Laramie. And I'm sure that's why you want to parade Claire out there; another Laramie, Tim's daughter."

Michael's lips tipped into a grin. "You better believe it. Tim's name means something in the structural and forensic engineering communities."

"Michael, I have never asked this firm to sponsor my animal shelter before now. It's in peril. I already lost my husband this year. I cannot lose my shelter, too. I'm asking you to do the right thing. You know that life insurance policy is but a fraction of what his salary over the next twenty years would have been, and we both know he would still be here at your age if he was alive."

"You are one hell of a negotiator," Michael said. "If Claire takes after her mom at all, maybe we have her in the wrong position."

"Just as long as that position isn't inside a collapsed structure. The firm does plenty of work with architects during renovations. Her impressive engineering knowledge can be put to good use there as well. Or she can continue to do in-office backup for the engineer on-site to help investigate the collapse, as she did for Tim. Now back to the donation?"

Michael smiled and shook his head. "I'm impressed, Elyse. Yes, Kensington-Laramie will make a cash donation. What's the highest level of corporate donor you have?"

"That would be our Platinum Level Sponsor, which provides a minimum donation of twenty-thousand dollars. This sponsor level gives the sponsor organization their logo on our website with links directly to that partner organization's website. We acknowledge their rise to the Platinum Level at the gala. We also do a write-up in our monthly newsletter as well as a prominent placement of that sponsor organization on all AHS social media as well as any and all printed material for one year."

"Fine, one year only, Elyse."

Elyse smiled at him. "And Claire?"

"You have my word. I won't send her on-site to a collapse. She's going to be pissed."

"But she won't know that it came from me," Elyse said.

"Fine," he repeated. "Are you sure you don't want to come work for me? I could use you to negotiate contracts."

Elyse chuckled. "No, I think one Laramie at this firm is enough. As long as you don't send her on-site at a collapse, you have my word that you will never hear from my attorney."

"But I hope I will hear from you from time to time, just to say hi. I miss Tim and not just the work he did. He was a friend, too," Michael said.

Elyse nodded. "I know. The two of you probably talked more than he and I did over the last fifteen years."

"He was the best in the field. You were right about that."

"Yes, I was very proud of him. He did what he loved, a job that mattered to him," Elyse said.

"And you stuck by him. I didn't travel as much as he did, and my wife left me years ago because of it. I always admired you for that," Michael said.

"Thank you, Michael," Elyse said, coming to her feet. "Will I be able to be handed that donation before I go?"

Michael smiled and shook his head. "You are good! I'll write you the check right now. I assume it's tax deductible?"

"Yes, we are a 501c3 charity."

Elyse left the building with the check and an assurance that Claire would not follow directly in her father's footsteps. That was a win. She'd accomplished what she came to do. And she didn't run into Claire while she was there either. She knew that Michael had moved Claire into Tim's old corner office right after his death, another indication he had originally planned to push Tim's work off on her. Regardless of his age, Michael needed to put himself back out into the field while he trained someone else for the collapse investigations, anyone else but Claire.

Did she feel bad for practically threatening Michael? No, actually she didn't.

Michael Kensington didn't care that Tim was away from home so much, making Kensington-Laramie a prominent name in the industry and a lot of money. His own wife had left him because of the incredible strain the traveling put on their marriage, but he didn't think to help Tim, his friend, avoid the same outcome. And he was prepared to inflict the same strain on Claire's family. The fact that Kensington-Laramie had a larger life insurance policy on Tim with the organization the beneficiary than the policy that would take care of Tim's family showed how much Michael cared about Tim's family.

• • • •

ELYSE HAD ALREADY CANCELLED dinner with Claire before driving into Norfolk to meet with Michael Kensington, just in case she was to see her there or if Claire was to find out about the meeting. She knew Claire would be livid, and time to cool off before they would talk would help. She knew her daughter well. Her dinner plans instead were to meet Jake at her favorite pizza place.

He was seated when she arrived. He stood as she approached the table, and he greeted her with an embrace and a kiss. She slid into the booth opposite him. The server approached with a beer in her hand. She set it in front of Jake.

"What can I get you to drink?"

Elyse's eyes flashed to his drink. "A glass of your house cab, please."

"I already ordered the pizza," Jake said.

"Thanks. I suppose it's okay to drink before our support meetings."

"It's not like we're going to an AA meeting."

Elyse laughed. "No, it isn't."

"How did your appointment go?"

Elyse filled Jake in on the entire meeting. "Twenty-thousand dollars," she told him proudly.

"Congrats," he said with a big smile. "Definitely a reason to celebrate with a glass of wine."

"I do enjoy a glass of red with my pizza."

When the server brought it, Jake held his beer up. "To you, Elyse Laramie. Fundraiser extraordinaire."

She laughed at his description. "More like blackmailer extraordinaire, but I'll take it." She took a drink of her wine. Jake chuckled at her statement. "Seems almost sacrilegious to have literally just blackmailed Michael and drank a toast to it before going to church."

Jake laughed a full belly laugh. "You're not going to church, just a meeting in one of the conference rooms. But if you do need to go anyplace to look for absolution of your sins, I think the church is a good place to try."

"Well then, while I'm at it, let's add one more sin after tonight's meetings."

"Why, Elyse Laramie, are you inviting me to come over tonight?" he began.

"Yes, I am," she answered quickly with a smile on her face.

He roared out in laughter.

The rest of their dinner was fun, overflowing with inuendo. Elyse had a wonderful time with him, as always. As they left the restaurant, he leaned into her up against her car and kissed her in a way that made her want to skip the meeting and just go back to her house. But they planned to talk with Eddie Brown during the break. Securing entertainment for the gala had to be more important than what she would rather be doing.

As always, Elyse found value in the topics discussed during the meeting. She was forming close friendships with several of the women in the group and she did like chatting with them every week. She wasn't sure if that would be enough to keep her coming to the meetings for too long, however. She'd play that by ear.

At the break, she helped herself to a cup of lemonade and grabbed a cookie. Jake's meeting wasn't out yet. She approached Eddie Brown alone as he exited the men's room.

"Eddie, can I have a word with you?" she asked with a smile.

"Of course," he said. "Let me just get a cup of coffee first."

As Eddie headed back towards where she waited for him, the door to Jake's meeting room opened. He came straight to her and Eddie. First, she told Eddie about the shelter and the number of dogs they rescued each year. Then she told him about the annual gala and that it was their one big fundraiser each year. Finally, she made her pitch.

Eddie Brown looked thoughtful for a moment. "What's the date of the event?"

"Saturday August twelfth," Elyse answered.

He pulled his iPhone from his pocket. It was turned so neither Elyse nor Jake could see it.

"My calendar says I'm free that evening," Eddie said. "Just tell me where and when to be there and I will be."

"That's fantastic! Thank you," Elyse said.

"I normally get four-fifty for an appearance such as this. Just provide me with that receipt and my fee is donated to your organization."

"I really appreciate that," Elyse said.

"I like to support charities that help children, the elderly, and animals," Eddie told her.

• • • •

AFTER THE MEETING, as Elyse drove home, knowing Jake was somewhere behind her, her mood soared. It had been a good day. He was staying the night. It would be a good night. She had missed him over the past few days. They had settled into a routine over the last three weeks they'd been together.

He'd come to her place Wednesday evenings after the meeting and spend the night. He had physical therapy at eleven on Thursday morning. He'd leave to drive back to Norfolk by nine-thirty. He'd drive back out on Saturday and spend the night, leaving early Sunday morning because he had duty all day every Sunday. She'd have to ask him sometime exactly what that meant.

After they made love they held each other, talking as they always did after. It was time spent together that Elyse appreciated. The physical aspect of their relationship was exciting and fulfilling, but the conversation they shared was bonding and sustained her in a different way. Both aspects were needed, and both had been lacking in her life for a long time.

"Jake, how is this schedule, so to speak, working out for you?"

She heard his soft chuckle, felt his chest shake. "Schedule? Is that how you see our time together? That sounds extremely boring."

"Okay, let me rephrase that. We've been spending two nights a week together."

"Two wonderful nights and mornings a week," he added.

"I know you have PT and duty through the week and duty on Sunday. Do you have any other time available, and would you have the desire to spend more time together any other time during the week?" She drew circles on his chest with the tip of her finger.

"Let me tell you, when a naked woman lying next to you asks you if you have a desire for anything, the answer is always, yes, ma'am."

They both laughed.

"It was a serious question," Elyse said.

"And I gave you a serious answer. The question is, how fast do you want to take this? I promised slow and steady."

Elyse laughed again. "If this has been slow and steady, I'd love to see what all ahead full is like."

After they both laughed again, Jake rolled her over and pulled himself atop her. His face hung over hers. "Are you ready to hear that, in the span of a little over a month, I have fallen in love with you? And all I can think about is a life with you in it?"

Elyse's heart thumped wildly in her chest. She was sure he could hear it. "Only if you're ready to hear that when I go to bed and you're not here, I miss you. And when I wake, I reach over and am sad you're not there."

Jake's kiss was soft, slow, passionate.

"I've fallen in love with you," he whispered.

"I know that I'm in love with you, too," she replied.

"Let me see what I can switch around so I can spend the night a few more nights a week."

"Do you have any inkling yet if or when you'll be returned to active duty?"

"My next appointment for an evaluation with the doc is in two weeks."

She nodded, feeling a sadness sweep over her. She knew that if he was returned to active duty and deployed, she'd miss him terribly. It would be worse than how she remembered missing Tim. She also knew she couldn't end this relationship. The time they spent together was too amazing.

July

Chapter 23 – The 4th of July
Fireworks Aren't Just in the Sky

Elyse cringed as she read the returned text message from Claire in the group text. Why did everything with her have to be so difficult? It was a simple request. Come to the house and go through your boxes of childhood memories and toys at some point over the holiday weekend. Take what you want, donate what was still usable but you didn't want, throw the rest away. It was a long holiday weekend. Certainly, Claire could carve out one day to come do it. Although Elyse would love for all three of her children to be there and do it together, as many things in the bonus storage room were joint property of all three of the kids, she knew their schedules may not allow for it.

It made little sense to her for Kade to move the boxes to the garage or basement to just sit there collecting more dust. It was time those boxes left her house; except for Kade's as he would be living there for possibly the next year. Even so, it was time he went through his things as well. And for him and Mel to use that room as their living room, all that stuff she stored in that bonus room had to be moved out.

"Mom, what's the hurry? That stuff has been sitting there for years. A few more months won't hurt anything," Claire texted next as a follow up to her first text of, *"I can't. The holiday weekend is so busy for me."*

"Claire, I need that room. Why can't you come for a few hours?" Elyse texted back.

The phone rang. It was Claire.

"Hello, Claire," Elyse answered.

"Mom, you're being ridiculous. What do you need that room for?"

Her tone and words caught Elyse off-guard. And Elyse was done putting up with this. "And I think you're being ridiculous. It's literally a four-day holiday weekend for you, as I know you have Monday and Tuesday off with the fourth falling on Tuesday."

"We have plans three of the days and Lizette has five days off, Saturday through Wednesday. Remember I told you I thought she has a boyfriend? Well, she does and they're going away. We had to give her vacation or I'm sure she would have quit. So now, I probably have to find a new nanny." Her tone indicated how annoyed about it she was.

"Good for her having a boyfriend. Claire, she's an employee of yours who deserves time off," Elyse said. "So, you have plans three of the four days. Come the day you have no plans."

"That would be Monday."

Perfect! That was when Kade, Kelsey, and Ash were coming.

"And the problem is Matthew is working that day. I'm trying to figure out what to do to keep the kids occupied. I was thinking that morning my friend, Jenna, who you met at the Starbucks at church, and I could take our kids to that Playworld place. We have taken our kids there a few times and they love it."

Of course, she was considering going there. Elyse had seen the ads on TV for Playworld. They had employees to supervise the kids. Claire and Jenna could get a cup of coffee and visit while the kids played. "I have a better idea. Bring them with you out to the house. There may even be some things up there that you guys no longer want that your kids would love to play with." *And we could leave them here for them to have toys to play with when they come to visit,* Elyse thought.

"Oh, that just sounds like so much fun trying to clean and go through all my stuff with Aiden and Emma under foot."

"I think they'd have a great time, and if they're in the way I can certainly entertain them."

Clear sighed loudly. "You still haven't told me what you need that room for."

Elyse considered it for a moment. It wasn't her place to tell Claire that Kade was going to be a father, nor was it her place to tell her that he was moving home. But, then again, when would the two of them talk? As far as she knew, Claire and Kade didn't text each other or talk on the phone like he and Kelsey did. If they were not there on the same day to clean the room out, it could be Thanksgiving before they would be together. Elyse pondered for a moment how that scene would go, Claire coming into the house to find Mel obviously pregnant. Claire would be livid she didn't know.

"When's the last time you talked to your brother?"

"Kelsey's graduation, why?"

"If you want to find out why, I suggest you come over on Monday to go through your things. I'll have some special activities planned for Aiden and Emma," Elyse said, proud of herself.

"Oh no you don't, Mom!"

Elyse laughed. "Kade plans to be here Monday all day to work on that room for me. He has some good news and it's his to share, not mine."

"I'm sure he won't mind."

"You can ask him yourself on Monday."

"What if I can't get there?"

"I'm having everything cleared from that room and a Goodwill pick-up scheduled for the seventh." No, Elyse would not give her stuff away. But she'd let Claire think she would.

"Are you kidding me right now? This is ridiculous! You're not even giving me a week's notice."

• • • •

"PREGNANT?" CLAIRE REPEATED, staring at Kade with her mouth agape. She couldn't believe her mom thought this was good news. They weren't even married.

"Yes, and Mel and I are moving in to save money. Mel got accepted to the Paramedic Program. Moving back home will allow her to go to the training," Kade said.

"Moving back home?" Was Kade crazy? And he was smiling. How did he not get that this was the mark of failure in his adult life?

"We're taking over your old bedroom. Mine will be the nursery. And we're using this room as our living room," Kade said, opening a large box marked 'toys'. "We'll spend time with Mom downstairs, too, I'm sure, but it'll be nice to have our own space."

"Do you think Mom needs the company? Has she confided in you that she's lonely?" Claire asked.

Kade smiled a grin she couldn't decipher. "No; trust me, Mom's not lonely. But she's very generous to share her home with Mel and me, and the baby when it comes." He wondered when Claire would find out about Jake.

Claire thought that was an odd statement. Share her home? It was their home, where they'd grown up. "How long do you plan to live here?"

"As long as we need to," Kade said to get her more riled up. It was obvious from her clipped words and wild eyes that she was shocked and didn't approve. "And Mom said she'd help with the baby as much as she can to help lessen the cost of daycare. Plus, she said she's looking forward to spending time with her new grandchild."

Claire was dumbfounded. She wasn't sure how her mom and Kade saw all this as good news. "You're going to have an hour-long commute, both ways, every day. That's going to suck."

Kade shrugged. "Other people do it. And we'll be able to save to buy our own house. It's worth it. If we stay in the apartment we'll never be able to afford to buy a house, and Mel wouldn't be able to take the time off from work to do the Paramedic Program." He pointed to the box he'd just opened. "This has all our old board games in it. I think we should go through it when Kels gets here. She and Ash should be here soon." He moved the box out of the way and grabbed a plastic bin, one of six that were stacked high.

Claire's mood plummeted further. Great, Ash was coming with her. This day was just getting worse and worse. And now her children would be meeting him, too. She'd hoped he would be out of Kelsey's life before her kids would have the opportunity to meet him.

"Mommy, Grandma made us popsicles!" Aiden yelled, running into the room with a red popsicle melting in his hand. His lips and chin were red. At least there was none on his shirt, yet. Mister Quack was tucked under his arm. It already had a few drops of red on it.

"Aiden, the napkin, remember?" Elyse called after him. She entered the room a few beats later, holding Emma on her hip. Emma, too, had a popsicle melting in her hand. She at least had a napkin wound around it. She handed a napkin to Aiden.

"Mom, popsicles before lunch?" Claire asked. "Let me have Mister Quack so he doesn't get dripped on any more. I don't think you want a red Mister Quack." She took the stuffed animal from under his arm and set it on the shelf beside the door, low enough for Aiden to reach.

"I made them out of only fruit, no added sugar," Elyse said.

"Fruit's one hundred percent sugar," Claire replied.

"And a vital part of a healthy diet," Kade added, coming to his mom's aid. "And she used red fruit, which provides important antioxidants in addition to vitamins and minerals."

"Thank you, Kade," Elyse said.

Claire sighed. Her gaze fixed on Aiden, who was licking ferociously to get each drip of the juice. He was obviously enjoying the treat. "Just try to be careful, Aiden, and don't let it drip all over. Mom, maybe they should sit in the kitchen or outside while they have them."

"That was the plan," Elyse said. "But Aiden wanted to show you."

Claire leaned down and pressed a kiss to the top of his head. "You should go back to the kitchen with Grandma."

"Hey, is everyone upstairs?" Kelsey's voice faintly called. She and Ash were climbing the stairs.

"Yes, in the bonus room!" Elyse yelled, turning her head towards the doorway.

A few seconds later the two of them stepped into the room. "Yay! The munchkins are here," Kelsey said. She took Emma from her mom's arms. "Hello, Emmie-bear," she greeted, giving her a hug.

"Auntie Kels," Aiden said, running over to her and greeting her with a hug.

"A-man," Kelsey greeted him. "How's the broken wing?" She examined his casted arm.

"It's fine," he said with a shrug.

"No more jumping from things, my man," Kelsey said.

Both kids' eyes went to Ash, who stood beside her. "Hi," he greeted Aiden, squatting down to his level and presenting his hand to the boy. "I'm Ash, your Auntie Kelsey's friend." He then repeated the greeting with Emma as Kelsey greeted both her siblings. "Hi, Claire. It's nice to see you again," he said.

"You, too, Ash." Her tone stated that, no, it really was not nice to see him again.

Elyse took the kids back downstairs and the others got to work, determined to put a big dent in the many boxes and bins full of everything imaginable from their childhood. They worked for a solid hour and had gone through at least half of the boxes.

Ash carried many downstairs and stacked up the boxes in four separate areas of the garage. One near the right side of the second open garage door were Claire's items to be loaded into her vehicle to go home with her. He would have loaded the back for her, but her doors were locked. The second, Kade's belongings, was near the back of the garage. He loaded anything that was Kelsey's directly into the back of his pickup truck. Trash was piled near the trash cans, and the last stack was near the left side of the second open garage door. It was for the items that would be donated.

"Mom wanted a few toys moved to the sunroom that I thought Aiden and Emma might want to play with here. I have this box over here," Claire said, pointing to a large, open, awkwardly bulky box.

Ash had just re-entered the room from his last trip downstairs. The room was beginning to be cleared out. They were making progress. Kade and Ash hefted the overfilled box into their arms and left the room.

Claire had been dying for a word alone with Kelsey since she'd arrived. "Kels, what do you think of Kade and Mel moving home and about her pregnancy?"

Kelsey knew her sister well enough to know that Claire was not thrilled with the news. "I'm so excited for them, and I know Mom is excited that she's going to be a grandma again. Ash and I are going to get a crib and help with the baby when we can, too. It takes a village, and all that."

"Yes, with their work hours, they're going to need a lot of help," Claire agreed.

"Maybe you could help, too, or your nanny, I mean?"

Claire looked unpleasantly shocked at her suggestion. "Um, no, I have to pay her per child, and it would be a lot more than Kade could afford."

Kelsey inwardly snickered. Of course, Claire wouldn't offer to help in any way. "Of course, well, maybe just occasionally."

"I'm concerned how much this is going to be for Kade," Claire said. "Work, a long commute, taking care of a baby."

Kelsey doubted she was that concerned about Kade. "I think he's going to do great. I can't wait to see him as a dad."

"And they aren't even married," Claire said.

"Kade bought her an engagement ring," Kelsey said.

"He did?" Claire knew their marriage would be doomed from the start.

"Yes. It's pretty."

"Well, I hope you're using good birth control," Claire said. "As obviously they weren't."

Kelsey laughed. "I would like to think this was God's doing to give us all a new life in the family and something happy to focus on after the last few months of sadness."

Claire hugged her. "Isn't that the truth. You're always so positive and optimistic."

Kelsey smiled at Claire's words. No one would ever accuse Claire of being either. Ash and Kade came back into the room. They worked until Elyse called up the stairs that lunch was ready. She had gone to the store early, before they were due to arrive, and picked up the pre-made fried chicken, macaroni and cheese, fries, and a garden salad. She just had to reheat it.

Elyse thoroughly enjoyed the time spent with them all at the table. It was a rarity that Aiden and Emma were at her house. She hoped that would be changing. And as close as Kelsey and Ash were with Kade and Mel, she hoped they would be over more often, too. When the kids were in school, hers had been the hangout house. Having everyone there reminded her of it and made her realize how much she missed it.

"One more thing before you get back to work," Elyse said as everyone finished up. "Saturday August twelfth is the Animal House Shelter Black and White Gala. We have a formal theme this year with a catered sit-down dinner and entertainment as always. Claire, Eddie Brown from Flowing Waters is donating his talent to the event." She glanced at the others. "He's an incredible musician. We'll have dancing after dinner. There'll be a silent auction again this year, and I'm in the process of gathering items to put up for bid. It should be a really fun evening. The tickets are two hundred a plate, with half of that going to Animal House. The rest covers food, beverages, and the waitstaff. The hotel is not charging us a rental fee on top of their exact costs, as their donation to the rescue. It would mean a lot to me if you were all there. And I'd also like for you to see if any of your friends would buy tickets and join you for the night."

"That sounds like fun," Ash said. "I just finished a set of really cool swords. I'd normally charge five or six hundred for them. Would you want anything like that for your silent auction?"

"Ash, that would be great! Thank you," Elyse said. "As beautiful as your work is, I'm sure they will get us a good price at the auction."

"They're yours," he said. "And Kelsey already has the date on our calendar."

"I'll put in to see if I can get off, Mom. I'll be honest, though, four hundred a couple is probably out of any of my friends' budgets, but I will ask, and if nothing else see if I can get some cash donations for you," Kade said.

"Thank you, Kade. I hope you can get off work and you and Mel can come. It's so nice she'll be going to school during the week days and you two will be available more than you have in the past," Elyse said.

"Can I come, Grandma?" Aiden asked.

"I'm sorry, sweetie, it's for adults only. But how about I plan something better for you and Emma another day? Maybe Playworld after your cast is off."

The two kids reacted excitedly to that.

Claire felt all eyes at the table settle on her. "I'll have to check my calendar to see if Matthew and I are free that evening," she said, not committing.

"If anyone's friends can afford to drop four hundred on the evening, it's yours, Claire," Kelsey said.

"And it would be a really fun night for you to have together," Elyse said.

Claire forced a smile and nodded. She couldn't believe her mom expected this of her. It was bad enough her mom expected her and Matthew to pay and to come, but to expect her to rope her friends in as well, was extremely presumptuous.

After lunch, Claire finished going through her boxes quickly. Aiden and Emma were with her mom, playing with the toys they'd moved downstairs. She had Kade and Ash help load her boxes into the back of her car. "Thanks for throwing me under the bus with Mom, Kels. If anyone's friends can afford it, it's Claire's," she said in a way clearly trying to imitate Kelsey.

"It's true. Why can't you support Mom? Do you have any idea how many dogs a year Mom saves from kill shelters? And she runs completely on donations. This is her one big fundraiser of the year. Why is it so inconvenient for you to come and invite your friends, who would probably have a really good time?"

Claire didn't know what to say. She wasn't used to Kelsey disagreeing with her and vocalizing it this strongly. "It's her expectation we all come."

"She said it would mean a lot to her if we all came. She didn't say she expected it, Claire," Kelsey replied, setting her straight. Her sister was really making her mad.

"I was reading between the lines," Claire said.

Kelsey shrugged. "Whatever. Just remember, you get back what you give. Karma's a bitch."

"Okay, the car's all loaded, Claire," Kade said, coming back into the bonus room. "I already said goodbye to the munchkins." He gave her a hug. "Hopefully I'll get off and see you at the gala."

"Yeah," Claire said, her eyes shooting daggers at Kelsey.

"I'm going to run down and say goodbye to Aiden and Emma, too." She left the room before Claire.

Claire followed her down. She said her goodbyes to Ash and her mom and rushed her kids out of the house. The more she'd thought about her mom's request and Kelsey's lecturing her, the angrier she got.

Ash and Kade moved the existing furniture around, readying all three rooms he and Mel would take over for their furniture. Kelsey and Elyse helped by vacuuming and other cleaning as they worked. The four of them put in two more hours after Claire and the kids left. All Kade would have to do on moving day would be to move their belongings in.

When they finished, they all gathered on the driveway near the two pickup trucks.

"I'll see you Saturday at the adoption event," Kelsey told her mom, giving her a hug. "I'm working late at the shop Friday night, so I probably won't get there until close to ten."

"No worries. I'll see you when you get there," Elyse said. She hugged Ash next. "Thank you for coming and helping today. They got through it quicker with you here." She knew he'd carried the majority of the boxes out to the garage.

"You're welcome. Anything to help," Ash said.

After they drove out of the driveway, Elyse turned to Kade. "You guys got a lot done. Have you started to pack anything at the apartment?"

"No, not yet, but soon. Thanks again for all your help." He wrapped his arms around her and tightly embraced her. "And I really am okay with Jake being here when I am. It'll be weird, I'll admit that, but I'll get used to it."

"Thanks, Kade," Elyse said. "I'm sure it will feel very weird to you, but I appreciate that you're good with it. I really enjoy spending time with him. We have fun and we talk about just about everything. I'd forgotten what companionship felt like. Your dad and I lost that in our relationship a long time ago."

"I'm sorry, Mom."

"Yeah, me, too," she said.

"So, when do you plan to tell Claire about him? It was hard for us to not mention anything in front of her. Someone is going to screw up and let it slip sooner or later."

"I know," Elyse said. "I have to do it soon. I may try to broach the subject Wednesday evening at her house while I'm there for dinner."

"Good luck," Kade said sarcastically. "I better take off, too." He gave her another quick hug. "I'll talk to you later."

"Goodbye, Kade." She watched him disappear behind the wall of purple leaf plum trees and flowering quince shrubs at the end of the driveway.

In Ash's pickup Kelsey was on a roll, ranting about Claire.

"Babe, from what you and Kade have said about her, why would you have expected anything different from her?"

Kelsey let out a frustrated sigh. "I know you're right. I guess I just hope she'll surprise us and change at some point. I don't understand how she got so selfish. She wouldn't volunteer any help with the baby. And I know she was lying. She's not paying her nanny per kid. She could easily ask Lizette to watch their baby one day a week if necessary."

"Maybe she'll change her mind and offer after the baby comes. Right now, it's so far off."

"Not so far off that you and I haven't already talked about it and committed to help," Kelsey said.

"I was more surprised by her reaction to your mom wanting all of you at her gala."

"That was disappointing. Believe me, four hundred dollars for a night out is nothing for her and her friends," Kelsey said. "It really made me mad. My mom asks so little of her."

• • • •

JAKE PULLED INTO THE garage, which had become normal since that first rainy night. Elyse met him at the door into the laundry room and greeted him with a smile and a kiss. She'd also picked up steaks for them to cook on the grill when she was at the store earlier that morning. She looked forward to a leisurely evening with him. He'd moved some things around in his schedule as promised and could now spend Monday evenings with her.

They cooked dinner together and shared a bottle of wine while talking about their day. After dinner they even took Charlie for a walk together. They retreated to the bedroom before nine and made love. As Elyse snuggled against him, she marveled at how comfortable it was for her to share her home and her bed with Jake.

• • • •

BEDTIME AT CLAIRE'S house was not comfortable or peaceful. Aiden could not find Mister Quack. He deteriorated into a panic with tears. "Where did you last see him, Aiden?" Claire asked.

"You had him, Mommy. Remember, at Grandma's house, you took him when we were upstairs," Aiden whined.

"Oh," Claire groaned. Yes, she had. She set him on the shelf in the bonus room. "Baby, I know right where Mister Quack is, and I'll get him tomorrow for you."

"No!" he wailed. "I can't go to sleep without Mister Quack!"

"What the hell is going on in here?" Matthew asked, barreling into the room.

"Aiden left Mister Quack at my mom's house," Claire said.

"You had him, Mommy! You left him! I need Mister Quack!"

Matthew did a palms up. "Claire?"

"He's having a sleepover with Grandma. You have other babies you can snuggle with tonight. Grandma has no one. Let's let Grandma have Mister Quack tonight."

"I want Mister Quack!" Aiden cried with the dramatic flair of stomping his foot and a torrent of tears streaming down his face.

"How about my special bear from up on the shelf in my room?" Claire offered. She had a good-condition Brown Bear Beanie Baby in its original packaging on a shelf in her room that Aiden always wanted to play with, which she of course would never allow. He was worth a few thousand dollars.

Aiden wiped his cheeks. He nodded.

"Okay, you get in bed, and I'll bring Brown Bear to you."

"Are you nuts?" Matthew asked as she removed the stuffed animal from its package.

"I'd give him anything right now to shut him up and get him in bed," she shot back.

"You should have made sure he had it when you left your mom's house."

"Look, you have no idea what it was like over there today. Between acting happy that Kade got his girlfriend pregnant and they're moving back in with my mom and dodging my mom's expectations that we not only attend her stupid gala but we get our friends to spend two hundred dollars a plate and come, too, it was exhausting. And that didn't even include the hours of work it took to go through all the boxes of the shit my mom saved from when we were kids. I'm sorry I didn't realize Aiden didn't have Mister Quack."

"If he doesn't go to sleep, you're going to have to drive back out there and get it. We have a fun day planned tomorrow and we don't want it ruined by Aiden being tired and crabby," Matthew said.

She ignored him and brought the bear into Aiden. "Brown Bear is very special. You need to be careful his tag doesn't get ripped off. It will hurt him if it does," she told him, handing him the bear. "He needs a lot of love from you tonight."

She kissed him and tucked him in. Then she left his room. She discovered that Matthew was in his office with his door closed. This made her even angrier with him. He hadn't been any help dealing with Aiden's melt down over the missing Mister Quack. And when she'd told him about

Kade, the baby, and him moving home he seemed to be barely listening. He shrugged and said it really didn't affect them, so what did it matter. He did, however, agree with her about her mom's expectation about the gala, though he admitted the formal dinner and dancing could be a fun night out.

As usual, Claire went to bed alone. One thing that her mom may have been right about was the need for her to have a private, honest conversation with Matthew about their relationship. Their problems went far beyond his lack of enthusiasm about spending time with the kids.

Chapter 24 – Claire Gets More Than Mister Quack

C laire put the car into park, aggravated that she had to drive out to Franklin to pick up Mister Quack. Had she not been mentally so thrown for a loop the day before by Kade's news and her mother's insistence they all attend her silly gala, she would have made sure Aiden had it. He was almost five years old. Certainly, he wouldn't need his comfort items much longer.

And, to be honest, she was still angry with Matthew over the whole situation as well. Aiden slept very well the night before, but that didn't stop Matthew from giving her grief this morning, beginning with the alarm he'd set for her to get up early enough to drive out here and back before the kids would be up so she'd have time to get everyone ready to leave for their friends' beach house. After all, she'd committed to joining them at their beach house without consulting him, and he wasn't going to let her forget it.

She unlocked and opened the front door. She glanced up the stairs and saw her mom's bedroom door was open, and she smelled the wonderful aroma of coffee coming from the kitchen. She walked back, expecting to find her mom either in the sunroom or sitting at the kitchen table.

What she found was some man she had never seen before, barely dressed, pouring two cups of coffee. "Who the hell are you?"

Jake smiled, amused by her question. He recognized Elyse's oldest daughter immediately from the pictures in the entry. "I'm Jake. You must be Claire," he said. He took a step closer to her and presented his hand. "It's nice to meet you."

Who the hell is he? Claire thought. She shook her head no and did not grasp his hand, which hung awkwardly between them. "Where's my mom?"

He dropped his hand and stepped back to the coffee maker. "She's still in bed," he said, stirring in the odd concoction of powders her mom flavored her coffee with. Claire stepped over and grabbed one of the cups. "I'll take this up to her."

"Trust me, that's not a good idea," Jake said. "She's not dressed for a visit from anyone, especially her daughter." He took the cup from Claire's hand. "Wait here. I'll tell her you're here. I'm sure she'll be down as soon as she's dressed."

Claire watched as he ascended the stairs like he owned the place. *Who the hell is he? Dressed?* Claire thought. *What. The. Hell?*

"Houston, we have a problem," Jake said as he came into the bedroom where Elyse still lay naked beneath the covers. After they'd awoken to his alarm, they made love. Jake had duty from eight until noon. He took a quick shower after he started the coffee. Elyse remained in bed.

"Did I hear voices downstairs?"

"Yep, you sure did. I just met your daughter, Claire, and she's not too happy."

"Oh no," Elyse moaned, wondering why Claire would be there.

Jake smiled. He waved a hand, Vanna White style, over his bare torso. When he'd gotten out of the shower, he had just pulled his jeans on. "I don't think she was awestruck with my impressive physique."

Elyse couldn't help but laugh. "I'm sure with the wet hair and bare feet you were quite the sight to her in the kitchen. There was no way she could have misconstrued what you were doing here."

Jake chuckled as well. "I'll give you a few minutes before I come down."

"Thanks," Elyse moaned. She took a quick drink of her coffee and then pulled on a pair of underwear and her jean shorts. She made the effort and donned her bra before slipping a t-shirt over her head. She also pulled her hair into a ponytail. Then she took another drink of her coffee, stalling as long as she could. She stepped towards the door. "Charlie," she called. He lifted his head, glanced at her, and then dropped it back to the bed. It was too early for even Charlie to get up.

She descended the stairs to find Claire standing in the doorway to the kitchen, a glare of outrage on her face. "Good morning, my daughter. What are you doing here so early?" She tried to keep her tone of voice light.

"Who the hell is that man?" Claire demanded.

"I don't know," Elyse joked, shaking her head.

"Mom!"

Elyse smiled, proud of herself. "His name is Jake Tanner and he's a good friend of mine."

"What the fuck, Mom?"

"Claire, please. Language."

"Mom, you have a half-naked man in your house at six-thirty in the morning!"

"Would it be better if it was closer to noon?"

"What? No!"

Elyse laughed. "I'm sorry you met this way. Jake is a really good friend I've been seeing."

Claire's eyes were wide.

Elyse looped an arm around her. "Come into the kitchen and have a cup of coffee."

Claire reluctantly let her mom lead her into the kitchen. "Seeing? I don't understand."

"Sure you do," Elyse said.

"You're sleeping with that man?" Claire demanded.

Elyse chuckled for a moment. "Claire, yes, I'm sleeping with that man. He's a very nice person, a good friend, and I enjoy his company."

"How could you?"

Elyse handed Claire the cup of coffee she poured for her. "I loved your father, Claire, but he isn't here any longer. I've gotten to know Jake over the last few months. Our relationship started out as friends, and it evolved into more."

"This soon?"

"Sweetie, life is unpredictable with no guarantees of tomorrow for any of us. If your father's death taught me anything, it was that. Yes, this soon."

"Where did you meet him?"

"At Flowing Waters during the Wednesday night meetings."

"He's a widower, too?"

"No, he attends the wounded veterans' meeting in the room next to the widow and widowers support group meeting."

"Wounded veterans?" Claire repeated. "Do they even require proof a person is a wounded veteran? He could be any guy off the street."

"He's not. He's attached to the base at Norfolk, still active duty. He was injured in an accident a few months ago. He's still going through physical therapy. The Navy will decide if he's able to remain or if they will give him a medical discharge."

"So he says," Claire said.

"Claire, there is no proof to him either that I'm a recent widow, unless he searches through obituaries."

"You told him you're a widow?"

Elyse smiled. "I am."

"Mom, men prey on widows, assuming they have had large insurance payouts. You have to be careful."

"Your mom is very careful," Jake said as he came into the kitchen. "And you are correct that there are some scumbag-scammers out there who prey on widows. I'm not one of them." He was half dressed for duty, with his crisp white t-shirt tucked into his khaki slacks, his shiny black corfams on his feet. He never donned his dress shirt until he arrived on base, for fear of spilling coffee on it or even wrinkling it.

Claire didn't even act remorseful that he heard her statement. She just stared at him with suspicion. She watched him pour himself a cup of coffee in a travel mug.

He held the pot up. "Anyone need a refill?"

"Not yet, thanks," Elyse said. "Claire, Jake volunteered to help at the rescue, and he helped to recruit several other injured vets to help as well. We got to know each other and became friends."

Oh jeez, not the rescue again, Claire thought. *The way to Mom's heart, through her silly rescue.* Claire was still pissed her mom expected her to get her friends to buy tickets for the gala, and also expected Matthew and her to attend.

"And then we obviously became more than friends," Jake added. "Claire, I'm not out to take advantage of your mom. I admire and respect her. And she's great companionship, something my life at sea has lacked. I enjoy helping with the dogs and it's nice to have someone to go to dinner with that I can have an intelligent conversation with."

And nice to have someone to have sex with, too, Claire thought. "Yes, I'm sure."

Jake's gaze flickered to his watch. "I'm sorry I have to go. I'll call you when I'm off, Elyse, and we can decide what we're doing this afternoon. Claire, I'm glad I finally met you. I look forward to meeting your husband and children." He stepped up to Elyse and gave her a quick kiss on the lips.

"See you later," Elyse said.

He smiled and nodded at Claire. Then she watched him disappear into the laundry room. Only then did she realize he must be parked in the garage, as there were no strange cars in the driveway. "How long has this been going on, Mom?"

"I met Jake the first night I went to the grief support meeting. There are four different groups that meet in the four meeting rooms in that wing of the complex, and we all take a break together halfway through our meetings. It's really nice, they have coffee and tea out, and cookies."

Claire shook her head. She didn't care about the coffee and cookies.

Elyse laughed. "He heard me talk with one of the women from my meeting who was asking about adopting a dog, and then he came and volunteered. Claire, reserve judgement until you get to know him. He's a good person and I enjoy spending time with him. Just like him, I've enjoyed going out to dinner and talking. He's provided companionship to me."

"At least tell me he's bought dinner," Claire said.

"Yes, every time. He won't let me pay for a thing when we're out together. He's a gentleman, Claire. And he respected that I was recently widowed. We didn't go right from pass me a chocolate chip cookie to let's get into bed."

"How come you didn't tell me anything about this?" Claire asked, hurt that her mom would keep something like a boyfriend from her.

"Out of respect for your dad's memory. I loved him, Claire, and his passing leaves a hole in my heart as much as yours. Jake can never replace him, and he isn't trying to. But he's company for me. We have fun together. We talk and we laugh."

Claire understood that her mom would be lonely. She was still worried this guy was out to take advantage of her, though. Then she remembered Kade would be moving in. He'd keep an eye on the situation. "What about Kade moving in?" Then she remembered Kade's statement about Mom not being lonely. "Wait, he knows, doesn't he?"

"Yes, Claire, he does." Elyse didn't elaborate on the how or when. "I asked him not to mention it to you for the same reason, honoring and respecting Dad's memory. I'm sorry you found out this way. I'm sure it was a surprise."

"More like a shock," Claire said.

Elyse wrapped Claire in a hug. "I'm sorry for that shock, sweetie. Now, why are you here this early?"

"Aiden left Mister Quack here yesterday. He had a meltdown at bedtime. I almost thought I had to drive back out here last night." She laughed nervously. "I'm sure I would have had a surprise then, too."

Elyse laughed as well. "Yes, you would have. I didn't see his duck anywhere."

"It's up in the bonus room. I'll run up and get it, then I have to get back. We're going out to my friend Jenna's beach house for the day; though with Aiden's cast he's not going to be able to swim, so that's going to be a problem."

"Wrap his cast tightly with plastic wrap and use waterproof tape all around it and then tightly secure a plastic bag over it, adding another layer of the waterproof tape. I did that several times with Kade's casts, and he was able to go in the water. Tell Aiden that he can't do anything crazy."

"Yeah, like jumping off a chair pretending to parachute. I still can't believe he did that," Claire said.

Elyse chuckled as Claire ran up the stairs. She made the mistake of glancing into her mom's bedroom as she passed the open door. The unmade bed with the covers pushed back from both pillows screamed, 'we slept here'. She cringed inwardly and plowed on to the bonus room. Mister Quack was right where she left him. "Damn it," she cursed aloud as she grabbed him.

Elyse waited at the foot of the stairs. She saw Claire's eyes flicker into her bedroom as she passed the open door before she descended the stairs. Claire had a disturbed look on her face when her gaze met hers. Elyse gave her a pleasant smile. "Have a great day at the beach. I love you, Claire." She gave her a hug.

"I love you, too, Mom."

Chapter 25 – Denied, Chickened Out, and Called Out

E lyse once again made the drive into Norfolk for dinner with Claire and the kids, to be followed by the grief support meeting. Claire never did bring up her visit to Michael, so Elyse assumed she hadn't heard about it. Jake had made a point of calling her after his doctor's appointment that morning to tell her that the doctor extended his medical hold another month and ordered more PT. Twelve weeks was the usual recovery time after ACL surgery to engage in running and other tests required to return to full active duty. That would push it out until the middle of August.

She planned to tell Annie this evening that she would be stepping away for several weeks or more. Besides seeing Jake there, she felt there was no reason for her to attend. She left earlier than usual and had an appointment scheduled with the three partners at DWJ, Donnor Woods Jeffries, her son-in-law Matthew Jeffries' firm. They were financial planners and investment managers. She and Tim had several investment accounts with them, and she had set up a self-employed IRA with Matthew years earlier. She was a client.

However, when she checked in with the receptionist, Matthew greeted her and ushered her to his office. "Elyse, a meeting with all three partners is highly unusual and unnecessary; a waste of everyone's time, actually. I'm at a loss as to why you'd do that," Matthew said.

"Am I or am I not a client of this firm?" Yes, she was immediately put off by his words. "Tim and I have had money with DWJ since you joined this firm, Matthew."

"What's this meeting about?"

"This meeting has two purposes. First, I want your advice on financial ramifications for me personally as well as to Animal House Shelter in the following scenario." She told him of the possible plan to either sell or donate a portion of her land to the rescue. She needed him to tell her how each would affect her and the rescue in each situation.

He was surprised by the plan. "Have you had a realtor give you the fair market value of that portion of land and the barn?"

She had.

"Your tax adviser can calculate your income tax savings by you donating the property, though from just a quick onceover of your finances I don't see too much tax liability for you this year. Especially since Tim's income stopped at the end of April. Elyse, I don't see enough income or funds that you'd want to draw on to get you through the rest of your life. My personal opinion is that you need to sell the property, not donate it. And have you considered a paying job at any point in time?"

"Tim and I have enough funds with you and in other accounts that I can live comfortably for the rest of my life without working a paying job," she said, dismayed by his statement.

"Technically, yes, if you draw on the accounts. But that's not wise. We never advise our clients to draw on their savings until after retirement. Certainly not at the age of fifty."

"By our investments and savings activity, this is one of the scenarios we planned for. I know there's enough there for me to live on. I do plan to draw money out. I'll let you know how much each year I'll need, and you can advise which fund to take it out of." She left no room for debate. This was what she was going to do.

Matthew nodded. "If I can't talk you out of it."

"You can't. The second reason I came in, and the main reason for wishing to schedule this meeting with all three partners, is that I'm looking for corporate donations to Animal House Shelter. I'm sure Claire told you about our big fundraising event, our Black and White Gala on Saturday August twelfth. I hope your calendars are free. I would really like all my family there."

"Yes, she did, and she's checking our calendars," he said.

Elyse wondered how long that could possibly take. "We have several corporate sponsors who have given direct cash donations. We list those sponsors prominently on our website and on all printed material. It would definitely provide exposure for your firm and help you acquire new clients."

"You're here to ask us for money?"

"For a tax-deductible donation." She slid the flyer she had made in front of him. It detailed the three sponsorship levels. "I'm approaching several businesses I'd like to promote."

He glanced at the flyer.

When his gaze again met hers, she could see his answer was no. "We are also looking for businesses to buy a table. Each table seats ten and the cost per plate is two hundred dollars, or two thousand for the entire table. You could give the tickets to employees or clients, and of course you, Claire and your other partners or friends could use them as well. We are collecting high-end items to put up for bid in a silent auction. We have an amazing emcee and entertainment as well as a delicious meal. It should be a really fun night."

"I'm sure it will be," Matthew said, sliding her info sheet back across his desk to her. "The thing is, Elyse, we as a firm don't make donations to any charities. It's something the partners decided on a while ago when we were approached by another local charity. I'm sorry."

Elyse nodded. She retrieved her info sheet. She really wanted to close all her accounts with him. "Well, hopefully I'll see you at the gala. I did ask Claire to reach out to some of your friends and invite them as well." She stood. "It will be a fun evening. I'm off to your house now to have dinner with Claire and the kids."

She saw herself out.

• • • •

ELYSE'S MOOD LIFTED as soon as Aiden and Emma squealed excitedly when she stepped into the house. She gave them both big hugs. She wondered if Matthew had contacted Claire about her visit, because her greeting was much colder than usual.

"Looks like the plastic wrap worked on the cast," she said to Claire.

"Yes. Matthew didn't think we should try it, but I had a vague memory of Kade swimming with casts on and I trusted you knew what would keep it protected."

"Good. So did you all have a good time at the beach?"

"Yes," Claire said in a clipped tone of voice. She turned her attention to the kids. "You have five minutes until dinner if you want to finish playing. We're going to clean the room up after dinner, after Grandma leaves for her meeting."

Her manner was brusque, Elyse noted. Both kids ran towards their playroom. Claire walked into the kitchen.

Elyse followed her in. "Is something wrong, Claire?"

Claire didn't want to tell her that, no, they didn't have a good time at her friend's beach house. The kids did, but she and Matthew fought. And she planned to talk to her mom about this Jake character. The more she thought about it, the less she liked the situation and the less she trusted him. Her mom had to be more careful.

"Mom, I've still been thinking about what I walked into last Tuesday. He may be legit. He may not be out to take advantage of you, but he could have been, and it makes me very worried about you and that you're not being careful enough."

Elyse read between her words. Claire did still question if Jake was legit, and she thought he was out to take advantage of her. She'd been worried. So, in other words, Claire questioned her judgement. "Is it just him, or are you bothered by the fact that I have a boyfriend?"

"Yes, obviously it bothers me." She didn't make eye contact as she said it. She busied herself taking a casserole dish from the oven. "Just as if you died, I'd be bothered if Dad had a girlfriend this soon."

Fair enough, thought Elyse. "I know you feel it's too soon. I don't. What you don't understand is that your father hadn't been home since Christmas. He wasn't home much throughout our marriage. I never thought I was lonely until I met Jake. I've met a lot of people over the years, but don't misunderstand and think that I've felt lonely and without friends all these years because that's not true. But it was different with Jake. There was a comfort and a spark I felt with him that I haven't with anyone else. I'm sure it partially was because your father was gone, and I could feel that with him. If your father had been alive I never would have gone to dinner with him, and I'm sure the dynamics of how I approached him would have been different, too."

Claire really tried to understand. But she couldn't get past how soon it was since her dad died.

"How long do you think I should've waited?" Elyse asked when she said nothing.

Claire shrugged. "I don't know, Mom."

"Will you at least admit that it would depend on who the person is and the situation?"

"I guess."

"Claire, I understand this is hard for you," Elyse said. "But spending time with him makes me happy."

"I'll try to be okay with it."

"Thank you." Elyse gave her a quick hug. "Should I get the kids for dinner?"

"Yes," Claire said. She plated the food, choking back her feelings.

No, she wasn't okay with it. And thinking about it piled on more to her emotional plate, which was already full because of the ongoing friction with Matthew. And she was pissed that Michael had told her he would be grooming one of the new hires to go on-site to investigate collapses. It wouldn't be her.

When Elyse drove away from Claire's house after dinner, she knew nothing was resolved and she still believed there was something more to Claire's mood. She couldn't help but wonder if Matthew had told her about her visit to his office. If so, why didn't Claire mention it?

Her mood instantly lifted after she'd parked and walked into the lobby of the meeting room wing of the church. It wasn't the anticipation of the meeting that brought a smile to her face. It was Jake standing directly in front of her.

His eyes locked on her as she approached. A smile was on his lips.

"Hi," she greeted. "You don't know how much I needed to see you right now."

His smile became a worried expression. "What's wrong? Was it Claire?"

She shrugged. "It's complicated. I went to see her husband today, was supposed to see him and his two partners. He derailed that meeting. I made my pitch for his firm to provide sponsorship to Animal House and he turned me down flat. Wouldn't commit to anything personally either. And something was definitely off with Claire."

"You haven't talked to her since she walked in on us," Jake suggested.

"I think it was partially that. But there was something else. Jake, I'm really getting concerned about what I feel is wrong in that house." She had talked with Jake previously about her feelings of something just being off. And she had shared what Claire had disclosed about Matthew's apparent dislike of spending time with the kids as well as his late nights out.

"Did the kids seem happy?" he asked.

"Yes, they were their normal selves. But my kids never knew what was up in my marriage."

Annie Eddison appeared in the doorway to her meeting room, and it was only then that Elyse realized the lobby had cleared out. Everyone had already gone into their rooms. "Are you coming in, Elyse?" she called as she was about to shut the door.

"I'll see you at break," Elyse said to Jake, wanting to give him a kiss or an embrace.

Annie stopped her within the door. The room was noisy with the participants talking and settling into their seats. "Elyse, I don't mean to pry, but I've noticed you and that man are spending a lot of time together. Tonight, when we split into groups, one of our groups will talk about how to communicate with a new significant other when you need time alone or with your other family members on days that were important with your deceased spouse. Dates like their birthday or the anniversary of their death, or the date that would have been your wedding anniversary are days that could give you pause with a new person in your life."

"Oh, shit," Elyse cursed, a rarity. That's why Claire was so off. Tomorrow was Tim and her wedding anniversary. How could she forget?

Annie's eyes went wide.

"I'm sorry," Elyse immediately said. "I had dinner with my daughter, Claire, and her family before I came here. Claire was moody and just off. And you just made me realize that our wedding anniversary is tomorrow. I can't believe I forgot."

Annie looked even more surprised.

"We hadn't celebrated it in years. The last two years, Tim didn't even acknowledge it when he called." Elyse felt tears gather in her eyes. She closed her eyes for a second to collect her thoughts. "Honestly, not many personal things were on Tim's radar. He was so focused on his work. I always reminded him when the kids' birthdays were so he could call them and wish them a happy birthday, otherwise he wouldn't remember."

"Not all marriages were the same. Some were very happy, and the spouses spent a great deal of time together. Others were not at all. We've had some members of this group that felt a sense of relief when their spouse died, either because their spouse had been ill for some time or because it had been a distant or an abusive relationship. But they still mourned the loss of life in their own way, and I'd like to think that these meetings helped the surviving spouse during their time of grief. As we've said before, grieving comes in all shapes and sizes."

"I know that but, still, you have to think I'm callous."

Annie took hold of her hand. "Not at all, Elyse, and I'm not here to judge you. I'm free after the meeting if you'd like to go get a cup of coffee and talk."

They planned that Jake would once again come to her house and spend the night after tonight's meeting, but Elyse now felt the need to be alone tonight and tomorrow morning. "Yes, I'd like that," Elyse said. "Thank you."

They took their seats, and the meeting began. Elyse did break off with those who had a new person in their lives, much to the surprise of a few of the ladies she had gotten to know since coming to this meeting. The discussion was valuable. One member even expressed going overboard to acknowledge the important days just to be sensitive of other family members' feelings, even though she personally didn't feel the need to any longer.

This reminded Elyse that grieving Tim's loss was something that Claire, Kade, and Kelsey were all doing in their own way and there was a side to it where, collectively, they as a family shared in the grieving process together. She had to let them know that these dates were important to her.

At break, she invited Jake to step outside with her where the smokers normally gathered. They stepped past them and sat together on one of the concrete slab benches. Even though Elyse was armed with the way to say she needed to be alone the next morning from the discussion in the meeting just minutes before, she felt uneasy about talking with Jake about this.

"What's the matter, Elyse?" Jake asked her after she remained silent for too long.

"I need to uninvite you to my house tonight." Her lips formed into a disbelieving small grin. "I'm not as insensitive of a person as you are going to think I am, and I'm embarrassed to admit it, but I was just reminded in my meeting by way of the topic we discussed, that Tim's and my wedding anniversary is tomorrow." She shook her head.

Jake took hold of her hand, which clutched the edge of the bench between them. "I could never think you're insensitive."

She heard him chuckle and only then did she make eye contact with him.

"A little forgetful maybe, but never insensitive." He grinned an amused smile at her.

"This isn't funny to me. I forgot or, moreover, maybe it didn't matter to me. Thirty-two years. Not that it was champagne and roses every year." She shook her head. "It wasn't."

"I didn't think it was, which is the greatest travesty if you ask me. I don't like to ever talk ill of the dead, but for him to have let the romance with you die makes me wonder what the hell his problem was. Work gets in the way; believe me I understand that. It's not like he was deployed, his life belonging to the U.S. military. I have to believe that he could have structured his travel to be home for things that were important. And for me, to be home to show the woman I love that I do on our anniversary, that would rate. He was a fool and that's on him."

"I let it die, too. I never insisted he be home, and I mean early on in his career. And that set the expectation. In a way I mourned the death of our romantic relationship years ago and that included acknowledging our anniversary."

"Then don't beat yourself up over it."

"Annie, one of the moderators of the bereavement group, invited me out for coffee after the meeting to talk. I think it could be valuable for me to go and talk with her. I'm sorry, Jake. It's not that talking to you isn't valuable."

"I understand. It's that she's been through it, losing her husband. It's okay, Elyse. Don't feel bad. And I understand that you need to wake up alone tomorrow morning."

"I really don't know if I do or not, but it seems the right thing to do."

"Elyse, can I ask you a question?"

"You know you can ask me anything," she replied. At least she hoped he did.

"Did you ever consider divorce?"

"And if not, why not?" she added. "That's usually what follows your question." She glanced out over the cars in the parking lot. "I'd be lying if I said I never considered it. But I never seriously considered it. It was a brief passing thought on occasion. My stock answer has been I was Catholic and took my vows seriously. But, to be perfectly honest, I stopped going to Mass a long time ago. So, no one would confuse me with a devout Catholic."

Jake chuckled. "That doesn't mean certain aspects of the religion don't mean more to you than others."

"No, and at first, it was the vow. But our marriage became something neither of us intended. And it was still comfortable. There was no cheating, no harsh words. I raised my kids how I saw fit. He barely commented on it unless I pushed him to contribute to a decision. And after he was making a decent living, it was financially comfortable as well. His long absences became normal, but up until four years ago I had the kids, well Kelsey at home after both Claire and Kade were out on their own. There were times I felt the loneliness of not having a true partner. And part of me foolishly thought that he'd retire someday, and we just may

336

rekindle that romantic passion." She paused and shook her head. "I almost wish it had been a bad marriage with fighting or cheating, as I certainly would have divorced him had that been the case."

"I'm glad that wasn't the case. Believe me when I tell you I've seen so many men I've served with go through the drama of a really bad marriage."

"At least drama-filled ends to relationships have passion and life. Mine died with a whimper years ago."

"Then you absolutely shouldn't beat yourself up for not being focused on the date tomorrow. I know your focus is on the gala, as it should be. It's a huge undertaking and is important for the future of the rescue."

"Yes, it is."

"I'll see you Saturday then," Jake said. "Can we plan on spending the day together after the gala planning meeting?"

Elyse nodded and smiled. "And the night, too. Bring a bag and plan on staying."

Jake smiled. "Yes, ma'am."

· · · ·

AFTER THE MEETING, Elyse followed Annie to a nearby diner. They sat at a table along the windows that gave a beautiful view of the river that was lit beneath the nearly full moon. Annie ordered coffee and a piece of cake. Elyse ordered tea and a chocolate chip muffin. The server brought them quickly.

"Elyse, tell me if I'm wrong. I sense you feel like you should be grieving more outwardly than you are."

Elyse glanced out at the water. "I'm not sure if I'm really even grieving. And I don't feel like I'm in denial."

"Your situation with the long separations is a unique one. When was the one time or the times when your late husband was a presence that you'll miss?"

"I guess Thanksgiving and Christmas are the only times that he had been home consistently for the last ten or fifteen years. Otherwise, it had been at random intervals. He used to make it home for Easter. He hadn't in a few years." She took a bite of her muffin.

"That had to be incredibly lonely for you," Annie said.

"It didn't seem to be at the time. I've talked about loneliness more in the past few months than I ever have. And I think that's because I don't think I realized how lonely I was until I had dinner with Jake, and we talked. We spent more time together and I appreciated the male companionship. I have many friends, female and male. The feeling with him was much different." She said the last sentence shyly.

"Have you gone through your husband's belongings yet?" Annie asked.

"No. I want all three of my children there so we can do it together. There may be items they want."

Annie nodded. "Tell me about how you found out Tim was dead. Where were you, how did you feel? Tell me everything you remember."

"I haven't really told anyone about that. I was alone when the call came." Elyse wasn't sure why she wanted to know. She took a second to put herself back in that moment. She took a sip of her tea. "It was a beautiful morning. I took my dog to a nature preserve where I liked to walk him. It had rained overnight and some of the clouds lingered, so when the sunrise touched the sky it cast this incredible color through the clouds. Pinks and purples that matched the speckling of wildflowers that had already bloomed in the grasslands. The trees were vibrant greens, the new spring leaves had already popped. It was quiet and peaceful. I'm sorry, I also paint landscapes, so I was looking over the scene, memorizing it with the intention of painting it."

Annie smiled. "It sounds beautiful. I'd love to see that painting."

"Thanks," Elyse said. "And then my phone rang. You know, I always thought that if someone I loved had left this world, that somehow I'd know. I'd feel it. I didn't think that news could ever come on such a glorious morning when I felt so at peace with the world, but it did. It was his partner, calling to tell me he was dead."

"That's how he said it?"

"No, but I knew something was wrong when I heard Michael's voice. It was strained, not the strong, confident voice I knew. He asked if I'd watched the news that morning and if I'd heard about the additional earthquakes India had been having. I hadn't. He told me another one jolted the region as we slept, and that Tim was on-site within a building, trying to measure the stability as the quake hit. It was a quake, not an aftershock. The building came down, with my husband inside. He was killed instantly. They'd already recovered his body. There was no doubt."

"What did you do?"

"I stood there and cried. And then I called each of my children."

"From the forest preserve?"

Tears had filled Elyse's eyes as she told Annie the story. "Yes. They're all adults. And I wanted them to come home to be with me right away. It was always just the four of us, and we needed to be together to come to grips with it."

"You're crying as you tell me about it. Right now, what are you saddest about?"

Elyse wiped the tears that had leaked onto her cheeks. "I'm sad for Tim. We may not have had a romantic relationship for years, but he was a good person. This world was better off when he was in it. I'm sad for each of the kids, losing their dad. Even though he wasn't a constant in their daily lives, he was their father. Well, he wasn't in Kade and Kelsey's lives much. But he was in Claire's."

"And for yourself, Elyse?"

Elyse breathed out hard. "I'm sad that I'll never know if Tim and I could have rekindled our romantic relationship once he retired, if he ever retired. I'm sad that I'm left feeling like a fool that I spent the last fifteen years, maybe even thirty-two years, in this relationship that didn't fulfill me. Kelsey, my youngest, has been away at school for four years. I asked Tim if I could go on-site with him twice in the last four years because they were in amazing places I really wanted to see. But it was so lonely while I was there. Tim worked at the jobsite long hours. And when he was at the hotel, he slept. He ordered room service. I couldn't get him to even go to the hotel restaurant. I knew then that our marriage had been over for a long time, but stupid me, I kept thinking just maybe that spark could come back. But it had been snuffed out years before."

"Do you feel he chose work and his career over you and the kids?" Annie asked.

Elyse took another bite of her muffin. She washed it down with a drink of tea. "I don't think it was a conscious choice on his part. I don't think he had the capacity to do both. What I'm going to say is going to sound terrible, but I'm not saying it to be mean-spirited, just factual. I think Tim fell someplace on the autism spectrum."

"Like Asperger's?"

Elyse shrugged. "He had a genius range I.Q. but he had difficulty relating to people, especially in new social situations. At first I thought he was just rude, or he lacked social graces. But that wasn't it. Then I thought it was because he was so smart that his brain was evaluating everything so much differently than the rest of us, or that his brain was stuck in whatever problem or equation he was working on. He had the ability to be warm and loving, but not while he focused on anything else. Everything he did, he did with a total focus on that one item."

"It certainly sounds like it could have been something like that. And back then they didn't evaluate kids like they do now, and they rarely put names to issues fifty years ago."

"No, they didn't. And he was smart and never a behavior problem in school."

"Elyse, I think you need to be very careful that you don't move on without putting the past to bed. You seemed genuinely distraught that you forgot your anniversary was tomorrow. The first year after a spouse passes brings many different emotions at different times."

"Do you think a person needs to put their life on hold during that year?"

Annie chuckled. "Not on hold. I think they just need to be cognizant that there will be emotional ups and downs. And if they are involved in a new relationship, that person needs to know it will happen. I'm not here to tell you if your relationship is a smart thing to get into at this time, I just want you to realize that you'll need to be able to communicate where you are emotionally to this man at any given time. You need to be able to say you're having a rough day and you need a hug. Or you're having a rough day and you need to be alone. And he needs to be able to receive it and give you what you need."

Elyse watched her as she'd spoke. "You don't believe I can do that, do you?"

Annie frowned. "Elyse, going strictly from what you've told me about your past relationship with your husband, it doesn't sound like you communicated well. You allowed a relationship that didn't fulfill you. You didn't speak up with your needs. You adapted, you enabled, you made your own life for you and your kids. I'm not saying any of that is good or bad. It just speaks to your history of communicating with your partner."

Elyse nodded. Annie was right, she had done those things. But Jake was a different man. She was in a different phase of her life, and she'd like to think that she'd gotten more assertive over the years. "I appreciate you pointing that out. I agree, communication is vital and, no, I didn't do it well in my marriage. It's something I'll need to be cognizant of in my current relationship."

Chapter 26 – T Minus Four Weeks and Counting

E lyse was happy that Jake arrived an hour earlier than the other members of the gala planning committee. His car pulling up in front of her house brought a smile to her lips. She and Charlie met him as he got out of his car.

"Hi," she said, pressing a kiss to his lips.

He circled his arms around her and pulled her into a lengthy kiss. "I missed you the last few days," he said when their lips parted.

"I missed you, too," she said.

He respected her need to be alone on her anniversary on Thursday. He text messaged a few times to check in on her. They didn't talk on the phone. Elyse started her morning with an individual text to each of her kids, personalized, with her thoughts of the day sprinkled with memories of their wedding. Then she took Charlie for a long walk in the forest preserve.

During the walk, she ended up in the same general area she had been in when she'd received Michael's call advising her of Tim's death. Negative feelings hit her hard. "Damn you, Tim," Elyse swore aloud. She felt intense anger and a crushing pain in her chest. Tears spilled from her eyes. She sat where she stood. The dew-soaked blades of the long grass tickled her bare legs, dampening her skin. "This wasn't how our lives were supposed to be. You missed most of your children's lives. You left me alone and without a partner more times than not. I loved you, but even that lessened over time. Your death didn't devastate me. I barely noticed you gone. That's not how it was supposed to be. Your life mattered. You mattered, but there is no hole where you were supposed to be."

She cried long and hard for the first time in months until there were no tears left. She sat, emotionally depleted, with no motivation to get up. The intense emotions slowly turned into a calm. She admired the brilliant colors of life all around her. It was still and peaceful. And she felt a burden lift when she forgave herself for not missing Tim.

It was a beautiful day, though by the time she and Charlie returned to her car in the lot, the temperature had climbed quickly, and it was hot and sticky. She treated them both to an ice cream cone as a lunch appetizer. She worked in her flower garden when they returned home. Then she took a cool shower. Throughout the entire day, she thought about her conversation with Annie the night before. Even though she had come to a peace earlier, she knew that it would take time to resolve all her feelings from her marriage and Tim's sudden passing. Her thoughts had pinged all over the place that morning.

She allowed herself to reminisce about the good times with Tim when they were young and newly in love. She had been Tim's focus then. The fear, embarrassment, and excitement that she felt when she discovered she was pregnant with Claire played through her thoughts. Their wedding, planned in just a few weeks, saying 'I do' with no understanding what it would take to make a marriage work. That was a long time ago.

She was a very different person now than she'd been then. From the outside, anyone looking in would think she had a storybook life. Married to the same man for thirty-two years, three beautiful children, running a charity, her rescue, her passion. And she had been happy. She'd been fulfilled in all aspects of her life but her marriage. This realization was powerful. Why had she never changed anything in her marriage? Why hadn't she demanded more from Tim?

The answer seemed quite simple. Besides the lack of having a partner, she was very happy. It was a tradeoff. And while the kids were growing up, it was worth it. She pacified herself over the last few years with hopes that that spark could return, even though she knew it would not. But it was comfortable.

"Thank you for understanding that I needed to be alone with my thoughts for a few days," she said, her arms still around his neck.

"I may not know what you're going through, as I've never lived it, but I would like to think I have the capacity to be sensitive to what you need," he said. He nodded to the house. "Are we going to stand in your driveway making out, or should we go into the house?"

She smiled. "Is that what we're going to do until the others arrive for the meeting? Make out?"

He chuckled. "Well, those were Wednesday night's kisses. We still have Thursday morning and Friday night's kisses to make up for."

She laughed as well. "I'm not sure we'll fit them all in before the meeting. We may have to continue after."

"I'm counting on it, up in your bedroom."

"That sounds perfect. I was planning that, myself." She kissed him again. "Bring your bag in." She nodded towards the house.

He ran it up to the bedroom and then joined her in the kitchen. She'd made a pot of coffee for the meeting. She also had a tray with cookies out. He helped himself to a cookie as she poured them both a cup and spooned her concoction of powders into both cups.

"I'm getting spoiled. And I don't like black coffee so much any longer."

"You say that like it's a bad thing."

"I'm getting attached to you. I really care about you, Elyse. And I really did miss you the last few days."

"I'm not going anywhere. I care about you more than I thought was possible. I like my life with you in it, Jake. Do I have some ghosts to clear out from my marriage, and some grieving left to do from the loss of my husband? Yes, but I hope you feel I'm worth it, to stick by me while I'm doing it."

"You're definitely worth it," he said.

"You're going to have to understand that there will be days that are rough for me, that I may need to be alone. And then there will be other days that will be rough that I may need you to hold me, so I'm not alone. I'll try my very best to communicate with you where my thoughts are and how I'm feeling as I move through these emotions that may hit me out of nowhere. That's what happened Wednesday night."

"I'll try my very best," he said. "I hope you have more of the rough days that you need me to hold you than the ones you need to be alone."

She emitted a short laugh. "Me, too." She took a sip of her coffee. "I did a lot of thinking over the last two days, a lot of reconciling different aspects of my life, my past with Tim."

"Did you come to any epiphanies?"

"Yes. I'm ready for this relationship with you. You're not a space-filler, because there was no tangible space to be filled. I built a life without Tim in it many years ago. You're a new addition to my life, not a replacement. But still, there are ghosts that linger that need to be dealt with."

He held her to himself. "Cancel the meeting and let's go up to bed right now," he whispered.

She laughed again. "You know I can't do that. But hold that thought."

The other meeting attendees arrived. Elyse poured coffee and iced tea. The cookies got passed. Everyone took a seat. They started with a recap of the last meeting and what had been accomplished on each point since then. Cassie Eischen delivered on everything she'd promised at the last meeting. She had no fewer than fourteen sets of tickets to great local sporting events and concerts. She even had a one-week stay at a luxury condo on Virginia Beach to include in the silent auction.

"I'm still waiting on a couples' massage at a local spa and the deluxe wine tasting package for four at one of the local wineries. I can't say which one yet. That was a promise to the owner," Cassie added.

"And I have promises of several great gift baskets from a few friends who know we're looking to get several hundred dollars out of the auction items," Pam said. "Not quite the high-end items that Cassie secured."

"But every donated item is appreciated," Elyse said. "Thank you, Pam."

"I also have six bottles of wine donated for the wine pull," Pam added.

"Great!" Elyse said. "I'm sure as we get closer the other volunteers will inundate you with bottles. Thank you for taking on this portion of the event."

"You're welcome."

"Cassie, where are we with the list of possible corporate sponsors? I approached both I thought of. I secured a twenty-thousand-dollar donation from one. The other one was a flat-out refusal."

Cassie pulled a handwritten list from her folder. "I have the organizations grouped by the ones I know donate to charities in one section, those who need tax deductions in another, and those that need a big-time image booster in the last. I'll take the last batch. Tom has agreed to take the businesses that need tax deductions, and Elyse, I thought the other one could be yours."

Elyse took the list from Cassie and glanced over the sixty-some business entities that were listed out. A few were high-profile businesses whose names she recognized. There were many she didn't but, by their names, they appeared to be sole proprietor entities, accountants, attorneys, small, unaffiliated medical practices, a small trucking company, and a car dealership.

Elyse didn't find any names on the list objectionable. "Our first goal will be trying to secure a large donation. If that's a no go, sponsorship of a table at the gala. If nothing else, a great silent auction item that will bring in a nice bid."

Everyone at the meeting was confident that they were on track. There were two more short meetings planned in the upcoming weeks, just to touch base leading up to the gala. Elyse had to admit that she felt much better at the conclusion of this meeting than she had after the first.

After all the other meeting participants had departed, Elyse locked up the first floor and then led Jake by the hand up the stairs to her bedroom. Now that all three of her children knew about this relationship, she doubted that anyone would just pop by without giving notice. They could spend time in bed without worrying they'd be interrupted. Elyse wasn't sure how it would go with Kade and Mel living there, but she'd worry about that later. Today, she needed this connection with Jake. She needed to physically express her feelings and desire for him.

Chapter 27 – Coming Home

K ade brought the last of the boxes into the apartment from the back of his pickup truck. He guessed they were ninety-five percent packed in all rooms with only a few things left. The next day was moving day. Kelsey and Ash would come help, as would Cletus. Three men and two women should get the job done in a few hours. They didn't have that much stuff.

He stepped over to the kitchen where Mel worked, packing food and dishes from the cabinets. "I hope we don't need more boxes," he said.

"The dishes are taking more boxes than I anticipated; but I have to wrap them good, as they'll be stored in the boxes for the foreseeable future."

She had a tone to her voice that Kade read as on-edge. He wrapped his arms around her. "You're not having second thoughts about moving in with my mom, are you?"

"Even though I'm counting down until my leave of absence begins, I'm just dreading the long drive from Franklin into Norfolk and back."

"I'll help you by recording some of your lessons so you can listen to them while commuting." He nuzzled her cheek with his. "I just may record some naughty stuff on there, too, to get your attention."

Mel laughed. "I love you, Kade. And I'm excited to start the training. I appreciate you asking your mom for the loan so I can."

"So why the mood?"

"I don't know," she shrugged.

"Don't think about the drive. Aren't you excited to have more space? And you said you love the openness and views at my mom's house. We'll have our own little suite there, which is bigger than our whole apartment here, plus the use of the rest of the house."

"It's nice and quiet out there. Are you sure you're okay with her boyfriend?" Mel asked.

"You know, Mel, for as long as I can remember I don't think I ever saw my parents really kiss, you know, lips on lips. They'd give a quick peck on the cheek, but that was it. They never held hands or showed any physical affection. I was shocked when I walked in to see what I saw. But now that I think about it, my mom deserves to have a man that she does those things with. It's uncomfortable as fuck for me, but this isn't about me. It's about her and her enjoying life. She had to be lonely over the years with my dad gone all the time."

"What's he like?"

"Nothing like my dad. I only talked with them for a half-hour or so, but this guy was more engaging in five minutes than my dad ever was."

"Hm," Mel sighed. "I always wondered about your parents. Your mom is outgoing and personable. Your dad always struck me as either preoccupied or shy."

"More like anti-social," Kade said. "It'll be weird, but I can adapt to my mom's boyfriend being there sometimes." He let go of her and scanned the half-empty cabinets. "What can I do to help in here?"

They got back to packing.

Cletus arrived at seven the next morning. He and Kade went to pick up the U-Haul. Ash and Kelsey weren't due until nine. They got all the boxes of the items that would be stored and not unpacked at his mom's loaded before Ash and Kelsey arrived. Once they did, the three men loaded the furniture next. Kelsey helped Mel empty the contents of the refrigerator and freezer into coolers. They had purposefully consumed as much of the food they could since deciding to move.

"My mom is excited you two are moving home," Kelsey told Mel. "How are you with it? It's not your house and she's not your mom."

Mel smirked. "Thank God she's not my mom. My mom wouldn't have let us move in. It would have been too much of an inconvenience." Mel didn't know if Kelsey knew about the money Elyse had lent them, so she didn't mention it. "I'd never have asked my mom."

"I'm sorry," Kelsey said. "My mom is pretty awesome."

Mel laughed. "Yes, she is. How do you feel about the whole boyfriend thing?"

Kelsey shrugged. "He seems nice, and he makes my mom happy. She's been alone a long time. I guess my parents' marriage wasn't exactly what I always thought it was, what I romanticized it to be. I just assumed they were madly in love and happy, because I never saw them fight and they stayed together."

"Yeah, just because two people stay together doesn't mean they're both happy."

"You know what's the craziest part?" Kelsey asked.

"I think most of it's crazy," Mel said.

Kelsey laughed. "Yes, it is. I think about Ash and me and I can't imagine their relationship with all the long separations and us living that way. But what I was going to say is that my mom said she and my dad never argued about it. They never talked about getting a divorce."

"Count yourself lucky. My parents had loud arguments often and they both threatened the other with divorce. By the time they finally did call it quits, I was almost relieved," Mel said.

"Yeah, I cannot even imagine my parents yelling at each other," Kelsey said. "So, when are you and Kade going to get married?"

Mel's gaze flashed to the ring on her left hand. "I'm in no hurry. I know Kade loves me. That's enough for me." She shrugged. "I don't need a piece of paper to know that. Maybe after the baby's born."

Kelsey wasn't surprised by Mel's attitude. But she knew her brother and she knew he wanted to get married before the baby came. "Yes, Kade does love you very much," she agreed. "I'm excited to be an aunt again. Kade did tell you that I'll help however I can. Ash and I are going to get a crib to keep at our house."

"We appreciate it, Kels. I'm honestly still overwhelmed with everything. School's going to be a major challenge, but at least I can focus on it and not try to do it while I'm still working full-time. I can't tell you how much I appreciate that Kade worked that out for me. I'm not ready to think about how we're going to take care of a baby, too."

Kelsey wrapped her arms around Mel. "With your family's help. My mom, Ash, and I are all here to help. I hope when the time comes, Claire will step up and help, too." Even as she said Claire's name, she doubted it.

Mel laughed sarcastically. "Claire? Whatever you're smoking, share some with me!"

They finished filling the coolers. The men came in and took them and the remaining boxes to the truck. The apartment was empty. Kade and Mel would come back and clean another day. They had a few more days before they had to turn the keys in.

They drove the vehicles to Franklin. Mel's new residence, home for Kade.

Elyse sat in her living room, watching for Kade and the others to arrive. Jake wasn't there. He normally spent Saturday afternoons with her. And he normally spent the night on Saturday night, too. After discussing it, though, they agreed that it would be better that he wouldn't be there the first night Kade and Melanie moved in.

Elyse hopped up when the first vehicle pulled into the driveway. It was Kade's pickup truck, driven by Kelsey. Ash's pickup was next. They backed up to the two farthest garage doors, leaving plenty of room for the U-Haul to pull up in front of the front door, which it did moments later. Cletus and Melanie brought up the rear of the procession in their own vehicles.

Elyse happily greeted everyone with hugs. Melanie hung back and appeared unsure as Elyse made her way to where she stood. Elyse embraced her as she had everyone else. She had not seen or talked to Melanie since Tim's memorial service. "Welcome. I hope you'll feel comfortable living here. I'm happy to help you and Kade, and my grandchild. This is just what this family needs, new life and a reason to be excited."

Mel smiled and nodded. She hadn't considered that. "Thank you for letting us move in, and Elyse, thank you so much for the loan for me to be able to go to the paramedic training."

"It's an investment in your future, in the future of Kade's and your family. When I got pregnant with Claire, all my dreams for the future were put on hold. It was all about Tim finishing his education and establishing himself in his field. That isn't the way it should be. Your career is just as important as Kade's. And the more successful you are, the better off your family will be."

"Thank you, Elyse. I wasn't sure how we were going to afford for me to do the program, and that was before I realized I was pregnant. And after, it seemed like the universe was conspiring against me."

"I'm glad Kade came to me. I would have been really mad if I found out you had an issue I could help with if he hadn't. Even though you and Kade aren't married yet, you're family, Melanie."

"Hey, you going to talk all day or are you two going to help?" Kade jokingly called from the door.

Everyone else was already inside. They joined them. Mel followed Kade up the stairs to help decide where each piece of furniture would go. Elyse went into the kitchen to begin unpacking the coolers of food into the refrigerator that Cletus and Ash had brought in. She had Charlie confined to the sunroom so he wouldn't be under foot.

"There's three more in the truck," Ash told her. "I hope you have a lot of room in that fridge."

"We'll see," Elyse said. "Do you know if anyone checked expiration dates as they packed these?"

"I'll send Kelsey in. She'll know."

Elyse didn't need to wait for Kelsey. The first item she pulled from the cooler, a jar of mayonnaise, had expired over a year earlier. She hoped they hadn't been eating it. As she unpacked the coolers, she lined up the expired food on the counter. She wouldn't throw anything away. That was up to Kade and Melanie.

It took a few hours, but they got everything unpacked. Cletus headed home. Kelsey and Ash stayed for pizza that Elyse ordered for everyone, but then they had to head to the shop. Ash had a few clients scheduled that evening. Kelsey again drove Kade's pickup, following the U-Haul as he returned it.

Elyse wandered up the stairs to find Melanie unpacking boxes in Claire's old room, which would be her and Kade's room. She knocked on the door jamb. "Hi, can I come in?"

Mel looked surprised by her question. "Of course," she said. "It's your house."

"The rest may be, but these rooms are now yours and Kade's and I respect your privacy. I won't intrude. But I'm free right now and if there is anything I can help you with, like unpacking, put me to work."

"You've done so much already," Mel said.

"And please don't feel you have to stay in these rooms. I hope you will make yourself comfortable and use the whole house."

"I really like the patio. I can see myself sitting out there reading and studying."

"Yes, that's one of my favorite spots. I also wanted to remind you that you are free to invite friends and family over. Kelsey's old room is set up as the guest room. If you have any overnight guests, they're welcome to use it."

Mel laughed. "We didn't have that at the apartment. It was the living room couch. Thank you."

"Have you told your mom you moved in here or that you're pregnant?"

Mel shook her head and frowned. "Not yet. I will eventually."

"I know you're not close with your mom, but I'm sure she'd like to know she's going to be a grandmother."

"There's time for that." Mel was thoughtful for a moment. "She's not like you, Elyse. I know she didn't give a shit when my brother became a dad."

"That's too bad, and I'm sorry," Elyse said. She would make sure that she was even more supportive towards Melanie. She knew Kelsey and Ash would be involved. She'd have to talk to Claire. "Just maybe she'll feel differently that it's her daughter's child."

"Yeah, I doubt it, but thank you for trying to make me feel better about it." She paused and thought for a moment. "I'm glad we have you and Kelsey and Ash. I'm sure between the five of us we'll be able to take care of this baby. Kelsey was so excited when Kade told her. She and Ash are going to get a crib and set up a room at their house for when she watches the baby."

Elyse smiled and nodded. She wasn't surprised. Kelsey had a big heart. And her assessment so far of Ashley Vincent was that he did, too.

August
Chapter 28 – The Gala, A Night to Remember

"Claire, I don't care if Matthew is coming or not. I want and need you there," Elyse said into her phone. "This is important to me." She stood alone in the hotel room, dressed in a beautiful black-beaded gown. Her shoes and the little beaded purse were on the foot of the bed. She'd driven into Norfolk earlier that day to set up the venue. They had over fifty great donated items for the silent auction that she and Julia set up in a beautiful display. Seventy bottles of wine were donated for the wine pull, including two bottles valued at over two hundred dollars. She'd also conferred with the caterers one last time. Other volunteers helped to decorate the venue and transform it into a beautiful and elegant setting.

"Mom, I'm super pissed at him right now about this and I won't be very good company. I sold a table to all my friends. Isn't that enough?"

"This isn't about you, Claire. And won't your girlfriends wonder where you are?"

"And what am I supposed to tell them about why Matthew isn't there? That he forgot and made plans with his partners that he won't break?"

"It's the truth. Why not?" Elyse asked, disgusted with her son-in-law. She wouldn't forget that not only was he a no-show at the event, but he turned her down flat to sponsor a table or donate to the rescue.

"Hold on, he just pulled back into the driveway. I'll call you back." Claire hung up.

Elyse threw her phone onto the bed. She took a deep breath and let it out slowly to calm herself. "The gala, that's what's important. It doesn't matter if Claire is there or not," she said aloud.

She slipped her shoes on and took one last look at herself in the mirror. Hair and makeup looked great. Jewelry was on. It looked sparkling and stunning. She slipped her lipstick into her little beaded bag as well as her phone and room key, and then she left her room.

· · · ·

"I DON'T WANT TO FIGHT, Claire," Matthew said, coming into the house through the front door.

She stood on the stairs in her white gown. "Just so you know, I'm going without you."

"I'm coming with. I called Troy and told him I fucked up and had other plans I forgot about. Give me five minutes to change into my tux."

After he went upstairs, Claire sent her mom a text advising her that Matthew was coming after all.

Elyse was in the elevator when Claire's text arrived, telling her that Matthew would be attending the gala. After reading it, she decided not to reply. She just hoped there would be no more drama with the two of them this evening. She would admit she was on edge. The future of the rescue hinged on the turnout and funds tonight's event would raise.

Getting the news that the warehouse was being sold the day before put so much added pressure on her. Not only was the building they currently used to house the dogs about to be condemned, but now the free location for their public events was being taken away as well.

If tonight didn't raise enough money to secure a location, she'd have no other option than to finish the barn and house the dogs there, opening herself up to liability. Public events would be more difficult. She took a deep breath and tried to push it all from her mind. She didn't need to stress about any of that tonight.

Elyse could hear voices as she approached the banquet rooms. Either it was later than she thought, or their guests were arriving earlier than planned. When she rounded the corner, coming into the atrium area where their cocktail and appetizer reception was set up, she stopped, unable to fathom the scene before her.

Gazing over their faces, every single volunteer was there except for Miles Maitland, who'd offered to stay with the dogs during the event. Upon seeing her, they stopped whatever they were doing and gave her an exuberant round of applause. They were all dressed in the requisite black or white, so it was clear they planned to attend this evening.

"Elyse, we've done the work. Now it's time to enjoy the evening," Julia said. "We all agree that whatever happens, Animal House will survive. The rescue isn't a physical location. It's you and it's all of us. So, tonight we are going to party and enjoy the food, the drink, and the dancing."

"And we are going to watch the guests open their wallets and bid way too much on the silent auction items that we all worked our asses off to acquire," Trevor Ferguson said.

Elyse couldn't help but laugh.

"So, no stress. Tonight is about having fun," Julia added.

Elyse hugged her. Leave it to Julia to say exactly what she needed to hear. "Thanks, Julia." She glanced over the faces of all the volunteers. "Thank you, all of you. Yes, I agree. Have a great time tonight. Thanks to all of you, we will have a record number of attendees. I hope that translates to a record amount in donations. One way or another, we will work it out."

As if on cue, the bartender opened the bar. Several waiters entered the area with trays loaded with champagne flutes and wine glasses. Elyse took a glass of champagne. Conversations rose in volume. By the time she made one more loop of the venue to check the placement of every silent auction item, the table of the gift bags containing the wine for the wine pull, and then a quick look into the banquet room set up for the formal dinner, the guests had begun to arrive.

Servers circulated with appetizers. Very quickly, the atrium area became crowded with guests looking over the silent auction items, talking with each other, eating and drinking. Elyse kept an eye on the front doors. Jake was usually punctual. She wondered why he wasn't there yet. She checked her phone, which was in her bag. He had sent a text a half-hour earlier that he was running late. He promised to be there by the time dinner was served.

Her consideration of Jake's text was halted when Kelsey and Ash entered. Elyse greeted them with hugs. "You both look very nice," she said. Kelsey wore a simple white gown that looked stunning on her.

"We had to quickly run and get Ash a suit today. He thought the one he had would work, but it was way too tight," Kelsey said.

"I'm so sorry you had to buy one," Elyse said.

"That's okay. I needed one," Ash said. "You never know when you'll need a suit for a wedding or a funeral." He motioned to his suit coat. "And black works for either."

Elyse laughed. She couldn't argue with that. "The cocktail hour offers complimentary wine or champagne, so make sure you have a few glasses. The table cards are near the door into the banquet room, but you're seated at my table, table number one."

Kelsey glanced around. "You have a great turnout, and this foyer area looks so elegant and amazing. I'm proud of you, Mom."

"Oh, Kels, thank you," Elyse said, tears flooding her eyes. She really hated that she felt this emotional and couldn't seem to get it under control. It was just that tonight was so important to the survival of the rescue. No matter how she tried to get her mind to stop thinking about it, she couldn't.

Kelsey and Ash moved away, Kelsey greeting other volunteers she knew, eager to introduce Ash to them. Elyse continued to greet the arriving guests. Claire's friend, Jenna, came through the door. Elyse smiled and greeted her. Jenna introduced her husband. "Are Claire and Matthew here yet?"

"I believe they're running a few minutes late," Elyse told her. "But please, until they arrive have a glass of wine or champagne and take a look at the fantastic silent auction items we have on offer. We have about twenty minutes left of the cocktail hour and we'll then head into the banquet room to enjoy the evening's events as well as the delicious meal we have planned."

"Thank you. Yes, we did take a look at the silent auction items on the website. We've already bid on a few of them through the app." Jenna patted the lapels of her husband's suitcoat. "Jerry is quite competitive. This may get ugly," she said with a laugh.

Elyse laughed as well. She loved to hear that. The more competitive the bidders were, the higher the price would go. Kade and Melanie came through the door a few minutes later. Kade always looked good dressed in a suit. He owned just one, the black one he wore. Her thoughts went back to Ash's comment, and she chuckled. She'd never seen Melanie dressed up. The black dress she wore was beautiful on her. It was not a maternity dress, but it was high waisted with enough blousing over her belly and hips that her tiny baby bump was camouflaged. She greeted them with hugs as well.

Julia approached from the direction of the banquet room. "Where's Jake?"

"He's running late," Elyse said. "Was there a problem?" She pointed back towards the doors into the banquet room.

"No, I was just getting John, our emcee, set up."

"I didn't see him come in," Elyse said.

"He came in through the back, through the employee's entrance. He texted me when he arrived. Don't worry about a thing. He's all set up. The music is ready. The slide show is ready to go. It'll all be on when the guests all take their seats. The room in there looks amazing."

"Thank you for taking care of all of it," Elyse said. Just then, Claire and Matthew entered. Claire wore a beautiful white gown, which looked gorgeous on her with her dark hair and darker coloring. Matthew wore what was obviously an expensive black tuxedo with a white shirt and a black tie. They looked glamorous, the perfect couple, except Elyse knew there were problems tarnishing the image they projected. "Claire, you look beautiful," she greeted her daughter with a hug.

"You, too, Mom. Your gown is stunning!" Claire said.

"Thank you for changing your plans, Matthew." Elyse greeted her son-in-law with a brief embrace, tucking away the ambivalence she felt towards him. He was here, wasn't he?

He nodded. "I know this event is important to you, and it meant a lot to Claire that we attend."

"Yes, and several of your friends are already here," Elyse said.

Elyse continued to man the door, greeting their guests. Before long, it was time to head into the banquet room to be seated for dinner. Elyse nervously looked around, searching for Jake. This was so unlike him to be this late. She entered the room with Kelsey and Ash. The room was stunning. The lights were low, creating a dramatic candlelight effect and silver sparkles were cast all around the room, projected from the ceiling. Kade and Mel were already at the table.

She glanced over her shoulder at the table behind them where Claire and Matthew were settling in with the four other couples seated there, their friends Claire had invited to the gala. Claire had filled a table, which helped tremendously. Hopefully they would bid on the auction items, buy into the wine pull, or just offer up cash donations.

As she sat, facing the stage directly in front of her, Elyse glanced around her table. Kade and Ash were talking, as were Kelsey and Melanie. The four of them were laughing and appeared to be having a good time together. Her heart was happy that their relationship was what it was. Julia was not at the table. She glanced around the room, looking for her. She and volunteer Trevor Ferguson were also sitting at her table. Tom Wallace, the volunteer who served as Animal House's accountant, and his wife, rounded out the seating of ten at the table.

The voice of John, their emcee for the evening, came over the PA system in the room as a spotlight lit him in the center of the stage. "Welcome, guests of Animal House! Please find your seats. We have a full schedule of entertainment for you this evening and a delicious meal. And of course, we have a lot of updates on the future of Animal House, contingent upon your generosity this evening! So please settle in and we'll get started shortly."

Soft music rose as planned. The four large screens throughout the room began the rotation of the slides they'd planned. Elyse kept her eyes on the screen to the right of the main stage. On the edge of the stage, Eddie Brown, the keyboard player, and vocalist from Flowing Waters Church was set up. He played a soft classical melody that Elyse didn't recognize, but he played it beautifully.

As the remainder of the guests streamed into the ballroom, every table filled. The voices of all the conversations rose above the music. After a few minutes, the lights flickered. Blue and white spotlights circled the room, getting everyone's attention and quieting their chatter. The soft music again dominated. Both of the spotlights converged, focusing on John at the front of the stage.

"Ladies and gentlemen, your music for the evening is being provided by the incomparable Eddie Brown." He motioned toward Eddie and the blue spotlight shifted to him. "Eddie has played with many of the great legends at blues and jazz clubs up and down all of the Eastern Seaboard."

Applause sounded through the room. The guests were all lively and in a party state of mind. Elyse was relieved. That was the vibe she had wanted, and had been secretly afraid the formal nature of the evening may make their guests reserved or stuffy.

"He plays many genres of music and I'm sure you will enjoy the music he's donating to Animal House Shelter very much!" John continued.

Applause interrupted him.

"We have many donation opportunities for you this evening in addition to the music and the wonderful meal. Also, please keep your eyes on the screens where the video presentation will repeat several times through the night, highlighting the financial need of the rescue as well as entertaining you with the pictures of the success stories of the dogs who have found their fur-ever homes. We'll also sneak in pictures of the dogs that are still waiting to be adopted. Hopefully, some of you are considering opening your homes and your hearts. If you are, there may be a few people here who can help you with that."

The audience laughed.

"But first, I'd like to bring Animal House's founder, Elyse Laramie, up onto the stage," John announced.

Elyse was taken aback. This wasn't part of the planned order of events. She was supposed to address the guests as dessert was served. Those at her table cheered her on as she rose and stepped onto the stage. She could just as easily give her thank you speech now as after dinner. She smiled, ready to take the microphone from the emcee.

"Elyse, you are the driving force behind Animal House, the heart and soul of it," he said, keeping his hand tightly on the microphone. "But there are many volunteers and many patrons who have supported the rescue with their time, their talents, and their monetary donations. Which is why we are here tonight, to secure much-needed funds to ensure the continuation of Animal House Shelter."

Elyse was even more confused. Who wrote this script for him? This wasn't at all what was planned for this portion of the evening.

"With that said, we will enjoy a wonderful meal with entertainment, followed by dancing. There are fifty great items included in the silent auction that were donated, including a ski trip, a condo on the beach for a week, professional sports tickets, concert tickets, and even a handmade twin blade set of Japanese swords. They're absolutely beautiful. Guests, please go on your phones and bid on these great items if you haven't yet. The bidding will remain open until ten p.m. There is also a link on the website to make a direct cash donation. All funds go directly to the Animal House Shelter."

Elyse smiled and nodded. Those who knew her could see the confusion behind her smile.

"But there has been one donation to the rescue that is so amazing, we are highlighting it right now. Elyse, one donor was made aware of the need for a permanent building to house the dogs that would also be open to the public to facilitate meeting and adopting the dogs taken in by the rescue. This donor stepped up to fill that need. Permits have been approved by the city. You are good to go once this donor closes on the purchase of the property." He clicked the button on the transmitter to change the picture on the screens around the room. "Elyse, here is the new permanent facility for Animal House Shelter."

A picture of the warehouse they'd been using was displayed, further confusing Elyse. *There must be some mistake,* she thought.

"Elyse, your donor initially wanted to remain anonymous, but those closest to you convinced him to let his generosity be known right now. Ladies and gentlemen, providing this permanent space is only the beginning. Substantial costs to build out the warehouse to be a fully functioning Animal House Shelter are still needed. So please, give with your heart tonight to enable the space to be completed."

Elyse now stared at him without the forced smile she'd put on to show some semblance of grace. She was beyond confused, and was sure someone had made a big mistake.

"Ladies and gentlemen, a round of applause please for our incredibly generous donor, Lieutenant Commander Jacob Tanner, United States Navy," John announced.

Elyse froze, shocked to hear Jake's name. At that moment, Jake stepped out onto the stage from behind the curtain that flanked it. One of the spotlights shifted to him. He wore his dress white uniform, adorned with ribbons and medals. He looked incredibly handsome. His eyes were fixed on hers. She was so numb she didn't notice he approached until he was directly in front of her, bringing the spotlight with him.

"You're buying the warehouse for us?" she squeaked out. Her vision was distorted from the tears in her eyes and the bright light.

Jake wiped a tear that slid down her cheek. "Yes. I believe in you, Elyse."

She wrapped her arms around him, not caring that everyone at the event saw that she hugged him. And she cried tears of absolute joy. He single-handedly had just saved Animal House Shelter. Jake held her for several long, comforting seconds.

Jake, on the other hand, felt uncomfortable and slightly embarrassed by the new applause thundering through the room from the guests who now stood at their tables. When he'd decided to buy the warehouse, he had intended to remain anonymous. But he couldn't do it alone and had talked with Julia and Tom Wallace, who were the ones who encouraged him to go public this way with the truth of his purchase.

"Well, I hope she's wearing waterproof makeup, or his nice white uniform is going to have a couple of black spots, but at least it will stick with the black and white theme of the evening," the emcee joked, garnering him wild laughter from the audience.

Hearing the emcee's joke, Elyse regained her composure. She pulled away, inspecting the front of his uniform. She'd pressed her cheek to his shoulder. No makeup stains were left, thank God. She wiped her cheeks and smiled. "Thank you so much for your very generous donation," she said, her gaze still locked on Jake's.

"You will hear more from Elyse later in tonight's events," the emcee said, motioning to her. "Until then, Elyse, Commander, please take your seats as I see our wonderful event staff are beginning to serve the first course of tonight's delicious meal."

Jake took Elyse by the hand and led her down the few stairs and to their table. As they reached it, Kelsey rose and embraced her mom. Then she hugged Jake as well. "I can't believe you did this for my mom," she said to him.

"I believe in her and the rescue," he said.

Kade and Ash also rose and shook Jake's hand.

Julia circled around from the back of the stage and also gave Elyse an excited hug.

"You were in on this," Elyse said to her.

"Guilty as charged. Tom and I both were," Julia admitted. "This couldn't have happened without Tom in on it."

Elyse circled the table and also embraced Tom and his wife. Jake followed and shook his hand, again thanking the accountant for his help in pulling off this surprise.

As Elyse and Jake took their seats, she again gazed at him in his uniform. If she hadn't been completely in love with him by then, seeing him dressed in his uniform would have done it. "A lieutenant commander, huh?"

Jake smiled. "You never asked."

Elyse chuckled, still completely overwhelmed by his donation. "Your rank didn't matter to me. I didn't care if you were the ship's captain or the man cleaning the toilets."

Jake chuckled as well. "I've done both. As the ship's XO, I have the conn in the captain's absence as second in command. I've also cleaned toilets on the ship. I've supervised and been responsible for everything in between."

"I haven't even begun to process any of this," she said, still gazing into his beautiful green eyes.

"Process it later. Tonight, just enjoy yourself. You've worked so hard to make this happen, and the night is now on cruise control."

Jake was right. Elyse had worked so hard to plan tonight. She sat back, ate, drank, enjoyed the company of those at the table, and delighted in the jokes and narrative coming from the lively emcee. He told stories of the dogs they'd saved and their new lives with adoring families. He showed pictures of spoiled hounds stretched out on couches or beds, and one even lounging on a float in a swimming pool. A litany of pictures showing dogs dressed up in human clothing posing with the children of their adoptive families came after. Laughter and oohs, and aws, rose from the crowd. The emcee's colorful commentary of course garnered the audience's reaction as much as the cute pictures displayed.

As dessert was served, their emcee called Elyse back to the stage. Giving speeches wasn't her forte, but talking about her shelter was. She focused her gaze between Jake and Kelsey while she gave her speech, which she now had to modify on the fly because of Jake's incredible gift.

"Ladies and gentlemen, thank you for attending tonight's gala. As John already told you, I'm Elyse Laramie, the founder of Animal House Shelter. I discovered the need for a rescue in this area by accident just over six years ago. At the time, I had two German shepherds, named Thor and Jane Foster. I used to take them for walks out in a large nature preserve near Franklin. One day while we were there, we came across a scared and lost black lab mix. He looked like he'd been out there for some time. Even though he was scared he came up to me and trusted me. Well, I slipped a leash on him and we brought him home. While trying to find a shelter to turn him over to, I discovered there was only one no-kill facility within forty miles and they were full. That was the start of Animal House Shelter. I called my vet," she said pointing to the table to the left of hers. "Ladies and gentlemen, Animal House's official vet, Doctor Lesley Montgomery."

One of the spotlights shifted to her. She stood and waved. The audience clapped.

"And I had the dog checked out. I couldn't keep him with two big dogs of my own, but I was determined to find him a good home. Well, one thing led to another. I met some of the wonderful volunteers who are in this room with us, and somehow, I acquired several more strays. Before I knew it, I had ten stray dogs in my barn, and I was setting up a 501c3 charity I named Animal House Shelter."

Laughter and applause reverberated off the walls.

"Within a year, we were gifted a small home by one of our early volunteers at the time of his death." A picture of that man, eighty-two-year-old Roger Barone, was displayed on the screens. "Roger was a great friend to Animal House. Unfortunately, that home was already aged and it was out of compliance with electrical and plumbing codes at that time. It has served us well, but we now find that we have severely outgrown it as well, and the costs to bring the electrical and plumbing current would cost us more than the value of the home and the land it sits on. With Lieutenant Commander Jake Tanner's generous gift we have a new facility, the warehouse we have used for the last year to hold our public meet and greets with potential adoptive families. Ladies and gentlemen, we thank the owner of that warehouse, Sal Giovanni, for letting us use it for so long."

She paused and motioned to him. He sat at the same table with Doctor Montgomery. As the spotlight focused on him, he too stood and waved to more applause. This, too, had been pre-planned.

"And for selling it for such a great price," Elyse added. "Lieutenant Commander Tanner has just told me that Sal is selling it way below market value because it's going to Animal House. Sal, I hope you get some kind of write off on your taxes for your generosity to us. See Tom if your own accountant isn't directing you on it," she said, garnering laughter from the audience.

"In closing, I again want to thank each of you for joining us this evening. I hope you enjoyed your meal and stay to enjoy the entertainment. Please join me in a round of applause for this evening's emcee, John Harris, and the incredible Eddie Brown," she said, motioning to them both.

The audience clapped and whistled.

"Oh, and that black lab mix I found that day, his adoptive family named him Warlock." His picture sitting in a chair cuddled with two small children displayed on the screens. "He enjoys lounging on the furniture with the kids he guards and protects, and he goes in the car just about everywhere the family goes. He was the first of Animal House's success stories, but with your generosity tonight I'm sure there will be many more."

She handed the microphone back to John and then stepped from the stage, relieved that her speech was done. She breathed out a heavy sigh and took a drink of her wine once she returned to her table. Everyone at her table congratulated her on her speech.

Jake wrapped his arms around her and held her. "I'm so proud of you. You looked so relaxed and natural as you spoke, like you were just talking to a friend at your kitchen table."

Elyse chuckled softly. "I'm just glad I remembered the speech and didn't trip walking onto or off of the stage." She felt his embrace tighten around her and a kiss press to her forehead. She should have been embarrassed by this public display of affection, but she wasn't.

"Ladies and gentlemen, I'm happy to tell you that every single item in our silent auction has bids on them. Please continue to check the app for the current bid and continue to bid as you can for the items you are interested in. Also, I'm thrilled to tell you that the cash donations for the event through the link on the app is currently at twenty-five thousand dollars. For anyone who hasn't given a cash donation yet, please consider it with all your heart. Funds are needed to build out the warehouse, constructing pens, and runs. Walls need to be built. Signage needs to be constructed. No amount is too large or too small. Oh, and we are about to begin the wine pull. The cost to buy in is seventy-five dollars. You can buy in on the app as well and it's now open. As soon as you have confirmed your purchase, stay in the app and hold your phone up. Volunteers will come around with the wine, confirm your purchase, and hand you a gift bag with your bottle. There are seventy bottles of wine that have been donated. Two of them are valued at two hundred dollars each. The minimum value is fifty dollars."

Hands with lit cell phones began to raise all around the venue. Every woman at Claire's table, including Claire raised her phone. Kelsey and Tom's wife did as well. It didn't take long for all seventy bottles to be claimed.

Eddie Brown took over, rocking the venue with slow as well as fast dance music. The first number was of course a slow song to encourage the couples to enjoy a romantic slow dance. He did a beautiful version of 'Wonderful Tonight', by Eric Clapton, a request from Elyse. It was immediately followed with a rousing rendition of 'Who Let the Dogs Out', by Baha Men, which brought laughter from the packed dancefloor.

As the evening continued, Elyse checked in periodically with the app's live feed that provided an accounting of funds donated and the status of the bids on the silent auction items. The guests were actively bidding. At five minutes till ten, John made an announcement that there was only five minutes left to bid. The bidding picked up. Jake excused himself to use the restroom.

Elyse went over to Ash and Kelsey. "Ash, how much would you have sold that Japanese sword set for?"

"What I had listed as its value," he answered.

"The bidding is at quadruple its stated value right now, and with only a few minutes left the bidding is going crazy," she told him.

"Really? That is crazy," he said. "I'm glad it's raising you some good funds. Kelsey and I tried to get some of our friends to buy tickets for the dinner, but at two hundred dollars a pop no one was down for it."

"I get it," Elyse said. "But the two of you are here, which is what's important to me. And you made and donated that sword set which is bringing in as much as a table would. Thank you, Ash."

Elyse moved away from them, heading towards the lobby to use the restroom herself. Claire watched her leave the room. She excused herself from their group of friends. Except for when they'd arrived, she hadn't talked to her mom all night. With the revelation of Jake's rank and generosity, she'd been proven wrong about what kind of man he was and she knew she owed her mom an apology.

Claire caught up with her mother and Jake in the lobby. She swallowed her pride and approached them, all smiles.

They returned her smile. "Mom, congratulations. This evening has not only been a success for Animal House as far as I can see, but everyone is having a wonderful time. All our friends at our table are already asking what date it will be next year."

"I'm glad they've enjoyed the evening," Elyse said. "And yes, the fundraising portion of the event has netted us higher donations than past years. I was just showing Jake the side of the app from the silent auction and donations I get to see."

Claire shifted her gaze to him. "Jake, I owe you an apology, which I want to do in front of my mom. I questioned your motives. I told my mom that I thought you were out to take advantage of her, the lonely widow, which you clearly are not." She now looked her mother in the eye. "And I disrespected you and your ability to judge his motives for yourself. I apologize to you both. I'm sorry. My motive was only to protect my mom. I hope you can both forgive me."

Elyse wrapped her in an embrace and held her tightly. "I love you, Claire, and I know you were only looking out for me. That's why I couldn't get too mad at you for it."

When they parted, Claire presented her right hand to Jake. "Friends?"

Jake smiled warmly and shook her hand. "Friends."

Pleased with Claire's apology, Elyse pointed to the ladies' room. "I'll be back out in a minute. Wait for me, Jake?"

"Yes, ma'am." After she disappeared behind the closed door, he turned back to Claire. "Does this mean that you're okay with your mom's relationship with me?"

"I'm getting used to it," Claire admitted. "It's nice to see my mom happy. She deserves it."

"Yes, she does," Jake said. "Claire, your mom is one smart lady. She built all of this, the rescue, the network of volunteers, the financial supporters. And this gala, she planned it as well. She deserves your respect professionally as well as personally. Just because she doesn't put her efforts towards a for-profit organization, don't assume that she doesn't have the same skills as or better than her peers in the corporate world. What she's built here is pretty amazing."

Claire felt embarrassed and put off by his statement. She had done that, hadn't she? She'd referred to her mom's rescue as silly on multiple occasions. But she didn't need him pointing it out to her. And she certainly didn't appreciate that he was trumpeting her mom's accolades when it should be her doing it.

"Yes, it's quite amazing," Claire agreed. "My mom has always quietly done so many remarkable things, making it look easy. When we were kids, she parented us alone. And until I became a parent, I didn't know how much of a feat that was. This rescue is no different. She poured herself into it and made it look easy. So, it's not that I haven't respected her," Claire lied. "It's just that I have only recently understood the weight of her undertaking."

"Her relationship with you means a lot to her," Jake said. "I'm sure your apology tonight has meant the world to her."

Elyse re-entered the lobby and stepped over to them. She judged that they were having a pleasant conversation. "So, what do you say, Commander? Would you like to join me on the dancefloor? I like this song that just started."

"I would love to join you on the dancefloor," he said with a smile, offering Elyse his hand.

"I'll talk to you later, sweetie," Elyse said to Claire.

Claire watched them walk away, holding hands. Yes, she could be okay with this relationship, she'd try very hard to be. Her mom was very happy. Her sister approached, exiting the ballroom through the other set of doors. Kelsey also watched their mom and Jake enter the ballroom.

"Mom is killing it tonight," Kelsey said, reaching Claire. "Her speech was so good, and everyone looks like they're having a great time. I'm really proud of her."

"Yes, I'm proud of her, too. It's great to see her so happy. I'm glad she has Jake with her tonight, given that Dad couldn't be here," Claire said.

"Dad wouldn't have been here. This wouldn't have rated with him to be home for," Kelsey replied. "He never came to any of the galas over the last three years." And neither had Claire. Her mom had never insisted like she had this year.

"I'm really struggling to accept Jake as her boyfriend," Claire admitted. She wasn't sure why she told her sister this. "I guess I'm just struggling to accept that she has a boyfriend this soon, period."

"That looked like a friendly conversation between you and Jake," Kelsey said. She'd seen them talking and waited to approach, not wanting to interrupt their conversation.

"It was. He thinks a lot of Mom," Claire said.

Kelsey nodded. "I still can't believe he bought her a warehouse!"

Claire laughed. "That is pretty amazing."

"Mom is happy, Claire. As far as I'm concerned, if Jake being in her life makes her happy it doesn't matter how soon it is since Dad died. Life is too unpredictable for there to be a time table associated with when it's okay for her to have a boyfriend."

"I know you're right about that," Claire agreed. "What about you? How are things going with Ash?"

Kelsey's smile answered the question with no words needed. "You know how good you feel when things in your life are just going how they're supposed to? That's how it is being with Ash."

No, Claire didn't know how that felt at this point in time. She had a vague memory of it. She nodded anyway. "I'm happy for you, sis. I didn't understand your decision not to go to grad school, but you're obviously happy and that's all I want for you."

The sisters embraced.

If Claire was being honest, she still didn't understand or support Kelsey's decision to become a tattoo artist and move in with a man like Ashley Vincent. She knew her father wouldn't have supported it at all. But he wasn't here, and she wasn't him. Kelsey was happy and that was all that mattered after the horrible sadness they'd all felt when he died.

Maybe that was the best peace that could come about from any of this, Claire thought. *Life is continuing for us all, but it will never be the same without Dad. If we each find a way to be happy again, that's all that matters.*

As the sisters released each other, Kelsey saw tears in Claire's eyes. "Claire, what's the matter?"

"I just miss Dad, or maybe, I'm just sad for him that he's no longer here. Life is going on for all of us and he isn't a part of it, will never get to be a part of it again."

Kelsey hugged her again, deciding against pointing out that she felt he hadn't been a part of her life when he was alive. "Claire, Dad wouldn't want you to be this sad."

"I know," she said. She let out a breath and looked up, blinking her eyes to try and blink the tears away as she stepped out of Kelsey's arms. "Anyway, you're right about Mom. Having Jake in her life makes her happy. We need to accept it and support her." She sounded like she was telling Kelsey she was the one who needed to.

"Yes," Kelsey agreed, again deciding against telling her that she had. Claire was the one who needed to.

"Okay, I'm going to hit the ladies' room and then go back in and have more fun with my friends, get Matthew out on the dancefloor for at least another slow dance, and I'll probably have another glass of wine or two."

"Sounds like a good plan," Kelsey said. She followed Claire into the bathroom, her reason for coming out to the lobby to begin with.

Chapter 29 – More Memorable

E lyse embraced Jake as the elevator rose. He would spend the night in her hotel room. Charlie was with Miles at the rescue, out in the office area not in the kennel portion. Since they were alone and she was flying high from the success of the evening, as well as the multiple glasses of champagne she'd drank, she initiated a kiss, pressing him against the wall.

Jake chuckled at her. "I like after-gala Elyse."

"Tonight was fabulous! I had such a great time," she said. "Jake, are you sure about the warehouse. That's a lot of money."

"I had a few hundred thousand lying around I wasn't doing anything with," he said with a chuckle.

"Not funny," she said. "That's a lot of money."

"Yes, it is," he agreed. "I made some investments years ago that have performed incredibly. And I didn't make the decision to buy it lightly."

"It's not like it's an investment. There'll be no return on it."

Jake's lips tipped into a flirty grin. "That depends on how good the sex is tonight."

She laughed and slapped his shoulder. She knew he was joking. The elevator chimed and the doors opened on her floor. He drew her by the hand into the hallway. Elyse pulled her room key from her bag and pointed him in the right direction.

Once behind the locked door of her room, she turned back to him. "Jake, I'm serious about the warehouse and the money."

Jake wrapped her in an embrace. "And I'm serious that I considered it carefully. Elyse, you don't get it, do you?"

"Get what?"

"I told you that I'm in love with you. I want a future with you, or maybe I should say I see a future for us. Animal House Shelter is your baby. I want to help with that baby and, dare I say, be a part of it with you. I'd like for it to be something for us to focus on together. Elyse, we haven't talked about the future. I haven't gone there out of respect for how recently you lost your husband."

Elyse felt overwhelmed by so many emotions boiling inside her at his proclamation. "I know, and I haven't brought it up either."

"I figured you were waiting to see if I'm going back to sea or not."

She shook her head. "You have to know that won't matter to me. I know I said I'd never be in a relationship with long separations again, but that was before I fell in love with you."

Jake's lips pulled into a grin. "Some men buy the woman they love an engagement ring when they propose. I thought I'd buy a warehouse instead."

Elyse's eyes went wide. "Propose?" She'd never been this shocked in her life. She felt lightheaded, though that could be all the champagne she'd drunk or the fact that she suddenly wasn't breathing.

"Yes, propose. I could be satisfied with loving you and leaving things as they are. But I want something permanent. I want to be more to you than just your boyfriend who sleeps over a few nights a week. I want to make a commitment to you." He could see what he interpreted as indecision in her eyes. "Obviously not right away. After what you deem the appropriate amount of time to wait."

She nodded, too stunned to speak. She smiled. There was no containing it.

"You're smiling," Jake said. "Did you forget to say yes?"

Elyse laughed, her eyes filling with tears. "I love your engagement ring." She flung her arms around his neck.

The embrace turned into a kiss, which turned into making love in a way they never had. Intense emotions and a promise for their future together made the coupling they shared more meaningful, more potent. Each caress, each kiss linked them together beyond boyfriend and girlfriend. This physical intimacy they shared was about the promise of his proposal and the affirmation of her acceptance.

Chapter 30 – Claire Flies and So Do Words

O n the Wednesday following the gala, Elyse made the drive into Norfolk to have dinner with Claire and the kids and to attend the grief support meeting. Unless something came up, she probably wouldn't be coming every week. She'd just pop in on a meeting whenever she felt she needed it. She did want to talk with Claire about scheduling visits to spend time with her and the kids now that she wouldn't be coming regularly for the meeting. She also wanted to talk with her about all the drama between her and Matthew the night of the gala, as well as her apology regarding Jake. She didn't plan to tell her about Jake's proposal.

Jake called as she exited the interstate. "Hello," she greeted, pulling her thoughts from her agenda items to talk with Claire about. "How did your doctor's appointment go?"

Jake sighed heavily. "The final decision has been pushed out another month. Medically, I'm not where I need to be to even attempt a physical fitness evaluation. More PT."

He sounded frustrated. "Okay, another month for your ACL to heal. But the doctor is confident it will heal more, isn't he?"

"I don't know. I'll admit I was so irritated that I didn't hear much after he said I'm not there yet."

"It's one more month I won't have to worry about you deploying. I like that."

Jake chuckled softly. "True. I like that, too."

"Will I see you tonight?"

"Tonight's going to be your last time going to the meeting, right?"

"Well, unless I feel I need to for some reason," Elyse answered.

"Are you heading to Claire's house?"

"Yes, and I'll tell her that I won't be coming on Wednesdays for the meetings any longer. I do want to work out another time every week, if I can, to see her and the kids. Who knows, maybe on Wednesdays I'll still be driving in to see them. She's quite attached to her schedule."

Jake chuckled. "Yes, she is. And to answer your question, yes, I'll be there tonight, and I plan to come to your place after. My bag is already packed and in my car."

"Good," Elyse said.

"Good luck with Claire. I have to go. I'll see you at the church."

"I love you, Jake." She smiled as she spoke.

"I love you, too, Elyse."

She put the car into park in front of Claire's house. She really had enjoyed spending Wednesday of nearly every week with Claire and her grandkids the last few months. If Wednesday was the only day that would work for Claire, she'd continue to make the drive every week. Though she hoped Claire would agree to bring the kids out to see her at least once a month.

Elyse knocked on the front door and waited and waited. After a few minutes, she pulled her phone out and sent Claire a text telling her that she was there. Claire's reply came via text. *I'm on the phone. Will come let you in but will still be on the call.*

The lock clicked and the door swung open. Claire, phone held in one hand, waved her in without a word. Elyse saw the Bluetooth earpiece in Claire's right ear. Claire turned her back on her mom and headed back to her office.

"That's bullshit, Michael! I've earned it and I have more collapse knowledge than he has."

"That's why he needs to be the one to go on-site, to learn," Michael said. "With your support from the office. You're an expert with the software. Tim always said the models you programmed were vital, and unearthed more stresses to the structures than a site survey after the fact."

"No, the models only confirmed what my father determined on-site. By cataloguing exactly how the structure settled after it failed, I then backtrack to determine which wall, support column, or beam failed. I'm really fucking pissed off about this, Michael. Send the kid to Seattle for the refurb instead of me and assign me to the collapse in Bolivia."

"Cody isn't up to the refurb. He has no experience with high-rise redesigns. One wrong wall removal and we'll have a new collapse to investigate. I need you there, Claire, and I need you to pull double duty working on both that and supporting Cody while you're there."

"I'll do it this time, but we need to talk about this more. My dad was prepping me to be the collapse expert. The Laramie name is respected in the industry. We both know using me for collapses will be more advantageous to the firm."

"We'll talk when you get back, Claire. I'll have Tara finalize your travel plans. She'll have them in your email within the hour."

"Fine," Claire huffed. She ripped the Bluetooth out of her ear and threw it onto her desk. She took a second to calm down before she left her office. She found her mom in the playroom with the kids. "Sorry about that. Work." She rolled her eyes.

"I'll be back in a bit to play," Elyse told the children. "I'm going to step into the kitchen with your mommy and help get dinner finished." She motioned to Claire. She'd heard enough to know Michael had dropped the news on Claire and Claire was not happy about it.

"I've got dinner in the oven. There's nothing for you to do, Mom," Claire said, following her mom from the playroom. She'd prefer her mom entertain the kids while she had a glass of wine and took a moment to calm down.

"I couldn't help overhearing your call with Michael."

"Yes. I'm so pissed at him. I'm being sent on-site to a damn redesign of a building and he's sending this kid he just hired, fresh out of college, to a collapse in Bolivia. And get this, Michael hasn't been in the field in years, but he's going with him. And he's leaving Chris Barton in charge of the office." She threw her hands into the air. "What the hell?"

Elyse was pleased. Claire obviously didn't know that she and Michael had spoken. Good. Michael was keeping his word. "What kind of redesign?"

"An old high-rise in Seattle. The architects are working on a substantial lobby redesign to make it look more modern."

"Is the building occupied?" Elyse asked.

"Yes."

"That sounds far more important that it be reviewed by an experienced engineer than a collapse. If it's not done right, isn't it possible it will collapse?"

"You sound like Michael," Claire spat. "Anyway, I leave tomorrow. I agreed this time, but he and I are going to have to talk about my assignments. Dad was teaching me everything he knew. I know more than Michael does at this point."

"You're going out of town tomorrow? How long will you be away?" Elyse asked.

"I should be home late Friday night or sometime on Saturday." She poured a glass of wine and then held the bottle up, offering her mom a glass.

"Yes, thank you," Elyse said. "Will Matthew be able to spend more time at home with the kids while you're gone?"

"Lizette will take care of them," Claire said dismissively.

"If you don't make it back on Friday, I could come get them to spend a few days at my house. And I could meet you at church with them on Sunday. I think they're old enough for a sleepover at Grandma's house."

Claire glared at her like she was nuts. "Aiden maybe, but Emma isn't old enough yet. I haven't even had the chance to tell Lizette she can't have Saturday off yet. If she throws a fit, could you come here to help?"

"Is Matthew busy Saturday?" Elyse asked. This was the perfect jump-off point to bring up the drama between them the night of the gala.

"I haven't even told him about my trip yet. It just came up this afternoon. But I'm sure he'll want Lizette or you to be here."

"Claire, what's going on with him? The last time we talked, you were going to see if his spending one on one time with each of the kids would work better for him. Has anything changed?"

"That discussion didn't go so well. He has spent a few hours with them, but he acts like it's a huge ordeal for him. Honestly, Mom, I don't know what the problem is."

"Was that the cause of the issue last Saturday before the gala?"

"No, Matthew claimed he didn't know the gala was that night, that it wasn't on his calendar, but I know I sent him an invitation that he accepted. So, I don't know how it got deleted. He'd made other plans with his partners and initially wasn't going to break them. We fought and he left the house in a huff. That's when I called you. But knowing I'd invited other couples, he realized how bad that would look if he didn't come."

Elyse was surprised, well, by all of it, beginning with Claire sending calendar invites to her husband for social engagements. "He looked like he had a good time."

"He did once he was there. He gets along with all the couples that were there. That reminds me, Mom, my friend Jill, who was at the gala, went on your website Sunday morning to look at the available dogs, and she noticed you have Strickland-Heinz Financial Services listed as a sponsor."

"They are," Elyse said.

"What about Matthew's firm. Why aren't they listed? That's free advertising you're giving their competitor."

"Because Matthew turned me down flat for a donation, said his firm makes no charitable donations as a standing policy. Strickland-Heinz was happy to donate."

"You asked Matthew for a donation to your shelter?"

Elyse couldn't tell if Claire was outraged that she'd asked, or that Matthew declined. It was clear this was news to her. "Yes. I made an appointment, as I'm a client, and went in to see him."

"And when he said no you went to his competitor?" Claire asked, genuinely outraged.

"No, Strickland-Heinz appeared on a list our fundraising coordinator prepared of businesses in Norfolk that give to charities for the tax write-off. I met with John Heinz, and he was most gracious with the generous donation they gave."

"Kensington-Laramie is on your website?" Claire asked in a questioning tone of voice even though her friend had told her it was.

"Yes, when I met with Michael, he was generous as well."

"You met with Michael? When?"

"It must have been late June or early July," Elyse answered.

"Why didn't you just talk to me about it?" Claire demanded.

"Only a partner can authorize donations."

"I could have brought the request to him. And duh – I'm a Laramie at Kensington-Laramie."

"That's your father's name on the company letterhead, not yours!"

The expression on Claire's face couldn't have been more shocked had Elyse slapped her. "I'm there with Michael every day. I could have asked and saved you a trip," Claire practically stammered.

"I wanted to see Michael. We hadn't spoken since your father's memorial service."

The timer on the oven buzzed. Claire busied herself taking the casserole out and setting portions onto the kids divided plates. Elyse went to the refrigerator and brought fruit to the counter for Claire to add. Without a word she then went to the playroom to get the kids. She helped them wash their hands and got them settled in their chairs.

"So, how long does Matthew's Wednesday night golf league run?"

"It never ends," Claire said. "But he enjoys it." She put on an obviously fake smile. "And now you guys both know where Daddy is on Wednesday nights, as he's taken you both to TopGolf."

"Daddy says when my cast is off, I can really play," Aiden said with excitement.

"The pretty girls sit me on the counter," Emma said.

Elyse's questioning stare went to Claire.

"The bartenders." She rolled her eyes. "But Daddy has also taken you to the zoo and the hands-on museum."

Elyse was glad to hear this even though Claire had said he acted like it was an issue. She sure hoped he didn't convey that feeling to the kids. Claire was cold for the remainder of dinner. Elyse was sure Claire was angry that she pointed out that the Laramie in the company name was Tim and not her. Oh well, it was true.

After they ate, Elyse gave her grandkids a hug and kiss goodbye. Claire walked her to the door. "Oh, I forgot to tell you tonight is probably my last meeting at the church. I don't feel I need it. But I've enjoyed spending time with you and the kids, and I don't want that to end. We need to come up with days and times we can get together."

"Are you kidding me? I set the schedule with Lizette based on you coming for dinner on Wednesday."

"I can still drive in on Wednesdays if that's the best day for you, but I was thinking, now that Kade is living at home and Kelsey is spending more time there, maybe you could bring the kids a few times a month when everyone is there."

"Why is Kelsey spending more time at home?"

"She and Ash are close to Kade and Mel, and they've been around more. I've really liked it, but would like it even more if you and the kids were there too."

"And what about Matthew?"

"Sure, him too, if he wants to come. He's just met Ash the one time at the gala, and they didn't even get the chance to talk."

Claire made a sarcastic sound. "I was hoping he'd be out of Kelsey's life before we got to a holiday that would necessitate Matthew having to sit down and really talk to him."

"Ash is good for your sister. She's very happy. Why would you wish him out of her life?"

"Come on, Mom! Can't we hope she aims a little higher than a guy who is way too old for her, and a tattoo artist of all things?"

Elyse held herself back from saying what she wanted to, but when she spoke her voice was harsh. "And he's a bladesmith who does beautiful work. He owns the strip mall his shop is in. And a house. Did you know that? And he really cares about your sister. In case you didn't notice, she's happy with him."

Claire held her hands up in a surrendering gesture. "Fine, she's happy."

"Okay, we can talk over the next week, and I can plan to drive in next Wednesday for dinner. Let me know if you need me to help with the kids while you're away. Claire, your dad missed so much of your lives traveling for work. You need to really give it some serious thought before you talk to Michael. I think Chris Barton is smart for putting limits on his travel. I wish I would have put my foot down with your father. It wasn't worth it, the sacrifices we made, sacrifices that you have no idea about. Those kids need their mother." She pointed back towards the playroom, where the kids were.

Claire felt the heat burn up from her chest and into her cheeks. "My kids are just fine. They have their mother, and even if I travel some, they are well cared for while I'm away. You're a sexist, you know that? You'd never say to a man that his kids need him."

"Yes, now I would. I wish I'd said it to your dad. Claire, a nanny can't replace a mom. Your kids have to come before your career."

"That's the difference between your generation and mine. My generation doesn't settle. We know a man and a woman are equal. Your generation accepted that a mom had

396

to be this long-suffering doormat who had to sacrifice her career, dreams, and goals. Well newsflash, Mom, a woman doesn't, nor should she."

Elyse wouldn't address any of what she'd just said, not now anyway. "Please just think about what I said, Claire. I love you and I love the kids. Try to believe that I'm coming from a perspective of experience." She gave Claire's rigid form a hug, and then left.

By the time she reached the church, Elyse's anger at Claire's words had spread through her entire body. She was aware that her breaths were short, rapid draws. Her pulse rate was elevated. Her hands squeezed the steering wheel so tightly her knuckles were turning white. And emotionally, Claire's words had felt like knives slicing through her. Is that what Claire thought of her, that she was a doormat who'd sacrificed her dreams and goals? How did Claire not understand that after she became a mom her dreams and goals changed?

Her thoughts were interrupted by a tapping on her window. She jumped in her seat, startled to see Jake standing beside her car. She turned the car off and opened the door.

"Are you okay?" he asked.

She slowly shook her head. "Claire and I had words."

Jake pulled her into an embrace. This was foreign to her, a comforting hug and soft caresses to her back when she was upset. When her kids were at home, it was she who provided the shoulder and the embrace to ease hurt feelings, sadness, or pain.

"I'm sorry," she apologized.

Jake pulled away just far enough to look her in the eyes. "Nothing to be sorry about. Do you want to talk about it?"

She frowned and nodded towards the building. "We should probably go in."

"There's nothing that says we have to. If you'd rather go get ice cream and talk about the words you had with Claire, I'm up for that."

Elyse kissed his cheek. "I'm always up for ice cream."

"Same place?"

"Yes."

"I'll meet you there," Jake said.

· · · ·

AS ELYSE TOOK THE LAST bite of her ice cream, she leaned into Jake. They sat atop one of the picnic tables overlooking the river. She'd told him about her evening, including overhearing Claire's harsh words while she was on the phone with Michael right through to Claire's last words to her before she left. She even confided her part in Claire's not being assigned to the Bolivia trip.

Jake folded his arms around her. "Well, all I can say is you had better hope this Michael doesn't let it slip that you kind of blackmailed him into ensuring that Claire wouldn't go to collapse sites. I have a feeling she wouldn't understand, and she'd be pissed. But I understand why you did it."

"She doesn't understand the negative impact it would have on those kids if she was traveling all the time. And believe me, Michael would send her out as much as he could had I not said something to him. And their father is not going to step up and be the parent I was all those years Tim was gone."

"I've seen first-hand how hard on families it is when a parent is away for long periods of time. In the military, that's what they sign up for and they have no choice. Claire has a choice. I could casually bring it up next time I see her if you'd like."

"That's a nice offer, thank you. I probably won't see or hear from her for a few weeks. That's Claire's normal M.O. when someone says something she doesn't like. She once didn't talk to me for a month when I said something about her nanny she didn't like."

Jake tightened his arms around her for a moment, giving her a hug.

"I'm sorry to dump all this on you. I'm sure my drama with my daughter is the last thing you wanted to hear about tonight."

"No apology needed. Your family comes with you, just like the Navy comes with me. I wish I had a family that created baggage you'd have to deal with, but I don't."

Elyse laughed. "Be careful what you wish for."

"I'm sure things will work out with Claire. If she takes some time to think about what you said, she may realize that you're just concerned about the kids. How can she not appreciate that you love your grandkids so much that you would say something to her that you'd know she wouldn't want to hear?"

"Sounds logical, maybe."

"If it matters to you, I think you did the right thing by telling her what you did."

"I couldn't stay quiet."

"And I think she was way out of bounds by what she said to you."

"Claire is Claire. I love her dearly, but she can be trying."

"You're a good mom, Elyse. And you have good kids, successful adults all three of them. I know that doesn't happen by accident."

"Thanks, Jake. I appreciate that."

"Let's head back to your house." He kissed her cheek. "We can get to bed early tonight." He nudged her and smiled suggestively.

Elyse smiled and nudged him back. "Sounds good."

September
Chapter 31 – Finally Unpacked

On Labor Day Monday, Kade had a rare day off. Jake did not. He had duty, and now, Elyse knew exactly what that meant. He was the officer in charge in the main office of his destroyer group, where he was assigned. And of course, Mel didn't have class. Kelsey and Ash came over for an impromptu end of the summer barbecue. Elyse loved when the kids were home. Even though she and Claire weren't really talking, she texted her and invited them over.

She received a two-word reply: "*We can't.*"

They all gathered on the back patio as Ash cooked the meat on the grill. Elyse watched him flip burgers as he and Kade laughed and drank a few beers. Ash had turned out to be a pleasant surprise. He fit into the family well, and Elyse was happy at the confidence and growth she saw this relationship continue to bring out in Kelsey. And Kelsey was genuinely happy. Kade was happy. Elyse was sure that Claire was not. This fact hurt Elyse's heart. No matter how old her children were, Elyse would always worry about them and want them to be happy.

She'd enjoyed dinner every week with Claire and the kids, but since the last few weeks she hadn't gone to the grief support meeting she hadn't gone in to have dinner with them either. And she missed seeing them once a week. But she wasn't sorry she told Claire her thoughts, knowing that Claire wouldn't want to hear it. So, she wasn't surprised that Claire wasn't talking to her. This wasn't the first time. Claire would eventually get over it and she'd reach out. There would be no discussing it, no apology, just the normal glossing over that it happened and a statement by Claire that she would agree to disagree on the topic. Elyse expected nothing else.

After they ate Kade brought up his father's two suitcases, which were still in the garage, untouched. He knew his mom needed to be pushed to deal with them. It bothered him every time he saw them while taking out the garbage or returning the bins to their place in the garage, a childhood chore he automatically resumed when he and Mel moved home.

"I'm just not up to dealing with them yet, Kade. Dad also has one drawer up in the bedroom with a few articles of clothing." She shook her head.

"Mom, all I'm saying is that Jake is staying here, what, four days a week? Don't you think it's time you go through and donate Dad's stuff to clear some room for Jake?"

"I wanted to wait until Claire was here, too, so we could all go through his stuff together," Elyse said. "I wanted to give you all the opportunity to take whatever you would like."

"So, we wait until Thanksgiving?" Kelsey asked. "Let's face it, Mom. Claire won't be here with us all before then."

Elyse knew they were both right. She relented and the three of them went to the garage. Ash and Mel stayed behind and cleaned the kitchen up, giving them time alone to go through the memories. Inside the suitcases were the same clothes they'd all seen him in the last few years. Tim had been a plain dresser, favoring comfort over style. He didn't have any cool clothes collections with pictures or the names of the many places he'd traveled, no band t-shirts, nothing designer.

Kade held up one of the long-sleeved black t-shirts they'd seen him in on a regular basis. He in fact had three of the exact same shirt in his bag. "This one piece of clothing was so versatile in Dad's wardrobe. I don't recall a time he wasn't wearing it alone or under another shirt." He gave a little laugh. "There's three, so no one should have a problem if I take one."

Kelsey grabbed one as well. "Me, too."

The three of them looked through the remainder of his things. There was nothing else anyone wanted to keep. They repacked the suitcases and Kade put them in the back of Elyse's car. She'd drop them at Claire's and give her the opportunity to go through them as well. It would give her an excuse to drop by Claire's house on Wednesday.

Then the three of them went up to her room. Might as well deal with the few items of Tim's left up there as well. Elyse scooped the pajamas, underwear, and socks from the drawer. Beneath the pajamas was a five by seven envelope with 'Elyse' written on it. She held it up to Kade and Kelsey. "It's your father's handwriting."

Elyse slowly opened the envelope, not sure what she expected to be inside. It was a note in Tim's handwriting. Inside the envelope were three other envelopes, each addressed to one of the kids. She left them inside for now, opting to silently read her note first.

Elyse,

MARGARET KAY

I wrote this note to you after a close call in Thailand that made me realize that my job and traveling to it are hazardous. Between going into collapsing buildings, flying all over, and not always in aircraft that have been well maintained, and climbing into any car that pulls up to transport me, often traveling on roads and bridges that are not safe, with drivers behind the wheel who should not be driving, I'll eventually run out of luck. I hope this note has sat here for some time before you are reading it.

I have notes for each of the kids as well. It's my wish that Claire reads hers as soon after my death as possible. Please give Kade his on the day he becomes a father. Kelsey's should be presented to her the day she gets engaged.

Elyse, I loved you and I loved our life together. You have always been my best friend. You allowed me to do a job that mattered, a job I loved, and one I poured myself into. You understood me, that I couldn't do this job and be present as a true husband or an active father. Neither are who I am. You gave me a comfortable place to come home to in between jobs and made no demands on me, which was what I needed. And you reminded me of the important dates I needed to acknowledge, the kids' birthdays, even when to be home for Christmas. I guess I'm the epitome of the absent-minded professor.

But I know it wasn't easy for you. I know I never told you I understood that. I should have, but I feared you would demand I change if we talked about it. It was easier for us not to talk. I knew you handled everything at home. And you did it better than I ever could or would want to.

404

I've often wondered if, had you not gotten pregnant with Claire, if we would have ended up together. I hope you have no regrets regarding your life with me. Was a home and three children enough for you? You always seemed happy. I pacified myself with the knowledge that if you were unhappy, you would have left me. That was an option. I'm glad you never did.

It may not have appeared by my words or actions, but I was always proud of our family. It was something that I never felt a true part of, though. You told me the events, but I wasn't there to feel the reality of them for myself. It was like I was watching a movie of someone else's life. This wasn't your fault. It's just the way I'm wired. Even as I write this, I'm not sure if I would have changed anything if I had my life to live over.

I'm not sure if this note will give you the closure, I meant it to. But I hope it sets you free. I know you will continue to be the rock for our family you've always been.

Love, Tim

Elyse wasn't sure how she felt after reading it. Closure? Is that what she was supposed to feel? Was this letter nothing more than Tim admitting he'd been selfish and disconnected and he'd do nothing differently, but hey, Elyse, thanks for being such a good sport?

"Mom, are you okay?" Kade asked.

Elyse forgot that he and Kelsey were in the room. She swiped the tears from her cheeks. "Yes." She pulled the three other notes from inside the envelope. "Dad wrote you each one as well. He didn't want you to have yours until you became a father," she said, her gaze sweeping to Kade. Then she shifted it to Kelsey. "And he said to give you yours the day you get engaged. It's up to you if you want to read them now or wait but I think you should read them now since he wanted Claire to read hers right away. I don't think you two should have to wait if she can read hers now." She handed each of their envelopes to them.

Kade and Kelsey exchanged unsure gazes. Kade opened his.

Kade,

You're a father now. It's hard for me to believe you're not that little boy any longer who was a daredevil, jumping from roofs and trees. I know I never told you, but I'm proud of the man you've grown into. I'm glad you chose a safer career than what I envisioned you'd choose. Truth be told, I know the man you are was your mother's doing, as I was not around enough to be a role model for you as I should have been. And that's something I regret. I hope you will be there for your child more than I was for you. I'm sure you won't be able to understand when I say I didn't have the capacity to do my job and be home enough to be a father. My job consumed me, my time, my thoughts, my energy.

I'd ask you to take care of your mother, but I know you already do. You and Kelsey, even as adults, are just what she needs. Claire, unfortunately, is too much like me to be there for her. Please do me a favor. If your mom finds a man she wants to be with, accept him. She deserves a happy life.

I'd also ask that you don't give up on Claire. The two of you are very different people, but you are family. It may not have seemed it over the years, but our family meant a lot to me, even though I was rarely with you. Being home nurtured me in ways I cannot put into words.

You have always taken care of Kelsey, more than a big brother. I know the two of you will always be close. Walk her down the aisle on her wedding day in my place.

Live the best life you can, son. Be the best, most involved father you can be. And do the things that make you happy. Those are the things I want for you.

Love, Dad

After Kade read the note, he dropped onto Elyse's bed and sat, staring at his father's handwriting across the page. "That's the most he ever said to me, my entire life." He shook his head, feeling so many emotions from his father's last words to him. "I wish he had said even one of those things to me when he was alive."

"What did he say?" Kelsey asked.

"Read yours first, then we can swap notes," Kade said. He was curious what his father would say to her, if it would be a near duplication of the note to him. That would help define how he'd feel about his note.

"Okay," Kelsey said with hesitation. She climbed onto her mom's bed and sat cross-legged. She pulled the handwritten note from the envelope.

Dear Kelsey,

You are engaged to be married. I hope he's deserving of you and will make you happy. I will miss walking you down the aisle. I missed out on much of your life, my career taking dominance. I know you will never let that happen in your life, as I know how you feel about the fact that it did in mine. Your mother raised you better than I ever could. Please try to understand that I didn't have the capacity to be the father you wanted. It didn't mean that I didn't love you, though. Because I did. And I'm very proud of the young woman you've become.

I know you will do great things in life. And you will do them with compassion and warmth. You are your mother's daughter in every way, a loyal and trusting soul. Maybe too much so. This is my warning to you: don't ever put your dreams and your goals on the backburner, not for anyone, not even the man you love. And please allow Kade to walk you down the aisle in my place. Also, if he doesn't approve of your groom, give that consideration. He's a good judge of character. He's always looked out for you, and I know he always will. Live your best life and don't ever let anyone overshadow you.

Love, Dad

Kelsey threw the note onto the bed. "Fuck him!"

"Kelsey, please. Language," Elyse said, shocked. "Was it that bad?"

Kelsey pointed to it. "Read it for yourself." She glanced out the window, fuming, hurt, so many negative emotions boiling through her. He didn't even know her at all. How dare he tell her how to live her life and issue any sort of warning! And what a copout, he didn't have the capacity to be a dad. Fuck him!

Elyse held the note. She and Kade read it together. They exchanged glances when they'd finished.

"There is a lot of positive in that note, Kels. He loved you and was proud of you. He acknowledges that he missed out on a lot of your life. I read his regret into that. He wants you to follow your dreams and live your best life. That tells me he'd be happy you spoke up and didn't go to grad school. I have to think he'd approve that you're giving tattooing a try."

"And pointing out that I should approve of the man you're with, well that's the seal of approval for Ash," Kade added.

"Not his place to approve or disapprove, and certainly not his place to delegate that to you," Kelsey argued.

Kade took a seat beside Kelsey and pulled her into an embrace, practically putting her head in a headlock. "He told me in my note, too, that he didn't have the capacity to be a father and do the job he did. Seeing what I see as a paramedic, I think I understand what he meant. I basically have to check my emotions at the door when I go to work. But you never really turn them off. You internalize a lot that you see, and that stays with you. And it can be hard to turn them back on and express what you feel. I think that's what he meant."

Elyse couldn't help but wonder if putting her dreams and goals on the backburner was what he thought she had done. And wasn't that a similar sentiment to what Claire had said in the heat of anger to her? "What about his note bothered you the most?"

"He didn't even know me. How dare he give me any advice!"

"I think he knew you better than you thought. You are my daughter, in appearance and temperament. You're compassionate and giving. You're loyal and trusting. And you are going to do great things in life. Maybe he shouldn't have phrased his warning the way he did that it came across as a negative. Had he said something to the effect of I know you'll stand firm in the pursuit of your goals, it wouldn't have sounded so condescending."

"And you know, whenever the day comes, I'll be honored to walk you down the aisle," Kade said, hugging her more tightly.

"Let me read yours," Kelsey said.

After she read through the note she handed it to her mom, who also read it. Both women had tears in their eyes when their gazes met Kade's.

Elyse really had to wonder what he wrote to Claire. Telling Kade not to give up on her. Acknowledging that Kade and Kelsey were close. He did have a greater grasp on the relationships in the family than she thought he had. He had regrets. She was glad he didn't blatantly say he'd do nothing differently in the two notes to the kids. Though it wouldn't hurt for Claire to hear it.

"Can we read Claire's note?" Kelsey asked.

"No, we can't!" Elyse said. "If she wants to share it after she's read it that's her decision, but whatever your father wrote to her is her business."

"How do you feel about what he wrote you, Kade?" Kelsey asked.

"I feel good about it. I'm glad I read it now and didn't wait until the baby is born. It's good to hear all he told me, because honestly, I'd never think he was proud of me. And knowing he had regrets and knew he missed out will be a good reminder for me to deal with my own work stress, so it doesn't interfere in my life as a father."

"You wouldn't let it, regardless," Elyse said.

"Yeah, you're going to be an amazing father," Kelsey added.

"Yes, you will be," Elyse seconded.

Chapter 32 – The Door is Open

"Do you think Claire will tell you what's in the note from her dad?" Jake asked.

It was late afternoon on Wednesday and Elyse was making the drive into Norfolk. She hoped to catch Claire at home with the kids. She had spoken to Tara Britton at the office to confirm that Claire wasn't out of town, and she'd left the office for the day around four. She had sworn Tara to secrecy regarding the phone call.

Elyse let out a heavy sigh. "I don't know. I doubt she'll hand it to me to read like Kade and Kelsey did. I'm honestly not even sure she'll let me in the door. We really haven't even talked since we had words. That was, what, three weeks ago?"

"Yes, exactly three weeks ago."

"I plan to leave Tim's suitcases and the note even if she won't talk to me. We'll see."

"Good luck," Jake wished her. "I'm proud of you that you haven't opened the note from her dad to read it for yourself. It had to be tempting."

"After what he wrote me, Kade, and Kelsey, I'm more than curious." She turned into Claire's subdivision. "I'm just getting here. Will you be available for the next fifteen minutes or so if I end up leaving right away?"

"I'm ready to head to your place whenever you let me know that you're heading home."

"Okay, I'll call when I leave Claire's house." Which she hoped would be in several hours. Even if Claire didn't want to talk to her, she hoped Claire would let her in to visit with her grandkids.

Elyse put the car into park and popped the back. She took Tim's two suitcases out and pulled them up the walkway. It was still hard for her to fathom that Tim basically lived out of these two bags. He had four pair of jeans, one pair of blue Dockers, those three long-sleeved black t-shirts, two dress shirts, and four short-sleeved t-shirts, a sweatshirt, plus socks and underwear. His shave kit and two pairs of pajamas plus one sports jacket, two pairs of shoes, and three different weight jackets completed his wardrobe. *That was a hell of a way to live,* she thought mentally using a rare curse word.

Elyse rang the bell. Claire answered the door a minute later, her surprised gaze scanning from her mother's face down to the two suitcases that she recognized at her feet.

"Hi Claire," Elyse greeted with a reserved smile. "We went through your father's things on Monday while everyone was at the house. Kade and Kelsey both took one of your father's long-sleeved black t-shirts. There's a third one in here if you want it. They wanted nothing else. I thought for sure Kade would want his leather jacket, which is in here," she said as she patted one of the suitcases. "But he didn't."

Claire was flustered and confused. "You want me to go through Dad's things?"

"If you want to. I wouldn't just get rid of his stuff without you having a look." Elyse noted that Claire had not invited her in.

Claire's eyes shifted to the suitcases, where they stayed. She knew she was not up to looking through them today.

Was that her mom's plan? Bring the suitcases in and force her to go through them? "Yes, may I hold on to them? I won't today, but maybe this weekend."

"Sure. Take them and go through them whenever. Keep what you want and donate the rest. Kade, Kelsey, and I are done with them."

Claire dragged her eyes back up her mom's body until she locked eyes with her. Her mom sounded so cold about it. "I might keep that leather jacket."

Elyse nodded, waiting to see if she'd be invited in and what Claire would say, if anything.

"Are you going to the meeting at the church tonight?" Claire asked after an awkward silence.

"No, I just drove in to bring these to you, as I knew this was the one evening I could catch you at home. I didn't want to just drop them off with the nanny or drop them to you at work."

"Did you want to come in and see the kids?" Claire finally offered.

"I would," Elyse said. "And I wanted to talk with you for a moment, too."

"Mom, let's just agree to disagree about our last conversation."

Elyse reached into her purse and pulled out the note from Tim to Claire. "When we were going through your father's things, I found notes addressed to each of us. We read ours on Monday. Here's yours." She handed it to Claire. "I can keep the kids occupied in the toy room while you read it. We all felt quite emotional after reading ours."

Claire stared at her father's handwriting on the envelope. A lump settled in her throat and tears came to her eyes. She'd recognize his writing anywhere. She nodded. "Yes, thank you. If you would, I would appreciate it."

Claire stepped back from the door and let her mom in. They left the suitcases in the entry, and she watched her mom walk towards the kitchen and on through to the playroom. She sat on the couch and pulled her feet beneath herself. She opened the envelope and pulled the handwritten note into sight.

My dear Claire,

Or as I called you as a small child, my Claire-Bear. If you are reading this, I'm no longer there. Don't be sad. I lived a good life. I had a dream job and a wife who allowed me to have it. But that job didn't come without sacrifices, namely my family as I didn't have the capacity to do both well. I love you and that you have worked with me. Passing my knowledge on to you has been a highlight of my life. But my job hasn't come without an enormous cost, one you should weigh fully before making the decision to follow any further in my footsteps. I purposefully shielded you from it while I was alive, but I'm most certain that, left unchecked by me, Michael will immerse you in that role. And Matthew is not your mother. Your marriage will end, and you will become estranged from your children. This is a natural consequence of so much travel and seeing the death and destruction that comes with collapse sites. What you have provided me from the office has been invaluable. Do not misconstrue the functions and the value each role brings.

It's also my wish that you reach out to your brother and sister more than you do. One day your mother, too, will be gone, and it will be the three of you left. Speaking of her, you have no idea the sacrifices she made out of love, for me to do the job I did and to raise the three of you alone and handle life's every-day stresses and emergencies. She deserves respect, Claire, and happiness. If she meets a man that she wants to move on with, accept him. I know it will feel wrong for you to do so, but you must. You will not be betraying me, and your mom deserves happiness.

Please know as you read this that our daily chats meant the world to me, but I'm glad they were with you safely in the office. I would never have allowed you on-site with me for fear of losing you. Don't be mad at me for this. It's a father's job to protect his children.

Love, Dad

Claire cried, ugly cried. Tears poured from her eyes. She hugged a throw pillow to her chest as if it were her dad. She didn't know how long she sat there sobbing, but when her mom came into the room, alone, she welcomed her comforting embrace.

"It's okay, sweetie," Elyse said, hugging Claire.

"Dad didn't want me to work in the field on collapses," Claire said. "He knew it was unsafe."

"Yes," Elyse said. "He told me in my note that he wrote our notes after a close call he'd had. He didn't elaborate on what that close call had been."

"He told me to accept a new man in your life if you find one. I'm sorry about how I was regarding Jake."

"You were looking out for me. I know you love me, Claire. It's just the way you come across sometimes can be trying. You're so much like your father in all ways. But I think you have a greater capacity to be in the moment with your family than he did while doing this job. He didn't have it in him. And I never demanded he try harder."

"What did his notes to Kade and Kelsey say?"

"That's for them to tell you if you want to all discuss your notes. Kade and Kelsey read each other's. Kelsey was initially quite mad at your father from what he wrote her. Kade and I helped to point out the positives in it."

"They shared their notes with you?"

"Yes," Elyse said. "And I was surprised what a good grasp on their personalities he had. I was also impressed that he understood the relationships between the three of you, as he wasn't here much to take it in. And lastly, I was amazed that he admitted to being absent and missing so much of their lives. He obviously put a lot of thought into each note. How do you feel about yours?"

"I wish he had told me to my face what he wrote. I wish I knew that he was the reason I never got to go on-site with him. I begged him so many times to let me come but this note confirms he didn't want me there."

Elyse didn't know that. "Kade told Kelsey that, as a paramedic, he checks his emotions at the door, but he can't ever turn them off and has a hard time turning them back on when he gets off shift. I had a really hard time being in Dubai and Singapore with your dad when I went. He was distant and moody when he wasn't at the jobsite. He wouldn't even go to the hotel restaurant with me for a meal, insisted on ordering room service and eating while he updated his notes. I think that was his way of coping with the loss of life the collapse created, in the same vein as Kade described. It put a wall between us, though, because I didn't understand at the time."

"How did you feel about what he wrote to you?" Claire asked.

"It's been two days and I'm still digesting it. He said he hoped I gained closure from it. I'm not sure if I have. I didn't need a note from him to know he loved us in his own way and that he was proud of his family. I was surprised, though, that he said he hoped I'd been happy all the years we were married. He'd avoided us talking about it for fear I'd demand he change. He should have known I wouldn't, because I never did at any point over the years."

"Why not?" Claire asked.

"I somehow knew that your father didn't have the ability to do his job well and be an active part of the family. The relationship your dad and I had wasn't what either of us set out for it to be, but it wasn't something either of us could change. And that was because he wouldn't have been able to. I loved him, Claire, and I accepted him for who he was."

"You couldn't have been happy," Claire observed.

"You three made me happy. Being the very best mom I could be to the three of you was my dream job. No, that wasn't my goal when I was eighteen and found myself pregnant with you, but after I held you and then your brother and then your sister," she said with a little laugh, "I knew a different type of love, and making the best life I could for the three of you was a goal that instantly took hold."

Claire was quiet. "Why don't you just let the contents of his note roll around in your head for a few days and take time to process your feelings."

"Do you want to stay for dinner?" Claire asked.

"I'd like that," Elyse said.

"We'd better check the kids. They've been quiet for too long."

"They're fine. They're both on their iPads."

Claire groaned. "Mom, you know I carefully control how much iPad time they get."

"Not today. I knew you'd feel emotional no matter what your dad wrote. They'll be fine. It wasn't you who gave them the iPads, it was me. They'll know your rules still stand. Grandmas can get away with a few things."

Surprisingly, Claire smiled and nodded.

Chapter 33 – The Summer of Love Transcends the Seasons

The Autumnal Equinox fell on September twenty-second, marking the official change of seasons from summer to fall. The weather in the evenings would get cooler, quickly. Kelsey only had a few cool-weather staples in her drawers and the closet. Under the bed in a flat storage box were the rest. Her warmer clothes like her fall flannel, several pairs of yoga pants and sweats, and her heavy sweaters, needed to be unpacked.

It was nearly noon on Wednesday. The shop was closed on Wednesdays. She and Ash had both worked until midnight the night before. She was getting more comfortable with the process and flow of tattooing. Not surprisingly, Ash was a patient and fun mentor. The other artists in the shop were cool and they treated her well, and not just because she was the boss' girlfriend. As she learned the art, she helped to do a lot of the prep for everyone as well as the cleanup. She enjoyed returning customer calls and setting appointments, too. Nothing was beneath her.

Ash came up the stairs. He'd been out running errands while she worked in the bedroom on her clothes. She'd also done their laundry that morning and she had it in folded piles on the bed.

"Hey," she greeted.

He glanced over the many clothes on the bed. "Looks like the closet threw up." He laughed.

"We didn't do any laundry in the past two weeks. I was out of underwear. Plus, I was cold when we left the shop last night. I wanted to get a few more of my fall clothes out." She held up her favorite flannel shirt, an oversized soft shirt in pinks and purples.

"Nice," he said.

She noticed a small brown paper bag in his hand but didn't think anything of it. He had just gotten back from running errands. "Help me put the clothes away?"

"In a second," he said, stilling her from moving towards the closet with a stack of clothes in her arms.

"You're acting weird. What's up?"

"I was talking with Kade earlier. Did you know that Mel doesn't want to get married until after the baby is born? Some bullshit about wanting to lose weight and save money for a honeymoon."

Kelsey was taken aback by his statement. "Yes, I knew Mel wanted to wait and I was sure Kade wouldn't be too crazy about the idea."

"Talking with him made me think of something. Babe, I have to ask, are you on something that prevents you from having a period?"

Kelsey heard his words, but they didn't register at first. Then she realized she didn't remember when her last period was. She brought up the calendar on her phone and scrolled through the weeks. She kept scrolling. "No, no, no, this can't be." Panic overtook her as the realization came to her that she hadn't had a period in months.

Ash pulled a pregnancy test from the small brown bag. He held it up between them, his eyes locked on hers. "That's kind of what I thought."

Her eyes darted between the box and his eyes. "Okay, I'll do it in the morning."

Ash grinned and shook his head. "Now. We need to do it now, Kelsey."

She nodded in resignation. He followed her to the bathroom and stood in the doorway as she sat on the toilet and peed on the stick. The blue lines indicating 'pregnant' were already present when she pulled the test stick into view. She stared at it in disbelief, barely breathing.

After a few silent seconds, Ash took it from her and wrapped it in a Kleenex and set it on the counter. She wiped, stood, then pulled her pants up and washed her hands, all without looking him in the eyes. She felt him press his body behind hers and her tear-filled eyes met his in the mirror.

The tears spilled out of her eyes. "I'm sorry, Ash. I don't know how this happened. I was careful. You saw me take my birth control pills every morning."

Ashley smiled a genuine, big smile. He wrapped his arms around her, a hand coming to rest on her lower abdomen. He snuggled in close, nuzzling his bearded cheek against hers. "You have nothing to apologize for." He pressed a kiss to her cheek. "We're having a baby, Kelsey." His smile grew wider. "We're having a baby."

"How come you're not totally freaked out by this?"

"Because I love you."

She turned and embraced him, wrapping her arms around his neck. She held on for dear life. "I don't think I'm ready for this."

Ash held her tightly. "I've got it for us both until you are."

"I love you, Ash."

"I know." He kissed her with one of those long, passion-filled kisses that always made her melt right into him. After the kiss, he gazed into her eyes. "I've got you. And I'm never letting you go." His voice was soft.

She nodded against him and clung more tightly to him. She couldn't understand how this had happened. She had been so careful, never missing a pill. "I can't believe I'm pregnant. I haven't had any symptoms, no nausea, nothing. Mel was throwing up and thought she had the flu on and off for weeks. And Claire said she was exhausted, that's how she knew. I don't feel that way."

"They say everyone is different."

"Yeah, my mom even said all three of her pregnancies were different. Oh shit, I'm going to have to tell her, tell my whole family."

Ash chuckled. "Yes, you are. I don't think your mom is going to be anything but happy." He was a bit worried about Kade. He'd promised Kade he wouldn't be reckless with his sister. Well, he planned to marry her, so he couldn't be considered too reckless, could he? He pulled the ring box from his jeans pocket and opened it. "Marry me. Right away. None of this waiting till the baby is born bullshit."

Kelsey's eyes took in the beautiful set of three rings in the box. They were forged from steel with incredible matching scrollwork around all three bands. The man's ring was thick and would look perfect on Ash's finger. The two smaller bands were narrow and dainty, but still had that gorgeous scrollwork around them. The solitaire diamond rising from one of the bands sparkled under the bathroom vanity light like it was under the special lights at a jewelry store.

"They're beautiful, Ash. You did an amazing job on these. And they're more meaningful because you made them."

"I measured your finger one night while you slept," he said with a smile.

"When did you do that?"

Ash grinned a guilty smile. "A month or so ago."

"You were planning to ask me to marry you?"

"Yes. I knew I wanted to spend the rest of my life with you shortly after you moved in and started working at the shop."

"How soon do you think we can pull a wedding together?" she asked with tears gathering in her eyes, a smile on her lips.

He shrugged. "I don't know, a couple of weeks. I guess that depends on what you want your wedding to be like."

She wrapped her arms around his neck. "As long as I'm marrying you, and my family and friends are there, I don't care. I'd love it to be in the backyard, and even into mid-October that should work."

"That's what I was thinking, too. We don't need to rent a place and spend a fortune."

"No, that sounds like a waste of money."

"And I want to put the money into the addition to the house. Now seems like a good time to do that. Remember those plans I showed you?"

"Yes." She kissed him. "And that was the yes that I'll marry you."

Ash slid the engagement ring onto her finger. He moved a few piles of clothes to clear one side of the bed and then drew her over to it. The 'we made a baby' sex they shared was incredible. The love and anticipation they expressed through meaningful caresses and passionate kisses were declarations of their commitment to each other as well as a celebration of the new life they'd created.

It was later that afternoon that they drove out to her mom's house. Kelsey had texted her mom to be sure she was home. Kade was off work all day, so they were sure he'd be there, too. Kelsey proudly wore the ring. The sunlight streamed through the windshield casting sparkles from the diamond in all directions. She couldn't keep her eyes from it.

"You're quiet. Are you nervous to tell your mom?" Ash asked.

"No, not at all. I was until you told me when you started making the rings. And for the record, whenever you would have asked. I would have said yes."

Ash took hold of her hand and raised it to his lips. He pressed a kiss to the back of it just below the ring. His eyes momentarily took in the sight of it on her finger. He knew that she'd appreciate the ring he'd made, just because he made it. She supported him in all ways, and that was something he didn't have to wonder about.

"What about you? Are you nervous to tell my mom and Kade?"

Ash chuckled. "No. Call it old-fashioned, but I would have liked to have asked your mom and probably Kade before I asked you."

Kelsey laughed. "I shouldn't be surprised you would want to be chivalrous. But I don't think you need to try to score points with either of them."

"It's not about making points. I see it more as a show of respect for your mom. If your dad was alive, I'd ask them both. I find it outdated and sexist that only the father would be asked."

"Especially in my case, as my mom raised me practically alone."

"Are you feeling any better regarding your dad's note to you?" Ash asked. They hadn't talked about it anymore since the day she read it and had such a visceral response to it just over two weeks earlier.

Kelsey shrugged. She still didn't feel too good about the note's contents. "All I can say is I would have asked Kade to walk me down the aisle regardless of what he wanted."

"I plan to ask Kade to be my best man. He can walk you down the aisle and then take his spot beside me," Ash said. "Will you ask Claire to stand up for you?"

"I'd ask Mel before Claire. But Cathy Kay and I always promised we'd be each other's maids or matrons of honor. I would like to have Aiden and Emma be our ring bearer and flower girl, though." She laughed out loud, a short burst. "I can't believe we're sitting here planning our wedding like this as we drive to my mom's house."

"How and where are we supposed to do it?"

"I don't know," Kelsey said with a sigh.

"If you want it to be over a nice dinner or something, we can do that," Ash offered.

"That's just silly," Kelsey said. "We're talking about it now, so we should keep planning. It'll be nice to tell my mom the plan right away, as it will take place soon. I know she'll help plan it if we want her to."

"I'd like to also ask Eric to stand up for me."

Kelsey laughed out loud without saying anything.

"I thought you liked him. Why is that funny?"

Kelsey reined it in long enough to talk, but then continued to laugh hysterically. "I'm envisioning Claire being partnered with him. Walking up the aisle, her arm linked with his."

Ash joined her in laughter. "We so need to do that. I need to come up with a third groomsman."

"It will serve her right for the reaction she's going to have to our news," Kelsey said when they'd stopped laughing.

"I know she's not a fan of mine. That's too bad," Ash said.

"She's too closed-minded to have given you a chance. I think when she gets to know you, she'll know she was wrong. But I don't need her approval, so whatever. She can feel however she feels. I'm not going to go out of my way to try to convince her I love you and am happy with you. She can see that for herself if she ever cares to look."

"I'm really proud of you. It wasn't that long ago that you were worried about telling her you weren't going to grad school."

"Yeah, it's funny. I feel like a completely different person than I was then, and it's only been a few months."

Ash pulled into her mother's driveway, and something suddenly spiked in Kelsey's system. Adrenaline, anxiety, or excitement. She wasn't sure. Maybe a mixture of all three. There was an anticipation element swirling through her thoughts, too.

Ash parked and Kelsey had to laugh and feel comforted by the parking lot in front of the house. It looked like it had when Kade and Claire were teenagers, and both had a car. Plus, their house was the hangout house for their friends, so there were normally a few other cars belonging to their friends parked there. Today it looked no different. Besides her mom's car and Mel's car, which were seen in the garage through the open doors, Kade's pickup truck, Jake's, and Julia's cars were there, too. It was a full house. That was crazy at three-thirty in the afternoon on a Wednesday.

Ash kissed her before they entered the house to find her mom, Jake, and Julia in the kitchen, going over Animal House stuff. They would close on the warehouse the next day. Her mom's laptop sat open on the kitchen table. Kelsey kept her left hand behind her back as she greeted each of them with a hug. Ash shook Jake's hand and gave her mom a hug.

So now that they were standing in front of her mom, yes, Kelsey would admit she was nervous to share her news. "Mom, can you come into the living room for a second?"

"Sure," Elyse answered. She exchanged a gaze with Jake before she followed Kelsey and Ash to her living room.

"Elyse, it will come to no surprise to you that I love your daughter," Ash said. "Over a month ago I started to work on wedding bands for us." He paused and chuckled. "I measured her finger one night while she slept. I planned to ask you before I proposed to Kelsey, but today after talking with Kade I realized she hasn't had a period for several months."

"I took a test a few hours ago. I'm pregnant, Mom," Kelsey said with a smile, feeling very happy by sharing the news. She pulled her hand into view. "He proposed right after the two blue lines appeared."

Elyse was stunned. She took hold of Kelsey's hand and gazed at the beautiful hand-crafted ring on her left ring finger, knowing right away that Ash had made it. She engulfed Kelsey in a hug. "Oh, my goodness! I couldn't be more surprised or happy." When she released Kelsey, she embraced Ash. "That ring is beautiful. I recognize your style."

"It is," Kelsey said. She smiled at Ash. "I love it."

"Does Kade know yet?"

"No, you're the first we told," Kelsey answered.

Elyse went to the stairs. "Kade! Melanie! Come downstairs please!"

Jake came from the kitchen. "Is everything okay?"

"Yes, everything's good," Elyse answered. "We have good news to share."

Kade and Mel descended the stairs. Kade knew something was up. His mom and both Kelsey and Ash were all smiles. Ash met him at the foot of the stairs. Looking over Ash's expression, his smile, his overall demeanor, Kade guessed it. "Kelsey's pregnant, isn't she?"

"Yes, and I proposed," Ash answered with a big smile. "We've got a wedding to plan."

Kade embraced Ash and then he hugged Kelsey. "When will I be walking you down the aisle?"

"Soon. We're thinking in a couple of weeks."

"A couple of weeks?" Elyse repeated. "How will we pull it together that soon, and why the rush?"

Both Mel and Julia congratulated Kelsey. Over-hearing the conversation in the entry, Julia had joined them. They all took a seat around the kitchen table, and Kelsey and Ash laid out their rationale for the rushed wedding and the plans they had discussed so far.

"We'd rather put the money into the addition on the house than on some swanky reception. A good party and bonfire in the backyard are more our style," Ash said.

"And we only have a few weeks to a month that the weather will be warm enough for that," Kelsey added.

"That sounds like fun," Julia said. "I sure hope I'll be invited."

"Of course you will," Kelsey said. "You're one of my mom's best friends, and we've known each other and worked alongside each other at the shelter for so long."

"I think I should call Claire and tell her she needs to come over right now," Elyse said. "This is wonderful family time that she's missing out on. We need to purposely involve her, and she has some contacts who may help us pull it together so quickly."

Kelsey rolled her eyes. "You can try. I'm not opposed."

Elyse lifted her phone from the table. She hushed everyone before she dialed.

Claire answered on the third ring. "Hi, Mom."

"Hi, Claire. I need you to come over right now. Bring the kids."

"What? It's late afternoon. I was just starting to plan dinner."

"We'll order out. Kelsey is here and we have a family situation I need you here for. I rarely make demands like this, Claire. It's important you come out."

"Now you're worrying me. What's wrong?"

"Nothing serious, but we need to be together as a family this afternoon. Matthew, of course, is welcome, but not needed if he has his golf league tonight like usual. You'll be back home by the kids' bedtime."

"Won't you give me a clue?" Claire asked.

"Not till you get here. I'll see you in about an hour." Elyse disconnected the call and then gazed at everyone's stunned expressions.

"She's coming?" Kelsey asked.

"She didn't say no. We'll see if she calls back," Elyse said.

• • • •

AS CLAIRE DROVE WEST towards Franklin, all the potential issues that would necessitate her presence ran through her mind. Had Kelsey broken up with Ash and it was messy? Maybe she needed someplace safe to stay. Ash had no idea where she and Matthew lived, and it was a gated community. Had Mel lost the baby? Kade would be devastated. Yes, the family would need to be together if that was the case. Neither, though, were appropriate situations for her kids to be there for, and her mom was clear the kids needed to come. So, it could be something happy, like maybe a video from her father for the entire family was found. No one would want to wait to view it.

She honestly couldn't think of another reason. If Kade and Mel were having an impromptu wedding, surely her mom would have insisted Matthew come, too. Maybe Jake had proposed to her mom. Surely, she wouldn't marry him without talking to her children. Could that be it? Or was her mom planning to sell the house and move someplace with Jake? Had he received orders and was moving away? Oh, that would not be good!

She pulled into her mom's driveway, surprised by the number of vehicles she saw. Ash's pickup was there, so that ruled out her thinking regarding him. As she and the children walked into the house, they heard voices and laughter coming from the kitchen. They entered and were all greeted with hugs and smiles.

"What's going on? What is the big situation I had to drop everything and rush out for?"

Kelsey came in front of her. "Ash and I are having a baby, and we're getting married in just over two weeks!"

Claire was shocked. And they all were smiling. "Congratulations," she forced out.

"And I want you to be one of my bridesmaids, and we want Aiden to be our ring bearer and Emma my flower girl," Kelsey continued. She knelt down to their level. "Will you two be in my wedding?" she asked them and gave them hugs. "I can't get married unless you're there."

Both kids squealed with excitement.

"We're pretty much planning the whole thing today," Elyse said. "We knew you wouldn't want to miss being in on the planning, and we could use your help, too."

Kelsey stood up with Emma on her hip. "Yes. We need to go shopping for my dress this weekend. We'll go whichever day you don't have any plans. It'll be you and me, and Mom and Mel. We'll make a day of it! I need to call Cathy Kay still. She's working overnights so I'm not sure of her availability either day."

"You're never going to get a dress in two weeks," Claire said. "And bridesmaids dresses." Her gaze went to Mel, who was at the stage that she just looked fat, not pregnant. Of course, the clothes she wore, yoga pants and an oversized long-sleeved t-shirt didn't do much for her figure, which was boxy to begin with. No surprise, Mel often wore clothes Claire wouldn't be caught dead in.

"All the stores have the floor model dresses they sell outright on clearance. I'm a common size. I shouldn't have too hard a time finding something that will need minimal alterations. And I'm not too picky, but I do want a nice gown from a bridal shop even if we're having a backyard wedding. As far as bridesmaids, you can all get together and decide on a color dress you already own. Nothing fancy. And it could be you all wear different shades of the same color. I'm great with that, too."

Claire mentally groaned. How was it her little sister didn't want better for her wedding day? Had she not dreamed of this day her entire life? "You're the bride, you certainly can dictate a color," Claire said cheerily.

It was as though Claire could read her mind. "Well, if blue works for you all, that would be my preference. But I really don't have this grand vision. Even the decorations for the day. The only thing I can say I want is a lot of lights strung all over after it gets dark. We'll do a bonfire, which will be fun."

"I'd love to help with the decorations," Julia volunteered.

"We can plan them together," Elyse said.

"Thank you both," Kelsey said. "I'll leave that to you two."

"We'll need a caterer. Claire, you have more experience with hiring a caterer in Norfolk. I hope you'll have some suggestions and contacts," Elyse said.

"We're not picky on the food," Ash said. "We'd even be fine with a couple of food trucks."

"Food trucks?" Claire repeated, horrified. Her little sister's wedding was not going to be serviced by food trucks!

Ash laughed, prompting everyone else to as well. "I'm just pulling your leg. Or am I?"

"Seriously, it doesn't have to be fancy," Kelsey said. Her gaze flashed to Ash. "But not food trucks." Then it shifted to Claire. "Unless there's no other choice."

"Okay, so you're having the wedding in his backyard in two and a half weeks, and you expect us to find you a dress this Saturday and find a caterer who isn't booked yet. Anything else?" How could she be the only one in the room who saw how ludicrous this was? "Bartender? DJ? Chairs and a tent to rent?"

"Yes! Thank God you're here. We need chairs and a tent," Kelsey said. "I didn't even think of that."

"I can help with that," Kade piped up. "I know a guy from the department. His brother owns that rental place out on I-64."

"Okay, chairs and tent are assigned to Kade," Jake said. He was making a list on a pad of paper. "Julia and Elyse are on decorations. Claire, can I assign the food to you?"

Claire's gaze swept around everyone's faces. "Yes, sure. I'll even pay for it, my wedding gift to you two."

"That's awesome!" Kelsey surrounded her with her arms. "Thank you!"

Ash joined, making it a group hug. "Claire, that is so nice of you."

"You're welcome." Claire wouldn't tell them it was to ensure that they had decent food at their reception. And she was sure they wouldn't be willing to pay for something nice to be served. Could a party in someone's backyard be called a reception? And then a thought came to her. Matthew was not going to be happy about her volunteering to pay for the food. Oh, well.

"Really though, Claire, nothing fancy. And please don't spend a fortune on it," Kelsey said, breaking the embrace.

"I do need to know how many people you're expecting," Claire stated.

"We haven't talked about who all we'll invite yet," Kelsey said. Her gaze went to Ash. "I'd think just family and close friends, the guys from the shop and their girlfriends."

"Yeah, probably the same people who were at our Memorial Day party and who we hung out with on the Fourth of July. With such short notice, probably only fifty-ish," Ash said.

"I've never even asked, Ash. Do you have family in the area or some who will be able to travel to be here for it?" Elyse asked.

"I have a brother in Florida. I haven't called him yet, but I know he'll be able to make it. He's not working. I'll have to send him the plane ticket, though. I have two cousins in the area I'm close with. I'll invite them. That's pretty much it. My mom passed away five years ago, and I haven't spoken to my dad since."

"I'm so sorry to hear that," Elyse said.

Ash shrugged. "I've always figured the people you choose to surround yourself with become your family."

"Well, that was a great group of people at your Memorial Day party, so it should be a fun wedding reception with them there," Elyse said.

"You went to their Memorial Day party?" Claire asked, the surprise evident in her voice.

"Yes, I wasn't going to, but your sister talked me into it. It was a lot of fun."

"And Mom somehow became this crazy Bags champion, beat me three games in a row," Kade added with a laugh for Claire's benefit.

Elyse ordered Chinese and they all took seats at the kitchen table. Elyse showed her grandchildren the toys in the sunroom, and they played while the adults planned the wedding. Kelsey and Ash wanted the reception to resemble more of a backyard party, informal and fun. Kelsey even planned to change into jeans after the ceremony.

• • • •

HOURS LATER WHEN CLAIRE left, the wedding was planned. An account on a wedding website was set up and e-invitations were sent. A client of Ash's was an ordained minister and she committed to performing the ceremony. Everyone was excited. Claire had wanted to have a conversation alone with Kelsey, but the opportunity never presented itself. Maybe it would when they went dress-shopping. She'd promised to let Kelsey know the following day which day worked best for her. She didn't want to admit it, but she'd have to see which day Lizette would work for most of the day when it was her day off. Matthew absolutely would not agree to be home alone with the kids for five or more hours.

Claire arrived home and put the kids to bed. They had a great time at Grandma's house. She would admit that it warmed her heart how attentive to the kids her mom, Kade and Kelsey were, which she had come to expect, but Ash and Mel were, too. She'd never noticed Mel paying any attention to her kids before tonight.

Claire enjoyed a glass of wine and stayed up, waiting for Matthew to get home. She couldn't wait to tell him about everything that happened that day, all of which were swirling through her thoughts like a bad dream. What had happened to her little sister? First, throwing her life and education away by deciding against grad school and choosing to be a tattoo artist, of all things. And her crazy relationship with Ash, a man clearly too old for her, which was reckless, dating your boss. And now this, an unplanned pregnancy and rushed wedding. Their father's death must have hit Kelsey way worse than Claire thought.

Only then did Claire remember that her mom had said the note to Kelsey from her dad made her angry. Claire had meant to reach out to her and Kade about their notes, but she just hadn't had the chance. She needed to do that in the next few days. Maybe she could take Kelsey out for lunch before the dress-shopping day, just the two of them to celebrate and then she could talk to her about everything.

Matthew arrived home around eleven, as usual. Claire had been sitting in the living room, surfing the internet on her phone, when she saw his headlights through the front window. She met him in the kitchen. "How was your night?" she asked him with a smile. She was trying to support him and what he'd described as his needed night out that he enjoyed. She'd given a lot of thought to the recent fights they'd had and was trying everything she could think of to save her marriage.

"It was good. What are you still doing up?" he asked as he reached into the refrigerator and pulled out a bottle of beer.

Claire still had wine in her glass, but she added another inch. She told him about her day from the point of receiving the phone call from her mom all the way through until she left her house after all the plans were made. "It was like I had walked into a weird cult, full-group insanity. They all lost their damned minds, planning a wedding to take place in just over two weeks. And they were all overjoyed my little sister is pregnant and going to marry this guy who is way too old for her and all wrong for her. I don't even recognize my own family any longer."

"And they expect you to stand up for her and for us all to be there?" Matthew asked.

"Aiden is going to be the ring bearer and Emma will be her flower girl."

"We can get through one night. I know neither of us is thrilled that we're going to call Mel our sister-in-law, either. Kade could have done better than her. I don't think she's ever said more than two words to me."

"She was actually more tolerable tonight," Claire said. "And they haven't set a date. It'll be after the baby is born, so we may luck out and it might not happen. Oh, and get this, they're not going to find out the gender of their baby. Mel wants to be surprised when it's born! How in the hell are we supposed to get them an appropriate gift? I was going to get them those great sleepers we loved with the magnetic closures in all sizes for the first year," she said. "They don't have many gender-neutral ones, and the ones specifically for boys or girls are so cute."

"So, get them the first two sizes for the gift and add the others later after the baby is born," Matthew suggested.

"Oh, and I have to tell you what I did. I agreed to book the caterer for the wedding, and I said we'd pay for it as our wedding gift to them."

"Why would you do that?" Matthew asked.

"Ash said even a couple food trucks would be okay. Can you even imagine what they'd pick? I felt the need to step in and take it on, so they have decent food at their wedding, and I was sure they'd cheap out and not pay to get something nice. They're doing it in his backyard, so I assume they can't afford too much."

"You're probably right," Matthew agreed. "Okay, we help with the food for the wedding."

Claire wrapped her arms around him. "Thank you."

Chapter 34 – A Tale of Two Lunches

"I'm so glad we could do this today," Claire said, opening her menu. She beamed a smile at Kelsey, who sat across from her.

The server approached the table. Kelsey glanced around the opulent restaurant with its crystal chandeliers and rich tapestry-upholstered chairs. An expensive restaurant in downtown Norfolk was not where she would have picked for this celebratory lunch. But it was close to Claire's office and her sister had made the reservations and invited her.

"Two glasses of champagne, please," Claire ordered.

"I didn't think I was supposed to drink," Kelsey said.

"One glass of champagne is not going to hurt anything. And we have to celebrate. My little sister is getting married and having a baby," Claire said, oozing sweetness with a smile.

"Thank you, Claire," Kelsey said, somewhat stunned at Claire's exuberance. She was singing a different tune today than she had been on Wednesday.

"So, you had your first prenatal appointment this morning?" Claire asked.

"Yes, Ash and I went. They confirmed I'm pregnant and set a schedule for my appointments."

"Ash went, that's sweet," Claire remarked. "Matthew came for the first few appointments when I was pregnant with Aiden, too."

Kelsey just forced a smile. She wasn't surprised. She wouldn't say anything, but she knew Ash would be there for all of the appointments. He had already promised, plus he was so excited about the baby. He'd been so incredible that morning. He brought her a protein shake he blended up for them while she was still in bed because he had done a lot of reading on a healthy diet for a pregnant woman. He asked the doctor a whole litany of questions regarding diet and exercise. On the drive home, he promised to quit smoking because it would be healthier for her and the baby. Even though she didn't smoke, she hadn't ever complained about it.

"So, when is your due date?" Claire asked.

"March thirtieth."

Claire reached across the table and took Kelsey's hand. "I have to admit, when you told me Wednesday, I was so surprised that I may not have expressed my excitement. I mean, you're a smart girl. You know how to prevent an unwanted pregnancy."

"I can't believe you just said that," Kelsey exclaimed, cutting her off. "No birth control is one hundred percent effective."

"And if you'd let me finish, I was going to say, so as you had said about Kade and Mel's oops, this too had to be God intervening to bring us another new life into the family. We so need more good things to celebrate and focus on."

"Oh," Kelsey said.

"Anyway, I know this is so much to process. How are you?"

Kelsey eyed her suspiciously. "I'm good. I'm happy, Claire."

"Mom said you weren't so happy when you read Dad's note. I wasn't when I read mine, either."

"You weren't?" Kelsey asked, quite surprised.

"No. I'd been begging Dad for the last few years to let me go on-site with him to investigate the collapses in the field. He made it out to be that the company could only send one engineer and I was needed in the office to do the part of the work where we created simulations and graphics to pinpoint the part of the structure that failed. He admitted in his note he didn't want me on-site because it was dangerous. He said he intervened with Michael to keep me in the office. And Michael won't let me go even now, so I can only deduce that he and Dad had some agreement he's sticking to."

"I'm sorry, Claire. But you know, Dad was right about the danger. I mean, he did die on-site during an investigation. In the note to Mom, he also told her that he thought flying all over, and sometimes in aircraft that he doubted had been maintained well and driving to the locations was dangerous, too. He said something about the roads and bridges, as well as the drivers themselves having no business driving. I understand you feel betrayed by him, but he was protecting you."

"I guess he was. It still hurts, though, and makes me so angry. What about you? What did he say in your note that bothered you?" Claire asked, dying to know.

"Well, evidently, Dad thought I'm too much like Mom. I'm too loyal and trusting. He warned me, and yes, he said his warning to me was to not give up my dreams for anyone, not even the man I love. Is that what he thought Mom did?

What a hypocrite. If she gave anything up, it was for him and for us."

"Mom told me that after she held us as babies, her dreams and goals changed to being the best mother she could be for us and to give us the best lives," Claire said.

"Didn't Dad understand that she would have divorced him if she had been any other way? And it's not like he was going to be there to let Mom be anything other than a single parent."

"I have to ask, and please don't get mad at me. Did you decide to skip grad school after you met Ash?" Claire asked.

"No. I went with Kade for him to get the tattoo that I drew to honor Dad. I had already decided I wasn't going to grad school. I told Kade that day, in front of Ash. I honestly had no idea what I was going to do, but I wasn't going to do that or any other formal education for a while. Ash suggested I do something with my art, that it was good. I was really surprised when Ash called me a few days later to see how my tattoo was healing and offered me the job."

"What tattoo?" Claire asked.

"Oh, I got it that day. Kade and I were going to try to talk you into getting it too, to honor Dad and match us."

"How come I didn't know?"

Kelsey shrugged. "I thought I told you. I've gotten two more in the past few months." She smiled. "It's kind of addictive."

Claire's lips curled in disgust. "Yeah, not a fan of tattoos."

Kelsey laughed. "I know. It's okay. You don't have to be."

The server brought their champagne. Claire raised her glass. "To you, Kels. I love you and I'm happy that you're happy."

Kelsey tapped glasses and drank. "Thanks, Claire. I'm happy you and the kids will be in our wedding."

"Of course," Claire said. "But I have to ask, Kels, why the rush?"

"We want to have it in the backyard, and we don't have much time until it will be too cold. And, unlike Kade and Mel, I don't want to wait until after the baby is born."

"Is having it in the backyard to save money? I know a rented hall costs so much," Claire said. "But haven't you always dreamt of your special day differently?"

Kelsey wanted to say something rude as an answer. Claire was insinuating something she didn't like. She took a drink of her champagne to give herself a moment to craft the perfect response. "I actually always dreamt of a wedding at the beach, my bare toes in the sand. It's getting too cool for it here. We could do a destination wedding to Florida, a resort in Mexico, or some Caribbean Island, but that's so inconvenient for everyone. I'm sure neither you nor Matthew would want to take off work to go, and I doubt Kade would be able to. Plus, many of our friends wouldn't be able to go. Ash and I have this amazing group of friends who are as casual about things as we are. Our Memorial Day party at the house, and the beach party we had on the Fourth of July were a blast. And that's the kind of atmosphere I want for my wedding. I want us to say 'I do' and then I want a fun party! And we don't need to pay for a room someplace to do that. Besides, both Ash and I would rather put the money into the addition on the house right away."

"Addition?" Claire asked.

"Oh, that's right. You've never been to the house. It's currently a small Cape Cod, just over a thousand square feet including the attic that Ash transformed into the master bedroom. Several years ago, Ash had plans drawn up for an addition that would double the size of the kitchen and add a large family room off the back on the first floor. It would add two large bedrooms and two bathrooms upstairs and have entry into the current upstairs bedroom. It would also link to the garage, creating an attached garage. It will bring the total size of the house to more than double what it is now. But then the strip mall the shop is in was for sale, and Ash bought it instead."

"I see," Claire said thoughtfully. "Is it a configuration you like? It's his house and his addition, after all, but you'll be living there so I hope you like it."

Kelsey groaned inwardly. "He's been amazing about that. It's not just his house. He calls it ours and my name will be on the deed and the mortgage. And he has asked my opinion on the plans, would gladly have the architect redraw them if I had different ideas, but I love it just as it is. He did a great job with it. Anyway, the builder is pulling new permits, and if all goes well they'll break ground on it within a week after the wedding."

"That soon?"

"Yes. They have time to pour the foundation and get it under roof before the winter weather hits. It's really so exciting. I can't wait for the bigger kitchen and the family room is going to have a fireplace and some big windows to take in the beautiful view at the back of the property. You'll see when you're there for the wedding. The whole yard is surrounded by trees. It's very private and I love it."

"Well, that all sounds just wonderful," Claire said. "I can't believe my little sister is excited about a kitchen." She laughed. "I really am glad you're happy. I've already begun to reach out to caterers. I'll make sure I run the menu by you before I finalize anything. And I'm sure Mom and Julia will come up with some beautiful decorations to make your wedding pictures look like you were someplace amazing. What are you doing about a photographer?"

"One of Ash's clients is a professional photographer. She said she'll take pictures as her wedding gift to us. She'll have our pictures on a website we can all view and choose from, and we can all download the digital pictures for free and get them printed up someplace at our cost if we want to." She wouldn't address Claire's comment about the pictures looking like they were someplace amazing. She happened to think the backyard, surrounded with trees would make beautiful pictures.

"Wow, that's very generous of her."

"Well, she'd be at the wedding anyway. We told her we don't need tons of formal pictures, just a few and some candid pics throughout the night. She'll definitely have time to be a guest as well and have fun."

"You seem to have everything covered. I still can't believe you're going to pull this together in two weeks. I hope we find you a dress tomorrow!"

"Did you know Mom and Grandma planned her wedding this fast, too?"

Claire had known but had forgotten. "That's right."

"By the way, Mom and Jake closed on the warehouse yesterday. Animal House Shelter now has a new home. They figure it will only take about a month to do the buildout and have it ready to be occupied by the dogs," Kelsey said, changing the subject.

"I still can't believe Jake turned out to be a lieutenant commander and bought her that warehouse!"

"I know, crazy, isn't it?" Kelsey agreed.

"Dad also told me in my note to accept a man that Mom may have a relationship with, that it wouldn't be betraying him."

"He told Kade that, too," Kelsey said. "He didn't tell me that, though. I guess he figured I would, or he was too busy issuing me warnings to get to it."

"Was Kade mad about anything in his note?" Claire asked.

"No. The tone of his note was very different from mine. It was all 'Kade, I'm so proud of you and you're going to be a great dad as long as you're not like I was.'" Kelsey shook her head. "He told me he didn't have the capacity to be the dad I wanted. What a huge copout! The only thing I can say, Claire, is I hope you don't parent like he did while doing his job. I hope you'll be there for your kids more than he was there for us. I know Kade will be a very different father, as will Ash."

Claire didn't know what to say. She didn't want to argue the point. She and her siblings had silently agreed to disagree on their father years before. And she knew she had a much different relationship with him than either Kade or Kelsey did.

Thankfully, the server returned and they placed their orders. Claire changed the topic immediately after and the remainder of the meal was pleasant.

• • • •

A ROUND OF CHAMPAGNE for the group at the table was ordered by Claire. It was eleven-thirty. They were starting their day with lunch out. Kelsey would have liked to visit one of the bridal shops earlier, but Cathy Kay couldn't join them until eleven-thirty due to her overnight work schedule. And, given that Cathy Kay was her maid of honor, Kelsey didn't want to start without her.

Kelsey had a twelve-thirty appointment for them at the bridal shop around the corner. The shop knew she needed a floor model dress and what her size was. They were to have all available dresses in the changing room when they got there. She had told them the wedding was in two weeks. She was promised there would be at least five gowns to choose from. They had a second appointment at another bridal shop at two o'clock. Kelsey hoped she found a nice dress at the first shop, and she'd be able to cancel the second appointment.

The five champagne flutes arrived. Claire stood. "A toast to Kelsey."

They clinked glasses and drank.

Elyse lifted her glass next. "Kelsey, I'm sure we will find a beautiful dress today that you will look stunning in for your wedding day. I love that you are flexible, and it's about you marrying Ash, a man I know you will have a lifetime of happiness with, and not about the perfect dress."

They again tapped glasses and drank.

Mel lifted her glass next. "Kelsey, I may not have married your brother yet, but you have always made me feel like I was already your sister-in-law. I'm thrilled to be standing up for you as you marry Ash and add him to our family."

Cathy Kay raised her glass. "I guess I'm next. Kelsey, you have been my best friend for four years, since our first day rooming together at college. You're the sister I never had. I have never seen you happier than you are right now. Congrats on marrying your Mister Right and on your baby, who will be lucky to have you as its mom."

Kelsey was warmed by this outpouring of love from the four women who meant the most to her. Her eyes settled on her mom. "I wish Grandma could have been here for this. The two of you planned your wedding this quickly. I would have loved her to help with mine."

"Me, too, sweetie," Elyse said.

Elyse's mom had died the year before. Kelsey had always been close to her even after she and her grandfather moved to Arizona when he'd retired. Her grandfather was the first person in the family that she was close to who passed away. They had never seen her grandparents on her father's side much. They were both college professors and after their children were grown and gone, they became world travelers who didn't let anything such as family or holidays interfere with their pursuit of knowledge. They died in a crash in a God-forsaken third-world country, on their way to dig up bones at a long-forgotten burial site, for a long-dead civilization.

They made it to the dress shop at the appointed hour. As promised, there were eight dresses hung in one of the salons. It turned out Kelsey was a little pickier than she thought she'd be. The first dress she looked at was a mermaid style with a tight skirt along the hips and legs. She told the woman assigned to them to put that one away.

"I don't like that style at all," Kelsey said. The next had yards and yards of lace fabric cascading from the dress. "This one can go, too." She glanced at the price tag. "Yuck, especially at that price." She arranged the six that were left in order by price, lowest to highest.

"Kels, you shouldn't even be looking at the price tags yet," Claire said. "This is about finding your special dress."

"I just want to be mindful of the price. I'm only going to wear it for all of a few hours."

"Claire's right," Elyse said. "See if you like any of them first before looking at the price."

They had fun, watching Kelsey try the dresses on. Or rather, they had fun laughing at her reactions to them. The fifth dress she put on, though, everyone in the room gasped, including the store employee helping them. It fit perfectly, everywhere including length. It was a plain dress compared to several of the others, with just the bodice beaded and hugging her curves. The tapered sleeves ended just past her elbows, coming to a subtle point. The skirt flowed to the floor, sleek and elegant. The back echoed the square neckline in the front. It looked stunning on her.

"Oh my goodness," Elyse breathed out. "Kelsey, you look gorgeous."

They all agreed this was the dress.

"Yes," Kelsey said. "It didn't look like much on the hanger, but oh my God!"

"And it's fifty percent off," the store employee said, showing Kelsey the price tag.

It was a designer dress, and even with the fifty percent off, it still was more than Kelsey was thinking she'd want to pay. Elyse could see the indecision in her face as she stared at the price tag. Elyse stepped up beside her and took a look at the tag. "We'll take it," she said to the clerk, handing her credit card over.

"Mom?" Kelsey asked.

"My gift to you, sweetie."

They left the store with the dress in a carrying bag. Kelsey insisted she didn't want a veil. And she had a pair of white sandals that would work fine. She cancelled the second appointment, and the group instead went to a coffee shop known for their delicious pastries. Plans were made for the day of the wedding. Claire invited Kelsey to stay at her house the night before and for them to all get ready at her house.

"I'll have to talk with Ash," Kelsey insisted. "There'll be a lot to do at the house the morning before the wedding. I can't say I believe in any of those superstitions of the bride and groom not seeing each other the day of the wedding before the ceremony. We can just as well all get ready at my place."

October

Chapter 35 – Before the 'I Dos'

The morning of the wedding, Elyse, Jake, Julia, Kade, and Mel helped Kelsey and Ash, his brother, and several of their friends set everything up and decorate the backyard for the wedding. Basically, everyone but Claire and Matthew helped. It was a time filled with fun and laughter, an indication of the event yet to come. They had a beautiful day for it. The high was forecasted to be seventy-two degrees, with sunny skies, and little wind.

Not only had Kelsey declined Claire's offer to have everyone get ready at her house, but she also didn't stay the night there either. She couldn't very well be the only one besides Claire not helping to set up for the wedding. Even Cathy Kay, who had worked the night before was there helping. She'd go home after set-up, get a nap, and would arrive back at Kelsey and Ash's house in time to get ready with the others, which they'd do in the master bedroom. Ash and the guys would dress casually in jeans and white dress shirts. The groomsmen would wear gray vests they'd all bought at a men's clothing store. Ash's vest was black. They'd gather in the garage before the wedding while the women got ready in the house.

Kelsey grinned, her face lighting up, as she surveyed the backyard scene when the set-up was completed. "This is perfect, just what I envisioned!" She hugged her mom and

Julia. "Thank you so much for taking care of this and making it such a beautiful place for our wedding."

The back yard had been transformed. Her mom and Julia had reused many of the decorations from the gala and had added thousands of lights; they were strung all over the yard, framing the house, garage, and the shed where Ash's forge was. Chairs were lined up in rows facing an elaborately decorated arch. White fabric was draped over it, with greenery and flowers adorning it as well. Lights were also strung on it that would be lit when it got dark. Rows of tables were on and near the patio, with an empty table for the chafing dishes the caterer would bring, set up, and serve from. Claire arranged a sit-down dinner, not a buffet, which would have been fine with Kelsey.

Ash embraced her and pressed a kiss to her lips. When the embrace ended, he glanced around at those who helped. "Thank you all again for helping set this up."

"And we'll take it all back down again tomorrow afternoon, when you come back from, where did you say you were spending the night tonight?" Ash's brother, Wren, asked.

"I didn't and I'm not," Ash said. Wren had landed the previous day, flying on the ticket that Ash had provided. He and Kelsey had picked Wren up at the airport. He and Kelsey had spoken on video calls, so he wasn't a complete stranger to her.

"I mean, I'm responsible for your house tonight. I should be able to reach you," Wren said with a coy smile.

"There's this thing called a phone," Ash said.

Wren shrugged and laughed. "You can't blame me for trying."

"So, tell me again about this tradition your family has of crashing a couple's wedding night?" Kelsey prompted.

Both Ash and Wren laughed. "It goes back a few generations and often involves a prank of stealing the bride," Ash said. "It's a tradition that has come to an end."

Wren chuckled. "You didn't think that way when you and Grandpa crashed my wedding night. Though if I knew then how that marriage would end, I would have told you to take her and keep her."

"Yeah, she turned out to be a piece of work," Ash agreed with a snicker.

"Okay, we're done with the yard. Can everyone be back about an hour before the wedding?" Kelsey asked. "And by the way, no one is stealing this bride."

Laughter erupted from those who stood in the yard. Everyone dispersed shortly thereafter. Kade and Mel would be staying to take showers and get ready there. Elyse and Jake left with plans to get ready at his quarters on base, a small one-room efficiency officer's guest apartment he occupied. It would be the first time that Elyse was there. Julia drove back to Franklin. She had a plus one she was bringing with her for the wedding, but had not said who it would be.

As Jake drove towards the base, he noted that Elyse seemed uncharacteristically quiet, almost sullen. "What's up, Elyse?"

"Huh?"

"You're quiet."

"I'm just thinking."

"I thought you liked Ash for Kelsey. Are you second-guessing this wedding?"

"No, it's not that. This is one of those moments I'm thinking about Tim not being here. He would have helped with the yard, not that he would have enjoyed it like we did. Kelsey is getting married without her father there. She has said it doesn't bother her, but I know it has to be on her mind. It just makes me sad is all."

Jake reached across the seat and gently squeezed her leg. "So, is this one of those times you need to be alone? Or do you need a hug?"

"Definitely the hug," she said, putting her hand atop his. "I'm glad you're here."

"Me, too. I had a good time this morning. Your daughter is a special young lady."

"I'm going to assume you mean Kelsey and not Claire," Elyse said with a smile.

Jake chuckled. "Yes. Claire is unique. But I am giving her the benefit of the doubt. Her apology at the gala goes a long way with me."

"Claire has always been independent, headstrong, and at times, difficult. Trust me when I tell you her wedding was quite different from what Kelsey's wedding today will be like."

"Let me guess. It was an over-the-top affair."

"Oh yes, she arrived at the church by a horse-drawn carriage decorated with flowers and bows."

"The horse or the carriage?"

"Both."

Jake laughed. "Why am I not surprised."

"But she's also a high achiever, always has been. She's firm in her mind what she wants and how she's going to get it. I always told myself that as long as she was channeled in the correct direction, that it was a great quality that would serve her well in life."

"Are you having second thoughts about that belief?"

Elyse sighed. "I know there's something very wrong with Matthew's and her marriage. My youngest two children are happy. I can't say that about her. She was unarguably the closest with Tim, so I fear what her mood will be today. If I'm sad he isn't here for Kelsey, she's going to be downright surly because of it."

"So, you fear how she'll act today?"

"Yes, I don't want her to ruin her sister's day. I'm going to have to have a private conversation with her. I knew she wouldn't show up to help decorate. I'm thinking of calling her to see how she's feeling, under the guise that I am sad, too, and we need to put on brave faces for Kelsey, but that seems manipulative."

"Your motive for doing it may be manipulative, but it's not completely dishonest."

"I know. I'm also angry I even have to think about this today. Today isn't about Claire. It's about Kelsey. But here I am, having to consider Claire."

"You're a good mom, Elyse. Thinking about all aspects of making this Kelsey's special day with no drama, *is* about Kelsey. I think you should make that call to Claire and try to head it off."

"Thanks. I'll do that when you're in the shower."

THAT FIRST YEAR

. . . .

AS CLAIRE CORRALLED Aiden to slip his legs into his blue jeans, she grunted. "Come on, Aiden. Will you please cooperate?" He was a wild man this afternoon. And the thought of him wearing jeans to be in his aunt's wedding didn't sit right with her. It was little surprise, though, that Ash would wear jeans for his own wedding, which was just ludicrous. He owned a suit. She'd seen him in it at the gala. She helped Aiden put on a white t-shirt. She'd wait to dress him in the white dress shirt and vest until right before the ceremony. Why risk a stain? Emma was in her light blue dress, sitting in her room playing with her dolls. Claire had a medium blue dress hanging in her room ready to be put on right before they would leave to drive to Kelsey's house. It was probably fancier than Kelsey intended, most certainly fancier than anything Mel owned. She wasn't sure about Cathy Kay.

Against her better judgement, Claire also had a bag packed with warmer clothes for them all, with jeans and hoodies. She and Matthew had discussed it and immediately after dinner they would make an excuse and depart early. She descended the stairs to go to her room and finish her makeup. She was surprised when her phone rang, an incoming call from her mom.

"Hi, Mom," she greeted.

"Hi, sweetie. I'm just calling to tell you we finished the set-up for the wedding and the backyard looks amazing. Kelsey is very happy with it."

Claire rolled her eyes. "That's good."

"I'm also calling to check on you. I know I'm sad your dad isn't here today. How are *you* feeling?"

Claire's eyes welled up with tears. "Oh, Mom, thank you for thinking of me. I've been thinking of my own wedding day all morning. I'm sad Dad isn't here for Kelsey." She was touched that her mom understood how she'd feel.

"This is just another of the times we're going to feel this way. We loved your dad, and we miss him. It's okay to feel this way. We do need to make sure we put on brave faces for Kelsey, though. I spoke with her, and she misses him, but she knows he wouldn't want the fact that he's not here to overshadow her day. She deserves smiles and tears of joy on her special day. We all need it."

"You're so right. I know I'm going to try my best to be nothing but supportive towards her today. I've had my cry this morning, and upon reflecting after I get home later tonight, I will probably cry again, but while we're there, I agree, we have to try not to let it overshadow her day," Claire said. "You said you're sad. How are you, Mom?"

"Thank you for asking, Claire. Thanks to that grief support group at the church, I understand there are going to be days like this. I know how to approach them and how to communicate with Jake about how I feel, too. He understands that it's going to be both a happy day for me and a rough day."

"Oh, yes, it will be, for all of us. I'm going to have to have that conversation with Matthew, too."

"Okay, sweetie. I have to get going and take a shower so I'm ready on time. Kelsey would like us all at her house by three o'clock if you're getting ready there, four if you come dressed for the ceremony."

"We'll come dressed and ready. I'll see you at four."

"Okay. Love you, Claire."

"Love you, too, Mom." She was in her bedroom now, where Matthew sat, reclined on the bed reading something on his phone. "That was my mom. She was calling to see how I was doing, knowing I'd be thinking about my dad today."

"Of course you are. Why would today be different from any other?" His eyes flickered up at her from his phone for a moment and then returned to the screen.

"Especially today. And I'm sure Kelsey is too." Deciding to ignore his inflammatory remark, she climbed onto the bed and sat close beside him, wrapping her arm around his middle. "Whenever we go to a wedding, I can't help but think about our day." Her gaze swept over the screen of his phone. "You're checking your work email?"

He clicked to turn his screen off. "I won't be on it all day."

"I was just surprised. I thought you took today off completely."

Matthew shrugged but didn't answer. "What time do we have to be there?"

"Four. The wedding starts at five. Kelsey said it should only last about fifteen or twenty minutes."

"Thank God you arranged some decent food or the whole thing would have been a joke. Your dad has to be rolling over in his urn."

"My dad was Catholic and would not have approved that they're getting married outside of the Catholic Church, that's for sure."

"And I'm pretty sure he wouldn't approve of this tattoo artist either," Matthew said. "He put me through the wringer. I don't think he thought anyone was good enough for his little girl."

"Dad approved of you and liked you. But you're right, he wouldn't have been happy about Ash. I think my mom is focused too much on her new man to have a clear head about everything going on in this family. Two unplanned pregnancies and this hurried wedding," Claire said, shaking her head. "And she's celebrating it all. The only thing I can say is that I know she's thrilled she'll have two more grandbabies."

"Yeah, well, if this relationship with her lieutenant commander continues, we'll see if it's really that important to her," Matthew said. He glanced at his watch. "I guess I'd better get into the shower." He got up and went to the bathroom, closing the door to seal himself within.

Claire patted herself on the back for not overacting to him reading work emails. They'd had a nice conversation and no words were exchanged. She was trying to be cautious to start no arguments.

• • • •

ELYSE HAD ONLY SHOWERED at Jake's. Her dress was at Kelsey's house, a beautiful silver-gray knee-length number she'd bought years earlier for some event she ended up not going to and she'd never worn the dress. It still had the tags on it. One of Kelsey's friends was a hairstylist. She was at Kelsey's house to do anyone's hair who wanted it done. Elyse definitely wanted someone to do her hair. She usually wore it quite plain, ponytails, straight and long, or long with some product scrunched in it to give it a wave. But she really didn't style it often.

Elyse and Jake arrived back at Ash and Kelsey's house at three o'clock. The guys were in the garage, visible through the open door. Music played, and as Elyse and Jake approached, they saw the four men were dressed for the wedding. They sat on chairs, drinking beer.

"The girls are up in the master bedroom. Go on up, Elyse," Ash said. He handed a beer to Jake.

"Thanks," both Elyse and Jake said in unison. Jake stepped further within the garage and joined them as Elyse headed into the house.

Upon climbing the stairs into the master bedroom, Elyse recognized Kelsey's friend Jeanie. They'd known each other since the sixth grade. Kelsey and Melanie were there, of course, as was a woman behind the camera that Elyse had met at their Memorial Day party, but Elyse was surprised to see Cathy Kay. "Hi, Jeanie," she greeted with a smile.

"Hi, Missus L," Jeanie answered. She was arranging Kelsey's hair in a half-up.

"Cathy Kay, I thought you weren't coming back until right before the ceremony," Elyse said.

"I went home and took a shower, meant to catch a short nap, but I couldn't sleep. I was just too excited for Kelsey!"

Elyse nodded. "Today should be a lot of fun. Do you have your vows written out someplace, Kels?"

"I have them memorized," she answered.

"Kels, you may be surprised you have a failing memory when you get up there, which is natural when a person is nervous. You may want to have them written out someplace, just in case."

"Nah, I'm good, Mom," Kelsey assured her.

Elyse smiled and nodded. She doubted that.

Music played softly in the room. There was a mimosa bar set up on the counter in the bathroom. Jeanie finished Kelsey's hair, curling the section that hung down into one large curl off the side, that set off the front and back neckline on her dress. And then Jeanie did Elyse's in a simple updo that looked sleek and sophisticated. The photographer snapped random pictures the whole time. Mel was next to take the seat for her hair to be done. She opted for a braid from one temple, over the side of her head to the back with the rest of the hair curled. After her makeup was applied, Elyse couldn't believe how beautiful she looked. And then Cathy Kay took the chair and Jeanie flat ironed her hair, giving her a mature, polished appearance.

The girls talked and laughed throughout. It reminded Elyse so much of all the times Kelsey and her friends hung out at their house. It felt like home, but Elyse knew this was Kelsey's home and she was sitting on Kelsey and Ash's bed, and Kelsey would soon be a mother herself. Life was changing for her and her kids. It was the natural progression of things, but Elyse couldn't help but long for the past when her kids lived at home, just a little bit.

Elyse and the other girls helped Kelsey put her dress on, at the photographer's direction as she took photos. Elyse had tears in her eyes as she gazed at her daughter, hair and makeup done, wedding gown on. "Kelsey, you look stunning."

Tears filled Kelsey's eyes as well. The tears were the first of many that would fall that day. She hugged her mom.

Claire arrived as they embraced, following her two children who ran ahead of her up the stairs. "Oh my God! Look at you. Kelsey, you look beautiful." She embraced her sister. "No more tears. You'll ruin your makeup."

"It's waterproof," Kelsey said, returning Claire's embrace.

"Why is Auntie Kelsey crying?" Aiden asked.

"Because she's so happy," Claire said.

Aiden scrunched up his face and cocked his head to one side, not understanding.

Shortly after, another set of footsteps was heard climbing the stairs. A woman with long black hair worn straight, cascading over bare shoulders and a black dress, came into view. She had tattoos visible on her chest and one, a vine of some sort, climbing up her neck. She smiled at everyone as she came into the space. The skirt of her dress hung long with a slit high up her thigh.

"Hi everyone," she greeted with a Southern accent thicker than Mel's. "Kelsey, I need you in the kitchen by the back door for a few minutes. Ash is in the garage, where he's been told to stay."

"Sure," Kelsey said and then followed her down the stairs.

"Who the hell was that?" Claire asked.

"That's Sabrina. She's their wedding officiant," Mel said. "She's one of Ash's clients and a friend."

"Elvira?" Claire asked. "They're being married by fucking Elvira?"

"Claire, language. Please," Elyse whispered.

"Mom, come on. I know it's October, but we're not nearly close enough to Halloween yet for that."

"Do not hurt your sister's feelings," Elyse warned. "A lot of ministers wear black."

"Not off their shoulders and low cut, revealing their breasts and neck tattoos, nor do they have a slit half-way up their thighs," Claire replied.

"Well, it's not what you're used to," Elyse said.

"You've got that right. I'm not used to an Elvira hoochie-momma performing a wedding ceremony. Won't their wedding pictures just look amazing." Her voice couldn't have held more sarcasm.

"Enough, Claire," Elyse reprimanded, her voice sounding as it had when Claire was a child. "That woman is an invited friend and guest of your sister and Ash."

"Yeah, of Ash." Claire huffed out a sigh. "But I will go along with this show of support for Kelsey, no matter what my thoughts are."

Just when Elyse thought Claire couldn't disappoint her more, Claire always sank lower. When Elyse spoke again her voice was an uncharacteristic growl. "You will either stop with your unacceptable comments or you will leave. If you can't support your sister, no one is forcing you to stay."

Claire was shocked by her mom's words and tone.

• • • •

THAT FIRST YEAR

THE GUESTS WERE ARRIVING. Peeking through the sheer curtains on the back door, Kelsey saw them milling around the back yard. Her enthusiasm spiked her adrenaline making her entire body buzz. Kade came in from the door that led to the garage.

"Ash isn't with you? Is he?" Kelsey asked.

"No. Don't worry. He won't see you until I walk you down the aisle," he said, giving her a hug. "You look incredible."

"Thanks," Kelsey said.

Samantha pointed out spots in the yard and advised when to send each of her bridesmaids down the aisle. "And wait until your maid of honor is at the arch before you two come out. It'll be just like we talked about. Kade, you'll hand her off to Ash, shake his hand, and then take your place beside him."

"Samantha, I changed my mind. I'd like Kade to seat our mom," Kelsey said.

"That will work. And then the two other groomsmen will walk down the aisle followed by Ash and me as Kade is making his way back to the house," Samantha said.

"Yes," both Kelsey and Kade confirmed.

"Okay, we're set," Samantha said. "Let's call your mom and the other girls down. I'll get everyone seated and then go get Ash and the other groomsmen from the garage."

"I'd like to have a few minutes with my mom before the ceremony. Give me just a second," Kelsey said. She went to the stairs and called for her mom. Elyse came down, followed by the others. Kelsey brought her into one of the small bedrooms on the first floor and closed the door. "I wanted to have a few minutes with you, Mom, to say thank you for always being an amazing role model for me." She took hold of her mom's hands. "The person I am is because of you. I hope I can be even half the mom you are. I love you so much and I am so thankful you are in my life," Kelsey said, new tears in her eyes.

Elyse engulfed her in a hug. "You are an amazing young woman who I'm incredibly proud of. I have no doubt that you will also be an amazing mom and wife. And for the record, I think your dad would have approved of Ash. Since you've been with him you have definitely become more confident, and it's apparent how happy you are with him. Being with him brings out the best in you."

Chapter 36 – They Do

Through the sheer curtain, Kelsey watched Kade escort their mom to her seat. As he headed back towards the house, she saw Eric, followed by Wren walk towards the arch. She caught sight of Samantha and Ash walk past, just as Kade was arriving back at the patio door. Her breath caught in her chest, seeing Ash's profile for the brief moment before his back was turned and he and Samantha walked together down the short aisle.

The patio door was open, and she could hear the classical music drift in. Kade re-entered the house. Then the melody changed, the signal for the first bridesmaid to go. Kelsey had another wave of tears come to her eyes. Mel gave her a hug before picking her bouquet up from the table where the flowers were laid out. Then she exited the house. When she reached the halfway point, it was Claire's turn.

Claire gave her children last-minute instructions, and then she too exited the house. When she reached the half-way point, Cathy Kay swallowed Kelsey in an embrace before pushing the sheer curtain aside and following.

"Okay, guys. It's your turn. Just like we talked about," Kelsey told Aiden and Emma. She knew Aiden wouldn't have any problems performing as asked, but she was worried about Emma freezing when she got outside the door.

Kade stepped out with them and sent them along, giving them a quick embrace. Emma held Aiden's hand and they walked down the aisle, receiving coos of 'aww and 'oh my', from those assembled.

"Are you ready, kiddo?" Kade asked, offering Kelsey his arm.

Kelsey's tears were continuous. "Thank you for Ash, Kade. If it weren't for you, I wouldn't have found him."

"He's a good guy, Kels. I wouldn't want you with anyone but him, and that's not just because one of my best friends is becoming my brother-in-law."

Kelsey laughed through her tears. "I'm glad our babies will be born around the same time. I want them to grow up together."

"They will. Remember, you're helping Mel and me out with our kid."

Just then, the music changed to the Wedding March.

"Okay, that's our signal," Kade said.

"I'm ready," Kelsey said with a teary-eyed smile.

Kade whisked the sheer curtain aside and then she stepped out onto the patio with him. Everyone stood as they approached the rows of chairs. Kelsey's eyes swept over everyone until they landed on Ash's face, where they became locked. The smile on his face matched her own. She even saw tears in his eyes.

They reached the arch quickly. Kade kissed her cheek and then shook Ash's hand before taking his spot beside him as Ash's best man. Kelsey stood, facing Ash, looking at only him. At that moment, she didn't care who else was there or who was not. She was marrying the man she loved. That was all that mattered.

"Well, here we are," Samantha said, glancing between Ash and Kelsey. Many seated in the chairs facing them laughed. "I have to admit that I knew this day would come quickly after I first met Kelsey and saw the two of you together. For those of you who don't know me, I have been a client and a friend of Ash's for many years, and I've gotten to know him well. All the ink I have, he's applied. That's a lot of time in his chair getting to know him. When Ash met Kelsey, I saw that he was immediately restored to the full being God created him to be. He found the one person in this world who God had made just for him. It was obvious. And the other thing I noticed was the relationship also brought out the best in Kelsey. I didn't know her well, but as I got to know her, I saw a woman coming alive, drawing energy and confidence from the relationship she and Ash have. I saw a closeness and a friendship between them. It's a relationship that nurtures them both. They have trust in each other. They laugh together. And they also have the magnetic attraction, the passion in their relationship that is the difference between friends and lovers. It's why we are here today, for them to make a lifelong commitment to each other, to become husband and wife. Many would argue in today's world marriage is no longer relevant. But Ash and Kelsey do not believe that. The commitment they will make here today, in front of their family members and friends, holds great meaning to them both. And since it does, they have each written their own vows."

Kelsey handed her bouquet to Cathy Kay.

"They will exchange rings as they say their vows. Their rings are the outward symbol to the world that they are husband and wife." She handed Ash's ring to Kelsey.

Kelsey positioned the ring on the tip of his ring finger on his left hand. At that moment, everything she planned to say got jumbled in her thoughts. "Ash, the day I met you, my world became this incredible place where anything was possible. I remember when you first held my hand that day, the smile on your lips and the life in your eyes as you shook my hand. I was in awe of you and completely enamored. I saw how special you were that day, but I had no idea just how special you were. It was the day I confessed to Kade, and you, that I wasn't going to grad school. I was upending my entire life and turning my back on everyone's expectations of me. But instead of feeling lost, not knowing what I was going to do, you threw me a lifeline and gave me the incredible gift of your confidence in me and my artwork. It's because of your confidence in me and your love for me that I feel I have achieved so much personal growth. My mom has even told me that she likes the confidence and happiness she sees in me since we've been together. And it's true. Because of you I am a better person, a more confident person, a happier person. I love you with all that I am. Samantha just spoke about our relationship and how it nurtures both of us. We nurture each other, each other's dreams, each other's passions. What we have is special and that's only because, at the heart of it, you are my best friend. I can be myself with you, my true self. And the first time you kissed me, I discovered what passion felt like. Ashley Vincent, I promise to love you every day like I do today. I promise to never let the passion between us die. I promise to be the best friend, partner, wife, and mother of your child or children that I can be. I promise to always trust in you and talk with you about any of life's struggles, knowing that together we can handle anything that comes our way. I take you, Ashley Vincent, as my husband to love and to cherish until death do us part." She slid the band completely onto his finger. Then she swiped at the happy tears that cascaded down her cheeks.

Ash gently helped her wipe her tears away. Then he placed a kiss on her lips.

"Ash, your turn. And you're not supposed to kiss her until after I pronounce you married," Samantha said, handing him Kelsey's rings, which he'd soldered together the previous evening.

"Oh, that wasn't *the* kiss. Just wait till you say we're married."

The laughter from all was loud.

He placed the rings halfway on her finger, admiring how beautiful they looked there. "Kelsey, I asked you to take my hand and jump off a cliff with me when you first met me. I was blown away that you did. You were never lost. You were searching. There's a difference. And you were searching with courage and strength, running towards your future, not away from anything. I fell completely in love with you immediately because you wowed me just by being the person you are. You have this gift of kindness and faith. You see the world's opportunities. You make my world better just by being in it. You are my best friend. I don't remember what my life was like before you wrapped me in your love." He paused and glanced at those seated. "I'm not talking sexually. I'm talking metaphorically." His eyes locked with Elyse's. "You get that, Elyse, right? We're good?"

She smiled and nodded, amused by his reaction. "Yes, we're good."

Many laughed.

His eyes came back to Kelsey's. He switched his grip on her hand, holding it more than poised to slip the ring completely on. "I promise to always hold your hand as your hand holds my heart, which belongs to you today, tomorrow, and always. I promise I will always nurture your dreams. I promise to always be your best friend, partner, and husband, and I promise to be the best dad to our children I can be. Life may not always be easy, but it will be far easier with us facing it together. Kelsey, with this ring, I take you as my wife, to love and to cherish until death parts us." He slid the ring all the way on and then placed a kiss on the back of her hand.

"Kelsey and Ash have spoken their vows and pronounced to the world that they take each other in the bonds of holy matrimony. What God has put together let no one trespass on. I challenge you, Kelsey and Ash's friends and family, to help nurture this new family. We'll raise glasses in toast. We'll share a meal to celebrate this marriage, this joining of two lives. This is a monumental occasion, a date Kelsey and Ash will always remember, celebrate, and cherish. By the power vested in me by God and the State of Virginia, I now pronounce you husband and wife. Ash, you may now kiss," she said, but stopped before she finished her sentence as Ash had already embraced his wife and kissed her like he would never kiss her again.

Kelsey was vaguely aware of claps and cheers as she and Ash enjoyed their first kiss as husband and wife. He held her tightly to himself and the kiss was passionate, tongues wrapping around each other in a sensual dance, every part of her body and numbed mind responding to the fire his kisses ignited. Their lips didn't part until someone yelled, "Get a room!" And when they did break from the embrace, they were both breathless.

"Yes, a room, soon," Ash joked, garnering him more laughter.

He offered his elbow to Kelsey. She took it as Cathy Kay handed her bouquet back to her and they walked back up the little aisle and waited a good few feet behind it for the rest of their wedding party to join them. They were greeted with hugs as each person reached them.

Elyse held Jake's hand as she stood.

"That was a very nice ceremony," Jake said.

"Yes, it was," Elyse said. She felt more emotional about it than she thought she would, more emotional than she had after Claire's wedding. It was probably because it was her baby, her Kelsey.

As Aiden and Emma ran around them to go to their mom, Jake leaned in close. "Are you okay?"

"Yes. This hit me harder than I thought it would. My baby, my youngest, is married."

"He's good for her," Jake said.

"I know. And he fits well into the family."

Jake raised an eyebrow. "Would Claire say that?" he whispered.

"She doesn't get a vote," Elyse muttered before flashing him a smile.

They walked up the aisle, reaching the back where the wedding party was still congregated just as Matthew shook Ash's hand. *This is promising*, thought Elyse. Elyse hugged both Kelsey and Ash. She smiled, watching Jake do the same. After more congratulations from all their guests, the photographer took the wedding party back over to the arch for formal pictures.

Elyse and Jake wandered over to the bar and she picked up a glass of red wine and then she joined Julia and Trevor Ferguson, the volunteer with the prosthetic left arm. She noticed they looked very close, intimately so. "Hi," she greeted them. They exchanged small talk about the beautiful wedding ceremony.

As several of Ash's friends began to move the chairs the guests had been sitting in for the ceremony over to the tables where dinner would be served, Jake and Trevor assisted in the effort. Elyse noticed that Matthew didn't help, not that she'd expect him to. No, Matthew Jeffries was not raised by his affluent diplomat parents and well-paid nannies to pitch in and help with anything.

Elyse pinned Julia with a stare. "Trevor?"

Julia smiled. "Yes, Trevor. He's a really great guy."

Elyse smiled, happy for her friend. Yes, Julia was more than a few years older than him, but if they were both happy, what did that matter?

Jake and Trevor rejoined them when the job was done. Jake got himself a glass of red wine as well. Beside the bar was a large tub filled with ice and many different brands of beer. Trevor grabbed a bottle of beer. As did most of Ash's friends, who Elyse had previously discovered were nice guys, not what one might expect from their appearances of multiple tattoos and piercings.

She glanced back at the arch in time to see the photographer snap a picture of Claire and Wren. She was so glad that Kelsey decided to pair Claire with Ash's brother rather than Eric, as she'd first intended. While she found Eric to be down to earth, with a heart of gold, she knew Claire would never see past his appearance. Little did Claire know that Wren was an ex-con, grand theft auto.

The photographer finished with pictures of the wedding party and would take a few more of only Kelsey and Ash and a few with Samantha, posed shots to recreate portions of the ceremony. The others moved away and joined the guests on the patio.

"Your sister is the biggest bitch," Mel whispered to Kade.

"Claire?"

"Of course Claire," Mel said. "You should have heard her make fun of Samantha's appearance."

"Well, Samantha is unconventional, to say the least, not that I'm defending Claire," he said. "A lot of people would raise an eyebrow or two in reaction to her if they didn't know her. We know her and know that she's a sweetheart."

"Yeah, and Claire would never give her enough of a chance to get to know her."

"Claire's loss," Kade said. "Really, Mel, why would you expect anything else from Claire?"

"Then I think it's only appropriate we have Samantha marry us as well."

A smile spread over Kade's face. "I like hearing you talk about us getting married."

Mel wrapped her arms around him. "I am so sorry for my initial reaction to the pregnancy and your proposal. I love you, Kade. It was never that."

"I know," he whispered, embracing her tightly. "So, when might this wedding be?"

"In the spring when the weather is nice enough for an outside wedding. I wonder if your mom would let us have it in her back yard. This worked out nicely. We'll have a larger guest list with so many of our friends from the department, and spending a fortune renting a hall is a waste of money."

"I agree, and I'm sure my mom would love for it to be in her backyard." He would have preferred to get married sooner, even if it meant by the justice of the peace with just a few people there. He didn't need any fuss or fanfare. He just wanted to marry the woman he loved who was pregnant with his child.

Before long, Elyse and Jake joined Kade and Mel. And then Claire and her family wandered over as well, because who else would they mingle with? Claire didn't really know Kelsey's friends. And neither she nor Matthew would have any interest in getting to know Ash's friends.

Shortly thereafter, all were called to the tables. There was no assigned seating. Everyone just sat where they wanted. Before dinner was served, Samantha said a prayer. It was short, sweet, to the point, ending with 'everyone let's eat'. And then the servers from the caterer that Claire hired swept in with meals plated on heavy white 'Chinet' dinner plates. They placed a garden salad and a roll on the table in front of each guest and asked each if they wanted a meat or a pasta and vegetable, and then set the requested meal in front of them. The meat option was a grilled chicken breast. They had the fifty meals served quickly. Seconds were available for self-service in the chafing dishes.

After only a few bites, Kelsey glanced up at Claire. "This food is amazing!"

Claire smiled proudly. "I've used them for a few events. They always do a good job."

"This chicken breast is the juiciest, most tender I've ever had. I can practically cut it with my fork," Kelsey said. "Thank you, Claire. I really appreciate you taking care of the food." Her words were as heartfelt as the expression on her face was.

"You're welcome. Only the best for my little sister," Claire said.

"The pasta is really good, too," Kade added. Claire had hit it out of the ballpark with the caterer. "We're probably going to do an outside wedding like this in the spring. We'll want the contact info for this caterer."

"Certainly," Claire said. "Just wait until you taste the wedding cake. You're going to want the bakery's contact info, too." She was glad she had taken over the food. This was one hundred percent better than anything Kelsey and Ash would have come up with on their own. A food truck, of all things!

As everyone was finishing their meals, Kade stood. "Kelsey and Ash said they didn't want any traditional toasts or speeches. They're not going to do any hokey bouquet or garter tosses, which would have been rigged like they always are. Mel and I will be married in the spring. We would have won the tosses, so we're just saving everyone time and disappointment if you were hoping to catch one or the other."

Laughs were the reply he received.

"But I want to do one toast. It's not every day that one of your best friends becomes your brother-in-law." He raised his beer bottle. "Ash, Kelsey, I didn't see the relationship between you two coming, but I should have. You're perfect for each other. I know you two will have a happy life together. I look forward to our kids growing up more as siblings than cousins, and I hope that when Mel and I can afford to buy a house it's near yours. Much happiness always." He brought the bottle to his lips and took a drink.

Everyone else took a drink as well. Kelsey had new tears gather in her eyes. After a kiss to Ash's lips, she went around the table to where Kade sat and gave him a hug. "That was nice," she said.

As the dinner portion was wrapped up, the caterers transferred uneaten portions into containers that would be left in Kelsey and Ash's refrigerator. Then they packed up and departed. The bar became self-serve. With the waning daylight, Ash lit the firepit and switched on the many lights that were strung all around the backyard.

Then he approached Claire. "Can you help me with something, Claire?" Ash queried, putting her on the spot.

Claire glanced around at the others who stood nearby, as if to silently communicate that she didn't know why she was being asked and not them. "Of course, Ash."

He smiled and then led her into the house. He brought her to one of the two small bedrooms on the first floor and closed the door with them inside the room. He uncovered something which was atop a desk, by pulling the sheet from it. "I made this as a wedding gift for Kelsey."

It was a large metal sculpture of polished steel. It had multiple kites intersecting as they waved in an imaginary breeze. Upon closer inspection, Claire noticed that each kite partially intersected and was attached by the thin strings of metal to the two human figures holding the spool of twine, who were cuddled up together. Each kite was etched with names. Some had dates. She saw her father's name on one of the kites, along with his date of birth, and the date of his death.

"Oh my God! That's you and Kelsey, isn't it?" she asked, pointing to the two human figures.

"Yes. After the baby comes, I will add him or her to the sculpture."

"Ash, this is beautiful. You are a true artist," Claire said.

"Do you think she'll like it?"

"She'll love it," Claire said. She loved it, so, she was sure Kelsey would, too.

"It's not a traditional gift a groom would give his bride," Ash said. "But, then again, neither Kelsey nor I are traditional. I wanted you to see it first, though."

"Why?"

"Because I know you don't care much for me," Ash said.

Claire stared blankly at him, completely taken aback that he had said it. "I never said that, Ash."

"You didn't have to say it to my face. I know you don't like tattoos, and you're disappointed this is the direction Kelsey has chosen for her life. But I love her with all my heart. I'll always take care of her, and I'll never hurt her. That asshole she last dated is going to school to be a doctor. He's going to be successful, richer than me, and respected. But he cheated on her, and hurt her which is something I'd never do."

"I never said you would," Claire defended.

"But you'd rather see her with someone like him."

"No, Ash. I wouldn't want her with anyone like him. She chose you, and you're married now. I don't understand why we're having this conversation."

"You're Kelsey's sister and she loves you. And she loves her niece and nephew. She wants our child to grow up knowing you and playing with his or her cousins. It's about family, Claire. This sculpture and this conversation. Elyse is good with me, as is Kade, obviously. That leaves you."

Claire busied herself reading the other names that were on the sculpture. Matthew's and her names and birthdates, and both their children's info were beautifully etched. Kade's and Mel's names were etched on nearby kites, as well. "I will tell you that you really surprise me. You are definitely more than you appear on the surface. Kelsey loves you. And I love my sister. I can't imagine my life without her in it and without her family in it, her child, and her husband."

"I know you and I are very different people, but I'd like to think that since we both love Kelsey that gives us something in common to go from in having a relationship," Ash said.

"Yes," Claire agreed. "It certainly does. And I think this is the perfect wedding gift for you to give Kelsey." She meant both the sculpture and the conversation he'd just had with her. In that moment, Claire adopted a newfound respect for Ashley Vincent.

Ash smiled. "Okay, will you help me bring it out? I want to give it to her so everyone else can see it, too. I'm really pleased by how it came out. I'm thinking of adding things like this to what I make to sell at the shop."

"You should. And I think you should make wedding bands and other jewelry to sell, too," Claire said. "Thank you for this conversation, Ash."

He nodded and then re-covered the sculpture. Claire opened the door as he lifted it from the desk. Claire also slid open the kitchen's patio door so Ash could step out onto the patio with it. He set it onto the closest table.

"Kelsey, come over for a minute," he summoned. "I want to give you my wedding gift before anyone leaves."

Kelsey viewed the large sheet-covered item on the table. She was sure it was going to be something amazing he'd made in the forge because he'd spent a lot of time in there over the past two weeks. She had suspected he was making something for her, as he wouldn't share with her what he was working on. The size of it surprised her, even though she didn't know what was beneath the covering yet. She smiled and gave him a hug. "I can't wait to see what it is!"

Ash helped her remove the covering.

"It's beautiful!" she exclaimed once it was in full view.

She heard gasps and murmurs from others as well. It sparkled and reflected not only the white lights decorating the yard but the last rays of sunlight and the flames dancing in the firepit as well. She became more impressed with it the more closely she examined the details etched into it.

Many other voices overlapped, voicing their congratulations to Ash on his sculpture. Kelsey's heart swelled with the pride she felt. Her husband was an amazing artist, and she wasn't the only one who knew it. She turned back to him and embraced him. "Thank you, Ash. I love it."

He took the opportunity to kiss her, as she was in his arms. "If you don't mind, I may display it at the shop for a little while."

"I would be proud if you did. It would be selfish not to share it."

"Are you ready to blow out of here?" Matthew whispered in Claire's ear.

"Not yet. Let's stay for a little while longer. You should take a look at the sculpture. He even has one of the kites etched with each of our names."

Matthew shot her a questioning look. It was clear he was ready to go, as they had agreed they would.

"Aiden and Emma will melt down if we take them home before the cake is served," Claire explained. But the truth was, she wasn't ready to go yet. She wanted to stay and see what kind of evening this gathering would bring. So far everyone had talked and there'd been much laughter between the other guests and the wedding couple. She enjoyed seeing her sister so happy. Her mom had been right that after so much sadness after their dad's death, they all needed this.

"You're probably right." Matthew's gaze went to the children, who were with Elyse and Jake, examining the sculpture. "When do you think they'll cut the cake?" His gaze then went to his phone's screen. "And can you help hurry that along?"

Claire pushed away her aggravation at Matthew. He was, after all, just trying to stick with their original plan. "Check out the sculpture. I'll talk with Julia and her maid of honor about the cake. I think they're responsible for it." Though she didn't plan to hurry them to cut it as Matthew had asked her to do.

"Yeah, and what's with your mom's friend, Julia, and the amputee guy?" Matthew asked. "Isn't she way too old for him?"

"I say good for her!" Claire whispered.

"I think it would be gross, to be with a woman that much older. But maybe that's just me," Matthew said.

"But it doesn't bother you when it's reversed, an older man and a way too young woman? Then it's more like, way to go, dude." She saw in his eyes that this would cause a fight between them, so she backed off. "Either way, it's irrelevant to us. Let me go see about hurrying along the serving of the cake so we can take our leave as planned." She rushed over to where Cathy Kay stood, talking with a few others. "Hi, any idea when Kelsey and Ash are going to cut the cake?"

"Soon, I'm sure," Cathy Kay answered.

"I've been wondering, is Kay your middle name?" Claire asked her to prolong the time away from Matthew, to make it look like she was prodding the process along.

"Oh," she laughed. "There are four Cathy's in my family. Kay's my middle initial. There's my aunt, Cathy, who I'm named after, and my Uncle Pete married a Cathy shortly after I was born. Everyone calls her Cathy Anne, and my Uncle Paul married a woman with a daughter named Cathy, too. She's Cathy Em because her last name is Emerich."

"Interesting," Claire said. She glanced back at Matthew. He was near the sculpture, examining it. Her mom and Jake had just taken seats near the firepit. Emma sat on her mom's lap. Her mom wrapped Emma in her sweater and she looked so happy, hugging Emma. Jake held Aiden on his lap. She wasn't sure how she felt about that.

"What's that look?" Kade asked Claire, startling her.

"Oh Jesus, don't sneak up on people like that!" Claire gasped.

Kade chuckled. "Sorry. I thought you saw me."

"No, and there's no look."

Kade glanced at the firepit area. "It's okay if you're bothered that Jake is sitting with Mom over there rather than Dad," he whispered.

Claire looked away, almost feeling ashamed. She hadn't been necessarily thinking about her dad's absence, more Jake's presence. "Kelsey's wedding and he's not here. It's just so fucked up," Claire said.

Kade wrapped an arm around her. "I know. It's life, Claire. People sometimes are just suddenly gone. And there's not a damn thing we can do about it but support each other when it happens. I'm happy Mom has Jake in her life, especially today. I mean, you have Matthew, Kelsey has Ash, and I have Mel."

"Yeah," Claire agreed, feeling suddenly emotional. "It's just startling to see him and Mom holding my kids like she and Dad did. Dad always held Aiden."

"Jake's willing to step up and play Grandpa," Kade noted. "Another point in his favor. If my kid won't be able to know Dad, I'm glad he or she will have Jake as that grandfather figure. Given that he bought Mom that warehouse, I'll bet that Jake will be around for a long time, and I think that's a good thing," Kade said.

"You're living there. And he's over a lot, isn't he? How weird and uncomfortable is that?" Claire asked.

Jake chuckled. "It was only weird and uncomfortable at first, and that was only when I ran into him coming or going from Mom's bedroom. But honestly, Mom's sex life is none of my business and I try not to focus on what may or may not be going on inside her room. It's better that way."

"Yeah, no kidding," Claire said. "The thought of Mom having sex..." She paused and shuddered.

Jake laughed again. "As I said, I try not to think about it. But what I will tell you is that it's very comfortable having dinner or hanging out. And he helps Mom with things. She's happy with him, Claire, and that's all that matters to me."

Claire glanced back at her mom and Jake holding the kids on their laps. She was sure they'd keep the kids safe that close to the fire, and Kade was right. Her mom looked thrilled to be fussing over Emma. Aiden was talking Jake's ear off and he looked attentive. Then her gaze met Matthew's, and she saw the expectation that they hurry and leave. She turned her back to Matthew, keeping her gaze on her brother. "Kade, Mom said you were good with what Dad wrote to you in his note. Could I read your letter sometime?" Claire asked hesitantly.

"Yeah, but it's no big deal what he wrote," Kade said, knowing he would not let Claire see that letter given what their father had written to him about her. "He told me he was proud of me, which he never said while he was alive, not even once. He also told me not to be the type of father he was. He knew he hadn't been there when he should have been. He asked me to walk Kelsey down the aisle when she got married, and he asked me to accept any man Mom would date. That was really about it."

"Was Kelsey's as bad as she interpreted it, or do you think she over-reacted?"

"I think there was a lot of positive messages in his letter to her, but he wrote it in a condescending tone, like he was talking to a fifteen-year-old, and maybe that was how old she was when he wrote it. I don't know."

"I wish there had been a date on the notes to tell us when he wrote them. Did you read Mom's note?"

"No," Kade answered. "Whatever was in it weighed on her right away, though. I could tell. She tried to not let on, but she was, I don't know if bothered is the right word or not, but it was something. And given what he wrote in our three notes, I'm sure there was something that had to have rubbed her the wrong way. Why?"

"It's been more than a month since we got those notes, but I can't stop thinking about what he wrote in mine. Dad purposefully limited my career. He said one thing to my face, but his actions at work and what he said in that note were contrary. I'm having such a hard time with it."

"Claire, you're going to drive yourself crazy if you don't let it go. Of the three of us, you had the closest relationship with Dad. I think the only thing the three of us should take away from those notes is that he loved us, and he knew he should have been more present as a father, but he just didn't have it in him. With that being said, I don't think Dad did anything maliciously, and that would include holding you back in your career. If that was what he was doing. He could have thought he was protecting you."

"I'm sure you're right," Claire murmured. "I should let you go check out that sculpture."

"I already saw it. I helped Ash move it into the house. Isn't it something?"

"Yes, he's an amazing artist. I will admit I underestimated him." And she hadn't just underestimated his artistic talent.

"Why, Claire Laramie-Jeffries, are you admitting that you were wrong about something?" Kade teased.

"Shut up," she said with a teasing smile. "I've never said I can't be wrong, though it happens rarely."

Kade laughed. "Watch it, next thing you know you'll be getting the ink to match Kelsey and me."

She laughed with him. "Yeah, don't hold your breath on that!"

Kade put her in a playful headlock like he did when they were kids. By middle school he was already taller than she was. "Come on, let's go over by Mom and Jake. Looks like they're getting ready to make some s'mores with the kids."

Claire knew she'd never get her kids into the car without them both suffering massive meltdowns–cake, s'mores, and attention from their grandma–would be too tempting to leave. After checking in on the kids, and seeing their excitement, she knew they couldn't leave anytime soon. She checked her watch. It was only seven-thirty. Their normal bedtime was eight. They would probably be good without too much crabbiness until eight-thirty. If they left in an hour, the kids could fall asleep on the way home. Her gaze shifted to Matthew. His facial expression was still urging her to hurry up.

Kelsey intersected Claire's path back to Matthew. "Hey, we're going to cut the cake in just a few minutes," Kelsey said with a big smile. "If you don't want the kids to mess up their good clothes, this might be a good time to change them into whatever you brought. I can feel it's already getting cooler."

Claire glanced back at the kids. "They'll be fine. They're warm enough by the fire with Mom." Claire smiled. "I don't think I'm getting them away from there until we go. S'mores with Grandma is more exciting than anything else going on."

Kelsey laughed with her. "I'm glad to hear you're not leaving already. I know they normally go to bed at eight."

"They can fall asleep in the car on the way home." Claire gave Kelsey a hug. "My sister's big day is more important than bedtime tonight."

Kelsey embraced her tightly. "I'm so glad to hear you say that. We have some fireworks we're going to shoot off after it's good and dark."

Claire cringed. Fireworks at home were so unsafe. Matthew would not like this at all. "Kels, can you hold off on the fireworks until after we go? Emma is so afraid of them."

"Oh, poor munchkin," Kelsey said. "Yes, I'll tell Ash. I wouldn't want to scare her."

"We'll go around eight-thirty, if that's okay?"

"Sure. I'm just glad you'll stay that late."

After the sisters broke their embrace, Claire walked over to Matthew. "Kelsey really wants us to stay another hour."

Matthew sighed in frustration.

"And the kids are enjoying the time with my mom. I think it'll be fine. With all the sugar from the s'mores and the cake, there's no way they'll go to sleep before eight-thirty. If we wait until then, it's likely they'll fall asleep in the car, and we can transfer them right to their beds when we get home."

Matthew shrugged. "Sure. I'm going to grab another drink. You're the DD tonight," he informed her.

· · · ·

WHEN ELYSE AND JAKE got home, while Jake let Charlie out, Elyse went to the front door to ensure it was locked. They'd come in through the door from the garage. The intention was that they'd head up to bed. A small fire was lit in the fireplace in the living room. Kade kneeled in front of it.

"Kade, what are you doing?" Elyse asked.

"I'm burning my note from Dad."

When his gaze lifted to hers, she saw tears in his eyes that had also slipped down his cheeks. Elyse went to him and bent down beside him. "Why did you do that?"

"Claire asked me tonight if she could read it. I told her what was in it, less the things he'd said about her. She can't ever read those things, Mom. It would hurt her."

"You could just keep it hidden from her," Elyse said. "Kade, those were your last words from your dad."

"I took a picture of it on my phone, which I'll send to my computer and put it in a password-protected file. That won't ever accidently end up in her hands like the actual note could."

Elyse embraced him, with more pride in her son than she had ever felt. He wanted to protect Claire. "Why were you crying?"

"Because I read it again. It's like he knew he wouldn't be here to walk Kelsey down the aisle. Claire was upset tonight, said how fucked up it was that Dad wasn't here, and she's right. But tonight was just another thing that he wasn't here for. My kid's not even here yet, but I can tell you I love him or her more than Dad could have loved us. I would never miss anything that was within my power to be there for." He rocked back on his heels and stood up.

"I don't think it had to do with love, for your father," Elyse said, standing back upright. "Kade, I truly think your father fell someplace on the Autism spectrum. He even talked about not having the capacity to do both his job and be present with his family in his notes to us. Even without a diagnosis, he knew his limitations."

Kade looked like an 'a-ha' moment had just struck him. He nodded. "You know, that makes perfect sense. His intellect was in the genius range, but he had no emotional intelligence and was clumsy socially. He hid it well, but the signs were all there."

"His notes proved that he picked up on the relationships between the four of us, but he said in his note to me that he felt like an outsider."

"Jesus, that's sad," Kade said.

"He never tried to change it," Elyse said. "He never told us to our faces what he said in his letters. I think he just couldn't. I'm sorry you grew up without him, Kade."

Kade wrapped her in a hug. "Mom, you have nothing to apologize for. You were there for everything, and you made up for the fact that he wasn't there. You taught me what a mom and a dad are supposed to be. I'm the man I am because of you."

"And I am very proud of the man you are. Your father was proud of you, too."

"Thanks, Mom. I believe he was, as he wrote in my note." He paused and smiled. "On another subject, Kelsey's wedding was a lot of fun, wasn't it?"

"Yes. She and Ash are good together. Your toast was nice, by the way. And I know she really appreciated that you walked her down the aisle. You've always been such a good big brother to her."

Kade chuckled. "You always told me to look after my baby sister. I guess I always thought that was my responsibility."

"Well, it's Ash's now. You can consider yourself relieved of duty," Elyse said.

"I think you've been spending too much time with Jake." Kade laughed.

Elyse snickered. "I guess he has rubbed off."

"That's not a bad thing," Kade said. He closed the glass doors on the fireplace. The note had burned itself out and all that was left were ashes. "I'm going to head up to bed. Goodnight, Mom."

"Goodnight, Kade," Elyse said. Just then, Jake and Charlie came through from the kitchen. "How much of that did you hear?" she whispered.

"Enough," Jake confirmed. He wrapped an arm around Elyse. "That's one fine young man you raised."

"Yes, he is."

Chapter 37 – Mixed Gifts

Not quite a week after Kelsey and Ash's wedding was Elyse's birthday. Fifty-one years old and a widow. Her youngest daughter married. Two more grandchildren due in the spring. She tried to drive those thoughts from her mind, which weighed on her negatively, even though she was truly happy for the new lives and for Kelsey's marriage.

She was alone in her bed. Jake had had duty overnight. She wondered to herself if that created her less than stellar mood, rather than the details of her life upon turning fifty-one. The truth was, she awoke beside Jake more often than not since the gala. He kept his room at the officer's quarters, but was rarely there. A junior officer who had been scheduled for the shift overnight had called in sick, otherwise Jake would have been there beside her.

Checking her phone, she saw the text from him wishing her a happy birthday. It brought a smile to her face. Charlie stirred, seeing that she was awake. He lazily stepped over to her and then hung his face in hers in silent greeting.

"Good morning, boy," she said, reaching up to pet him. "Okay, let's get up."

She pulled on yoga pants and a sweatshirt. The mornings were cool, in the low fifties, but would warm to the mid-seventies throughout the day, so she hadn't turned the heat on yet. She always tried to wait until November first before she turned it on. She ran into Kade in the hallway, who was just coming back up the stairs with a cup of coffee in his hand.

"Good morning, Mom. Happy birthday," he said.

"Thank you."

Kade peered past her into the bedroom. "Is Jake here?"

"No, he got called in for duty overnight," Elyse answered. "Kade, are you okay with him being here so much?" She hadn't asked him in almost a month, after he'd insisted that he was.

Kade stopped and gave his mom a hug. "I promise you, Mom, I'm okay with him. It was an adjustment at first, but I'm good with it now. I was only asking because I'm off today and I wanted to see if he was free, if he'd give me a hand with some work I want to do on my truck."

Elyse was filled with warmth and pride, pride in both Kade for accepting Jake as he had and pride in Jake that he had established a friendship with Kade enough that Kade felt comfortable asking him to work on his truck with him. It wasn't a relationship that Kade had with his father, not that Tim ever seemed open to spending that kind of time with his son. Kade's assessment previously, that if you weren't a collapsed building you didn't get his attention, had been correct.

"He's due back after lunch," Elyse said.

"If he worked all night, I'm sure he'll want to catch a nap," Kade said.

"You have his number. Shoot him a text and ask him. I know if it's not busy he can sleep while at the office."

"I'll do that," Kade said. "I'll see you later this morning. I'm working on recording notes for Mel to listen to as she commutes to and from class. The next test she has to take is a killer."

"With your help, I'm sure she'll ace it," Elyse said. "I'm really proud of you both, Kade. She studies constantly, and you help her as much as you can."

"You loaned her the money for the program, Mom. Of course we're both going to make sure she does well. Did I ever tell you that when I told her you gave me the money for it that she cried, unable to believe that you'd do that for her?"

"No, you didn't tell me, but I'm not surprised. Melanie has a big heart and I know she's not used to people, other than you, making her life easier. I've been meaning to ask, has she told her mom yet that she's pregnant?"

"No, she hasn't had any contact with her mom since we found out. Do me a favor and don't mention it to her. She's in a good place right now. She doesn't need the negative thoughts associated with her family to mess with her mind."

"I promise I won't," Elyse assured him. Then she proceeded down the stairs.

The aroma of the freshly brewed coffee filled her nose as she entered the kitchen. That was another plus of others living in the house. Lined up on the counter beside the coffee pot were four envelopes with her name on them and one small, wrapped gift sitting partially atop the envelope with Jake's handwriting on it. A large bouquet of flowers overlapped the envelopes with Kade's and Kelsey's writing on them. The fourth envelope had a dog paw written on the front. Kelsey always gave her cards from the dogs.

She lifted the envelope with Kade's writing on it first, opened it, and read the beautiful card. Sentiments of thanks and appreciation were written in by both Kade and Melanie. She opened the envelope with Kelsey's writing on it next.

It, too, was a beautiful birthday card which both Kelsey and Ash had signed.

"The flowers are from both Kelsey and me," Kade said from the doorway into the hall.

Elyse hadn't seen him standing there, nor had she heard him come down the stairs. "They're beautiful. Thank you."

"You're welcome. Kelsey and Ash will be over for dinner. They're bringing steaks for us to grill. I checked with Jake to be sure he didn't make dinner plans yet."

"Did anyone invite Claire and her family?" Elyse asked.

"On a school night?" Kade asked with a laugh. "Or rather a pre-school night? No, we didn't, as we already knew what her answer would be."

"I think your sister might surprise you."

Kade cocked his head and the expression on his face said that, no, he didn't believe that. "Well, call her if you want to. We could always message them to pick up more steaks."

"Even if they can't come, it's always nice to be invited and included."

He wouldn't comment on that. "What's in the box from Jake?"

Elyse opened his card first and read it. Besides the sweet birthday wishes, he handwritten in his personal thoughts of celebrating this first of many more birthdays to come. It was signed 'Love J'. She opened the box. Inside was a little statue of a warehouse.

She showed Kade. "It's kind of a joke between us." With her birthday approaching, she had warned Jake not to get her a gift. He'd already spent far too much by buying the warehouse.

Then she opened the last envelope. It was, as expected, a birthday card from Charlie. She showered attention on Charlie and then let him out to do his business before getting herself a cup of coffee. Kade returned to his room to work on the recording for Mel.

After she let Charlie in and fed him breakfast, she sat at the kitchen table and tapped out messages of thanks to Kelsey and then Jake for remembering her birthday. She glanced around, feeling a little lost. What should she do this morning? She hadn't planned on going to the shelter today. Julia had it handled with volunteers scheduled to give her the day off to enjoy her birthday. With just moving into the warehouse, she had spent a great deal of time there every day since they'd closed on the property.

Normally, she'd take Charlie for a walk in the forest preserve. But the grass was saturated from the heavy dew overnight. She'd wait until later when it was dry before taking him.

She lingered and drank another cup of coffee. Several friends, including Julia, sent her birthday wishes via text message. She acknowledged each, feeling an odd sense of restlessness. Her spirits instantly lifted when her phone rang an incoming call from Jake. "Hello."

"Happy birthday," he greeted.

"Thank you for the beautiful card and the statue. I appreciate that you didn't buy me anything."

"I'm sorry I wasn't there to hand them to you myself," he said.

"That's okay," she said. "Were you able to get any sleep overnight?"

"Why? Do you have plans I need to be up for this morning?"

She chuckled at the inuendo in his voice. "Maybe, but Kade also was wondering if you'd have time to help him fix something on his truck today."

"I could probably work you both into my busy schedule," he joked.

"When do you think you'll be back?" She stopped from referring to her house as home in her question to him. But that was exactly the way she had wanted to ask. In that moment, she was finally able to identify her mood, or rather her issue today. She missed him this morning. She had been excited at the prospect of waking with him beside her on her birthday. When he'd gotten called into work the night before it hadn't bothered her that much, but her mood this morning was definitely off.

"I'm heading to my doctor's appointment right now," he answered. "I should be out of here in about an hour."

"Did you eat yet? I could meet you in Suffolk. Buy this birthday girl breakfast?"

"Are you going into the shelter this morning?"

"I'd like to stop by, but my primary motivation is getting you to buy me breakfast," she joked.

"That's fair, given you didn't want me to buy you a proper gift. I'd like to swing by and visit Frick and Frack. Elyse, I may find out at this appointment if I'll be restored to regular active duty or if I'll be given the medical separation. I've been giving this a lot of thought. If it's the latter, I want to move completely in with you. It makes no sense for me to get my own place. I'd never be there."

"I've been thinking the same thing."

"And I'd really like you to think about us seeing if Charlie would accept Frick and Frack. I know you think it would be too chaotic for us to adopt them, too, but if I'm out of the Navy. I really want them, Elyse."

Elyse knew he did. She smiled at the thought of him moving in. "We'll talk."

"That wasn't a no," Jake said.

She laughed. "It wasn't a yes, either."

"I'll call when I'm leaving base."

"I'm going to get dressed and head into Suffolk now. I'll probably be at Animal House when you call."

"See you soon, birthday girl. I'll meet you there and then we can go to breakfast."

"Sounds good," she said.

With that she got moving. She downed the rest of her coffee and then ran back upstairs to make herself presentable. She was behind the wheel of her car less than thirty minutes later, heading towards the warehouse in Suffolk that they had completely moved in to. There was still some construction to be completed, but it was functional. That weekend they would have their grand opening ceremony and would post their new open to the public hours that would begin immediately. It would also mean that she would be spending more time there than she did now until they got the new volunteers all trained. Jake had come through yet again, the military referring twenty new volunteers to Animal House Shelter.

"You weren't supposed to come in today," Julia complained when Elyse pushed through the unlocked front door of the shelter, coming into the new reception area. Julia and Trevor sat at the front desk together.

"I'm meeting Jake for breakfast in about an hour," she said.

"Happy birthday," Trevor said.

"Thank you," she said. "Is all quiet this morning?"

"Yes. Everyone is fed and the pens are clean," Julia said.

"I didn't see the electrician's truck outside, so I'll assume he isn't here yet," Elyse said.

"No, but he did call. He should be here within the hour," Julia said. "It's getting there. We'll be ready by our grand opening."

"I guess I'm just anxious," Elyse admitted.

"The last few things we have to finish aren't show-stoppers," Julia said.

"And this warehouse, even not at one hundred percent, is a hell of a lot better than the old facility," Trevor chimed in.

"I know you're both right." Elyse stepped behind the counter. Julia was making updates to the website. "Hey, do me a favor. Take Frick and Frack off the website for now."

Julia shot her a questioning stare.

"Jake wants them. He may find out today if he's getting that medical separation."

"Damn," Trevor cursed, shaking his head. "That's gonna be tough for him to accept. I know he doesn't want it."

"I'm not saying the dogs will make it all better, but knowing they will be his should help a little," Elyse said.

With a few clicks of the mouse in her hand, Julia had them removed from the active listing on the shelter's website.

. . . .

ELYSE TOOK CARE OF a few tasks at the shelter for well over an hour, waiting for Jake's call. She kept checking her phone to see if she had a signal or if it had somehow turned itself off. It had a signal and it was on. It had been over two hours since Jake had called and said he was heading to his doctor's appointment. What was taking so long?

Finally, about an hour later, she received a text from him. *"I'll meet you at that brunch place on Main, in Suffolk, in ten minutes, if that's okay."*

"Sure, see you then," she messaged back. That was odd. She wondered why he hadn't called when leaving the base.

She checked one more time on the electrician, who had arrived shortly after she had. He was high on a ladder, finishing the job of adding power to run another garage door opener. She wanted to be able to open a newly installed door to give one of the playrooms outside access and fresh air. Not vital, but a great feature she wanted to incorporate into the space.

"I'm heading out to meet Jake for brunch," Elyse told Julia and Trevor as she came back into the reception area. "We'll probably stop by after we eat."

Then she drove to the restaurant. When she pulled into the parking lot, there stood Jake in his khaki uniform, leaning against his car. As she parked he met her by her car door, holding a bouquet of flowers.

"For the birthday girl," he said, handing her the bouquet before she exited her car.

"They're beautiful. Thank you." She placed them on the passenger seat before she got out of the car.

He greeted her with an embrace and a kiss.

When they separated, she saw the smile on his lips. "You're in a good mood."

"I passed the medical evals, Elyse. I've been returned to regular active duty, effective today," Jake announced with an even bigger smile.

Her smile fell. Even though she was tremendously disappointed, she forced the smile back to her lips. "Congratulations, Jake." Her words were hollow. This was not the news she wanted, especially on her birthday.

"This doesn't mean I'm deploying," he reminded her.

"I know."

"I know you're not thrilled with this news," he admitted. "My days won't change too much, and I still plan to spend every non-working hour with you, Elyse." When she didn't say anything, he continued. "If anything, I should get more time to be with you since I won't be going to doctor's appointments or PT any longer. With a shore duty billet, Navy life can nearly mirror civilian life."

"But you're not really on shore duty, are you? You said yourself they'll be looking for a boat to assign you to." She closed her eyes tightly for a second. "I'm sorry, Jake," she said when she reopened them. "I didn't mean to not celebrate your good news with you. I know this is what you've been praying for. I'll adjust to it. I love you and I always knew this was a probable outcome, so it's part of the territory."

"Do you want me to resign my commission?"

Elyse's breath caught in her chest. She knew he would if she asked him to, but she would never be that woman. And even if he said he was going to do it on his own, she would argue with him about it. She'd never want him to give up his career for her before he was ready to for himself. "No. You've said from the moment I met you that you're not done with your career yet. You want to command your own boat. You've worked towards it all these years."

"I love you and don't want to lose you, Elyse," he whispered.

"You're not losing me, Lieutenant Commander," she said. "Remember, you gave me an engagement warehouse and I'm holding you to that."

Jake chuckled. "Yes, ma'am. And for the record, I don't want out of that commitment. I'll marry you any day, anywhere of your choosing."

"How soon do you think they'll assign you to a boat?"

"Let's go eat while we talk," Jake suggested, pointing to the restaurant. Once they were seated, orders placed, he answered. "I don't think I'll be deploying within the next three months unless something unexpected happens to knock out a CO or an XO currently assigned to one of our ships."

"But you think the possibility of it happening is likely in four months?"

"I didn't say that. I was only able to analyze assignments and schedules going three months out and it looks unlikely during that timeframe, unless something unexpected comes up."

Elyse digested his statement. "So, assignments are normally set in stone then?"

"Yes. Advancement and executive staff assignments go through a rigorous review."

"But they have to keep some sort of list of who they'll assign in case of an accident, like when yours happened."

"Yes, and I am now at the top of that list."

"That doesn't exactly reassure me. Whoever was at the top of that list when your accident happened suddenly deployed."

"That sort of thing happens very rarely. In general, unplanned executive staff replacements happen very rarely. I said three months because that timeframe was all I could analyze this morning. It's possible I could sit on that wait list for the next year."

"I'm sorry I'm making this an issue," Elyse said, taking hold of his hand.

"It's an issue for you. I understand. You don't want to sign on to another relationship with long separations."

"No, that wasn't my plan," she agreed.

He grasped her hand and brought it to his lips. "I love you, Elyse. And I don't want this to ruin your birthday. We can talk more about it if you want or we can table it until another time, if you prefer."

"You're here with me today, so my birthday isn't ruined. I love you, too, Jake. We'll work through it when it happens. Until then, you're not deployed, and I'd like us to try and have as normal of a life as possible together."

"I'd like that, too," Jake said.

. . . .

LATER THAT NIGHT, WHEN they snuggled beneath the bedcovers, their kisses and tender strokes declared the love they each felt for the other. They'd enjoyed a full day together. After brunch they did return to the shelter, where Jake played with Frick and Frack while Elyse checked on the electrician and door project. Elyse didn't tell him she'd had Julia take the dogs down from the website. She didn't tell Julia to put them back up either. She wanted to think on it.

As Jake helped Kade with his truck, Elyse's heart warmed from watching the interaction. She observed them through the front window, seated on her living room couch, holding Charlie on her lap. Was she really ready for three dogs? And would it be fair to Charlie to bring the two high-energy dogs into his territory?

Dinner with Kelsey and Ash was enjoyable, the food amazing. Elyse truly enjoyed spending time with all of them. Not only did Ash fit into the family well, but so did Jake. This new, expanded family was comfortable. The six of them even made plans to get together to play cards the next Sunday night Kade was off, and the tattoo shop closed early on Sundays. Now that Jake was back on normal duty, he'd rarely work evenings or overnights. As expected, Claire had declined the invitation.

"Did you have a good birthday?" Jake asked after he'd made love to her.

She smiled at him, his face sharing her pillow and visible in the moonlight that streamed into the room through the sheer curtains on the windows. "I woke this morning feeling off and realized what I was feeling was missing you. I didn't doubt before today that I loved you, but had I, that realization would have convinced me."

"I'm sorry I had to work overnight. I wanted to be here with you when you woke."

"I know you did, and it's okay. I don't mean to sound whiney. Honestly, today was the best birthday I've had in many years because I spent it with you. Dinner with Kade and Mel and Kelsey and Ash made it special, too. I wish Claire and the kids had come. That's the only thing that would have made it better, but we'll see them Saturday night." When Claire had declined the dinner invitation, she then set up a dinner date with them for Saturday evening.

"Thank you for saying that spending your birthday with me made it a good day. And I am sorry I got my medical clearance today of all days."

She pressed her finger against his lips to hush him. "No apology needed. We'll work through whatever comes with your career."

"I've hesitated to say this, as I didn't want to sound insensitive, Elyse. But I'm not Tim. I promise you I won't handle any separations the same way he did. I will never let the passion between us die. I will never let you think that you are not the most important thing in the world to me."

Elyse replied by covering his lips with hers.

Chapter 38 – The Boys Come Home

The next weekend was the open house and grand opening event at Animal House Shelter. Ninety-five percent of the work on the to-do list had been completed by the contractors. Many of them reduced their normal hourly rates to conduct the work in exchange for tax deductible receipts for their donations.

Elyse had put in a lot of hours every day at the building since closing on it. It had slowly taken shape into her vision, right down to the color the newly constructed walls were painted. Julia and Trevor had been constant fixtures at the shelter as well, not only tending the dogs once they were moved in but painting, building runs, and unpacking boxes, basically anything that needed doing.

On the day of the event, Elyse and Jake arrived several hours before the doors would open to the public to find several dozen volunteers had beat them in. Directing their activities, Julia coordinated the chaos masterfully. Elyse was beyond grateful.

"You pulled this off, El; today is your day to shine, not to work your ass off," Julia said. She smiled as she hugged her friend. "I may have taken the liberty to call the volunteers in to make your day just a little easier."

"Oh, Julia, thank you. I don't know what I'd do without you," Elyse said, returning her embrace.

The foster parents arrived with the dogs in their care a half-hour before the doors opened. There were special pens for them, as many of them did not do well in groups with other dogs. While directing where a few should go, Julia pulled Elyse aside.

"Hey, just a reminder, Frick and Frack are still off the website. If Jake isn't going to take them, do you want me to reactivate them?" Julia asked.

Elyse looked down the row of pens to theirs. Jake was in with them. "He loves those dogs."

"But it would basically be you taking them on if he adopts them," Julia said.

"Yes," Elyse said. "I can't decide yet."

Julia watched Jake play with the two wild-men. "They're still such high-energy dogs. If they get adopted, I doubt it would be together. It'll take someone special to take them both. Double trouble," she said with a laugh.

"And they've been together their whole lives. It would be cruel to separate them at this point," Elyse agreed. "Let's put a sign on their pen that says 'adoption pending' and to enquire with staff about a waitlist. I'll decide within the next week."

As soon as all the volunteers and foster parents were there, Elyse conducted a short meeting. She began by handing out champagne in plastic flutes. "We did it!" Elyse said, holding her glass in the air. "Animal House Shelter is about to open its new public facility because of the work we have all done. I appreciate you and your efforts more than you will ever know. We will be open seven days a week and be able to house triple the number of dogs we did at the old facility." She turned to Jake. "And of course, none of this would have been possible without your generosity of buying this facility for us, Jake, so thank you."

Jake raised his glass high. "Cheers to Elyse and Animal House!" After he took a sip, he leaned in and kissed Elyse's lips. "Congratulations, Elyse. You did it."

"We did it," she replied.

The day was a success. They had invited all the families who had ever adopted a dog from Animal House and everyone who attended the gala the last two years. They invited all of their donors and put notices out to the general population. Several local radio stations ran ads regarding the grand opening.

Hundreds of people attended the event over the four-hour open house. A donation box on the main counter was full by the end of the event. Twenty dogs were adopted. All of the Laramie family dropped by. Claire even brought the kids, much to Elyse's surprise. Since she and Jake were going to Claire's for dinner that night, a belated birthday get together, she had not thought that Claire would come. Aiden and Emma had a great time and even begged their mom for a dog.

"How about this," Claire said. "Instead of us bringing one home, we can come play with the dogs here and help Grandma with her shelter one day every other week."

Not knowing that only equated to two days a month, Aiden and Emma cheered with excitement.

After the foster parents left to bring home their charges that weren't adopted, Jake made another trip back into the kennel area to say goodbye to Frick and Frack. He came back to the reception desk, where Elyse was talking to the last of the volunteers who were there, including Miles Maitland, who had just arrived and would stay overnight with the dogs.

"Elyse?" Jake asked, holding the sign that had been on their pen in his hand. "Adoption pending? Who's taking them? And why didn't I get introduced to whoever wants them? I should have. I hope it's one family taking them both."

"Jake, no one will ever love those two dogs as much as you do. They're your dogs," Elyse said, making the decision in that moment.

"We're taking them home?" he asked, his shock apparent by the expression on his face.

"I propose we do so slowly, for Charlie's sake. We can treat Animal House like a doggy daycare for them. When you're working, if I can't be at home with them or if I'm here, we'll bring them here to play like they're used to. At night, if we aren't going to be home, like tonight, they can hang out in the office with Miles, like Charlie does sometimes." Her gaze shifted to Miles. "That's okay with you, isn't it?"

"Yes, it's fine, ma'am. I often work with them while I'm here and I often bring one or two of the dogs up here to hang out with me overnight."

"Thank you, Miles," Elyse said.

Jake wrapped her in an embrace. "Thank you, Elyse. I would have been heartbroken if someone adopted them, even though I know it would have been good for them."

"I know. I took them down from the website a few days ago, when you weren't sure if you were going to be given that medical separation."

"Miles, we need to work on potty training them. They're used to just going in the pen or the play area. Can you start with that tonight and tomorrow morning, please?" Elyse asked.

"They never go to the bathroom when they're in the office with me. But I'll work on teaching them to notify me when they have to go out," he replied. "I think you'll be surprised how smart those two are."

• • • •

DINNER THAT EVENING at Claire's was at five-thirty. Elyse and Jake drove straight there from the shelter. That was another benefit of Kade and Mel living at the house. Someone was usually home to feed Charlie and let him out. Elyse hoped she'd made the right decision about Frick and Frack. She didn't want to upend Charlie's world. The chaos of the shelter had been too much for him. That was why she'd taken him to begin with. If Frick and Frack could calm down, all should be fine. And she knew that Jake would play with them and work with them daily.

They were surprised when they arrived at Claire's house to learn that she and Matthew had made dinner reservations out. Elyse thought they were eating there. She was happy, though, that the reservations were at her favorite pizza place and Claire was bringing the kids.

"We could have met you guys at the restaurant," Elyse said.

"We wanted to give you your birthday gift here," Claire said. "The kids helped to make it and they're very excited. We were going to bring it today to Animal House, but when I found out how busy it would be, I didn't want to risk it getting ruined."

Elyse was curious as Claire and the kids left the room to go get it.

"And we thought we could have a drink before we went," Matthew said. He already had a highball glass in his hand, drinking what Elyse assumed to be rum and Coke.

Claire had a glass of red wine in her hand when they arrived. Both Elyse and Jake accepted a glass of red wine from Matthew while Claire and the kids were gone.

They came back into the room with a sign that had to be five feet long by three feet wide. It read "Animal House Shelter Rocks' written in bright colors. Pictures of dogs framed it along with handprints in many different colors, hands that Elyse recognized as Aiden and Emma's.

"Oh, my goodness," Elyse exclaimed. "It's perfect! And I love it!"

"Those are our hands, Grandma," Aiden said, placing one of his hands over one of the prints. Emma followed suit.

Elyse gave them both hugs. "That makes it even more special to me!"

"Julia helped me get the pictures from your website. They're the dogs you have now and those you adopted out over the last year."

Upon closer inspection, Elyse and Jake saw Charlie and both Frick and Frack among the many familiar faces on the sign. Elyse gave another round of hugs. "Thank you for this amazing gift. It means so much to me, and I will always treasure it because you guys made it for me."

The gift set an amazing tone for dinner. It was one of the best times spent with Claire and her family that Elyse could remember. Although Matthew drank more rum and

Cokes than Elyse had ever seen him drink, he was more relaxed than usual, too. Thankfully, Claire drove when they'd finished the meal and said goodnight.

• • • •

ON SUNDAY, ELYSE AND Jake worked at the shelter for a few hours in the morning. After putting the sign up that Claire and the kids made in a prominent place in the main office, Elyse worked on administrative tasks. Jake worked with Frick and Frack, determined to tire them out before they would bring them home. Miles reported that they'd been good all night in the office with him.

After a bath for each of them, they slipped on the boys' new blue collars with bone-shaped nametags, complete with Elyse's address and Jake's and her cell phone numbers, and they hooked the boys to their new blue leashes. They loaded them into the backseat of the car.

"What do you think of us fencing in an area of the backyard or maybe out by the barn so we can take them off leash and let them run?" Jake asked as he turned onto Route 58, the car pointed towards Franklin. "It'll help tire them out every day and we won't have to worry about them running off."

"I think it's a great idea," she said. "We'll figure out where this afternoon." They were both hopping side to side in the car, alternating sticking their heads out of both of the windows. "Even though you played with them for two hours, they still have way too much energy. I think a nice long walk this afternoon will be in order."

"Aw, they're just excited. I bet you they'll crash hard after we get back to your house."

She doubted that. "Can I ask you a favor?"

"Of course, Elyse. Anything."

"Can you stop thinking of it as my house? You're living there. I'd really like of you to think of it as home if you can."

He took hold of her hand and raised it to his lips. "I already do, Elyse. But I didn't want to sound presumptuous."

"Presume away. Remember, you bought me an engagement warehouse and I'm holding you to it."

Jake beamed a smile at her. "As far as I'm concerned, a ceremony will be a formality. I couldn't be more attached or committed to you, Elyse Laramie. My dogs and I are excited to be going home today."

Chapter 39 – Halloween Tricks or Treats

"Hi, Mom," Claire's voice came through the speaker on Elyse's phone. "What are you doing?"

"I'm at Animal House, making a batch of dog food. What are you doing?" It was odd for Claire to call her on a Tuesday in the early afternoon.

"I'm at work. I'm waiting for Tara to get my reservations made for my next trip."

"When is that?" Elyse asked. It was October thirtieth. Halloween was the next day. Elyse hoped Claire would not miss Halloween and her kids' opportunity to go trick-or-treating. Sure, she could have the nanny take the kids, but those are memories that Claire and her children would never get back.

"I hope on Thursday morning. I told Tara I don't want to go tomorrow. There's trick-or-treating at the church tomorrow afternoon. I want to take the kids. That's why I'm calling, to see if you would like to come with."

Elyse's heart squeezed in her chest. "Oh, Claire, that would be wonderful. Thank you for calling. I would love to come with."

"Great. I was thinking we could take the kids out for dinner after. They'll have a lot of fun going in their costumes."

"Is Matthew coming as well?" Elyse asked, already suspecting she knew the answer.

"Tomorrow is Wednesday, Topgolf night. Of course he isn't. He made a commitment joining that league," she said sarcastically.

"I'm sorry to hear that," Elyse said.

"You and me both," Claire said. "Mom, he asked for a little space to work through things, which I've given him. But..." Her voice trailed off.

"I get it," Elyse said. "I can stay after the kids are in bed tomorrow night, if you want to talk."

"Yes, maybe," Claire answered. "At what point do I tell him, shit, that's a call I need to take. I have to go. Be at my house at four tomorrow." Then Claire disconnected to switch over to the business call coming in.

Elbows deep in shredded sweet potatoes and ground meats with chunked apples and bananas, Elyse wondered what Claire's next words would have been. Tell him what? She was thrilled, though, that Halloween and trick-or-treating with the kids was important to Claire.

Over dinner at the microbrewery around the corner from the shelter, where they'd eaten their first meal together, she told Jake about her conversation with Claire. It was incredible to have someone to talk with about, well, just about everything. "I'm really encouraged by the changes I've seen in her," she told Jake. "You know, when Kade said not long ago that Claire is just like her father, he wasn't exaggerating. But for her to let the kids stay up past their rigid bedtime for Kelsey and Ash's wedding, and now her inviting me to come for trick-or-treating with her kids, which she'll have to leave work early for, shows a flexibility I haven't seen much in her."

"I'm glad to hear that," Jake said. "Obviously, I know nothing about raising children, but I would think you have to be flexible. Rigid rules and kids just don't seem to mix."

"They don't," Elyse agreed. "So I'll be late tomorrow night getting home. After trick-or-treating we're going to bring the kids out to dinner, and I told Claire I'd stay after the kids are in bed if she wants to talk."

"I hope she does," Jake agreed. "I just can't understand her husband. He has a beautiful wife and two beautiful, healthy kids and, from what you've said, he wants little to do with them. Do you think he's having an affair?"

Elyse's stomach dropped. "I've been trying to not think that."

"Does Claire suspect he may?"

"She hasn't said anything. I'm sure she's trying not to think it either," Elyse said. She took a drink of her wine. "I'm just really angry, that whatever his issue is, he doesn't seem to care about the important things with his kids. They're getting old enough now to notice that their dad isn't present for so many things."

Jake took hold of her hand. "How did your kids handle that?"

Elyse rubbed her forehead with her free hand. "I hate that it's being repeated with my grandchildren. I'm just glad their mom finally woke up to what's important. I hate that their father is still oblivious."

"Elyse, I think you should tell Claire to put her foot down, if that is what she's thinking of doing. I know you regret letting things be as they were."

"Yes, I regret a lot and I'm angry with myself for a lot, too. I don't want Claire to have to wrestle with those feelings at any point in her life."

"You need to forgive yourself and let that anger go. It's not serving any purpose," Jake said.

She squeezed his hand. "I know, and I'm really trying to.

· · · ·

ON HALLOWEEN AFTERNOON, Elyse put her car in park in Claire's driveway in front of the far garage bay where no car was kept. The one thing she noticed as she'd driven into the subdivision was very few houses were decorated on the outside for Halloween. It was three-thirty on Halloween and there were no kids in sight. Maybe they didn't trick-or-treat in this neighborhood. The houses were quite far apart, as were they in her own neighborhood. Her kids only trick-or-treated to a few neighbors when they were young. And after, she'd drive them to a friend's house in a subdivision where the houses were closer together and there were more of them. The group of four or five moms would take their kids in one large group out to trick-or-treat. Elyse had fond memories of it.

Claire opened the door as she approached. Both kids ran out in costume. Aiden was dressed up as Woody from the movie *Toy Story* and Claire had Emma dressed as Jessie, Woody's cowgirl sidekick.

"Oh, my, it's Woody and Jessie!" Elyse exclaimed. "Does Andy know you're here?"

Aiden lifted his cowboy hat from his head. "No, Grandma! It's Aiden." He took Emma's hat off, too. "And Emma."

"Oh, wow, I wouldn't have known." She smiled at Claire.

They drove to the church together in Claire's car. Elyse hadn't been there in several months. Claire put the car in park in front of the main entrance into the church. The lot had to have several hundred cars in it. Only then did Elyse get a sense of how big an event this was.

Inside the church, the lobby area and hallway leading towards the food court was packed with hundreds of families. Elyse could see that not only the outreach booths were manned with people giving out candy, but other little stations were set up along the way, many with families including children in their costumes giving out candy. It was noisy and chaotic, and everyone appeared to be having a good time.

Annie Edison and Eddie Brown were at the booth for the Widow and Widower Support Group. They were both in costume as were many who handed out candy. "Hello, Annie, or should I say Missus Potato Head! It is great to see you!" Elyse greeted.

"Hello, Elyse," Annie said, giving her a hug. "And who do we have here? Oh, it's Woody and Jessie!" She gave both the kids a hug as well.

"Hello, Elyse," Eddie said. He was dressed as a pirate with the eye patch and even a stuffed bird on his shoulder. "It's great to see you. We've missed you at our meetings."

"Hi, Eddie, thanks. I've missed all of you. I'm sure as we get closer to the holidays, I'll pop back in. I've been swamped with getting the new public location for Animal House up and running."

Eddie smiled and shook his head. "I still can't believe Jake's generosity, buying that warehouse for Animal House. That was quite a night!"

Elyse chuckled with him. "Yes, it was. It earned him a spot on the board of directors for AHS."

"Make sure you keep me in mind for next year's gala. I'd love to provide the entertainment again."

"Thank you, Eddie," she said. "If you want the job, it's yours."

"Great, yes, put me down."

He and Annie then made a big show of doling out candy to the two kids. Everyone at all the booths was great, handing out candy, showering attention on the kids. They all appeared to be having a great time. The kids were worn out before they'd made it to the food court area where even more people were stationed to give out candy.

"This was so much better than going house to house trick-or-treating with the little ones," Elyse told Claire as they left the church a few hours later. "It was so much fun!"

"Yes, that's one of the many reasons I love this church. It's a community. I feel safe bringing the kids here for trick-or-treat." With the kids buckled into their car seats, Claire pulled out of the lot.

"I remember taking you kids to a few neighbors and then we drove into that one subdivision where the houses were close together. Your friend Molly lived there."

"Yes, I remember the fun of that whole big group going out trick-or-treating together," Claire said.

"I miss certain things like that from your childhood years. Thank you for inviting me to come today. It was fun for me and brought back great memories from when you three were all at home."

"I can't even imagine them grown and gone," Claire admitted.

"It happens faster than you'd ever guess," Elyse said. "One minute they're strapped into car seats. The next they're driving. And before you know it, they've graduated from college. I know you've heard it before, but don't blink. The time really goes so fast."

"I can't believe that next year Aiden will be in kindergarten," Claire said.

They arrived at the little diner in a strip mall just down the street from Claire's house. It was a family-friendly place with a fifty's theme. The owner was a grandmotherly woman who was always there. They walked in and she made a big fuss over the kids in their costumes.

The food was always good. Tonight's special was meatloaf with mashed potatoes. They had a large children's menu. Claire ordered chicken strips and fries for the kids. "I would get them something healthier, but I just want them to eat tonight, and I want peace at the table." She dropped her voice and leaned to whisper in her mom's ear. "We've all of a sudden started having these stupid food battles at mealtime."

"Sometimes it's just not worth it," Elyse agreed

It was a fun dinner and the kids enjoyed eating out. Elyse got the impression it was something they didn't do often. She knew that Claire and Matthew went out often. She could understand that it was more work and could be less enjoyable to bring the kids, but they had to be brought out and taught how to behave in a restaurant.

After they returned home, Claire let the kids each pick one piece of candy as their dessert. And then it was right up to bed, on time. And here Elyse had thought that Claire had lightened up some, as she'd kept them up past bedtime for Kelsey and Ash's wedding.

Then Claire poured two glasses of wine and invited her mom to sit with her on the living room couch. "I'm glad they had such a good time today," she said.

"I've been thinking about our conversation yesterday, about Matthew," Elyse said. "Did you even remind him today was Halloween and invite him to come?"

Claire shrugged. "No. He has a calendar. He knows what the date is."

"One of my biggest mistakes with your father was not speaking up about what I wanted from him, or what I expected from him as a father and a husband for that matter. I did what I did to provide a good home for you, Kade, and Kelsey. In the moment you don't realize you're setting a precedent, but you are."

"Why would I think he'd want to come, Mom? He bitches about coming to church once a month or on holidays. He doesn't want to spend time with the kids. He loathes dinners with them because someone melts down, cries, and moans they don't want to eat their green beans or one of them spills their plates, and that drives him crazy." She rubbed her temples and then took a drink of her wine.

"Do the kids know he feels this way?" Elyse asked.

"I think they're oblivious to it. They're kids."

"How does this resolve, Claire?"

"I wish I knew. He's asked I give him space to work through his issues, or whatever it is he's needed to work through. I have, but I'm coming to an end of my patience. We have three meals a week as a family, and I can tell he would rather be anywhere but our kitchen table. He has spent two hours a week with each of the kids alone since I laid out that expectation, so I have voiced my expectations of him."

Claire's voice sounded defensive. "If he's acting pissy when he's doing it, that's worse than not doing it," Elyse said.

"Pissy?" Claire laughed. "Mom, did you really just say pissy?"

Elyse laughed. She shrugged. "I guess I did."

Claire laughed again. "Is it Jake, or Kade moving home that's had the bad influence on you and your language?"

Elyse smiled. "I'm going to go with Kade. Though I really like having him and Mel living at the house. I wish you'd come over more with the kids, with or without Matthew. Kelsey and Ash are over about once a week and it's nice, like on my birthday."

"Mom, that was a weeknight. That's so hard for me. Franklin is an hour's drive each way."

"I understand, sweetie," Elyse said. "But maybe on the rare occasion for something special. You have good kids that are on a good schedule, which should allow for occasions off that schedule. That won't mess them up too much."

"I know. It's just a lot on me. I'm practically doing this alone."

Elyse was stunned by that statement. She had a full-time, live-in nanny as well as a weekly housekeeper. Surely, she didn't believe that she was doing it alone. "I know it's hard when your husband is not involved. Can you lean more heavily on Lizette, maybe switch around her hours to give you support when you're not getting it from Matthew?"

Claire sighed. "She has the boyfriend, remember? I've already had to rearrange her schedule to give her more time in the evenings and weekends off. I'd hate to think I'm going to have to hire a second, part-time nanny."

Elyse was having a hard time keeping herself from replying to that in the way that she wanted to. She made a show of looking thoughtful for a moment. "How many weekday evenings is Lizette off?"

"If I'm not traveling for work, three. And that includes Sunday evening. That's more than half the week!"

"And if she's off in the evening, what time is she here by the next morning?"

"Seven. I wanted her here by six-thirty, but she said seven is the best she can do."

Elyse nodded. "But if you're traveling for work, she's here the entire time?"

"Yes," Claire answered.

"I think that's more than fair. Especially because she's flexible and will cover a twenty-four-hour period whenever you're traveling; plus, will work any weekend you need her when you and Matthew have plans."

"And the kids are comfortable with her. That's what's stopped me from replacing her entirely."

"Yes, their comfort with her is very important," Elyse agreed, hoping to drive the point home. With all that Lizette did to help them, she couldn't believe that Claire had even entertained the idea of replacing her. "I think you should look at this time as temporary. As you said, Aiden will be in kindergarten next year and you'll probably bump Emma up to the three day a week preschool program, won't you?"

"Yes, but I don't see why that's relevant."

"Every phase that comes with your kids' ages is temporary and ever-changing, Claire. And so, the help and supervision you need with each age and phase your kids will go through will be ever changing as well. The help you need now contrasted with the help you'll need when both the kids are in school full-time will be vastly different. And them both being in school full-time is not that far away."

"I still have to get through the next year, Mom. And the next few months and holidays are going to be difficult with Matthew not wanting to spend time with us as he works through whatever his issues are."

Elyse noted she was getting agitated. "You said on the phone yesterday something to the effect of when do you put your foot down. I wish I had earlier, but it could have led to divorce. But that was your father and me. We didn't talk, Claire. In your father's note to me, he even said he avoided talking about anything, even acknowledging how much I did alone for fear that I would demand he be more involved or change. Do you and Matthew talk, or I guess I should ask, can you talk and share how you each feel, compromise, and come to agreements?"

"About some things," Claire said. "Matthew doesn't fight, just like Dad. His favorite tactic is to say let's let this rest for now. But we never get back to it. Let it rest is the same as not talk about it."

"What you want matters, too, sweetie. I let things rest when I shouldn't have, and I have regrets because I did. From what you've said, a lot of what bothers Matthew will resolve when the kids get older. It sounds to me like he needs some coping strategies to get through and maybe even a reality check as far as what behaviors are perfectly normal in kids. If he won't go see a counselor himself, maybe you could go on his behalf and pass the info along to him. I'd be willing to come and stay with the kids if it's at a time Lizette can't be here. Kelsey would help you, too. You know, you have family that's willing to help you if you ask."

"Thanks, Mom," Claire said.

"You're welcome. Think about the counseling," Elyse repeated, knowing it would help Claire greatly.

November
Chapter 40 – Give Thanks

Thanksgiving was a day that Tim always made it home for. Even if he was working an active jobsite, he would fly home the day before and stay for at least a few days when Elyse reminded him what day the holiday was. Thanksgiving and Christmas were the two days out of the year that everyone in the family had an emotional attachment to that involved Tim. Elyse was conscious of this. So, when Jake told her he had duty until four that afternoon and would make it just in time for dinner, she was relieved. He of course was invited, and Elyse had a conversation with each of her kids about his presence.

The Laramie clan always gathered by noon, ate munchies, and watched football. Dinner was always during the half-time of the second game that started at four-thirty, and then everyone except for Kelsey left to go home when the second game was over so they would be home to watch the third game that started at eight-twenty. Kelsey always spent the night at home. This year and all going forward would be different.

Claire's in-laws were rarely in the United States. If they were, she and Matthew would spend the holiday with the Laramie's and then see his parents on Friday or at some point that weekend, which often involved flying to whatever city they'd be in. Claire advised Elyse early in the month that they would be there for dinner with the family like usual.

Claire also conveyed how heavy her heart was with the approach of the holiday. The holiday would just not be the same without her dad home.

Kade could always get off from work on Thanksgiving if he volunteered for Wednesday overnight and on the Friday after. The night before Thanksgiving was one of the busiest nights of the year. News to Elyse, but that Wednesday, also known as Thanksgiving Eve or Blackout Wednesday, was one of the biggest drinking and going out nights of the year. With a spike in alcohol sales, there was naturally a spike in EMS calls.

Kelsey, of course, never had a scheduling conflict for the holidays. And Elyse was glad that her marriage to Ash wouldn't change this. Ash usually got together with his cousins, who lived in the area and had attended the wedding, on the Sunday following Thanksgiving. So Thanksgiving Day would continue with the Laramie tradition that Ash would now be a part of.

Elyse was sad for Ash that he hadn't spoken with his father since his mom died, not even on the holidays. Kelsey had shared with Elyse Ash's issues with his dad to explain why he no longer talked to him. Ash was angry with how his dad had handled his mother's terminal cancer, which was basically leaving her in a hospice facility to die alone while he climbed into a bottle and hid. He didn't even call his sons to tell them their mother was near death. Ash was denied the last moments with his mother to say goodbye. That was something he would never forgive his father for.

Elyse found it heartbreaking that all three of her children's significant others were so estranged from their families. She had to wonder if it was really that prevalent in modern culture that families were so fractured. In Mel's case, her parents' divorce and subsequent serial relationships displayed her parents' selfishness, putting themselves and their new partners ahead of their children. Elyse didn't blame Mel for keeping a distance between herself and the family situation that only brought her bad feelings.

Mel was surprised early in the month on Kade's birthday, the fuss Elyse went to acknowledge it. While her kids slept, Elyse had always decorated the house with balloons, streamers and banners announcing their birthdays each year. She did the same that year for Kade. He had a good laugh that she did, and Elyse knew he appreciated it. Mel's birthday was in May. She'd do the same for her.

Elyse was happy she would be Mel's mother-in-law and give her the attention and acceptance she deserved but didn't get from her own mother. She began that morning by inviting Mel to help prepare the many munchies that would be out for them to enjoy during the first game. Kade had gotten home at five and joined her in bed. It was now ten o'clock. Kade still slept, but Mel had ventured down for coffee and breakfast. Mel had never joined them, as she normally worked Thanksgiving Day every year.

"I am so glad you are here this year and I know Kade is, too," Elyse said to her. "And next year with the two new babies, the holidays will be so much fun." Elyse handed her the cutting board and the vegetables to make the veggie tray.

"I can't believe we're going to have a ten-month-old baby next November," Mel said.

"You'll be surprised how fast the time flies after you're a parent. And you and Kade are going to be phenomenal parents."

"Why do you think that?" Mel asked as she began to chop carrots.

"You're both paramedics. By the very nature of your job, you can handle stress and chaos and are used to juggling schedules, not to mention the lack of sleep. And you're both caring and compassionate. You wouldn't be in your chosen profession if you weren't. Those are all qualities that make a person a great parent. Oh, and you have me." She flashed Mel a smile. "A grandma who is excited to help in any way I can."

"You've already done so much, Elyse. You know, I really admire you. Even though your children are adults, you still are a concerned and involved mother."

"Do you think that's a bad thing?" Elyse asked.

"No, I didn't mean to phrase it like it was. A lot of our friends at work who have children have families that help with their kids. I always assumed that was when their moms got back involved in their lives. I assumed they weren't before then. I never had that kind of mom, not my own or my stepmothers who I would ever ask or would help even in an emergency. It's just the way it is. I've pretty much been fending for myself since I was fourteen. I guess before I met Kade I didn't think most families were that tight."

"Some are, some aren't," Elyse said. "I happen to like who my children are, and I like to spend time with them. I also think family bonds are important, no matter how old a person is. My mom worked full-time when the kids were young, so she couldn't help me too much. And then when my dad retired, they moved to Arizona. I always knew I wanted to be different, more involved and able to help my kids when they needed it. I think distance is a major reason for families not staying tight. Life is busy and people usually get focused on their own little family, often letting the relationships with extended family deteriorate."

"Or in my parents' case, they focused on the new love in their life rather than their kids. I haven't even met my child yet, but I can't imagine that he or she wouldn't be the most important person in my life until they were grown and out of the house."

Elyse was glad to hear her say this. "Yes, I will admit I don't understand it."

"Did you help Claire before she got the nanny?"

"Claire had already decided on nannies when she was pregnant with Aiden. She didn't ask me to help her much. I would have helped her more, but I wouldn't intrude either. I may not agree with all her choices, but I respect that she's an adult and free to make them."

Mel laughed. "Yeah, Kade doesn't agree with many of her choices either."

Elyse laughed, too. "With him and Claire only being two years apart, you'd assume they would be closest. Kelsey is eight years younger than Kade, and the two of them have always been much closer. He was the sweetest older brother to her when they were kids. When Kelsey was four, Claire was fourteen and couldn't be bothered with her little sister. But at twelve, Kade looked after her and took care of her. The divide was even worse by the time Claire was sixteen, but

Kade and Kelsey were really close. I remember how hard it was on Kelsey when Kade moved out of the house."

"Yes, he's always felt protective of her," Mel seconded. "Honestly, I'm glad that she and Ash hit it off. I don't think Kade would have accepted any other guy marrying her. He loathed that last guy she dated and when Kelsey told him he had cheated on her I think Kade wanted to go have a word or two with him."

"I'm glad he didn't," Elyse said.

They finished getting the food ready and Mel went upstairs to wake Kade before Kelsey and Ash arrived. Jake had brought Frick and Frack to Animal House on his way to work that morning. They would stay the night there. They were settling in, but Elyse knew with all the family and the food that would be out, it would be too chaotic to have them there. At noon, they all settled in front of the family room television to watch the first game and eat the game-time munchies Elyse and Mel prepared.

With the game on in the family room, no one heard the front door open. It wasn't until Aiden came running in that anyone realized they had arrived. It was twelve-thirty. When Claire's family hadn't arrived at noon, Elyse silently wondered if they were coming.

"Some watchdog you are," Elyse said to Charlie, setting him back onto the couch cushion after she'd stood. She greeted Aiden, who then went and got hugs from his uncles and aunts. Elyse met Claire, who carried Emma, in the kitchen. "Happy Thanksgiving!"

"Happy Thanksgiving, Mom," Claire said, followed by Emma's attempt. Normally her speech was well vocalized, but she had a hard time getting the long word out. "Go to Grandma, sweetie," Claire said, angling Emma towards her. "I have to make a trip back out to the car to get the desserts."

Elyse looked back towards the front door. "Isn't Matthew with you?"

Claire forced a smile. "No, he actually flew to JFK this morning to meet his parents. They flew in from Turkey and have a five-hour layover before their connection to, I don't even remember where. Seattle, I think it was."

"What are they going to Seattle for?" Elyse asked.

"I have no idea," Claire replied, shrugging. "I'm sure his parents are going to be disappointed the kids and I didn't go along, but that was just too much to ask, and I told Matthew I wasn't going to drag the kids through two airports just to have lunch with his parents."

"Yes, I think that is an unrealistic expectation," Elyse agreed.

"Daddy left with his suitcase," Emma said.

"And it's not like they ever make an effort. It's always, here is where we'll be. Can you come meet us. I don't understand why they couldn't plan their trip to swing through Norfolk to come see us on their way to Seattle."

Elyse nodded. She agreed. Matthew's parents were extremely self-centered. They probably didn't even realize it was Thanksgiving. "I'm glad you and the kids are here. Is Matthew staying over in New York?"

"No, why would you think that?" Claire said.

"Emma just said he left with his suitcase," Elyse said.

Kelsey came into the kitchen. "Hi, Happy Thanksgiving." She gave Emma a hug and took her from Elyse's arms.

"Kels," Elyse said with a head nod back towards the family room. Once Kelsey and Emma were out of the kitchen, she turned back to Claire. "What's going on, Claire? Why did Matthew leave the house with a suitcase?"

Claire's stomach did flip flops. She hadn't planned to tell her mom or anyone else. Damn Emma! "Well, you know we've been fighting a lot and Matthew asked for space. I'm giving it to him, and we're taking a bit of a pause."

"A pause?" Elyse repeated. "It's called being separated, Claire."

"It's not like he moved completely out. He just took one suitcase and is going to stay at one of those Extended Stay places for a couple weeks. He'll still come by the house a few times a week to see the kids. I told him he has to spend at least half a day alone with each of the kids and a half a day a week with them both."

"Claire, he just left today? On Thanksgiving? On a holiday?"

Claire nodded, fighting to keep her composure. "He says he doesn't want a divorce. Him taking a pause was my idea. He actually expected the kids and me to fly to New York with him and was shocked when I said no. I'm really just sick of all the fighting."

"Are you going to marriage counseling?"

"No, Matthew won't commit to that."

"Then you need to go without him."

Claire shrugged. "I haven't really thought it through. When I told him to take a few weeks away, I thought he'd argue. He didn't. He just said he's tired of fighting, too."

Elyse wrapped her in a hug, the only thing she could think to do. She was so sad for Claire and the kids. "I'm so sorry, sweetie. Let me know if there is anything I can do."

"Just don't say anything to anyone. I don't want the kids to know. They won't understand."

"No, they won't," Elyse agreed. "Your kids are so young, Claire. I really hope this time away makes Matthew realize what he has. I really do think you need to keep trying to get him to go to counseling. If you two don't talk, you're never going to resolve anything."

"Resolving things isn't anything he's familiar with. For him, it's better we just let it lie and hope it will go away."

"And for you?" Elyse asked.

"I just can't do this anymore. That's why I asked him to stay someplace else for a few weeks." She blew out a loud breath. "But enough of that. I don't want to talk about it. This is a hard enough day for me, a Thanksgiving without Dad. I've been thinking about him all morning."

"I think we all have, sweetie," Elyse said. "Today and Christmas were the only two days of the year that we knew he'd be home."

"He didn't care about the football game like the rest of us, but he sure liked your turkey," Claire said.

"Turkey, stuffing, and all the trimmings was his favorite meal," Elyse said. "Speaking of football, we have the game on." She pointed to the kitchen table, set up as the buffet.

"And we have all our favorites out. I'll make plates for the kids. Do you need help with the desserts?"

"No, I'm good. Thanks, Mom."

· · · ·

AT DINNER, PER THEIR family tradition, after a dinner blessing, they went around the table, each of them reciting what they were thankful for. Elyse started as she'd said the blessing. "I'm thankful for all of you. This has been a rough year. But we've faced it together. I'm thankful for the new people in our lives, Jake and Ash, and the two new family members we'll meet in the next few months. I'm thankful I've been able to spend so much time with Aiden and Emma," she said, shifting her gaze and smiling at them as she spoke. Then her gaze swept to Jake. "And I am very thankful that, because of you, Animal House has a new home. We've tripled the number of dogs we can house, and with it open to the public we have had multiple adoptions every single day."

Kade sat to her right. They always went clockwise. "I'm thankful to Mom for welcoming Mel and me home. There is something comforting about being home. I'm thankful that Mel and I will be welcoming our child in a few weeks, and I'm thankful to Kelsey and Ash, as well as Mom, that they'll help with the baby." His focus went across the table to where Claire and the kids sat. "I'm thankful for family and that we are all together today."

Mel looked uncomfortable that it was her turn. "I am so incredibly thankful to Kade, my rock. I'm thankful for this family that I have been welcomed into, and for you, Elyse, who made it possible for me to go to the paramedic training and have our baby."

Kelsey sat beside her. "I am so thankful for my family, for every member of this family seated at this table today." She smiled at Jake as she spoke, to communicate that she included him in that family. "I know thoughts of Dad are with us today. I'm thankful how we've come together over this past year to get through losing him," she said as her gaze went to Claire. "I feel in the last few years our family drifted a bit apart. If anything good came out of losing Dad, it's that we've spent more time together the last six months than we have the last two years."

All eyes went to Ash. "I'm thankful for this family, too, and for having been welcomed into it. I'm most thankful for Kelsey and our baby." They'd been holding hands under the table. He lifted her hand and kissed her knuckles.

"Aiden, it's your turn," Claire said.

Aiden held up his duck stuffed animal. "I'm thankful for Mister Quack, my mommy, and my daddy."

"Thankful my," Emma started and then stopped, not knowing what to say.

Claire leaned down, her lips to Emma's ear. "For your family, sweetheart."

"My family," Emma echoed. Everyone at the table smiled or chuckled.

Claire knew it was her turn. "I'm thankful this family came together and supported each other when Dad died. As Kelsey said, we've spent more time together in the last six months than we have the last two years. Our family has added a few members and will add a few more when both of the babies arrive. I'm also very thankful that Aiden and Emma will have two new cousins, and I look forward to seeing them all play together, when the babies are old enough to."

Claire's gaze went to Jake, who sat beside her, indicating it was his turn.

"I have so much to be grateful for. First of course, was meeting Elyse. I was extremely lucky that I wasn't injured worse in the accident, but had I not been injured I wouldn't have met her. I am thankful that my injuries did heal, and I was not forced out of the Navy. I'm not quite done with my career yet, and I am thankful that Elyse did not ask me to make a choice. I'm thankful for this new family that has welcomed me at a time that I know has been difficult for you."

"Before everyone digs in," Kelsey said, getting everyone's attention. "Ash and I have an announcement. We are very happy to share that we were at the OB on Monday, and we found out the gender of our baby. We're having a boy!" She smiled, the joy across her entire face.

Ash held up the pictures from the sonogram. "He was in the perfect position that we saw it. There's a stem on the apple!" he announced proudly.

Laughter and congratulations sounded from everyone at the table. Even Aiden and Emma clapped along with the others, not really understanding what they were celebrating. The response would have been the same had it been a girl.

"Have you thought about names yet?" Claire asked. "Are you going to name him after Dad, be it his first or middle name?"

Kelsey and Ash looked at each other. Kelsey was tactful in her reply. "Ash's family has a tradition that Ashley is alternated as first and middle name in their kids. Ashley will be his middle name. We're still discussing first names."

"Timothy Ashley Vincent has a ring to it," Claire said. "Or his middle name, David. David Ashley Vincent. Now that really sounds good."

"Sorry, Claire, not naming him after Evil D," Ash said.

"Who?" Claire asked.

"David Vincent, also known as Evil D. of the band, Morbid Angel."

Claire shrugged and shook her head. She didn't know who that was.

"Morbid Angel is a heavy metal band. David Vincent was the front man of the band for many years," Kade informed her.

"Oh, okay," Claire said. She smiled. "I guess not David Vincent."

"You have a lot of time yet to come up with names," Elyse said.

"But you two only have about six weeks," Claire said, pointing to Kade and Mel. "Are you sharing your possible names?"

Both Mel and Kade smiled. "No, not sharing until after he or she is born," Kade said.

"I don't know how you cannot want to know if it's a boy or a girl," Claire said. "I couldn't wait!"

Mel and Kade both laughed. "Yeah, we want to be surprised. We have a few names picked out and we'll decide when we meet our baby," Kade said.

They lingered and ate. After dinner Jake invited Kade and Ash to clear the table and give Elyse a break in the kitchen. He washed the pans and large dishes in the sink as Kade loaded the dishwasher after Ash had filled plastic storage containers with the leftovers. If this would become a new tradition, Elyse would be elated. Kelsey, too, was happy to be off dish duty as usually it was her mom and she who cleaned up the kitchen.

After dessert, Elyse walked Claire and the kids out after everyone had given them goodbye hugs. After securing the kids in their car seats, Claire turned to her. "Mom, I just don't get it. Jake's not anything like dad was."

"That's the point, Claire. I'm not trying to replace your dad with someone just like him. I'd never be able to. I like Jake for the person he is. And it's okay that he's nothing like your dad. It doesn't mean anything, so don't try to read anything in that isn't there. It simply is that Jake is the person I'm attracted to now."

Claire nodded and smiled. "I was dreading today, no Dad, no Matthew, but it was okay. The family, including Jake, made this a good day for the kids and for me. It's not the same as it was, but it was all right."

Elyse embraced her. This was progress. Maybe, just maybe, Claire was dealing with the loss of her father and working through her grief.

December
Chapter 41 – The Words Fly, But Claire Doesn't

O n the first Wednesday in December, Elyse drove to Norfolk to have dinner with Claire and the kids. Matthew had been out of the house for nearly two weeks. She'd talked with Claire on the phone or via text more in the past two weeks than at any point in the past few years. And not all of the interaction had been initiated by her. She judged that Claire had to be lonely and missing Matthew, given how many times she'd reached out.

They had so far merely told the kids that Daddy was away for work on the days he wasn't there. He came by on Tuesdays and then also on Saturday and Sunday during the day, as required by Claire. She held the threat of divorce over him to come by those three days, otherwise she wasn't sure he would. In the thirteen days since she'd asked him to take a pause, he hadn't asked to come home.

This concerned Elyse, as she knew it would be so much easier for Matthew to not have to deal with the family more than three days a week. He could easily get used to it and opt for the easy path. Claire wouldn't come out and say she missed him. But she did say several times that the kids didn't understand why Daddy was working so much.

When Elyse got to the house, Claire let her in but was on her phone, Bluetooth in her ear. She motioned Elyse in and pointed her towards the toy room. Elyse found her grandkids playing in an uncharacteristically messy playroom. It looked like it had been weeks since the toys were picked up and put away.

After giving the grandkids hugs, she began to sort and pick up some of the toys to help. It wasn't long before Claire came in.

"Mom, you should have Aiden and Emma help with that."

"I just thought I'd get the puzzle pieces put back in their boxes," Elyse said.

"Aiden, help Grandma with that," she directed. "He and his daddy did the puzzles last night but didn't clean up."

"That sounds like fun," Elyse said to Aiden. "But I agree with your mommy. If you get the puzzle pieces out, you should put them away when you're done with them."

"Yes, I will be mentioning that to Daddy," Claire said. "Mom, can you help me in the kitchen for a minute, please?"

Elyse placed the last few pieces of the dinosaur puzzle in its box and then closed the lid and placed it on the shelf where it belonged before joining Claire. "That's promising that Matthew was doing puzzles with Aiden last night."

"Yes. I gave Lizette Tuesday nights off, and while Matthew is here I get two hours to myself after a family dinner." She paused and rolled her eyes at her own statement. "He does bedtime with them and then he leaves. I told Matthew if he couldn't commit to three hours at home every Tuesday for dinner and a few hours with his kids he better find a permanent place to live with bedrooms for the kids, because it wouldn't be here. I took your advice and have rearranged Lizette's hours to help me more as Matthew is not here to help. Right now, she's being very flexible. I gave her all day off today because she'll be here alone with the kids for the next two days. I leave for Seattle for a work trip for a few days early tomorrow. Lizette will be here by five tomorrow morning."

"You're going out of town tomorrow morning?"

"Yes."

"When will you be home?"

"Late Friday night. As you know Aiden's birthday party is Saturday, which is going to suck as I'm sure I'll be tired. My flight home doesn't even land until eleven-thirty Friday night."

Even though Elyse knew that telling Claire her thoughts would anger her, this time it had to be said. She couldn't remain quiet. "Claire, you can't go on this trip." Her voice was unwavering. "Matthew just moved out two weeks ago, and Friday is Aiden's birthday. He's going to feel completely abandoned."

"If we don't tell him it's his birthday, he won't know. His party is on Saturday, and I'll be home late Friday night. It's not that big of a deal."

"Listen to yourself. Yes, his birthday is a big deal, or at least it should be for you. You're a mother, Claire, and whether you like it or not your kids have to come before your career." Did Claire not remember waking up on her birthday to the signs, balloons, and streamers that Elyse had lovingly put up after Claire was in bed? Or had it not meant anything to her?

"Oh, no you don't. Don't try to dump that guilt on me! What I do, I do for my kids, so they'll have a good life. I work hard to provide them with everything they need."

"Really? They need the McMansion and the nanny? They need a ninety-thousand-dollar Escalade? They need a toy room that rivals the toy section of most stores? No, Claire. They need their parents in their lives as caring, attentive, and nurturing role models. They need their parents to spend time with them and make a fuss over things like birthdays. But mostly they just need their parents to spend time with them, especially their mom when their dad has just moved out."

"So, I'm supposed to tell Michael that I'm not going to travel? I'm fighting for my career, Mom. Laramie is on the company letterhead, and I have worked so hard that I should be made a partner. Michael's considering Chris Barton for it. Chris of all people! And he won't even travel more than fifty percent."

"Exactly," Elyse said. "Michael doesn't give a shit about you and your family, just like he didn't give a shit about your father." Elyse could see the shock on Claire's face at her statement. She wasn't sure if it was because she cursed or if it was her declaration of Michael's character. "Did you ever stop to think that Michael's making you jump through hoops for his benefit? He's using your Laramie name with clients, maximizing on your dad's good reputation. I suspect he'll offer you that partnership, regardless of how much you will travel or not. It would cost him a lot to change the company name to Kensington Laramie Barton. You better believe he won't take Laramie out of it. It has name recognition in the industry."

"I don't think Michael is using me, Mom."

"Has he given you a raise since Dad died? More compensation for the travel? Kensington-Laramie had a very large life insurance policy out on your father. And Michael even admitted to me the salaries for the two new associates he hired doesn't even total what your father's salary was. He has the money to properly compensate you for the work and travel you do. But even if you are compensated, Claire, you're a mom. Nothing and no one can replace you with your kids. But if the day Aiden was born holds no meaning to you, maybe you need to re-evaluate your priorities. When was the last time you praised him for building the worst LEGO building ever, or even read him a book? You don't get this time back."

Claire wasn't sure what she was angrier about, her mom's words or the possibility that Michael was using her. "I read him a book every night I tuck him in bed."

"Really? The nights I've been here, I've never seen that," Elyse said. "When asked about his bedtime routine he says Lizette reads him books. Not Mommy or Daddy. But that's, what, three nights a week you tuck him in? Trust me, I get it, Claire. By eight o'clock bedtime you're exhausted. You just want to get the kids in bed. Especially the last two weeks that Matthew hasn't been here."

Claire had tears in her eyes.

Elyse reached out and embraced her. "I get it. I lived it, Claire. It's exhausting. I promise you it won't always be like this. They'll get older and you'll wish for this time back so you can spend time with them, snuggled in bed reading them a book or two. Before long they'll be fighting you about bedtime, lying that they brushed their teeth when you both know they didn't, and slamming the door in your face when you say good night to them because they're mad you're making them go to bed earlier than they think they should."

"My God, I did do those things," Claire said.

"You all did," Elyse said, pulling back to look her daughter in the eye. "I didn't take any of it personally."

Claire straightened and pulled from her mom's embrace. "I believe that mothers can be different. Not all mothers have to be the same. You were the type of mother you chose to be. Please respect the type of mother I need to be. My career is important to me. I cannot give it up, Mom. I provide a good nanny to my kids to be there when I cannot."

"Claire, I'm not asking you to give it up. I'm only asking that you put your children on the same level of importance as your career. Is this job in Seattle so urgent that pushing it off until Monday is going to impact anything?"

Claire felt anger surge through her. She didn't want to admit it, but her mother was right. No, there was no urgency to the Seattle trip. It certainly could wait until next week. It was her internal desire to prove to Michael and Chris Barton that she was dedicated to the firm and its work. That she was partner material.

"A partner is an equal. I guarantee you that Michael will respect you more if you act it rather than acting as a subordinate. Isn't that what Chris Barton did? He spoke up and set his terms."

"Fine, I'll push the trip off until Monday." Her tone of voice was belligerent.

Elyse knew Claire didn't like to be told anything. She'd always been that way. She also knew that Claire hated to be proven wrong. The fact that she backed down and would change her trip, Elyse took as a win. "I think that's best all the way around. You don't want to be exhausted hosting your son's birthday party. I can't believe he's going to be five," she said, changing the subject.

"Me either," Claire agreed. "Can you go back in with the kids and prod them to clean some of the toys up? I'm going to call into the office to push my trip off until Monday. And I guess I should call Lizette too and let her know my plans have changed."

"Absolutely. Let me know if you want any help with dinner."

"I'll get it after I'm off the phone," she said, and then left the room.

Elyse returned to the playroom, where she made a game out of picking up the toys. By the time Claire called that dinner was ready, more than half the toys had been sorted, picked up, and put away. Elyse praised both the kids for their effort and gave them high fives as they left the playroom.

Claire remained distant but cordial towards Elyse throughout dinner and during the remainder of the evening. She did read two books to the kids as the two women tucked the kids into bed that night. Elyse knew Claire's feelings were hurt by the words they'd exchanged. She also knew her daughter would think about what was said. She may never admit her mom was right, but she'd evaluate what they discussed. She already had, as she changed her travel plans.

When they returned to the kitchen after the kids were in bed, Elyse hoped that Claire would want to have a glass of wine with her, but Claire declined.

"I just want to go up and take a long, hot bath and relax, if you don't mind," Claire said.

"Of course, sweetie," Elyse said. "I love you, Claire. You are a very good mother. Please don't confuse my concerns about your traveling with me thinking you're not. I think, though, when you're in the middle of something like fighting for your career, you can't see the whole picture. And Michael Kensington is certainly going to take everything from you that he can get."

As Claire lounged in the bathtub with a glass of wine, she thought about her conversation with Michael earlier that evening when she'd called in to change her travel plans. She may have just committed career suicide. After speaking with Tara and asking her to change the travel plans, she had Tara transfer her to Michael.

"Hi Michael, I had Tara push my travel arrangements for the Seattle trip off until Monday morning," she had said. "Tomorrow is Aiden's birthday, and you know what? It always bothered me when I was a child that my father wasn't home for mine. So, I've decided that I won't be traveling on my kids' birthdays, or Matthew's, or our wedding anniversary. In addition to holidays, there are some days that are too important to me to be away for work. I'll update those days on the master calendar tomorrow when I'm in the office."

"I'm disappointed to hear you're delaying this trip, Claire."

"It impacts nothing. There really is no rush to be there tomorrow. And we were trying to cram the job into basically one day on-site, when we both know two full days is more realistic. This way I can leave Monday morning and stay until Wednesday, which will allow me to do a better job for our clients. I already called them, and they know not to expect me until Monday."

"You know very well that travel is required in this job, Claire."

"And I have no problem with travel that won't negatively impact my family. You've asked me to step up, and I have. Since I won't be going on-site to collapses I'm fine with traveling up to fifty percent of the time, same as Chris."

"In the early days of this company, your father and I both traveled all the time," Michael had said.

His statement angered her when he'd said it, and it still angered her now. He hadn't traveled much in the last ten years, until recently when he'd decided to personally train Cody, his new boy-wonder, as the new on-site collapse lead for the firm. Yes, she was still pissed off that the position hadn't gone to her, even though it would have meant she'd be traveling constantly.

"How'd that work out for you, Michael?" she had asked him in a tone of voice that wouldn't be misconstrued. "My mom stayed with my dad all those years. You did me a favor by giving that position to Cody. I know it would kill the relationship between Matthew and me, and my marriage and my family are more important to me than any job. With that being said, I will continue to work my ass off for Kensington-Laramie. My father gave everything to make this firm what it is, and I'd never disrespect his memory by not giving it my all. Within reasonable limits."

"Very well," was Michael's reply.

Claire took another sip of her wine and added some hot water to the tub. She prayed her mom was right that Michael would take the lazy and cheap course. Kensington-Laramie needed a second partner. Her name was on the company letterhead. And she'd earned it. She didn't relish the idea of looking for a new job, but if Michael didn't offer her the partnership, then fuck him. She'd leave and take as many clients with her as she could. Maybe that was what she needed to do.

The world was changing. A lot that she did on-site could be done remotely. If her marriage couldn't be repaired, maybe that should be the direction she should go. She could work completely from home, hire a small staff to work with her out of Matthew's vacant home office, and be there more for her kids.

"Oh, Dad, I hope this is what you would have wanted me to do," she said aloud.

· · · ·

JAKE SWEPT THE STRAY strands of hair from Elyse's face. He pressed a kiss to her lips. "Are you still thinking about the words you had with Claire?"

She stroked his bare shoulder. "I'm sorry, yes."

Jake's lips cracked a small smile. "No apology needed. For what it's worth, I think you did the right thing by speaking up. You know better than anyone that once someone's work takes over their life, their family comes second. You don't want that for your grandkids, and you don't want it for Claire either."

"I thought she would have gotten that on her own. I know it bothered her when she was little that Tim was never home for her birthday. How she was about to repeat that with Aiden, I can't fathom."

"But the good news is she was able to switch her trip. That means it wasn't urgent, and hopefully she'll think about those kinds of things in the future."

"We'll see in February when Emma's birthday rolls around," Elyse said.

Jake pressed another kiss to her lips.

"I'm sorry. You had to think when you got involved with me that you wouldn't have to hear all this drama because my kids are grown and gone."

"I love you for who you are, Elyse. We talked about this before. The Navy comes with me. Your family with you. Kade and Mel needed to move home, and you'll help with the baby after it's born. Claire needs a little nudge to get her priorities straight and you have to give her that nudge. You've lived it and made it look easy to her. She needs to know it wasn't, and she needs to know what the probable outcome will be if she travels too much for work. And you need to be able to talk with me about it because I know it's tearing you up inside."

"I let it stay on my mind while we were together," she said. "I'm sorry I couldn't push it from my thoughts while you kissed me."

Jake chuckled. "If you're thinking of anyone else while I'm kissing you, I'm just glad it wasn't another man. That would be a problem for me."

Elyse laughed, too. "Never any other man. You're the only one I want to kiss me and to be with me in my bed."

"I like the sound of that," Jake said.

"You have my thoughts on you and only you now." She gently grasped his jaw. "Let's try this again."

Chapter 42 – A Christmas Miracle

C hristmas Eve was upon them.

Elyse and Claire hadn't really talked since their words earlier in the month. Even at Aiden's Playworld birthday party, they didn't. They both knew it was neither the time nor the place to talk about the words they'd exchanged. The whole party was very uncomfortable. Matthew was there and tried to be involved, even though he clearly had not been in on the planning. He didn't say two words to Claire, instead hung with the husbands of several of the couples who were their friends while the kids played.

Jake had duty and didn't go with Elyse. She talked mostly with Kelsey and Ash at the party. She'd confided in both Kelsey and Kade that Claire was mad at her again. Kade was at work. Mel didn't come without him. She claimed she had tons of homework and had to study. Elyse was sure it was because she avoided uncomfortable family situations, a coping mechanism from her volatile childhood.

During the month, Elyse had tried to call Claire several times. Claire let the calls go to voicemail. She had text messaged her. Claire's reply was she didn't want to discuss it. She'd agree to disagree with her mother's opinion. They did text about Christmas gifts, but Claire had not committed to coming home for Christmas Eve, even though getting together for dinner and gifts on Christmas Eve was their tradition. She said that she and Matthew had not figured out their time with the kids for Christmas yet.

At noon on Christmas Eve, Kelsey and Ash came through the door with two large laundry baskets full of wrapped gifts. Kelsey's stomach had really popped now that she was six months pregnant. Her due date was in just three months. She looked so cute pregnant, Elyse noted. She had enjoyed a very healthy pregnancy.

In contrast Mel was large, carrying low, and very uncomfortable. The baby was due in two weeks and the drain on her was apparent. Her instructors for the paramedic program were working with her to set alternate schedules for class content, tests, and labs that needed to be completed with her impending due date. She was planning to take a month completely off, and then during the second month after giving birth she would complete modules remotely before returning to the training facility to complete her labs when the baby was eight weeks old.

Kade had worked overnight and had been up in their room sleeping since he'd gotten home at five. Instead of going up to wake him, Mel called him on the phone to tell him that Kelsey and Ash were there. She just didn't have the energy for another trip up the stairs. He came downstairs several minutes later.

"Are Claire and the kids coming?" Kade asked after he'd made himself a cup of coffee and taken a seat at the kitchen table.

"Good question," Elyse replied. "Has she replied to any of you regarding their plans?"

"Last time she replied to me she said she wasn't sure. She and Matthew were trying to figure out what they were doing for Christmas with the kids. He's refused to go to marriage counseling but is still saying he doesn't want a divorce, yet he hasn't lived at the house for almost a month. It's very confusing to me," Kelsey said.

"Someone in that house needs to grow a pair," Kade said, getting a response of laughter from all.

Jake laughed the hardest. "I thought you said before that Claire is your father without a penis."

Kade laughed. "Dad didn't have a pair either." His gaze swept to Elyse. "Sorry, Mom."

Elyse covered her laugh with her hand. "I am quite surprised Claire has given him this much time."

"I'm not sure how either of them thinks anything can get resolved. They're not talking about their issues and trying to come to an agreement," Kelsey said.

"I'm sure neither of them wants to confront whatever their problems are," Mel said. "That's how my dad and his second wife handled things. The problem with that is that little problems that don't get discussed and worked out become big problems that no one can fix. I hate to say it, but I don't know how they will reconcile. The other thing I saw happen with my parents is that once someone moves out, a trial separation becomes permanent."

The mood in the room instantly crashed. Elyse had had the same thoughts but hadn't wanted to voice them to even Jake during the month. She tried to be optimistic that Claire and Matthew would come to some sort of resolution for their kids' sake. But she knew Melanie was right. Trial separations often became permanent ones.

• • • •

THAT FIRST YEAR

AT ONE IN THE AFTERNOON, after waiting several hours for a response from Matthew regarding what time he planned to come see the kids, Claire decided she was done waiting. She packed up the gifts for her family in the back of her SUV. Then she loaded the kids into the car and sent a text to her mom that they were heading over. She hoped her mom would agree to disagree about the words they'd exchanged before Aiden's birthday, as she'd asked her to. She'd changed her plans and had opted not to go out of town. Hopefully, her mom would let the subject drop. She was stressed out enough without having to go through any of that again.

The kids were excited to be going to Grandma's house. But Aiden was still asking when Daddy would be home. As they drove towards Franklin he asked again if Daddy would be at Grandma's house. Her heart ached. When she'd asked Matthew to stay elsewhere, she thought it would only be for a week or two. Certainly, he'd come to his senses in that amount of time and miss his family. Certainly, he'd be home by Christmas at the latest. It was very confusing to her that he swore he didn't want a divorce and swore he wasn't having an affair, but he didn't want to talk with a marriage counselor, her only stipulation that would allow him to come home.

Her phone chimed a new text message that displayed on the console of the car. Hoping it was from Matthew, she glanced at it and was disappointed to see that it was from her mom acknowledging her message. Mom said they were all excited to see them and were glad they were coming. She hoped the attention the kids would get would distract them from the fact that their father had so far been a Christmas no-show.

The kids were excited when they arrived at her mom's house. They ran ahead of her towards the kitchen when Claire opened the front door. "Merry Christmas," she greeted everyone, who were all in the kitchen standing around sampling plates of munchies from the kitchen table.

Kelsey already had Emma on her hip. Her mom held Aiden in an embrace. Her family was exactly what she and her kids needed today. She was glad she came, which at one point that morning she wasn't so sure she would. Claire went around and hugged each member of her family. Yes, Ash and Mel as well as Jake had become members of the family. That didn't lessen the love she had for her father or how much she missed him. Their presence was separate of him. And she realized accepting Jake wasn't being disloyal to her father's memory.

At Jake's feet sat his two dogs, obediently staying. He held a finger an inch from each dog's nose, his command to them to stay. "Wow, you have really gotten them trained well since the last time I saw them," Claire said to Jake after she'd embraced him.

"He also had them out running for a few hours this morning," Elyse said. "The first chance they get, they'll sneak up to our bed and nap for hours." She laughed, but Claire was right. Jake had put in so much time working with the dogs to get them trained. He had enlisted Miles Maitland's help as he was an experienced canine handler. The boys were still wild-men with a lot of energy, but now, they were well-behaved wild-men.

"Mommy, is Daddy coming here?" Aiden asked Claire.

"I'm not sure when Daddy will be here, or maybe you'll see him at home tomorrow. Remember I told you that Daddy is away for work. He loves you and he misses you."

Elyse nodded to Kelsey. She knew what that meant. "Hey, let's go into the family room, guys. I've been waiting for you to watch some Christmas shows."

Ash scooped Aiden up. "Come on, A-man."

Elyse ushered Claire to the front room to be as far away from the kids as possible. Jake followed. "Claire," Elyse said. "What's going on with Matthew? When is he going to see the kids for Christmas?"

Claire shrugged, feeling so sad. "I don't know, Mom. He isn't responding to my calls or text messages since yesterday afternoon about when he wanted to spend time with the kids for Christmas." She hated to cry but the tears flooded her eyes. "He's mad at me because I asked him to leave for a few weeks to get his head on straight. I can deal with him mad at me, but the kids..." She paused, her words strangled with emotion. "The kids don't understand why Daddy isn't with them today. If he had wanted for us to pretend nothing was wrong today for the kids, to make it a good Christmas for them, I would have been okay with that. But he's hurting his kids and I don't know what to do about that."

Elyse sat on the couch and patted the cushion next to her, inviting Claire to sit. Jake took a seat in the chair across from them. When Claire sat, Elyse wrapped her in an embrace, her heart hurting for her daughter and grandkids. "And you have no idea at all what his problem is?"

"Besides not wanting to spend time with us, no." With this admission, Claire cried harder. She took a few deep breaths to calm herself and then continued. "I've been seeing a counselor like you suggested. I've sent her info to Matthew and invited him to our sessions. He told me once that I didn't approve of his parenting and he couldn't do anything right in my eyes, so I told him I don't want it to be like that. I invited him to come help me work on myself and change that. He never replied. Not a yes, or it's too late, not even a go fuck yourself. Nothing."

"I'm sorry, sweetie," Elyse said. She hated to hear how isolated Matthew had made himself, but she was encouraged that Claire was seeing a counselor and was open to explore that maybe some of her actions had caused a rift between them. Admitting you're wrong and asking for help to change isn't easy. She was proud of Claire for taking the step. "I'm glad you're seeing someone. No matter what happens with Matthew, it will make you a stronger person."

"Ever since Dad died, everything at home has been so fucked up," she said. "I'm sorry, I know, language."

Elyse chuckled. "It's okay. But why do you think everything went so sideways then?"

"I don't know," Claire said. "I needed Matthew to step up but he didn't. Not with the kids, not with asking me how I was. He acted like he was tired of hearing me say how much I missed Dad or how sad I was right away. I needed him to ask me how I was, but he never did."

Elyse's gaze focused on Jake, who sat across from them. She hoped he had some wisdom to share.

"I know a lot of men in my command, when they have been away on a deployment, have a hard time reintegrating into their families when they return. If the kids and the nanny have always been your territory, he may not feel like he's allowed to step up and invade that realm. That's how many men returning from deployment feel," Jake said. "And if he ever did make a wrong decision that you had to call him on, he may feel cautious. No one wants to get their knuckles slapped multiple times."

Claire nodded. "I know he has never had a really close relationship with his parents. He was raised by nannies. But I would have thought that he'd have had a good role model in the nannies at least, as obviously he didn't with his own father. His dad is such an ass. When Matthew met them on Thanksgiving, he told me that his parents were really pissed the kids and I didn't come. It was fine that we did it when we didn't have kids, or when it was just Aiden. But to drag two young children through two airports to visit with them in the airline's club room for a few hours is an unrealistic expectation. His dad actually told him that he expects us to be there next time and Matthew promised him we would be. Oh, hell no, we won't!"

"Claire, do you think your marriage is salvageable?" Elyse asked, sad that she was asking.

"I don't know," Claire admitted with new tears flowing down her cheeks. "Matthew keeps saying he doesn't want a divorce. But I don't want this marriage to continue as it is. And his nonresponse to me since yesterday afternoon and not committing to when he will spend time with his kids makes me so mad at him."

Through the windows that faced the driveway, they all saw Matthew's car pull up and park.

"Oh my God! He has some nerve just showing up," Claire said.

"Claire, go out and talk to him. Don't attack him. See what he has to say," Elyse said. "We'll keep the kids in the back of the house so they don't know he's here."

Claire stood and rushed out the front door.

"Do you think she can do that, not attack him?" Jake asked Elyse.

"I doubt it."

Claire met Matthew as he pulled himself from behind the wheel. Matthew looked hung-over. His hair was as disheveled as his clothes. It looked like he hadn't shaved in a couple of days, which was very unlike him. "You look like hell," she told him.

He ran his fingers through his hair, trying to smooth the wild locks which were grown out and desperately needing a trim. "I feel like hell."

"I've been trying to reach you since yesterday afternoon."

"I lost my phone."

"Why didn't you just drive over to the house?"

"I did this morning after I woke up and you weren't home. I figured you had to be here."

"It's the afternoon. Not the morning. Are you hung-over?"

Matthew rubbed his temples with both hands. "Yes, very."

"What the fuck, Matthew? What's going on with you?"

"Claire, I need to come home," Matthew said.

"Only if you come to a few counseling sessions so we can figure out why we're fighting so much," she said.

"We don't need a counselor. We just need to let everything rest."

"We've been doing that for a month. And obviously things are only getting worse."

"You won't understand," Matthew said.

"No, I don't, because you're not telling me anything."

"Things are kind of fucked up, Claire."

"Have you been having an affair?" she demanded.

"I promise you on our kids' lives, I haven't had an affair. I told you, I don't want a divorce. There isn't anyone else." His voice was pleading.

"Then what is it?"

"I can't go into it now, today of all days when I feel like shit."

"Yeah, and on Christmas Eve when your kids have been asking when they'll see Daddy."

"I know I've failed you; I've failed them. I want to do better, Claire."

"Actions speak louder than words. What exactly are you going to do in order to do better?"

"For starters, I'm going to be there. I showed up today, didn't I?"

She didn't point out that he showed up hungover as hell and looking like shit. "Yes, you did."

"I love you, Claire. I love us. I love our family and I want to do better. But please, can we let it sit for today and tomorrow and give the kids a good Christmas?"

Claire nodded.

"And can I stay at the house tonight to be there for Christmas morning with the kids?"

"You can stay in the guest room."

Matthew nodded with a deep frown on his face. He nodded at the house. "Can I come in? Will your family welcome me?"

Claire wasn't sure if they would, and she wasn't sure if she wanted them to see him looking so bad. But if they could reconcile her family would have to allow him back in and she knew they would. She knew her mom wanted them to work through their issues for the kids, if nothing else.

"Claire?" he asked when she hadn't answered.

Elyse and Jake watched from inside the house. "He looks like he slept in his clothes and just woke up."

"He looks really hungover," Jake said. "Do you think alcohol or drugs could be his problem?"

Elyse hadn't considered that. "Maybe. I don't know."

Claire told him, "Wait here. I want to feel my mom out on it. We could tell the kids you're sick." She rushed back into the house and was met in the entry by Elyse and Jake.

"He looks terrible," Elyse said.

"He's hung-over," Claire said in a whisper. "He wants to come in and see the kids. He said he lost his phone yesterday."

"What do you want, Claire?" Elyse asked.

"I want a normal and happy Christmas for my kids."

Elyse nodded. "Invite him in. Tell the kids that Daddy was up all night traveling or working, sick, whatever. Let him see the kids for a few minutes and then we'll encourage him to go up and take a shower. He can take a nap in Kelsey's old room for a few hours until dinner. Maybe if he sleeps it off, he'll feel and look better."

"Thank you, Mom," Claire said. She went back outside to where Matthew still stood beside his car. "You can come in and see the kids. My mom even said you can take a shower and a nap for a few hours until dinner."

"That would help."

Claire shook her head and sighed. "I'm doing this for our kids."

"I want things to go back the way they were, Claire."

"No. I want things better than they were. I'm telling you right now, you need to either step up and be who we need you to be or we need to make our separation permanent."

"Claire?"

"We'll talk about this when you're not hung-over." She turned and walked back to the house. He followed.

"Elyse, Jake," Matthew acknowledged them as he came through the door.

"Merry Christmas, Matthew. I'm glad you're here for your kids," Elyse said.

"Yes, me, too," Matthew said. "And thank you. I'll take you up on the offer of the shower and a bed to nap in for a few hours."

"See your kids for a bit first. They've missed their daddy," Elyse said.

The others were clearly taken aback by Matthew's appearance. Their greetings to him were subdued. The kids, however, welcomed him with exuberance. After a few minutes of Matthew getting through his kids' loud voices and animated conversation, which noticeably were hard for him to handle, he gave his kids one last hug and then stood.

"Daddy didn't sleep last night. I was away, traveling home to see you. I'm going to go upstairs to one of Grandma's spare bedrooms and take a nap so I'll feel good for dinner."

Claire walked with him to the stairs. Kade followed. "I can lend you some clothes if you want," he offered.

Matthew glanced down at what he wore. "Yes, thank you."

The three of them went upstairs. While Kade went to his own room to gather a change of clothes for Matthew, Claire and Matthew went to Kelsey's old bedroom which was set up as a guest room. Matthew unpacked his pockets, placing his wallet, car keys, and a package of breath mints on the dresser. He unbuttoned his shirt, which he noticed only then was stained with mystery substances in addition to being wrinkled.

"Here," Kade said, coming into the room. He held a pile of clothes that included a pair of holiday-themed flannel pants and a dark green Henley shirt, plus a towel. "Feel free to use any of the products in the shower."

"Thanks, Kade," Matthew said. He placed the pile on the bed. He pulled out the flannel pants and the towel and then moved to the door to leave the room.

"Thanks, Kade," Claire repeated.

After both Kade and Matthew left the room, she opened Matthew's wallet and looked through it. She prayed she wouldn't find any hint of an affair on his part, not that she knew what that would be. What she didn't expect to find was a little package of a white powder. She held it in her hand, staring at it with shock, when Kade re-entered the room. He had a bottle of water and two ibuprofen tablets in his hand.

"Oh, shit," Kade said. He set the water and pills on the dresser and took the packet from Claire's hand.

"Do you know what it is?" Claire asked.

"Looks like coke to me," Kade said.

"Coke as in cocaine?" Claire repeated.

Kade nodded.

Claire wasn't sure if she wanted to cry, scream, or throw up. "Drugs. He's doing drugs, too." Her voice was sad, flat, and bordering on angry all at the same time.

"That would explain a lot," Kade said.

Tears filled Claire's eyes and her bottom lip trembled.

Kade put his arm around her and drew her in close. "Easy, sis."

"I'm going to kill him," Claire said.

"Let me deal with this," Kade said. "Go downstairs and ask Ash to come up."

"He's my husband. I should confront him."

"And this is my territory. I see the effects of drugs on people every day. Let me deal with this, Claire."

She nodded and left the room because, honestly, she didn't know how to deal with it. She wanted to scream at Matthew and demand he answer why. She wanted to tell him he couldn't be anywhere near their kids. She wanted to fist her hands and hit him until she felt better.

Matthew re-entered the bedroom wearing only the flannel pants. His hair was wet but clean. From just the shower, he felt so much better. He was sure after a few hours' sleep, he'd feel fine. He stopped his forward momentum, coming face to face with Kade, who held up a packet of his coke.

"You brought drugs into my mother's home? You sat on her couch, hugging your kids, with drugs in your pocket?" Kade charged.

"I'm careful. I'd never let them get their hands on it."

"No one is careful when they're high. Where's your phone? I heard you lost it. Yeah, that's being careful," Kade said.

"That's different. I've never used that near my kids."

"Just having it near them is stupid. Do you have any idea how many children accidently get a hold of this shit and die every year?"

Matthew looked at him blankly.

"I'll tell you how many. Too many. I had a call just last week where a two-year-old little girl somehow accidently got her hands on her mommy's heroin. Two years old, just like Emma. It was in a really nice neighborhood, just like yours. I worked on that little girl, bringing her back every time she coded. Administering Narcan in kids is tricky. Especially little ones. Child Protective Services was called in as were the police. Nothing in that house will ever be the same again."

"It's only coke. It's not heroin or meth. Jesus, you make it sound like I'm an addict. I'm not." He pointed at the package of coke, still in Kade's hand. "That's a one-off."

Kade's eyes shifted to the doorway, where Ash now stood. Matthew's gaze followed.

"Ash, will you dispose of this?"

Ash nodded.

Kade handed the packet to him. "Do you have more anywhere? Pockets? Your car?"

"No," Matthew said.

Kade picked his keys up from the dresser and threw them to Ash. "Search his car to be sure. Then hold on to his keys." His gaze swung back to Matthew. "I bet if I had you blow, you'd still register over the limit. I could smell the booze oozing out of your pores when you stepped into the family room." He pointed at the bed. "I brought you a water bottle and a couple ibuprofen. Take them and sleep it off until dinner. We're going to give your kids a normal Christmas in every way. We'll deal with this later." His voice was firm.

Matthew said nothing because, really, what could he say? Kade watched him drink some water, swallow the pills, and then drink more water. He left and closed the door behind himself when Matthew pulled the covers back on the bed. He found his mom standing outside the door in the hallway.

"How much did you hear?" he asked her.

"Enough," Elyse said. She put her arms around her son. "You handled that well, better than any of us could have. I'm proud of you, Kade."

"That stupid fucker," Kade swore.

Elyse didn't comment on his language. Unfortunately, she agreed with her son's assessment. "Claire's in my room. She's pretty upset."

"I'll talk to her," Kade volunteered. He entered to find Mel seated beside Claire.

"There's a way back from this," Mel said. "Don't make any snap decisions today."

"That's right, sis," Kade said, taking a seat beside Mel. "You talk about this after he's sober. But not today or tomorrow. The kids deserve a normal and happy Christmas."

"I know," Claire said. "If it weren't for the kids, I'd kick him out and file for divorce right now." She couldn't believe this had happened. She was angry and so embarrassed.

"Let's see first if he'll get help and get sober. He's got a road ahead of him to fix all he's fucked up, but he needs to have a reason to want to get sober," Mel said. "Kade and I see this kind of thing on the job with the calls we get all the time."

"Unfortunately, we do," Kade seconded. "Mel's right, Claire. He has to have a reason to get and stay sober. And that reason is you and the kids."

"This doesn't have to mean the end of your family. If he's willing to change, this will be nothing more than a speed bump," Mel said.

"Have Mom take the kids and have that talk with him then. Let me know if you want one of us there with you. And if he wants to go to a meeting, let me know. A friend of ours goes to one almost daily. I'm sure he'd take Matthew."

"I'd make it a condition of him staying in the house," Mel added.

Jake joined Ash to search Matthew's car. They didn't find any more drugs. They did, however, find a pack of cigarettes in the cup holder and Matthew's dead cell phone under the seat with a wadded-up Taco Bell wrapper that also had sand in it. The cigarettes were left in the cup holder after the pack was searched and no drugs were found in it. The phone and

Taco Bell wrapper were placed on the kitchen counter the phone to charge, the wrapper to ask Matthew about.

Claire would have loved to look through his phone, but she didn't know the passcode. Likewise, Matthew didn't know hers. If there was any chance of their marriage surviving, that would have to change. She needed proof that he wasn't having an affair because from where she sat, she couldn't think of any other reason for his recent behavior.

Determined to keep things normal for the kids, the family continued with their normal Christmas Eve festivities while Matthew slept. Claire put on a brave face for her kids, even though all she wanted to do was cry. Her family's support meant the world to her. She appreciated Kade and Mel's experience dealing with this sort of thing. But she was also incredibly embarrassed.

A half-hour before dinner would be ready, Matthew woke. He felt more rested. The physical ails of his hangover were waning, but now he had to face Claire and her family; though he knew, for the sake of the kids, they wouldn't treat him too badly. Had Kade not taken his keys, he probably would have quietly slipped from the house and driven away. He finished the water bottle and brought it with him from the room.

"Daddy!" Aiden called as he walked into the kitchen, bringing all eyes to him.

The family all sat at the kitchen table playing some game with playing cards and larger cards akin to bingo cards with chips on them. Even Aiden and Emma played, obviously with one of the adult's help.

"Hey, everyone," Matthew greeted sheepishly. "I can smell the ham all the way upstairs. It smells great."

"Do you feel better, Matthew?" Elyse asked.

"Yes, thank you. I still need a few more hours of sleep, but the nap helped a lot."

"If your stomach is unsettled at all, there's some Seven-Up in the fridge, as well as bottles of water to hydrate," Kade said.

"Thanks," Matthew said. He opened the refrigerator and pulled out a bottle of water. Then he noticed his phone and the Taco Bell wrapper on the counter.

Jake walked over and grabbed a bottle of water from the refrigerator too. He came in close to Matthew and dropped his voice to a whisper. "If you want to prove to Claire that you aren't having an affair, I suggest you unlock your phone and hand it to her to look at whatever she wants." Then he retook his seat at the table.

Matthew stood near the counter, drinking his water. He watched those at the table for a moment. Ash shuffled the cards. It looked like they were in between rounds. He grabbed his phone from the charger. He turned it on and then walked over to the table. He kissed Aiden's head and then Emma's.

"Claire, can I speak to you in the front room for a moment?" Matthew said.

"When the game is over. I'm already in for this round." Her voice was cold.

"I'll do your card," Elyse, who sat beside her, said.

"And I'll help Aiden," Kade, who sat beside him, said.

Claire breathed out heavily. "Sure."

She got up and followed Matthew to the front room. "What?" she whispered in a demanding and unfriendly tone.

"I'm so sorry," Matthew said slowly. He unlocked his phone and handed it to her. "My birthdate is the passcode. Look at anything you want. Keep it for as long as you want. I promise you I haven't had an affair."

"Jesus Christ, Matthew. It's Christmas Eve and I haven't heard from you in twenty-four hours. You came here hungover as hell with drugs in your wallet. You thought you lost this," she said as she held up his phone. "But it was dead under the seat in your car with a Taco Bell wrapper. Since when do you eat Taco Bell? And there was sand in that wrapper. Were you at the beach?"

"I deserve that. Yes, I was at the beach. I drove out to the hotel we stayed at a few months ago. I was drunk, which is the only time I eat Taco Bell."

"You drove around drunk. Do you have any idea of the liability? We could have lost our house if you hurt or killed someone."

Matthew held his hands up. "I know. I sat watching the waves. I considered walking into them," he admitted.

Claire's anger turned into an ice-cold shock. Had he really just said he thought about killing himself?

"But I couldn't do it. I couldn't let a bean burrito be my last meal." He paused and frowned. "No, of course that isn't what stopped me, but it went through my mind. How fucked up is that? I do love you and the kids. That's what stopped me. I've been a shitty father and a shitty husband. Things have been really fucked up for the last six months or so, and I just couldn't be what you needed me to be. Look through the text messages. Listen to the voicemails. You'll figure out what's been going on."

"I'd rather you tell me," Claire said.

"I can't." He shook his head and then left through the front door.

Claire watched him reach into his car. Not knowing that Kade had taken his keys away, she was convinced he was about to drive away. When he produced a pack of cigarettes and lit up, her jaw dropped open. Since when did Matthew smoke cigarettes? But then again, since when did Matthew do drugs, drink so much he was still hung over at one o'clock the next day? She didn't even want to think about his admission that he considered killing himself.

While keeping one eye on him she scrolled through his text messages, at first just looking to see the names of those who messaged him. Her unanswered text messages were at the top. There were also unread messages from both of his partners and also his father. And there were a few from his college roommates. There was a name up in the top six that she didn't recognize. Don S. She clicked on that message.

The new message read: *"We need you to come in on the twenty-sixth at nine a.m. We're ready to move forward with the case."* Matthew hadn't replied, but it showed read.

Case? What case? she thought. That didn't sound like something with one of his clients. It sounded official. She scrolled back to the beginning of the messages with him. There were only about a dozen messages between the two of them, dating back to June.

"Thank you for coming in. I'll be in touch after my initial investigation," Don S. stated in his first message in the thread.

"Just appreciate the risk I'm taking. This is a long-established relationship I'm jeopardizing," Matthew messaged the same day.

"Understood. We'll be discreet," Don S. answered.

The next message was from Don S. in the beginning of August. *"Sorry for the delay. There was much to go through. We need statements of each client's transactions in the High-Yield Stock Index Fund. You have my secure email address to send them to."*

"I just sent them," Matthew replied four days later. *"I had to access his personal files. He may detect the intrusion. Can you speed this along?"*

There was no reply for a week. *"We have a problem. You're implicated in those files."*

"I had nothing to do with that fund," Matthew replied immediately.

"You need to come in. Tomorrow at nine," was the response from Don S.

The next text came the beginning of November. *"I received your voicemail. No, we are not ready to formally lay out charges yet. Do not disengage. We need you in place. But you are correct. You have been thoroughly framed. You look guilty as hell."*

Matthew replied with one word. *"FUCK"*

Claire's head was spinning as she continued to read the messages. Guilty of what? And whose files had he accessed? It had to be one of his partners. Don S. had to be some sort of law enforcement. Stock funds had to be some investment his firm offered. And that last message indicated someone framed him. Dread settled over her.

Don S. didn't reply until the day before Thanksgiving. *"Testimony before the Grand Jury is conducted in secret. Fowler can wait in the hall, and you may leave the room to consult with him before answering any questions. Don't be late."*

"Grand Jury?" Claire said aloud. Fowler had to be Kerry Fowler, Matthew's college roommate and frat buddy. He was in the yearly golf group. He was also an attorney.

The last text before the one asking him to come in at nine a.m. on the twenty-sixth was sent by Matthew a week earlier. *"I need an update. I left you two voicemails. Why aren't you responding? I'm getting the feeling you're going to fuck me over. I came to you, remember?"*

Claire's stomach dropped. She glanced back out at Matthew, who leaned against the car, puffing away on a cigarette. Then she opened the text string with Troy Donnor, one of his partners. She read as she scrolled back over the last months' messages. It was all about golf, client meetings, martinis, and Troy's love life.

She opened the message string with the other partner, Ken Woods. There were many more messages going into specifics of offering certain funds to certain client profiles in addition to messages about golf, and graphic comments from Ken regarding Troy's sex life. In the last month she saw at least six messages referencing the High-Yield Stock Index Fund and minimizing the risk associated with it. It was Ken who was saying how to minimize that risk.

Claire realized her hands were shaking. She thought she had a pretty good idea of what was going on from the text messages. She checked his call log quickly and also checked his voicemails. She played two. One was from Kerry Fowler from the day before. He was arranging to meet up with him prior to, to accompany him to Don Schehl's office on the twenty-sixth. The second was from Don S., reiterating the need for him to come in on the twenty-sixth.

She went out the front door and stood in front of him, her back to the house. "Tell me if I'm right. You went to the authorities with suspicions that one of your partners was doing something illegal. But the documents you turned over to them implicated you."

Matthew nodded. "I have to go in there on the twenty-sixth. I'll either be arrested on the spot for something I didn't do, or I'll find out I was instrumental in getting one of my friends, my business partner, arrested."

"Ken?"

Matthew threw the cigarette to the ground and crushed it out with his foot. "Yeah. Back in May, I was looking into this new fund he started to represent. Something about it waved red flags at me. The returns weren't adding up. They were too high. When we were on our yearly golf trip, I mentioned something about it to Kerry. The next thing I knew he messaged me for drinks after work one night and this guy from the SCC was there."

"Don," Claire said.

"Yes."

"You testified before the Grand Jury," Claire said.

Matthew nodded. He reached into the car and pulled the pack of cigarettes out. He lit another.

"Why didn't you tell me any of this?"

"I hoped I was wrong about it and it would turn out to be nothing. You were grieving your dad's death. You didn't need anything else to worry about. But the stress of this has been terrible. I was relieved when you asked me to move out. I couldn't do it, Claire. We were fighting all the time and I couldn't tell you why. I was told to tell no one, including you, about this."

Claire wasn't sure how she felt about that. Betrayed? No matter what this Don person had told him to do or not regarding who he told, surely he should have told her and swore her to secrecy too. "So, there was something illegal going on?"

"Yeah, it's a Ponzi scheme."

"Does Ken know it is?"

"Yeah, Claire. There's no way he thinks it's legit."

"Is Troy involved in it, too?"

"Only on the paperwork that Ken falsified to implicate him, same as me. Troy's too concerned with reliving his single twenties right now. Committing fraud isn't on his radar," Matthew said with a sarcastic laugh.

"Okay, so best case scenario, their investigation comes to the correct conclusions and only Ken is arrested."

"Our firm is toast, Claire, regardless of who is indicted and who isn't. Donnor Woods Jeffries will be in the news as a firm associated with a Ponzi scheme, with the arrest of one of the partners. Investors will never trust the firm again or any of its partners. My career is done. And Troy, the poor oblivious son-of-a-bitch, doesn't even know what's coming."

"You're a hero, Matthew. You went to the authorities and reported what you suspected was illegal acts being committed by your partner, your friend. You're saving your firm's clients from losses."

"That's not going to matter, Claire."

"That's not fair. You did the right thing. It has to matter." She wrapped her arms around him and held him. "We'll deal with this in counseling, why you didn't tell me and how I feel about it. You can come home, but we have to go to counseling regardless of what happens on the twenty-sixth."

Chapter 43 – What Families Are For

"That looks promising," Elyse said to Jake, who stood beside her at the window, gazing out at Claire and Matthew in the driveway.

"He had to have quite the explanation to get her to wrap her arms around him after what he's done," Jake said.

"If she forgives him, we'll also have to," Elyse said. "Without a good explanation, I'm not sure Kade's going to be able to."

"Without him proving he can change, I won't," Kade said from behind them. "Words are cheap. It's actions that matter. And he better pick his own butts up. I don't want to get blamed for them."

Elyse chuckled. "On the up side, looks like you have a new smoking buddy to step outside with after a meal."

"Yeah, that's not going to fly with Claire too long," Kade remarked.

When Matthew and Claire headed back to the house the three of them moved away from the window, but they didn't make it out of the entry in time before the front door opened and the pair stepped in. "I'm glad you're here," Claire said. "Step back into the living room."

Elyse knew she should feel guilty having been caught leaving the living room as they entered. It had to broadcast they'd been watching them. But neither Claire nor Matthew seemed to notice.

"Mom, something very serious is going on," Claire said. "I can't tell you what yet, but we need this family's support."

"You know you have it," Elyse assured her. She gave Matthew a sympathetic grin.

"I promise you," Matthew began. "I'm sorry for coming here in the state I was in, and I'm very sorry I brought drugs into your house." His gaze shifted to Kade. "Thank you for what you did. As Claire said, we're going to need your help. We'll let you know how in a few days."

"You're being very cryptic," Elyse said, getting the feeling there was more going on than what appeared.

"I'm sorry, Mom. We can't say yet," Claire repeated. "Just knowing you'll be one phone call away and will help with whatever we need means so much."

"Claire, come on. This is ridiculous. A hint?" Kade asked. This went beyond Claire's normal drama.

"In a few days, please, Kade. I'm asking you guys to trust me. Let Christmas for my kids be good." Her voice was pleading.

"We can let this rest until after Christmas," Elyse said. "Claire's right. We need to let this rest for her kids."

They returned to the kitchen and put on happy faces for the kids. The game was already put away and the table was set for dinner. Ash had the ham out of the oven and he and Kelsey had put all the sides in to bake. Elyse omitted putting the bottle of wine on the table for dinner, opting instead for a bottle of sparkling water and a plate of cut lemons and limes. If alcohol was a problem for Matthew, they could omit it and support him.

They all made it a good, friendly dinner for the kids. But there was an underlying tension, which could easily have been due to the fact that it was the first Christmas since Tim had passed away. That wasn't the cause, though, and they all knew it.

Claire appreciated that her family did this for her kids. If Matthew was to get wrongly arrested and convicted of the crime, this could be his last Christmas at home with his family for a long time. She was keenly aware of this as she watched her kids eat the Christmas dinner that she barely tasted. She wasn't aware that there were tears in her eyes until Matthew took her hand and squeezed it, bringing her eyes to his. He gave her a supportive nod and mouthed, "I love you."

"I love you, too," she whispered back as she fought the tears that now flooded her eyes.

This exchange didn't escape the rest of the family, minus the kids.

After dinner the men once again cleaned the kitchen, Jake directing Matthew to help Ash clear the table. He took his position at the sink to wash the larger pans and plates, anything that Kade couldn't fit into the dishwasher.

Then the family settled in front of the Christmas tree, which was in the family room, to open gifts. The undercurrent dissipated as gift wrap was torn from boxes revealing gifts that the giver had thought out to bring the most joy to the receiver.

The last gift picked up from beneath the tree was one that had been pushed farthest into the corner. Kade held it up. "To Tim's family, from Jake," he read.

Seven pairs of adult eyes went to Jake, questions on everyone's lips.

"I hope a new tradition," Jake said. He nodded to Kade. "Open it."

Kade slowly opened the wrapping paper. Inside was a candle sitting atop a glass jar and a small pad of multicolored paper with a pen. Kade read what was written on the top sheet of paper. "I don't get it." Kade said.

"Read what I've written aloud," Jake prompted.

"Tim, I never had the pleasure of meeting you. Thank you for the gift of your wonderful family. My gift to you is that I will love and care for them. Jake."

"You write him a note, thanking him for a gift he gave you, and you give him one back," Jake said. "The notes get folded up and placed in the jar, and the jar doesn't get opened until next year. You add a new gift at that time. You can all decide if you want to share yours or not, either now or next year."

"Jake, that's lovely," Elyse said. "I've never heard of this to honor a family member who's no longer with us, but I think it's a beautiful way to do so."

"We could keep the jar with the notes near his urn," Claire said. "This is a wonderful gift. Thank you, Jake."

"Kade, please place it on the counter in the kitchen and everyone can have privacy while writing out their gift. We'll get desserts out and I'll make some coffee," Elyse said as she stood. "I'm sure Claire and Matthew will want to get the kids home soon. Afterall, it is Christmas Eve, and they need to get to bed so Santa can come tonight."

"Within the next hour or two is fine," Claire said, much to everyone's surprise. "It's Christmas Eve and we're with family. Santa doesn't come this early. If they get to bed a little later than usual, maybe they won't wake so early tomorrow."

They enjoyed dessert, and each member of the family wrote out their gift and added it to the jar. By unanimous vote, they decided to not share what they wrote today. They planned to open the jar and read the notes on the anniversary of his death. It would fall on a Sunday, and they all committed to gather for a meal that day.

Claire's family did stay later than usual. It was nearly eight-thirty before the family gathered in the driveway to say goodnight to them as they strapped the kids into their car seats. By this time Matthew had sobered up. Kade returned his car keys to him.

"Mom, are you free on the twenty-sixth?" Claire asked as she gave her a goodnight hug.

"Yes, I just plan to be at Animal House."

"Keep your phone on you. I may need you to come over, okay?" she whispered.

"Claire?" Elyse asked.

Claire shook her head.

Elyse let it drop. She gave Matthew a goodbye hug as well. "Merry Christmas. Drive safely."

"Thanks for everything, Elyse," Matthew said.

After the two cars had driven away, the rest of the family returned to the family room. They put on another Christmas movie and all settled in, the six of them and the three dogs. Kelsey and Ash were staying the night. While Elyse was thrilled with the house being full, she couldn't help but have worried thoughts regarding what was going on with Claire and Matthew. And it sounded like whatever it was would get worse in a few days.

After Claire and Matthew got the kids into bed, they took care of getting the Santa gifts beneath the tree. And then Claire wrapped her arms around Matthew. "Come to bed," she said.

Matthew embraced her back. "I am so sorry for everything the last few months, Claire. Thank you for allowing me to come home. Not knowing what's coming, I need to be here with you and the kids."

"We'll deal with that later. Tonight, just hold me. And let's not think about anything unpleasant or stressful until we find out what's going to happen with Don and the case. We can speculate and worry all we want. But that isn't going to help anything." She wouldn't tell him that was where her thoughts had been since the truth came out. She wasn't sure if she could put it from her mind or not, but she would surely try for the kids. This Christmas had to be good for them.

· · · ·

ON CHRISTMAS DAY, IN the late afternoon, Kade's pickup truck pulled into the driveway of Claire's house. He and Ash got out of the cab and walked up to the front door. Claire was surprised when she opened the front door to find the two of them standing there.

"Hi, sis," Kade greeted. "Can we come in?"

"Sure," she said. She stepped back and invited them in even though she was confused by their visit.

This was the first time that Ash had been to their home. "Nice house," he said.

"What are you doing here?" she whispered to her brother.

"Trust me, Claire," he said. "Is Matthew here?"

"Yes, of course he is. It's Christmas Day."

Matthew came into the room from the kitchen. He stopped and viewed them with the same surprised and suspicious expression on his face as Claire had. "Hi, did we forget something at Elyse's house last night?"

Kade stepped up to him and embraced him. "We've come to take you to an AA meeting. Our friend Eric will take you. He goes daily."

"Thanks, but really, I'm good," Matthew said.

Ash stepped up to him. He and Kade had planned this before they arrived. "I'm asking you to come with us and go to the meeting for Kelsey and our unborn child. We want him to know his Uncle Matthew."

"And I'm asking you to go for Mel, our baby, me, and our mom. You're a part of this family, Matthew, and we care about you."

Matthew's surprised gaze settled on Claire. She nodded in agreement. Even though she didn't know they were going to do this, she agreed. "Please, Matthew," she said.

"You'll be back home in less than two hours," Ash said.

Matthew nodded. He went back into the kitchen, where the kids sat making gingerbread houses. He gave them both a hug and kiss, telling them he'd be back before dinner. He grabbed his coat from the closet and then he gave Claire a kiss as well.

Claire watched Kade's pickup back out of the driveway and pull away before she joined the kids in the kitchen. She wasn't sure how she was going to make it through the day and evening. Every nerve was on edge, dreading what might happen the next morning.

She appreciated Kade and Ash coming to take him to a meeting, knowing nothing except he was drinking and using drugs. A meeting was a logical way to help him. She had asked for the family's help, hadn't she? And if she was this nervous waiting, Matthew had to be going crazy. If he did have a problem with alcohol or drugs, a meeting was just what he needed.

She wanted to go with Matthew the next morning. He convinced her it was best she didn't. He promised that either he or Kerry would call her as soon as they knew what would happen. He made her promise that she would stay home with the kids until she heard from him or Kerry. If she needed to join him after they knew, she would call her mom to come stay with the kids. Lizette was on vacation with her boyfriend until January second.

· · · ·

LATER THAT NIGHT, IN bed, Claire held Matthew. He'd made it home by dinner and seemed to be in a better place, mentally. She didn't ask, as the kids were there. They had one of the most enjoyable dinners as a family they'd had in a long time. They both tucked the kids into bed that night, reading each of them two books. Then they went to bed, themselves and made love.

"That Eric guy is actually pretty nice," Matthew said. "He's a widower. His wife died a year and a half ago and he misses her every day. She's the one who inspired him to become sober, says he won't dishonor his wife by drinking or using drugs ever again. He does go to a meeting every day, says the urge to use is still there." He paused and shook his head. "He offered to be my sponsor if I want one. I don't even know if I have a problem or not. If I'm not arrested tomorrow, I'm going to try to not drink. If I can't, I plan to call him."

"I think that's a good plan," Claire said. "I have a counseling appointment on January second already scheduled. Lizette is back to work that day. If you can, I'd like you to come with."

"If I can," he agreed. They both knew that meant if he wasn't in jail.

"Okay, so if it's the best-case scenario, have you thought out your next steps for the partnership, or just the office in general?"

"If Ken gets indicted, I have to be the one to tell Troy what happened. Then I guess he and I will need to meet with Kerry and figure a few things out." He sighed loudly. "Let's not jump ahead to any of that yet, though."

"I think you need to," Claire said. "You need to have a clear plan, no matter how it goes tomorrow morning. I have to believe that the truth's going to win out. Neither you nor Troy had anything to do with it, and you have been working with the authorities for six months. That has to count for something. I've never met this Don person, but I hate him for leaving things up in the air, leaving you to worry."

Matthew kissed her. "How's this for a plan? If it plays out in the best-case scenario, we take the kids to Disney World like you talked about before. We just go as soon as we can."

Claire nodded. "That sounds nice." She wouldn't tell him she had no idea about her own career. She may well leave Kensington-Laramie by then. Then neither of them would have a job. An expensive vacation would be reckless, but maybe just what they needed.

Chapter 44 – Breaking News

"**O**h my God. Mom, have you heard the news?" Kelsey asked through the phone, without even greeting her mom after she'd answered.

"No, what news?" Elyse asked. She was at Animal House, updating the website. It was ten-thirty a.m. on the twenty-sixth of December.

"Matthew's partner, Ken Woods, was just arrested for being involved in some kind of securities fraud and investment advisor fraud. I'm looking at the TV right now. There are FBI agents leading him out of the office in handcuffs. Holy shit, Mom. Do you think Matthew was involved or will be arrested too?"

"Oh no," Elyse said. She quickly launched another browser and brought up the live newscast from the network's website. The action was taking place in front of Donnor Woods Jeffries, all right. This explained what had been up with Matthew on Christmas Eve, she was sure.

"They said he invested city pensions including the police and EMS in a scam," Kelsey said. "That's probably the only reason it's getting such news attention."

Elyse knew that included Kade and Melanie's pensions. "This is really bad," Elyse said.

As Elyse watched, her heart pounding in her chest, her call waiting sounded. It was Claire. "Kels, Claire is calling. I have to go."

"Call me back and let me know what she says," Kelsey said.

Elyse clicked over. "Claire, I'm watching the news."

"Matthew has been working with the authorities for six months. He went to them when he suspected Ken was doing something illegal," Claire said. "Mom, I need you to come over right now."

Even though Elyse felt relief from Claire's first statement, Claire's tense voice and insistence she come right away kept her on edge. "I'm on my way. I'll be there in about a half-hour."

"Don't tell anyone else yet."

"I was on the phone with Kelsey when you called," Elyse said. "She's the one who saw the news first and called me. Claire, you have to tell your sister. She's worried. And when Kade hears, he will be, too, especially since the EMS pensions were involved."

"I'll call them. Please head over. I need you here, Mom."

Claire's hands shook as she hit 'End' to disconnect the call. She re-opened the text message from Matthew that she'd received an hour earlier. *"Best-case scenario, baby. Formalities to work out here. Will call when I can. Ken will be arrested this morning."*

She thought about Ken's ex-wife and wondered if she knew. They'd been divorced nearly a year. Maybe that was why they'd divorced. Had it been Matthew doing something illegal and she knew, would she stay with him? If Ken's ex didn't know, she was about to get one hell of a shock.

Matthew hadn't called yet and she was a nervous wreck, waiting to talk with him. She needed to be sure he was okay. She knew how badly this was affecting him. And she wondered what kind of formalities there were to work out that involved him. She prayed this Don person had been honest with him.

She checked in on the kids. They were happy, playing on their iPads. She brought up Kelsey in her contacts and hit dial.

"Claire, what's going on at Matthew's office?" Kelsey answered.

"I'm swearing you to secrecy," Claire said.

"I swear."

"Matthew suspected Ken was doing something illegal and reported him to the authorities. He's been working with them for six months as they investigated."

"Holy shit! Are you kidding?"

"No. He found out on the twenty-third that they concluded their investigation and was ordered to report this morning. Ken tried to frame both Matthew and Troy. Matthew wasn't sure which way it was going to go. Kels, he could have been arrested this morning, but he wasn't. The truth won out." As the words left her mouth, the tears freed themselves from her eyes.

"Are you okay, Claire?" Kelsey asked, hearing her sister cry. That was something that didn't happen often.

"I'm just so relieved," Claire said. "Mom's coming over. I don't know if Matthew is going to need me, and I want to be available if he does." Plus, she didn't want to tell Kelsey that she just didn't want to be alone. She felt on edge, worried, relieved, anxious, just a wound-up bundle of raw nerves.

"Where is he now?"

"I'm not sure. He said he wanted to be the one to explain everything to Troy after Ken was arrested. He's sure this is the end of the firm, doesn't think it can recover from this even though he did the right thing."

"That sucks," Kelsey said. "What's he going to do now?"

"I don't know, Kels. I just don't know." Her phone notified her of a call waiting. "Kels, Matthew is calling. I have to go." She disconnected and switched over. "Matthew, are you okay?"

"I–I'm not sure."

Claire waited a few seconds. He said nothing more. "Where are you now?"

"At the office. After I met with the SCC and the EDVA, I came to the office and confirmed with Don that Ken was here. Then they moved in and arrested him."

"I saw it on the news," Claire said. She didn't know that the Eastern District of Virginia federal prosecutors were involved. That would explain why the FBI made the arrest. "How did this become a federal case?"

"They found evidence in Ken's emails that he was working with some investment broker in New York that was also being investigated for fraud. I gave them access to DWJ's servers a week ago."

"How did Troy take it?" Claire asked.

"Not well," Matthew said. "I think he's pissed at me for going to the authorities and keeping him in the dark."

"You did what you thought was right."

"He would have wanted to deal with it between the three of us. He'd never have allowed the authorities to be called."

"Ken broke the law. He was basically stealing people's money, stealing their future financial security," Claire said. "How does Troy not see that?"

"I don't know, but his judgement has been skewed for over six months now. I didn't see it before, but I clearly see it now. I have to go, Claire. Kerry and I have a meeting with Troy to see what we can salvage. I'll call you later. I love you."

"I love you, too, Matthew."

• • • •

ELYSE CALLED JAKE'S cell phone as she drove towards Claire's house. It went to voicemail. He was at work. She wasn't sure that if he saw the news he'd connect the dots to Matthew from Donnor Woods Jeffries. "Hi, I'm not sure if you've seen the news or will realize it's Matthew's firm they're talking about. I'm on my way to Claire's house. She called. Matthew's partner was just arrested for some sort of financial crime. Claire says Matthew has been working with the authorities for six months on it. She couldn't tell me more, said not to tell anyone. Call me when you get this. I'll try to answer, depending on how Claire is. She sounded panicked when she called."

And Claire was indeed not herself when Elyse arrived at her house. Claire tried to project a collected and calm front but, knowing her daughter, Elyse knew it was a facade. After greeting the kids, they went to the kitchen where Claire put the tea kettle on. Elyse swallowed her in a hug and held her, not unlike she did when Claire was a child, insisting she was fine, when Elyse knew she wasn't.

And like when she was a child, it didn't take long for Claire to break down and cry, telling her mom how she felt. She needed the release and was so thankful her mom was there. "I'm so worried about Matthew, Mom."

"Has he stayed sober the past few days?" Elyse asked.

"Yes, Kade and Ash actually came over here yesterday afternoon and took him to go to an AA meeting with that weird tattooed guy from Ash's shop. Matthew said he's a nice guy, though." She paused and laughed. "I actually think Matthew liked him, plans to go to more meetings with him. Can you even imagine Matthew choosing to hang out with a guy like that?"

Elyse couldn't help but laugh. "That would be Eric, and he *is* a nice guy."

"Matthew believes his firm is done, no matter what. Between Ken's arrest and Troy being mad at Matthew because he thinks that he and Matthew should have dealt with Ken's illegal activities between the two of them, Matthew doesn't think any part of the firm and his partnership with Troy can be salvaged."

"Matthew did the right thing. Certainly, Troy has to know that."

Claire shrugged. "Well, Troy just found out about this today. Maybe after he has some time to think about it. I don't know. I'm just so relieved that Matthew didn't get arrested. Mom, Ken tried to frame both Matthew and Troy. If Matthew hadn't given the authorities access to their computer system and servers, they may have arrested him, too."

"No wonder he was a mess on Christmas Eve."

"He's been a mess for the last six months he's been working with them. I wish I'd known what his problem was. I told him we'll deal with my anger over him not telling me any of this in counseling. But in his defense, they told him he couldn't tell anyone. Including me."

"I think counseling is a good place for him. You may want to suggest to him that he gets individual counseling as well as the marriage counseling with you. I'm so glad you started going."

"Me, too, Mom. Thank you for that suggestion." As the tea kettle whistled, Claire embraced her mom. "Thank you for being here. I don't know what I'd do without you."

Warmth filled Elyse's heart. "I love you, Claire. I'm glad I'm here and I'm glad you called me to come over. Anything you need, let me know. I think things are going to be up in the air with Matthew's firm and future for a few months. You need to be prepared for a marathon. This isn't a sprint."

Claire focused her tear-filled eyes on her mom. "I'm sure you're right. I think as soon as things are relatively stable for him we're going to go on a vacation for a week, just to get away. I think the kids deserve a trip to Disney World." She smiled. "Funny, just a few months ago, Matthew would have considered that hell on earth, but now, he's actually the one suggesting it."

Elyse was glad to hear that. "I think as long as the two of you face this together, you will come through it just fine."

January
Chapter 45 – A Not So Routine Shift

It had been an uneventful shift. Kade and Cletus had just made a run to the hospital with a minor injury from an accident at a construction site. They were heading back towards their assigned territory when the call came in. An MVA on the 264, two vehicles with rollover and entrapment at one of the off ramps. Kade switched on the lights and sirens. Cletus took the next on ramp to the 264. Through the radio, Kade heard a second ambulance get dispatched.

Kade and Cletus arrived first on the scene of several police cars all with their lights on. A crumpled red SUV of some type lay on its roof on the shoulder of the expressway. It was clear that it had rolled down the embankment due to the damage along the hill. At the top of the hill, also on its roof, was a white SUV. It was off to the side and looked to have struck the guard rail and careened into the culvert on the right side of the off-ramp. Cletus pulled up beside the cop who was directing traffic.

"You're needed up top." He pointed to the red car. "That's a fatality. The coroner will come back with the driver being impaired, I'm sure. When I opened the door to check on her, a cloud of smoke surrounded me. I'm high just from checking her out. You got an unconscious woman and two young kids at the top of the hill. We haven't moved anyone yet. The boy was unconscious when we arrived but he's conscious now."

Cletus drove up the hill. Kade's mind was already planning what may need to be done based on the types of injuries he'd likely encounter. The other ambulance was five minutes out. He hoped the kids were at least in car seats or boosters. He hoped the driver had been wearing her seat-belt as well.

Another officer met them at the back of the truck as they grabbed their gear. Two kids crying and yelling for their mom from within the vehicle was heard, which made Cletus' gut clench. For Kade, their cries set off alarm bells in his head. He recognized their cries, their voices. He grabbed his bag and took off running towards the familiar overturned vehicle.

Coming along the driver's side door, his fear was realized. The driver's side window was shattered. He saw black hair that was saturated with blood and the face that he would recognize anywhere, even though it too was streaked with blood. Claire. She was unconscious. Her side of the car had sustained the worst damage. From inside the vehicle, he could hear Aiden and Emma crying and desperately calling for their mom.

One of the cops was inside the vehicle near the kids. It looked as though he'd entered through the rear hatch area, which was open. It was standard practice for the police to leave kids in their car seats so the paramedics could evaluate them and place C-collars on their necks to prevent spinal injuries after an accident, especially a rollover. The driver's side was crunched in on the driver and with crushing damage along the entire side of the vehicle.

"The doors are jammed," the officer told them. He pointed to the passenger side up along the wall of the culvert. "And the hill is obstructing entry from that side. We called in the entrapment."

"Cletus, it's Claire and the kids," he called back to his partner, who had the gurney and was approaching quickly.

"Oh shit, man," Cletus swore under his breath. He picked up his pace.

Kade mentally shifted back into paramedic mode, stowing the initial shock that it was his sister and her kids in this vehicle. The kids were both crying. Good signs. Though the fact that Aiden had lost consciousness was concerning. Through the smashed window, he was able to check Claire for a pulse. It was there. She was breathing with minor difficulty. He suspected she wasn't far from consciousness. Her entire left side appeared to have impacted the side of the SUV, which was crunched into the passenger space, pinning her to the center console. He opened his bag. First, he slipped a C-collar on her.

He peeled back the windshield and climbed into the cab of the car. Normally, when an overturned vehicle settled, it fell onto the hood even if the roof maintained its structural integrity and didn't collapse, leaving its trunk area in the air. Because of its positioning in the culvert, Claire's car did not. It settled flat, allowing easy access to the car through the windshield area. He, Cletus, and the officer freed her from her seat-belt, laying her on the board which was right outside the car.

She came awake and moaned in pain as they moved her. "My kids?"

"They're both fine, Claire," Kade said, his face in hers. "You're all okay."

"Kade?" she said in a weak, moaning voice. "What happened?"

"You were in a car accident. I've got you, sis. The kids are fine," he said, even though he hadn't checked them out yet. "Where do you hurt?"

"Everywhere," Claire moaned.

She was losing consciousness again. "Hey, stay with me!" he commanded to her.

He performed a physical assessment. The lacerations on the left side of her head appeared to be superficial. He bandaged them. Her face was spared any lacerations. The blood had merely run onto it from the head wound. She responded with painful reactions all along her left side, shoulder, arm, hip, and leg. Her left arm appeared broken near the wrist, but her hip and left leg showed no abnormalities. He immobilized her, securing her to the board. He still didn't care for her breathing sounds. They were a bit too labored. He called it in as a trauma activation.

The other unit and the fire department had just arrived. Kade performed a quick turnover of Claire to the other unit. They would transfer her to the trauma center immediately. The fire department popped open the passenger door within two minutes. Cletus had just removed both kids from their car seats after placing C-collars on them. Still inside the vehicle Cletus cradled Aiden, who had calmed and was quiet. The cop who was in the SUV extricated himself with a still-wailing Emma in his arms, followed by Cletus with Aiden from the third-row seat.

Kade took Aiden from Cletus and brought him near Claire, who was barely conscious. "See, Claire? He's fine."

"Mommy!" Aiden cried.

"It's okay, A-man," Kade said. "Mommy is going to be fine."

"Emma I hear Emma crying," Claire said with tears in her own eyes.

"She's just afraid. She's not hurt." Kade looked over his shoulder. Cletus now held Emma in his arms. Emma still clutched her soft dolly. She hadn't let go of it during the rollover or after. "Cletus, bring her over."

"Mommy!" Emma screamed upon being brought near her mom's face. Emma reached for her, but Kade held her back.

"Mommy's going to be fine," Kade said. "You're all okay. I promise." Emma still cried. Aiden was too quiet. Kade was concerned. He made eye contact with the other paramedic. "I'll contact her husband and our mom to meet you at the trauma center."

Kade glanced back into the overturned vehicle, through the back door, which hung open. On the floor he caught sight of the yellow Mister Quack. He retrieved it and handed it to Aiden. Then he and Cletus hurried to their own unit. Both of the children would be transported and checked out. He was most concerned about Aiden, as he'd lost consciousness and was a little too sedate, possibly in shock.

Once he and Cletus strapped Emma into the car seat in the back of the unit and secured Aiden to the gurney, Cletus ran to the front of the unit to drive them to the trauma center as well. Emma had quieted and Aiden was stable. Kade pulled his phone out of his pocket. He dialed his mom. She answered on the second ring. He heard the unmistakable sounds of her answering through the mic on her car. "Hey Mom, are you driving?"

"Yes, I just left the shelter. I'm running a few errands. What's up? You're at work, aren't you?"

"Mom, I want you to pull off the road into a parking lot or something. Tell me when you've put the car in park."

"What's the matter, Kade?"

"There's been an accident, but everyone is okay. Let me know when you're no longer driving." He heard his mom's breath leave her lungs.

"Okay, my car's in park."

"Claire and the kids were in a car accident."

"An accident? How bad was it?"

"Mom, I need you to stay calm," he said in his professional voice, which was even and authoritative. "The kids are fine. They were in their car seats. I have them in my unit. They'll both be checked out at the ER to be sure there are no injuries that we can't see." He wouldn't tell her over the phone that Aiden had lost consciousness and he was concerned about him. "Claire was injured. She was conscious when she was transported to the trauma center, so that's a good sign. I need you to call Matthew and I need you both to meet us at the hospital. They're all being transported to Sentara General up on Gresham Drive."

"I know where it is at. I'll call Matthew," Elyse said. "You're sure everyone is okay, Kade?"

"I didn't see any life-threatening injuries, Mom. Make sure you tell Matthew that. I'm sure Claire will be admitted, for observation if nothing else. She has a head wound."

"Oh, my God," Elyse repeated. "Okay, I'll hang up and call Matthew right away. I'll see you in probably about a half-hour or so."

"Come in through the emergency entrance and ask for me," Kade said. He disconnected the call. "Grandma and your daddy are going to meet us at the hospital. The doctors will check you both out just to be sure you're not injured at all and then you will be with me, your daddy, and Grandma while the doctors make your mommy all better."

Emma made a whimpering sound, still hugging her dolly. She was calmer now and didn't cry. Aiden stared at him but didn't reply.

Kade took his hand. "Are you all right, A-man? You're very quiet."

"I'm just trying to be brave for Emma," he whispered. His voice cracked and he suddenly looked like he was on the verge of tears.

"And you're doing a great job. I'm sure it was scary, but it's over now and you guys are safe." He took Aiden's pulse, blood pressure, and listened to his heart. Nothing jumped out at him as off, but Aiden just was.

• • • •

ELYSE TOOK A SECOND to calm herself and then she dialed Matthew. It went to his voicemail. "Damn it," she

601

swore aloud. She called the main number for his firm. The receptionist answered. "This is Matthew Jeffries' mother-in-law. I need to speak with Matthew right away. There's been an accident involving his family. Pull him off any call or out of any meeting he may be in."

"Yes, ma'am," she said.

Less than a minute later, Matthew came on the line. "Elyse, what happened?"

"Claire and the kids were in a car accident. Kade called me. He has the kids in his ambulance. Claire was transported in another. He said there are no life-threatening injuries, but Claire has a head wound. He's sure she'll be admitted."

"Oh Jesus Christ!" Matthew exclaimed. "And the kids?"

"Kade said they were in their car seats so they are unhurt but will be checked out by the doctors at the ER. I think that's standard after an accident."

"What hospital are they at?"

"They're being transported to Sentara General on Gresham Drive," Elyse answered. "I'm on my way, too."

"Okay, good, thank you," Matthew said.

They hung up and then Elyse called Jake to tell him. She assured him that she didn't need him to come. She'd call if she needed him. She wasn't going to call Kelsey yet until she was at the ER and knew herself the extent of everyone's injuries. If either or both of the kids were injured, too, they'd need Kelsey there. She wasn't sure if Kade could stay or if he'd be back to work right away.

She arrived in less than thirty minutes, driving way above the posted speed limit. She parked in the ER parking lot. She could see several ambulances parked off past the doors into the Emergency Room that the ambulances used, which was separate from the entrance the general public used. She rushed through the front doors. Neither Kade nor Matthew were in sight, and certainly, Matthew would have beat her there. His office was closer than she'd been out in Suffolk.

She approached the front desk where patients checked in. "My adult daughter and two grand-kids were brought in by ambulance. My son, Kade, is a paramedic and was in one of them with the kids."

The woman gave her a compassionate grin. "You must be Missus Laramie. Kade told me you were on your way."

"Yes, I'm Elyse Laramie."

The woman handed her a 'Visitor' sticker to put on her shirt. Then she ushered her through the doors to the back area with the treatment bays. She saw Kade and Cletus standing outside one of the rooms. "There's my son," she told the woman and then charged ahead. "Kade!"

"Mom, it's okay," he said, wrapping her in an embrace.

"Hi, Missus L," Cletus greeted, giving her a hug as well.

"Hi, Cletus."

She noticed blood on both their shirts, and she recalled he said Claire had a head wound. "How is everyone?" She looked around but didn't see Matthew. "Is Matthew here?"

"Yes, he went with Aiden to Imaging. They're doing an MRI. He lost consciousness for a few minutes after the accident. They're just ruling out any injury."

Elyse's heart dropped. Aiden had been injured. "And Emma?"

Kade pointed to the room behind him. "She's in with the nurse. The doctor will be in soon. She seems fine. They'll just verify there's no injury and probably release her. Claire is in X-ray. It looks like her left shoulder is dislocated and her arm may be broken. It's not a compound fracture, but there could be a break in her ulna or radius. Her left wrist is likely sprained, and she has some tenderness to her hip, leg, knee, and down to her foot all on that left side. The impact was to that side of the car. She probably hit her entire left side against the frame of the car. They'll check it all out and make sure there are no injuries there."

Elyse held back tears of concern. "I'm so glad you were there, Kade."

"Me, too, Mom. Why don't you go in with Emma. I'll be in when the doctor comes. I'm waiting to hear from my supervisor. It's nearly the end of the shift and I've requested he clock me out so I can stay here and help."

"That would be great if you can. How did the accident happen, Kade? Do you know?"

"It looks like an impaired driver entered the off-ramp the wrong way as Claire was exiting the interstate. It looks like she swerved to avoid a head-on collision and struck a guard rail. Her car then flipped and rolled down into the culvert," Kade said.

"An impaired driver? Like drunk?" Elyse asked.

"Most likely under the influence of something," Kade said.

"At three o'clock in the afternoon?" Elyse asked, surprised.

"Yes, impaired drivers are on the road at all hours of the day and night, Missus L," Cletus said.

Elyse shook her head. She shouldn't have been surprised but she was. "I'll be in with Emma."

She slid open the door and went in. A young woman in scrubs was fussing over Emma and her dolly. Emma wore her normal clothes. She sat upright on the bed.

"Grandma!" Emma exclaimed when she entered.

"Hi, sweetie. Are you okay?"

Emma nodded.

"She's been very brave," the nurse said. "She understands that her daddy is with her brother and the doctors are taking good care of her mommy. And her Uncle Kade and I have been here with her."

Elyse went up to the other side of Emma's bed. She hugged her granddaughter and then took her hand. "I'm sure you're being brave. It had to be scary though."

Emma nodded again.

"Did having Uncle Kade there help?"

"Yes," Emma said.

"Kade is the best," the nurse said.

"Yes, he is," Elyse agreed.

It wasn't long before the doctor came in, followed by Kade. He was a likable man with a good bedside manner for dealing with children. He showed Emma what he was going to do on the dolly first, and then on her, feeling over every joint and bone, her tummy, and her back. He even shined his pen light into the doll's eyes before doing so to Emma.

"She's fine," he proclaimed, his eyes going between Kade and Elyse. "No tenderness anywhere and her pupils reacted normally. I won't admit her, but I will send home a list of symptoms that, if they present, she'd need to be brought back to the ER. She should be watched closely over the next twenty-four hours."

"She will be," Elyse promised. She'd take her home with her and watch her like a hawk!

"Okay. And after I review Aiden's imaging, we'll go from there. I am concerned he lost consciousness and by what you," he said, his eyes focusing on Kade, "described as his overly sedate manner when you arrived on the scene and during transport. I suspect a mild concussion at the very least. Even if the scan is clear, I'm leaning towards keeping him overnight for observation."

"Are you also my daughter's doctor?" Elyse asked.

"No, Doctor Jernigan is her doctor. She's in good hands. Jernigan is thorough."

"Thank you," Elyse said.

"After he's done in Imaging, Aiden will be returned to the bay next door. I'm going to process the paperwork to get Miss Emma out of here. Sit tight for about fifteen minutes and then she can go."

After he left, Kade viewed the text message that pinged his phone while the doctor had been in. It was from his supervisor. His request was approved. He would be clocked out and wouldn't need to return to the EMS headquarters building. Cletus had gone out to clean the unit. "I'll be right back, Mom. I have to go get my backpack and touch base with Cletus. I'm off as of now, so I can stay and help here. I was thinking, though, if Aiden is being admitted, maybe we should ask Kelsey to come get Emma. Someone needs to stay with both Aiden and Claire tonight."

"You're right. I'll call Kelsey. What do you say, Emma? Would you like to have a sleepover at your Auntie Kelsey's house tonight?"

Emma smiled.

Kade nodded to Emma. "I'll call Kels on my way out. I'll be back in a few." He slipped out of the room and then exited the hospital. With long strides he closed the distance between the door and the ambulance, where Cletus was in the back, disinfecting and cleaning. "Hey, thanks for taking care of this. The captain got back to me. He's punching me out and I'm approved to stay here. You'll drive back alone. It's nearly the end of the shift anyway."

"Good. I'm glad you can be here with your family. I'm glad they're all going to be okay."

"Do you got this, or do you want help?" Kade asked, motioning to the inside of the unit.

"No, man, I've got it."

"Thanks. I owe you one. I'm just going to grab my backpack." He appeared in the open door again. "I left my radio on the seat."

"I'll get it signed in. Don't worry. Let me know how everyone is, okay?"

"Yeah, for sure," Kade said. Then he stepped over to the smoking area behind the building and lit up. He took out his phone and dialed Kelsey.

"Hi, Kade," she answered.

"Hey, Kels. What are you doing?"

"I'm at the shop."

"Are you real busy?"

"No, never too busy to talk to my brother. What's up? You sound overly serious."

"Do I?" he asked. "Yeah. Kelsey, can you take the night off? There's been a car accident; Claire and the kids, no life-threatening injuries. Claire's pretty banged up. She'll definitely be admitted. Aiden will probably be kept overnight for observation, but he'll be fine I'm sure. Emma was checked over and is being released."

"Oh my God!"

"They're all going to be okay, Kels," Kade stated calmly.

"Does Mom know?"

"Yes, she and Matthew are both here. We need you to come and take Emma, though. Can you do that?"

"Yes, which hospital are you at?"

He gave her the details, including to come in through the ER entrance and ask for him when she arrived. After he finished his smoke he unbuttoned and took off his work shirt, which he had noticed was saturated with blood. It had soaked through to his t-shirt. He wadded both shirts up and stuffed them into the plastic bag he kept in his backpack for soiled clothing. Then he pulled a black t-shirt with the department emblem on before returning to the ER. He arrived back just as Aiden and Matthew were returning to the area.

"How'd it go, A-man?" Kade asked, coming up to the gurney. Aiden still looked out of it.

"He did good, didn't you, Aiden?" Matthew replied as the attendant wheeled him back into the bay he'd been in.

Kade motioned Matthew back into the hallway. "The doc checked in on Emma while you were gone. She's being released. Mom's in with her. I called Kelsey to come get her," Kade told Matthew. "He also said he'd be keeping Aiden overnight for observation, no matter what his scan showed. He's processing both orders now."

Matthew sighed and rubbed his neck, the strain already showing. "Okay, yeah, good you called her. Emma will be fine with her."

"Yes she will, Matthew," Kade said confidently. "Both the kids and Claire will be fine."

"Yeah, thanks," Matthew said. He made eye contact with him. "Thanks, Kade."

"You're welcome. Mom can stay tonight so that someone is in with both of them."

Matthew rubbed his temples. "Sorry. I'll admit I'm out of my element. I don't even know what to do."

"You let your family help you. That's what you do. Just be here for Claire and Aiden. That's all you need to do. Claire was worried about the kids. You'll need to reassure her they're both fine."

Matthew nodded. "Is she back from X-ray yet?" The room she'd initially been treated in was on the other side of the circular-shaped ER department.

"No," Kade confirmed. He would admit that he was getting worried. His gut instinct was that they'd sent her for a CT or an MRI after X-ray. If anything was found, she may go directly to the OR prep area if staff was available. If an operation wasn't needed, the doctor would be arranging a room for her. This hospital usually tried to keep the ER clear after a patient had been triaged. "I'm sure her doctor will be back shortly to tell us what's up." He pointed to Aiden's room. "Why don't you stay with Aiden. I'll make sure Kelsey brings Emma in to say goodbye before she takes her, and I'll watch for Claire's doctor."

"Thanks, Kade," Matthew said for the umpteenth time.

Twenty minutes later Kelsey passed through the doors from the ER waiting room. Recognition of Kade, who still stood in the hallway outside the kids' rooms, had her quicken her pace. She greeted him with a hug. "Any updates?"

"Emma will be released with observation instructions. Aiden is being kept overnight for observation. Claire will be admitted. I haven't heard what any of the test results are yet."

"Oh my God!" Kelsey said. "Where were Claire and the kids going?"

"Dentist appointments for the kids," Kade said.

Aiden and Emma's doctor approached. He had discharge papers for Emma and the paperwork that would hold Aiden overnight for observation. He'd be transferred to the pediatric floor. He went over all of it with Matthew, Kelsey, and Kade. A nurse stayed in with Aiden while they talked. And Elyse stayed in with Emma.

"Hey, Emmie-bear," Kelsey said with a smile, poking her head into the room. "Are you ready to come have a sleepover at my house?" Her gaze shifted to her mom. "Hi, Mom." She stepped all the way into the room and gave Emma a big hug. "Matthew is going to come outside with me, and we'll transfer the car seat from his car to mine. Mom, can you stay with Aiden while we're outside? Kade will remain in the hall, watching for Claire's doctor."

"Where's Mommy?" Emma asked.

"Remember, sweetie?" Elyse said. "Your mommy's head and arm got an ouchie on them and the doctors are going to make her better."

Emma rose onto her knees, her arms out to Kelsey. "I want Mommy."

"I know, sweetie," Elyse said as Kelsey scooped her up.

"How about we stop in and see Aiden before I take you home. And if your mommy comes back down to her room like this one, you can see her. If not, we'll need to wait and maybe FaceTime with her once she's done with the doctor and in a bed to take a nap."

"Aiden coming home, too?" Emma asked.

"No, sweetie," Kelsey said. "The doctor needs him to stay over here tonight to make sure he's okay. But you and I are going to go get you a Happy Meal and we're going to have a fun night at my house."

Emma dropped her head against Kelsey's shoulder.

"Thank you," Elyse said, her eyes locked on Kelsey's. She knew Kelsey would take good care of Emma.

They left the room together and went into Aiden's room. Matthew stood at the head of his bed, holding his hand. "Ah, there's Emma," he said. He stepped to meet them and took her from Kelsey's arms to give her a hug. "You are going to have such a fun night with your Auntie Kelsey and Uncle Ash."

"I told her that as soon as her mommy is able, we'll do a FaceTime call with her," Kelsey said.

"That's a great idea," Matthew said. "And I'm sure Mommy will love that."

Elyse noted that Aiden didn't seem quite his normal self. They had him reclined at a forty-five-degree angle. He just laid there, holding Mister Quack, his eyes scanning them all. "How are you feeling, Aiden?" she asked him, coming up beside him.

"I'm okay, Grandma," he said. "I don't want to stay here. I want to go home."

"I know," Elyse said. "I'm going to stay all night with you. Your daddy will be here too, probably in with your mommy, but I'm sure he'll come in to tuck you in when it's time for bed. And I know it's almost dinner time. They'll get you something to eat, I'm sure. Are you hungry?"

Aiden shrugged. "I don't know."

Elyse found this concerning. She was glad they were keeping him tonight. He was way too calm, which wasn't like him. "We'll see when we get to your room. I happen to know that hospitals always have ice cream or popsicles," she tempted him, which brought a smile to his face.

Kelsey and Emma said goodbye to them and then, as planned, Matthew accompanied them to the parking lot to transfer Emma's car seat to Kelsey's car. Matthew returned just as Claire's doctor was filling Kade in on her imaging results.

"To recap," Doctor Jernigan said, "Claire's left shoulder is dislocated. Her left ulna is also broken near her wrist. There is a second fracture at the base of her fifth metacarpal. Surgery is needed to repair both breaks. We have already transferred her to the surgery prep area. We'll have forms for you to sign. We'll reset the shoulder once she's sedated for surgery. Her head wound, while it did bleed a lot because head wounds do, is not serious. She has a concussion, which we'll monitor, but Imaging revealed no brain bleed and no skull fracture. There was no damage to her spinal column. And there were no fractures anywhere else on her body, just some bruising along that left side that most likely impacted the frame of the car during the accident." Doctor Jernigan was a woman in her early fifties with an even voice who spoke in a matter-of-fact tone. "She was very lucky."

"Surgery?" Matthew echoed. He nodded. "Okay."

"Is she conscious?" Kade asked.

"Barely. The morphine has her pretty out of it. But you can see her before surgery if you'd like," she offered.

"Yes, thank you," Matthew answered. He was grateful Kade was there. He wouldn't have even thought to ask.

Kade gripped Matthew's shoulder. "I'll stay with you until she's out of surgery. Mom will stay with Aiden."

Matthew blew out and nodded. "Yeah, good."

• • • •

KADE WAS EXHAUSTED by the time he made the drive home to Franklin. He came through the front door and went straight to the kitchen. He was also thirsty and hungry. He was surprised to find Mel at the kitchen table, studying.

She rose and rushed over to him, greeting him with a silent embrace. She understood. She just held him and waited for him to either pull away or speak. After a few comforting minutes, he drew away just far enough to press a kiss to her lips. Then he dropped his head onto her shoulder. He breathed out heavily before he pulled away and went to the refrigerator, where he plucked a beer from the shelf. After a long drink he finally spoke.

"How goes the studying?"

"Good," she said, watching him closely.

"How do you feel? Any more contractions?"

"Just Braxton Hicks."

Kade had of course messaged Mel with what was happening as the afternoon unfolded. After taking an Uber from the hospital to where he'd parked for work, he called her and gave her a quick verbal update. Then he blasted the music in his truck as he drove home.

"I was surprised you were coming home. I thought you might stay."

"I thought about it," Kade said. "But there was no need. Mom and Matthew are both staying all night so someone will be with both Claire and Aiden. They're both going to be okay. Besides, I'm on at four." He checked his watch. "I'll get to bed soon. Should be able to get at least five hours."

"If you can get right to sleep," Mel said. She knew that was unlikely.

Tears filled Kade's eyes. "When I heard the kids crying and calling for their mom when we first arrived on-site, I knew it was Aiden and Emma. Even on its roof, I recognized that it was Claire's car."

Mel took him back into her arms as he broke down and sobbed.

"Claire can be a pain in the ass but she's my sister, and the thought that she may not make it was hard to keep from my mind. I had to treat her first. The kids had to wait, but they cried and screamed until Cletus got C-collars on them.

They were suspended upside down in their seats and I'm sure they didn't understand why the police didn't get them out of their seats. Even though I knew they were fine, their screams and cries broke my heart."

Mel held him. "I know, baby. You had to treat the worst-injured first."

"I don't want them to hate me because I didn't help them."

"They'll understand you had to help their mommy first," Mel said. "And you did. You did your job and stowed the rest away, like you're supposed to. You're a true professional, Kade, and the best paramedic I know. I'm sorry you had to go through this, but if anyone had to take care of the scene there's no one better than you. I'm sure when she realizes what happened, Claire will be so glad you were there."

Kade took a few more minutes to shed the tears he needed to and purge the stress and emotions from the day from his body. Even though everyone survived, he knew that call would never leave him. He'd carry the moment that he knew it was his family in that overturned car with him always.

"Thanks, Mel," he said. He straightened out of her hold and then finished his beer. He grabbed a bag of chips and another beer. "The dinner of champions."

"I think there's still some chocolate chip cookies if you want dessert."

"Yeah, I just might."

Thirty minutes later they let Charlie out for the last time and then took him to bed with them. Mel wrapped Kade in an embrace, his hand coming to rest on her abdomen. His child was due in just two weeks. He'd be a father soon.

Chapter 46 – Aftermath

Claire felt as though she was pulling herself from a deep fog. Her whole body hurt, and it was a struggle to open her eyes. When she did, the brightness in the room blinded her. She tried to raise a hand to shield her eyes but her left arm felt heavy and unresponsive, and she instantly felt pain when she tried. Her right felt odd, but she was able to raise it. Cracking her eyes back open, she saw her forearm taped with what she recognized to be the tubing and a needle beneath indicating an IV was in her arm.

"Claire, you're awake," Matthew's familiar voice said and then his face appeared in front of her. She then realized she was in a hospital bed. "How do you feel?"

"My whole body hurts and I have one hell of a headache. Matthew, what happened?" Her throat was scratchy, and she sounded hoarse even to her own ears.

"You were in a car accident. Don't you remember?"

"No," Claire said, searching her memory. "The kids?"

"They're fine," Matthew assured her. "Emma is with Kelsey and Ash, and your mom is with Aiden. They kept him overnight for observation and he should be released this morning. Your mom promised to contact me if he had any issues overnight. I haven't heard from her, so I'm confident that Aiden slept well."

"Why didn't you stay with Aiden?"

"I couldn't leave you, Claire. He was okay. You weren't. I was so afraid I was going to lose you."

She saw tears in his eyes and genuine concern etched deeply in his face. "How bad was it?"

"It was bad, Claire. I've never been so afraid in my life. When your mom called and told me you and the kids had been in an accident, my heart seized. I feared I'd lost my whole family. You three are all that matters to me. Then she told me that the kids were okay, but that you were hurt. I didn't find out that Aiden had lost consciousness until I got here. You were already in Imaging by then. Kade stayed with Emma, waiting for your mom, but I went with Aiden. They did an MRI on him to check his brain. But they didn't find anything wrong. He seems fine."

"I don't remember the accident. What happened? How bad is the damage to my car?"

"Kade's sure it's totaled," Matthew said.

"How did the accident happen?" She didn't understand why she couldn't remember.

"It looks like a drunk or high driver drove down the off-ramp, the wrong way and you swerved to avoid the head-on collision. Kade told me the entire side of the car on the driver's side scraped the front driver's side corner of her car. Her car careened one way, down an embankment; yours flipped around and hit a guard rail before rolling down into a culvert of some sort."

Claire breathed out the heavy breath that had gotten stuck in her chest, frightened by that description. Why couldn't she remember it? "You promise the kids are both okay?"

He took her hand and kissed her knuckles. "I promise. Both Aiden and Emma are fine. And you're going to be fine, too. You had a head wound. It's bandaged and they didn't even have to shave your head." He paused and smiled. "Your mom was glad about that. It looked bad because it bled a lot, being a head wound, but you didn't have a skull fracture or any brain bleeds. Just a concussion. That's why you have a headache."

She looked down at herself. She wore a hospital gown. Her left arm was in a splint and wrapped in a bandage. "Is my arm broken?"

"Yes, in a few places. You had surgery yesterday. They had to put some plates and screws in near your wrist. It's in a splint right now, but the doctor said it will be in a cast after the surgery incisions heal."

"How long will it have to be in the cast?"

"I don't know. The orthopedic surgeon will be in sometime this morning. I'm sure we'll get more information then."

She reached her right hand to her face and gripped her forehead.

"Are you in pain?" he asked, ready to go get the nurse if she was.

"A little." Her eyes took in the IV needle taped in her arm. Her gaze traveled up the tube to the pole where they had two bags hanging and dripping into the vials that then sent the fluid into the tube. "What are they giving me?"

Matthew shrugged. "I don't know. I think one is a pain killer."

"Well, it's not working or I need more," Claire said.

"I'll call the nurse," Matthew volunteered. He leaned over her and pressed a kiss to her lips while reaching for the call button on the bed. He pressed it. "I love you," he said, his head hovering over hers. "I'm so sorry for the last six months. For everything."

"Shh," Claire said. "None of that matters right now."

"I'm all in, Claire," he said, still gazing into her eyes. "Just like we talked about with the counselor the other day. You can count on me to be here with you and the kids all the way. I'm not going to step back and retreat into my own thoughts. I'm not going to drink or use drugs to turn off the worry like I did. I promise."

"I believe you," she said. "I love you, too, Matthew. I want you to call the counselor today and tell her what happened and reach out to her if you need to talk to her. I shouldn't be in here too long, should I?"

"I don't think so," he said. "We should be able to keep our appointment with her next week."

"Did anyone call Michael to let him know?"

"Yes, I took care of that last night," Matthew assured her. "Don't worry about work. That doesn't matter right now. Your recovery is all that does."

"Yes, but what about your firm? I know that you, Kerry, and Troy are trying to sort out the mess Ken made."

Matthew shook his head. "I don't care about any of that right now. You and the kids are all I care about. I called Troy and Kerry last night, too. They know not to bother me for the next few days, unless it's an emergency. Kerry has been a lifesaver, though. I'll tell you when you're up and around what he's done to try to save the firm."

"I may be leaving Kensington-Laramie," Claire said. "I've been contemplating it."

Matthew smiled. "We could be unemployed together. Your mother has a few rooms left at her place. Maybe we could move in with them, too," he joked.

Claire laughed softly as the nurse entered. She was an older woman, closer to her mom's age.

"This looks promising," the nurse said with a smile. "How do you feel, Claire?"

"I'm in a little pain," she answered. "I understand I have a concussion, so that explains the headache. And my arm, especially my shoulder and my wrist, really hurt." She paused and let out a sigh. "I just feel like a truck hit me. I'm achy all over."

"What kind of car do you drive?" the nurse asked.

"An Escalade."

"You *were* hit by a truck, honey. An Escalade," she said with a smile as she patted Claire's shoulder. "It impacted the entire left side of your body as it rolled over."

Claire smiled at her description. "Can I get something for the pain?"

"Yes, the doctor left an order for it. I'll go get it. Do you think you can swallow a couple of tablets?"

"Yes." Claire's eyes went to the IV bags. "What's in those?"

"One is just fluids. The other is an antibiotic so your surgery site doesn't get infected," the nurse said. "My name is Darcy, by the way. I'll be here until three this afternoon. Are you hungry?" She handed Claire a piece of paper, one of the many on the tray table. "Here's the menu. Your doctor hasn't given you any restrictions. You can order whatever you want." She pointed to the extension number. "Just dial it on the phone. They'll know your room number." She pulled the room phone onto the tray table. "I'll also get you a fresh water."

"Thank you," Claire said. After she left the room, she made eye contact with Matthew. "She's efficient."

"She came on duty at seven. The nurse who'd been here overnight with you brought her in and introduced her to me. You were still sleeping from the strong painkiller they gave you last night."

"I hope whatever she brings me doesn't knock me out."

"No, the doctor did say you'd be given a lighter painkiller beginning today. He doesn't want you sleeping all day. And I'm sure when that nurse comes back, she's going to make you get up and use the bathroom."

She looked down at both arms. "I'm not even sure how I'll do anything between the splint and bandages on this arm and the needle in the other. I hate IVs."

"Hopefully you'll get out of here today," Matthew said.

"I hope so." Claire looked over the tray table in front of her. "Where's my phone?"

Matthew pointed behind her. "It's charging."

"Can you get it for me? I want to call my mom and see how Aiden is."

"And when you're up for it you should call Kelsey too and talk to Emma. She was pretty upset leaving you and Aiden yesterday."

"Did Kelsey take her back to our house so she could sleep in her own bed?"

"No, she brought her back to her house. I'm sure she's fine, Claire."

"Did you hear from Kelsey on how she did going to bed last night?" Claire asked. Emma had never spent the night anywhere but her own bed.

"No. I assumed no news was good news."

Nurse Darcy returned with a tablet in a small cup and a large Styrofoam cup of ice water. After Claire had taken the painkiller, Matthew had been correct; she helped Claire get up and use the bathroom. She got her settled back in bed. sitting up.

Claire hated to admit it, but she felt lightheaded. The nurse assured her she'd feel better after she ate something. With the nurse's prompting, Claire placed the order for her breakfast and then typed out a text to her mom to see how Aiden was. Her phone rang immediately.

"Hi, Mom. How is he?"

"Aiden is doing good. How are you?"

In the background Claire heard Aiden. "I want to talk to Mommy."

"Mom, can you put him on the phone?"

"Can we do a FaceTime call?" Elyse asked. "I think he'll feel better if he can see Mommy."

"Do you think the bandage on my head will scare him?"

"No, he saw it bloody yesterday, so he knows it was bleeding. He and I already talked about your injuries. He knows you have a big band-aid on your head. I also told him you have a broken arm like he had," Elyse said.

Claire initiated the FaceTime call. As Elyse accepted it, she moved the phone to show Aiden. He sat upright in his own hospital bed. He looked tired, but otherwise fine. "Good morning, Aiden. How do you feel?"

"Mommy!" he greeted with a big smile. "I'm okay. Grandma stayed with me all night. I wanted to be with you and Daddy, but they wouldn't let me."

"I know, sweetie. I wanted to be with you, too. But they only let one person be in a bed and only one person can stay in the room with them. Hopefully both of us will go home today."

"Yes, I want to go home, Mommy."

"Did you have breakfast yet?" Claire asked.

"No, Grandma just ordered it for me. I'm going to have pancakes, and I had ice cream for dinner last night!"

"Yum," Claire said. "I just ordered mine, too." She moved the phone to include Matthew on the screen when he leaned in close beside her.

"Good morning, Aiden. You look like you slept well. I know yesterday was scary. But you were so brave for your sister," Matthew said. "I'm proud of you."

"It was scary. Mommy, Emma cried and wouldn't stop until Uncle Kade brought her to you. He and Cletus had you on the ground and you were bleeding. They put these icky things on our necks that hurt, and I didn't like it. But we got to ride with Uncle Kade in his ambulance and he called Daddy and Grandma."

Claire's eyes went to Matthew. "Kade?"

"Yes, he and Cletus were the first unit to respond to your accident. He transported the kids, but another ambulance brought you. He was really amazing, Claire. And everyone in the emergency room knew him. He took care of everything."

Claire was shocked. Her gaze went back to Aiden on her phone. "I'm so glad Uncle Kade was with you," she told Aiden. "I'm sure that had to make you and Emma feel better."

She couldn't imagine how Kade felt. If it were her coming upon her family in an accident, she didn't know how she'd handle it. She would call Kade as soon as she could, after she called Kelsey so she could see Emma. She owed a huge thank-you to her entire family.

"Aiden's breakfast just came," Elyse said, pulling the phone so she could see Claire. "How about we hang up so he can eat, and we'll call you again after. Matthew, I'll let you know when the doctor comes in so you can be here. The nurse anticipates that he will release Aiden when he comes in. I can bring him home to your house and have Kelsey bring Emma home, too. And I will stay with them until you get home, Matthew, hopefully with Claire. When is Lizette due to come back from her vacation?"

"Not until Monday," Claire answered.

It had been a long two weeks without Lizette. Claire wondered if Lizette had gotten married over her vacation with the boyfriend, who she had yet to meet. If she had, that would bring a new level of complication. This was not the situation Claire wanted to interview and hire a new nanny under.

"Both Kelsey and I can be there to help with anything you two need," Elyse offered.

"Thank you, Elyse. I owe you both so much for yesterday," Matthew said.

"You're welcome, and you owe us nothing. This is what family is for." Elyse gave them a smile and then shifted the phone so they saw Aiden. "Aiden, say goodbye to your mommy and daddy for now."

He already had a fork in his hand and was preparing to take a bite of his pancakes. "Bye," he said, completely unfazed.

"Bye sweetie. Enjoy those pancakes," Claire said. "Thanks, Mom," she said before she disconnected the call. Unlike Aiden, she felt very emotional. Seeing the tears in her eyes, Matthew embraced her. "I don't want to cry. My head is finally feeling better." She dropped her head against his shoulder and enjoyed the sensation of safety his embrace brought. "Do you really think they'll discharge me today?"

"I think so," Matthew said. "There's really no reason for you to stay in here."

"I think we will need to take my mom and sister up on their offers to help. Taking care of me and the kids will be a lot on you."

"Don't worry about anything, Claire. We'll get whatever help you need if I can't handle it. I'm sure the hospital can help arrange a visiting nurse for a few days. I'll reach out to Lena and see if she can come a few more days a week to clean and maybe do some meal prep. If she can't, maybe she'll know someone who can. And as far as help with the kids, if your mom and Kelsey can each come for four or five hours on opposite days until Lizette is back, that would help."

Claire wiped the tears from her cheeks. "Yes, that will all help." She blew out a cleansing breath. "Let me calm down and then I'll call Kels."

Matthew pressed a kiss to her lips. "Take your time. It's early. I think there's a good chance Kelsey and Emma are still asleep."

"I want to call Kade, too," Claire said.

"I'm sure he'd appreciate that."

. . . .

KELSEY LAY AWAKE, SNUGGLING with Emma in her bed. It was early, nearly eight. Ash was still asleep on the other side of Emma. He'd gotten home from the shop around midnight, long after Emma had fallen asleep. That was after Kelsey laid down with her. Once she was asleep, Kelsey crept downstairs. She never went to bed that early. She relaxed on the couch under a cozy blanket and read a book she'd been wanting to read but never had time for. She sipped herbal tea and tried not to think about what could have happened to Claire and the kids in the accident. They were all going to be fine, no permanent damage done to anyone. But still, the what-ifs were storm clouds that wouldn't clear.

Emma had been so afraid. After getting her a Happy Meal, Kelsey drove to the shop and brought Emma in to see Ash. She sat Emma up on the counter and everyone showered her with attention, even the clients. That had helped to calm her. By the time Kelsey got her home it was nearly bedtime. It became clear immediately that Emma wasn't going to lie down alone, so Kelsey joined her and snuggled with her until she was asleep.

Kelsey's phone rang. She rolled over quickly to answer it before it woke Emma and Ash. Too late. Seeing it was Claire, she answered it with a whispered voice as she rolled back to see both of them had their eyes open. "Hi, Claire. How are you?"

"I'm good this morning. How is Emma?"

"Just waking up. Here, let me switch this to a FaceTime call." After the screen showed Claire's face, Kelsey brought the phone to hover over Emma.

"Mommy!" Emma squealed.

"Hi, baby. Is Auntie Kelsey taking good care of you?"

Emma rolled up to a sitting position and hugged Kelsey. "We had Happy Meals and went to her work." Emma grabbed the phone and pointed it at Ash, who was awake, lying on his pillow. "Uncle Ash didn't come home with us for bed. He's here now."

Claire was taken aback seeing them all in bed together. She surely hoped Ash had clothes on his bottom half, given that his torso was bare and covered with tattoos. "That's good, sweetie," she said. "Put the phone back on you." When she did, Claire continued. "Mommy and Aiden are just fine, baby. We'll probably both be coming home today. We'll have Auntie Kelsey bring you home later this morning. Are you okay, sweetie? Daddy told me you were afraid yesterday."

"I was," Emma said with a pouty lip. "Auntie Kelsey hugged me better."

Claire smiled. That was a thing her mom used to say to them whenever they were sad or hurt. She'd forgotten it until now. "I'm sure she did, baby. Auntie Kelsey is good at that."

Kelsey swiveled the phone screen so she could see Claire. "Do you really think you'll be released today? That's great!"

"Yes, we think so. Aiden definitely will be. Mom stayed with him all night. I really owe both of you a huge thank-you for being here."

"Aw, Claire, no thanks needed. And yes, just let me know when you want me to bring her home."

"We may need you and Mom to alternate helping out for a few hours over the next few days until Lizette is back from vacation, if you can," Claire said.

"Sure, whatever you need," Kelsey assured her. "Okay, now that Miss Emma is awake, I'm going to get her to the bathroom and make her some breakfast," Kelsey said.

"Okay, sounds good," Claire said. "Let me say goodbye to Emma."

Kelsey spun the phone so the screen was on Emma. "Say goodbye to your Mommy. We'll talk to her more later, Emma."

· · · ·

KADE AND CLETUS WERE mid-way through their shift. The morning rush hour saw the normal number of calls for MVAs. Claire's was still on Kade's mind. They only made one run to the ER at the hospital where Claire and Aiden were, and it was too early for him to pop into their rooms. He'd thought about it, though. He was sure there would be a few more transports that morning, and he'd go see them then.

They'd just completed a call that didn't warrant transport and had called themselves in as clear from the scene, when his phone rang. "It's Claire," he said holding his phone up to Cletus. "Hi sis. How are you doing this morning?"

"I'm good, Kade," Claire said. "Matthew told me you were there yesterday. I can't thank you enough. He and the kids told me how you took care of everything."

Claire sounded emotional. Kade's chest constricted with so many different memories of the previous day running through his thoughts. He'd never tell her how afraid he felt, approaching her overturned car. Or how the cries that he recognized belonged to Aiden and Emma hurt his heart.

"No thanks needed, Claire. I was just doing my job."

"I don't think so," she said. "Matthew told me that you arranged to get off early and stayed at the hospital with him even after I was taken to surgery. You helped him so much just by being there." She started to cry again.

"Of course I did, sis. I wouldn't leave until things were settled there and I knew you were all going to be okay."

"Thank you, Kade. You took care of my babies when I couldn't. I don't even remember the accident."

"That's normal, Claire. Don't worry that you can't remember it. Cletus and I were glad it was us who were on-scene. And we're both so happy all three of you are okay. We will probably be at the hospital a few more times today with transports. I'll try to pop up to your room during one of them."

"I'd like that," she said. "I'm hoping to be released today. I'll text you if that happens to save you the trip up to my room."

"Okay," Kade said. "Also let me know when Aiden gets released. The doctor was sure he'd only be there overnight."

"I will," Claire promised. "And thank Cletus for me, too."

"I will. I'll talk to you later."

"Bye."

"Bye." After disconnecting the call his gaze shifted to Cletus. "She sounded good. She said to tell you thank you from her."

· · · ·

BOTH AIDEN AND CLAIRE were released later that day. Kade never did make it back to the hospital before their discharge. Before they left the hospital, Matthew was able to arrange for a home visit from a nurse for the three days following her release. Matthew drove Aiden and Claire home in his car. Elyse followed.

Once they arrived home Claire called Kelsey, who promised to bring Emma home right away. Claire's splinted and bandaged arm was in a sling. She had an appointment in four days with the orthopedic surgeon who would cast it then. She'd most likely have it on for ten weeks, maybe twelve.

"I'm trying not to complain about the length of time the cast will have to be on," Claire told her mom. They sat on the white couch in the front room, waiting for Kelsey and Emma to arrive home. "I just don't know how I'm going to function with only one arm."

"You'll manage. You'll figure out new ways of doing things," Elyse said. "And it sounds as though you will have a lot of help here at home. I'm glad your house cleaner can come twice more a week."

"Me, too. And I trust Lena. I really didn't want someone new that I'd have to worry might steal something. Though, with all the fallout from Ken Woods' arrest, this is probably the worst time for us to be spending money on all these extra things. And at some point, we have to get me a new car, too."

"Does Matthew still think this is the end of his firm?" Elyse asked in a whisper. Matthew was in the play room with Aiden.

"He's not sure. And even if some clients can be kept, he's not sure that he and Troy Donnor will stay in a partnership. Troy is still pretty pissed at him for going to the authorities, and Matthew is pissed at Troy for not seeing the bigger picture. Plus, Troy has been unreliable since he had his midlife crisis when his wife divorced him and he started to party like a madman. Matthew said he was able to get by not bringing in new clients for the last nine months because he and Ken were holding up the business."

"It sounds like a mess. Matthew might be better off if he severs all ties with Troy," Elyse said. "But it's only been a week since everything happened. I'm sure a little time will help calm everyone's frayed nerves."

"Yes, I'm sure you're right," Claire agreed. "He's been a different person this last week. A better person. That whole situation had really eaten at him. I can't imagine being in that situation, suspecting a partner and friend was breaking the law. He went to counseling with me earlier this week and was so open about his feelings regarding it all."

Elyse patted her leg. "I'm glad to hear that."

"Yes. And Matthew actually stepped out of my room earlier to talk with that Eric guy because he said he thought about having a drink. He told me that he's considering taking Eric up on his offer to be his sponsor." She paused and smiled. "I have to say I can't see the two of them as buddies, but if it keeps Matthew sober I'd welcome him for dinner here at the house any day of the week."

"Yes, I got to know Eric at Ash and Kelsey's Memorial Day party last year. He's not at all what you'd expect from his appearance. Then again, neither is Ash."

"No, he isn't," Claire said. She saw Kelsey's car pull into the driveway. "Oh, there's Kels." Her smile spread. "I can't wait to see my baby."

Elyse stood. "You stay seated. I'll let them in and remind Emma to be gentle with you."

Even with Grandma's warning to be gentle to Mommy, Emma ran in and practically jumped on her as she pulled herself onto the couch.

"Oh, baby, I missed you so much," Claire said. "But I knew Auntie Kelsey was taking good care of you, so I wasn't worried."

Emma patted her arm and then the bandage on her head. "You have owies." She wrapped her arms around Claire's neck. "I hug you better."

Elyse's heart warmed. Someone remembered that from their childhood. She suspected it was Kelsey, as she'd never heard Claire use those words.

Claire wrapped her right arm around Emma. "So much better. You know, Grandma used to hug us better, too, when Aunt Kelsey, Uncle Kade, and Mommy were kids."

Matthew and Aiden came into the room and greeted Emma and Kelsey. "Elyse, if you can stay for a few hours, I'd appreciate it," he said. Then his gaze went to Claire. "If you don't mind, I called Eric because I want to go to a meeting. I think it will do me good. The last twenty-four hours have been trying and I don't want to drink."

"Of course," Claire said.

"Yes, I was planning to stay as long as you both wanted me here," Elyse said.

Matthew kissed Claire and hugged the kids. Then he left to go meet Eric. Kelsey took the kids back to the playroom.

"I'm glad he said he needs to go, but I guess I didn't realize it would still be an issue," Claire said. "He hasn't had a drink since Christmas Eve. He even boxed up all the alcohol in the house and took it into the store room in the garage. Out of sight out of mind."

"The last twenty-four hours have been hard on all of us," Elyse said. "He was strong through it and accepted all the help we offered. He had to be worried sick about you, though. He's being smart, going to a meeting when he's stressed."

"He said Kade took care of everything. He really appreciated that Kade was there," Claire said. "I don't remember the accident or him being there, but I am so grateful he took care of Aiden and Emma."

Chapter 47 – Pink or Blue

I t was exactly a week after Claire's car accident. Kade's dreams were still haunted with Aiden's and Emma's cries. He woke with wide, startled eyes after another dream that warped and twisted the outcome of that day. In this alternate rendition, Claire's overturned car was shrouded in dense fog and the scene he approached was silent and lifeless.

He checked his watch. The alarm would go off in fifteen minutes. When he sat, he realized Mel wasn't beside him. He knew getting a full night's sleep had become difficult for her. She was so uncomfortable. He couldn't believe that he would be a father any day now. And then getting a full night's sleep would be impossible for them. He turned the bedside light on, and his gaze went to the bassinet across the room.

Mel had been to the OB the day before. She was dilated to three centimeters and twenty percent effaced. The baby had dropped several days earlier and his or her head was down where it needed to be for delivery, fully engaged. Mel had described it as feeling like the baby was a watermelon that wanted to fall out of her, which she'd welcome. The doctor had said that he wouldn't be surprised to see them within the next forty-eight hours.

Kade used the bathroom and splashed cold water on his face, his normal tactic to wake himself. He brushed his teeth and got dressed for work. It was two-thirty. He was scheduled to be in at four. He'd found that at this hour of the morning the commute into the EMS hub, where he clocked in and got issued his ambulance, took less than forty-five minutes most days. Thankfully, there wasn't much traffic on the roads at four in the morning.

He quietly descended the stairs, planning to relax and have an extra cup of coffee while scrolling through the news on his phone. He had a half-hour before he would leave for work. What he didn't expect to find was coffee made and Mel holding her abdomen with one hand, the counter with the other, doing controlled and intentional breathing as she stared at the coffee maker.

"Mel?" he said, rushing over to her. He knew what a woman in labor looked like. He had delivered a dozen babies over the years. He placed one of his hands beside hers on her abdomen, the other on her back. He felt the tightness of the contraction in both hands. "That's good; slow, deep breaths."

When it ended, she focused her gaze on his. "Are you ready for this?"

Kade kissed her. "I love you. We're ready for this. How far apart are the contractions?"

"Relax; they've been at eight minutes apart for the last hour. But they've gone from lasting thirty seconds to a full minute now. They're not bad in intensity."

"Why didn't you wake me?" Kade asked.

"I knew you'd be up soon. There was no use in both of us being up in the middle of the night. Besides, when I first got up I didn't realize I was in labor." She pointed to the coffee maker. "It's ready. You might as well have a cup before we drive into Norfolk. Oh, and I already called into work. Smitty was on. He wished us good luck and will probably have the news of our little one's impending arrival spread across both shifts. So, you better remember to call in after this baby is born."

Kade chuckled. He was officially on his week-long vacation. He pulled his phone from his pocket and typed out a quick text message. After he pressed send, he looked up at Mel. "Cletus." After all, he couldn't let his partner and best friend find out from Smitty.

She smiled. "Yes, I figured. I called the doctor's line too. I do want to stay at home as long as we can."

"Do you want to go up and take a shower?" Kade offered.

"No, I honestly don't want to go up and down the stairs again. Maybe after we get to the hospital. We'll see." She paused and flashed him a smile. "I can't believe we're going to meet our baby today."

Kade embraced her and held her until her next contraction hit. Then his training kicked in. He timed it, coached her, felt the tightness in her abdomen and across her back. It lasted one full minute. She easily breathed through it. He wanted to do an exam and check how dilated she was. He wasn't sure if she'd go for that.

She had also timed it. "Still at eight minutes apart."

Kade chuckled. "Your OB does realize that both of us have delivered babies at work, doesn't he?"

Mel also laughed. "Yes, I mentioned it. I warned him that we're probably going to drive him nuts."

Kade laughed again. "I can't tell you how badly I want to do an exam and see how dilated you are."

"No, you are not the paramedic today. You're the father of the baby. That's your role in the delivery room, just as my role is the birthing mother."

Kade laughed and pulled her close. He sipped his coffee, with his eye on his watch, waiting for the next contraction. He was able to have a second cup of coffee before the contractions jumped from eight minutes to every five minutes. He wrote a note and left it by the coffee maker for his mom and Jake. And then the pair quietly left the house for the drive to the hospital in Norfolk. They took Mel's car as they already had the infant car seat installed in it.

Upon arriving at the Emergency Room entrance, Kade parked at the rear of the ER lot and they walked in. Her contractions were still five minutes apart, but they had increased in intensity. He knew after sitting for fifty minutes the walk would do her good.

She was mid-contraction when they passed through the double sliding doors.

"In active labor, need a wheelchair please," Kade told Payton Campbell, the attendant at the check-in desk. That was the thing about his job. He knew everyone who worked at any of the hospital's ER departments.

"Certainly," she said, jumping up from her chair to grab one. "How are you doing, Mel?" she asked as Kade helped her to sit.

Mel blew a long, solid breath out as the contraction ebbed. Then she gave Payton a smile. "Hoping things are progressing quickly. I'd love to have this baby as soon as we reach the floor."

Payton laughed. "And how are you doing, Dad?" she asked, focusing her gaze on Kade.

Kade's smile was telling. "It's much different when it's your own baby on the way."

"Let me just print your forms, then you can bring her up to the Family Maternity Center."

Shortly thereafter, Kade pushed the wheelchair down the corridor and into the elevator. He pressed '4'. His excitement rose with the elevator. He hadn't been exaggerating when he said that it was much different when it was your own baby on the way. He was so happy, he would describe himself as giddy. He couldn't wait to meet his child. And underneath that excitement there was a palpable nervousness, knowing what all could go wrong during a delivery. Until they got a monitor on the baby and he heard the heartbeat, he wouldn't relax.

The check-in at the reception desk was remarkably fast. They were in their room within minutes. Mel changed into the gown and was directed to sit in bed by the nurse so she could check her vitals and how far dilated she was.

"How long did you say it was in between contractions?" Nurse Eva Gomez asked.

"Still five minutes, for the last hour," Kade answered.

"Well, they're doing their job. You're dilated to eight and I'm calling it nearly one-hundred-percent effaced."

She hooked up the monitor to the baby and they all saw and heard there was a strong heartbeat.

Kade leaned in and kissed Mel. "You're doing great, babe. Let's get you back on your feet and walk this kid out of you."

Mel laughed just as another contraction hit. It had been just three and a half minutes since the last, and this one was much stronger. The nurse started an IV and they breathed through another contraction and then Kade helped her back to her feet. The nurse left. She would notify the doctor of the progress.

At the next check when Mel reported she felt the need to push, she was fully dilated. The doctor was called. It was a textbook delivery. Mel only pushed for twenty minutes before Kade saw the dark curly hair of his baby crown. One more push and the head was delivered. The baby's perfect reddish-purple skin came into view with the next push.

"You have a daughter," the doctor announced. Their daughter answered him with a loud cry from her healthy lungs.

Seconds later she was placed on Mel's chest. Both Mel and Kade cried tears of relief and joy. Kade held her tiny hand, marveling as he always did at the miracle of new life. His eyes traveled to Mel's. "You did it, babe." And then he kissed her lips. "I love you," he whispered. He checked his watch. It was six-thirty a.m. on January twelfth, a date and time that would be one of the most important dates to him for as long as he lived.

"Love you," Mel answered. Her eyes then returned to her daughter. She vowed in that moment that she'd never be like her own mom. She wanted to be the kind of mother that Elyse had been to *her* children. And she knew that this baby would take priority in her life over everything else. "We have a daughter, Kade."

The baby weighed in at eight pounds, two ounces. She was twenty inches long. Kade took a picture of her and typed out a text message to his mom, Kelsey, and Claire, announcing her arrival. Then he sent a similar text with her stats and picture and sent it to Cletus. Lastly, he sent one to the EMS coordinator's email box. Smitty would be off shift by now.

Congratulatory text messages from their coworkers pinged both Kade and Mel's phones within minutes.

• • • •

JAKE FOUND THE NOTE left by Kade when he went to the kitchen to get coffee for Elyse and himself. Kade had not written what time they'd left for the hospital. The coffee maker was off, but the coffee was still hot. He turned it back on and then let Frick and Frack out into the backyard from the slider in the kitchen. They had fenced in the main backyard area to make it convenient to let the two dogs out. Charlie rarely left the immediate area, would do his business, and return. Frick and Frack, not so much. After he let the boys in, he brought the note and the two cups back to the bedroom.

"Hey, Kade left a note. Mel's in labor. They left for the hospital sometime this morning." He handed the note to Elyse and then her coffee cup after she'd sat, propping herself up with pillows at her back.

Frick and Frack jumped back onto the bed, trying to provoke Charlie into getting up. They knew there would be no breakfast served until Charlie was up.

Elyse's eyes scanned the note. "Well, the doctor did tell Mel yesterday that it could be any day now. I'm so excited for them."

"And for you," Jake said. "I know you're excited, too. They're lucky to have you. I know you'll be a big help to them and get a lot of baby cuddle time." He chuckled. "I never thought I'd find a grandma so sexy." He leaned over and kissed her.

"That just sounds wrong. Some days, I don't think of myself as old enough to be a grandmother."

"Ah, not addressing me calling you sexy," Jake said.

"No, not going there," she said with a smile.

"I've got to get into the shower," Jake said, stepping into the bathroom with his own cup of coffee.

Elyse sipped her coffee and thought about the day ahead. A trip into Norfolk to meet her new grandchild would be on her agenda. She'd drop Frick and Frack off at Animal House to go play, that way she wouldn't have to rush to get back. While she was in Norfolk she'd visit Claire and see if she could help with anything, though it seemed like Matthew had it all covered. She was so pleased with how he'd stepped up since the end of December when the news of Ken Woods' arrest broke. And in the last week since the car accident, he had *really* stepped up. He was the husband and father he'd never been in the past but Elyse had always hoped he could be.

Her text message chime startled her. She picked her phone up from the nightstand. It was six-thirty. The text was from Kade. "*Our daughter has just arrived. Eight pounds, two ounces, twenty inches long, perfect! Mom and baby are both doing great. I'll message later when you can come see her if you want to.*" And there was a picture of a perfect little baby, with a headful of dark curly hair wrapped in a pink blanket.

Tears filled Elyse's eyes as a smile curved her lips. A little girl; perfect for Mel to have the relationship with that she'd never had with her own mom. She tapped out her reply, congratulations, well wishes for all three of them, and a promise to come visit later that morning.

When Jake came back into the room he was greeted with her wide grin.

"We have a little girl," she said.

"That's great," he said. "Is everyone doing well?"

"Kade texted. He said Mom and baby are both doing great. I'll drive in and visit later this morning. Let me know what your day looks like and if you have any lunch plans. Maybe we can meet for lunch before I head over to Claire's house."

"You have a full day scheduled," Jake said. "Do you want me to drop Frick and Frack off at Animal House?"

"Ah, great minds, Commander," she answered with a smile. "I'll drop them on my way. I plan to pop in on my way to Norfolk."

· · · ·

CLAIRE AWOKE TO THE aroma of coffee. She was off all painkillers and had the first good night's sleep since the accident. Her left arm was still bandaged and splinted. The orthopedic surgeon was waiting to put a cast on it until the incisions healed and the swelling went down. In the splint it was completely immobilized. She would try to convince him to leave it as it was to heal. She didn't want the weight of a cast.

Matthew entered the room from the bathroom. He had a towel wrapped around himself. She hadn't heard the shower run. "Ah, you're awake. Good morning," he said. "Do you want any help to sit up?"

"Good morning," she replied with a smile. Matthew had been wonderful since the accident, and especially since she'd come home from the hospital. He'd brought her coffee every morning and helped her to place the pillows behind herself so she could sit comfortably. He'd also taken care of everything with the kids and Lizette. "Let me do it myself this morning," she said. "Thank you for bringing me coffee." She reached for her cell phone which was on the nightstand beside the coffee. "What time is it?"

"Just past seven-thirty," he said.

Viewing her phone, she saw the text messages from Kade and her mom. She'd had the phone silenced overnight. "Kade and Mel's baby came this morning," she announced. "They had a girl." She was so happy for them. "It says Mom and baby are both doing well. Wow, my brother's a dad."

She tapped out a reply to Kade, congratulating them. She promised they'd get over to their mom's house to see them as soon as they came home, knowing the hospital wouldn't let Aiden and Emma in to visit.

● ● ● ●

KELSEY AND ASH AWOKE around ten that morning, as usual. They hadn't gotten home from the shop until close to one and they stayed up for an hour, reviewing the update from the builder. The addition was progressing. The builder assured them it would be done within the next month. Plenty of time to decorate the nursery before the baby came.

Kelsey grabbed her phone, the first thing she always did when she woke. "Oh my God! Kade and Mel had the baby this morning," she told Ash, who still laid flat on his back, staring at the ceiling. "They had a girl. He sent a picture. She looks just like Kade!"

Ash rolled to his side to face her. He took the phone and viewed the picture. He knew that Kade and Mel would be amazing parents. He had secretly been hoping they'd have a boy, too, as their two kids would be so close in age. "Yes, she does look like Kade. As both he and Mel have green eyes, I'm sure she will, too."

Kelsey took the phone back and hit dial. Kade answered on the second ring. "Hi."

"Hi! I'm so excited for you guys. Both Mel and the baby are doing good, right?"

"Yes, they're both great," Kade said.

"Put it on speaker," Ash said.

"I have you on speaker, Kade," Kelsey said.

"Hi man, congrats! She's beautiful," Ash said. "When can we come by the hospital?"

Kade laughed. "Mom is on her way now. So, any time after she goes is fine. They only allow two visitors in at a time. I'll let you know when she's getting ready to go."

"Perfect. We probably won't come until this afternoon," Kelsey said.

"Okay, I'll see you later," Kade said.

Kelsey sat up and caressed her belly. "I'm almost jealous they had their baby today. I can't wait till he comes."

Ash sat up beside her and pulled her tightly against himself. "Two and a half more months, Kels. We're in the home stretch," he said, his hand joining hers on her belly.

. . . .

EXCITEMENT RAN THROUGH Elyse as she walked into the hospital. It had been just a week earlier that she'd entered the Emergency Department of this hospital. Her mood was much different today. She rode the elevator to the fourth floor and checked in at the registration desk of the Family Maternity Center. She was given her visitor's badge and pointed towards Mel's room.

The door to the room number she'd been given was a jar. She could hear voices and laughter from within. She knocked on the doorjamb and cracked the door open another few inches. "Knock, knock," she called into the room.

"Mom," Kade said as his head appeared around the partially pulled curtain. "Come on in."

Elyse entered with a bouquet of flowers for Melanie in her hand. Kade embraced her. Cletus stood in front of Melanie's bed. She'd recognize his uniformed back anywhere. All she saw were Melanie's legs.

Cletus turned to face her. "Hi, Missus L," he greeted her with a hug.

"Hi, Cletus," she said.

"Much better reason for us all to be here today," he said as they broke their embrace.

"Yes, so much better," Elyse agreed.

"Mom, meet your granddaughter, Elle Anne Laramie," Kade said with a grin. "We'll call her Ellie."

Tears filled Elyse's eyes. They clearly named the baby after her, and they used Kelsey's and her middle name, too. "She's beautiful." Her eyes flickered to Melanie. She handed the bouquet of flowers to her. "For you."

"Thank you," Mel said as she took the bouquet from her.

Kade placed the tiny bundle in his mother's arms. Elyse held her in a gentle embrace and gazed into her wide, alert eyes. "You are absolutely beautiful and perfect, Ellie," she said. "And you are one lucky little girl to have the mommy and daddy that you do." She pressed a soft kiss to the top of her head.

"And she is lucky to have the grandma she has," Mel added.

Chapter 48 – Not Dropping the Ball this Time

Even with all the activity at the beginning of the month, and the wonderful upheaval in the house of baby Ellie coming home, Elyse remained focused on the date that was quickly approaching. Tim's birthday. Elyse gave Jake plenty of notice of the date and admitted that she wasn't sure how she'd feel on the day. It fell on a Sunday. She planned to cook Tim's favorite meal of lasagna and invite everyone over for dinner. She assured Jake that he was part of the family, welcome, and expected for dinner.

Kade was aware of the date when his mother mentioned it to him. He would make sure he was off work for the dinner. His father's birthday had been a non-issue for him since he became an adult. When they were children, his mom would make sure the kids made him cards and she'd send them to wherever he was, if they had enough notice to mail cards there. Often, it was just a phone call during which they'd sing 'happy birthday' to him. His mom would have a birthday cake for him at home, which was really for the kids.

One year, after that high-rise apartment collapse in Florida that his dad remained on-site, investigating for several months until it was fully demolished, his mom, Kelsey, and he took an impromptu vacation and flew down to have dinner with his dad on his birthday. Claire and Matthew were away, on vacation themselves, and Claire was mad the rest of the family decided to go and she couldn't. That portion of the trip had been a waste. His dad didn't seem to care that they were there. When his dad went back to work the next day, the three of them went to the beach for two days before flying home. That part of the trip had been fun.

His mom always tried to keep their dad a part of the family which, now that he was a father, Kade appreciated more than he had before. He also understood his father now, in a way he hadn't previously. That too made him be grateful for his mom. And with this dinner she planned she was actually still doing the same thing, acknowledging his father's birthday and inviting them all to celebrate it. Old habits died hard, he supposed.

Claire and her family arrived first, in her brand-new Cadillac Escalade, white, identical to the one Kade had last seen upside down in that culvert less than a month before. He had hoped she'd get a different make and model of car or at least a different color. His nightmares from that day had finally stopped. He hoped seeing them drive up in that car wouldn't reactivate them.

Kade put out his cigarette and helped Emma from her seat in the middle row, where she'd been that day. Aiden, the big five-year old, took off his own seatbelt and walked forward. "Hey, A-man," he greeted with a high five.

Aiden high fived him and then jumped down from the car, Mr. Quack in his arms. "See Mommy's new car?" he said.

"I see it," Kade said, his questioning gaze on Claire. He greeted her with a hug. "Hi, sis; got your new car, huh? Looks just like the old one."

"It is new. You were right that the old one was totaled."

MARGARET KAY

Matthew approached Kade and shook his hand. "Can
you give me a hand? We have a couple of boxes of Emma's
outgrown clothes for Ellie."

"I had Lizette wash them in gentle, hypoallergenic
detergent. They can go right into her drawers and closet,"
Claire said.

"That's great, thanks," Kade said. He and Matthew
brought them right upstairs.

Claire and the kids went inside. Out the back door she
saw her mom and Jake standing on the patio. All three dogs
were in the yard. "Come here, Emma," she said. She used her
right arm to help her take her jacket off. Aiden already had
his off. She picked it up from the floor where he'd dropped
it. Both kids ran into the sunroom and began to play with
the toys that were there for them.

Elyse saw movement in the house and turned to see
Aiden and Emma digging into the toys in the sunroom. "Ah,
Claire and her family are here," she said to Jake. "I'd better
go move a few of my paintings before the kids knock them
over." She went in and gave each of the kids a hug as she
moved her canvases out of the way. Then she greeted Claire
in the kitchen with an embrace as well. "Where's Matthew?"

"We brought a bunch of Emma's outgrown clothes for
Ellie. He and Kade took the boxes up to her room."

"Oh, that's so nice, and will help them a lot."

"We brought a couple boxes of Aiden's baby clothes for
Kelsey, too."

"I know they both will appreciate it," Elyse said. "How's
the arm feel?"

650

Claire's left arm sported a dark blue cast. "I've gotten used to it. I was incredibly lucky. A head-on collision and I walked away from it with only a concussion and a broken arm. It could have been so much worse. And both the kids were okay. God was really watching out for us."

"Yes, he was," Elyse agreed, happy Claire could see it in those terms. "Any updates on Matthew's firm?"

"Yes," Claire said with a frown. "I think he wants to tell all of you when Kelsey and Ash get here."

Matthew and Kade descended the stairs. Matthew greeted Elyse. "The lasagna smells incredible. I hope you have garlic bread, too."

"Of course I do," Elyse said with a smile. She also had a salad made, but there would be no wine served tonight. They were doing all they could to support Matthew's sobriety. Claire had shared with her that Matthew was going to a couple of meetings a week with Eric. He hadn't had a single drink since Christmas Eve. Elyse was proud of him. It had been nearly a full month, and it had been a month full of intense stress.

"And a salad, too, I hope, Mom," Claire said.

"Yes, I have a salad, too. Oh, I also have a birthday cake for Emma," Elyse said. "I know you aren't having a birthday party for her, so I thought we could celebrate it today, a few days early."

"I thought we were celebrating Dad's birthday," Claire said.

"We'll toast him at dinner and remember him. But I wanted to have the cake for Emma. She's here. Your father isn't," Elyse said. "But I still think it was important we all gather to remember him."

Clair hugged her mom. "Yes. And thank you for thinking of Emma."

"I really think we should try to pull off something with a few of our friends that have kids her and Aiden's age; maybe just a visit to Playworld," Matthew said.

"I plan to decorate the house on her birthday and make a big deal of it. And we'll take her to Playworld for pizza. Just with everything going on, Matthew, I didn't want to overwhelm you."

Matthew wrapped his arm around her. "It's fine, Claire. I'm doing okay."

Elyse was so glad to hear that Claire was going to make a big deal of Emma's birthday. And she agreed with Matthew that Emma should have some sort of party. Yes, the family would celebrate it today, but she was turning three and had friends she should have at a party.

Kelsey and Ash arrived, and Jake brought the dogs in. After they greeted the kids, the kids returned to the sunroom to play. The adults stood in the kitchen while Matthew filled them in on what was happening with the firm.

"My attorney and friend, Kerry, advised us on how to dissolve our LLC. Troy and I voted to dissolve it, the first step. What Ken wants is irrelevant, and legally we are two to dissolve which carries the motion. Kerry is helping to file the firm's last tax return and we're filing the Article of Dissolution. We just need to divvy up the accounts and cover the last expenses incurred by Donnor Woods Jeffries. Elyse, you have accounts with me. You and all the clients will be getting a letter in which they get to choose who will keep their account."

"I'm sorry, Matthew," Elyse said.

"This was why I cancelled your meeting with the other partners before your gala last summer. I didn't want Ken anywhere near you. He would have tried to talk you into buying into that fraudulent fund. I was already working with the authorities at that point."

Elyse and Jake were both shocked to hear that. With everything that had happened since Christmas, they had forgotten about it. "Thank you for protecting my money," she said. "What are you going to do now?"

"Troy and I are still talking to see if we will go back into business together. I think it will depend on what happens with all our clients' accounts. Many have already had their accounts transferred to other brokers. I'm not sure if there will be a business left to salvage."

"You're still working with the regulatory agencies, aren't you?" Kade asked.

"Yes. That might actually lead to a new career for me–investigating fraudulent security sales," Matthew replied.

"Do you know what's going on with the EMS pensions?" Kade asked.

"I'm not really supposed to say, but I will tell you not to worry about yours. Public sector pensions are being protected."

"Thank God!" Mel said.

"I hope it all works out as you want it to, Matthew," Elyse said.

"The thing is, I'm not even sure what I want. Some days I want the firm in some shape or form to survive, other days I want to just say screw it, let it be done, and let me figure out what to do with the next chapter of my life. Working for the SCC, EDVA, or some branch of law enforcement to investigate financial wrong doing sounds appealing. Kerry, has said I should think about teaching classes on finance and business ethics at the college level."

"That would be a great fit with your real-world experience," Jake said. "When I was faced with my possible medical separation last year, I looked into teaching as well. When I do retire, I very may well try to get a part-time teaching job at one of the universities or colleges in the area."

"I've told Matthew that he doesn't have to make any decisions yet. He has options," Claire said. "Even if he cobbles together two or three part-time jobs, that works. Through Kensington-Laramie I provide the medical and dental benefits, so he doesn't have to worry about that."

"If you stay at Kensington-Laramie," Matthew said. "Working for one of the regulatory or law enforcement agencies, I would get good benefits and you would be free to leave Kensington-Laramie, Claire."

This was the first Elyse was hearing of this possibility, and she'd spent a lot of time at Claire's house since the car accident. "I didn't know you were considering leaving, Claire."

"I plan to have a talk with Michael next week," Claire said. "He still hasn't decided who he'll make a partner. He's been stringing Chris and me along since Dad died. And because of my accident, I realized that if something was to happen to Michael I don't know what would happen to the firm. I don't know if he has any provisions in place regarding it. There are ten families relying on Kensington-Laramie. I think it's irresponsible of him that he hasn't offered the partnership position to me or Chris."

"What'll you do if you leave Kensington-Laramie?" Kelsey asked.

Claire laughed. "I don't know. Get a job at another firm? Start my own? I don't know."

They all knew her attitude was very uncharacteristic of her. She always had a plan. "I'm sure the right path will present itself to you. To you both," Elyse said.

· · · ·

"HAPPY BIRTHDAY, DEAR Emma, Happy Birthday to you!" they all sang to her. The rainbow-colored cake with three candles lit was in front of her.

"Make a wish and blow out the candles, sweetie," Claire said.

She blew them out and everyone clapped. Claire and Elyse cut the cake and passed servings around the table. Afterwards, birthday gifts were brought out from the laundry room, where they'd been kept out of sight so Emma would be surprised. Claire and Matthew also were. Everyone had gotten Emma a gift. There was even one from Baby Ellie to her.

"Mom, thank you for arranging the birthday surprise for Emma," Claire said quietly as she came up beside her mom as she cleaned up the kitchen.

"You're welcome, sweetie. We thought it was only right that she received so many gifts, given that you weren't planning a birthday party with her friends. Though I agree with Matthew, if you can pull something small off with just a few friends, that would be nice."

"Yes, I think we'll try. I just wasn't sure if Matthew was ready. Between the news about his firm and the drinking issue, I didn't think he wanted to get together with any of our friends yet, and I didn't think he would want it to be in public."

"You haven't gotten together with any of your friends in the last month?" Elyse asked.

"No. I haven't even gone to church. I've had a few short conversations with my closest friends, Jenna and Jill, but we haven't gotten together, and Matthew hasn't spoken with their husbands."

"Claire, sweetie, this is a time when you need your closest friends around you," Elyse said.

"I've had you guys, my family. That's all I've needed."

February

Chapter 49 – Valentine's Gifts

Claire didn't feel the slightest bit nervous as she pushed through the door to the office suite. Maybe it was that all the events over the last month had numbed her, or perhaps in the scheme of life over the last month, if she was made a partner or not held less meaning that it had just a few months prior. She noticed the gold print on the door, spelling out Kensington-Laramie, more than she had in a long time. But as her mom had reminded her, it was her dad's name. Not hers.

She'd worked from home several days a week since the car accident, which had worked out well for her. And she'd gotten all her work done. If Michael didn't make her a partner, and if she stayed, she would push for the same schedule going forward.

It was eight-thirty. Tara didn't get in until nine. She walked through the hall, past the conference room and bathroom, kitchenette, and storage room to the office area. Only one light was on, in Michael's corner office. The others usually got in after nine as well. Chris was out of town. She dropped her bag and coat in her office and then went to Michael's.

"Hi, Claire," he greeted when she appeared in his open doorway.

"Hi, Michael," she said, entering his office. She took a seat in one of the two guest chairs in front of his desk. He also had a table and four chairs off to the side. "How are you today?"

"I'm okay, Claire. How's the arm?"

She nodded. "It's okay. You know, Michael, my accident reminded me how any of us could be gone at any time. You'd think my dad's death would have really driven that home, but for some reason it didn't. There are ten families relying on Kensington-Laramie, plus all of our clients, and you have yet to name a partner or partners since my father died. Do you at least have arrangements made for the continuation of the business, should something happen to you?"

Michael steepled his hands in front of himself. "I have given it a lot of thought, Claire. I do have a plan in place in the event of my death."

"And what happens if you're in an accident and unconscious, or in a coma? Is someone named who can sign checks and contracts? Hell, even if your appendix were to rupture, you'd be in the hospital several days to a week. Would payroll be made?"

Michael frowned.

"This firm needs a business continuity plan that senior staff are aware of. It can't be a secret, Michael. And, ideally, senior staff should be several people. You and my dad, when he was alive, were the only ones with authority at the firm."

"I know you're right. I've hesitated to give anyone signature rights, especially to our bank accounts."

"It could be two signatures are required. Mort has been the accountant the firm has used for as long as I can remember. Perhaps if it's not your signature authorizing expenditures, it could be two senior members plus Mort's signature that's needed. But there has to be a plan, Michael."

He nodded. "Thank you for bringing this to my attention, Claire."

She couldn't tell how her statements had been received. He didn't seem angry. Moreover, he seemed surprised that she was talking with him about it. And he seemed a little embarrassed that he didn't have a business continuity plan. At least he hadn't argued the need for it.

"Also, I uploaded all of the revisions to the Grand Park Project into the file share for the client to review. I plan to have a video call with them this afternoon to go over them. I don't think an on-site visit will be needed."

"I can appreciate you don't want to travel with your cast and with everything that happened with Matthew and his firm. I could have sent another associate," Michael said.

"That expense is completely unnecessary, Michael. With the ability to do file shares and video calls, the drawings can be shared and the information can be told face to face without having to physically be in the same room and without the expense of traveling, thus reducing overall business costs. New technologies can replace the way business was once done. I think this firm should look at its practices and evaluate if how we've conducted business in the past are still the best practices."

Michael slowly nodded.

Claire came to her feet. "Okay, I'm going to get to work. It was nice chatting." Claire smiled and then left his office. She had a satisfied grin on her face when she walked into her own office. She glanced around at it. It was Dad's old office, the other corner office. She would give Michael a little time to think about what she said. If she didn't sound like partner material who was taking responsibility at the firm, nothing she could do or say would make him see it.

• • • •

A WEEK AFTER CLAIRE had the conversation with Michael, he popped his head into her office. It was three in the afternoon. He'd been on the phone most of the morning, she'd noticed. "Hi, Claire. Can I have you step into the conference room for a minute?"

"Sure, Michael," she said.

She checked her Outlook Calendar to ensure she had no meetings scheduled. She didn't. As she walked to the conference room, she found it odd he'd invited her there rather than just speaking with her in her office, where they both already were.

Coming into the conference room, she found a full house. Not only was Michael there, but so were Chris Barton, Tara, Mort, the firm's accountant, and Harrison Wells, the firm's attorney. She greeted Mort and Harrison warmly, even though she didn't know the context of this meeting. For all she knew, she could be getting fired. That would be just her luck. It was February thirteenth; getting fired would be a hell of a Valentine's Gift.

"Thank you all for attending this meeting. I've been quite busy this last week trying to get things lined up. Mort and Harrison, I want to thank you both for all the time you've put in to help take care of this." His gaze swept to both Claire and Chris. "Claire, I want to thank you for the conversation last week and reminding me that we do not have a clear process in place for the continuation of the business, should something happen to me. I have been meaning to get to this, and I will admit that with all of the business demands it just kind of slipped."

Claire smiled and nodded. She figured with that intro to the meeting, she probably wasn't getting fired. She certainly hoped that this meant that Michael was ready to offer a partnership. She was disturbed, though, that Chris was present. She also wondered why this meeting wasn't on her calendar. Michael very easily could have sent a meeting invitation.

"Anyway," Michael continued, "I have worked with Mort and Harrison to get new partnership terms drawn up. Kensington-Laramie started out as Kensington Britton Laramie." His gaze went to Tara. "Your husband was a good friend and I still miss him. Claire, Chris, you probably aren't aware of this, as it was before your time with the firm, but the terms of the agreement that was made with Tara guaranteed her position for as long as she wanted it to remove Britton from the firm name with no funds transferring. The firm was not profitable back then, but all three original partners put funds into the business to get it started and keep it operational that first year before we turned a profit."

Claire did in fact know it, as her father had confided it in her.

"Claire, Chris, I would like to offer both of you the position of junior partner. If something should happen to me, the firm would transfer to the two of you equally. If you both accept my terms, the name of the firm will change to Kensington-Laramie-Barton."

Claire forced a pleasant facial expression. Junior partner? Was he joking? She deserved full partner. She had to wonder what Chris had done to deserve a position equal to her.

"The terms you will find are quite favorable, with no upfront cost to either of you," Michael continued. "As senior partner I would retain final decision-making authority, unless I am unavailable, and if that is the case the two of you would have to be in complete agreement and both sign off on said item. This holds for contracts and any other items that decisions need to be made on. The same holds true for the finances, but an added layer would be that Mort has to approve any expenditures that the two of you agree on. Travel would be scheduled so that one of the three of us is in the office at all times."

The attorney handed agreement paperwork to both Claire and Chris. "These do need to be signed and notarized to be binding. Tara is a notary."

Chris and Claire both read over the document. Chris signed it immediately. Tara notarized it and it was handed back to the attorney. Claire noticed that Michael had already signed it on his designated line. Claire had brought her leather portfolio in with her. She tucked the paper into the folder and closed it. Michael and the attorney exchanged surprised glances.

"Claire, is there a problem with the document?" Michael asked.

"Not at all. I want to reread it in my office and digest the content, possibly make notes on any items I may want clarification on. And then I'd like to discuss it with my husband. With all the upheaval with his own firm we had discussed all possibilities for our family's future, which also involved a potential move out of state."

The others in the room all looked horrified. All except Chris Barton, who gave her a smile. Either he figured out it was a ploy on her part to get something more out of it, or he was happy she may be leaving, hoping if that was the case that perhaps he'd get a better deal.

"I assume twenty-four hours to read it over and think about the offer isn't too much to ask. Tara could notarize it tomorrow and we could courier it back over to Harrison's office," Claire said.

"We could," Michael agreed. "I would like an answer by end of business tomorrow."

"Let's schedule a meeting for the two of us tomorrow morning, Michael, just in case I have any questions and for me to give you my answer." Claire stood. "And if you would excuse me, please, I do leave the office at three-fifteen on Wednesdays. You can reach me on my mobile for the remainder of the evening, as usual." She smiled at Mort and Harrison. "It was nice to see you both." Then she slipped out of the room.

• • • •

KADE'S ALARM WENT OFF at two-thirty. He had been working the shift that began at four a.m. since he'd returned from his week-long vacation when Ellie was born. He'd only been asleep for an hour since Ellie had last woken. They'd settled into a nice routine in the month since her birth. Even though he was working, and Mel currently was still on her maternity leave, when Ellie woke while they both slept, Kade would get up, change her diaper, and then bring her to bed for Mel to nurse. Then he'd go back to sleep and rarely heard Mel return her to her room. They'd already moved her into his old bedroom, which they'd turned into the nursery so she wouldn't wake to his alarm and so he could sleep when he needed to, when Mel or his mom were tending her.

He got up and quietly left the room so he wouldn't wake Mel. His clothes waited in the bathroom. After completing his morning routine to get ready, he crept past his mom's and Jake's room. Yes, he thought of it as theirs now, and then he silently descended the stairs.

In the kitchen he found several cards on the counter beside the coffee maker with his name on them. Two were written in Mel's handwriting, the third in his mom's. There was also one to Mel, Jake, and Ellie all in his mother's handwriting and one to his mom and Jake that also had Mel's handwriting on it.

He smiled as he lifted one in Mel's handwriting to him addressed to 'Daddy'. He opened it to find a cute Valentine's card to Daddy from Ellie. Tears filled his eyes. The emotions that overwhelmed him with the realization on days like this were powerful. He was a father; he had a daughter. Mel had written in it from Ellie, that he was the best daddy ever. He'd sure try with everything he was to be the best father. He opened Mel's card next. It was sappy and sweet, and unlike any cards they had exchanged in the past. He figured her emotions were running wild, too. His mother's card professed her pride in the man and father he was.

He opened his backpack and pulled the three cards and little box from inside, stashing the cards to him in their place. He had gotten both Mel and Ellie cards, as well as one for his mom. He'd stop on his way home after work and bring Mel a bouquet of flowers. He'd bought her a necklace with Ellie's name and hearts incorporated into the chain. It was unique, dainty, and a custom order. That's what was in the box. Mel had seen it advertised shortly after they brought the baby home, and he'd ordered it right away for her. He set them out onto the counter and then made himself a cup of coffee. When done, he poured it into the to-go cup. Then he quietly left to head to work.

• • • •

"ARE YOU SURE ABOUT this, Claire?" Matthew asked.

She rolled towards him. They lay in bed. They had just made love and exchanged Valentine's gifts. Matthew had gotten her a pair of diamond earrings she'd wanted. Claire gave him a watch he'd had his eye on, even though they both agreed they probably should be watching their money, with Matthew's firm in jeopardy.

She pressed another kiss to his lips. "Yes, it's how I want to play this. Chris Barton is an idiot, agreeing to Michael's terms with no counter. Michael isn't going to want to remove Laramie from the firm name. That'll cost him more than simply adding Barton to the end. And if I'm only going to be a junior partner, I'm going to work half of the time from home and have a few more demands."

• • • •

KELSEY AWOKE TO AN empty bed at eleven. They'd gotten back from the shop around midnight. She couldn't believe she'd slept so long. She sat up and as she did every morning, she caressed her abdomen. "Good morning, little guy."

Then her gaze went to the bassinet. She couldn't believe that he was due in a month and a half. Ever since Ellie had arrived, she'd gotten even more excited and impatient to meet him. She'd gone over to her mom's house three times to spend time with the baby and let Mel sleep. Plus, she wanted her niece to know her since she would be one of her babysitters.

She got up and went down to the kitchen, which was mid-construction. Thankfully the wall with the sink and the stove was not being touched with the addition. It was taking shape and would look great when it was done. Already, the openness into the addition transformed the room. The kitchen would be more than double the size it was, and the kitchen space would flow right into the family room. The plastic was down. The wall of sliding glass doors from the family room to the outside were installed, and the stonework on the large, raised fireplace at the far end of the room was mid-installation.

Glancing out one of the new sliding glass doors, she saw the doors to Ash's forge were open. That explained where he was. She opened the refrigerator and found a bouquet of flowers and a card. She laughed that Ash had placed them there. Her card and Valentine's gift to him were up in their liquor cabinet.

She opened the card. Ash was so open with his emotions, and the love expressed in the card brought tears to her eyes. It was what she'd come to expect from him. And she appreciated him for it more than she could ever say to him. He taught her how to be unafraid and how to open her heart. She smiled as she set the card onto the counter. She retrieved a vase and filled it with water before she placed the flowers in it. She set the vase beside the card. Then she got his gift and card down. She'd give it to him as soon as he returned to the house.

• • • •

ELYSE ARRIVED HOME from Animal House at three in the afternoon with Frick and Frack. Most days, she took them with her but left Charlie at home. She was surprised to find Jake sitting at the kitchen table. The dogs excitedly ran to him, and he gave them pats and rubs.

A bouquet of roses was on the table in front of him. Elyse picked it up. "Should I be jealous someone gave you flowers for Valentine's Day?"

Jake laughed. "No, they're for you. I stopped at a flower shop and bought them myself."

"I'd never know if someone else gave them to you, though," she teased. She sat on his lap and wrapped an arm around him. "Thank you." She kissed him. "You're home early." By the looks of it, he hadn't been home long. He was still in his khaki uniform, which he usually changed out of promptly. Then she noticed he looked overly serious. "What's wrong?"

"I got my orders today."

Elyse sucked in a breath. She nodded her head and then her gaze scanned his attractive face. She pressed a kiss to his lips, holding back her tears. "We'll deal with it."

"The Gravely will be back in port in a few weeks. There will be a thirty percent new crew assignment and a complete shakedown of her with some new systems installed. New sea trials of the systems and the crew will last for about a month. Then she'll return to Norfolk for a few weeks before deploying, probably around June first."

"June first," Elyse repeated.

Jake took a piece of paper from his breast pocket and unfolded it. "My assignment to the Gravely is to be the executive officer. The current CO will remain with her. The current XO is getting his own boat. He's a good officer, he's earned it."

Elyse glanced at the words on the paper in his hand. "Surface Reserve Component?"

"The reserves. Surface Warfare Officers who are considering leaving active duty are highly encouraged to consider transferring to the part-time Surface Reserve Component, the drill reserves. They're flexible, have drills on weekdays and weekends to meet the annual commitment right here in Norfolk. It will allow for the maximum time home while I still earn credit towards retirement. And they love ranking officers to transition to the reserves rather than separating."

"Reserves? Is that something you really want to do? I know you want your own boat."

"Honestly, Elyse, if I'd been given my own boat this would have been a more difficult decision. Assignment to the Gravely takes me out of the line of succession to my own boat for at least the next year, maybe two. Plus, I don't want to leave you, Frick, Frack, and the family."

"Couldn't you just separate?"

"I can file my intent to separate, but I wouldn't officially separate prior to June first. They likely would have me deploy and could possibly extend me. Transitioning to the Surface Reserve Component will happen faster and will negate the possibility of me deploying."

"I don't want you to sacrifice your career and what you want for me."

A smile tugged at his lips. "You weren't listening to me, Elyse. I don't want to leave you. It's not that I'm afraid I'll lose you, I don't want to be apart from you. I love you, Frick, Frack, Charlie, your family. I feel I have a home here, and I don't want to leave my home."

She wrapped her arms around him and held him tightly. "You do have a home here. I love you, Jake, but I don't want you making any decisions you may regret. How long do you have to make your decision?"

"I have the transfer form filled out, ready to submit tomorrow. I just wanted to run it by you first."

"What will likely happen after you file it and how quickly?" she asked, which surprised him.

"You'd speak up if you didn't want me to do this, wouldn't you?"

"The only other option is you staying active duty and deploying, right?"

"Yes. Do you want me to deploy, Elyse?"

"No, Jake. Why would you think that?"

"You aren't as happy as I thought you'd be that I'm resolving this so I won't have to deploy."

"I feel you're settling or doing the lesser of two evils for my sake, and I don't want that."

"Elyse, I don't feel like I'm settling. When I got the orders, I felt no excitement. I knew it wasn't what I wanted. I knew staying here with you was what I wanted to do. I checked the regs on filing my separation and retirement, and that course brought me out too far past the Gravely's deployment. I'll earn a small salary while serving in the reserves, but nothing close to my pension. I may have to live off my sugar-momma for a year until I can retire and draw my pension."

Elyse laughed. "Is that what I am to you, your sugar-momma?"

"After buying you that engagement warehouse, I'm kind of tapped out of accessible funds."

"Oh, so maybe Claire was right after all. You are after me for my money," she said with a smile.

Jake laughed. "Guilty as charged, ma'am. I'm looking to sponge off you, a free place to live, food and doggie daycare services for my dogs, sex. What more could a man want?"

"This is the best Valentine's Day gift you could have given me," she said.

"Do you have a gift for me?" he asked with a quirk of his eyebrows and a suggestive smile.

Elyse stood and pulled on his hand. "Come up to our room and let me see what I can think of."

· · · ·

MATTHEW WAS HOME AT five-thirty when Claire got home from work. After greeting the kids, who were in the playroom with Lizette, she joined Matthew in his home office.

"How did your discussion with Michael go?" Matthew asked.

Claire smiled. "Four of my six counters were accepted with no discussion. In the end he agreed that I could work from home when appropriate, up to fifty percent of the time, but I had to drop my additional compensation request, agreeing to not revisit it for six months."

"I think the time to work from home is more important right now," Matthew said.

Her eyebrow rose. Her work situation was now resolved, his was anything but. The extra money may indeed be more important as he may very well be without an income in a matter of weeks.

Chapter 50 – An Unconventional Interview

Matthew's gaze scanned the many students in the ascending rows in the lecture hall. This room was one of the university's largest, and it was packed to capacity. Off to his left in the front row sat his family. He was humbled they all came at such short notice. And besides Claire, none of them knew the importance of this lecture. He knew Kade had traded a shift to be there. Kerry Fowler sat in the front row on his right with administrators from the university who he'd set up this guest speaking event with.

"Good evening. My name is Matthew Jeffries. Yes, *that* Matthew Jeffries. I was a partner at the financial services firm of Donnor Woods Jeffries, a firm that is no more because of one of my partner's illegal acts. It seems like something so basic that we shouldn't have to teach a course on it. Don't break the law. Don't rip off your clients, be honest, and do the right thing. I'm aware that this seminar counts towards your ethics credits or grades for graduation. I'll try to make it worthy of the weight your professors have placed on it to mandate your attendance here this evening, as well as make the content valuable so you don't feel like you sacrificed one of your precious Friday nights." He paused and shook his head. "Like who really wants to attend the equivalent of a class on a Friday night?"

He was rewarded with laughter from the audience.

"Okay, a few basics to keep in mind. First off, any returns on investments that are too good to be true, use your heads, people, they're too good to be true and there is probably something shady going on." He wrote 'ROI Too Good = Shady' on the board. "Secondly, pressure to sell an investment and a directive to minimize its risk to your clients is a huge red flag." He wrote 'Pressure + Minimize Risk = Red Flag' next. "And lastly, a person, be it your boss, your friend, or your partner, not showing you forms or answering questions to your satisfaction, using avoidance language like, 'it's me, don't you trust me?' should be the biggest red flag to get your attention." He wrote 'Refusal to Answer' at the bottom of his list.

He'd only had a few days to think about what he'd say in this lecture and the order he would present it in. He still didn't know if college professor was a job he wanted. If the administrators liked his presentation, it would be a part-time position, but it would be a paying position, which he needed.

"So, that's what I was faced with, the red flags that first got my attention and made me suspect that my friend and partner was doing something illegal. I was sure enough that I confided my suspicions in another friend, an old college buddy of mine, who happened to be an attorney. After that, things moved quickly. Every professional job you will hold carries with it a set of professional ethics that are binding. There was no question in my mind that reporting the illegal activities was the right thing to do. But it cost me friendships, partnerships, and my firm. I've only retained about a third of my clients. I'm basically starting from scratch. I thought my life was at its lowest point."

He paused there and his gaze settled on Claire. She smiled proudly at him and gave him a nod of her head, urging him to continue. He had run his lecture for her to practice it. She gave him a few pieces of advice and helped add to his presentation, but mostly she'd just encouraged him to go with it.

"You saw it on the news, I'm sure. And you've talked about it in your classes here at Old Dominion. So, that all went down on December twenty-sixth. Merry Christmas. Fast forward a week later, I received a phone call from my brother-in-law, who is a paramedic. I was notified that my wife and two young children had been in a car accident and were all transported to the hospital. In that moment, I didn't care for a second about saving my firm or my reputation. When I walked through those emergency room doors it wasn't about the money or the status, the things we all think about as we're preparing for our careers. It was about my family, the most important thing in the world to me. The expensive house, the cars, all the trappings of a successful life, none of it mattered. We seem to get caught up in this thought that a certain type of life is somehow guaranteed if we study hard, get our degrees, and then put in a ridiculous amount of hours and hustle, hustle, hustle. But in a second it can all be gone. Do I regret notifying the authorities when I thought my friend and partner was committing a crime? No, I don't. I saved our clients from losses. I did the right thing. And even that, with my wife and kids in the hospital, it didn't even enter my thoughts when I held my wife's hand after she'd had emergency surgery."

His gaze again went to Claire. She had tears in her eyes. He was fighting to maintain his composure. Talking about the car accident still reminded him how it could have been worse. He could have lost all of them. As his gaze shifted over the rest of the family, it was the disturbed look on Kade's face that really drew his attention. Kade looked as though he was going to cry. It was only then that he considered how hard it must have been on Kade.

Claire fought to keep her tears from spilling down her cheeks. He must have added this part to his lecture after he'd rehearsed it by reciting it to her. She hoped it wasn't too emotional, as that could turn off the administrators. He hadn't decided if he wanted a job teaching here or not, but she hoped he'd at least get the offer. His ego needed it. And their family could use the small salary that would come with the job. When he had said he'd retained a third of his clients, the truth was the ones who stayed, accounted for a very small portion of his commission. They had already tapped into their savings to pay the bills.

Matthew returned to the board. On the side opposite of what he'd already written, he wrote 'Personal Life and Professional Life'. "So, here is what no one tells you when you're in college. There is a difference between your personal life and your professional life. With social media and everything you do, work and personal, on your phone, we tend to let those two things overlap. That is something I want to caution you against. And I think if you can keep it separate, it will be easier for you to remember the ethical choices you will be faced with daily in your career. Confronting a friend over something has different levels of responsibility than confronting a partner or coworker over missteps or outright illegal acts."

He paused and glanced at the young faces in the room. He was sure this was the first time they were hearing this. Good. It was an important message. Troy Donnor still hadn't realized it.

"I am only able to speak about any of this today because Ken Woods took a plea deal. This is no longer an active case for the SCC or the EDVA. Had it been, I would have been barred from discussing it. As the case was being built against Ken, I was working with the agencies and I was forbidden from discussing it with even my family. I couldn't even tell my wife. That was a tremendous burden. I even testified before the Grand Jury, in secret, which my wife was unaware of. I was threatened with prosecution if I discussed the pending case with anyone. And this brings me back to a question I already posed to myself at the beginning of this lecture. Did I and do I regret that I initiated this to begin with? No. I don't. Ken Woods was committing a crime. Ken Woods' actions were defrauding and stealing his clients' hard-earned money. There is absolutely no decision in that case but to do the right thing, ethically and legally."

As Matthew took questions from students, Elyse thought about what he'd said. Any anger or disappointment she still had regarding him evaporated. Him referring to it as a tremendous burden was an understatement. No wonder he'd acted as he had. And now, the growth he'd made, the acceptance of his own responsibility in their marital problems and his alcohol and drug use, showed strength. Speaking before this seminar showed honesty. And she'd seen for herself how he'd stepped up to be the husband and father Claire needed him to be. She was even impressed that he'd invited the entire family, begging Kade to trade a shift so he could attend. She realized that he'd finally transformed from Claire's husband into a member of the family.

Kelsey was in awe of Matthew's honesty. His lecture was amazing. She knew he was considering teaching business and ethics classes. He absolutely needed to as far as she was concerned, and she'd tell him as much after the lecture. The entire family was going out for dinner.

Kade choked back his own emotions after Matthew brought up the car accident. Matthew had learned what he and all his coworkers were keenly aware of. That life was about the people in your life that you cared about, not the money, the job, or the status that came with it. None of that matter. It was the people in your life who could be gone in a split second that mattered.

Mel squeezed his hand. His gaze shifted to her, and he knew she understood. She and Ellie were his world. Ellie was with Lizette, who watched her with Aiden and Emma tonight. Claire had already spoken to her nanny about helping out with Ellie a few days a week. He wasn't sure if Claire would be paying her more to do so, but Claire had promised him it would not cost him anything. She was glad to help. And he was grateful.

• • • •

A WEEK LATER, SUNDAY dinner at Elyse's was again on the agenda. This time, the birthday cake was for Claire. "Thirty-three," Claire said, gazing at her cake on the counter.

"This has been a hell of a year," she told her mom. They were getting the plates out to set the table. Claire had become quite adept at functioning with her arm in the cast. Aiden and Emma were upstairs with Kade and Mel, getting Baby Ellie up from her nap. They adored her and thought of her as a baby sister. Everyone else was in the family room visiting. "I hope we never have a year like this one ever again."

"There's been a lot of good things that happened this year, Claire. Don't forget about those things. And even things you list on the bad side, like your car accident, I'd list that you all walked away from it with minimal injuries on the positive side."

"I know. Oh hey, did I tell you that Matthew received a few job offers and decided?"

"The last you told me was that Old Dominion had offered him an adjunct professor position to teach up to four classes a semester, beginning in the summer."

"They did, and that could lead to a full professor standing within a few years. The administrators that were there for his lecture were very impressed with him."

"I was too," Elyse said. "That was a fun evening, his guest lecture and then dinner out, the whole family." That was a huge positive that came about that year, the amount of time the family had spent together. And that was a direct result of Tim's passing.

"And it meant the world to him that the whole family was there."

"I'm glad we were, too," Elyse said.

"He's planning to take that job. He's also been offered to be brought on as a contractor to the SCC to investigate financial crimes and securities fraud. It is a temporary part-time position, but he's accepted it too. It also could lead to a full time, permanent position. And of course, he has kept about a third of his original clients at the firm. We're setting up an LLC with him and his attorney friend, Kerry. They'll focus on family financial planning, including wills and trusts. He'll work on that out of his office at the house. They'll take any client meetings at Kerry's office."

Elyse gave her another hug. "That's fantastic, sweetie. He'll be busy with three jobs. He has to be relieved that everything is falling into place."

"Yes, he is. And I'm relieved he's completely separated himself from Troy Donnor."

"It's too bad that relationship couldn't be saved," Elyse said.

March

Chapter 51 – March Madness

J ust as the annual NCAA college basketball tournament got started, things for the Laramie family got hectic as well. Jake, Kade, Mel, Ash, and Kelsey all picked their brackets and made side bets with each other over Sunday dinner, which had become a new tradition for the family.

Kade tried to involve Matthew and Claire, but college basketball was one sport they didn't follow. Plus, Matthew was busy getting his two new careers off the ground and was focused on expanding his new family financial planning business. Claire didn't follow basketball either, and she was okay that it was something the rest of the family was engaged in that she and Matthew were not. She was happy with the new closeness with the family they were enjoying, and didn't need to join them in brackets and watching games she had no interest in.

Elyse insisted that she didn't have time to follow the games. Animal House Shelter had several litters of puppies arrive, which created all the March madness she could handle. Claire promised the kids she'd take them to Animal House to play with the puppies on Wednesday, which was still the day Lizette was off each week at four p.m. They'd be revisiting Lizette's schedule again as she had just informed Claire that she had gotten engaged.

Kade and Mel had settled into being parents. Mel was back to going to classes in Norfolk five days a week, Monday through Friday, with the occasional Saturday. She had a lot of clinicals to make up. Kade was still on the early shift that started at four a.m. He would be making the switch to the later shift, of noon until eight on April first. That would make it easier as he would be able to care for Ellie most mornings and drop her at Kelsey's or Claire's house on his way into work. Mel could then pick her up after her day was done, usually around five.

Kelsey had a crib at her house in a guest room for Ellie. Kade or Mel could drop her off as needed at any hour. She'd be taking a few months off work, a leave of absence from the tattoo shop, but she felt confident she could adjust to being a new mom and still help with Ellie. She really loved doing something with her art, though, so she didn't want to stop her training now. She'd continue the bookwork during her leave of absence. She planned to bring their son with her to the shop when she didn't have Ellie, but she primarily wanted to be a mom for now.

Claire supplied help with Ellie as well, promising up to two days a week that Lizette would watch her. And Elyse was already enjoying varied hours helping with the baby. It was time she never had with Aiden and Emma and wished she had. She also couldn't wait for Kelsey and Ash's baby to be born so she could enjoy time with him as well. Perhaps she'd be able to watch him one evening a week while Kelsey worked at the shop. She didn't want her daughter to give up her new career.

Jake had just started to help prep for the systems upgrades to the USS Gravely, which had arrived back in port the week before. Even though he wouldn't be assigned to her, he was temporarily serving as the XO until the permanent executive officer would check in, prior to sea trials, which were set to commence on May first. He was now working six days a week, eight to ten hours a day, with Sunday being his only day off. He was eager to transition to the reserves. That should happen around May first as well. Even though his days were long, he drove home to Franklin each night. Yes, this was his home.

Kelsey felt amazing at eight and a half months pregnant. She and Ash were excited to meet their son. She marveled that her due date was just two weeks away. The addition to their home was completed and it had turned out just as they'd envisioned. They'd decorated the baby's room a week earlier with mountains, bears, and other forest animals in blues and greens, some browns, and grays. All were subdued, calming colors. It was a serene space that Kelsey already enjoyed spending time in as she put away the clothes, books, and toys that she'd received at a baby shower. They'd bought a plush blue rocking chair that she knew she'd spend a lot of time sitting in with her baby. He just needed to hurry up and come!

As Elyse served the dessert of brownie pie and vanilla ice cream, she listened to the many conversations overlapping at the table and she smiled. Her family was closer to each other than ever. Their time together wasn't forced or centered around a holiday or birthday. The friendship she saw between Kade and Mel and Kelsey and Ash seemed to get tighter daily. And Claire and Matthew and the kids had become close to the family in a way they never had been. Even these Sunday dinners just seemed to come about with enthusiasm from all. It was Claire who had called her on Friday to ask if she was hosting dinner for everyone and what she could bring. That was the first planning for tonight's dinner there'd been.

"This brownie pie is good, Claire," Kelsey said. "Did you buy it or make it?"

Claire pretended to be offended. "I will have you know I baked it."

Matthew snickered. "From a Betty Crocker box," he teased.

"I still baked it," Claire insisted. She raised her casted arm. "And with only one arm."

"And I stirred it," Aiden added with a huge smile.

"And you did a fantastic job," Elyse said. "Thank you for helping with it, Aiden."

Aiden smiled proudly.

As the evening wrapped up, Claire and her family were the first to leave. With hugs all around they left in a flurry of activity. After Kelsey and Ash departed, Kade and Mel brought Ellie upstairs. The three of them would spend family time alone in their living room over the garage.

Jake snuggled in against Elyse's back as she locked the front door. He pressed a kiss to the top of her head. "I don't know about you, but I'm exhausted," he said. "How does an early night sound?"

"How exhausted are you?"

"Not *that* exhausted," he replied.

She turned and wrapped her arms around his neck. "Good." They enjoyed a lengthy, passionate kiss. When they separated, she could tell there was something on his mind. "You look like you're mulling something over."

"Have been most the evening. I'm set to officially transition to the reserves on May first. I'll probably have a few weeks off right away. Could you get someone to cover at Animal House for a week? I'd really like for the two of us to go away someplace, a vacation. If you can be away from the family and if they can do without your help with the kids for that long."

Elyse felt a glow spread through her. A real vacation sounded perfect. "I'd like that. I'm sorry you have to think of my family in asking the question. I bet when you started this up with me, you didn't expect my family to be an obligation you had to consider."

He shook his head at her. "I happen to like your family. And I admire your commitment to them. I don't think that has to end at a certain age or timeframe. Besides, I see the joy you get out of spending time with them and getting to know your grandkids."

Elyse nodded. "I've loved this time with Ellie because I didn't have it with Aiden and Emma. Even the time I've gotten with them over the last year is more than before Tim died. I appreciate and value that time. I've gotten to be the type of grandma I always wanted to be."

"I think Claire has changed a lot over the months since I met her. I'm sorry you were deprived of having that time with her kids when they were babies."

"I'm just glad I have it with them now, and that I have the time with Ellie and will have it with Kelsey and Ash's baby. And I appreciate that you understand."

"It's one of the things I love about you, Elyse," Jake said. "And I appreciate that they all welcomed me to the family and accepted me this soon after they lost their dad."

"You fit in with the family so well."

"Thanks," he said. "So, do you think you can get away for a week?"

She smiled. "Yes. I'd love to take a vacation with you. Where did you have in mind?"

"I thought we could go to an all-inclusive resort on the beach someplace, Mexico or Aruba. Your passport is current, isn't it?"

Her smile spread wider. "It is, and that sounds amazing. And your birthday is that week. You thought I forgot, didn't you?"

Jake chuckled. "I didn't think you'd forget. No need to make a big deal out of it."

Elyse laughed. "Maybe it can be our tradition to spend your birthday week away. I'll make a big deal of it in a way I didn't any of my kids' birthdays."

"Now that plan has potential."

"Can you let the dogs out for the last time and lock up the back of the house?" Elyse asked. "I want to go up and take a quick rinse-off."

Jake grinned. "Yes, ma'am. But first, one more thing. I was thinking the barn-space is nearly finished. It won't take that much to turn it into that art studio for you and a small office for me. I'd like to have a room that's mine, if it's not asking too much. I'm still giving my after-Navy life some thought, but I do think I'd like to try to teach part-time at one or two of the local colleges. My master's degree is in supply chain management. I'd think there'd be a few courses I'd qualify to teach."

So, that was the other thing that had been on his mind. Of course he wanted and needed his own space. How had she not realized that? "I think that sounds like a great idea. I want that space to be used, not just sitting unused like it is after I put money into it." She placed a kiss on his lips. "Don't be long. I'll be waiting for you."

Chapter 52 – Blue

At ten p.m. on March thirtieth Kelsey and Ash were at the shop, as they were most evenings when the shop was open. It was her due date, but so far there was no indication this baby had any intentions of coming soon. She had a few Braxton Hicks contractions occasionally, not nearly as many as Mel talked about having. What she did have, though, was terrible gas pains and heartburn. And tonight was no exception. She felt miserable. She and Ash had been to the obstetrician two days earlier and the OB was now talking about how long he'd let her go before he'd induce labor. He, too, didn't think the baby would come soon.

She stretched and rubbed her abdomen. "I'm going to be evicting you soon, little man. Why don't you just make things easier on us both and come on your own?"

Both Ash and Eric laughed. "I'm not sure it works that way, babe," Ash said. "You can't talk your body into going into labor."

"Well, we tried the spicy food and all that did was give me horrendous gas pains and heartburn tonight. I even did prenatal yoga this morning. That did nothing."

"I'm sure it did something; stretched your muscles, relaxed you," Eric said.

Kelsey shot a glare his way. And then she had the oddest sensation hit her. She experienced a sudden release of fluids down her legs. And she was sure it hadn't come from her bladder. She looked down and saw that her leggings were saturated. Her surprised expression met Ash's. "I think my water just broke!"

"Really?" Ash asked, doubtful. From where he was, he didn't see her wet pants.

"Well, I'm not sure. I've never felt anything like it before." She took a few steps closer to him, leaving a puddle and a trail of dripping water behind her.

"Damn," he said.

And then a tightening all around her abdomen hit, which she was sure was a contraction, a real contraction. More fluid leaked out. "Okay, yes, that was a contraction and I'm leaking water."

Ash jumped up from his seat and rushed to her side. "We have to time them to figure out when we're supposed to call the doctor and leave for the hospital." He had his phone out, running the timer.

The contractions were ten minutes apart.

They remained at the shop. They were closer to the hospital there than they would be at their house, so they decided they wouldn't go home. By midnight, the contractions were five minutes apart and getting stronger. Eric had remained with them even after closing time when they locked the door. He was more nervous than either Kelsey or Ash.

When they left for the hospital, Eric went home, but only after making them promise to text and send a picture of the baby no matter what time he came. On the short drive to the hospital, the contractions increased in intensity and sped up to three minutes apart. Ash would admit he was concerned. But he was proud of Kelsey that she didn't panic.

THAT FIRST YEAR

As they walked through the ER entrance, which was the only entrance into the hospital open that late, the most intense contraction yet hit and she understood what was described as the need to push. The ER staff quickly had her sit in a wheelchair and brought them right up to the Family Birthing Center. The nurse helped her into a gown and immediately called the doctor after a check showed that Kelsey was fully dilated and one hundred percent effaced. The baby's head was crowning.

Their son came into the world at twelve-fifty-two a.m. on March thirty-first, less than thirty minutes after they'd arrived at the hospital. He was healthy and alert. Kelsey and Ash cradled him between them, marveling at this perfect little being they had created. He had a shadow of light-colored hair on his head.

"He's so tiny," Ash said. He kissed Kelsey for the umpteenth time. "You did it, babe," he whispered.

"*We* did it," she corrected him. "He's perfect. Just like his daddy."

Speaking with the nurse, Kelsey discovered that the gas pains she'd experienced all night had actually been labor pains. She was glad her water broke, otherwise they probably would have gone home and wouldn't have left for the hospital early enough. He very well could have been born at home or on the drive there.

"No, he's perfect like his mommy," Ash said. "I'm so proud of you, Kels."

The nurse came back into the room to check on them. "Have you thought of any names?"

"Yes, we've known his name since we found out it was a boy," Kelsey said. "But we didn't tell anyone."

Ash beamed a smile at her. "I can't wait to tell your family about him."

"I hate that it's the middle of the night. I want to call my mom and tell her he's here, but it would be wrong to wake her up. I guess it's going to be a text with his picture and name," Kelsey said.

"We know that Kade will be up around two-thirty. He's still on the four a.m. shift. We could give him a call right before he leaves to drive into Norfolk," Ash said.

"Yes! So I'll just text my mom, if that's okay. We can let everyone else know after we talk to Kade."

Ash laughed. "You know, Eric is probably still awake. And Drew probably is, too."

"It would be wrong to call them and not my mom."

"More wrong than to wake her?"

Kelsey thought about it for a minute. "I say we send a group text to everyone after we tell Kade before he leaves for work."

• • • •

ELLIE AWOKE AT TWO a.m. Kade changed her and brought her to Mel and then just stayed up. He'd just be falling back asleep when his alarm was set to go off. He sat at the kitchen table and leisurely enjoyed a second cup of coffee. He was surprised when his phone vibrated a call. It was Ash with a FaceTime call. Given the date and time, he knew the baby had come.

He hit answer and the screen showed what he expected would greet him, a newborn baby. Kade smiled at the image. He looked just like Kelsey. "Hello there!" he greeted the baby.

The screen shifted and he saw Kelsey and Ash's smiling faces. "He's here!" Kelsey said.

"He looks just like you, Kels. Congrats! You look good, sis. How'd it go?"

"It went fast," Ash said. "We weren't even at the hospital for an hour before he was born. Kelsey was amazing."

Kade laughed. "Don't tell Mel that."

Kelsey shifted the baby so he was nestled between them. "Meet your nephew, Kaden Ashley Vincent."

Kade's vision became distorted with the tears that filled his eyes. "Kaden?"

Kelsey's smile grew bigger if that was even possible. "Of course we named him after you, though we may call him Denny if it's too confusing."

"I don't think it will be," Ash said. "Kade and Kaden are different names."

Kade felt emotional. "Wow, guys. I can't believe you named him after me. Are you sure you want to do that?"

Kelsey giggled. "Of course we are. Kade, you have to know you mean the world to me."

"And to me too, bro," Ash added.

$$\bullet \ \bullet \ \bullet \ \bullet$$

ELYSE ROLLED OVER AND picked up her phone from her nightstand. She had been checking it as soon as she woke for the last two weeks as Kelsey neared her due date. She saw a text from Kelsey and opened it in anticipation. The picture of Kelsey and Ash cradling their newborn in their arms, his beautiful face visible, greeted her. Below it said, *"Mom and baby both doing great, born on 3/31 at 12:52 a.m. 19" long, 7 lbs. 8 oz."*

"Jake," Elyse said, shaking him awake. "Kelsey and Ash's baby was born last night. He's doing great. He's beautiful." She held the phone up to Jake as he opened his eyes.

"Does it say what they named him?"

Elyse scanned back through the message. "No, it doesn't." She hit dial.

On the third ring, Ash answered. "Hi, Elyse. Kelsey is doing great. She's in the bathroom."

Elyse had to chuckle at his statement. "And how are you doing, Dad?"

Now Ash chuckled as well. "I'm doing great. I'm so proud of Kelsey. She was amazing, bringing our son into the world. She'll tell you herself, but we barely made it to the hospital in time. He was born less than an hour after we got here."

"Who's on the phone?" Elyse heard Kelsey's voice.

"It's your mom," Ash replied. "Here she is."

"Mom, when can you come to the hospital and meet him?" Kelsey asked, coming to the phone.

"I'm just waking up. It's only seven. I think visiting hours start at nine. How do you feel, sweetie, and did you get any sleep?"

"Yes, a few hours. And I feel fine," Kelsey said.

"Well, what did you name him?" Elyse asked.

"Kaden Ashley Vincent."

"You named him after your brother? I assume he knows."

"Yes, we called him early this morning before he left to go to work," Kelsey said. "He cried when we told him the name, Mom."

Elyse's heart swelled and tears filled her eyes. Of course he had. "I'm sure he felt honored."

"Then mission accomplished," Kelsey said. "And we're going to ask Claire and Matthew to be his godparents."

The tears spilled out of Elyse's eyes. Her three children were closer now than they'd ever been.

• • • •

CLAIRE AWOKE TO THE alarm on her phone. Upon turning it off, she saw the text from Kelsey announcing that the baby was born overnight. She studied his picture. He looked just like Kelsey had as a baby. He was beautiful. She decided immediately that she would take a long lunch and go to the hospital to visit. There was no way she would wait to meet her nephew.

When Claire entered the hospital room hours later, her mom was there, sitting in a chair opposite the bed where Kelsey sat. Her mom cradled the small blanket-wrapped bundle. First, Claire rushed to Kelsey and gave her a long hug and a bouquet of flowers. She marveled how fantastic her sister looked, not like she had given birth in the middle of the night. Ash was just coming out of the bathroom. She gave him a hug next. He looked tired.

"I'm so happy for you two," she said. "Well, you three! So, what did you name him?" Kelsey wouldn't tell her over the phone.

Elyse stood and handed the baby to Claire, flashing her a proud smile. Claire's eyes focused on his perfect little face. Yes, he looked just like Kelsey had as a baby.

Ash took a seat on the edge of Kelsey's bed. "First off, Claire, we'd like you and Matthew to be his godparents," Kelsey said.

"Oh, we'd be honored," Claire said, deeply touched.

"We've named him Kaden Ashley Vincent," Kelsey said.

"Kaden? You named him after Kade?"

"If our next child is a boy his middle name will be Timothy, after Dad," Kelsey said.

"And if we have a girl, her middle name will be Claire," Ash added. "We gave names a lot of thought."

"Kade has to feel very honored," Claire said, recovering from the surprise.

"I'm actually thinking Anna Claire or Hanna Claire," Kelsey said. "Sounds good, don't you think?" She flashed a big smile at her sister.

Claire nodded. "Yes, it does. I can't believe you're already talking about another baby."

Kelsey giggled. "Well, I doubt he's going to be an only child."

Claire's eyes went back to the baby. He was beautiful. Godmother, yes, that was an honor.

April
Chapter 53 – Eggs and Ink

On Easter Sunday, the entire family attended Flowing Waters for the eleven o'clock service. Kade had worked an overnight shift for the overtime pay. He was able to get a three-hour nap before Mel woke him to get ready for church. They brought Ellie in a frilly, pastel-colored floral dress, one that had been Emma's.

The pastor talked of resurrection and forgiveness, eternal life, peace, and hope. In her seat, Claire considered the message as she held Emma on her lap, her newly un-casted arm wrapped around her youngest as she listened to the Easter message, her heart taking his words in unlike she ever had before. Aiden sat in a chair between her and Matthew. The struggles their family had gone through over the last four months were just memories now. She was at peace. She had forgiven Matthew, truly forgiven him.

Her gaze swept to her brother. His wedding was in two weeks. She was excited to celebrate this milestone with him. He held his baby daughter in his arms. It looked good on him, being a father. She felt closer to him than she ever had.

She had a new respect for him and the job he and Mel did, and not just because he had probably saved her life in January when she'd been in the car accident. Kade could have gone to med school and become a doctor. But being a paramedic was a calling. And he was good at his job. When Matthew had told her how he handled everything that day calmly and confidently, she wasn't surprised. Mel had even grown on her, and she considered her a sister-in-law. They didn't need to take vows for Mel to be considered a part of the family.

Kelsey and Ash sat beside Kade with their newborn son asleep in her arms. Tears came to Claire's eyes considering Baby Kaden. Her little sister was a mom. She'd always felt close to Kelsey, but even more so now. And she was happy that Ash was a part of the family. He fit well and made Kelsey happy. He appeared to be a good father, as attentive to the baby as to Kelsey. She wished her father had been alive to meet him. He'd surely have approved.

Her mom and Jake sat at the end of the row. On this Resurrection Sunday, perhaps the relationship they had and the relationship she had with them was what Claire was most grateful for. Liking Jake had no bearing on her relationship with her father. She could love and miss her father and like Jake too. Her mom was happy. She had been an amazing mother all those years, doing the toughest job alone, something Claire had not realized at the time.

Elyse held Jake's hand as she listened to the Easter message. Tim was at peace. The sermon reminded her of that. Easter services were always her favorite, right along with Christmas. This was the first time in more years than she could remember that the entire family had been together on Easter Sunday. And this year was even more special with the additions to their family; the two babies, Ash, Jake, and the fact that Mel and Kade would marry soon.

Kade gazed into the eyes of his daughter. She had her mother's eyes. As the pastor spoke of peace and hope, his thoughts were centered on the baby in his arms. He and Mel would be married in two weeks. He would be a constant presence in his wife's and daughter's lives. He thought of his father and that note he'd written to him, that was safely hidden in a password-protected file as his gaze flickered to Claire. He made eye contact with her and smiled. He was happy that peace had settled over her household. She'd really changed over the last few months. He forgave her of past injustices and episodes of self-centered drama. As far as he knew, there had been no purposeful malice in her heart.

Kelsey felt emotional, listening to the Easter message as if she was comprehending it on a different level. And in a way she was. She was a mom now to a beautiful newborn baby boy. She knew that life would never be the same for her again. The pastor talked of eternal life, and that held a different meaning for her now, a renewed importance. Out of the corner of her eye, she saw Claire, looking in her direction. She smiled and felt an appreciation for her sister that she hadn't last year. She was thankful for the renewed closeness of her family, for the family her child would know. She recalled feeling that her family had spent too much time together the month following her father's death. But that hadn't been the case. That time together ushered in a new closeness between them.

After the service they all gathered at Kelsey and Ash's house. It would be Kelsey's first time hosting a holiday meal, a transition of sorts for her into true adulthood. She was a mom and the mistress of this house, welcoming her family. She'd planned the meal, communicated what each family member could contribute, and had shopped and prepared the dishes. This was a much different role than reporting to her mom or Claire's house at the appointed hour as she had in the past.

And she was proud to show off the addition that was completed, including the decorating she'd done. She was excited as she showed Claire and Matthew around her home, who hadn't been there since Ash's and her wedding. The rest of the family had been over throughout the construction, so they'd all seem it.

"Everything is decorated so cute," Claire said when the grand tour was concluded. "I'm proud of you, Kels. You even have a room for Ellie here, with a second baby monitor and everything."

Kelsey smiled. "Well, it's technically one of the guest rooms, but yes, she's here several days a week and I don't expect that to change. I want her to be comfortable and think of it as a second bedroom. When Mel returns to work, her schedule will be varied. They could both be scheduled on the overnight shift. I'm sure we'll have Ellie overnight some nights."

Claire felt even more pride in her sister. "Just don't give up your art and your new career. Even if you only do it one day a week, don't give it up."

Kelsey hugged Claire. "I won't. I really love tattooing. I've done some linework on people, real live people," she added with a laugh.

"And she's great at it," Ash chimed in. He unbuttoned the top few buttons on his shirt and pulled the fabric aside. He pointed out script lettering on his chest. "She did this. No hesitation in her lines, just a smooth flow of the ink."

Claire's eyes flashed from his chest to Kelsey's eyes. "You're practicing on him?"

"Yes," she answered with a shrug. "Who else would I practice on?"

"I don't know, I guess it's just weird," Claire replied.

"It's not like it's some kind of weird foreplay," Ash joked. "Or is it?" He grinned and raised an eyebrow.

Claire cringed and everyone else laughed.

"I will admit I'm getting more comfortable with the whole tattoo thing," Claire said. "Matthew is even talking about getting one, and I'm not opposed to the idea."

"Really? What are you thinking of getting?" Ash asked him.

Matthew looked embarrassed. "You'll think it's stupid."

"Never," Ash said.

"Well, with everything that's happened in the last year between the business stuff and nearly losing Claire and the kids, I saw this movie and the lead character had this chunky block writing kind of in the same place across his chest like you do. It was in a code to represent his wife's name and their wedding date, and his child's name and birthdate, without saying it outright. I'd have to think what that code would be, but I thought it was pretty cool."

"That *is* cool," Kade said. "And I'm sure your brother-in-law here will give you a good price."

Ash laughed. "The family discount, for sure."

Kelsey nudged Claire. "You could get a two for one price if you want to come in and get ink to match Kade's and mine to honor Dad."

Claire laughed. "I'll think about it."

Kelsey raised an eyebrow. She hadn't said no. She hadn't said tattoos were disgusting. Her gaze met her mom's, and she could see her mom was thinking the same thing.

• • • •

LATER THAT WEEK, MATTHEW had figured out the code that would represent his family. He and Claire went to Ash's shop on Friday evening while Lizette babysat the kids. Hearing of the appointment, Kelsey called Claire and teased her that since it was a date night, she needed to get a tattoo, too. She had her mom and Jake babysit Kaden and Ellie. Even Kade and Mel were at Ash's Ink and Blades when Claire and Matthew pulled up.

"Seriously?" Claire said, seeing everyone there.

Eric laughed as he approached them. First, he shook Matthew's hand and then he gave Claire an affectionate hug. "This is a huge occasion, Matthew's first tattoo."

"Um, first and only," Claire said.

Everyone laughed but her and Matthew.

"It's kind of addicting," Kelsey said. "I'll bet you a night of babysitting that he gets another within six months."

"I'll take that bet and double it. Two nights of babysitting," Claire said.

They shook. "Deal. Can they be back-to-back nights? Ash and I just might want to go away for a weekend," Kelsey said.

Claire laughed. "You are too confident."

Kelsey made eye contact with Eric. They'd talked and she knew that Matthew had mentioned to Eric that there were several more pieces he was thinking of. So, yes, she was very confident in her bet.

Matthew settled in, lying on the padded table. First, Ash shaved his chest where the lettering would be. "Normally, Kelsey would do this, but for some reason it seems wrong to have her shave it," Ash said.

Laughter filled the room.

"Yeah, thanks for that," Matthew said. "Not that it would be incestuous, it would be like too familiar a contact, I guess."

Kade laughed. He stood near the table. "And your brother-in-law shaving you instead isn't?"

"It's his chest. It's not like someone is shaving his balls," Kelsey said.

Louder laughter followed.

"This is great, keep it up. He'll never come back for another tattoo, and I'll win the bet," Claire said.

After he was shaved and cleaned up, Ash pressed the transfer to his chest to position where the ink would go. Matthew was pleased with the size of the letters and their positioning on his chest. Then Ash explained the process and the sanitization aspect.

Matthew felt very little pain from the inking process, didn't even wince. He laid there and carried on conversations with everyone. Claire watched intently, fascinated with a process she'd once thought was disgusting. She had to admit it looked sexy across his chest, especially because of the significance of what looked like random Roman numerals and capital letters in one continuous string.

When Ash was done inking him, they took pictures and Matthew was instructed on how to care for it. Claire was amazed that was it. It had been so simple and appeared to be painless.

"What do you think?" Matthew asked her with a smile on his face.

"I think it looks kind of sexy," she told him, returning his smile.

"Ooh," Kelsey teased. "Claire's liking his ink."

"It's addictive," Mel teased her. "You'll be the one mentioning new ideas to him that you think are cool for him to get."

Claire waved them both off. "Oh please!"

"Or you'll be wanting one of your own," Mel said. "That's how it started for me."

Kelsey went into a drawer of Ash's station. She pulled the transfer of the design that both she and Kade had and held it up between her and Claire. "It's here, waiting for you whenever you want it, sis."

Claire took it from her and studied it. "Show it to me again on you."

Kelsey pulled the front of her pants down just enough for her tattoo to be visible.

"Your stomach is already completely flat from being pregnant. I hate you," Mel joked. She was still struggling to lose the last ten pounds that she'd gained while pregnant with Ellie.

Kelsey smiled.

"That really is a nice thing to honor Dad with. Yours is much smaller than Kade's. This size it's actually cute," Claire said.

"I've got time. I could ink you right now," Ash offered, expecting an instant decline.

Claire smiled nervously. "Really, you could do it right now?"

"Now *I* will bet you a night of babysitting that you aren't going to get it," Kade said.

Claire presented her hand. "I'll take that bet. I bet you I am."

They shook. Claire stuck her tongue out at him and then hopped up onto the table. "Yes, let's do it."

Chapter 54 – Two Dates, One Week

T he one-year anniversary of Tim's passing was the Sunday before Kade and Mel's wedding. Elyse secretly wondered if Kade had planned their wedding date on purpose to help distract from the somber day that marked one full year since Tim had been killed.

As planned, the family gathered for dinner and she made his favorite meal of lasagna, which she hadn't made since the day that would have been Tim's birthday. They acknowledged him with a short prayer before the meal began. After it was eaten and Aiden and Emma were happily playing in the sunroom, Elyse invited each of her children to share any thoughts they had regarding this solemn milestone. She didn't specify what kinds of thoughts and was surprised when Claire began.

Claire recounted where she was and how she felt when her mom had called that morning. "I was still at home getting ready for work. I am thankful that it was Mom who called and not Michael. That was not news for him to share with me. It was appropriate it came from Mom. I still remember how shocked I was to hear the words. And a part of me didn't believe it."

"I remember I had just woken up when I got Mom's text, asking me to call her ASAP," Kelsey said. "Somehow, I just knew that something was wrong. It was probably because it said just that, no 'Hi Kels' starting the message. It wasn't that I didn't believe it, but I thought that there had to be a mistake. Something happened to someone, but not Dad.

And I was so thankful when Kade called and offered to drive me home."

Kade flashed her an understanding smile. "I called Claire, too, and offered, but Matthew was coming to Mom's with her. I was at work when Mom called me. You know, I deal with death at work. As I've said before, doing the job, you check your emotions at the door and deal with anything that gets to you later, off the job. I did the same thing that day. I don't think I let myself feel the shock of the news or absorb the reality that he was dead until a few days later. Then I broke down."

"Those memories will stick with you for the rest of your lives. I recall exactly where I was and how I felt when I got the news of my parents' deaths, too," Elyse said. "But time does help to heal. It's been a year and we've had a lot of good things happen this year, too. The amount of time we've all spent together has been the best part of the year, after the births of Ellie and Kaden. Ash and Jake coming into our lives is right up there, too."

"I know we planned to open our letters in the jar to Dad and read them today, but I don't want to," Kelsey said. "What I wrote was a private note to Dad."

Elyse was proud of her for speaking up. Kelsey from a year ago wouldn't have. She would have waited to see what Kade and Claire wanted to do first and then she would have sided with Kade if they were at odds or followed their lead had Kade and Claire been united.

"I agree," Kade said. "It's too soon. But on the other hand, it feels like so long ago that we wrote them."

Elyse chuckled. "That's because you're sleep deprived with an infant."

"It could be worse. I could be on overnights. I'm glad I finally build up seniority."

"What are your thoughts regarding the notes, Claire?" Elyse asked.

"I look at the jar and Dad's urn every time I pass through the entry. And I never think about reading those notes. They weren't written to me."

The conversation took a turn towards the wedding plans, and just like that the anniversary of Tim's death passed with the proper remembrance and sadness. A realization came to Elyse. There was nothing magical about the one-year mark. It was a milestone, getting past the first of every holiday and every tradition without him. The passage of time had lessened the hurt, or maybe it was that they had adjusted to living with it. Elyse knew that she and her children would continue to grieve in their own ways, collectively as well as individually. Gazing into the faces of little Ellie and Kaden proved that life went on, and change was a constant, the one thing you could count on.

"I think that sounds doable, don't you, Elyse?" Jake's question cut in on her reflections.

"I'm sorry. I was lost in my own thoughts for a second. I'm embarrassed to admit I wasn't listening," Elyse said.

"Are you okay, Mom?" Claire asked, concerned. That was so unlike her mother.

"Yes, sweetie, I'm fine." Her gaze swept back around the table, not knowing who said something that Jake thought was doable.

"I said that the weather forecast on Saturday is a ninety percent chance of rain in the afternoon," Kade repeated.

"And I asked how much work it would take to clean the inside of the barn to use for the ceremony and reception." Claire said. "That's all the rage now, you know, having your wedding and reception inside a barn. One of our friends rented one that is used for weddings, and it was really beautiful."

"I really don't want anyone to go to that much trouble," Mel said.

"There has to be a Plan B if it rains," Claire said. "You have guests that are invited, and food, chairs, and tables have been ordered and paid for, or have balances due. You originally planned a backyard wedding, but it has to get moved indoors now, and I think the barn is the logical choice."

"And if we all pitch in and help clean the inside of the barn, I think it would work just fine. But we need help to make it look presentable," Kade said.

"And decorations will be easy," Kelsey said. "The white string lights from my wedding and some flowers and greenery will transform it into a beautiful room."

"Please, you don't need to go to that much trouble," Mel said.

"It's no trouble, sweetie," Elyse said. "Just a few hours of everyone's time."

"And I have about a dozen volunteers lined up to come over Saturday morning and set everything up," Kade said.

"I know you already bought white plastic table cloths to go over all the tables," Claire said. "But I saw the easiest and cheapest addition to that on Pinterest that would make the barn look rustic and amazing. They went to a fabric store and bought bolts of material from the clearance table, and had it cut in long strips that they used as table runners, leaving the edges raw," Claire said. "And the weight of the material also helps hold down the plastic table cloths if it's windy at all."

"Sure, whatever you want to do," Mel conceded, knowing that everyone just wanted to help. "And thanks, Claire."

• • • •

KADE AND MEL'S WEDDING day arrived with a beautiful spring morning, the rain completely removed from the forecast, but the work had already been done to make the barn the perfect wedding venue. The day began with Jake running Frick and Frack to Animal House, where they'd spend the day playing. They would be under foot if they remained home. Charlie could easily be confined to the house, and he'd happily sleep the day away.

Jake returned home and got busy helping to set up the barn for the wedding. By ten, an army of friends and family descended on the property to set up tables and chairs for the catered meal. It was decided the guests would sit at their dinner tables during the wedding ceremony, as they'd all have a good view of the wedding arch that would be set up at one of the two wide-open doorways.

Lights and other decorations were strung on the walls and a beautiful chandelier that had once hung in the entry of the house had already been hung from the rafters in the middle of the barn. The entire Laramie family, including

Claire and Matthew, had worked every evening in the barn to clean it up enough for the timber structure to host the wedding.

Somehow, this informal celebration became a big undertaking. The reason of course was the guest list. No one from EMS could be omitted. And every last one of Kade and Mel's coworkers who were not on duty during it responded that they were coming, most bringing a plus one, and many their children, who were also invited, which added to the numbers. In order to keep them entertained a bouncy house was rented, as were a couple blow-up slides. Bags, a volleyball net, and horseshoes were also added outside of the barn.

Claire once again took care of arranging for the meal, but this time Elyse split the cost with her. And it would be set up buffet style and include kid's favorites like chicken nuggets, fries, and macaroni and cheese. The adult side of the menu was summer picnic favorites that included a garden salad, burgers, grilled and breaded chicken breasts, and gourmet pasta salads. Large plastic tubs would hold beer, wine, and other canned or bottled beverages. It would all be self-serve, with no bartender at any point.

Had it been a month later, the party could have been a Memorial Day summer kick-off party.

After all the set up and decorating was completed, Mel stood back and her uncomfortable gaze swept over the barn. "I really didn't want anything this elaborate."

Elyse hugged her. "It's not over the top. I'd call this comfortable and relaxed. It celebrates the occasion but also invites your guests to have a good time."

"Just a big party with a bonfire would have been fine," Mel said.

"We have the bonfire built outside to light later!" Ash yelled, from across the room. He and Kade were just getting ready to put the two ladders away that they'd used to reach the rafters to string lights.

"I truly think you're a pyromaniac," she called back, teasing Ash.

Claire stepped in front of Mel. "You have over a hundred guests, including children. It's about controlling the situation." She waved her hand around the room. "This is control. Tables and chairs. A place for the food to be set up. Lighting because the sun will go down during the party. And entertainment outside. No one spent a fortune on any of this. Your table-cloths are bolts of fabric from a clearance table over plastic, and the lighting is primarily from Mom's Christmas box. There's nothing elaborate about it. Mom's right. It's a comfortable and relaxed atmosphere that just happens to look amazing."

"Don't forget there are porta-potties and ample parking," Matthew added with a laugh.

"Okay, okay," Mel conceded. She turned to Elyse and gave her an unexpected hug. "Thank you for letting us have the wedding here. And thank you for being an amazing mother-in-law and grandmother to my daughter."

"You're welcome, sweetie," Elyse said.

It still bothered Elyse that Mel hadn't told her parents about Ellie, nor had she told them she was getting married. She hoped Mel wouldn't grow to regret it. But that was Mel's relationship to manage, not hers. All she could do was be the best mother-in-law and grandmother she could and make sure that Mel knew that she was a welcomed and valued member of the family.

. . . .

IN TRUE KADE AND MEL casual fashion, they entered the barn and walked arm and arm through it and up to the wedding arch at the far end of the barn where Samantha waited. Their guests stood and clapped as they walked through, creating the music that was omitted. Mel wore a simple white dress she'd bought at a department store. It was loose-fitting and the skirt flowed to mid-calf length. It was nothing fancy, but she looked very feminine. Kade wore blue jeans with a white dress shirt topped with a dark blue sports coat. Mel didn't carry a bouquet. There was no maid of honor or best man.

Samantha was dressed in dark blue to officiate this wedding, a low-cut halter style dress that clung to her curves and draped to the ground. Kade thought back to what he was told Claire had said about her appearance at Kelsey and Ash's wedding. There was no slit this time and, based on how Samantha usually dressed, he'd consider this conservative. He laughed at the thought.

"That was quite an entrance!" Samantha said. "We are all of course here to celebrate Kade and Mel and their love. What a fabulous day that God has given us for this momentous ceremony. Marriage." She paused and glanced over everyone in the barn. "Marriage is a holy union created by God. It is a space to love and to grow, for each person to become the best version of themselves with the support of that one person who loves them the most. Please pray with me," she invited. "Heavenly Father, Kade and Melanie come before you in the presence of their friends and family, those who mean the most to them, and seek to be joined in the bonds of holy matrimony. Bless their union with many years of happiness." She paused and raised her gaze to the couple standing before her. "Mel and Kade have written their own vows and they will exchange rings."

Mel had Kade's ring on her finger. She placed it on the tip of his. When she spoke, it was quiet and laced with more emotion than anyone but Kade had ever heard in it. "Kade, with this ring I take you as my husband. I promise to love and cherish you, forsaking all others until we are separated by death. You have taught me what true love is, true friendship, and what a partner is supposed to be. You've given me a life better than anything I would have dreamt for myself. You've given me a precious daughter, a tiny being who, along with you, is my world. But most of all, you have given me an amazing future that I am thrilled is before us." She slid the ring completely onto his finger.

Kade had tears in his eyes, matching those in hers. He pulled her ring from his pocket. "Mel, with this ring I take you as my wife. I promise to love you and cherish you, forsaking all others until we are separated by death. You are my best friend, my partner in all ways. You are an amazing mother to our daughter, and I wake up every morning knowing that I am blessed to have you and Ellie in my life. I look forward to our amazing future. I can't say it will always be smooth, but together we can handle any bumps we encounter." He kissed the back of her hand after he had pushed the ring all the way on.

"Melanie, Kade, may love and laughter remain in your hearts and in your home for all the days of your lives. May you remember to turn to each other in difficult times and face those times as you do the good, hand-in-hand, knowing that with God's grace you can conquer all obstacles together. And may you always remember why you fell in love with each other and celebrate that love in big and in little ways every day of your lives. I now pronounce you husband and wife in Jesus' Name. Amen," Samantha intoned.

Kade and Mel kissed. Watching them, Elyse smiled with the true joy she felt. Even though they'd been in a committed relationship and were good partners to each other, which she'd been able to observe for herself, she believed in marriage and was glad they'd felt it was important, too. She gazed down at Ellie, asleep in her arms. She knew that Mel and Kade would give her a good life.

Mel and Kade approached their table. They would take seats at the table with Elyse and Jake. It was a long rectangular table that sat five on each side, and one on each end. Kelsey and Ash, Claire and Matthew, and both of the kids were seated there, as well as Cletus and his wife Valarie. They had left their son with her mom for the night, so they could have a rare adult evening out. But first Kade and Mel made the rounds, greeting their guests.

Now that the ceremony was over, Kade felt relaxed. He knew that Mel was uncomfortable with how big, and in her mind, fancy, the event had become. It was no longer just the relaxed little party with their friends that she wanted.

But glancing around the barn, at everyone there, with the backdrop of the lights and decorations, he was glad they'd made the effort. And they were married now. Mel had said the piece of paper meant nothing to her, but it did to him, and he knew it mattered to his mom. And what mattered to his mom was important to him.

Ash's friend and client, Nikki, was hired to take pictures of the wedding and the party after. She'd again set up a website that would allow anyone to download pictures from the wedding for free. It was one of Ash and Kelsey's wedding gifts to them. She had been snapping pictures during the ceremony and after as Kade and Mel greeted their guests as they made the rounds to every table.

The volume in the barn increased with the many conversations. Kaden stirred in Kelsey's arms. She and Mel had a changing table with a comfortable chair to use to nurse arranged in the finished area of the barn, in one of the back rooms near the bathroom. The caterers were using the front part of the space to unbox and get the food ready to be served.

She hoped Kaden would go back to sleep so she could eat before he woke and she'd have to nurse him. She had a Moses basket behind her chair to put him in if he was asleep and no one wanted to hold him. It was large enough that Ellie could also use it if they were asleep at the same time. Kelsey laughed to herself, considering how the two kids were more like twins than cousins, twins that were nearly three months apart.

The caterers arranged the food on the buffet table so lines could be formed on both sides of it. There was no speaker or microphone set up, as they weren't having a DJ or dancing. So once the food was ready, Cletus held a rotating light up and activated a hand-held siren that sounded like the siren on their ambulance units to get everyone's attention. As the room quieted, Samantha moved to the center of the room from the table she'd been near, where she'd eat. She had a bottle of beer in her hand.

"Friends," she called. "I first want to say a prayer to bless the food, and then make a toast to Mel and Kade."

Only a few children could be heard, otherwise the barn was silent.

"Father God, we thank You for this beautiful day and this gathering of those who are closest to Mel and Kade, to enjoy this first meal they will have as husband and wife. Bless this food and the hands that prepared it. May they enjoy many more meals shared with loved ones over the years. We pray for safe travels home for all from this event tonight in Your Son's Name Amen."

Murmurs of 'Amen' sounded through the barn.

"And now the toast. Friends, please raise your glasses to Mister and Missus Kade Laramie!" Applause and whistles resounded. After she took a drink and the noise in the room quieted, she continued. "The food is now served. Kade and Mel's family table will go first, followed by the table to their right. One of the catering staff will prompt each table when it's your turn."

Kade insisted everyone else at their table take their food from the buffet before he approached it. He held Ellie as they all selected their food. She was awake and he knew that Mel would need to feed her soon. He'd hold her while Mel ate. He glanced around the table at his family. He counted Ash as both family and a friend now. And Cletus was a friend so close he also counted him as family at this point. He spent more time with his partner than anyone else.

They were all seated now and eating. Kade raised his beer. "Hey," he called loud enough to get their attention. "Join me in a toast to my beautiful wife and mother of my child, with a huge thank-you to all of you at this table for helping to make today happen. I love you guys." His gaze swept over everyone's faces.

All glasses raised.

• • • •

SEVERAL HOURS LATER, the sun had dipped below the tree line and the deep blue of the night sky had crept in. The temperature had dropped. Kade and Ash were preparing to light the bonfire, which was situated out a good hundred yards from the barn, downwind. A heavy dew would keep the surrounding grasses moist, so a stray spark wouldn't be an issue. They stood beside it, drinking their beers while enjoying a cigarette over a private conversation.

Jake approached. "Hey, Elyse and I are going to take the kids back to the house. It's getting too cool out and Elyse figured this will give you guys some time to enjoy the party without worrying about them. We'll spend some time with them and then put them to bed. If we can't get Ellie to take the bottle we'll text you and Mel, so keep your phone where you'll hear it or feel the vibration," he told Kade.

"Sounds good. Thank you." Kade surveyed the play area. Only a few kids were left. Their other guests with children had departed as it got dark. It would now shift into an adult party.

"Are Claire and Matthew getting ready to go now, too?" Ash asked.

"No, we're taking Aiden and Emma up to the house. We'll put them to bed in the guest room. Claire said they can just move them to the car whenever she and Matthew decide to go," Jake said.

"Claire isn't taking them home? It's nearly their bedtime!" Kade said with an exaggerated expression of shock on his face.

Jake laughed. "They actually might just leave them here tonight; depends on what time they decide to head out."

"Who would have guessed?" Ash joked.

Kade turned to Ash. "Give me a second with Jake, will you?"

"Sure. I'll go get the lighter fluid and then we can light this bitch up!"

Kade and Jake chuckled at him as they watched him walk back towards the barn. "I wanted a second to thank you for all your help to get ready for the wedding."

"You already did," Jake told him. "And it's unnecessary."

"I also wanted to tell you that I'm glad my daughter will grow up with you as her grandfather."

Jake was touched by his declaration. "You know your mother and your family mean a lot to me."

"So, when do you plan to marry her?"

Jake nearly laughed. "The warehouse for Animal House was an engagement present."

"Kelsey, Claire, and I talked about it. We're all okay with it. All we ask is that we be there. Please don't do it on your vacation next week."

"We weren't planning on it. And your mother would never get married without her family there. We were waiting to be sensitive to the three of you."

"There's no need to wait any longer. Set the date whenever you and Mom want to. Just give me enough time to request off work." Kade took a last drag from his cigarette and tossed the butt into the bonfire pile. "Oh, and enjoy Aruba next week. Maybe in about a year we can leave the babies with you and Mom, and we can go on a honeymoon trip." He paused and laughed. "Not conventional, but it would be a blast if we went with Kelsey and Ash since they didn't take a honeymoon either."

Jake laughed with him. "I'm sure your mom and I could do that."

Kade reached his hand to Jake to shake.

• • • •

THE PARTY WAS STILL in full swing in and near the barn. The glow of the bonfire could be seen from the bedroom window. After taking one more peek out the window Jake settled into bed and turned on the television, muting the sound as the bedroom door was open. Ellie had stirred and Elyse went back to her room to replace her pacifier. She should sleep until Kade and Mel returned to the house after the party wrapped up.

Elyse poked her head in. "Mission accomplished. She's back to sleep. I peeked in on the others and they're all out cold. I'm going to the kitchen to get a bottle of water for the night. Do you want anything?"

"No, I'm good, thanks," Jake answered. After they were lying together, he'd tell her about the conversation he'd had with Kade. He was sure that Elyse would appreciate it as much as he had. It was quite a step for her children to make. An entirely different level of them accepting him into their family.

Chapter 55 – Notes in the Jar

A s Elyse passed through the entry, she turned on the battery-operated candle which sat on a little shelf beside the front door. It cast a warm glow throughout the entire space. On the table beside the urn, its light touched the decorative jar with the folded-up notes within, written four months earlier. Written on those colorful pieces of paper were the sentiments of healing, promises for the future, and acknowledgements of the past. They were the gifts from the living, recognizing the gifts they received, a conversation of sorts with a man no longer able to speak. They professed that grief was as much of a journey as life. It was a personal as well as a shared experience. But mostly, they confirmed that grief was unavoidable when you loved.

On the purple slip of paper, the thoughts from the oldest daughter.

Dad,

Thank you for the gift of the career we shared, for the time we spent together making a difference, and thank you for protecting me from danger. My gift to you is my sincere thanks. I understand why you did what you did. It was your job to protect me, and you did. You realized that I am a mother and I need to be here for my kids, both physically at home now while they are young and alive in the world as they grow into adults.

I love you and miss you every day.

Claire

On one of the blue notes, her husband contributed.

Tim,

Thank you for the gift of Claire. Had she been on-site with you and died beside you, I would have been left with a hole in my heart that would never heal. You protected her. My gift to you is that I will always love and protect her as well, to the best of my ability. I have some repair work to do with her and I pray I get the chance.

Matthew

The other blue note was from the son.

Dad,

Thank you for the gift of your words in your final note to me. I needed to hear those things from you. My gift to you is my forgiveness. I now understand who you were and why you couldn't tell me those words to my face. I am about to become a father, and I will make sure I am present in my child's life in a way that you couldn't be. I will continue to make you proud of me.

Love,

Kade

The green note was from the woman who felt as though she barely knew him even though she had met him on numerous occasions.

Tim,

Thank you for your gift of Kade. You wrote in your note to him that you had nothing to do with the man he became. My gift to you is to tell you that you most certainly have helped to shape him into the incredible man he is. I know he will be an amazing father. Kade is responsible, caring, and able to handle anything that life throws at him. He's always looked out for Kelsey, the mature older brother he wouldn't have been had you been there daily. Your absence made Kade the man he is, the man I love, the man who I know will take care of our family.

I hope you have found peace,

Mel

On one of the two pink notes, the youngest daughter wrote her last note to the father she thought barely knew her. She'd realized that he did.

Dad,

Thank you for the gift of your love and confidence in me. My gift to you is that I have let go of the anger I felt towards you for not being here. My heart is free, a weight has been lifted that I didn't even realize had been there. I'm happy, Dad. I'm married to a wonderful man and we're expecting a baby. You said in your note to me that you believe I will do great things in life. You're right. I will.

Love,

Kelsey

One yellow note had been read on Christmas Eve: Jake's note. The other yellow slip of paper was from the other newcomer to the family.

Tim,

I wish I had met you. Thank you for the gift of Kelsey and this incredible family that I am now a part of. My gift to you is that I will always love her and take care of her. I will nourish her dreams so she will soar. She will never give anything up for me.

Ashley

And finally, the other pink note was written with much thought given to it by the widow.

Tim,

THAT FIRST YEAR

Thank you for the gift of our family. Each of our children are the unique people they are because you are their father. It's not just the DNA that created their bodies, it's the parts of your personality I see in each of them. Claire is the spitting image of you in all ways; her intellect, her unwavering surety in her abilities, and her dedication to go after what she wants from life. Kade chose to be a paramedic when all career choices were open to him with the salary you provided that would have paid for him to become a doctor had he wished. He definitely has the intelligence and the stamina to go the distance. But he needed to be on the front lines, making a difference. That has always reminded me of you. You say you had nothing to do with the man he became, but I beg to differ. Kelsey, while she is me in so many ways, is also humble and unafraid, which are traits that she gets from you. She will go far in life. You were right about that. My gift to you, Tim, is that I will never let your memory die with your family. I have found a wonderful man who understands that you will always be a part of this family and he's okay with that. I've found that closure you spoke of in your note to me. You can rest in peace, Tim. Your family is on course.

    Love,
    Elyse

The End

• • • •

IF YOU WOULD LIKE TO read more from Margaret Kay featuring real, well-developed characters with interesting relationships telling their stories in unique plots, check out Margaret's Best-Selling Shepherd Security Series. As of

November 2023, there are 14 books published out of 24 planned in the series with thousands of Five Star reviews. It is realistic, with adult language and content on the way to the happily ever after. Even though the story continues from book to book, each is a stand-alone story and can be read without reading the prior book(s), but they are best enjoyed in order.

That First Year is the first book written outside of Margaret Kay's Shepherd Security Series, the first of many stories she has planned that explore family and sibling relationships, family drama, marriage, divorce, loss, starting over, and moving on.

Please visit our website to see all our books and follow links directly to where they can be purchased. All of Margaret Kay's books are available as eBooks and paperback books.

An audiobook version of That First Year is available on Audible and Amazon.

https://www.sistersromance.com/

Acknowledgements

I truly say thank you to you, the reader, for choosing this book. If you enjoyed it, would you please recommend it to your friends and family who read? And please leave a review, so others might find this book to enjoy, as well. As an Independent Author, without a publishing house to help advertise my work, I rely on reviews from readers such as you and followers on social media to promote me.

Thank you! I would greatly appreciate it.

Thank you to my sisters, RK Cary and Charlie Roberts, who are writing their own Romance books. RK has finished up her Destined & Redeemed series and has several other Science Fiction/Fantasy stories in the works. Charlie is working on a contemporary romance series, the Stevens Street Gym Series. Both have been wonderful friends with the honesty and encouragement that only a sister can give. Check out their work on Amazon! Links directly to all our books on Amazon can be found on our website. The link is below.

Thank you to my wonderful and supportive husband for his patience and love while I spend hours upon hours to research and write my books. And for being a sounding board to bounce story ideas, characters, and dialogue off of. He has been my best friend for forty years! Thank you to both my adult children who are my biggest cheerleaders!

Thank you to my mother, who shared with me her love of books. As a child, the wonderful example my mother set for me as an avid reader led my sisters and me to write our stories. She encouraged me to publish, and she was very proud of me. I miss her every day.

My friend, photographer, and graphic artist, Harry R., took the beautiful picture on the cover at a nature preserve he frequents and allowed me to use it. Thank you, Harry!

A big thank you to my friends who have encouraged me and made me feel I could do this at the times I felt insecure in my ability to accomplish this. You hold a special place in my heart.

Thank you, Kimberly Huther, editor and proofreader (www.wordsmithproofreading.wordpress.com) for guiding me where those pesky commas belong and where they do not, besides so many other suggestions. She improves my writing. And to my ARC Team, willing to read this story, which differs greatly from the stories they normally read of mine.

About the Author

Hello! I am Margaret Kay is a wife, a mother of two adult children, and a grandmother who has been fortunate enough to turn the passion of daydreaming about characters and storylines into books that people read. I am humbled that my books have been read in forty-five countries and have ranked on Amazon's Best Sellers Lists in their genres.

Her dogs have always been family members and with this book, she is am thrilled to include a storyline involving an animal rescue. All but one of our family pets over the years were adopted from a shelter.

Early in our marriage, my husband proudly served eight years in the United States Navy in the 80s. I was a veteran of more than a few deployments. That was before cell phones and the internet. They say being a military wife is the toughest job in the Armed Forces even though there is no MOS for the position. I must agree. And so, some part of every book I write has something to do with the military.

My husband honorably separated from the Navy and easily transitioned to civilian life, but I never forgot what it was like while he served. Many of our returning servicemen and women have not had it so easy. Please keep them in your thoughts and prayers as they recover from physical and emotional injuries. Many struggle to find employment. If you have the ability in your work to encourage the hiring of a Vet, please do.

Our military members are special! I honor all past, present, and future members of our military with my stories. Salute the flag, stand for the national anthem, and thank a Vet for their service. Freedom is not free. A lot of people sacrificed for the freedoms we enjoy.

Don't ever forget!

Margaret

www.ingramcontent.com/pod-product-compliance
Lightning Source LLC
Chambersburg PA
CBHW020240030726
47499CB00001B/5